The Chocoholics Series

by Tara Sivec

Other books by Tara Sivec

Romantic Comedy

The Chocolate Lovers Series:
Seduction and Snacks (Chocolate Lovers #1)
Futures and Frosting (Chocolate Lovers #2)
Troubles and Treats (Chocolate Lovers #3)

The Chocoholics Series:
Love and Lists (Chocoholics #1)
Passion and Ponies (Chocoholics #2)
Tattoos and TaTas (Chocoholics #2.5)
Baking and Babies (Chocoholics #3)

The Holidays Series:
The Stocking Was Hung (The Holidays #1)
Cupid Has a Heart-On (The Holidays #2)

Romantic Suspense

The Playing With Fire Series:
A Beautiful Lie (Playing With Fire #1)
Because of You (Playing With Fire #2)
Worn Me Down (Playing With Fire #3)
Closer to the Edge (Playing With Fire #4)

Romantic Suspense/Erotica

The Ignite Trilogy:
Burned (Ignite Trilogy Volume 1)
Branded (Ignite Trilogy Volume 2)

New Adult Drama

Watch Over Me

Contemporary Romance

Fisher's Light
Worth the Trip

Romantic Comedy/Mystery

The Fool Me Once Series:
Shame on You (Fool Me Once #1)
Shame on Me (Fool Me Once #2)
Shame on Him (Fool Me Once #3)

Psychological Thriller

Bury Me

The Chocoholics Series
Copyright © 2016 Tara Sivec
Print Edition
ISBN: 9781682306789

All rights reserved. No part of this book may be reproduced or transmitted in any form or by any means, electronic or mechanical, including photocopying, recording or by any information storage and retrieval system without written permission from the author, except for the inclusion of brief quotations in a review. The characters and events portrayed in this book are fictitious. Any similarity to real persons, living or dead is coincidental and not intended by the author.

License Notice
This book is licensed for your personal enjoyment only. This book may not be resold or given away to other people. If you wish to share this book with another person, please purchase an additional copy for each person you share it with. Thank you for respecting the hard work of this author.

Disclaimer
This is a work of adult fiction. The author does not endorse or condone any of the behavior enclosed within. The subject matter may not be appropriate for minors. All trademarks and copyrighted items mentioned are the property of their respective owners.

Cover Design by Tara Sivec

Interior Design by Paul Salvette, BB eBooks
bbebooksthailand.com

Table of Contents

Love and Lists	**1**
Gavin	**2**
Chapter 1 – The List	3
Chapter 2 – Hold Her Hair When She Pukes	12
Chapter 3 – Make Her Jealous	24
Chapter 4 – Make Her Think You're a Sex God	33
Chapter 5 – Take Her to The Cheesecake Factory	42
Chapter 6 – Show Her Your Penis	48
Chapter 7 – Gag the Groin Ferret	55
Chapter 8 – Stick Your Tongue Down Her Throat	61
Chapter 9 – The Telephone	70
Chapter 10 – Make her Feel Sorry for You	78
Chapter 11 – Show Her Your Nuts	84
Chapter 12 – Here's to You, Mrs. Robinson…er, Ellis	89
Chalotte	**96**
Chapter 13 – Spiderman	97
Chapter 14 – Cat Fight	105
Chapter 15 – You're a Labia	112
Chapter 16 – Children of the Corn	119
Chapter 17 – Numb Vagina	126
Chapter 18 – Just Say No to Weird Sex	132
Chapter 19 – I Wanna Get the Craps	139
Chapter 20 – Old Man Balls	145
Chapter 21 – Run Virginityman!	153
Epilogue	158
Passion and Ponies	**163**
Chapter 1 – Prancing Pony	164
Chapter 2 – A Happy Vagina is a Happy Life	169
Chapter 3 – Suck on those Giblets	174
Chapter 4 – You are NOT the Father	181
Chapter 5 – Dick Nipples	188
Chapter 6 – Accidental Anal	194
Chapter 7 – Ass Captain	199
Chapter 8 – Pinky Pleasure or Butt Tower	205

Chapter 9 – Dolphin Rape	212
Chapter 10 – I Like Mushrooms	217
Chapter 11 – I Will Not Have Sex With Tyler	222
Chapter 12 – Hot and Juicy Wiener	228
Chapter 13 – Wood Chipper	233
Chapter 14 – Hoity Toity	238
Chapter 15 – Stripper Glitter	243
Chapter 16 – Pulsating Posey	248
Chapter 17 – Genital Flogging	253
Chapter 18 – Sparkly Penis	258
Chapter 19 – Interstate	263
Chapter 20 – Fisting – For the Win	269
Chapter 21 – All the Feels	274
Chapter 22 – No Kink? No Problem.	281
Chapter 23 – I Made a Poopy!	287
Chapter 24 – Merry Kiss My Ass	293
Chapter 25 – Whinny Like a Horse	299
Chapter 26 – When You Wish Upon a Dildo	304
Chapter 27 – Friendship is Magic	310
Chapter 28 – BronyCon	316
Epilogue	323

Tattoos and TaTas	**327**
A Note to Readers	328
Prologue	331
Chapter 1 – Go Ducks! Rrraaawwwr!	333
Chapter 2 – Who Wants Blistex?	339
Chapter 3 – Sex and Cookies	345
Chapter 4 – Hello, My Name is Zoltron	352
Chapter 5 – Non One-Night Stand	359
Chapter 6 – Shaved Pussy	365
Chapter 7 – Cow Ass	371
Chapter 8 – Rack of Ribs	376
Chapter 9 – Meat Curtains	381
Chapter 10 – It's All About You	387
Chapter 11 – Balloon Fucker	392
Chapter 12 – Say Cheese!	398
Chapter 13 – Atom Machine, For the Win!	404
Chapter 14 – Aggressive Vagina	410
Chapter 15 – Porn Star Tits	418
Epilogue	423

Baking and Babies	**425**
Prologue	426
Chapter 1 – Can I Get A Woohoo?!	428
Chapter 2 – Satisfaction and Sugar	438
Chapter 3 – Soup	447
Chapter 4 – Toxic Spooge	456
Chapter 5 – Thug Mug	467
Chapter 6 – Cream Puff Balls	479
Chapter 7 – Meat Sweats	491
Chapter 8 – Bag of Dicks	497
Chapter 9 – Pee Hand	507
Chapter 10 – Titillating Tube Socks	518
Chapter 11 – Handy	529
Chapter 12 – Dammit, Ian	539
Chapter 13 – Shocker Honor	546
Chapter 14 – I Have a Vagerie	555
Chapter 15 – Ganja Grandma	563
Chapter 16 – Fuck Betty White	573
Chapter 17 – Lips, Tongue, Penis, Suck	581
Chapter 18 – Hairball	589
Chapter 19 – Poop Sex	597
Chapter 20 – Pez Penis	607
Chapter 21 – Drunk Babies	617
Chapter 22 – Pumpkin Roll Punany	625
Chapter 23 – Smell the Meat	638
Epilogue	655
Acknowledgements	666

Love and Lists

(Chocoholics #1)

by Tara Sivec

Gavin

Chapter 1
- The List -

CAN SOMEONE DIE *from a severe case of blue balls?*
Yep, that just happened. I just typed that exact phrase into the Google search engine.

My mother always warned me to stay away from Google. She told me it was the devil. I'm twenty-five years old and I still don't listen to my mother.

According to Wiki, the answer is NO. Just, no. Period. The end. No explanation whatsoever. You would think the person answering these questions could have elaborated just a little bit. Like, "No. You cannot die from blue balls, you fucking moron. Why the hell are you even asking this question? You do realize your internet history can and will be seen by everyone you know at some point in your life, right?"

Note to self: delete internet history. I need to consult my mom on this. I believe I came across a contract between her and my Aunt Liz a few years ago ...

You're probably wondering why I'm curious if someone can die from blue balls. You're probably also wondering how in the hell I can possibly be twenty-five years old when just yesterday I was four. I know, it's a tough pill to swallow. I'm not a foul-mouthed, cute little kid anymore. I'm now a foul-mouthed, cute adult. I take after my parents, so obviously I'm good looking. That might sound conceited to you, but oh well. I'm not one of those guys who are all "Awwwww, shucks. You really think I'm good looking? Naaaaah,

I'm just me."

Fuck that.

I walked around for most of my childhood talking about my penis to anyone who would listen. Owning it when people say I'm hot isn't conceited. It's me being comfortable with who I am.

So anyway, where were we? Oh, right. Penis. Blue balls. Death by blue balls. There's only one reason for my earlier Google question: Charlotte Gilmore. The most beautiful woman I've ever met and my best friend. She's the oldest daughter of my parents' best friends, Liz and Jim Gilmore. She has long, dark brown hair, big gorgeous brown eyes, and a body that takes my breath away. Since we're only three years apart in age, we grew up together. I've been told that we used to take baths together when we were little. Obviously the times we were naked in the tub never left a lasting impression on her since no matter how hard I try, I can't get her to see me as anything other than a friend. The kiss of death. The "friend" curse.

It's all her fault that I even have blue balls, although to be honest, I really shouldn't blame her. It's not like she knows she's causing me extreme pain. She has no idea that every time I'm within three feet of her my penis perks up like a meerkat when it hears a noise. It's fucking Meerkat Manor in my pants. My penis is like a magnet and she's a hot piece of steel. As soon as she walks into a room, the magnetic pull begins and I feel like I have to hold on tight to something. Otherwise, my penis will drag my body over to her and slam itself up against her, like a dog grunting and humping some poor, unsuspecting person's leg. I'm like a fucking dog in heat when it comes to her. My poor penis wants to hump her leg and she just wants to be friends. I feel bad for my penis. He's had a rough life. I love my penis and he's totally getting the shaft. Ha! See what I did there?

Anyway, I know what you're thinking. Who doesn't love their penis? But this is serious, yo. My mom still tells me stories about when I was a little boy and how much I talked about my penis. I'm an adult and I have to worry about inviting my mother to public events for fear she'll tell everyone the story about how I got my first boner to Barney the Dinosaur. Do you have any idea how mortifying that is? A fucking purple dinosaur. Why couldn't I be normal and get excited about the Victoria's Secret catalog like all my friends? To this day, when I see a dinosaur, no matter what I'm doing, my penis instantly retracts itself up inside my body in fear. Even my penis is ashamed.

So, anyway, where was I? Oh yeah, my penis. I get it. I'm a guy and guys think about their penises a lot. Maybe I'd feel better about this obsession if I had someone touching it other than myself. I grew up surrounded by girls. All of my friends are girls. Everywhere I look there are girls. And yet, I still go home alone every night and touch my own penis.

Okay, I don't touch it every night. That's overkill. Maybe once a week.

Okay FINE! Every *other* night. I think the problem is my job. I love my job, I really do. It's not something I grew up dreaming about doing, but I'm good at it, and I make a pretty decent living doing it considering I've only been out of college for a few years.

As some of you know, my mom is a pretty famous person. She owns a huge chain of bakeries around the world. She taught me everything I know about cooking and covering things in chocolate. I always knew I would go into the family business when I got older, and I did. No, not that family business. The *other* one. Are you sitting down for this? Maybe you should be sitting down. I, Gavin Ellis, am the Creative Director for one of the largest sex toy stores in the world. I may have forgot to mention that the chain of bakeries my mom owns is connected to a chain of adult toy stores called Seduction and Snacks. Charlotte's mom, Liz, owns that side of the business.

So, while I don't actually work in a store selling dildos, I'm in charge of the entire product development process for every single item Seduction and Snacks sells. Considering the fact that my job has made me a genius when it comes to pleasuring a woman, and I know the inner workings of every single toy ever made, you would think that women would be throwing themselves at me. Yeah, so not the case. You try being in a bar flirting with a chick and see the look on her face when you tell her you touch rubber penises all day. They all think I'm gay. Or a creeper. Like I'm going to just whip a dildo out of my back pocket and chase her around the room with it. That only happened once, and I was really drunk. I swear.

And that's me in a nutshell, since the last time you heard about me. Tonight, I spent three hours with Charlotte and let her cry on my shoulder because she got into a fight with Rocco, her boyfriend.

"SO DID YOU guys break up or something?"

Please say yes, please say yes.

Charlotte cried harder and pressed her face into the side of my neck while I wrapped my arms around her and held her close.

Is it wrong that I'm thinking about pushing her back onto the couch and making out with her instead of consoling her? I suck.

"He just doesn't understand me, you know?" Charlotte whimpered and burrowed closer to me.

You're right. He doesn't understand you. I'm the only one who understands you. ME!

"Did you just say *me?*" Charlotte questioned, pulling her face away from my neck and staring up at me.

"Uh, yes. Me totally understand that he doesn't understand you. Me understand."

I patted her back lamely and tried to think of something un-caveman-like to say next.

"What did you guys fight about?"

I couldn't care less but I'm a good guy and good guys ask these sorts of questions.

Charlotte sighed and scooted away from me on the couch, brushing her long brown hair out of her face. "I don't know. I don't even remember. It was something stupid. I shouldn't have come over here and unloaded all of this on you. He really does love me and he's a great guy."

She looked up at me with wide, expectant eyes, waiting for me to agree with her that he's a super human being. Yeah, not gonna happen.

He's a troll who gets to touch her whenever he wants. He can burn in the fiery pits of hell for all I care.

Charlotte kept looking at me with those gorgeous eyes, and I caved under the pressure.

"You're right. He's awesome. I'm sure you guys will be fine."

Someone get me a bucket to barf in.

I'M JEALOUS, IRRITATED, and horny after holding her so close to me all night and smelling her skin. She always smells like cherry almond. And since I'm slightly obsessed with her, I know that's because of the lotion she uses: Jergens Original Scent. No, that's not weird at all. Shut up. It's probably weird, though, that I stroke the snake using Jergens Original Scent. How about we just pretend I never shared that little tidbit, okay?

My best friend, Tyler Branson, called me when I was on my way home from consoling Charlotte, and he could tell by the sound of my voice that I needed help, so he made an emergency trip to my apartment.

"I think what we need to do here is make a list," Tyler tells me after he swallows a mouthful of beer.

Tyler was my college roommate. I met him on my first day when I moved into the dorms. I walked into our room with my mom and dad carrying boxes of my crap behind me, only to find him standing naked in the middle of his bed, hanging a poster of Megan Fox on his ceiling.

Tyler likes being naked. Tyler thinks everyone likes *seeing* him naked because he's under the impression he has the body of a Greek God. Tyler learned within seven seconds of meeting my mother that women will point and laugh at him when he's naked. Tyler has been in love with my mother ever since.

"Seriously, bro. We need to make a list. I'm tired of seeing you moping around on your period every single day. You have the most epic job in the history of the world, and that alone should make you happy, but I get it. You need the girl. We'll get you the girl," Tyler reassures me as he rummages through the junk drawer in my kitchen for a piece of paper and a pen.

"How's a list going to help Charlotte fall in love with me?" I question him as he finds what he's looking for. He smoothes out a crumpled piece of paper on my countertop and writes in big, bold letters across the top: **How to Make Charlotte Bang Me**.

"That is so not the purpose of this. I don't want her to bang me," I complain.

Tyler stares at me with one eyebrow raised.

"Okay, fine!" I relent after a few seconds of his stare-down. "That's not the ONLY purpose. I can't just come right out and tell her I love her; she'll have a heart attack. We've known each other since birth and this is going to come out of left field. I need to figure out a way to ease her into it."

Tyler sighs in annoyance and crosses out the last part of the title and scribbles on the paper again. He turns it around to show me.

How to Make Charlotte ~~***Bang Me***~~ ***Love Me. And Turn into***

a Giant Pussy.

"You're such a dick."

Tyler shrugs. "Whatev. You're still a pussy. Okay, item number one..."

He pauses, tapping the end of the pen against his chin while he thinks.

"Ooooh, I've got it! Show her your penis," he says aloud as he writes on the paper.

"What?! No! That is not going on the list," I argue as I try to take the page from him.

He jerks away, rolling his eyes at me.

"This is absolutely going on the list. Chicks need to test out the merchandise before they can make a decision. Do you honestly think she's going to love you if she thinks you might be harboring a pinky-peen in your pants?"

There's really no use in arguing with him at this point. Tyler is going to do whatever the fuck he wants. It's best to just humor him. It's not like I'm ever going to really use the list so who cares?

"Fine. But it's not going as number one."

Tyler smiles in victory and crosses out what he wrote, moving further down the page and rewriting it with a number five in front of it.

"There. Not at the top, not at the bottom. It will give you plenty of time to work up to the showing of the penis and then plenty of time to recover after you show it to her and she starts rocking back and forth in the corner, weeping silently."

Reaching across the counter, I punch him as hard as I can in the arm.

"Fucker! I bruise easily! What would Claire say if I told her you were abusing me?" Tyler questions as he rubs the spot on his arm where my fist connected.

"Shut up about my mother."

"No can do. She's going to be mine one day. You should just start calling me dad now," he says nonchalantly.

Ever since the day he met my mother—naked—he's been in love with her. For seven years I've had to endure him leering at her, making inappropriate comments, and imagining all the different ways my dad could die so he could console the grieving widow.

"I'm going to punch you right in the ball sack if you don't shut up," I warn him.

"Don't take that tone with me, young man."

I decide against beating the shit out of Tyler at this time. The faster he makes this stupid list, the faster he'll go home—to his parents' basement where he currently lives. No, I'm not kidding. He's a walking, talking epitome of a guy that refuses to grow up. He has a bachelor's degree in Japanese studies (a surefire way that he will never get a real job), works part-time at The Gap, and has never had a serious relationship.

Remind me again why I'm even thinking of taking advice from him?

"Okay, I've got a better idea for number one. Go shopping with her."

He writes out his new number one while I stare at him questioningly. When he looks up after writing it down, he stares at me like I'm an idiot.

"Bro, chicks love shopping. If you go and *ooh* and *ahh* over every pair of shoes she picks up, you'll be in her pants by the time you get to Auntie Anne's Pretzels," he informs me.

I don't even bother explaining to him, yet again, that my main purpose in life isn't to get in Charlotte's pants. Sure, it's something I dream about. Well, wet dream about. And the reason for my earlier Google search, but it's not the ultimate goal. I want her to love me. I want her to see me as something other than a friend. I want her to realize that we're soul mates.

Fuck. Maybe I am getting my period.

"Alright, item number two. Take her to The Cheesecake Factory," he states as he continues to write.

"Why The Cheesecake Factory?"

Tyler shrugs as he taps the pen against the counter. "Chicks dig The Cheesecake Factory. It will show her that you can be all fancy and shit. Oooooh, oooooh, oooooh! Tell her she can order whatever she wants. That's a total cool-guy move," he tells me excitedly.

Alright, so this isn't too bad. I can handle a day of shopping as long as I'm with Charlotte. And The Cheesecake Factory is delicious.

"What else?" I ask as I go around the counter and stand next to him as he writes furiously.

"Dude, this is going to be epic. I am such a fucking genius. You better name your first born after me or something," he tells me as he continues making the list, quickly coming up with ten things that he swears will have Charlotte in love with me by the time I finish all of them. We work together, crossing things out and moving them around until we have a pretty good list of things for me to do to win Charlotte over.

I know I'm going to regret this. Somehow, some way, this is all going to come back and bite me in the ass, but I'm desperate. I know I'm a chickenshit and should just come right out and tell her, but that's not happening. This needs to be handled delicately. Tyler is the only person who knows how I feel about Charlotte. If anyone finds out about this before I'm ready ... Well, let's just say having my mom tell my eighth grade English teacher at conferences that when I was little I used to walk around telling strangers my dad had a huge wiener will seem like the best day of my life.

Yep, totally going to regret this.

Chapter 2

– Hold Her Hair When She Pukes –

CHARLOTTE GRADUATED FROM college a few weeks ago. She had a few make-up classes to do during the summer session, but she's finally finished. She majored in Communications at Ohio State University, my alma mater. Today, her parents are throwing her a small graduation party at their home, and I can't deny the fact that I'm a little bit excited to get started on *The List*. After several six-packs of beer last night, this idea became more and more awesome. I mean seriously, what woman wouldn't love it if a guy started doing a shit ton of awesome things to prove to her how much he cares? And these aren't just everyday, common sense things like buying her flowers. These are the things women *want* men to do, but never come right out and ask for. I'm going to be a God among men when this is all said and done.

"Alright, bro. Are you ready for phase one? I mean, it will probably take a little while since it's early in the day, but you got this," Tyler reassures me as we get out of my car. I cock my head from side to side to crack my neck and shake out my hands.

"I can do this. I can TOTALLY do this. Phase one to commence by 9 pm," I reply.

Tyler gives me a high five and we make our way around to the backyard of Aunt Liz and Uncle Jim's house. My ears are immediately assaulted with the sounds of very bad, very off-pitch singing. Glancing under the tent they have set up, I see my Uncle Drew and Aunt Jenny doing karaoke. They're singing Sonny and Cher's "I Got

You Babe," but they've changed up the lyrics just a bit.

"I'VE GOT YOU, BITCH!"

"I'VE GOT YOU, ASS!"

In case you've never met my Uncle Drew and Aunt Jenny, let me just tell you that this is pretty typical behavior. To put it nicely, they are bat shit crazy. Not crazy like *One Flew Over the Cuckoo's Nest*, crazy like ... I don't know, picture the most insane porno you've ever seen and then add in an episode from the Cooking Network with a couple of Oompa Loompas watching and you have a day in the life of Drew and Jenny Parritt. Uncle Drew is completely inappropriate one hundred percent of the time, and Aunt Jenny is a few fries short of a Happy Meal.

There's an awful, screeching feedback from the speakers as they stand facing one another, screaming into the microphones, and I wince as my mom greets me with a kiss on the cheek.

"Save me. Please, with all that is holy, save me. Get up there and sing something in tune." Her face is contorted in pain as Aunt Jenny continues to screech.

I used to sing in a band in high school. I'm not going to brag or anything, but I was pretty good. The band, not so much. I only joined the band to impress Charlotte because she made a comment once about how guys in a band are "so hot." Our one and only gig, was at Keystone Point Senior Center's annual Christmas party—I know, contain your excitement—and after we finished our set that consisted of a death metal version of "Silent Night" and a moving rendition of "Head Like a Hole" from Nine Inch Nails, I realized quickly that the whole band thing worked. Just not for me. Charlotte came running up on stage, flew right past me, and into the arms of the base player. It turns out guys that are in a band *who play the guitar* are "so hot." And that was our only gig because we were asked not so nicely to never play in public ever again.

STANDING IN THE middle of the stage clutching my microphone, I tried not to throw it right at DJ's head as he lifted Charlotte up in the air and she wrapped her legs around his waist.

"You looked so hot playing that guitar!" Charlotte gushed as she peppered DJ's cheeks with kisses.

DJ looks over Charlotte's shoulder and smirks at me. Before I knew what was happening, the microphone sailed through the air, slamming against the back wall and barely missing DJ's face.

"Dude, what the fuck?" DJ shouted as he set Charlotte down on her feet and looked behind him at the dent that was now in the wall and the microphone rolling to a stop on the ground.

"Uh, it slipped." I shrugged.

Charlotte looked back and forth between us before calmly walking over to the back wall and scooping up the microphone. She turned and brought it over to me.

"Are you mad about something?"

I'm mad that you don't think singers are totally hot!

I took the microphone from her hand, trying not to look like an idiot when I felt her fingers brush against mine. "Nope. Not mad at all. I'm perfectly fine."

"Is this part of the show? Can I throw something? I want to throw a speaker," one of the old people in the front row said to a nurse.

"I don't want to eat peas for dinner anymore!" an old guy piped up from the back row, getting up from his wheelchair and kicking one of the tires.

Uh-oh.

"Sorry, folks! That wasn't part of the show. How about we play some Jingle Bells next?" I asked the crowd hopefully.

"SCREW JINGLE BELLS! AND SCREW BINGO! BINGO IS

A SHITTY GAME!" a lady in front of the stage screamed.

Before I knew what was happening, thirty old people were getting up out of their chairs and wheelchairs and chanting "BINGO SUCKS," advancing on the nursing staff.

DJ came up next to me and whispered in my ear while we watched the chaos unfold in front of us. "Dude, I think we should make a run for it."

"It will be fine. Let's just play something low-key to settle them down."

DJ quickly started strumming the first few bars to Silent Night and suddenly thirty pairs of cataract eyes turned in our direction. "NO! WE WANNA HEAR METALLICA!"

DJ immediately stopped playing and clutched on to Charlotte's arm as the group of blue hairs started advancing toward the stage.

"Oh Jesus. Forget the equipment. RUN!" I screamed.

"MAYBE IF YOU'RE lucky I'll sing a song or two later," I say with a sympathetic smile as Aunt Jenny butchers the words some more. I haven't sang on stage since that dark day at Keystone Point, but I'm all for doing whatever I can to help my mom out.

"I guess that's Joe, we don't have pot, but at least I'm sure of alllllll the snot."

"Hey there, Claire. You're looking especially lovely today," Tyler says as he leans in with his lips puckered for a kiss.

My mom holds her hand up in front of her, and Tyler's face is smooshed against her palm. She's only five foot four and a hundred and five pounds soaking wet. Tyler towers over her at around six foot, but she will kick anyone's ass if they piss her off.

"Stop calling me Claire or I will neuter you."

Tyler pulls back with a huge smile on his face and shoves his hands in his pockets.

"I look forward to our time together, honey."

"Make him stop," mom deadpans.

"Tyler, stop."

Tyler sighs happily and continues to smile at my mom until she finally shakes her head in annoyance and walks away.

"What is wrong with you?"

Tyler shrugs. "I can't help it. Every time I look at her, all I can think about is sex."

"I'm very uncomfortable with this conversation right now," I complain.

"It's your fault for marketing a dildo called *The Claire*."

I shudder and grab him by the arm, dragging him over to a table where my dad and Uncle Jim are sitting. "That thing was invented when I was six. You can't hold me responsible for that."

It's true. My company manufactures sex toys named after each female member of my family: *The Claire*, *The Liz*, and *The Jenny*. Do you have any idea how disturbing it is that the highest grossing product for the last eighteen years is one named after my mom? I have to read daily emails from customers that say things like, "*Claire* is the only one that can get me off," and "I was able to have multiple orgasms with *Claire*!" and "My wife screams *Claire* when she orgasms, and I'm perfectly fine with that!"

I want to puke just thinking about it.

"Hey, Uncle Jim, Dad, what's going on?" I ask as we walk up to the picnic table where they're sitting.

My dad and Uncle Drew met Uncle Jim ages ago when their job transferred them to another city. Uncle Jim had worked for the same company for a few years and was in charge of showing my dad and Uncle Drew the ropes on their first day. Uncle Jim invited them over for dinner that first night and they've been friends ever since. My dad and Uncle Jim are a lot alike. They have the same sense of humor and are great family men. They used to look similar when they were younger, but my dad has definitely aged more gracefully. Or should I say not aged at all. He's like Dick Clark. You know, before the whole dying thing.

My dad still works out regularly and stays in great shape. There isn't one gray hair on his head. Uncle Jim is tall and lean, and I'm pretty sure has never worked out a day in his life. The guys like to tease him about how he should dye his brown hair since it's started graying at the temples, but Aunt Liz always puts her foot down. She says it makes him look sophisticated. I think she just tells him that so he doesn't cry himself to sleep at night.

"Your Aunt Liz said you guys had a great production meeting the other day. Something about a contest you decided to do to name the new sex toy?" Uncle Jim asks.

"You should name it *The Beaver Banger*. Or *The Tyler Tickler*," Tyler says with a laugh.

"Tyler, you get more and more annoying every time I see you," Dad says with a shake of his head.

"Thank you, sir! How's your cholesterol? Can I get you something fried and dipped in butter?" Tyler asks as he takes a seat across from him.

"Stop trying to kill me off Tyler or I'm going to shove my foot up your ass."

"Very good, sir!" Tyler nods.

I hear a commotion over by the deck and all the breath leaves my lungs when I turn and see the sliding glass door open and Charlotte step outside.

She's wearing a pale yellow strapless dress, and with her hair up in a ponytail, I can see so much of her sun kissed skin that I unconsciously lick my lips.

We should have put "lick her skin" on the list. It wouldn't be weird at all if I just walked up to her and ran my tongue across her shoulder, would it? I could tell her she had a piece of food there or something. Totally normal.

Our eyes meet across the yard and a huge smile lights up her face. She squeals and comes running down the stairs of the deck in my direction. I can't keep the excitement from my face as I start walking to meet her halfway.

When she's a few feet away, I start to lift my arms to grab her in a hug.

"Hey, Gavin," she says as an afterthought, running right past me and throwing herself into Rocco's arms.

Rocco, who's standing right behind me and I hadn't even noticed.

Dejected, I stand there and watch as he swings her around in his arms and peppers her face with kisses.

Fucking Rocco.

I walk back over to the table and stand behind my dad and Uncle Jim. While I'm busy trying not to throw up in my mouth from the PDA going on right in front of me, let me tell you a little bit about Rocco. Charlotte met Rocco three months ago at her sorority mixer. Rocco is a year younger than her and had just pledged the brother house of her sorority. Rocco has blonde hair that he regularly gets highlighted. Rocco always wears khakis and pastel-colored polo shirts with the collar popped and loafers without socks. No, I'm not kidding. I met Rocco once and I wasn't impressed. This is the first boyfriend Charlotte has had that lasted longer than a few weeks and therefore, I want to kill Rocco. Today is the first time the family is meeting Rocco, so I'm hoping everyone else will see that there is something wrong with this guy. He probably seems okay to you right now: nice hair, swanky dresser, and member of a fraternity. But just wait. You'll see what I'm talking about.

"Oh, sweetheart, it's been too long! We should never spend this much time apart ever again. I had to watch the last two new episodes of *The Kardashians* all by myself," Rocco complains with a pout as he sets Charlotte back down on her feet.

Charlotte laughs a little uncomfortably and I watch as she pinches him in the arm and he shoots her a dirty look. I doubt anyone else notices that little exchange, but I do because I'm obsessed with everything she does.

"Did I say *The Kardashians*? I totally meant ... football. I had to watch FOOTBALL all by myself."

She grabs Rocco's hand, turning him to face Uncle Jim.

"Dad, this is my boyfriend, Rocco. Rocco, this is my dad, Jim Gilmore."

Uncle Jim stands up and extends his hand out to Rocco. Rocco ignores the hand and throws both of his arms around Uncle Jim and squeezes him in a hug that lasts entirely too long by the uncomfortable look on Uncle Jim's face.

"Charlie has told me so much about you! Can I call you *Dad*? It's okay if I call you *Dad*, right?" Rocco asks excitedly as he finally lets go of Uncle Jim and steps back to Charlotte's side.

"If you call me *Dad* I will chop off your dick and leave you for dead on the side of the road," Uncle Jim states before sitting back down.

"Oh, Charlie, you were right! Your dad is quite the character! I already feel like part of the family. Dad, you have a lovely home," Rocco gushes as he wraps his arm around Charlotte's waist.

"Someone get me my shotgun," Uncle Jim mutters to himself.

"What's up, fuckers?" Uncle Drew asks as he walks up to the table. "What song should Jenny and I sing next, any requests?"

Rocco raises his hand excitedly. "Oooooh, I've got one! Do you know the words to 'Don't Rain on my Parade?' I love me some Barbara-OUCH!"

Rocco's hand flies to his ribs after Charlotte elbows him.

"I'm like, totally kidding, dudes. It would be some epic shit if you could sing Megadeth," Rocco adds in a weird, deep voice.

"Who is this tool?" Drew whispers in my ear.

"He's Charlotte's boyfriend. She met him at school," I whisper back as Rocco starts banging his head and attempting to sing death metal.

"What school did he go to, Closet State?" Drew mutters.

"Can I get you something to drink?" Charlotte asks Rocco, interrupting his singing.

"I would KILL for a white wine spritzer, sweetie. I'm so parched," Rocco informs her as they walk away, hand-in-hand toward the row of coolers back by the deck.

"What the fuck just happened here?" Uncle Jim asks as he watches the two of them walk away.

"I think your daughter is dating the president of Cum Guzzlers University," Drew informs him.

"I'm going to need Tequila for this," Jim tells us with a sad shake of his head.

THREE HOURS LATER, we're all sitting on the deck listening to Rocco tell the story of how he met Charlotte.

"And she had on a pair of the CUTEST shoes I've ever seen. They were black with white polka dots and had a little pink bow right above the kitten heel. I knew I just HAD to meet this woman."

Charlotte is sitting in between Rocco and me on a bench seat, and the only thing stopping me from throwing a temper tantrum in the middle of the deck is the feel of her leg rubbing up against mine every few minutes when she shifts positions. I watch as she brings a hand up to her forehead and rubs it with her fingertips, like she's getting a headache.

"Okay, by my count, she's had five glasses of wine. I think it's time to put *The List* in motion," Tyler whispers in my ear from the other side of me. "Ask her if she feels okay."

Giving him a slight nod, I lean closer to Charlotte and whisper right by her ear.

"Are you feeling okay? Do you want me to get you some water?" I ask her.

I feel Tyler flick my shoulder, and I know I shouldn't have asked her about water. The point is for her to throw up so I can be all gentlemanly and hold her hair back while she pukes. I don't want her to feel like shit if it isn't necessary.

Charlotte turns her face to mine, and I can feel her warm breath against my lips.

"Thanks, I'm good. Just think I had a few too many glasses of wine. They're starting to churn in my stomach."

Churning stomach equals puking! It's going to happen! It's totally going to happen!

She turns away from me and leans forward, resting her elbows on her knees while Rocco continues to talk about shoes and how Charlotte's lip gloss perfectly matched her dress.

I need to take action. Right the fuck now! Puking can happen at any time, without any warning. I need to be prepared. I NEED TO BE PREPARED, DAMMIT!

I quickly reach out and wrap the long ponytail hanging over her shoulder in my hand, pulling it back away from her face. In my excitement to be awesome though, I pull a little too hard and yank her head up.

"Ouch! What the hell? Did you just pull my hair?"

While she questions me, everyone on the deck suddenly turns their eyes in our direction and all conversation stops. And here's where I turn into a fucking moron. I can't let go of her hair. The silky strands are wrapped around my fingers, and it's like my hand has a mind of its own and won't let go. I squeeze tighter and pull harder, and this is now turning into a nightmare because she's glaring at me, not giving me the look of love I imagined when I saved her from puke-hair.

"Dude, too soon. Too soon! Abort!" Tyler whispers frantically in my ear.

"Ooooh, Gavin likes to pull hair. Kinky!" Uncle Drew says with a satisfied nod as he stares at me.

"I like having my hair pulled. Why haven't you pulled my hair lately, Drew?" Jenny questions.

Let go of her hair! Let go of her fucking hair, douche!

"Jesus, let go or say something!" Tyler whispers again.

I mutter the first thing that comes to mind as I continue to hold her ponytail in my hand.

"Your hair is soft. Did you switch conditioners?"

"Oh sweet Jesus," Tyler mutters.

"Seriously, Drew. Why haven't you pulled my hair during sex lately? My hair isn't soft enough for you, is it? Charlotte, what conditioner do you use?" Jenny asks.

"She uses Aveda moisturizing conditioner. I can get you some free samples from my stylist, Jenny," Rocco tells her.

"Can you let go, please?" Charlotte asks me softly.

"You shouldn't have puke-hair. Wine puke doesn't wash out easily. I use Herbal Essence and it smells like strawberries," I mumble.

All of the beer I've consumed under the blazing sun this afternoon, mixed with my mortification that I still haven't let go of Charlotte's hair, is starting to make me feel queasy.

"Drew, pull my hair," Jenny demands.

"Babe, I can't pull your hair. Pulling your hair makes me want to have sex with you. I pulled a hammy last night when we were on the swing set, remember?" Drew complains.

"Drew, seriously. Over share," my mom complains with a roll of her eyes.

"Should I escort him out for you, Claire?" Tyler asks my mom in a concerned voice.

Oh Jesus, here it comes. I'm going to puke.

Finally letting go of Charlotte's hair, I jump up from my seat and run down the stairs of the deck, over to the bushes on the side of the house, and empty my stomach of beer and shame.

A few seconds later, I feel a hand patting me on my back as I heave. When I feel comfortable that no more vomit is going to come out, I stand up and turn around.

"Are you done, or is there more? Want me to hold your hair back?" Tyler asks with a laugh.

Chapter 3

– Make Her Jealous –

"How about some ginger ale? Or some dry toast? Maybe I should take your temperature," mom says as she fusses over me and feels my forehead.

My mom and I have always been unusually close. And no, I'm not talking Norman Bates and his mom close. That's just sick. I think it's because she was a single mother for the first four years of my life. Or it could be that when I was little she used to joke all the time about how she hated kids. I think sometimes she overcompensates trying to make up for all of those jokes by doting on me now that I'm an adult.

"Mom, I'm fine. Really. It was probably just something I ate." The lie easily flows from my mouth as I swat her hand away from my head.

"I'm actually not feeling so hot myself, Claire. I could use a sponge bath," Tyler tells her.

"How about I take your temperature with a rectal thermometer the size of my fist?" Mom threatens.

"I'm strangely aroused right now," Tyler muses.

"Do you want me to throw up again?" I ask him angrily with a punch to his arm.

After my awesome projectile vomiting skills in the shrubbery, the party had started to disperse and Charlotte left with Rocco to go to dinner, explaining she would have invited me to come but she was afraid I might be contagious and she didn't want to get sick.

Super. Now she thinks I'm a leper.

We're sitting in Liz and Jim's kitchen while everyone else is outside cleaning up. I had come in here to get some peace and quiet and to get away from Uncle Drew so he would stop asking me if I could puke on command because he was sad he missed the show, and my mom and Tyler followed me in here to check on me. My mortification level is at an ultimate high right now. There's nothing else that could possibly make this day any worse.

"You know, if you want Charlotte to realize you're in love with her, pulling her hair and throwing up in her parents' bushes probably wasn't the best idea," Mom informs me.

I take that back. THIS could possibly make my day worse. Much worse.

"Oh my gosh, what?! What are you talking about? I'm not in love with Charlotte. You're insane. Where would you get that idea? That's just crazy. It's nonsense. Preposterous! She's like my sister. We used to take baths together."

If you ramble enough, people will think what you're saying is true, right?

"Yes, and you used to stand up in the middle of the tub and say, 'Hey, Charlotte, look at my big wiener!' I hope that's not what your next plan of attack is," Mom says with a serious look on her face.

Note to self: remove number five from The List.

"I'm not going to show her my wiener!"

"I really think you should show her your wiener. I'm not taking it off of the list," Tyler adds.

Everyone needs to stop saying wiener right the fuck now!

"Did someone say wiener? What list? What's everyone talking about?" Aunt Liz asks as she walks into the kitchen with an armful of dirty dishes that she piles in the sink.

"A list to get Charlotte to realize Gavin's in love with her," Tyler tells her.

"Dude! Shut the fuck up!" I yell.

"Oh thank God. It's about time you do something about it. I thought your mother and I were going to be old and gray before you manned the fuck up," Aunt Liz says as she walks over to the table and takes a seat next to my mom.

My mom and Aunt Liz have been best friends for all my life and for a lot of years before that. They've been through everything together, and sometimes I think they share a brain. It's hard to believe they aren't sisters with the way they fight. They talk more shit to each other than a book with "your mother is so fat" jokes in it.

"I think I'm going to wear blue to the wedding. I saw this gorgeous dress on sale at Macy's the other day. I think I have a coupon," Mom tells Liz.

"Oh hell no! I already told you I was going to wear blue, you whore. You can't wear the same color as me, that's tacky," Liz complains.

Oh my God, this is not happening right now.

"Fuck your mother. I'm wearing blue. I already found my dress," Mom argues.

"I'm the mother of the bride. The mother of the fucking bride! That means it's up to me!" Liz fires back.

"Claire, I think you would look lovely in blue," Tyler pipes in.

Mom turns to face Tyler and folds her arms on top of the table. "When I'm finished neutering you, I'm going to take your tiny little neuticles and light them on fire."

Putting my elbows on the table and my head in my hands, I try to tune out the conversation going on around me. How in the hell do my mom and Liz know I'm in love with Charlotte? How is this possible? And if they know, does Charlotte know? She can't know. There's no way.

"You should probably take hair pulling off of the list. Charlotte never even liked it when I brushed her hair when she was little. She has a sensitive head," Liz informs me.

"You should buy her flowers."

"Or jewelry. Women love getting jewelry."

"I never cared much for jewelry. I was happy if he just remembered to put the toilet seat down."

"True. Put down the toilet seat. Ooooh, make her a mix tape! Those are always fun."

"Nineteen-eighty-five called, they want their idea back."

"Suck my dick."

"This is better than watching porn," Tyler whispers in awe as my mom and Liz go back and forth.

"Can we all just stop talking about this right now? I am not in love with her, I'm not making her a mix tape, and we're not getting married," I tell them, finally looking up from the table.

"You're not in love with who? Are you dating someone now?"

Whipping around in my chair, I see Charlotte standing in the kitchen doorway with a look of horror on her face. Of course all of the idiots in the room with me choose NOW to not say anything, and the silence drags on for so long that I feel like I might puke again.

"Gavin? Are you seeing someone?" she asks again.

I should just tell her now. Tell her that there could never possibly be anyone else because I've been in love with her since I was six. Tell her that she's beautiful and sweet and amazing and I want to spend the rest of my life loving her.

But I don't. I sit here with my mouth open like a tool.

"Dude, didn't he tell you? He met this totally hot chick at a bar a few weeks ago. Seriously, we're talking super model hot. And she used to be a gymnast so she's real bendy. Nice girl. Huge rack."

I don't know what the fuck Tyler is saying right now, and I can't even do anything to stop him because I'm frozen in my seat. Charlotte looks like I did an hour ago when I jumped up and ran off the deck. She looks sick to her stomach and like she might cry at any second. She's probably completely disgusted with me right now. I pulled her hair, puked in her lawn, and now I'm dating a pretend woman with big boobs.

"What are you doing back so soon? I thought you and Rocco were going to dinner," Aunt Liz asks, and Charlotte finally looks away from me and goes over to the sink to pour herself a glass of water.

"We just got something quick. One of his friends called when we were finishing up and asked him to go shoe shopping, so I just had him drop me off," Charlotte tells her as she polishes off her water and puts the glass in the sink.

"I'm sorry, did you just say your boyfriend ditched you to go shoe shopping?" my mom asks her.

Charlotte sighs and crosses her arms in front of her. "He didn't ditch me. I told him he could go because I was tired."

"You don't really mean shoe shopping right? You meant to say shopping for sports equipment or a new surround sound system, right?" Aunt Liz asks.

"He told us his favorite book of all time was *Under the Rainbow: The Real Liza Minnelli*. I'm pretty sure shoe shopping would be right up his alley," Mom reminds her.

"Has Rocco gotten the memo yet that he's gay?" Aunt Liz questions her.

Tyler starts laughing hysterically and reaches his hand up to fist-bump my aunt.

"Seriously, Mom? Are you judging him? That's really low," Charlotte complains.

"I'm not judging him. Some of the best people I've ever met are gay. I just don't particularly want my daughter dating someone who's gay."

Charlotte stomps her foot and growls at Liz, and I have to tell myself not to get too excited. I love seeing her get fired up. Her cheeks turn pink and her eyes sparkle. Now is NOT the time to get a boner.

"He is NOT gay! He's just … he's in touch with his feminine side."

Tyler snorts and Charlotte shoots an angry look in his direction.

"Honey, he doesn't have a feminine side. He has a vagina," Aunt Liz informs her.

Before Charlotte can go completely ape shit on her mother, a loud banging sound comes from the living room followed by a bunch of cursing. A few seconds later, Aunt Jenny walks in with a scowl on her face.

"You really need to get that French door to the backyard fixed, Liz. All the humility has made it stick and it doesn't open very easily."

"Ahhhh yes, the *humility* in the air. We've humbled the door into not opening for people," Aunt Liz replies.

"I'm going to bed. Gavin, don't forget we're all going out tomorrow night. Make sure to invite this new girlfriend of yours so I can meet her," Charlotte says as she walks behind me and pats me on the shoulder before she leaves the room.

I hold my breath until I hear the click of her heels taper off down the hallway and the door to her bedroom close.

Turning around in my seat, I smack Tyler in the arm once again.

"Owww! What the fuck was that for?!"

"Girlfriend? Supermodel hot? Bendy?" I whisper through clenched teeth.

"The bendy part was a bit overkill, but it totally worked. She was insanely jealous," Aunt Liz says with a nod of her head.

She wasn't jealous. We're friends. Best friends. She's irritated because she found out about it from Tyler in a room full of people instead of directly from me. When she started dating Rocco, she sat me down and told me, just like a good friend does. I should have taken her aside alone and told her about my girlfriend.

Oh my God, what the fuck am I saying? I don't have a girlfriend!

"Gavin, you have a girlfriend?! Oh my gosh that's so exciting! I have condoms in my purse if you need them. They're the kind with insecticide so they totally work," Aunt Jenny tells me.

"*Spermicide*, Jenny. Spermicide. Sweet Jesus," Aunt Liz complains.

"Gavin's cock has roaches, pass it on!" Tyler laughs.

"It's all fun and games until you assholes start talking about my son having sex. Gavin doesn't need condoms," Mom informs everyone.

"Are you ready to be Nana Claire right now? Because I'm too young and pretty to be Gammy Liz. If he's going to be having sex with my daughter, he will damn well wrap his shit up!" Aunt Liz yells. "Jenny, give him your condoms."

Aunt Jenny starts to walk over to the counter where her purse sits but stops when my mom speaks.

"Jenny, you take one more step in that direction and I will rip out your ovaries," Mom threatens.

Aunt Jenny freezes again and holds her hands up in the air like she's under arrest.

"Throwing away all of the condoms you found in his top dresser drawer didn't stop him from having sex with Shelly Collins in the twelfth grade. Quit being a twat and let him have the damn condoms," Aunt Liz adds with a roll of her eyes.

You know, sometimes I think I'd like it better if my mom had absolutely no friends at all. Especially friends that she tells everything to and that also happens to be the mother of the woman I'm in love with. Talking about my one and only sexual encounter on prom night that only happened because I found out Charlotte lost her virginity the week before to the bass player in my band obviously wasn't my finest hour. And the fact that my mom and Aunt Liz have already picked out their grandparent names is disturbing. Gammy Liz???

"We are never to speak again of my son having sex. EVER!" Mom warns.

"Thank you," I mutter gratefully with a sigh.

"Instead, we should be talking about what his girlfriend will be wearing tomorrow night," she states.

Oh my God.

"Make sure she wears something totally slutty," Aunt Liz tells me.

"And make sure you watch Charlotte out of the corner of your eye so you can see the look on her face," Mom adds.

"Um, are we forgetting something here? I don't have a girlfriend," I remind them.

"I got your back, bro. I've got the perfect woman for you," Tyler tells me.

"You don't know any women. You only know hookers. You are not setting my son up on a fake date with a hooker." Mom glares at him and practically growls.

"Hey, that was one time and it was an honest mistake. She was right outside the bar asking people if they wanted to go on a date. Who turns down an offer like that?" Tyler asks.

"Someone who doesn't want to get VD," Mom tells him.

"I had Chlamydia once. It wasn't so bad. Antibiotics cleared it right up," Jenny says, still standing by the counter with her arms up in the air.

"Tyler, I am trusting you to find my son a nice girl that you DO NOT have to pay."

Tyler salutes her and then rests his hand over his heart.

"Your wish is my command, my beauty. Is there anything else I can do for you on this fine evening?"

Mom rubs her temples with her fingers and starts muttering under her breath about cyanide tablets and firing squads while Aunt Liz and Tyler discuss the girl he's going to hook me up with tomorrow night.

I was really looking forward to a night out with my friends, even if I have to suffer through more hours of watching Charlotte with Rocco—her flamboyantly annoying boyfriend. Now, I'm pretty sure I should just plan on leaving the country and changing my name. It would be less trouble.

"Meet me outside by your car in fifteen minutes. I'll slip you the condoms when your mom isn't looking," Aunt Jenny whispers in my ear. "Just make sure you don't use them with apple butter and grapeseed oil. It sounds like a good idea, but it's not. Trust me."

Chapter 4

- Make Her Think You're a Sex God -

"CAN YOU GET me the notes from last week's interactive design meeting? Also, book the conference room on the sixth floor for tomorrow morning at nine. We have those fifteen product testers coming in to give their opinions on the orange dreamsicle flavored massage lotion," I distractedly tell Ava as I sort through my emails.

Ava is Charlotte's sister and a year younger than her. Liz decided that her daughter should do something other than get spray tans and take naps on her summer break from school so she made her take an internship at Seduction and Snacks and work as my assistant. Charlotte and Ava share physical attributes. Just like Charlotte, Ava is slender with long dark hair, but that's where the similarities end. Where Charlotte is sweet, funny, thoughtful, and amazing, Ava is ... not. She's pretty much just a bitch. Charlotte and I used to argue a lot when we were younger, but Ava and I would get into all-out brawls. Punches were thrown, things were lit on fire ... it was anarchy.

I look up after a few minutes when she hasn't answered me and see her standing there pressing buttons on her iPad, concentrating furiously.

"Ava, did you hear me?"

She sighs in annoyance but still doesn't look up from the screen. "Yes, I heard you. Book the fifteenth floor and make notes about massages."

Ava is the worst assistant on the face of the earth. And I can't even say she means well because she doesn't. She couldn't care less about this job.

"Ava, you have an iPad in your hand for notes. Did you even type anything I said?" I ask her in annoyance.

I don't have time for this crap. I have a ton of work to do and an illness to fake before seven o'clock tonight.

"Oh my GOD this is so hard. I just can't do this," Ava whines and stomps her foot just like her sister. Except when Charlotte does it, I don't want to hurl myself across my desk and strangle her.

"It's okay, I know it's a lot to take in at once. Just take good notes and you'll be fine," I reassure her.

"Uuuughhhh! I don't understand how anyone passes level thirty-five of Candy Crush," she complains, still tapping away at her iPad.

I don't even bother replying to her. I just lean forward and bang my head against the top of my desk.

I'm still banging it a few minutes later when my phone starts ringing. After five rings, I lift my head and stare at Ava.

"Are you going to answer that phone or what?" she asks in annoyance.

I will not strangle her. I will not strangle her.

"Creative Development, this is Gavin," I say into the phone as Ava turns and walks out of my office without ever looking up from her iPad.

"You sound like a douche bag. Don't answer the phone like that," Tyler tells me.

"Shut up. What do you want?"

"Seriously, you should answer it 'Dicks for Chicks, how can I help you?'"

I ignore Tyler's suggestion and quickly close out my email when I see a customer comment about how "Claire can be taken up the ass."

"I'm bringing your girlfriend to the bar at six-thirty. We'll meet you in the parking lot so make sure you wear something pretty," he tells me.

"Actually, I think I'm coming down with something. I'm not feeling so hot."

I cough a few times into the phone to make it sound real.

"Suck it, dick nose. You're going tonight," Tyler states.

He doesn't even give me a chance to plead my case before he hangs up on me and I hear the dial tone in my ear.

"Son of a bitch," I mutter as I put the receiver back.

"Hey, Gavin, you want some coffee?" Ava yells from her desk right outside my door.

All right, maybe I've been too hard on her. I start to feel a little bad about getting irritated a few minutes ago. I'm nervous and frustrated about tonight. And what the hell am I supposed to do with a fake girlfriend? I'm probably taking it out on Ava just a little bit.

"Coffee sounds great," I yell back to her as I pull up my search engine and type in *twenty-four-hour illnesses that aren't contagious or make people think you're a leper.*

"Awesome. Can you get me a Venti nonfat double shot espresso while you're out?" Ava replies.

Abandoning my Google search, I smack my head against top of my desk and pray to God that tonight is better than today.

"I CANNOT BELIEVE you set me up with her. Of all the women in all the world, you had to pick *her*."

I'm standing in the parking lot of Wolfey's, the bar we all frequent when we have something to celebrate. I had pulled in at the same time as Tyler and my "girlfriend" and watched in horror as she stepped out of his mom's car that he borrowed for the evening.

Right now she's checking out her reflection in my passenger side window while I rip into Tyler.

"Dude, do you have any idea how hard it was to find a chick willing to pretend to be your girlfriend for the evening? This was the best I could do on short notice. What's wrong with her? She's hot," Tyler says as we both look over the hood of the car to find her staring at us.

"What's wrong with her is that I used to date her. And she's psychotic. Plus, my mom hates her. If she finds out I spent a night with *her*, even if it's pretend, she is going to lose her shit."

The *her* in question is Brooklyn Daniels. We went to school together from kindergarten through high school, and I dated her for exactly two weeks in eleventh grade. By day three I had met everyone in her family, including an aunt and uncle who flew in from Turks and Caicos just to meet me. By day ten she'd given me three photo albums filled with pictures of herself. No, not her and I together, just her. Pictures that to this day still burn my retinas when I think about them. Where was I? Oh, yes. By day eleven she'd tattooed my initials on her lower back, by day twelve she'd given me a wedding scrapbook filled with bridal magazine clippings of what she wanted our wedding to look like, and by day fourteen she'd suggested that we go to couple's counseling because she thought I didn't value her. By day sixty-eight she was history.

Yes, we only dated for two weeks, but it took fifty-two days after that for her to get the memo. Brooklyn Daniels is a stage five clinger. I almost had to move to get her to leave me alone. The only thing that worked was having my mom show up at her job at the local ice cream shop where she told Brooklyn that if she didn't leave me alone, she'd shove so many sugar cones up her ass that she'd be burping up chocolate and vanilla twist for the rest of her life.

"Can we go inside now? I need a drink."

Tyler and I continue to stare at her across the top of the car. She seems normal right now. Maybe things have changed and she's not bat shit crazy anymore. I mean, we all do stupid things in high school, right? She's twenty-five years old now. She's probably matured.

Brooklyn walks around the front of the car and comes up next to me, linking her arm through my elbow.

"It's nice to see you again, Gavin. So, what are we going for tonight? A little jealousy or total annihilation?"

"Jealousy."

"Make the bitch cry!" Tyler and I inform her at the same time.

"Well okay then. How about somewhere in the middle? Are you okay with that?" Brooklyn asks as we walk toward the door of Wolfey's.

"Nothing over the top. I just want Charlotte to get a tiny bit jealous and maybe see me differently."

"False. You need to make Charlotte think he's a sex God. So talk about his penis a lot," Tyler informs her.

Trying not to blush with embarrassment, I smack Tyler on the arm. "We do not have to follow the list exactly. No talking about my penis."

Brooklyn nods as Tyler opens the door for us. "Got it. No problem."

"I really appreciate you doing this for me, Brooklyn. I know we didn't end on the best of terms, and I apologize for my mom throwing chocolate sprinkles in your eye."

We make our way through the crowd of people to the back of the bar and the group of tables where the gang always sits.

"Really, it's fine. No hard feelings at all. That was a long time ago, and I'm a different person now."

I breathe a sigh of relief at her words and try not to be nervous when I see Charlotte standing next to Ava, staring right at us.

This is going to work. It's totally going to work.

THIS IS NOT WORKING AT ALL! CODE RED!

"Gavin, let's go into the bathroom so you can stick it in my ass again like last week. That was sooooooo good," Brooklyn slurs as she wraps her arms around my neck and drapes her body across my chest.

I try to shush her so she stops talking so loudly but that just makes it worse.

"GAVIN HAS AN AMAZING PENIS!" Brooklyn screams over the sounds of music and people.

For the most part tonight, no one has paid much attention to Brooklyn, which I think is part of the problem. She wants people to notice her. I just want her to sit next to me quietly and pretend to be a nice, sweet girlfriend. The first time I whispered that suggestion in her ear, she reached under the table and squeezed my nuts in a death grip. Obviously my recommendation wasn't pleasing to her ears.

Tyler, Ava, Charlotte, Rocco, Brooklyn, and myself have been here for exactly two hours. Within the first three minutes, Brooklyn has downed two dirty martinis and three shots of something called Liquid Marijuana. My sister Sophia couldn't make it tonight because she just started the summer session of her last year in college. I am thanking my lucky stars for that because she probably would have dragged Brooklyn by her hair into the bathroom and beat the shit out of her. Even though Sophia was only twelve when I dated Brooklyn, she still remembers. And she shares our mother's hatred of her.

Ava has been shooting her dirty looks all night, even before Brooklyn turned belligerent. I've seen her whispering in Charlotte's ear every time Brooklyn speaks, and I can only imagine what she's saying. Probably something along the lines of "I'd punch that bitch in the face if I wasn't afraid of breaking a nail or missing a text message when I had to put my phone down."

I wish Molly, Charlotte and Ava's youngest sister, was here. Molly is the peacekeeper in the family and can diffuse any situation. She probably would have been able to get Brooklyn to stop drinking eight shots ago with no problem. Unfortunately, Molly is only nineteen and therefore, not allowed in the bar. Same goes with both of Aunt Jenny and Uncle Drew's kids, Veronica, also nineteen, and Billy, sixteen. All they care about is being the life of the party and probably would be doing plenty of stupid things to take the focus off of Drunky McDrunkerson sitting here next to me.

"Dude, this plan is NOT working," I complain quietly to Tyler next to me.

"What are you talking about? It's totally working. Charlotte can't stand to see you with her."

"The entire bar can't stand to see me with her because she keeps yelling at random people that she's going to cut their mother," I complain.

"She'll be fine. Just make sure she takes her meds," Tyler tells me distractedly as he winks at a girl a few tables away.

"Meds? What meds? Should she be mixing medication with alcohol?" Panicking when I feel Brooklyn's head slump forward, I place my fingers against the side of her neck to make sure she's still alive.

Her head jerks up suddenly and she starts screaming. "OH MY GOD I LOVE THIS SONG! I WANT TO DANCE!"

I stare at her in horror as she laughs uncontrollably. She suddenly shoots up from her chair and points to a guy at the far end of the bar about twenty yards away. "Do you see that guy? He's staring at me. He's creepy and he keeps staring at me. That little Chinaman keeps staring."

Glancing over to where she points, I see nothing but a group of women talking to a fifty-something guy.

"I'm going to chase him," Brooklyn states.

"What? No. He's not staring at you and you aren't chasing anyone."

"I don't think that's a Chinaman. He looks Italian to me," Tyler muses, totally not helping the situation.

Brooklyn narrows her eyes at the poor unsuspecting man who isn't even facing our direction.

"Yep. This is totally happening. That little Vaginaman is going down."

Before I can stop her, she kicks her chair out of the way and goes running full sprint to the bar.

The guy she's aiming for looks up and sees her barreling toward him at full speed. A moment of panic flashes across his face before he slams his beer bottle down on the bar and takes off running in the opposite direction.

"RUN, VAGINAMAN, RUN!" Brooklyn screams as she runs after him. Everyone in the bar stares in shock and moves out of the way as she chases him right out the front door and into the parking lot.

I turn my head away from her and glare at Tyler who just shrugs. "Don't give me that look. She wasn't this cuckoo when I banged her a few months ago."

"Jesus Christ, you slept with her? What is wrong with you?" I scold.

"What? I like the crazy. Crazy chicks are needy and hot in bed. Don't worry, I'll go after her."

Tyler gets up from his seat and heads to the door. Out of the corner of my eye I see a flash of something and watch as the Italian-China-vagina-man streaks past the window outside with Brooklyn right on his heels.

Looking across the table, I catch Charlotte's eye and she gives me a sympathetic smile. Obviously making her jealous didn't work. And I'm pretty sure hearing Brooklyn shout about anal all night long didn't convince her I'm a sex God. All this evening did was make her feel sorry for me. I wanted her to see me with another woman and realize she has feelings for me. If I ever need another fake girlfriend again, remind me to never put Tyler in charge of finding her.

"I caught the Chinaman. He won't be bothering me anymore. Show me your penis," Brooklyn suddenly demands next to my chair before collapsing onto my lap and dissolving into a fit of tears.

Chapter 5

– Take Her to The Cheesecake Factory –

SINCE WOLFEY'S THE other night was a total bust, I'm moving down the list and forgetting all about it. Out of sight, out of mind. I know what you're thinking, I should just give up the list and come up with something else. Something like, oh, I don't know, just telling her the truth. Do you have any idea what it's like to be a dude and tell a woman you love her only to have her shoot you down? Neither do I, but I'm guessing it would cut me deep. Especially considering this is Charlotte we're talking about. It's not like I could just drop that bomb on her, walk away, and never see her again. Our families are practically related. I'll have to spend Christmas and birthdays with her while she looks at me with pity from across the room. Poor, lonely Gavin holding a torch for his best friend while she moves on, marries Rocco, and spends the rest of her life listening to Barbara Streisand and shoe shopping with him.

This list is my only hope of saving face. It has to work. So I'm moving on to one of my favorites on the list: take her to The Cheesecake Factory. Glancing down at my cell phone, I see a text from Tyler reminding me what to do.

> *Chicks love cool guys that order for them. Be cool, dude. Make sure she knows money is no object. Chicks dig it when guys say that.*

"Hey, Gavin, sorry I'm late. Traffic was a bitch," Charlotte says brightly as she kisses me on the cheek and then rushes over to take her seat across from me.

It takes everything in me not to vault over the table and tackle her to the ground. I'm guessing that would be frowned upon at The Cheesecake Factory.

"It's fine. I haven't been here that long. How was job hunting today?" I ask as I signal for our waitress so she can get Charlotte something to drink.

"Job hunting sucks. I should have just stayed in college for the rest of my life," she says with a laugh as she looks over the drink menu. "How was work for you? I heard you're doing some new promotional thing where you're letting customers vote on a toy name. That sounds fun."

"The customers seem to like it so far. We've gotten some great submissions and some creepy ones," I tell her.

"Creepy ones?"

"Well, the creepy ones have all come from Tyler. I need to block him from the company website."

Charlotte laughs and I'm instantly hard. I try to think about something other than the musical sound of her laugh, like cheesecake. But that doesn't help; I love cheesecake. And now I'm thinking about smothering Charlotte's body with cheesecake and then licking it off. I wonder if she would taste better with cherry cheesecake or blueberry? Does blueberry sauce stain the skin? I bet Uncle Drew would know the answer to that …

"I was asked to come to the grand opening of a new sex toy store in Cleveland this weekend. You should totally come. They want me to cut the ribbon during the opening ceremony," I explain.

"That sounds fun. I'll definitely be there. Just text me the address and when it is. Thanks for asking me to lunch too. I haven't been here in a while. Rocco brought me here on our first date and our bill was outrageous."

Fucking Rocco. I'll show him. My bill will be bigger than his bill.

"So how's Brooklyn?" Charlotte asks, checking a text on her

phone and then setting it to the side of her silverware.

I don't know. How *is* Brooklyn? I haven't spoken to her since she passed out at the table and Tyler drove her home. I told him if he gave her my cell number or told her where I lived, I'd tell my mom he still sucks his thumb at night when he sleeps.

"She's great. Just great. Wonderful and great."

Charlotte leans forward and puts her elbows on the table while I gush about Brooklyn.

Holy cleavage, Batman. Don't look directly at the cleavage. Look at the ceiling.

"They have a light burnt out. I should tell someone," I mutter as I stare above our table.

I feel Charlotte's hand cover mine on the table. Swallowing thickly, I will my penis not to make a fool of himself under the table. I can feel him perking up and that's all I need—him standing at attention, slamming against the underside of the table, and making the glasses and plates clang together. And now I'm picturing my penis rising up like a phoenix and repeatedly smacking against the table like he's knocking on a door. Maybe that would impress her. *"Hey, Charlotte, look what my penis can do!"*

Charlotte's thumb starts tracing small circles on top of my hand, and I'm pretty sure the clanging of the table is about to commence in two seconds.

"Brooklyn is really pretty. A little crazy, but pretty. Does she make you happy?"

She makes me happy when she's passed out cold.

"Totally happy. She's great."

When she's not speaking. Or breathing.

"That's good. I'm glad you've found someone who makes you as happy as Rocco makes me."

Why can't Rocco just die already in a fiery crash?

"Are you guys ready to order or do you need a few minutes?" Our waitress interrupts as she stands next to the table with her pen and notepad.

Charlotte takes her hand off of mine and moves it into her lap. I want her hand touching me again. It's such a casual thing for her to do, but it has me all tied up in knots. Now my penis has switched from a majestic, mythical bird to a fire-breathing dragon that wants to destroy the town. It's time for me to attempt the next item on the list, though, so I need to chill the fuck out.

"I'll have the Steak Diane and she'll have the Shrimp Scampi," I tell the waitress with a confident smile.

"I'm allergic to shellfish," Charlotte replies, giving me a funny look.

Shit! How could I forget that! Okay, be cool. Try again.

"I know, I was just making sure you remembered. Actually, she'll have the petite filet."

The waitress crosses it out and writes down the new order.

"I'm not really in the mood for steak," Charlotte states.

"Okaaaaay, she'll have the grilled chicken and avocado club."

Why is this so much cooler when guys do it in the movies?

"I don't like avocado. It's mushy and gross."

Son of a bitch!

At this point the waitress has crossed off and scribbled so much on the first page that she has to flip it over and start on a second page.

"Southwest chicken sandwich?"

Charlotte makes a face and shakes her head.

"Four cheese pasta?"

She shakes her head again and I start to panic. I already closed the menu and handed it to the waitress so I could look cool and smart. Now I look like a tool because I can't remember anything else on the menu. At this point it would probably be best if I could smack my penis into the table. It'd be more entertaining than this train wreck.

"What would you suggest?" I ask the waitress, trying to give her a look with my eyes that says "Help me the fuck out with this!"

"I would suggest you let her order for herself," the waitress replies in a bored voice.

She is so not getting a twenty percent tip.

"You can order anything on the menu!" I tell Charlotte with my best air of authority.

"Yeah, thanks. I was planning on doing that anyway. Are you okay?"

No! I'm not okay because I love you and you won't love me back if I don't even know what the fuck you want to eat!

"I'm great! Money is no object."

Now Charlotte and the waitress are both looking at me like I'm a douchebag, but I can't shut up.

"She'll have the most expensive thing on the menu."

"Seriously, I'm fine with just soup and salad," Charlotte states.

Soup and salad only costs ten dollars. That does not make me look cooler than Rocco.

"And she'll have a bottle of wine. I'll have a bottle too. As a matter of fact, buy those people a bottle of wine as well," I tell the waitress, pointing at two women sitting at the table next to us.

"You want to order wine for people you don't know?" the waitress asks.

Don't question me. The customer is always right, God dammit!

"We'll also have a cheesecake. A whole cheesecake. And so will those ladies over there."

"I'm pretty sure those ladies are already eating cheesecake," the waitress tells me.

Can you just help me the fuck out already?!

"Really, I don't need a whole bottle of wine. Or an entire cheesecake."

"We'll just have one of everything on the menu."

Take THAT, Rocco!

"I think I'll give you guys a few minutes," the waitress mumbles.

"No, no, it's fine. He'll have the Steak Diane, medium-well, I'll have the French onion soup with a side salad and Italian dressing, and we'll each have a glass of Moscato," Charlotte explains with a smile as she hands the waitress her own menu.

And just like that, the next item on the list dies a slow, painful, emasculating death.

Chapter 6

– Show Her Your Penis –

IT'S PROBABLY BEST if I take a few days off from the list. My mental state demands it. It's the last Friday of the month and that means Chicken Paprikash day. My mom makes the best Chicken Paprikash in the world and always invites a few people over when she makes it once a month. Tonight, my grandfather and his wife Sue are going to be joining us.

My grandfather George is pretty bad-ass. For the first few years of my life we lived with him, and I have some of the best memories ever from that time. He always let me watch whatever I wanted on TV, and I could swear as long as I never told my mom. My grandfather is the king of stringing together long, completely inappropriate words that hardly ever make sense but sound good coming out of his mouth when he's pissed off. He used to let me practice my run-on sentence curses until one day I said "Shit-poop-hell-freak-monkey" and I was banned from cursing. He shook his head at me sadly and told me he was disappointed in my lack of effort.

I haven't seen Pops in a few weeks, and since the entire freaking family is now aware of my love for Charlotte, I'm assuming he is too since my mom can't keep her mouth shut. Hopefully he'll be able to give me some good advice. He's been married twice; he's got to have *something* useful for me.

I walk into my parents' house without knocking and see my grandfather sitting on the couch watching the Game Show Network. What is it with old people watching game shows? When I'm old, please don't let me ever fall asleep in my recliner watching reruns of Family Feud.

"It's about time you got here. There's too much estrogen in this house," Pops complains as he lowers the volume on the TV.

"Where is everyone?" I ask.

"Sue's in the kitchen with your mother and Sophie."

"Dad's here, isn't he?"

"Like I said, too much estrogen," Pops deadpans.

Flopping down on the couch next to him, I let out a great big sigh.

When Pops doesn't say anything, I sigh again, hoping he'll get the hint.

"Just spit it out, kid. You know I don't do the whole touchy-feely thing, so don't expect me to ask you what's wrong."

I should be used to his crass bedside manner by now, but I'm not. Being subtle isn't one of his strong suits.

"So, there's this girl I'm in love with—"

"Yeah, Charlotte, I heard," he interrupts. "She's not out of your league, if that's what you're worried about."

Well thanks a lot. I wasn't thinking that at all until now.

"She doesn't know that I'm in love with her. We've known each other since birth, and it's a little hard to just come right out and tell her at this point," I explain.

"Stop being a pussy and just tell her," Pops replies.

"But what if she doesn't love me back?"

Pops shrugs and turns back to the TV. "Then grow a pair and get over it. Jesus mother of fuck Christ in a piss shithole, dick for brains, the answer is bathtub."

Well, this little talk sure helped to boost my confidence. As I get up from the couch to go in the kitchen and check on dinner, Pops grabs my arm and pulls me back down next to him.

"Sometimes I get a little nervous too. Here," he says, reaching into the pocket of his jeans and pulling out a bottle of pills. "Take one of these vitamins. They're good for brain stimulation and all that shit. Maybe they'll help you strap on a set and use that brain of yours to figure out a way to come clean with Charlotte."

Pops opens the lid and dumps two of the pills in my hand and then hands me his glass of water on the coffee table in front of him. Downing the pills in one swallow, I figure if they don't help stimulate my brain into coming up with a better idea for showing Charlotte I'm in love with her, maybe they'll calm my nerves about the ribbon cutting ceremony later tonight, or give me strong bones at the very least.

SOMETHING ISN'T RIGHT. Something isn't right at all. I want to have sex. I always want to have sex, but right now I want to have sex with the giant pair of scissors I'm currently holding in my hand and that wouldn't be good at all. Sex and scissors should never mix.

I could totally fit my penis into the finger holes, though.

I'm also contemplating having sex with the drainpipe attached to the building to my left. And maybe even sticking it to the Rhododendron bush to my right. I wonder if anyone would notice if I got down on my stomach and just started rubbing myself against the curb? Is it still illegal to have sex with trees in Ohio? I need to stick my penis in something right the fuck now.

I glance out at the crowd of people gathered in the parking lot of Minney's Adult Mart and wipe the sweat from my brow. Seduction and Snacks is the only distributor for Minney's, so this ribbon cutting ceremony is a pretty big deal. I don't have time for whatever is going on with me right now. I feel like I'm fifteen again and a gust of wind can get me hard.

"Dude, what's wrong with you. You look like you want to kill someone. Or rape the pair of scissors you're holding. Are you feeling okay?"

I glance at Tyler standing next to me and notice he's wearing corduroys. Those would feel really good right now if I rubbed my penis against them. All soft and rough at the same time. Like a ribbed condom, but better.

"Why are you looking at my legs like that? Stop it," Tyler scolds.

Shaking the dark thoughts from my head, I quickly turn away from him and try to think of something other than sex.

"I don't know what the fuck is wrong with me. I was fine at my parents' house but started feeling funny on the way over."

That woman has really pretty knees. I've never had sex with knees before.

"I hope that is a real fucking gun in your pocket and you're not excited to see me, otherwise this friendship is over. I don't swing that way," Tyler says in disgust as he stares at the crotch of my black dress pants.

Looking down, I realize I have the world's biggest hard-on tenting the front of my pants. I quickly turn away from the gathering crowd and un-tuck my dress shirt from my pants to try and cover it up.

"Oh my God, why won't it go down?!" I whisper yell.

"Try thinking about your mom naked. Wait, never mind, that just got me hard," Tyler says with a laugh.

"God dammit, shut up! Shit. Baseball, Pops taking a dump, puppies dying, Barney," I mutter, squeezing my eyes closed. "Holy fuck this is starting to hurt. Why won't it go away?"

"Wait, this is a serious problem? I thought you were just kidding," Tyler says after a few minutes of watching me mumble.

"It's a serious fucking problem! It feels like there's a penis inside of my penis trying to claw its way out and fuck everything in sight! I have to cut this ribbon in fifteen minutes. I can't stand in front of all of these people like this," I complain.

"Actually, this is probably the best place for you to be with this type of problem. I'm actually surprised there aren't people whipping it out in the parking lot. Try smacking it," Tyler suggests.

Before I can tell him that's a dumb idea, the palm of his hand smacks against my dick with the force of a two-by-four. I immediately bend over at the waist and start dry heaving and calling Tyler every name I can think of.

"Hey, Tyler! Is Gavin okay?"

Oh holy fuck, Charlotte is here!

I can hear her heels clicking on the sidewalk, bringing her closer and closer.

"Oh my God! She can't see me like this!" I panic, fumbling with the scissors and trying to get them to cover me.

"Hey, number five on the list is totally gonna happen right now!" Tyler says, clapping his hands together in glee.

"I'm not showing her my penis!" I whisper.

"Oh I'm pretty sure your penis has other ideas. He's like an angry armadillo trying to claw his way out of a bunker right now."

Staying hunched over, I turn around to face Charlotte, which is a really bad idea. Seeing Charlotte always turns me on. My face suddenly feels hot, and I'm lightheaded because all of the blood in my fucking body is now pumping through my penis. My angry armadillo penis.

"Are you okay? You don't look so good," Charlotte says as she puts her hand on my shoulder and starts rubbing small circles there.

"You might not want to touch him right now. That's probably going to make it worse," Tyler laughs.

"Shut the fuck up," I growl under my breath as I try to stand back and wince when I feel my penis shift against my boxer briefs.

"Do you have a stomach ache or something?" Charlotte asks.

"His ache is a little lower than his stomach," Tyler tells her with a smile.

"I have some Pepto in my car. I'll be right back," she tells me before turning away to rush back to her car.

"Mr. Ellis, we're about five minutes away from the ribbon cutting. The photographer is just finishing setting up his equipment,"

Chris Minney, the owner of Minney's Adult Mart, tells me as she walks up next to me.

Sucking up the pain in my groin, I stand up. Her eyes flash right down to my tented pants.

"Well, um, huh. It's good to see you're so excited about our grand opening. I think we have some things inside that will take care of that," she tells me with a pat on the back before walking away to talk to a few customers.

"Oh this is just awesome," I complain.

"How long have you had this problem?" Tyler asks.

Looking at my watch I'm shocked to realize just how long it's been.

"Almost two hours. I think my penis is broken. What if it never goes down? I can't walk around like this forever."

"Well, you've still got five minutes. Go around back and spank one out," Tyler says.

"I'm afraid to touch it. What if it gets worse?"

"Dude, you don't have a gigantor penis. It can't possibly get any bigger. Maybe it's stress. I get stress hard-ons sometimes. If The Gap gets really busy and I don't have time to fold all of my jeans, it can turn into a problem."

Sometimes I wonder why we're even friends.

"Fuck. It's probably those stupid vitamins my grandpa gave me before dinner. I knew I shouldn't have taken those on an empty stomach," I complain.

"Pops gave you vitamins? That doesn't sound like something he would do. He's not that nice. What kind of vitamins were they?"

I shrug and try to shift my weight to my other leg to alleviate some of the pressure. My penis feels like it's going to explode. And not in a good way. In a blood and guts kind of way.

"I don't know. He *said* they were vitamins. They were little, blue things."

Tyler's eyes open wide and he bursts out laughing. "Oh fuck, dude, Pops gave you Viagra!"

I shake my head back and forth in denial. "What? No. There's no way he would just slip me Viagra and not tell me."

Right? RIGHT?!

"Oh he totally did. But don't worry, it's not a problem until your erection lasts for more than eight hours I've heard," Tyler says with another laugh.

"Okay, here's the Pepto. This should help," Charlotte says, coming back up to us and handing over the pink bottle while I scramble to hunch back over and dangle my arms in front of me.

"That's probably not going to help. But I bet taking him around back for about thirty seconds would," Tyler tells her.

"What?" Charlotte questions.

"Nothing. Just ignore him," I tell her, taking the bottle of Pepto and swigging some of it for her before handing it back.

"Oooh, look. The photographer is ready to take your picture, Gavin. Make sure both your heads are smiling," Tyler informs me before putting his arm around Charlotte's waist and moving a few feet away.

Chris Minney walks back over and puts her arm around my shoulders. "This is so much fun. I'm so glad you were able to make it out tonight and do the cutting for us."

The crowd gathers close as Chris turns us to face them and gives a little speech, thanking everyone for coming out to the grand opening.

As I move the scissors up to the red ribbon hanging in front of the walkway to the store, Chris pulls me closer and forces me to stand up straight. Right as I make the first cut and the flash of the photographer's camera goes off, the snipped ribbon falls, draping perfectly on top of my hard-on.

The caption under the picture in the paper two days later reads:

> *"Employee of Seduction and Snacks was VERY Excited to Cut the Ribbon for Minney's Adult Mart!"*

Chapter 7

– Gag the Groin Ferret –

"HOLD HIS CALLS for the rest of the afternoon, Ava!"

I look up from my desk to see Uncle Drew barging through my office door with Aunt Jenny right behind him.

"I don't answer his phone, Uncle Drew. Someone else does that," Ava tells him from the doorway.

"Aren't you his assistant?" Uncle Drew questions.

"Yeah, so?"

Uncle Drew rolls his eyes and ushers her out into the hallway before closing the door and locking it.

"What are you guys doing here?" I ask as Uncle Drew walks up to my desk and perches on the edge of it while Aunt Jenny takes a seat in one of the extra chairs.

"Well, I was originally coming here to commend you on an awesome boner shot in the paper the other day, but we have more pressing concerns to deal with right now. Jenny, tell him what he's won!"

Jenny looks at Drew in confusion. "Did he win something? I thought we were coming here to talk to him about sex?"

Oh my God.

"Gavin, I just found out from your mother that you've got a thing for Charlotte. What the fuck, dude? I can't believe you didn't come to me first. This cuts me deep, real deep, little man."

I groan as I rest my elbows on top of my desk and put my head in my hands. It was bad enough that number five on my list actually happened by accident the other day and that I had to jerk off six times in one night before my fucking hard-on would go away. Now I have to deal with this. Aunt Jenny and Uncle Drew consider themselves sex experts ever since they started giving "Spicing Up Your Sex Life" classes at the local community college. They've even been approached by a publisher to write a "How To" book, and all of this has gone to their heads. Their sex life is unconventional to say the least. It usually involves props that defy nature and almost always ends in someone going to the emergency room. Why anyone would want to take advice from them is beyond me. There was an incident when I was younger that involved Skittles. I don't know much about it, but I know that whenever my mom sees a bag of Skittles at the store, she dry heaves a little.

"I hear there's a list. Why haven't I seen this list? I should have had major input for this thing," Uncle Drew complains.

"Should I bring out the condoms and the banana now or do you want to do that later?" Aunt Jenny asks him.

"Let's hold off on that, babe. First, I want to make sure this list he's using is in tip-top shape. Do you have 'tell her she has moist folds' on the list? That should definitely be on the list."

Drew reaches into the bag he brought with him and begins pulling out various items: a blender, a wheel of Vermont Cheddar cheese, and a jock strap are the first to land on my desk.

"Eeeew, that's … no. No that is not on the list, nor will it ever be," I reply with a shudder.

"It should really be on the list Gavin," Aunt Jenny tells me seriously.

"What the hell does a blender and cheese have to do with my sex life?" I ask, picking up the wheel of cheese from my desk and turning it over in my hands.

Uncle Drew quickly grabs it from me and sets it back down. "All in good time, little asshole. Leave the cheese alone. It needs to stay at room temperature."

He continues pulling other items out of the bag that I really don't even want to know what they're going to be used for. Seriously? A small United States flag on a stick and a potted fern?

"Tell me you at least have something with role-playing on there?" Uncle Drew puts his hands on his hips and raises his eyebrows at me.

"I don't think that needs to be on the list. The last time we played with rolls you got a yeast infection in your eye," Aunt Jenny reminds him.

"Seriously? That can happen?" I ask Uncle Drew.

"You are never to speak of my yeast infection again," he warns me before turning around to look at Aunt Jenny. "And, honey, I'm not talking about that night with the tubes of Pillsbury dough. I'm talking about the Brady Bunch thing. Where I'm Greg and you're Marsha and you accidentally touch my penis at the dinner table while Alice serves us spaghetti."

I'm going to throw up. It's happening right now.

"Oh, I don't like that one. The blow-up doll we use as Alice looks at me funny. I think she's judging me," Aunt Jenny complains.

"Yeah, Alice is kind of a bitch. I'll blindfold her next time. Anyhoo, give me the list. I need to make sure you know what you're doing," Uncle Drew demands.

"Really, it's not necessary. I've got it under control."

Uncle Drew laughs and shakes his head at me. "You've puked in front of her, wrapped your schlong in a bow, and showed it to the entire city. You don't have it under control. What we have here is a failure to know what the fuck you're doing when it comes to chicks."

Getting up from my desk, he walks over to the dry erase board on my wall and uncaps a marker. He writes *moist folds* in big, black letters across the top.

"Oh my God, erase that," I complain.

"Fuck your mother, I'm not erasing it. This is important," Uncle

Drew says before writing *role-playing* right underneath it.

"What temperature is your ball sack running at now?" he asks, turning around and narrowing his eyes at me.

"What? I don't know. Why are you asking me this?"

"Dude, to effectively produce sperm, your testicles need to be at least two degrees cooler than your core temperature. You should ice those little nuggets."

Is this really happening right now?

"Or he could just stick a pair of sunglasses on his little balls. That would be cute!" Aunt Jenny laughs and claps her hands together in glee.

"Ha-ha, totally! A little pair of Hello Kitty sunglasses and a bonnet for his un-fucking-cool testicles," Uncle Drew adds with a laugh.

"Can we please stop talking about my testicles?"

"You're such a buzz kill, dude. Okay, next. Gag the groin ferret," he states.

"I have no idea what that means," I complain, watching him write the words on the board.

"Um, hello? Whack off, gag the groin ferret, spank the monkey, bludgeoning the beefsteak, corralling the tadpoles, tweaking the toucan. You should be doing it at least eight to twelve times a day at this point."

I wince thinking about how I spent my evening after the ribbon cutting ceremony. I'm pretty sure I will never jerk off again.

"Can I bring out the condoms and banana now? Pretty please?" Aunt Jenny begs.

"I know how to put a condom on. There's no need for that," I tell her with a roll of my eyes.

"Are you sure about that? Last I heard, you were using them as balloons," Uncle Drew says with a laugh.

"Oh my God, I was FOUR when that happened. It stopped being funny twenty years ago!" I complain.

"I just thought of another one, Drew. Make sure you do hallucinogenics before and after sex. You don't want your muscles tightening up on you," Aunt Jenny explains.

"Are you saying I should take drugs to have sex with Charlotte? I don't even understand what is going on right now."

Uncle Drew shakes his head at both of us before turning back to the board.

"She means calisthenics. Although a little pot might be just the ticket for you. If you get really stoned, it won't even matter that you have a small penis and have no idea how to please a woman," he says with a laugh.

"Fuck off, old man. I don't have a small penis. And I know how to please a woman," I fire back.

"Really? Quick, what are the ten erogenous zones on a woman? GO!" he shouts.

"I love when Drew touches my erroneous zones," Aunt Jenny says with a sigh.

Ignoring her, I run through every article I've ever read in a magazine or online. "GAAAAH! Fuck! Um, neck, lips, feet, inner thighs—"

"BZZZZZZZZZZ. WRONG, FUCKER!" Drew interrupts.

"What? Those were totally right. And I wasn't done yet," I argue.

"Those are wrong. Want to know what the ten erogenous zones on a woman are? Number one: vagina. Number two: it doesn't fucking matter if you're touching her vagina right!" Uncle Drew shouts. "You are a disgrace. Your mother should have swallowed."

I give him the finger before he turns back to the board and begins scribbling furiously.

"Jenny, get the lawn darts and the graham crackers out of your bag. We're sending Gavin back to Sex-Ed. By the time we're done with you, Charlotte will be eating out of your hand. Literally. Jenny does this awesome thing with Nutella and a lint brush that will blow your mind."

Before my aunt and uncle walked into my office today, I had sworn off the list that Tyler and I made, vowing to never look at it again. Right now, that list is looking better and better.

Chapter 8

– Stick Your Tongue Down Her Throat –

THE ONLY WAY to forget everything I saw today is to bleach my eyes. But that really isn't an option since I'd still like to be able to look at Charlotte. Instead, I'm getting drunk.

"You know what word isn't used enough in the English language? Anal glands."

I nod in agreement, not even really paying attention to Tyler since I'm currently staring at Charlotte across the bar. She's so pretty and nice and pretty.

"I shouldn't have had that last shot of Crown. I can't feel my chalk," Tyler mumbles.

I haven't talked to Charlotte since Viagragate 2013 last week. She's been busy job hunting, and I've been busy being mortified. I knew she'd be here at this bar tonight because we've been coming to Fosters every Saturday night for as long as I can remember. My mom used to bartend here back when I was little, and the same couple still own the bar. Mr. and Mrs. Foster are in their seventies. They always let us drink for free and constantly ask us if we want to play P.O.R.N. I have no idea why they always ask that, and frankly, I don't want to know. Tyler swears that one of these times he's going to take them up on their offer because he thinks they'll take him into the backroom and show him their secret stash of old people porn.

All the alcohol I've consumed tonight hasn't erased my fear that I don't know how to please a woman. One sexual experience does not a master make. Ha! That rhymes with masturbate! Which I'm never doing again. What was I saying? Oh, yeah ... I know how to power up a Jack Rabbit and make a woman come three times within a minute, in theory. But what if I actually get the chance to be with Charlotte and I suck balls?

Not that I would suck balls. There shouldn't be any ball-sucking going on from my end of things.

Charlotte was already here at Fosters with a few of her girlfriends when we arrived an hour ago. I probably could have just gone over to her and pretended like she hadn't seen my giant erection the last time we were together, but instead, I waved to her and proceeded to act aloof, taking a seat on the opposite side of the bar.

I don't care if you saw me with a hard-on in public. It's totally cool. Happens all the time. I am totally secure with my penis pop-ups.

"I think I'm going to make a new list," I tell Tyler suddenly. "I'm going to use some of your ideas and some of Uncle Drew's ideas and it's totally going to work."

I finish off my Jack and Coke and slam the empty glass on top of the bar.

"That's a good idea, bro. You should totally drive the Honda to the Californias," Tyler agrees.

"I just need to get rid of the disturbing things on Uncle Drew's list. Did you know that goat testicles dipped in honey are an aphrodisiac? Or maybe it's just honey ..."

Tyler suddenly smacks me on the arm. "Dude. Charlotte is totally staring at you. Wow, she's got a lot of facial hair."

I look across the bar and see a guy waving at us a few stools down from Charlotte.

"That's not Charlotte, you dick. That's Brad Manginallo. We went to school with him." I wave back at Brad and signal for him to come over and join us.

"Didn't we used to call him Mangina?" Tyler asks.

"Yes. And he threatened to kick your ass, so you might not want to do that again."

Brad comes over to us and I give him a pat on the back and pull out the stool on the other side of me.

"MANGINA!" Tyler yells in greeting.

"I see you haven't changed at all, Ty," Brad says with a laugh.

Brad was in a fraternity in college and a pretty cool guy, even if he was in the same frat as Rocco. For some reason, I was always told by my parents to stay far away from fraternities. It was actually one of their rules for letting me go away to college. No fraternities and no beer pong. Obviously, I obeyed the first rule. Not so much the second one.

"I hear you're some big wig at a dildo plant or something," Brad says with a laugh. "You always looked like the type of guy who liked to play with penises all day."

I take that back. Brad is not a cool guy anymore.

"Yeah, he makes all those toys your mom uses on her huge vagina," Tyler retorts. "MANGINA!"

Brad doesn't look happy about Tyler's repeated use of his nickname, and this makes me happy.

"Anyway, I'm working for my dad's financial company. I'm pulling in about two-hundred K a year," Brad tells us.

Was he this much of a douche in college?

"You're so awesome, Mangina," Tyler tells him with a smile.

"Don't you still work at The Gap and live in your mom's basement?" Brad asks him with another cocky laugh.

"Yeah, I still work at The Gap. But now I live in *your* mom's basement and pay my rent with daily sperm deposits on her face. MANGINA!"

Brad is really getting pissed off now, but it's obvious he's trying to keep his cool so he doesn't look like an asshole for punching Tyler in the face. Normally, I'm all for letting someone beat the shit out of Tyler when he's saying dicky things, but this is too entertaining to put a stop to.

"Either of you dicks know who that hot chick is on the other side of the bar? She's totally checking me out," Brad informs us.

I don't even bother looking across the bar because I'm pretty sure he's talking about Charlotte, and the idea that she would find him even remotely attractive is disgusting.

Eventually, I look over at her just to see if she's really eyeing Brad, but she's not. She's staring right at me. She smiles at me and I watch as she says something to one of her friends and hops down off of her stool on unsteady feet. She wobbles a little bit and her friends cheer and scream her name as she walks away from them and over in our direction. I'm pretty sure I heard one of them scream, "Give it to him, Charlie!" but I'm too busy wondering if I'm sober enough to punch Brad in the face if he says anything inappropriate to her.

My eyes grow wide and Brad immediately stops talking about how awesome he is as Charlotte squeezes her small body in between the two of us. With her back to Brad, she inches in between my legs and closer to me until our noses are almost touching.

"Hey, Gavin, why don't you introduce me to your friend," Brad says over Charlotte's shoulder.

I ignore him and stare directly into Charlotte's eyes.

"I'm a little drunk," she whispers.

"Me, too."

We smile at each other, and I can see Brad staring at us out of the corner of my eye.

She frowns. "I got into a fight with Rocco tonight."

"I'm sorry," I tell her, even though I'm not.

"My name's Brad. I work for McDonald Investments downtown. I'm sure you've heard of it."

I can feel Charlotte's warm breath against my lips as she continues to stare at me. She's never looked at me like this before, and I really hope I don't do something stupid.

"Don't lie, Mangina. You really work at the drive-thru of

McDonald's flipping burgers. Do you want fries with that, Mangina?" Tyler says with a laugh.

"So, my girlfriends all dared me to do something to get back at Rocco. But I don't know if I should do it," she whispers.

I can't process what she's saying right now because she's moved in closer, and I can feel her breasts up against my chest. She's still a little wobbly on her feet, and since I'm such a gentleman, I place my hands on her hips so she doesn't fall.

"But I kind of have to do it since it's a dare, you know?"

I don't know. I don't know and I don't care about anything right now but keeping her exactly where she is and never letting her go. She fits perfectly in between my thighs and she smells amazing, just like always.

"We should all go outside so I can show you my new Porsche. It's parked right in front," Brad says loudly.

"No one cares, Mangina. Get in the kitchen and make me a Quarter Pounder!" Tyler tells him.

"I'm totally going to do this dare right now, okay? So don't freak out," Charlotte adds softly.

I nod in reply as I stare at her lips while they move. She has such pretty lips.

"Stop being a dick, Tyler," Brad threatens.

"At least I have a dick and not a MANGINA!" Tyler yells.

At this point, a few of the bar patrons have caught on to the shouting and join Tyler every time he yells Mangina. It's a fun word to yell, and I would totally be doing it if I wasn't so mesmerized by Charlotte's mouth.

Tyler and Brad are still arguing back and forth from either side of me, and before I can tell them to shut up, Charlotte suddenly leans forward and presses her lips to mine. I instinctively open my mouth on a surprised gasp and she takes the initiative, sliding her tongue past my lips and tangling it with mine. Her hands move to the back of my head, and she clutches the hair at the nape of my neck, pulling me harder against her mouth and deepening the kiss.

As half the bar starts chanting, "Mangina, Mangina, Mangina," I wrap my arms around her waist and hold her close, pouring everything I have into this kiss. Her friends dared her to kiss me so it means nothing to her, but it means everything to me and I want her to know that. All thoughts fly from my mind as our lips move together in perfect sync. She tastes like wine and I want to devour her. Her tongue glides against mine slowly, and I moan into her mouth, pulling her tighter against me. I move one of my hands up to her face, cupping her cheek as I deepen the kiss. I can't help myself; I slide my hand around to the back of her neck and grab a handful of her hair, clutching it in my hands. She whimpers against my lips and I'm instantly hard.

Charlotte suddenly ends the kiss and pulls her head back to stare at me. Her eyes are wide with shock, and I'm pretty sure she's completely mortified that she just kissed her best friend even if she's drunk. She probably thought it was a great idea at the time, and now she's regretting it because she can totally feel my hard-on pushing into her. A kiss between friends changes everything, even if it's just a dare.

She slides out from between my legs without saying a word, and I watch her walk back to the other side of the bar to her friends. They all start giving her high fives and scream her name in congratulations for a perfectly executed dare. They surround her, and in the midst of the chaos, she looks back over at me. She doesn't smile. She just stares.

Tyler smacks his hand against my back, and I break our eye contact to turn and look at him, hoping he witnessed what just happened so he can tell me it was real. It feels like a dream right now.

"Dude, that was the best thing I've ever seen," Tyler says in awe.

Thank God. He saw. It was real. I wasn't dreaming.

"Right? I'm freaking out a little bit right now. I can't believe that just happened."

Tyler nods his head in agreement and signals the bartender.

"We need two shots of Crown for me and my buddy here. The most epic thing in the entire world just happened and we need to celebrate," Tyler tells the bartender.

The guy pours us two overflowing shots of Crown, and when he walks away, we each grab our glasses and hold them up in the air.

"Tonight we toast to something amazing. A man was brought to his knees and will never be the same again," Tyler states.

I wasn't actually brought to my knees since I was sitting. But it works. If Charlotte had kissed me while I was standing, I probably would have lost all feeling in my legs.

We clink our shot glasses together, and as I bring mine up to my lips, Tyler adds, "To Mangina. Thanks for looking at some chick tonight and screaming 'WILD PUSSY!' at her. The punch she gave you to the face was the best thing I've seen in my entire life."

ROLLING OVER IN bed, I'm immediately assaulted with a pounding headache and the need to throw up. I groan as I move both of my hands up to my head and hold it in place. Slowly opening my eyes so that the bright morning sun doesn't make it feel like knives are stabbing through my skull, I scream and scramble up the bed until I slam against the headboard.

"HOLY FUCK WHY ARE YOU NAKED?!"

Tyler opens his eyes with a groan and glances up at me. "Will you stop shouting? It's too early for this shit."

I stare in horror as he reaches down and scratches his balls.

"Dude, WHY THE FUCK ARE YOU NAKED?" I yell again.

Tyler yawns and scoots up until his back is against the headboard next to me. I immediately move as far away from him as possible without falling off the edge of the bed.

He casually looks down at himself and then up at me. "Oh my God. I'm naked and you're afraid. It's the Ohio version of *Naked and Afraid*. You should be building a fire and trying to make a bikini out of palms right now."

"Why do we make such bad life choices?!" I shout.

"Naked … and afraid," he whispers menacingly with a laugh as he pulls one of legs up to rest his arm on top of it casually.

"What the hell happened last night? I don't remember anything after that last shot, except for a bunch of people screaming 'Wild Pussy' all night. Did that really happen?" I ask him as I get up out of bed and try to locate my cell phone.

"I roofied you because I wanted you naked … and afraid," Tyler says again in a sinister voice.

As I get down on my knees to look for my phone under the bed, I hear my front door open and close. Before I can yell at Tyler to put some fucking clothes on, my dad is in the bedroom doorway.

"Gavin, I brought over some of your mail that …"

He trails off when he sees me on my knees at the edge of the bed and Tyler casually lounging naked against the headboard.

"It's not what it looks like," I tell him with a sigh as he stares at both of us in horror.

"Yo, Mr. Ellis! Welcome to *Naked and Afraid*," Tyler says with a wave to my dad.

"I feel like I'm in *The Crying Game* right now," Dad mutters with a sad shake of his head.

Tyler swings his legs over the side of the bed and stands up, putting his hands on his hips. "Did you bring your lovely wife with you this morning? I should go and say hi." Tyler smiles.

"Tyler, for the love of God, cover your junk. I just had breakfast and I might puke. Gavin, your mail is on the counter. And just so you know, your mother and I will still love you no matter what life choices you make."

Dad turns and walks away as Tyler swings around gives me a big smile. "Naked ... and afraid, mother fucker!"

I don't know what happened last night, but at least I remember one thing. Charlotte kissed me. That means I have successfully completed one item on the list. I'm no longer oh-for-four. Game on, bitches!

Chapter 9

- The Telephone -

"SO LET ME get this straight. There's a secret testing room at Seduction and Snacks and I haven't been invited? Remind me again why we're still friends?" Tyler asks as he kicks back in his chair and puts his feet up on my desk.

"It's not what you think. Women don't go in there and actually USE the toys. Get your feet off of my desk." I reach over and smack the bottom of one of his shoes.

"You're totally lying to me right now. I bet you have a two-way mirror in this place somewhere and you can just sit there watching hot chicks diddle themselves. I can't believe you've kept this from me all these years," Tyler complains.

I made the mistake of telling Tyler that we had a product-testing group coming in today to give us their thoughts about our newest toy, *The Telephone*. Every time we come out with something new, we send out free samples to fifty customers who've signed up to be on our testing list. They agree to use the product for at least a week and then come in on a scheduled date to discuss the product with other customers and fill out a survey about it. We do it in small groups of ten, and today the first group for *The Telephone* is showing up in a half hour. Tyler called me to see about meeting for lunch, and when I declined and gave him the reason, he hung up on me. Fifteen minutes later he showed up in my office.

"I'm not lying to you. It's actually pretty boring. We do have a two-way mirror, but I just sit on the other side taking notes about people's opinions."

Tyler shakes his head, still not believing me. "Liar. Take me to the diddlers."

Ava walks into my office and places the form I gave her an hour ago in front of me. "Gavin, I can't figure out the copier, so you're going to have to get someone else to make copies of these surveys."

"Ava, you're looking particularly slutty today. How about we get out of here and—"

"Stop talking to me," Ava interrupts.

Tyler places his hand over his heart and pretends to look wounded. "That hurts, Ava. Really hurts."

"Just being in the same room with you makes me want to start taking antibiotics," Ava complains before turning back to me. "So, anyway, I can't make these copies. It's too hard."

Sighing, I grab the survey and get up from my desk. "Ava, all you have to do is punch in the number of copies you want and then hit *print*. It's not that hard."

I don't know why I even bother; she's already on her cell phone, ignoring me.

"So, Ava, did you hear that our boy here sucked face with your sister Saturday night?" Tyler asks as she walks past him. She stops in her tracks and looks up from her cell phone.

"I may have heard something to that effect. What do you know?"

I watch as Tyler slides his feet off of my desk and leans closer to her. "I heard it was pretty hot. I was there, but I was otherwise occupied making fun of a man with a vagina. What did you hear?"

Ava shrugs and takes a step toward him. "I heard the same thing. I also heard that both parties were pretty into it and haven't spoken of said event since it happened."

Tyler nods and rubs his chin with his thumb and forefinger. "Interesting."

What is going on right now? These two can't be in the same

room together without strangling each other, and now they're talking about me like I'm not standing right here.

"I think we should go somewhere and discuss this privately," Tyler informs her.

There is no way this can happen. I don't want Tyler divulging any of my secrets to Charlotte's sister. I'm sure I don't have to worry though; Ava hates him.

"I think that can be arranged," Ava replies.

Son of a bitch!

"Hello? I'm standing right here," I remind them.

They both turn around to look at me and then go right back to their discussion.

"I need to see a chick about a telephone. I'll meet you at Fosters in an hour," Tyler tells her.

"No one is meeting anyone in an hour. Ava, you don't get off of work until five."

Ava sighs and looks over her shoulder at me. "Gavin, I need to leave work early today for a doctor's appointment."

"DENIED!" I shout.

"I'll see you in an hour," Ava tells Tyler before walking out the door.

"She's a bitch, but she's got potential," Tyler muses as he stares at her ass while she leaves.

"You are not meeting up with her to tell her about the list," I demand as I head out the door to make copies of the survey. Tyler jumps up from his seat and follows behind me.

"I won't tell her about the list, vagina face. Give me a little credit here. She's got the inside scoop on Charlotte. I can feel her out, or up, and find out if that kiss the other night moved you up a few notches on Charlotte's love scale."

Sticking the survey into the copier, I slam the lid down and angrily punch the buttons for copies. "You can't even stand Ava. Why would you want to spend even a minute alone with her?"

Tyler shrugs and grabs the copies as they spit out of the machine. "I don't have to like someone to use them for sex. Seriously, it's like you've grown a vagina since the last time you banged a chick. How do you not know this information already?"

At this moment, I should probably threaten Tyler's life and tell him that Ava is like a sister to me and if he hurts her I will dismember him. But really it's Tyler I'm worried about. Ava is like a praying mantis on crack. She will not only chew off his head after she has sex with him, she will have sex with his headless body afterwards and then light it on fire.

I really don't want Tyler and Ava alone together where potential secrets could be leaked, but maybe Tyler can use his evil powers for good and find out what Charlotte is thinking.

We walk to the end of the hall and enter a room with a row of chairs facing the double-sided glass, and I take a seat in the middle. Tyler walks right up to the glass and puts his face against it.

"Holy hell, look at all those hot girls. And to think, right before they came here they probably had a few orgasms. Is this what Heaven is like?"

I roll my eyes at Tyler and check my watch. It looks like all ten consumers are in the room; we just need to wait for Aunt Liz to get here to start the meeting.

A few minutes later while Tyler is busy licking the glass, the door flies open and Aunt Liz comes rushing in, out of breath and looking frazzled. "Do you have the surveys?"

I hand them to her and she takes a moment to flip through them and catch her breath. "There was a breakdown on one of the machines in the plant and I've been on the phone with them for the past three hours trying to get it fixed. Of course it's the one producing *The Telephone* and everyone is freaking out."

Tyler turns away from the glass and walks up to Aunt Liz. "You're a busy woman. How about you go back to your office and relax. I'll take care of this meeting."

She looks up from the surveys and raises her eyebrow at him. "You know that none of those women in there are going to actually masturbate today, right?"

Tyler crosses his arms in front of him and glares at her. "Why is everyone lying to me today?! It's like you WANT me to cry."

Aunt Liz sighs and turns back to me. "Alright, I think I'll head in there and see what's what. A few of them emailed me questions that I need to answer. Mostly they just want to know why we made a toy shaped like a phone and called it *The Telephone*."

"Why *did* you make a toy like that? It doesn't exactly shout, 'Hey, let's have sex!' unless it's designed for people who call hookers. Or maybe sex phone operators. I knew those chicks weren't faking it," Tyler complains.

"Actually, Gavin should know the story around *The Telephone*," Aunt Liz says with a laugh.

I look at her in confusion and shake my head. "No, I don't know any story. I just know my dad surprised Mom for their anniversary with the specs for the toy. Should I know the story?"

Aunt Liz crosses her arms in front of her and cocks her head to the side. "You seriously don't remember *telephone calls* when you were little?"

Wracking my brain to try and remember what the hell she's talking about, I have a faint memory of my parents constantly talking about making phone calls. I guess now that I think about it, they used to always put a movie on for me and tell me they had important phone calls to make. My mom was always really busy getting Seduction and Snacks up and running so I assumed she just had a lot of business calls to make.

"Oh my gosh, this is the best day ever," Aunt Liz states happily. "So, yeah, when they said they were making *phone calls* they were really having sex."

I can feel all of the coffee I drank this morning churning in my stomach. I know everyone's parents have sex. I'm not stupid. But

MY parents shouldn't have sex. My parents should have only had sex to procreate, so twice. I'm going to vomit.

"Your dad really liked to make long distance phone calls. And pull his *antennae* out," Aunt Liz adds.

Covering my mouth with my hand, I shake my head back and forth.

"I'm pretty sure they made a phone call in your room while you were sleeping. Maybe even on your bed when you were gone. I bet they even made phone calls in the front seat of the car while you were oblivious in the back. You know, some *road calls* under the steering wheel."

Aunt Liz couldn't care less that I'm about to curl up in the corner, rocking back and forth.

"Claire is so awesome. I need to see if she'll add me to her friends and family plan," Tyler says. "It could be worse, Gavin. You think imagining about your parents having sex is bad, try thinking about your mom masturbating. Now THAT's disturbing."

Vomit in my mouth. VOMIT IN MY FUCKING MOUTH!

"Wait, that's not disturbing at all. Fuck, now I'm thinking about Claire flicking the bean."

"Hooker, the group is waiting for you in there. What's taking so long?" my mom asks as she steps into the room and closes the door behind her.

"Oh, nothing much. Tyler was just talking to your son about you masturbating, and I was telling Gavin about *phone calls*. I think he needs a minute."

My mom looks at me with sympathy and mutters, "Oh dear. This could pose a problem."

"When I was twelve, we went to Disney World and you wouldn't let Sophie or me go in the jacuzzi tub in our room because you said dad's phone broke in the tub when he was making a phone call. Tell me he was really using his cell phone in the tub!"

Mom bites her lip and then winces. "If by cell phone you mean penis, then yes."

"OH MY GOD, MOM!"

She shrugs likes it's no big deal. "The maid hadn't stopped by yet. The jacuzzi was still contaminated."

I shiver in revulsion as I imagine what exactly the tub would have been contaminated with.

"Claire, I need to talk to you about getting on your cell phone plan. I'm going to need a lot of extra minutes," Tyler tells her with a wink.

"Do you kiss your mother with that mouth?" Aunt Liz asks.

"No. But I'll kiss Gavin's mother with this mouth."

Everyone needs to stop talking right now before my brain explodes all over this fucking room.

"Speaking of kissing, Charlotte kissed Gavin the other night," Tyler adds.

"WHAT?!" Mom and Aunt Liz screech at the same time, whipping their heads in my direction.

"Oh my God, it's happening, it's really happening. We need to pick out a venue for the rehearsal dinner. Those things book fast," Mom states, pulling out her cell phone and clicking on Google.

"Jesus, Mom, it was just a kiss. Stop googling restaurants."

"Look up Stancato's, I love their salads," Aunt Liz says, standing behind my mom and looking over her shoulder.

"Fuck you, we're not doing the rehearsal dinner at Stancato's. Stop being such a whore for that place," Mom complains.

"Hello! Will you two cut it out?" I shout.

"I'm going to punch you right in the vagina if you don't pipe the fuck down," Aunt Liz argues with my mom.

How did I lose control of this situation so quickly?

"Ladies, could I interest you in a pool of Jell-O while you hash this out?" Tyler pipes up.

Perfect. Just perfect. I find out my parents never actually made any important phone calls when I was growing up and locked me in my room just so they could bang, and now my mom and my aunt are back to planning a wedding between Charlotte and me when I don't even know if she remembers that we kissed because she was so drunk.

This day can't possibly get any worse.

Chapter 10
– Make her Feel Sorry for You –

"JESUS, DAD, WHAT the hell happened?" I ask in a panic as I rush into the hospital room to find him in a gown, hooked up to a bunch of machines.

Toward the end of the testing meeting, my mom got a frantic phone call from Uncle Drew letting us know that my dad was rushed to the emergency room because he thought he was having a heart attack. My mom immediately hightailed it out of there, leaving Aunt Liz and me to quickly wrap up the meeting.

"The dragon on the ceiling has bingo teeth," Dad says in a serious tone.

My eyebrows rise in surprise at his response, and I turn to my mom as she gets up from his bedside and walks over to me.

"Um, you should probably just ignore everything he says at this point in time," she whispers.

"No, really. There are sharks on the planes in the window of the palm tree. My chin feels funny," Dad mutters, reaching his hand up and scratching his nose.

"What the fuck is wrong with him? Is he having a heart attack?" I question.

We both turn to look at him when he bursts out laughing, pointing at his feet. "There are kittens licking my toes! Look at the kittens! Hi, little kittens!"

Mom sighs and turns back to me. "The doctor is still running some tests, but right now it doesn't look like a heart attack or anything serious. He was at work and told Drew he felt funny—dizzy and nauseous. Then all of a sudden he told Drew he couldn't feel either of his arms so Drew freaked out and brought him here."

Dad continues to point and laugh at the kittens that aren't there, and a few minutes later, Tyler joins us in the room.

"I parked your car in the garage, Gavin. Saw Drew and Liz outside. They're going to call everyone and let them know what's going on."

Tyler tosses my car keys to me and I put them in my pocket. I was so worried when we got here that I jumped out of my car in front of the emergency room and told Tyler to go park my car.

"So what's going on with big daddy? Is he dying?" Tyler asks as he sidles up to my mom and puts his arm around her shoulder.

She elbows him in the ribs and moves away. "I'm going to chop off your arm and beat you with the bloody stump. Gavin, I'm going to go get some coffee. Keep an eye on your dad. Call me on my cell if he starts crying again."

Mom walks over to my dad and kisses him on the cheek before leaving the room. I move around to the side of his bed and take the seat my mom had been occupying.

"How are you feeling, Dad?" I ask.

"These chicken feet have pot whistles," my dad complains to the ceiling.

I sigh and look over at Tyler. He looks a little guilty. He's biting his nails and staring wide-eyed at my dad.

"Don't worry, I'm sure all of your wishes that he would die so you could make a move on my mom aren't coming true," I tell him with a laugh, trying to lighten the situation now that I know Dad isn't really having a heart attack.

"My penis is a pirate and I fight crime with a meat whistle sword. Who wants to pet my goat?" Dad asks.

"Oh, Jesus, you're going to kill me," Tyler moans.

"What are you talking about?"

Tyler stops biting his nails and begins pacing back and forth at the end of the bed.

"I need to tell you something, but you have to promise not to kill me," Tyler begs.

"Dad, I'll be right back," I tell him as I get up from my chair and move around to the end of the bed, grabbing Tyler's arm to get him to stop pacing.

"FAIRYDUST!! EVERYONE GETS FAIRYDUST!" Dad yells.

"Oh my God, this is bad. This is really bad," Tyler mutters as he stares at my dad.

"Tyler, what the hell is your problem?"

He sighs and turns away from my dad to look at me nervously, biting his lip. "So, remember yesterday morning, *naked and afraid?*"

"I thought we agreed to never speak of that again," I complain.

"Yeah, well, I just now remembered why I was naked. The night before, after you passed out, I made some chocolate candies in your kitchen. And then ate one."

I stare at him in confusion and then shrug my shoulders. "Yeah, and?"

Tyler bites his lip again and glances nervously between my dad and I.

"Shhhhhh, the puppies are making glue," Dad warns us.

"And, um, well, they were 'shroom chocolates."

He looks at me worriedly and I'm still not catching on so I shrug again.

"Hence the reason for my nakedness. I was high that night," Tyler adds.

Still not getting it, I stare at him in confusion.

"I made six chocolates and I ate one. But when I left your house that morning, there were only four chocolates left. Which means ..."

I turn my face away from Tyler slowly and stare at my dad who now has his leg bent and his foot in his hand, staring at it intently.

"There's no marshmallow in this. WHY THE FUCK ISN'T THERE ANY MARSHMALLOW? Tell the beaver to stop singing. I don't like that song."

Oh no. Oh my God. My dad stopped over that morning to drop off my mail.

"So yeah. I'm guessing this means your dad is tripping his balls off," Tyler mumbles. "Hey, at least it's not a heart attack."

Now that I have this information, I should be a little bit relieved. I mean, Tyler's right. At least it's not something serious. But now I have to tell someone, like my mother. And she is going to kick my ass. I could just take this information to the grave, but I can't let the doctors continue to test him for no reason. That's just cruel.

"Gavin, oh my God, I got here as soon as I heard. Is your dad okay? What's going on?"

Turning, I see Charlotte rush into the room and she throws herself in my arms. It feels so good to have her body pressed up against mine that for a minute I forget about the problem at hand. She squeezes me tightly to her, and I take a moment to just breathe her in. We haven't spoke at all since the kiss, which is really unusual for us. We talk every single day whether it's in person or via text. I'm not embarrassed at all by what happened between us at Fosters, but the fact that I haven't heard from her since then makes me wonder if *she* is. And if she is, at least she's able to put it aside and be here for me. At least the fact that she still cares about me hasn't changed. But if I tell her that my dad isn't really sick, and the reason for him being in the hospital, she's probably going to be pissed and no longer concerned for my well-being.

I know I'm an ass. Don't judge me.

Staring over her shoulder at Tyler, I give him a look that says "I really want to kick your ass right now, but I won't because I'm an awful person and I'm going to use this to my advantage."

"They think he might be having a heart attack. I'm so worried," I tell her, burying my face in the side of her neck and holding her tighter.

"I HAVE A MEAT WHISTLE!" my dad yells.

Charlotte pulls away from me and looks over at him.

"Did he just yell about his meat whistle?" she whispers.

"Um, yeah, just ignore him. It's the drugs they have him on to keep him comfortable," I tell her quickly.

Tyler laughs behind us and I shoot him an angry glare.

"Alright, I just spoke to the doctor down in the cafeteria and it looks like there's nothing—"

"MOM! Thank God you're back," I interrupt her quickly.

Stepping away from Charlotte, I pull mom over to the door and lower my voice.

"So, here's the thing. Dad accidentally ate a 'shroom chocolate that Tyler made at my place the other night so he's not having a heart attack. He's just really, really high. But Charlotte doesn't know that and she's worried about me, so we're just going to go with it, okay?"

I stop rambling and try not to wince at the wide-eyed look my mom is giving me. The look that says her head is about to explode.

"You have got to be fucking kidding me," she finally mutters. She leans around me and stares angrily at Tyler. Tyler just shrugs and waves at her while Charlotte steps over to the side of my dad's bed and grabs his hand.

"It's going to be okay, Uncle Carter. You just concentrate on getting better and I'll make sure Gavin is okay," she tells him softly.

I smile brightly at Charlotte's words but quickly wipe the happiness off of my face when I turn back to see my mom glaring at me.

"Charlotte, have you made any phone calls with Gavin yet? You're probably going to need to help him pull out his antenna, I don't think he knows how it works," Dad explains.

Mom laughs, patting me on the back when she sees the look of horror on my face before walking around me to go over to my dad. Charlotte moves out of her way and comes back over to me.

"Wow, I can't believe how out of it your dad is. I feel so bad.

Are you having a problem with your phone? Do you need me to take a look at it?" she asks.

"Gavin, pull out your phone and show her how broken it is," Tyler says with a laugh.

"There's nothing wrong with my phone. It works perfectly fine," I growl.

Charlotte holds her hand out in front of me. "Don't be stubborn. Put your phone in my hand. I'm really good with phones."

Tyler laughs again and I reach over and smack him in the arm.

"Really, my phone isn't broken," I reiterate.

"Dude, Charlotte is *really* good with phones. Let her touch it," Tyler snorts.

"Gavin, if you don't give me your phone right now, I'm going to reach into your pocket and take it out myself," Charlotte argues.

"I am so turned on right now," Tyler whispers.

"I have a better idea. Why don't we get out of here for a little while and give my mom and dad some peace and quiet," I tell her, trying to change the subject.

Charlotte sighs and looks back over her shoulder at my parents. "That's probably a good idea. Your dad needs his rest and you need to do something to take your mind off of what's going on with him."

Elated by the idea that I'm going to spend some more quality time with Charlotte, I tell my parents goodbye and leave Tyler with them. He deserves the punishment of my mother's wrath for the rest of the afternoon after what he did.

Charlotte grabs my hand as we head toward the door, and I try not to skip across the room in happiness when she laces her fingers with mine.

"We can do whatever you want today. It's your choice. But just so you know, I *will* have my hand on your phone by the end of the night," Charlotte threatens.

"MAKE SURE HE PUTS A PROTECTIVE COVER ON HIS PHONE!" my dad screams at us as we exit into the hallway.

Chapter 11

- Show Her Your Nuts -

"SO HYPOTHETICALLY, WHAT would you say if I told you I broke up with Rocco?" Charlotte asks.

We've been at my apartment ever since we left the hospital and we've consumed quite a bit of beer. All of our empties clang together as Charlotte leans forward and slams her bottle on the coffee table before curling her legs underneath her, sitting next to me on the couch.

For most of the afternoon, we watched mindless TV and didn't talk about anything important. It seemed like we were both trying to avoid the white elephant in the room. But now that we have some alcohol in our system, more important issues are being discussed.

"You broke up with Rocco?" I ask in shock, trying my hardest to keep the elation from my face.

"I said hypothetically," she reiterates.

Dammit all to fucking hell.

How do I answer this? How does she want me to answer this?

"Um, Rocco is a really nice guy."

BULLSHIT!

Charlotte sighs heavily and turns to face me on the couch. "That's not what I asked. I know Rocco is a nice guy. One of the best. I want to know how you would feel if I wasn't with him anymore."

Feelings? Fuck, she wants to talk about feelings? I feel like I want to go streaking through the streets if she's no longer with

Rocco. I'm guessing that's not what she's looking for here, though.

I need to talk to my dad. This is really sad that I'm a grown man and need my dad, but I do. Fucking Tyler and his 'shroom chocolates. If I call my dad now, he'll probably just tell me to eat the butter because the cornflakes are watching.

"Can you hold that thought for a minute? I just realized I forgot to send an email out for work. It's really important," I add when I see the disappointed look on her face.

"Fine, but hurry up. I'm feeling a little buzzed and I want to talk."

Standing up and walking backwards toward the doorway, I watch as she pulls her legs out from underneath her and leans forward to grab her beer bottle. The front of her shirt falls open and I have a perfect view of her red, lace-covered breasts.

Sweet Jesus. What was I doing? What day is it? Did I eat a 'shroom chocolate by mistake?

"Stop staring at my boobs and hurry up," she tells me with a smirk.

I flinch and look up into her eyes, a little shocked that she hasn't made any attempt to lean back so I can't see down her shirt anymore. It's like she WANTS me to keep staring at her boobs. I feel like it's my civic duty to continue staring at her boobs. Even *they* want me to keep staring, the way they're all pushed up in her bra and looking so amazing without even trying. I think one just winked at me. Do boobs wink? Does beer contain eleventy-seven thousand percent alcohol by volume now?

Remembering my purpose for suddenly getting up from my spot next to her, I start backing up again, my eyes never leaving her winking boobs.

Eventually, I have to pull my gaze away as I round the corner of the living room and into the kitchen. Turning around, I race across the room and wedge myself between the fridge and the cupboards, pulling my cell out of my back pocket and dialing the first number I can think of.

As the phone rings, I peek my head out from around the fridge to make sure Charlotte didn't follow me in here.

"This better be good. I have a naked woman on the roof and a jar of almonds toasting in the microwave," Uncle Drew answers.

"Charlotte wants to talk about feelings!" I whisper yell into the phone.

"Carrots want to dog above ceilings? Dude, are you stoned?" Uncle Drew replies.

Taking a quick glance around the fridge again, I raise my voice a little louder, cupping my hand around my mouth to contain my words.

"Charlotte is in my living room. I just saw her boobs. I repeat, I JUST SAW HER BOOBS!"

There's silence on the other end of the line and I wonder if the call dropped.

"Uncle Drew?" I whisper.

"I'm here, I'm here. Fuck! I wasn't expecting this phone call for at least another seven to ten days. Aunt Jenny hasn't finished making the bar graph, and we still have statistics to process. Shit! Okay, don't panic. Did you TOUCH the boobs yet?" Uncle Drew questions.

"No! But she wants me to tell her how I feel. What the fuck do I do?"

Uncle Drew sighs. "Fuck. Feelings. Damn, she's bringing out the big guns. Okay, here's what you do. You distract her. Chicks are like squirrels on crack. Throw a nut in their direction and they'll forget what they just wanted five seconds before," Uncle Drew explains.

"So, you're saying I should just change the subject when she asks me how I feel?"

"Fuck no! I'm saying, if she asks you some girly shit, you throw your nuts at her. Whip those puppies out, roll them around in your hands, and get her to focus on those bad boys instead."

Remind me again why I thought calling him was a good idea?

"I'm not showing her my balls!" I whisper angrily into the phone.

Uncle Drew laughs and before he can give me any other stellar advice, I hear Aunt Jenny in the background.

"Drew, did you just tell Gavin to show Charlotte his balls to avoid talking about how he feels?"

"Babe, why did you get down from the roof? The almonds are almost ready and the pickled relish is cooling on the stove," Uncle Drew pleads.

"Drew Parritt, are you telling Gavin not to talk about his feelings?" Aunt Jenny demands again.

I hear a rustle of fabric over the line and then Uncle Drew shouts, "Jenny, look at my nuts!"

Peering around the corner, I see Charlotte walk into the room and look at me questioningly.

"Ooooh, I love your nuts. Don't forget to grab the salad thongs. I'll see you on the roof."

A few seconds later, Uncle Drew comes back on the line as Charlotte walks right up to me and stands a few inches away, staring into my eyes.

"What did I tell you? Nut tossing works every time. Good luck. I gotta go. There's a few orgasms calling my name."

The dial tone sounds in my ear and I end the call, slowly lowering my arm down and placing my phone on the counter next to me, my eyes never leaving Charlotte's.

"Are you done with work stuff?" she asks.

I nod my head in response, unable to speak because of her close proximity. I want to touch her boobs. They're right in front of me, straining against the front of her T-shirt. They're doing this on purpose! They know I can't just reach out and touch them whenever I want. Fucking boob teasers.

"We kissed the other night," Charlotte whispers.

I swallow thickly and nod again, trying not to look directly at the boobs since it would be rude.

"What were you feeling right when we kissed?" Charlotte asks, leaning in closer so that her boobs are now pressed up against my chest.

I want to snuggle her boobs and I want to kiss her and never stop, and she wants feelings! I have feelings, dammit! I have all the feels! But what if my feels aren't the same as her feels and I look like an idiot because of my feels? I don't want to look like an idiot!

Staring down the front of her shirt, her warm breath on my face, I reach for the fly of my jeans without even thinking about what I'm doing.

"I HAVE NUTS!"

Chapter 12

– Here's to You, Mrs. Robinson...er, Ellis –

"YOU LOOK GUILTY. Why do you look guilty?" Tyler asks as soon as he hops into the passenger seat of my car and I take off.

How the fuck does he do that? Of course I feel guilty. My best friend stuck her hand down my pants last night and jerked me off. And when I tried to reciprocate and wound up ripping her underwear by accident, she left without saying a word. I'm way beyond feeling guilty. I'm fucking mortified.

My mom had a meeting she couldn't miss this morning and my dad is being released from the hospital. She didn't ask so much as tell me I would be picking him up today.

"You need to pick your dad up from the hospital. And take him wherever he wants to go. I don't care if he has to go back to the doctor for an enema, you will go with him and hold his hand."

Even though Tyler spent half the evening with my parents last night after I left the hospital with Charlotte, I didn't feel like that punishment was enough for him, considering he roofied my dad, so I told him he was coming with me.

"I have no idea what you're talking about. I don't feel guilty," I finally reply, refusing to look in his direction.

"Liar, liar, you're a fucking whore. Spill it," Tyler demands as I stop at a red light.

I can feel Tyler's eyes boring into me from the other side of the car, and I know my face is heating up and turning red.

"Oh my fuck. Is that a hickey on your neck?" Tyler shouts.

Craning my neck, I look into the rearview mirror, and sure enough there is a little red mark right below my ear. Hot damn.

"I think you have your answer right there, bro. When a chick gives you a hickey, she means business."

Looking away from the mirror, I glance over at him in confusion. "What are you talking about?"

Tyler shakes his head at me. "Dude. She marked you. Now, every chick that sees you is going to know you're taken. She should have just pissed all over you and been done with it. Golden shower, party of one!"

I'm sure that's not why Charlotte did it. It was the heat of the moment and all that shit. Tyler's insane.

"So, you made a move. Little Gavin is all grown up. It brings a tear to my eye. Under the shirt AND under the bra? Did you blow your load in your pants as soon as you touched her tits? Is that why you feel guilty?"

I scoff at him and roll my eyes. "What are we, twelve? Did you seriously just ask me that?"

I know, I know. I totally DID blow my load like ten seconds after she touched me, but I'm not about to tell Tyler that.

"Hey, it happens to the best of us. I once came in my pants when I was thirteen and Christy Collins made me play with her My Little Ponies."

I laugh and glance Tyler's way as I wait for a red light to change. "Was Christy Collins THAT hot when she was thirteen?"

Tyler shakes his head and pulls his cell phone out of his back pocket. "It had nothing to do with her. Have you ever played with My Little Ponies? They have such silky smooth hair and cute little butts. Twilight Sparkle is my favorite."

I can't form words right now, even if my life depended on it.

"Dude, did you jerk off to a My Little Pony?" I ask in disgust.

"See? I knew you'd judge me. It's not like that at all. It's all about her personality," Tyler argues.

"It's a fucking plastic horse! Holy shit, you don't bang animals do you?" I yell in horror.

"Oh my God, that's just sick, Gavin. Really, I expected better from you. Can we please change the subject? I really don't like discussing my Bronie status with someone who doesn't live the lifestyle," Tyler complains.

"Did you just say Bronie? What the fuck is that? Is this some sort of club or something?"

"Not that you care, but yes. Bronies are a select group of men who appreciate the beauty and personalities of My Little Ponies," Tyler explains.

"And by *appreciate* I'm assuming you mean *jerk off to*," I say with a laugh.

"IT'S NOT LIKE THAT!"

I just nod, trying to contain my laughter and overall disgust from this conversation.

"So, did you close the deal and fuck Charlotte?" Tyler asks, changing the subject.

"Stop. I would never fuck Charlotte. I would make love to her gently," I tell him.

"Alright there, McSensitive Pansy Ass. Did you make sweet, sweet love to your beautiful goddess?" Tyler asks, folding his hands under his chin and batting his eye lashes at me.

"No, we didn't get that far. I did rip her thong, though," I tell him sheepishly.

"BOOM! That JUST happened! Maybe you really do have a penis hiding between your legs after all."

Before I can call Tyler a My Little Pony-fucking freak, he puts his phone up to his mouth and speaks into it.

"Siri, where is the closest Victoria's Secret?"

"*I do not understand the question, Hot Lover Boy Big Penis Man Titty Tickler.*"

Listening to Siri spout off the name Tyler makes her call him, I roll my eyes and shake my head.

"Don't judge me. Siri speaks the truth," Tyler says distractedly as he presses the speaker button and talks into his phone once again. "Siri, my friend needs to buy some thongs for a chick he almost banged. Where the fuck is Victoria's Secret?"

"I do not appreciate your tone of voice, Hot Lover Boy Big Penis Man Titty Tickler."

Tyler curses at his phone.

"Why exactly do we need to go to Victoria's Secret for thongs?" I question.

"Um, hello? Item number seven on the list. Buy that bitch some lingerie."

Damn, I forgot about that one. Come to think of it, I'm surprised I even know my name after what happened last night with Charlotte. I don't even need to close my eyes to remember what it felt like to have her small, warm hand wrapped around me. Things escalated quickly between us in my kitchen, and I hope to God she doesn't have any regrets because I want a repeat performance as soon as possible. One where I actually last more than a few seconds. I have no idea what any of this means. Is she going to break up with Rocco now? Was last night a fluke because she was a little buzzed and it will never happen again? Why the fuck can't vaginas come with instruction manuals?

"Siri, you are a worthless piece of shit," Tyler complains.

"I could say the same about you."

"You fucking whore! Take a note, Siri. Go fuck your mother."

"This note has been recorded and added to your Notepad."

"FUCK YOU!"

"I do not understand your request, but I could search the web for 'fuck you.'"

"How about you search the web for why you're such a cunt cake?"

"I don't think you appreciate me anymore, Hot Lover Boy Big Penis Man Titty Tickler."

"I'm sorry, Siri. I still love you."

"Impossible."

"PIPE THE FUCK DOWN AND TAKE A COMPLIMENT, YOU WHORE FACE BAG OF DICKS!"

Tyler tosses his cell in the center console and crosses his arms angrily in front of him.

"You seriously need a girlfriend. The relationship you have with Siri is disturbing," I tell him as we pull into the hospital parking lot.

"She's a bitch, but she's the only woman who understands me. And anyway, do you know any single women who would call me Hot Lover Boy Big Penis Man Titty Tickler?" he questions.

"I don't know any single women who could even just think that in their heads without throwing up in their mouths a little," I reply as I find a parking spot.

"Exactly. So, anyway, I'm going to guess your mom never told your dad about the whole 'shroom chocolate incident since I haven't heard about any hits out on me."

"You're lucky my dad never found out. Your body would be buried in a ditch somewhere."

"Aww, I think Carter would take it easy on me. That's the best trip he's ever had. You're mom probably got laid in the hospital," Tyler says with a frustrated groan. "I knew I should have stuck around longer. She probably would have thrown me a bone."

"In what universe would my mother ever throw you a bone?"

"In Tylerverse. Where there are rivers of beer and naked chicks servicing me all over the land," Tyler replies.

"I'M GOING UPSTAIRS to take a nap. I still don't feel all that great,"

my dad tells us as we walk into my parents' house an hour later.

"I could make you a snack if you'd like. Maybe some delicious chocolates?" Tyler shouts to his retreating back as my dad makes his way up the stairs. I shoot him a dirty look as the front door opens behind us and my mother walks in carrying an armload of paperwork.

"How's your father?" she asks, handing me the paperwork so I can set it on the foyer table.

"He's okay. He just went upstairs to lie down."

Tyler walks up next to me and winks at my mom.

"Hello, Claire. You're looking beautiful as always," Tyler says with a cocky smile.

My mom, who normally looks like she wants to chop off Tyler's balls and feed them to the nearest shark tank, gets a sudden gleam in her eye. This is not good.

"Hey there, hot stuff. How about you come over here and show Mama a little sugar," my mom says with a sultry purr to her voice that I've never heard before. It makes me wince and gag a little.

"Um, I don't … what?" Tyler squeaks.

My mom saunters over to Tyler with a sway of her hips and stops right in front of him, letting her tongue skim her bottom lip.

I'm going to puke. I'm totally going to puke all over the floor right now. What the fuck is she doing?

Mom presses her palm against Tyler's chest and leans in close until her lips are grazing his ear. "You're heart is beating so fast, big boy. Want Mama to make it all better?"

Tyler's face immediately turns ten shades of red, and his eyes are so wide I'm surprised they haven't popped out of his head. His fantasy has come to life and he's realizing it's really a nightmare.

"What's wrong, Tyler-pooh? I thought this is what you wanted?"

Tyler shakes his head back and forth frantically, looking over at me in a panic. As disgusting as this is to witness right now, I'm pretty sure Tyler is going to be scared straight when it comes to my mother and his sexual comments.

Mom drapes her arm around Tyler's shoulder and smiles at him. "Don't be afraid. I'll be gentle with you. I'll make sure to use the small strap-on."

She runs her finger down Tyler's cheek, and I'm pretty sure if I look close enough I'll see that he's wet himself. I'm suddenly cured of my nausea and totally on board with whatever warped plan Mom has brewing in her head right now.

"Um, I think there's been a mistake," Tyler stutters as he looks back and forth nervously between my mother and me. I just shrug at him and slide my hands in my pockets. He's not getting any help from me. I'm actually kind of proud of Mom right now. She is one hundred percent committed to this performance and will do whatever it takes to make Tyler back off, including scarring him for life.

"Come on, baby. Mama wants you to take it like a good boy," she coos.

"What?! No! That's okay. I don't need Mama to give me anything. Seriously, stop saying that!" Tyler says in a rush.

"Gavin, you should go and give us some time alone."

"NO! DON'T YOU DARE LEAVE ME!" Tyler shouts, reaching his hands out to me.

Moving out of his reach, I walk toward the door with a laugh as my mom wraps both of her arms around Tyler and squeezes him tight. "Sorry, dude. This is something I definitely don't want to see."

As I open the door and step out onto the front porch, I've forgotten all about my disastrous evening with Charlotte, thanks to my mom. Maybe it's time to scrap the list and just tell her how I feel.

I look back over my shoulder as the door closes behind me, and it's like something out of a horror movie. Tyler is screaming and flailing his arms all around and my mom reaches around from behind him, smacks her hand over his mouth, and pulls him back away from the door right before it closes.

Chalotte

Chapter 13
— Spiderman —

"IT WAS A disaster, Rocco. A total disaster," I complain with a sigh.

"I'm confused. How was it a disaster when you touched his penis?"

I glare at Rocco and signal the bartender for a refill of my Moscato. This is going to take a lot of booze.

"I think I'm going to need you to start at the beginning because I really don't understand what the problem is. You've been following the list we made and things are moving along quite well, if I do say so myself," Rocco replies, giving himself a pat on the back.

I've done something stupid. Something really, really stupid and now that it's done, I can't take it back. And no, I'm not talking about shoving my hand down Gavin's pants last night. That wasn't stupid, that was genius. Contrary to popular belief, I've never touched a penis before. Wait, that sounds bad. That sounds like everyone thinks I go around touching penises. No one thinks I'm a slut. At least I hope they don't. But I'm pretty sure they think I gave up the goods to some idiot in high school that was in Gavin's band. Let me set the record straight here–I didn't. I just kind of sort of made people think that. And by people, I mean Gavin. I know, I know. I should be hanging my head in shame, but what the fuck was I supposed to do? Nothing else was working. I tried going out with a few guys, I tried kissing a few guys ... nothing got a reaction out of him. And telling a teensy, tiny, little white lie about losing my virginity only made him go straight into the arms of that whore, Shelly Collins. He took her to prom! It should have been me, God dammit!

Shit, I'm getting off track here. I should probably do what Rocco says and start at the beginning. But the beginning was a really long time ago. I don't even remember when I actually fell in love with Gavin. It feels like forever. The problem is that we grew up together and our parents are best friends. Our families have always done everything together, and I'm like a little sister to him. I'm sure he still looks at me and sees a girl in pigtails that used to suck her thumb. That is NOT a turn-on. Wait, actually I think it is. I'm pretty sure they have porn for that. And if I'm not mistaken, Rocco even put it on our list that I should dress up as a schoolgirl for Gavin. Fuck. I probably should have started with that instead of the easy stuff like making him jealous and forcing him to look at my cleavage.

So, let's go back to the middle instead of the beginning. I met Rocco a few months ago at a sorority mixer, and he very quickly became one of my best friends. Obviously, he didn't understand why I turned down every single guy who asked me out, so I had to come clean with him. I had to tell him that I've been in love with my best friend practically since birth. One night over Pink Poodle martinis, Rocco started to make a list on a scrap of paper from my purse of things I could do to get Gavin to notice me. One thing turned into twelve, and now here I am with a fake gay boyfriend, a few drunken kisses, and one sloppy hand job.

Gavin probably thinks I'm a drunken idiot. I've kissed him twice now after copious amounts of alcohol, and last night, I took the bull by the horns. Or the penis by the base.

"Rocco, I can't rehash what happened last night. It's too mortifying."

Rocco puts his arm around my shoulder and pulls me close, giving me a squeeze. "I know, sweetie. But I haven't gotten laid in months, and I need to live vicariously through you. Tell me everything."

The bartender sets down another glass of wine in front of me, and I grab it, taking a huge gulp before beginning.

"So, you know that I went to Gavin's place last night so he could get his mind off of his dad being in the hospital. And of course, since I had a few beers, I had the courage to actually ask him about that kiss last week," I start. "As soon as I asked him, he got up from the couch and said he had to do something really important for work."

"Let me stop you right there. What was Gavin wearing?" Rocco asks.

I scowl at him and smack his arm. "Cut it out. It's bad enough that you drool over him every time you see him. What he was wearing doesn't matter."

To be honest, though, I really can't blame Rocco for drooling over Gavin. He is definitely drool-worthy. Gavin is six feet tall and the hottest guy I've ever seen. I don't even know when it happened—when he turned from annoying little boy to hot as fuck. It's almost like he went to sleep one night as a little kid and woke up a man—a man with a great body and a gorgeous face with a dimple in each cheek that is to die for. He has short brown hair, chocolate brown eyes, and sometimes if I'm lucky, day old stubble that I want to lick.

Rocco shakes his head sadly at me. "It ALWAYS matters, Charlotte. I need to get the visual correct if I'm going to help you. Was his T-shirt molded to his well-defined chest? Did his jeans hug his scrumptious ass? Was he wearing that cologne that smells like a crisp fall day?"

Rubbing my fingers against my temples and closing my eyes, I ignore Rocco's stupid questions. Why the hell did I think it would be a good idea to enlist my gay friend to help me out with this?

"If you want me to tell you what happened, shut up. This is

serious. I touched a penis for fuck's sake! I touched GAVIN'S penis! In all of our talks about this stupid list, we never discussed the specifics. Like how to give a proper hand job. It was probably the worst thing he's ever experienced. How am I ever going to face him again?" I whine.

"Stop being so dramatic. It couldn't have been that bad. If you touch the penis, the penis will be happy. I did have one guy, though, who would only touch my penis with his thumb and forefinger. Like he was trying to milk a cow. I'm not saying I have a ginormous penis or anything, but it's definitely bigger than a cow's teat. Tell me you didn't milk his penis," Rocco begs.

"It probably would have gone better if I had. He actually said 'ouch' and 'be careful.' I think I pulled too hard."

"What the fuck were you doing with his dick? You know those things need to stay attached, right?" Rocco questions me in horror.

"SHUT UP! I told you, I have no fucking experience with this shit. I just reached in and started yanking on it."

"I think my balls just ran away in fear. Oh look, there they go, right out the front door. GOOD-BYE, BOYS!" Rocco shouts with a wave to the door of the bar.

"I hate you. I really hate you," I complain.

Rocco laughs and pats me on the back. "No you don't. You love me. You're just so cute when you get mad. I promise, no more comments about your inadequate dick handling. Carry on."

I down the rest of my glass of wine and take a deep breath, determined to get through this horrific story quickly so I never have to speak of it ever again.

GETTING UP FROM the couch, I walked into the kitchen to see what was taking Gavin so long. I heard whispering coming from the other side of the fridge, so I headed in that direction. I really should have stopped after three beers. Alcohol gave me liquid courage, but I maybe had a bit too much at that point. All I could think about was ripping Gavin's clothes off of him.

I heard Gavin say *balls* and figured he was on the phone with work. *Is it weird that I'm strangely turned on every time Gavin talks about what he does for a living?*

Walking around the edge of the fridge, Gavin looked up at me in surprise with his phone still pressed against his ear. He didn't say a word as I moved in closer to him, but I saw his eyes flash back and forth between my boobs and my face. Sweet! Maybe the list Rocco made was actually working. Showing more cleavage was a great idea after all. Wait. What if he wasn't looking at my boobs? What if he was looking at a mole I have on my chest? Did I have a mole on my chest? Son of a bitch, what if it was a hairy mole and he was so overcome with disgust that all he could think about was this fucking mole?! Or it could be food. Oh holy Jesus, what if I had a piece of leftover pizza stuck to my chest? I could play it off, tell him I put a slice of pepperoni there so he could lick it off.

I decided to do the most logical thing and just pretended like I didn't have a hairy piece of mole pepperoni sticking to my tits.

Gavin slowly lowered the phone from his ear and continued to stare at me without saying a word.

"Are you done with work stuff?" I asked.

He nodded his head.

"We kissed the other night."

Might as well divert his attention from my pizza boobs.

He nodded again.

Fuck! Why won't he just say something! At this point, I might actually prefer it if he points and says, "HOLY MOLEY!"

I tried again. "What were you feeling when we kissed?"

I leaned in closer, hoping to distract him by my proximity. It didn't work. He looked away from my face and right down the front of my shirt.

"I HAVE NUTS!" he shouted suddenly.

Glancing down, I realized he was unzipping his pants. *Well, this escalated quickly. I guess we can ignore the talk and just go right for the good stuff.* I wrapped my hand around the back of his head and pulled his face to mine, slamming my lips against his.

I took my other hand and quickly tried to shove it down the front of his pants, but with my eyes closed, I misjudged where I was going and punched him in the stomach.

"OOOF!" he blurts against my lips. "I'm sorry, I'm sorry! I shouldn't have unzipped my pants. I have no idea why I did that! Don't hit me again!" Gavin said in a rush.

Shit! I don't want him to think I'm offended!

"I totally didn't mean to do that. I'm going to stick my hand down your pants now," I warned him.

"Oh my God," he mumbled as I cut him off with my lips and slid my hand inside his boxer briefs.

Oh fuck. I'm touching his penis. My hand is on his penis. I was so excited I didn't even realize how hard I was squeezing his penis. And thinking about it just makes me squeeze it even harder.

"Ouch!" Gavin winced and pulled away from my mouth.

Instead of letting up, I jerked in surprise when he shouted, bringing his penis with me. So basically, I was choking the life out of this thing and trying to detach it from his body. *WHAT THE FUCK AM I DOING?!*

"It's okay. It's fine. Just be careful," Gavin said before pulling me back to him and kissing me.

Be careful. I can do this. Just pretend it's a cat. Nice kitty. Nice, soft kitty.

Gavin pulled away again and I growled in frustration. I wanted his lips on me and he kept moving them.

"You're petting my penis," he stated.

Well, I WAS until you stopped me. QUIT IT!

"Stop talking," I told him.

I couldn't think when he talked. The sound of his voice made me feel all warm and gooey, and I wanted to do this right. I wanted him to feel good and maybe realize that by touching his penis, I love him.

Picturing every porn I've seen in my mind, except that weird one that Aunt Jenny showed me with people dressed up as Smurfs, I wrapped my hand around him and started moving it up and down slowly. Gavin groaned and closed his eyes, letting his head fall back against the wall.

I realized that we were wedged between the fridge and the counter, and it wasn't the most ideal location to be doing this, but I didn't care. *This is happening right the fuck now.*

Leaning forward, I placed my lips on his neck and let my tongue taste his skin. He groaned again and I picked up the pace with my hand, moving it up and down his smooth shaft.

I wondered if that slut Brooklyn really did all the things she said she did with him? I wanted to cut that whore for ever laying a finger on my Gavin. I didn't realize I was channeling my anger to Gavin's penis until he whimpered in pain. *Dammit. Focus, Charlotte! There are better ways to mark your territory than by dismembering the man you love.* Securing my lips to his neck once again, I nibbled and bit his skin before sucking it into my mouth.

There, take that, you skanky piece of trash! He's mine!

"Oh shit, Charlotte. Slow down," Gavin begged, wrapping one of his hands around my wrist and sliding the other into the edge of my jeans by my hip.

I ignored his warning and moved my hand harder and faster, up and down his length. He tried to hold my wrist tighter to get me to slow down, but I wasn't having any of that. His hips thrust into my hand, and it was the hottest thing I ever felt.

I am NOT stopping.

"Charlotte ... Jesus .... I'm gonna ... oh holy shit fuck ..."

I felt his fingers graze the skin of my hip, and I wanted more than anything for him to just dive right in like I did with him. I wanted him to touch me, but I was pretty sure he was beyond rational thought right now. His fingers tangled into the fabric of my thong resting on my hip, and he clutched it so tightly the fabric ripped.

He's going to come! I'm totally making him come! This is the best day ever!

"OKAY, SO ASIDE from the fact that you pet his dick like a cat, I don't see what the problem is," Rocco says when I pause with my story. "You might be surprised to know that I've had my dick pulled by a few of the ladies back in the day. You're not the only one who has no idea how to use one of those things. At least you got the hang of it."

"Sure, I got into a nice rhythm and he finished pretty fast. That was awesome. But in porn, they don't tell you what to do when it's all over. The scene just ends and there's no cleanup involved," I complain.

Rocco stares at me for a few minutes and then the light bulb comes on and his eyes widen.

"Oh dear God. What did you do with the jizz in your hand? Charlotte! What did you do with the jizz?!"

Biting my lip and squeezing my eyes closed so I don't have to see Rocco's face, I blurt it out quickly.

"I pulled my hand out of his pants and then sort of whipped my hand in his general direction to get it off. Then I just turned and walked out of his apartment."

Opening my eyes, I see Rocco with his hand over his mouth trying to contain his laughter.

"Oh no you didn't. Oh, Charlotte. You Spidermanned the one you love."

Chapter 14
– Cat Fight –

"AVA, ARE YOU home?" I shout into my parents' house as I walk through the front door.

Moving into the living room, I see a flash of naked, white ass streaking down the hall to the guest bathroom and Ava rearranging her skirt on the couch. Not one piece of her long, dark brown hair is out of place, and she looks like she just stepped off the pages of a fashion magazine. Her make-up is flawless and her blue skirt and matching tank top are perfectly pressed. Not at all what someone should look like who was just doing what I KNOW she was doing.

"Oh my God. Ava! Were you having sex on mom and dad's couch? That's disgusting. I sit on that couch," I complain.

She rolls her eyes. "Fuck off, twat. I laid a blanket down."

Glancing underneath her, I see the blanket in question.

"Son of a bitch! That's the comforter from my bed!" I yell with a stomp of my foot.

"Ooooh, the older sister. This is like a porn dream come true. Can I be on the bottom?"

My head whips around to the door of the hallway and I see Tyler standing there buttoning his shirt.

"Oh my God. I'm going to have to burn that blanket now. And the couch."

Tyler finishes with his shirt and walks over to the couch, plopping down next to Ava and throwing his arm over her shoulder.

"Don't worry, Charlotte, I only got a little Tyler juice on your blanket. It's all good."

Ava shoves Tyler away from her and gets up from the couch. "I'm finished with you. You can leave now."

Tyler pouts and stares up at her. "Babe, that wounds me. I'm delicate after my run-in with Claire the other day. Be gentle."

Ava rolls her eyes and walks over to the door, opening it up and pointing outside. "Aunt Claire made you wash her kitchen floor with a toothbrush and mow the lawn with a pair of scissors. Go away or I'll make you gargle toilet water."

Tyler stands up and saunters over to her. "Ooooh, kinky. I like that. Until next time. Unless you gave me the clap. In that case, call first."

Tyler whistles as he walks out the door and Ava slams it shut behind him.

"I cannot believe you had sex with that thing," I tell her as she comes back into the living room.

"You should be thanking me right now, you whore. I took one for the team to see if I could get any information on Gavin after you threw a web of spooge on his shirt," she complains.

"God dammit! Will you stop bringing that up!"

Ava shrugs, gathers up the blanket, and throws it behind the couch before taking a seat. "I'm sorry, but that's some funny shit. You threw sperm at him. You're like the creepy guy in Silence of the Lambs, throwing goo through the jail cell bars. At least you didn't hit him in the face with it."

I should have never trusted Ava with this information. She's my sister and I love her, but she never lets shit go. She still brings up every single time I've ever tattled on her when we were growing up in casual conversation. She's got the memory of an elephant and can tell everyone who asks the exact date, time, and outfit we were both wearing when I told Mom that she drew a picture of a penis in crayon on the back of my bedroom door when she was twelve.

"Since you decided to be a slut for the cause, tell me you at least got some information out of Tyler," I beg, taking a seat next to her.

"Tyler shouts the names of My Little Ponies when he comes. And he makes horse noises with his lips when he's going down on me."

My mouth opens and I gag.

"I know. It's weird. But it was kind of hot. If you ever tell anyone I said that I will smother you in your sleep," she warns.

"Can we get back to more pressing matters please? What did he say about Gavin?"

Ava sighs and leans back into the couch. "He didn't say much. That boy is loyal; I'll give him that. Every time I asked him about Gavin he would just say, 'Well, what does Charlotte think?' It was annoying. I even tried asking him when his penis was in my mouth, figuring it would distract him."

Eeew, I really don't want to picture Tyler's penis in ANYONE'S mouth, especially my sister's. He's a good-looking guy I guess. Around six feet tall with surfer blonde hair and blue eyes, but as soon as he opens his mouth it ruins everything.

"How do you talk with a penis in your mouth?" I question.

"It takes some practice. You have to know how to roll your *r*'s and really enunciate. I'm pretty good, but he still thought when I asked if Gavin liked you I said, 'Muff diving dike harlot.' He thought I was telling him I'm a slutty lesbian. It took me fifteen minutes to get him to focus after that."

Fuck! How in the hell am I going to find out how Gavin feels about what happened between us? Tyler was my last hope.

"I have a great idea. How about you find some balls and just tell Gavin how you really feel?" Ava suggests with a glare at me.

"Yeah, because that would go over really well. 'Oh hey, Gavin. So, I know we grew up together and we've been best friends since we were little. We usually tell each other everything but here's something new. Every time I'm around you I want to climb your face like a tree. Oh and you know how all my friends dared me to kiss you at the bar last week? Yeah, totally false. I just made that up because I've been dying to stick my tongue down your throat since I was twelve. No, please, stop laughing so hard. I'm serious.'"

I end my tirade and stare back at Ava.

"Yeah, that's probably pretty accurate. Okay, so what's left on Rocco's list?" she asks.

I heave out a sigh and throw my head back against the couch. "Dress up like a slutty school girl, get a flat tire and call him for help, take him to a sporting event and pretend like I know what's going on, and take naked pictures of him. But obviously that suggestion was for Rocco's benefit."

Ava shakes her head sadly at me. "Rocco isn't going to be able to keep his gayness contained for much longer. Did you know he called Dad the other day and asked him if he wanted to go to a game? Dad thought maybe he'd misjudged him and felt bad. Then Rocco told him the game was drag queen bingo. I think Dad put a hit out on him."

I hear the front door open and a few seconds later my mom walks into the living room.

"Why does it smell like sex in here? Ava, shouldn't you be at work?" she asks with her hands on her hips.

"I'm on my lunch break," Ava says casually.

Mom looks at her watch. "It's four o'clock."

"Snack break?" Ava replies with a shrug.

"AVA!"

"Um, I'm sick," she says, adding in a cough for good measure.

"I swear to Christ if you left work to come home and have sex in my house, I will stop paying your cell phone bill," Mom threatens.

"Oooooh, not the cell phone bill!" I reply in mock seriousness. "Careful, Ava. Mom's got her stern face on."

Ava and I both giggle while Mom stands there tapping her foot angrily.

"You two are both adults, so I have no problem saying this to you right now. You're a bunch of dicks."

"Mom, you said that to us when we were eight," I remind her.

"Well, now I really mean it. Charlotte, how's the job search coming along?" she asks as she takes her shoes off and moves into the room to sit in the chair across from us.

"Lousy. No one is hiring," I complain.

"You know you can always come and work for Seduction and Snacks," she reminds me.

My mom has been asking me to work for her ever since I was old enough to know what sex toys were. A part of me would love to go into the family business. I love my family and it would be awesome to work with them. The only thing holding me back right now is Gavin. It's bad enough that our families are close and we see each other a lot. If whatever this is between us completely implodes, not only would I have to see him at family get-togethers, I'd have to work side-by-side with him every day. What if he marries Brooklyn and I have to watch her coming into the office every day for a quickie? I can't work under those conditions. It would be best if I just find a job elsewhere.

"Mom, I can't work at Seduction and Snacks," I tell her.

"Why? What's so bad about working there? Do you have vibrator anxiety? I thought we went over this on your eighteenth birthday when I bought you that starter kit," Mom says with concern in her voice.

Both an upside AND a downside to having a mother who owns a sex toy store: she always wants to talk to you about sex and buys you vibrators for every holiday. And usually whips them out at the dinner table when you have guests over.

"Mom, I am not afraid of vibrators. If I'm not mistaken, you used to put a vibrator under my crib mattress to get me to sleep when I was a baby. You're lucky I don't turn narcoleptic every time I hear one buzzing."

"Well, if that's not the problem, what is? Seduction and Snacks is a very good company to work for. There are so many options for you to choose from with a degree in Communications," she tells me.

"I think you should be more concerned with the fact that you and Dad forked over ninety-thousand dollars in tuition for this fuckernutter to get a degree in talking when she can't even manage to say three little words to a certain someone." Ava crosses her arms over her chest and looks at me smugly.

"AVA!"

"WHAT?!" Mom and I both shout at the same time.

"Oh for fuck's sake, Charlotte. This is getting annoying. Mom, Charlotte is in love with Gavin," Ava states, crossing her arms in front of her.

"WHAT?!" Mom shouts again, looking back and forth between us with wide eyes.

"I am going to reach down your throat and rip out your ovaries, you fat cow!" I yell at her.

"Oh, I'm sorry, was that a secret?" Ava asks me, batting her eyelashes.

"AVA HAD SEX WITH TYLER!" I scream, pointing my finger at her.

"WHAT?!"

Either Mom's head is about to explode or she's having a stroke and can only speak one word. Whatever it is, I'm not about to let Ava win this shit. I'm small, but I'm scrappy. Even when we were little and she would get pissed at me and pull my hair, I always finished the fights and had her screaming for mom within seconds.

"You fucking HAG!" Ava screams at me. "Charlotte tried to give Gavin a pearl necklace!"

"Ava likes it when Tyler shouts My Little Pony names instead of hers!"

Before I can come up with another insult, Ava launches herself at me and grabs onto my hair. She yanks it hard and I scream in pain, reaching my own hand up and clutching onto a chunk of her dark brown locks. We're smacking, pulling, biting, screaming, and kicking for only a few seconds before Mom dives on top of us, trying to pull us apart.

"GIRLS! That's enough!" she yells, grabbing onto both of our arms as they flail all around, trying to gain purchase.

"Hey, sweet thing, I think I dropped my wallet under the-"

All three of us immediately stop screaming and fighting and turn our heads to the door as Tyler stands there with his bottom lip quivering.

"Mom AND daughters ... I never thought this day would come. God does exist."

Chapter 15

— You're a Labia —

"Seriously, Charlotte. You need to watch this. It's goats screaming like humans," Molly tells me in a fit of giggles as she stares at her iPhone.

Molly is nineteen and the youngest out of the three of us girls. Where Ava and I take after our dad with dark hair and dark eyes, Molly is the spitting image of my mom with her long blonde hair and spitfire personality.

"I don't have time for that shit right now, Molls. I need a sharp object that will poke a hole in a tire," I tell her distractedly as I look through all of the cupboards in the kitchen.

After our catfight a few days ago, Ava and I called a truce and she suggested I go with the whole flat tire item on the list next. Guys like a damsel in distress. Rocco assured me that it would be a good way to make Gavin feel like a man. He's under the impression that Gavin is probably more embarrassed about what happened last week than I am. I find that hard to believe, but whatever. He hasn't called or sent me a text since it happened and it's freaking me out.

"No, really. Come here and watch this. It's a Taylor Swift video and during the chorus, goats scream. Oh my God, this is the best thing I've ever seen," Molly says in between hysterical laughter.

Opening the silverware drawer, I pull out the largest butcher knife I can find.

"Jesus, put the knife away. I'll stop playing goat screaming videos," Molly says in a panic as she comes up behind me, staring nervously at the knife in my hand.

Rolling my eyes at her, I close the drawer with my hip and grab my purse off of the counter.

"I swear to God you never listen to anything that goes on in this house."

Molly follows behind me as I make my way to the front door.

"Oh, I heard all about you trying to beat the shit out of Ava. Why do I miss all of the good stuff?" Molly complains.

"Because you're in school. Or you're supposed to be. Why aren't you at school right now?"

Molly is five years younger than me and from an early age, she loved helping Aunt Claire out in the kitchen. Right now she's in school full-time earning her degree in Culinary Arts so she can be a pastry chef for one of Aunt Claire's stores.

"It's midterms week. I only have to go to class for my tests. So, remind me again why you're taking a knife with you to meet Gavin? I don't think gutting him like a fish will convince him that he loves you," Molly says with a laugh.

"No, but hopefully slashing my tires will."

Molly shakes her head at me. "I still don't understand how you could possibly be in love with Gavin. I mean, this is GAVIN we're talking about. He used to take the heads off of all of our Barbie's and then staple them to the ceiling. And you two used to fight constantly when we were kids. How many times did Mom and Aunt Claire have to break you guys up before you killed each other?"

She's right. We hated each other as kids. I don't even know why we didn't like each other. Every time we were in the same room together, someone wound up crying.

"THAT DRESS LOOKS funny on you," Gavin told me, grabbing my favorite *I can be a teacher* Barbie from my hands and then throwing it across the room.

"You're a dumb stupid head. Go pick up my Barbie right now," I said with a stomp of my foot.

"You're such a baby. I can't believe you called me a dumb stupid head," Gavin replied with a laugh.

"I'm not a baby. YOU'RE a baby!" I shouted.

"I'm nine. That's practically an adult."

"Fine, then you're dumb stupid adult!" I yelled angrily.

"You're a labia," Gavin replied.

"What's a labia? That's dumb."

Gavin shrugged. "I heard it the other day. My mom said it's a rare fish that no one ever talks about."

"I want a labia," I told him.

"You can't have a labia. You ARE a labia. Labia face," he said, turning his back on me and walking away.

I was so angry that I hurtled my six-year-old body at him and wrapped my arms around him from behind, tackling him to the ground.

"GAAAAAAAAAAAAAH MY NUTS!" Gavin screamed in pain as we crashed to the floor and he flung me off of him.

I stood up quickly and stared down at him angrily.

"You're mean. I don't like you."

Gavin scrambled up off of the ground and before I knew it, he charged at me and slammed his head into my hip, knocking us both back on the ground.

We were both screaming and crying when my mom and Aunt Liz came running into the room.

"What the hell is going on?" Aunt Claire shouted as she picked Gavin up off of the floor and my mom helped me up.

"SHE HURT MY NUTS!" Gavin cried, pointing at me.

"HE CRASHED HIS HEAD INTO MY NOO-NOO-COW!"

I wailed, holding my hands between my legs.

"Jesus God. He head-butted her in the vagina," my mom muttered.

"I hope these two get married some day or this is just going to get worse," Aunt Claire replied.

Opening the door, I lift up my arm and wave good-bye to Molly with the knife. "Wish me luck. If this flat tire thing doesn't work, I might have to punch him in the nuts."

"I have no idea what that means, but have fun with that. Bring me home some mint chocolate chip ice cream."

THIRTY MINUTES LATER, after I called Gavin and told him my *dilemma*, I'm standing next to my car on the side of the road listening to the hiss of the air leaving the tire. I may have been a little overzealous in my stabbing. There's no way Gavin is going to believe my car just got a flat on its own. He's a guy. Guys know these things. I don't have time to worry about that, though. I see his car pulling off the side of the road right behind mine. Leaning against the hood, I try to look as sexy as possible. Rocco suggested I pretend like I'm in a porno. Ultimate guy fantasy: a woman having car problems on the side of the road.

Gavin gets out of his car and walks up to me with a smile. "Flat tire, huh?"

Shit. He already knows. Time to distract him.

"Hey there, handsome. I could use a little help pumping myself back up," I tell him in my best Marilyn Monroe voice.

Gavin looks at me quizzically. "Are you getting sick? You're voice sounds funny."

Fucking Rocco.

Clearing my throat, I turn away from him and walk up to the

front tire. "I don't know what happened. I was driving home when all of a sudden I had a hard time steering. My car was swerving all over the place. I was so scared."

Gavin glances down at the tire, then back up at me and doesn't say a word.

Son of a bitch! Do cars lose control when they get a flat tire?? I should have googled it.

"Aww, you're okay now. It's totally normal. Cars always do that with a flat tire," Gavin tells me.

Oh thank God.

"So, do you want a lift home or something?" he asks.

"Uh, I kind of thought you could just change the tire," I tell him.

Gavin nods his head. "Right, right. Change the tire. I can totally do that."

He turns and walks around me, opening up the door to the backseat and sticking his head in.

"What are you doing?"

Pulling his head back out, he turns and looks at me. "Changing the tire."

"I think the stuff's in the trunk," I tell him in confusion.

He laughs awkwardly and slams the door closed. "Oh, yeah. I totally knew that. I was just checking to make sure you didn't do any damage … to the … backseat and stuff."

While he quickly walks to the trunk, I reach in through the driver's side window and hit the trunk release button. Moving to the back of the car, I see him standing there just staring into the trunk.

"Everything is under that floor mat," I tell him, pointing to the middle of the trunk.

"I know. I was just … um … assessing the situation. Thinking about my plan of attack," he replies, reaching into the trunk and flipping back the mat.

I watch as he leans in and grabs the tire iron, flipping it up in the air casually as he turns and smiles at me. He reaches his arm out to catch it as it comes back down, but instead of catching it, he smacks his hand against it and the thing goes flying out into the middle of the road. His smile falls and he races over to quickly pick it up.

With his head down and the tire iron clutched tightly to his chest, he walks right by me and up to the tire. I'm pretty sure he's trying to look cool, and I am not about to call him out on it since I stuck a fucking butcher knife into my tire to get him here.

Squatting down on his knees next to the tire, he attaches one end of the iron to a nut and starts to turn it.

"Um, you need to jack the car up first," I remind him.

"I know that. I always loosen the screws first."

"They're called lug nuts."

"Well, where I come from, we call them screws."

"We both come from Ohio. I'm pretty sure they call them lug nuts everywhere," I say with a laugh.

"Are you trying to tell me how to change a tire? I know how to change a tire," he complains with a huff, grunting as he puts all of his muscle into trying to loosen the nut.

Oh my God. He doesn't know how to change a tire.

"You don't know how to change a tire," I mutter.

Shit! Rocco is going to kill me. This is so not going to make Gavin feel like a man. I need to shut the fuck up.

Gavin drops the tire iron to the ground with a *clang* and stands up, stalking over to me.

"I totally know how to change a tire," he argues, as we stand toe-to-toe.

"Fine. What's the part on the tire where the air goes?" I question.

He purses his lips and stares down at me. "It's an air-tube-put-inner-thing."

It's kind of cute that he's trying to act like he knows what he's talking about. But it's also a little irritating. I have a flat tire and he was supposed to be the big man and fix it for me so he could feel better about what happened the other night. My dad taught me when I was five how to change a tire.

"Actually, it's a valve stem," I tell him with a smile.

"Whatever! It has nothing to do with changing the actual tire so who cares?!" he complains.

"I can't believe you don't know how to change a tire. You're a guy and you have a penis. You should have been born knowing how to change a tire!"

Gavin puts his hands on his hips and glares at me. "Yeah, well you're a girl and you have a vagina. Does that mean you can waltz over to that field over there, squat down, and pop out a baby?"

The way we're arguing reminds me of when we were little. We haven't done this in a long time. It always pissed me off when I was young. Now it turns me on. Gavin is so hot standing here in front of me on the side of a deserted road. My eyes move away from his, and I find myself staring at his lips.

I open my mouth to fire off a smart-ass reply to his vagina comment when I'm suddenly pulled up against him and his mouth crashes down to mine.

Maybe this whole flat tire thing actually worked.

Chapter 16
— Children of the Corn —

GAVIN ENDS THE kiss before I'm ready for it to be finished and pulls away from me. He opens up the back seat of the car and jerks his head. "Get in."

I don't even hesitate. I have no idea why I'm getting in the back seat of my car, and I don't care as long as it involves more kissing. Quickly crawling into the car, I turn around to find Gavin getting in beside me. I grab onto the front of his shirt as he slams the door closed behind him and pull him against me, our mouths colliding so hard that our teeth clank together.

"Ouch!"

God dammit! Once again I'm putting him in pain. At least it wasn't his penis this time.

Moving back slowly this time, I press my lips to his. His tongue eases its way inside my mouth, and I can't stop the groan when I feel it slide against my own. One of his arms wraps around my waist and he slides my butt across the seat, leaning his body against mine to get me to lie back. All of this happens really quickly, though, and my head smacks against the window.

"Fucking hell!" I shout, reaching up to rub the back of my head.

"Shit! I'm sorry, are you okay?" he asks in a panic.

"I'm fine. Totally fine," I reassure him. I don't care if I have a head wound that is spraying blood all over the interior of my car; we aren't stopping.

Scooting myself lower onto the seat this time, Gavin turns his body and moves between my legs, bumping his own head on the ceiling.

Seriously? Can we catch a fucking break here?

Twisting and turning our bodies to try and get into a comfortable position, there's a bunch of swearing, more body parts smacking into various pieces of the car's interior, and the windows are starting to fog up from our exertion. This is so not as hot as it is in the movies. Why the fuck are back seats so small?

After ten minutes of us scrambling around, we're finally both on our sides facing each other, my back pressed up against the seat.

"I should turn on some music or something," Gavin tells me as he starts to move away from me.

Wrapping my arms around his neck, I pull him back to me. "Don't even think about moving or it will take us another hour to find comfortable positions."

Gavin laughs, moving his hand up to brush a strand of hair out of my eye.

"Are we going to talk about last week?" he asks.

I shake my head. "I really don't want to talk right now. You should just take your pants off."

Gavin stares at me blankly for a minute and I wonder if maybe that was too much. Before I can tell him I was just kidding so it's not awkward, he quickly reaches down and undoes his jeans, sliding them right off of his body and then ripping his shirt off of his head in five seconds flat, tossing everything onto the floor next to us. I feel like it's only fair that I do the same. I pull my shirt off and lift my hips, shimmying out of my skirt and kicking it up to the front seat.

"Oh my God. You're naked," Gavin whispers in awe.

At least I think it's awe. It could be shock. Or fear. Fuck, I hope it's not fear.

"Do you want me to put my clothes back on?"

"Don't you dare put your clothes back on. This is the best day EVER," he replies. He places his palm flat on my chest and runs it down the front of my body. I swallow nervously as he touches me. Gavin has never touched me like this. NO ONE has ever touched me like this. He's right. This is the best day ever.

Leaning up, I press my lips to his. He immediately deepens the kiss and pulls me underneath him. Wrapping my legs around his hips, I pull him against me and holy fuck is he hard. He's hard because of me. I mean, I know it happened before, but I was touching his penis. If a feather touched his penis he'd probably get hard. I haven't even touched him yet. He wants me and I want him and this is totally going to happen right now. I don't care if we're in the back seat of a fucking Honda.

Okay, I totally care that we're in the back seat of my shitty car. This is like the worst cliché in history. Girl loses virginity in the back seat. What if someone drives by? What if someone looks in the window? Gavin is still kissing me and his hands are pushing down my underwear and all I can think about is someone staring in the window. I stopped next to a cornfield. Are the Children of the Corn gathering around the car getting ready to kill us?! He who walks behind the rows!

"Did you just call me Malachai?" Gavin asks, pulling his head away from me.

It's never a good idea to call a guy by another man's name when you're about to have sex, even if it's a homicidal maniac dressed like an Amish kid.

"Ha! What? No! I said, 'May I lick..I,'" I fumble.

"If you want to lick yourself, go right ahead." He laughs. "That might be kind of hot."

Pushing all thoughts of Malachai staring at us with a bloody sickle in his hand, I help Gavin remove his boxer briefs, and then he helps me slide my underwear off. I quickly pull his body back down to mine.

This time when he kisses me, I stop thinking. All I do is feel. His hands run over every inch of my body he can reach, and before I know it, I feel his fingers sliding between my legs. While his tongue tangles with mine and his fingers ghost over my clit, I sigh into his mouth and try not to think about the fact that I've never gotten a Brazilian. I keep everything nice and tidy down there, so it's not like he's going to get his fingers tangled or anything, but maybe I should have taken my mother up on her offer to go with her when she went to *her* appointment the other day. Something about going somewhere with my mother where we're both naked from the waist down, spread-eagle on a table, and letting a stranger paw around down there with hot wax didn't sound appealing. Go figure.

Oh sweet Jesus his fingers ...

Working for a sex toy manufacturer has definitely given him some skills. He uses just the right amount of pressure as his fingers gently circle my clit, and I can't stop the sounds escaping from my mouth as he slowly pushes one inside me.

My best friend is diddling me. This is totally happening!

"Fuck, you feel amazing," Gavin whispers against my lips as he holds his finger still inside of me and moves his thumb back and forth right where I need him.

Keep talking. Holy hell, keep talking.

"You're so wet and soft and it's so cool you don't shave or wax."

Wait, what? That's not hot.

"Did you just say I'm hairy?" I question on a gasp as he adds a second finger to the first.

I have a hairy wildebeest vagina. That's what he's saying, isn't it?

"What?! No! That's not what I meant!" he quickly adds as his fingers continue sliding in and out of me.

This feels good. Fuck no, this feels AMAZING. But all I can think about right now is that he thinks my vagina feels like an English sheepdog. All that hair falling down over the top of its eyes so it can't see where it's going. You know, if my vagina had eyes. It could be a scary movie: If the Vagina had Eyes. Rogue vaginas pissed off because they're so hairy, hiding in abandoned houses, waiting to bring down their wrath on unsuspecting townspeople. Wait, didn't Big Bird have a dog like that named Barkley on Sesame Street? Gavin is going to start calling my vagina Barkley.

I'm so preoccupied with my sheepdog vagina that I don't immediately notice Gavin is reaching his one arm down to the floor; the arm that isn't busy reaching into the horror story that is my vagina. He fumbles around for a few seconds before coming back with a condom in his hand.

"I swear I don't always carry these around with me. Aunt Jenny gave them to me a few weeks ago and they've been in my wallet ever since," he reassures me as he sees me staring at the little foil packet in his hand.

"I'm fine. It's totally fine. Of course you should carry condoms. You need those for sex. The sex that you have. The sex that everyone has," I ramble.

Everyone but me. Oh shit, I should really come clean and tell him I've never done this before. I don't have time to confess that little white lie, though, because he's back to kissing me again and putting on the condom at the same time. This is happening.

He positions himself at my opening, and since his nimble fingers got me nice and wet before Barkley made an appearance, he starts to slide right in like it's no big deal. This is really happening and it's a big deal and oh my holy fuck JESUS MOTHER OF FIRE BURNING HELL THIS HURTS!

My thighs clamp down like vises on his hips, and I squeeze my eyes closed as he pushes the rest of the way inside me.

Ouch, ouch, ouch, ouch, fucking holy shit ouch.

"Holy shit. What the fuck? Oh my God. Charlotte, why the hell didn't you say something?!" Gavin curses as he holds himself still and winces like he's the one in pain. FUCK YOUR MOTHER! The only pain being had right now is by me and my vagina.

"Oh shit, oh shit, oh shit, oh my God I'm sorry. Are you okay? WHY DIDN'T YOU SAY SOMETHING?!" Gavin shouts.

"Telling you I'm a virgin is not exactly romantic," I fire back.

"God dammit! The only reason I even had sex with Shelly in high school was because I thought you had sex with DJ! Fuck! Your dad is going to kill me!" he complains.

"Can we NOT talk about my father right now?" I shout.

"We can't talk about your father, we can't talk about you being a virgin, what the fuck CAN we talk about?!" he yells.

"Are we really going to argue about this right now when your penis is inside of me?!" I scream back.

We lie there, breathing heavy and staring at one another, until Gavin's shoulders droop and he leans his forehead down against mine.

"You should have told me," he whispers before pulling back and kissing my cheek. "I hurt you."

He kisses my cheek, my nose, my eyes, and finally my lips. "We should stop. It shouldn't be like this … in the back seat of your car. You should have music and candles and flowers."

"We are not stopping. I'm okay now, I swear. The deed is done. I am no longer a virgin, thank you very much," I remind him.

"I want this to be good for you," he pleads.

"It IS good for me. I swear."

I pull him back to me and kiss him. After a few minutes, he begins to move against me and this time, I'm vocal with my *ouch*.

"Okay, maybe it isn't going to be THAT good. I'm sorry. It's not you, it's me. We're parked next to a corn field and I'm pretty sure there are killer children out there waiting to bust in the windows and stab us," I tell him.

"I knew you said Malachai before. And don't worry, I can totally fix this situation," Gavin says.

I start to protest as he moves away from me again, but he just reaches down to the floor and fumbles around again for a few seconds. He pulls his arm back and in his hand is the world's tiniest bullet vibrator.

"Did you just pull a vibrator out of your jeans?"

"Yes, yes I did. See? My job is TOTALLY awesome," he says with a smile as he presses a button and the little silver ball fires up.

"Don't guys feel like less of a man if they have to use a vibrator on a woman?" I question.

"If you have an orgasm, that's all that matters to me. And you WILL have an orgasm. Ten out of ten women surveyed got off with this little guy," he tells me, sliding his hand between us.

"It's so hot when you talk shop," I tell him with a groan as he gently presses the bullet to my clit.

"Holy hell, make that eleven out of eleven women," I moan as he holds the bullet in place and slowly starts to move inside me.

It only takes me thirty seconds to have my first orgasm with a guy. And not just any guy—Gavin. And luckily, he doesn't take after his best friend and shout the names of My Little Pony when he comes during sex; he just shouts my name.

Chapter 17
— Numb Vagina —

"I WANT TO try something," Gavin tells me later that night as we lie curled up together on his bed.

All in all, losing my virginity went pretty well, if I do say so myself. There was no awkward silence after it was over and nothing felt weird at all. It just felt ... right. Everything feels right, aside from the fact that I had sex with my best friend and I haven't come clean yet about what I did to get us to this point. Gavin assumes I broke up with Rocco. Gavin doesn't know Rocco is my gay fake boyfriend and that I used Rocco just to make him jealous. How in the hell does one even start an admission like that? I need more time to figure this out before I tell him. Not a lot of time, just enough to make him fall madly in love with me and not care about the fact that I deceived him.

Gavin's palm runs up the inside of my thigh and I forget all about my fake boyfriend.

"I'm pretty sure you already tried that and it was a success." I laugh as he pushes my skirt out of the way and runs his fingertips along the edge of my underwear.

Kissing my cheek, he scoots his body down the bed and situates himself between my legs with his chin resting on my thigh. I watch his face as he stares at his fingers that continue to lightly skim over my underwear. My breath catches at his fierce concentration. He places a kiss on the inside of my thigh and then kisses his way up my leg, his fingers working their way under the edge of my underwear.

"What are you doing?" I whisper, following it up with a soft moan when he pulls my underwear to the side and then presses his lips right to my clit.

"Shh, just close your eyes," he tells me.

I have no choice when I feel his tongue dart out and circle me. My eyes close automatically and I arch my back as he licks me slowly.

So this is what I've been missing all these years. Holy Jesus.

He flattens his tongue and adds more pressure as he laps at me, like he's licking an ice cream cone. A vagina-flavored ice cream cone. Dairy Queen should put that on their menu. I would buy one for Gavin every single day.

He leans in closer and his lips join his tongue as he sucks and licks at me. It feels amazing ... for about ten seconds. And then something weird happens. I know he's still down there because I've opened my eyes and I'm staring right at the top of his head between my legs, but suddenly, I don't feel him there anymore. I see his head moving, I witness his tongue darting out every few seconds as he goes to town on me, but I feel nothing. This isn't a dream is it? One of those weird wet dreams where you're just about to come and then wake up? What the fuck is going on?

Bringing my hands up to my face, I rub my palms roughly against my eyes, pulling them away and looking back down between my legs.

Okay, I'm awake and this isn't a dream. Am I suddenly paralyzed from the waist down? Oh holy shit, I've just gone paraplegic! I read about that happening to a woman in Brazil. She was just sitting there at the dinner table when all of a sudden she couldn't feel her legs, and now she's in a wheelchair. I DON'T WANT TO BE IN A WHEELCHAIR THE REST OF MY LIFE! Can oral sex cause paralysis?

Glancing over to the nightstand next to Gavin's bed, I see my iPhone. He's still busy so it's not like he's going to notice if I pull up Google on my phone. I can wiggle my toes so it can't be that bad.

Damn, I need a pedicure. I should schedule one for tomorrow.

I haven't made any encouraging noises in a few minutes; I should probably do that so Gavin doesn't think anything is amiss. I don't want him to never do this again. The first couple of seconds were mind-blowing. Maybe that's how oral sex is. You have to build up your tolerance for it. Maybe next time he does this, I'll feel it for thirty seconds. Then after that, a full minute.

Fuck, why did I put my phone so far out of reach?

"Oh yeah, just like that," I say, trying to keep the boredom out of my voice.

Do you have to wait a certain amount of time between orgasms? Maybe it's like swimming after eating. Lifting my arm up, I check my watch. It's been two hours since my last orgasm. Is that too soon to have another one?

"You taste so good, baby," Gavin says in between licks.

"Um, thanks?" I mutter.

It makes me feel all warm and fuzzy that he called me *baby*. Too bad that warmth doesn't travel to my vagina. What if it's broken? Did we break it when I lost my virginity?

"Mmmmm, yeah," I add in a breathy voice so he doesn't stop.

I've heard girls say that in pornos when they're getting oral. That sounds about right. I don't want to tell him to stop. What if he thinks I don't like what he's doing? I'm assuming I would like what he's doing if I could feel it. He's got a great tongue and he knows how to use it. I think.

Did I remember to turn off my straightening iron at home? Mom will kill me if I left that thing plugged in again.

Pretending like I'm really into this, I moan some more and start moving my hips, angling myself closer to the nightstand at the same time. Reaching my arm out slowly and making sure he's still preoccupied with my broken vagina, I grab my phone.

Gavin glances up at me and I quickly bring both of my hands to my chest, hiding my phone against me. "Oh yeah, that feels so good. Keep going."

He looks away from me and keeps on keeping on. I make sure to continue moving my hips against him as I pull up the message app on my phone and send off a quick text to Molly.

Can u make sure I unplugged my straightener? Thx.

Pressing *send*, I glance down at Gavin. Man, he's really working it. Lips, tongue, fingers ... if only I could feel it. My phone vibrates and I hide the noise with another loud moan while I check my messages.

It's unplugged. Whatcha doin? I'm bored. – Molly

"Don't stop," I mutter as I type a reply to my sister.

Eh, nothing much. I'm prob not going to be home till late. Wanna go shopping tmrw?

I wonder if those shoes I wanted are still on sale at Macy's? They were so cute. Rocco would love them.

"Does it feel good? Are you close?" Gavin asks.

Quickly hiding my phone next to my hip, I smile down at him and nod my head. "Oh, so good. I'm really close."

He dives right back in, and when I'm sure he's not paying attention to me, I bring up Google and type in *numb vagina*.

Hmmm, sitting for long periods of time can cause a numb vagina. I didn't really sit down today for more than a few minutes, so that's not it. Nerve damage? Oh fuck no! What if I have damaged nerves? That doesn't sound like something easy to fix. "Hey, Doc, so I have this problem with broken nerves in my vagina. Get your scalpel, STAT!"

Certain yeast infection remedies have ingredients in them that soothe and cause numbing. That sounds about right, but I don't have cottage cheese vagina so that isn't it either. Clicking on the ingredients, I see one right at the top called Lysine. I've heard of that before. It's in a few of my plumping lip-glosses. Looking away from my phone and down at Gavin, I ponder this for a few minutes while he slurps and licks away at my vagina. I look back at my phone and then down at Gavin. Back and forth, back and forth.

SON OF A BITCH!

Throwing my phone down on the bed, I reach down with both hands and grab handfuls of Gavin's hair, pulling his head up.

"Hey, I wasn't finished yet," he complains.

"Did you put chapstick on before we got in bed?" I question.

He starts to move his head back down between my legs, but I clutch tighter and hold him in place.

His face scrunches up in pain as he stares at me. "Ouch! What? Chapstick? I don't know. I think so."

"Give me the chapstick."

Gavin looks at me like I've lost my mind. "I'm kind of in the middle of something here."

"GIVE ME THE CHAPSTICK!" I scream.

He scrambles up on his knees and fumbles in the back pocket of his jeans, quickly pulling out the small tube of MEDICATED FUCKING CHAPSTICK.

Snatching it out of his hand, I read the ingredients.

"Active ingredients include camphor, cooling menthol, and phenol to relieve pain."

Gavin continues to stare at me while I shoot him a dirty look.

"What?"

Sighing, I toss the chapstick at his chest. "You put on medicated chapstick before you went down on me."

I can see by the perplexed look on his face; he still doesn't get it.

"Tell me something. How did your lips feel right after you put on that chapstick?"

He thinks about this for a minute before responding. "Tingly. And then they numbed a little. I don't see what the problem is. I wanted to make sure my lips were nice and smooth before I did this. You should be thanking me."

Pulling my skirt down to cover myself, I scoot back on the bed until my back is against the headboard. "Say that again, out loud."

"You should be thanking me," he replies.

"No! Not that part. Sweet fucking hell … the part about your lips."

He huffs at me and puts his hands on his hips. "Tingly. And then they numbed a lit … Ohhhhhhhhhh."

He scrunches up his nose and winces at me. "So the whole time you couldn't—"

"Nope."

"And you were just making those noises so that—"

"Yep."

He lets out a huge sigh, crawling up the bed and then sitting next to me, our shoulders touching as we both lean against the headboard and stare blankly at the wall across the room.

"So, you wanna watch a movie or something?" he asks after a few minutes of silence.

I shrug. "Sure."

Well, it's good to know there's no awkwardness between us.

Chapter 18
— Just Say No to Weird Sex —

"I CAN'T BELIEVE you had sex for the first time in the back seat of a car. You are such a whore," Ava tells me over the phone.

Even her annoying judgment can't put me in a bad mood right now. I had sex with Gavin. I had sex with Gavin and I had not one, but two orgasms. Whoever invented vibrators should be king of the world.

"Did you tell him you love him yet?" Ava questions as I pull into Gavin's driveway and check myself in the rearview mirror one last time before getting out of my car.

"No, not yet. There's one more thing I want to check off of my list before I do that," I inform her as I make my way up his front walk.

"Please tell me you aren't doing the food one," Ava begs.

"What? Why? That's a fun one. And now that we've got the whole virginity thing out of the way, it will be awesome," I explain.

"Alright, fine. But don't say I didn't warn you," she tells me ominously before I roll my eyes and end the call.

Taking a deep breath, I reach my hand up and knock on his door. It's been a few days since the whole losing of the virginity thing, but I am happy to say that it hasn't been awkward between us at all. Gavin has been busy with work but we've talked on the phone every day. Before I finally admit that I love him and that I've spent all these months using a list Rocco made of things that would get him to fall in love with me, I want to have some fun.

The door opens and Gavin stands in the doorway, looking me up and down. "Nice coat."

He smiles at me and pushes the door open wider so I can come in. I borrowed one of Molly's white chef coats for the evening. And I'm not wearing anything underneath it.

"Are you cooking me dinner?"

I laugh and slide my hand into his, pulling him through the apartment and into his kitchen. "Nope, you know I can't cook. I've got something better planned," I tell him.

Stopping next to the fridge, I turn around to face him and unbutton the front of the coat until it's draped open and I'm just standing in a matching black lace bra and thong.

"Never mind. That coat sucks," he mutters as he stares at me.

He moves to come closer and I hold up my hand in front of him. "Nope. You just stay right there and close your eyes."

Gavin does as I ask and I quickly turn to the fridge and open the door.

"Are you making yourself a snack?" he asks with a laugh.

"Shush! Don't move and keep your eyes closed."

Bending down to stare into the fridge, I have a moment of doubt as I stare at the vast emptiness in front of me. How the hell am I going to do this? I knew I should have stopped at the store before I came here. Glancing around quickly, I grab the first bottle I see and quickly shut the door. Pulling up on the lid, I squirt the best upside down heart I can manage on my chest.

"Okay, you can open your eyes now," I tell him.

Gavin blinks his eyes open and stares. "Wow. Okay. Still hot. But what is that?" he asks, pointing to the heart.

"It's mustard. And you're going to lick it off me," I tell him with a confident smile.

This was such a better idea when I imagined it with chocolate sauce in my head.

"Mustard ... I'm going to ... yeah. That's hot. That's totally hot. I'm okay with this."

He walks up to me and gulps before lowering his head slower than I've ever seen him move. He scrunches up his face like he's in pain, and I'm starting to get a complex here.

"Is something wrong? I have a heart on my boobs that needs to be removed with your tongue," I remind him.

His mouth is hovering a few inches from my boobs, and he shakes his head back and forth quickly. "Nope. Nothing wrong. Nothing wrong at all. You are totally hot and I am going to lick this ... mustard off of you. I'm going to do it and it's going to be awesome."

Right now it sounds like he's giving himself a pep talk instead of reassuring me that he's good.

I know it's not chocolate sauce, but come on! Half naked woman standing here! I close my eyes as he starts to move forward again and right when I feel his warm breath on my chest and anticipate the feel of his tongue against my skin, I hear a gagging sound. Popping my eyes open, I look down at him.

"Are you gagging right now? Oh my God, Gavin! You're totally gagging when your mouth is right by my boobs!" I shout.

"It's ... not ... your ... boobs! I ... love ... your ... boobs!" he yells, gagging in between each word as he backs away.

"I cannot believe you're gagging!" I tell him, stomping my foot.

"Oh God, I'm sorry! I hate ... mustard. Oh Jesus, I thought I could do this but I can't. It's ... mustard ... fuck ... mustard is ... uuugghh ... mustard."

"WILL YOU STOP SAYING *MUSTARD* IF IT MAKES YOU SICK?!" I shout, reaching for a towel on the counter and quickly wiping the mustard heart off of my chest.

"Why the hell do you have mustard in your fridge if you hate it?" I demand.

"I don't know! I'm a dude. Dudes always have mustard in their fridge!"

"There, is that better?" I ask, tossing the towel into the sink and holding my arms out.

"Yes, much better," he tells me with a sigh as he moves back toward me.

He wraps his arms around my waist and pulls me up against him. Just as soon as our bodies touch, he pushes me away and takes a step back.

"Nope, not better. I can still smell it. Oh Jesus, it's so mustardy!"

His hand is covering his mouth at this point and he's bent over at the waist. In an angry huff, I turn around and march back to the fridge, flinging the door open and grabbing random items. I take the lid off of the first bottle in my arsenal, whirl around, and start pitching it in his general direction. A-1 sauce rains down on his head and all over the kitchen floor.

His head jerks up as I empty the bottle and then toss it to the side, flipping up the lid on the squeeze-bottle of ketchup tucked under my arm before bringing it up above my head in both hands.

"You wouldn't."

"Oh, I would," I threaten before squeezing hard on the bottle. An arc of ketchup flies out and hits Gavin right in the chest.

He blinks at me in shock and then charges. Squealing, I throw the ketchup bottle to the ground and turn to run, but my foot slides right through a ketchup/A-1 mixture and I slip across the floor, landing right on my ass. Gavin jumps over me and opens the fridge, quickly turning around and dumping a jar of black olives and all the juice on top of my head.

"Eeew, eew, eew! Black olives are disgusting!" I screech.

"Yeah, how do you like it now, bitch!"

I stop screaming and glare up at him.

"Oops, my bad. Please don't kill me," he pleads.

"Gavin, you seriously need to get your mailing address changed. I'm getting tired of bringing over your—"

Uncle Carter stops at the doorway to the kitchen and looks back and forth between the two of us. I quickly pull the chef coat closed and avoid looking at him while I button it back up.

"Hey, Dad. So, what's new?" Gavin asks casually as he leans against the fridge.

Reaching over, I smack him in the leg and hold my hand out to him with an angry glare. He quickly grabs my hand and pulls me up off of the floor, moving me behind him so I'm not standing in front of his father, half-naked and covered in black olive juice.

"Well, at least you're not naked with Tyler again," Uncle Carter says with a sigh.

Gavin looks at me and whispers. "Don't ask."

Uncle Carter turns and walks out of the kitchen.

"Follow me," he shouts back to us.

Gavin and I stare at each other for a few minutes before he shrugs and grabs my hand, pulling me into the living room behind his dad. We find him sitting on the couch with his elbows on his knees and his hands clasped. I'm not going to lie, I'm a little freaked out right now. Uncle Carter is usually never this quiet. Is he going to yell at us? Be disappointed that we're kind of sort of together and haven't told the family?

"I was really afraid of this happening," Uncle Carter finally says with a sigh as we stand in front of him with our heads bowed like two kids at the principal's office.

Oh my God, here it comes. He's going to tell us what a bad idea it is for us to be together. He knows Gavin doesn't love me and that it's only going to end in disaster.

Uncle Carter raises his head and looks back and forth between the two of us. "Be honest with me here. How long has this been going on?"

My heart is racing a mile a minute and I kind of want to cry. I can't believe this is happening.

"Um, like a week? Or something," Gavin mumbles.

"A week. Okay. Okay, we can fix this. That's not enough for any long-term damage," Uncle Carter says reassuringly.

Except I am NOT reassured. I am not reassured at all. What kind of long-term damage is he talking about? It's official. I'm going to have to marry my fake, gay boyfriend and spend the rest of my life never having awesome sex with the man I love ever again.

"I don't think we'll need hypnosis. Maybe just some mind-altering drugs. I wonder if acid would work. I've never done acid. It should be perfectly safe in small doses," Uncle Carter tells us.

"Dad, what the fuck are you talking about? I love Charlotte. We're not taking acid and nothing needs to be fixed," Gavin argues.

Wait, what the fuck?!

"I know you love her. Love has nothing to do with this," Uncle Carter complains.

I say again, THE FUCK?!

"Love has everything to do with it!" Gavin shouts.

"Gavin, I don't think you understand the seriousness of this situation. Look at the two of you. You're so young. It's not a path you want to go down."

"Dad, are you high right now? Seriously. Has Tyler been to your house? Did you eat any little pieces of chocolate he might have left behind?" Gavin demands.

"Gavin, listen to me. Whatever Uncle Drew and Aunt Jenny have taught you, there's still time for you to unlearn it. There's still hope for both of you to live normal, happy lives," Uncle Carter pleads.

"Dad, you are talking out of your ass right now. We are already living normal, happy lives." Gavin wraps his arm around my shoulder and pulls me in close to him. A black olive covered in ketchup drops out of my hair and lands on the ground by my feet with a *splat*.

Uncle Carter looks back and forth at us. "But you're covered in food. First it's food, then it's Skittles and a trip to the emergency room, and the next thing you know, you're out on the streets begging strangers for honey and jumper cables. JUST SAY NO to weird sex, GAVIN!"

Gavin starts to laugh and I probably would too if I wasn't in complete and utter shock at the words that came out of his mouth a few seconds ago.

"Dad, we have not been taking sex lessons from Uncle Drew and Aunt Jenny. Don't worry," Gavin reassures him.

Uncle Carter gets up from the couch and rushes toward us, wrapping his arms around both of us and squeezing us to him.

Just as quickly, he lets go of us and backs away toward the door.

"Well, alrighty then. You two kids have a nice evening."

Chapter 19
— I Wanna Get the Cramps —

IT'S HALLOWEEN AND my favorite holiday of the year. I should be a little more excited right now, but I'm not. Gavin and I still haven't discussed the bomb he dropped on me last week. Well, *I* haven't discussed it. I've done everything I can to avoid talking about it, including taking advice from Aunt Jenny.

"If you ever want to distract a guy from talking about something serious, just mention your period. It works every time. When Uncle Drew asks me if his butt looks big in a pair of jeans, I just tell him I've got cramps and he runs away screaming."

We've spent almost every day together and it's pretty obvious at this point that I'm not ready to talk about the whole "love" thing.

"So, don't you think we should talk about what happened at my place the other night?" Gavin asked.

"My ovaries feel like their being ripped out of my body right now, and I'm losing so much blood it could kill a horse, and you want to talk?!" I shouted in panic.

"I just … I think my phone's ringing. At work. I'm going to get in my car and drive to work to answer my phone. The phone. At work," Gavin mumbled before turning and racing out of my house."

It's killing me not telling him I love him. But I have to figure out a way to get rid of my pretend gay boyfriend and still keep him as my friend without Gavin knowing what I've done. Piece of cake.

"Later."

"When later?"

"Just, later, alright?"

"But when? Isn't it time yet?"

"Jesus Christ, Drew, will you stop asking if it's time to go yet? We'll go when the pumpkins are finished being carved," Uncle Carter complains as I walk into Aunt Claire and Uncle Carter's kitchen.

Uncle Drew grumbles and flops down in one of the kitchen chairs.

Every year, we all go to a Halloween Walk in the Woods that the local Metro Park puts on. Uncle Carter always volunteers to carve a few pumpkins for their displays, and each year he tries to one-up the other volunteers on the level of pumpkin carving difficulty. This year, I think he's taken it to a whole new level.

"Sweetie, you should know by now to never tell Drew we're going somewhere. You just throw him in the car when it's time to leave," Aunt Claire reminds him as she comes into the kitchen. "Hey, Charlotte! Cute costume."

I look down at my knee high white socks, black four-inch Mary Jane's, short plaid skirt, and white button-down tied under my boobs, and I have to say, I'm pretty proud of myself. Rocco brought the outfit over earlier and helped me get dressed and even put my hair into pigtails.

"Where's Gavin?" I ask as I take in the scene in front of me. There are pumpkin guts everywhere, and Uncle Carter is so deep in concentration on carving the pumpkin in front of him that he doesn't even notice Uncle Drew has carved an extra piece of pumpkin into the shape of a penis and is currently pinning it to the back of Uncle Carter's pumpkin.

"Jenny's with him in the bathroom helping him finish up his

costume. Oh my God, Carter. Who's going to get the pumpkin guts off of the ceiling?" Aunt Claire asks as she stares above the table.

"Don't worry, I'll scrape them off. It's my fault. The electric drill had a mind of its own," Uncle Carter replies as he starts gathering up all of the newspapers from the table with piles of guts on them.

"Is there any particular reason why you thought power tools were necessary when carving pumpkins? Our kitchen looks like Home Depot covered in shit right now," Aunt Claire complains as she looks around the room and sees a drill, a sander, an electric nail gun, a circular saw, and a soldering iron, along with enough extension cords to plug something in all the way to China. "Oh my God, there's pumpkin on the curtains."

"What's up, bitches and hos?!" Tyler shouts as he walks into the kitchen with a five-year-old little boy in tow.

"Yay, Tyler's here," Uncle Carter deadpans.

"Who's the kid?" Uncle Drew nods in the little boy's direction.

"This is my little cousin, Josh. Josh, say hi to everyone," Tyler tells him.

"This is stupid. I hate costumes," Josh complains as he tugs on the neck of his Batman cape.

"Tyler, your cousin's a dick, dude," Uncle Drew replies.

"I know. But my aunt and uncle are out of town and I got stuck babysitting him so-OWWW! SON OF A BITCH!" Tyler screams as Josh kicks him in the shin.

"You're a dick," Josh tells him.

"Never mind," Uncle Drew says. "Your cousin is awesome."

Gavin walks into the kitchen then and we both stare at each other with wide eyes. Word hasn't seemed to have spread through the family yet that we're sort of together so for right now, we decided to just try and act normal when we're with everyone. That's going to be impossible with the costume he's wearing right now and the way he's staring at mine.

"Is everyone ready to go? We should probably leave soon so we can get a good parking space," Gavin finally says, tearing his gaze away from me.

"Dude, what the fuck are you wearing?" Uncle Drew asks, getting up from his chair and walking over to Gavin.

"What?" Gavin asks in confusion, looking down at his costume and then back up at Uncle Drew.

"Seriously, that's what you're wearing? That's embarrassing."

"What's wrong with what he's wearing? He's a cowboy and I think he looks very handsome," Aunt Claire replies.

"He looks like that homo from Brokeback Mountain. I JUST CAN'T QUIT YOU! That movie was like ten years ago, Muppet fucker," Uncle Drew says with disappointment.

Gavin is wearing a barn coat with sheepskin lining over a button-down blue jean shirt, dark jeans, and cowboy boots. On his head is a black cowboy hat.

I want to shove him to the floor and fuck his brains out. Jesus, he looks good enough to eat.

"Who the hell are you supposed to be?" Gavin asks, pointing to Uncle Drew and his T-shirt that says: *Don't scare me, I poop easily.*

Uncle Drew reaches over to the kitchen table and grabs a mask, sliding it over his face. "I'm Michael Myers, bitch!"

"I don't think Michael Myers would wear a shirt like that," Uncle Carter tells him.

"Fuck all your mothers. Everybody poops, even Michael Myers. Is it later now? Can we finally go?"

"EEEEEEEEEEEEEEEEEEEEEEK!"

The scream echoes through the forest and makes us all wince at the ear-piercing sound as we walk along the dark trail through the trees.

We've been listening to these screams for the past twenty minutes as we make our way through the Halloween Walk. There are jack-o-lanterns with candles in them lining the walkway and helping us see where we were going, but other than that, it's pitch dark until we come up on another Halloween display every hundred yards or so.

Since it's dark, Gavin and I have been able to steal a few hand-holding moments here and there, and while everyone was occupied with one of the haunted houses, he pulled me around the side of the house, pressed me up against it, and kissed me in the dark. My legs are still a little bit shaky from that kiss.

We pass the tree of skeletons. Over two hundred glow-in-the-dark skeletons hang down from a tree that has black lights shining on it to make them seem even more eerie. A man dressed in all black with glow-in-the-dark bones on his clothes jumps out and yells, "Boo," which is the most recent cause for the ear-piercing scream.

"I swear to God if he screams one more time, I'm leaving his ass in the woods," Tyler complains.

"Be nice. This walk is a little more scary this year," I tell him.

"EEEEEEEEEEEEEEEEEEEEEEK!"

I cringe as another shriek fills the night air and our small group trudges farther down the path.

"Seriously? You could see the mechanical arms on that thing," Tyler says with a roll of his eyes. "What a pussy."

I feel a tug on my hand and looked down at Josh, clutching tightly onto both Gavin and I as he walks between us.

"Hey, Charlotte. What the heck is wrong with the guy with the *poop* shirt? Why does he keep screaming so much?"

I laugh and shake my head at him.

"His name is Drew and he's a big baby, that's what's wrong with him," Gavin answers for me.

"Hey! I heard that," Uncle Drew yells from a few feet in front of us.

"You were supposed to hear that, dumbass," Gavin replies.

"Awwww, you said *ass*," Josh scolds.

"Yeah, so did you. So there!" Gavin sticks his tongue out at Josh.

We stop to look at a tombstone display while the others continue walking ahead.

"Are you ready to talk to me yet?" Gavin asks.

No! Distraction!

"Ha, look at that tombstone! It says *Bea A. Fraid*. Hilarious!" I say nervously.

"Charlotte, I lov—"

"MENSTRUAL CRAMPS!" I shout, cutting him off.

"What are men's tall craps?" Josh asks.

Shit, I forgot he's still with us.

"Do tall men get craps? I'm gonna be tall when I get bigger. I wanna get the craps," Josh adds. "Gavin, do you get the craps?"

Gavin looks down at Josh in horror and then back up at me. "I think I hear my mom calling us. WE'RE COMING, MOM!"

Gavin turns and walks away quickly, and I follow behind him with Josh.

"I'm gonna tell my mom I'm getting the craps. This is gonna be awesome!"

Well, at least kids are good for one thing.

Chapter 20
— Old Man Balls —

"EEEEEEEEEEEEEEEEEEEEK! SON OF A BITCH!"

We're almost finished with the walk when a man dressed up as the Grim Reaper is suddenly walking elbow-to-elbow with Uncle Drew, staring straight at him as he walks, not saying a word.

"Hey you! Mean guy! Get away from poop guy before he cries!" Josh yells.

We all laugh at the prospect of Uncle Drew breaking down in the middle of the woods crying, but Josh's shout stops the Grim Reaper in his tracks. He slinks back off into the woods to wait for the next group of unsuspecting walkers to come through so he can scare *them*.

There are a few more small houses set up along the path that they turned into haunted houses, and we come up to the first one. Aunt Claire didn't want to take Josh through it just in case it was too scary, but he insisted.

My dad bought him a light-up wand when we first got to the Halloween Walk, and he wields it in front of him as we slowly make our way into the house.

"Oh my God, oh my God, oh my God," Uncle Drew chants quietly over and over.

"Will you shut up?" Dad scolds him in a loud whisper.

Cobwebs hang from the ceiling, body parts with blood all over them litter the floor and dangle from the walls, and a strobe light flashes as the sounds of scary music is piped through the house. We twist and turn through the maze of the rooms, electronic bats falling down from the ceiling around one turn, a mummy popping up from a coffin around another, and a person dressed up like Freddy Kruger jumping out at us close to the exit.

As soon as the guy leaps out from behind the door and throws his razor fingernails up at us, Josh smacks him in the hand with his light stick.

"OW!" screams Freddy Kruger as he clutches his injured razor hand to his chest.

"Ha! Not so tough now, are you, Fred?" Uncle Drew laughs as he walks by the guy and out the exit.

"GAAAAAAAAAAAAAAH!" Uncle Drew screams as the Grim Reaper guy steps out from the side of the house directly into his path. Uncle Drew holds his hands to his throat and starts choking on his own spit from yelling so loud.

"Drew, for God's sakes, keep it together, man," Dad mutters as I stick a finger in my ear in an attempt to rub out the ringing going on from Uncle Drew's girly screams.

"I pacifically told him he shouldn't go with us if he was going to be too scared," Aunt Jenny mutters. "Baby, do you need the Heineken Remover?" she asks as she walks over and starts smacking him on the back.

"I DON'T KNOW IF HE DOES, BUT I COULD SURE USE A HEINEKEN RIGHT NOW, JENNY!" Tyler shouts.

"Dude, why are you shouting?" Gavin asks.

"Didn't your aunt have like a stroke or something? Isn't that why she's a little off? I figure if I talk loudly she'll understand me," Tyler explains.

"No, no stroke. She's just kind of ... special," Gavin adds nicely.

We continue down the path, following the lit jack-o-lanterns to the next haunted house. The Grim Reaper walks elbow to elbow with Uncle Drew the entire way, never once taking his eyes off of him.

"Okay, seriously, fucker. If you're going to follow me, at least say something. All this staring is wigging me out," Uncle Drew complains.

The man says nothing, just continues to keep pace with Uncle Drew. When he speeds up, the Grim Reaper speeds up. When he slows down, the Grim Reaper slows down. When he walks in a circle around our group as we stop to admire some of the carved pumpkins, the Grim Reaper follows right behind him.

At one point, Uncle Drew lifts his knee and holds his arms out to his side, touching his nose with each finger like he's doing a sobriety test. The Grim Reaper follows right along. Uncle Drew decides he's no longer just going to sit back and let this poor volunteer for the parks department get off easily. He hops like a rabbit for about two hundred yards and then sprints to the next haunted house.

The Reaper follows, mimicking his movements.

Eventually, Uncle Drew starts calling him Grimmy and invites the guy out for drinks after the walk but tells him he can only come along if he keeps the costume on.

Grimmy never answers.

I have to say, I've never seen a guy stay in character this well, especially with all the shit Uncle Drew is having him do. We go into a haunted house and the guy disappears into the woods. Then, a few minutes later, he's right back next to Uncle Drew, following him like a puppy dog.

And of course when we say something about that, Uncle Drew decides to crawl on all fours for a little while, barking every few feet.

Grimmy copies.

It takes about an hour to go through the entire Halloween Walk through the woods, so pretty soon, we're all kind of attached to Grimmy. When we walk over a small wooden bridge and look down into the water to see all of the jack-o-lanterns they place on pedestals in the water, Grimmy lifts Josh up so he can see over the railing.

When we come around a bend to see a graveyard setup on the hillside, Grimmy points out one of the big tombstones to Josh right before a ghost jumps out and tries to scare him. Josh walks right up to the ghost and kicks him in the shin.

If we could see Grimmy's face, I bet we would see him smile.

We come around the last corner of the walk and can see people milling about at the end getting hot chocolate and hot apple cider from some of the vendors.

Uncle Drew pats Grimmy on the back. "Well, Grimster, it's been fun. I'd say it was nice to meet you, but you scared the future children I might have had out of my nut sack when we first met."

"Future children? Your balls are too old to have any more kids," Dad laughs.

"I'll have you know that my sperm are in excellent condition and my balls are NOT old. I do NOT have old man balls. Honey, tell them." Uncle Drew looks over at Aunt Jenny.

"It's true. He doesn't have old man balls. They are still nice and soft and not wrinkly at all."

Grimmy puts his hand up over his masked eyes and shakes his head sadly.

We all wave at the guy as he stands in place in the middle of the path, and we make our way out of the woods. Gavin and I walk over to one of the stands, and he gets me some hot apple cider.

"I'm having a really hard time being with you tonight and not ripping every piece of clothing off of—"

"What are you kids talking about?" Aunt Claire asks as she comes up next to us.

"The weather."

"Astrophysics," Gavin and I reply at the same time.

Aunt Claire looks back and forth between us suspiciously.

"The direct correlation to the earth's atmosphere blending with the time space continuum to produce noxious gas on Mars," I ramble.

"Well, alright then. Have fun with that," she replies, turning around and walking back over the picnic table where everyone is seated.

"That was close. Nice save," Gavin says quietly with a laugh as we follow behind her.

"We need to be more careful or everyone's going to find out," I warn him as we walk.

"Who cares? You broke up with Rocco, right? So it doesn't matter."

ABORT! ABORT CONVERSATION!

"I think I need to change my tampon."

"Oh look, a squirrel!" Gavin says, rushing away from me and taking a seat next to Uncle Carter at the picnic table.

With a sigh, I take a seat across from him, next to Tyler and Josh. A man with a Metro Parks uniform walks up to our table and asks if we had a good time and enjoyed the walk.

"I beat up Freddy Kruger and kicked a ghost. It was alright," Josh replies with a shrug.

"I have to tell ya, man, that Grim Reaper you got walking around the woods deserves a raise. That guy scared the holy hell out of me," Uncle Drew tells him with a laugh.

We all chuckle and then notice the park worker looking at Uncle Drew in confusion.

"Grim Reaper? We don't have a grim reaper employed with us this year, do you mean Frankenstein?" he asks.

"Uh, no. I mean the Grim Reaper. Tall guy, wearing a black cloak that dragged on the ground and had a hood pulled around his face so you couldn't see him. And he had that big sickle thing in his hand that he walked with," Uncle Drew explains.

"I'm sorry, sir, there is definitely no one of that description that works here this year."

We all look around at one another in confusion, no one wanting to admit just how creeped out we are. But I know there has to be a logical explanation.

"It was probably just someone going on the walk like we were and he decided to have some fun with you," I tell Uncle Drew.

Once again, the park worker shakes his head.

"I was at the front gate collecting tickets from everyone tonight, and there wasn't anyone wearing a costume like that," he says.

The man talks to us for a few more minutes about the people that volunteer for the walk every year and how he's known them since the walk first opened twenty years ago. He walks away and our table stays silent while everyone processes what he'd said.

"Maybe he was a homeless guy or something. I bet he lives in the woods and just wanted to make some friends," Aunt Jenny says wistfully.

"Make some friends, yeah right. That guy wanted to ass rape me," Uncle Drew complains.

"Really, Drew? I'm surprised you noticed anything while you were humping trees and squatting over pumpkins so it looked like you were shitting them out." Mom gets a disgusted look on her face as she remembers Uncle Drew's actions in the woods.

"Oh believe me, I could tell. There was something squirrely about him," Uncle Drew says with a nod of his head.

"Wait a minute. You thought he was a squirrel? I thought he was supposed to be the Grim Reaper?" Aunt Jenny says in confusion.

Uncle Drew pats her hand. "No, baby. It's just a figure of … never mind."

"I still say he's homeless. It's a doggy-dog world out there. Poor guy was probably just trying to make some money," Aunt Jenny adds.

Tyler looks at her in confusion. "Don't you mean *dog eat dog world?*"

"Jenny lives in the puppies and rainbows part of the globe," Aunt Claire says with a laugh.

"Is there really a place like that?" Aunt Jenny asks.

"He told me what his name was," Josh says nonchalantly.

Uncle Drew looks across the table at Josh. "Dude, shut up. No he didn't."

"YOU shut up. He totally did," Josh argues, looking over his shoulder, back into the woods with a nervous look taking over his face.

We all turn our heads and stare in silence toward the trail entrance.

"What did he tell you his name was?" Aunt Claire asks quietly.

Everyone leans closer to Josh, no one saying a word, waiting for him to speak.

"He said ..."

Everyone holds their breath.

"His name ..."

No one blinks.

"Was ..."

My heart is beating out of my fucking chest and my knee is bouncing nervously under the table. I feel Gavin's hand reach under the table and clutch my knee.

"Death," Josh whispers seriously.

We all sit there staring at Josh with our mouths dropped, the silence permeating the air around us.

"Holy shit," Uncle Drew whispers.

"I'm going to find security and tell them," Dad says as he starts to get up from the bench.

"I'll come with you," Uncle Carter states, doing the same.

Josh scrambles off of the picnic table bench and starts laughing hysterically. "You guys are a bunch of sissies! He said his name is Bob and he was opposed to be dressed like a ghost but he got hot chocolate all over his costume and had to change!"

Everyone lets out the breaths they'd been holding as Josh continues to laugh and taunt everyone.

"Oh my God, we just got punked by a five-year-old," Uncle Drew says with admiration in his voice.

Well, after this fun-filled evening, telling Gavin about Rocco should be no big deal.

Chapter 21
— Run Virginityman! —

"SO, THE PLAN is you're going to just break up with me in front of Gavin? I don't know if I like this," Rocco complains as he stands in my living room.

"You will do it and you will like it, or I will never go shoe shopping with you ever again!" I threaten.

Rocco places his hand over his heart and pouts. "Now that's just mean."

I am such a chickenshit. I should have told him when we got back to his apartment after the Halloween walk last night. Instead, I dragged him into the shower and gave him a blow job. Blow jobs equal love, right?

My mom invited a few people over for dinner, so I figure this is the perfect time for a public break-up. I can just end things with Rocco, pretend like the list never happened, and we can all move on.

"Charlotte, your mom needs help in the kitchen," my dad says as he walks into the living room. He stops when he sees Rocco and glares at him.

"Oh, no worries, Dad. I'd be glad to help Liz in the kitchen. I could even whip up a soufflé if there's time," Rocco tells him.

"Seriously, dial down the gay a notch," I whisper.

"I mean, how 'bout we grab us a few brewskies and see if there's a fight on TV," Rocco tells my dad in a deep voice.

"How about I give you a five second head start before I get my shotgun," he replies.

"LIZ! Get your ass out here and help me carry these cupcakes," Aunt Claire yells as she walks through the front door. "Oh … hi, guys. Jim, stop staring at that poor boy like you want to slit his throat. LIZ!"

Mom comes rushing into the living room, wiping her hands on a towel. "What the fuck is your problem? Stop shouting already. Rocco, when did you get here? What are you doing here? Why is he here?"

"I really think your family is going to be crushed when you break my heart," Rocco whispers in my ear.

The front door opens again and in walk Uncle Carter and Gavin, both of them smiling and laughing until they see Rocco standing next to me.

Shit. Maybe this wasn't the best idea.

Rocco moves to stand behind me and clutches onto the back of my shirt. "Don't let them hit me! I just had a facial!" he whispers frantically.

"What's he doing here?" Gavin demands.

"Want to go help me clean my gun?" Dad asks him.

Aunt Claire smacks my dad on the arm.

Oh my God, Gavin looks pissed. He has every right to look pissed. I kind of sort of alluded to the fact that I was breaking up with Rocco a few weeks ago and haven't mentioned him once since Gavin and I started fooling around. This is bad. Very bad.

I quickly turn around to face Rocco. "Rocco, I'm breaking up with you."

"WHAT?! NOOOOOOOO!" Rocco screams. "Baby, please don't leave me!"

I widen my eyes at him and scowl. "Nope. It's over. I don't love you. I've never loved you. You should just go now."

"OH MY GOD MY LIFE IS OVER!" Rocco wails, throwing his arms around me and sobbing into my shoulder.

"OVER. ACTING," I say through clenched teeth.

He quickly pulls back and puffs out his chest. "Whatev, babe. It's cool."

With that, he walks around me and heads to the door, passing Ava as she comes in with Tyler.

"Oooooh, cute shoes!" Rocco says before walking out, the door slamming closed behind him.

"So, who's hungry? I'm starving!" I announce to the room as they all stand there staring at me.

"Hey, Charlotte, what's with this list I found on your desk?" Molly asks, walking into the room from the back hallway. "Show him your cleavage, make him change your tire, have him lick chocolate off of you ..."

Molly trails off when she finally looks up and sees me staring at her in horror. Gavin walks past me and right up to Molly, snatching the piece of paper out of her hands reading through it. As his eyes widen in what I assume to be horror while he scans the list, I seriously contemplate turning and running out of the house. Maybe leaving the country and changing my name.

"Gavin, I can explain," I tell him softly, trying not to cry.

Gavin doesn't say anything as he continues reading.

Tyler walks across the room and glances over Gavin's shoulder. "Ooooh, that's a good one. *Take him to a sporting event and act like you know what's going on.* He would have totally fallen for that."

Gavin puts his hand over his mouth, and I'm wondering if it's going to be the mustard episode all over again and he's going to start gagging. I see his shoulders start to shake and suddenly realize he's laughing. He's fucking laughing at my list.

"What the hell is so funny?" I demand.

I don't care if I'm in the wrong here. He's laughing at my misguided attempt to get him to fall in love with me. It's really not a laughing matter.

Gavin moves his hand away and laughs out loud. "Tyler, I think you should tell her what's so funny."

"Holy fuck, it's about time," Tyler complains, reaching into his back pocket and pulling out a folded up piece of notebook paper, handing it over to me.

I stare at it in confusion for a few seconds before Gavin speaks through his laughs. "You really need to open that."

With a sigh, I unfold the paper and scan the words written in Tyler's messy handwriting. I really don't need to read everything; the title at the top of the page pretty much says it all.

"Oh my God," I mutter.

Gavin comes up to me and places both of his hands on my cheeks, pulling my head up so he can look into my eyes. "I'm not crazy, right? This means you love me?"

I laugh and shake my head at him. "You idiot. Of course I love you. I loved you even when you were mutilating my Barbies and calling me a labia. I'm pretty sure giving you my virginity should have been clue number one."

Too late, I realize we're not alone in this room.

"Gavin, I love you like a son, but right now I want to punch you in your face," Dad tells him.

"Can you wait to kick my ass until after I kiss your daughter, please?" Gavin begs him.

"Fine. You've got ten seconds. And then I'm ripping off your dick and giving you your own labia," Dad threatens, crossing his arms over his chest.

Gavin doesn't waste any of those ten seconds. He swoops down and presses his lips to mine.

"Oh my God, I'm totally going to cry. Liz, get me a tissue," Aunt Claire says.

"Get your own fucking tissue, you whore," Mom sniffles.

"I'm still wearing the blue dress to the wedding," Aunt Claire tells her as I wrap my arms around Carter's neck.

"We are going to throw down right the fuck now. Jim, get the

Fight Club DVD. This is totally happening," Mom states.

"I'm going to punch you right in the ovaries."

"Yeah, well I'm going to be the first one to walk down the aisle, so you're going to look like a dick when you waltz down in your subpar blue dress."

"I'm going to make you wear a suck-for-a-buck shirt at her bachelorette party."

"Oh no you DIDN'T just say that to me!"

"Oh yeah, that JUST happened!"

"Their first born is going to be named after me."

"Your name is bullshit."

"YOU'RE BULLSHIT!"

Breaking the kiss, I pull back and look at Gavin.

"Are you sure about this? I don't know if our families are going to survive," I tell him softly with a smile.

"Jim, get me the basket of dinner rolls from the kitchen. There are twelve with Claire's face written all over them."

"Carter, get me the mashed potatoes and turn on the ceiling fan. This bitch is going down."

Gavin laughs and shakes his head. "Love and lists. Just remember, love and lists. Nothing else matters."

Pulling Gavin's mouth back down to mine, I forget all about the chaos surrounding us and just enjoy the moment.

"Alright, that's enough. Break it up. I've got a face to beat up," my dad announces.

Gavin looks over my shoulder and his smile instantly falls. "Oh shit. He's serious."

"Run, Virginityman, run!" Tyler shouts.

Epilogue
- Gavin -

HAND IN HAND with Charlotte, we walk around to the back of her parents' house. It's no longer her house anymore since she moved into my apartment last week.

Can I get a round of applause, folks?! Or maybe just a "FUCK YEAH!"?

"This is so weird. Just a few months ago I was making this same walk with Tyler, giving myself a pep talk about my list," I tell Charlotte with a laugh.

"Yeah, well I was inside the house at that same time freaking out about whether or not Rocco was going to be convincing as my boyfriend," she replies.

"I'm so glad I never killed him. He has great taste in shoes." I look down at her platform wedges that make her long legs look fucking hot.

"Don't even think about it, Gavin. We are not sneaking off into the bushes to have sex at my parents' house," Charlotte warns me as I continue to stare at her legs while we walk.

"That's probably a wise decision since I'm pretty sure my puke is still in those bushes."

Once Charlotte finally came clean that she and Rocco were never really dating, he and I actually became good friends. I've had to put him in his place a few times when he makes comments about my great ass, but all in all, having a gay dude as a friend is pretty awesome. I pretend like I never hated him or wished that a rabid infestation of crabs would chew off his dick, and he takes me shopping to pick out sexy shoes and lingerie for Charlotte. It's perfect.

I'm still working my ass off at Seduction and Snacks and loving every minute of it, especially now that I have a new co-worker. Charlotte accepted a position as the new Media Sales Rep for the business, and Aunt Liz couldn't be happier. We all decided that from now on it would be a good idea for *her* to do the ribbon cutting ceremonies at sex toy shops. Less chance of humiliating newspaper headlines that way since I'm pretty sure Charlotte won't be ODing on Viagra anytime soon. At least I hope not. I wonder what Viagra does to a vagina? I should ask Uncle Drew. I'm sure he knows.

As soon as we get to the back yard, we're immediately greeted by the sounds of screaming.

"GAAAAAAAAAAAAAAAAAAAAH!"

"What the fuck is that?" I ask Uncle Drew as he walks up to us.

"That, my little asshole, is a screaming goat. Molly showed me this awesome video on YouTube and I had to get one," Uncle Drew says with a huge smile.

"GAAAAAAAAAAAAAAAAAAAAH!"

Uncle Drew turns around and points proudly to a little black and white goat tied to one of Aunt Liz and Uncle Jim's trees. "Isn't she cute? Her name is Taylor Swift."

"GAAAAAAAAAAAAAAAAAAAAH!" the goat screams as she looks right at us.

"I don't even understand what is happening right now," I reply with a shake of my head.

"I've been trying to teach her—"

"GAAAAAAAAAAAAAAAAAAAAH!"

"How to sing a—"

"GAAAAAAAAAAAAAAAAAAAAH!"

"Song, but she never comes in at the right—"

"GAAAAAAAAAAAAAAAAAAAAH!"

"SON OF A BITCH, TAYLOR SWIFT! I TOLD YOU, NOT UNTIL THE CHORUS!" Uncle Drew yells across the yard as he turns and walks away from us.

"Do you think Uncle Drew is ever going to grow up?" Charlotte asks me as we watch him have a conversation with the goat, his arms flying in every direction as he tries to explain to her what she did wrong.

"Definitely not."

I turn toward Charlotte and wrap my arms around her waist. I start to lean down for a kiss, but of course we're interrupted.

"You two need to get a room. All of this PDA shit is disgusting."

Charlotte and I turn our heads as Ava walks up next to us, with Tyler right behind her.

"Oh, don't be jealous, sugar muffin. Some day you'll be able to save up enough money and pay a guy off to love you that much," Tyler says with a smirk.

"Hey, Tyler, want to know what it feels like to have a stiletto shoved up your ass?" Ava casually asks him while she examines her fingernails.

"You already had your finger in my ass, so I'm assuming it wouldn't be much different."

Ava continues to stare at the chipped polish on her thumbnail, but I can tell she's about ready to lose it. Her nostrils flare and she lets out a growl.

"Dude, you might want to start running now," I whisper to him.

Unfortunately for Tyler, Ava isn't about to make a scene in her parents' backyard by beating the shit out of him. She's going for complete and total mind fuck right now.

"Remember the last time you were in my car and you left that My Little Pony toy in the center console?" Charlotte asks him sweetly, finally looking up at him.

Tyler loses all of his smugness and his smile falters.

"You didn't," he whispers.

"Know what happens when you put My Little Pony in the microwave?" Ava asks.

Tyler's eyes widen and he clenches his fists at his sides. "No. Please, not Twilight Sparkle."

Ava takes a few steps in his direction until she's right up in his face. "She put up a good fight. She screamed until the bitter end."

Tyler grits his teeth and if I'm not mistaken, I think I see a few tears pooling in his eyes. He's quiet for so long that I wonder if maybe he's going to take the high road and just walk away. Too bad Ava sticks the knife in a little deeper by smiling brightly at him. That's all it takes to push Tyler over the edge.

"YOU CRAB INFESTED CROTCH ROT! I was lying about those jeans the other day. They TOTALLY make your ass look fat!"

"YOU FUCKER! Did you just call me a fat-ass? YOU HAVE A SMALL PENIS!" Ava yells.

"I don't have a small penis. Your vagina is just bigger than the fucking Grand Canyon!"

"I HATE YOU!" Ava screams.

"I HATE YOU MORE!" Tyler adds.

They both stand nose-to-nose, chests heaving and staring angrily at one another. I start to pull away from Charlotte to break up the fight when Tyler suddenly speaks.

"You're so fucking hot. Your car or mine?"

"Mine. I parked closer."

Ava grabs Tyler's hand and drags him across the yard to the driveway.

"Those two are going to kill each other." Charlotte sighs with a shake of her head as we watch them hustle away.

"At least they're going to maim each other in *her* car. Tyler borrowed mine today, remember? I don't think I can get severed head stains out of the upholstery."

Now that we're alone again, I turn back toward Charlotte and pull her close. There's nothing better than being able to touch her and hold her whenever I want. Except for having sex with her.

Having sex with her is definitely better.

Taking up where we left off before the tornado of Tyler and Ava came screaming through the yard, I lean my head down to Charlotte for a kiss. She quickly brings her hand up in front of my face to stop me.

"I know this whole thing is still kind of new with us, but I feel like I should tell you something really important. It might have a huge impact on our relationship," she tells me softly.

"As long as you don't tell me you have another fake, gay boyfriend somewhere, nothing else matters," I laugh.

"No. Rocco is the only fake, gay boyfriend I will ever have. You can count on that."

Charlotte takes a deep breath and spits it out. "The thing is, I never want to have children. I really like my vagina, and I'm pretty sure you do too. I have no desire to push a tiny little human out of it and destroy the poor thing forever."

I stare at her in silence for a few seconds before one corner of my mouth turns up in a grin.

Fuck, do I love this girl.

"Good. Because I can't stand kids. And the thought of your vagina turning into something that looks like finely sliced roast beef is not appealing to me at all."

"Eeeew, that's disgusting," Charlotte replies, scrunching her nose up.

"Sorry, I heard my mom say that once and it's always stuck with me," I tell her.

Charlotte wraps her arms around my neck and stands up on her tiptoes. "Well, it's a good thing your mom never felt like that about kids or you wouldn't be here with me right now."

I hear someone clear her throat and turn to see my mom standing next to us with a sheepish look on her face. "Yeah, about that …"

– The End –

Passion and Ponies

(Chocoholics #2)

by Tara Sivec

Chapter 1
— Prancing Pony —
Ava

MY EYES SUDDENLY jerk open when I feel the subtle shaking of my bed. For a minute, my sleep-addled brain wonders if we're having an earthquake and panic sets in. Then I remember I live in Ohio and the house is probably not preparing to crumble down around me. As my eyes adjust to the darkness in my childhood bedroom, I listen intently for sounds of heavy breathing or the distinct metallic clang of a knife sharpening, certain the shaking of my bed is a not-so-stealthy axe murderer preparing to slit my throat.

What? That could totally happen. Some dude could have broken into my parent's home and now he's sitting on the edge of my bed, sharpening his giant knife.

I hold my breath in fear. I begin to slowly turn my head and prepare to come face-to-face with a homicidal maniac when something kicks the back of my leg with the force of a two-by-four.

"Ouch! Son of a bitch!" I shout as I quickly flop over in bed. Unfortunately, I don't come face-to-face with a killer. What I do find in my bed next to me is much worse.

"Tyler! What the fuck are you still doing in my bed?" I whisper-yell, hoping my initial outburst didn't wake my parents, who are sleeping down the hall.

Tyler Branson, man-child extraordinaire and the guy I've been shame fucking for the past few months, doesn't even bat an eye at me. I listen in irritation as he lightly snores and watch as his legs jerk forward every couple of seconds. Pretty soon, his arms join in, reminding me of those stupid Youtube videos of dogs dreaming that they're running.

Almost immediately, a sound that can only be described as a *whinny* passes his lips as his arms and legs move at a faster pace, my bed bouncing with the force of his movements.

Oh, my God. Oh, sweet mother of Mary…

Reaching for my bedside table, I quickly turn on my lamp even though seeing Tyler swathed in any kind of lighting right now makes me want to puke. *This* is an image I don't want burned into my brain.

With my face scrunched up in disgust, I reach around his flailing arms and punch him in the chest. His eyes fly open in fear and he bolts up in bed, scrambling backwards until his back hits the headboard.

"What is it? What happened?" he asks frantically as he rubs the sleep from his eyes.

"What the hell were you doing?" I demand.

His eyes zone right in on my braless chest covered in a tank top. I quickly pull the sheet up to my chin and give him a dirty look.

"I was sleeping. What the hell did you wake me up for?" he complains.

"You kicked me and made a horse noise."

He stares at me blankly for a moment before scoffing at me in disbelief and sliding back down the bed until his head hits the pillow again.

"I was having a dream. Now leave me alone and let me go back to sleep."

When he rolls over, I shove my hand against his back. "Were you dreaming about horses? You were fucking *prancing* in your sleep."

Tyler looks over his shoulder at me and I watch his face redden with embarrassment. "What? You're delusional. I don't prance. I NEVER prance."

I just shake my head at him. "You were totally prancing in your sleep. Prancing and *whinnying* like a damn horse."

"You shut your face! Shut your face right now!" he shouts.

I shove my finger close to his nose. "No, YOU shut your prancing face, Twilight Sparkle, before my parents hear you. You're not even supposed to BE here. You were supposed to sneak out of my bedroom window just like always. Get out of my bed!"

He huffs in irritation and angrily flings the blankets off of him before getting out of bed. My already black soul dies a little more inside when I can't tear my eyes away from his perfect ass and his chiseled abs as he pulls his clothes on, muttering under his breath the entire time.

This was never supposed to happen. Sleeping with Tyler was supposed to be a one-time thing – a means of scratching an itch and quelling the boredom that has consumed my life lately. The first time we had sex and he sang the theme song from My Little Pony while he went down on me should have sent me running for the hills like my ass was on fire. He's immature, he constantly pisses me off and he's twenty-five years old and can't hold down a job to save his life.

But dammit, sex with Tyler was the biggest high I've ever had in my life.

It's official: I am clinically insane.

I am twenty-one-years old and I hate my life. Okay, maybe hate is a strong word. I'm *dissatisfied*. I took a leave of absence from college because wasting my parents' money when I had no idea what I wanted to do with my life was pointless. I've been working at my mother's company, Seduction and Snacks, as an administrative assistant for the past few months and hating every minute of it. My mother co-owns the business with her best friend Claire. Mom's side is the Seduction half of the equation. They sell all things sex from toys, porn and games to lingerie and costumes. Claire operates the Snacks side, where they make the best damn baked goods ever to hit the Midwest. Sounds amazing, right? I should love the fact that my family has made a small fortune over the years and that Seduction and Snacks is now located in twenty-eight states throughout the U.S. I should also enjoy working in the family business and take pride in the fact that my mother and my Aunt Claire started building this empire when they were only a few years older than me.

Maybe that's my problem. They were my age when they came up with this idea and they made it a reality only three years later. I don't have any earth shattering, groundbreaking ideas. I have nothing that's just mine alone, except a fashion blog where I talk about clothes and purses and other things that interest me. I'm expected to work at Seduction and Snacks and continue living *their* dream. It's not my dream, though. I have no fucking clue what my dream is aside from finding a good sale at Nordstrom's for those Michael Kors wedge pumps I've had my eye on.

Which brings us back to Tyler. And no, *he's* not my fucking dream either! He's just a way to keep my mind off of the fact that I'm in my early twenties and clueless about where my life is going. Obviously, it's going nowhere fast with Tyler and I need to nip this thing in the bud immediately.

Tyler pulls his shirt down over his head and I pretend like I'm not sad to see his naked abs go.

"I can't believe you're kicking me out at three-o'clock in the morning," he grumbles as he slides his feet into tennis shoes without bothering to tie them.

He walks over to my window and slides it open, looking back at me and smirking. "So, same time, same place tomorrow?"

Rolling my eyes, I shake my head. "No. Absolutely not. We're not doing this anymore. Leave and don't come back."

He's got one leg swung over the windowsill and his body halfway out before he jerks his head back inside and stares at me in surprise. "What? What do you mean 'don't come back'? Like, don't come back tomorrow, or ever?"

Seriously, how can he be so dense?

"Ever. This was a huge mistake."

He actually has the nerve to growl at me. Thank God he didn't whinny or I'd be puking right into my lap.

"Fine! But you'll be begging for another piece of Tyler, mark my words!"

"Jesus Christ, don't talk about yourself in third person," I complain.

"They come back, they always come back to Tyler," he mutters with another smirk, completely ignoring me.

"By 'they', I'm assuming you're talking about the ponies you were dreaming about?" I chuckle.

"Fuck your face! Fuck your face right now!" he demands.

"Get the hell out of my bedroom and don't come back, Prancer!" I fire back.

Sticking his tongue out at me in one poorly-executed, last ditch effort to put me in my place, he tries to smoothly exit my window but his head smacks against the frame. He lets go of the sill to grab his wounded head and loses his balance, falling out the window and into the shrubs on the other side.

"Mother fucking dick fuck ass cake piece of shit shrub!" I hear him whisper from the yard.

Getting out of bed, I rush over to the window, slam it closed and secure the lock. I climb back into bed, turn off my light and try to think about anything other than Tyler Branson and his stupid tongue.

I can totally quit Broke Back Moron, piece of cake.

Chapter 2

– A Happy Vagina is a Happy Life –
Tyler

"MY LIFE IS over," I wail, plopping myself down in the chair across from Gavin's desk.

He looks up from his computer and cocks his head. "So you got fired from The Gap? You didn't like that job anyway."

I stare at him in confusion and shake my head sadly. "I'm sorry, have we met? Who gives a shit about The Gap? I'm talking about Ava. I'm pretty sure she's not going to have sex with me anymore."

In all honesty, I am kind of pissed about getting fired. It's not like working at The Gap was a dream job, but it paid for porn and strip clubs so it had some perks. I gave those assholes two of the best months of my life and what do they do? Get audited by corporate and tell me the copy of my birth certificate I gave them when they hired me was a fake. As if!

"I thought you couldn't stand Ava?" Gavin asks in confusion.

"I can't. All she does is bitch at me. But man alive, that chick's got a mouth like a Shop Vac."

Gavin winces and mimics dry heaving. "Seriously dude, stop. Just stop."

Gavin and I have been best friends ever since we met our freshman year in college. It's unfortunate that I was naked during that first meeting, but what can you do? Sometimes the boys just like to dangle while you're hanging pictures around your dorm room.

Anyway, as soon as we got to talking (after I put pants on), I knew this was a guy I wanted in my corner. He's a good-looking dude, so he's always had a plethora of hot chicks sniffing around him. Lucky for me, he's been in love with Charlotte, his childhood sweetheart, since birth and I, therefore got all his castoffs.

Some dudes would probably be offended at being the second-best choice. Those dudes are obviously dumb fucks who don't know rule number one in the guy handbook – you never, ever turn down pussy. Gavin's feelings towards Charlotte are obviously not brotherly, but he's always looked at Ava as a little sister. Needless to say, talk about our sexcapades grosses him the fuck out.

"I guess I shouldn't let it get to me. I mean, how can I bang a chick that has no appreciation for animals?" I ask in irritation as I kick my feet up on his desk.

"I'm pretty sure Ava loves animals. I think the problem is that she didn't expect to sleep with one," Gavin replies with a smirk.

I knew I shouldn't have told him about that whole horse incident the other night.

"So what's on the agenda today, dick licker? Are we going to watch some chicks masturbate, maybe construct a mold of my penis for a new sex toy?" I ask, quickly moving the conversation away from my embarrassing evening with Ava.

Gavin has worked in Product Development for Seduction and Snacks ever since graduating from college. Lucky bastard.

Shaking his head at me, he gets up from behind the desk and heads towards the door. "How many times do I have to tell you that no one masturbates inside this building?"

"And how many times do I have to tell you that I don't like it when you lie to me and crush my dreams," I remind him as I follow him out into the hall.

Luckily, Ava isn't at her desk right outside Gavin's office. She works part time as his secretary and I made sure to stop by today when she was on her lunch break. Actually, regardless of what time I stop by, chances of her ass being in that desk were miniscule. That chick is hot as fuck and the best lay I've ever had, but working is not her strong suit.

"Our tour guide for the warehouse was in a pretty bad car accident over the weekend, so I'm stuck taking over the tours until we can find a replacement," Gavin explains as he pushes open the double doors to the warehouse.

I've strolled through the warehouse and even participated in a few tours, but each time I walk through those doors is like the first time. I swear as soon as I set foot in this place I can hear a choir of angels singing. As far as the eye can see, row after row, aisle after aisle, box after box – are sex toys. Metal shelving from floor to ceiling filled with boxes of beautifully crafted love machines.

I don't even realize I'm mumbling until Gavin punches me in the arm.

"Were you just chanting 'This is my home; this is where I belong'?"

I just shrug and follow him over to the first aisle, where a group of about ten women ranging in ages from twenty-five to sixty-five stand, anxiously awaiting their tour of Mecca.

"No talking, no crying, no sword fights with the dildos and please, for the love of God, do NOT lick the Chocolate Thunders on aisle twelve again," Gavin warns me under his breath.

Is it my fault they named a sex toy after chocolate? How the fuck was I supposed to know it didn't taste like chocolate? That's false advertising, if you ask me.

"Ladies, welcome to Seduction and Snacks! My name is Gavin and I'm the head of Product Development. If you'll just follow me, we can start the tour."

"THIS ONE HAS slow pulses along with intense vibrations. It's got an easy two-button functionality and you'll be happy to know it's made from durable, phthalate-free plastic. I would highly recommend this toy for any of you first-timers who just aren't sure how to start when building your toy collection. It's one of our most popular models and I guarantee you'll enjoy it."

Gavin was called away from the tour a half hour ago for an emergency conference call. I felt bad for all these bitches standing around waiting for him, so I figured I might as well carry on with the tour.

Placing the toy back into its bin on the shelf on aisle fourteen, I look up from the crowd of women surrounding me and see Gavin and his Aunt Liz standing at the edge of the group. Gavin is smiling and Liz has a look of complete shock on her face.

I excuse myself from the group, leaving them to chat amongst themselves as I make my way to Gavin and Liz.

"What the fuck was that?" Liz asks as soon as I reach her.

Awwww shit, now I'm in trouble. I should have just wandered over to the flavored lube on aisle seven and had a snack. The funnel cake flavored lube really is quite filling.

"That was the Eighth Wonder of the World. You know, one of the toys you sell here?" I remind her.

I barely finish my sentence when her hand flies out and smacks me up side the head. "I'm well aware of toy's name, dick face. I meant, how did *you* know so much about it? You sounded like you could have written the fucking product description for it."

Oh, is that all?

"Well, I'm kind of a connoisseur of sex toys, if you will. I like to keep myself informed for the ladies. A happy vagina is a happy life," I tell her with a smile.

"Eeew, that's disgusting," Liz complains. "I can't believe I was actually thinking about giving you a job."

Gavin's face lights up and he turns to face her. "Seriously? Aunt Liz, that would be awesome! Finally, something better than that stupid clothing store."

I gasp, placing my hand over my heart. "That hurts, Gavin, that really hurts. Have you ever taken off all of your clothes and curled up in a box of cotton blend t-shirts? It's like floating on a cloud."

"Forget I said anything," Liz mutters, turning to walk away from us.

Gavin grabs her arm, forcing her to stop. "Wait, Aunt Liz, just hear me out. Tyler might be an idiot, but he really does know a shit ton about our products. He could recite the specifications for everything we carry in his sleep."

Liz raises an eyebrow and looks at me.

"It's true. I've been known to talk about twirling beads, rotating shafts and cock rings during a night of peaceful slumber," I admit.

"Oh my God, this is the worst idea in the history of the world. I must be high," Liz mutters.

"Hey, what a coincidence, so am I!" I tell her with a smile.

Gavin punches me in the arm and I scowl at him.

"I cannot believe I'm actually considering this," Liz sighs. "Here's the deal. I just found out that our guy who usually gives the tours won't be coming back. He hurt his knee pretty bad in the accident and he's not going to be able to stand for the long periods of time that tours require. Right now, I just need someone to fill in until we make a more permanent decision. You have to be friendly, informative and you absolutely CANNOT have sex with anyone on the tour."

"Fuck it, I'm out," I complain.

That earns me another smack from Gavin. Seriously, does he really expect me to work in a sex toy warehouse, playing with toys all day long and not have sex with anyone? I wonder if that includes myself. It better not include myself, that's just wrong.

"He'll take the job," Gavin answers for me.

And just like that, I'm a working man again.

Chapter 3

— Suck on those Giblets —

Ava

"YOU DID WHAT?!"

I realize my voice might be a little high when my mother winces and covers her ears. But seriously, she must be joking.

"Please tell me you did NOT hire Tyler to work at Seduction and Snacks. Are you insane?" I ask, abandoning the email on my iPhone announcing a seventy-percent off sale on Coach purses that I should be writing a blog post about right now. Only something this insane could tear my eyes away from the new coral colored Peyton leather satchel.

It's so pretty I want to pet it.

"According to the doctors, no, I am not insane. Borderline, with homicidal tendencies towards my children, but that's understandable," she replies with a smile.

Before I completely lose it and start throwing a hissy fit, I should probably warn you that my mom, Liz, is not like other moms. She says whatever she thinks and has no filter. We have an unconventional relationship in that she doesn't hesitate to call my sisters or me assholes and my sisters and I are content to continue acting like assholes just to get her riled up. Sometimes it's fun to watch my mom lose her shit. She's obviously determined to turn the tables today.

It's no secret that my mother doesn't really like Tyler, which makes it even more alarming that she actually hired him to work for her company. *I* don't even like Tyler. I'm still trying to figure out why in the hell I ever slept with him in the first place. And then repeated that mistake. Eighteen times.

"You have to fire him. Immediately. Tell him you made a mistake or something," I beg.

There is no way I can go to work at that place every day knowing he's going to be there. It's bad enough he shows up unannounced all the time to hang out with Gavin; this would be much worse and make me hate that job more than I already do.

My mom rolls her eyes and takes a seat at the kitchen table. "If you're going to continue sleeping with him, he needs a better job than folding sweaters at the mall."

"I am NOT sleeping with him!" I argue, stomping my foot and putting my hands on my hips.

Technically, I'm not lying. I'm not sleeping with him right this second.

"Oh, please. I heard barnyard animal noises coming from your room the other night and someone shouting 'Pull my reins, bitch!' I realize you're twenty-one-years old and theoretically an adult, but if I have to hear that shit one more time when I'm trying to sleep, I will beat you like a red-headed step child," she warns.

Did I also mention my mom is sort of the coolest mom ever and has never threatened my life the many times she's caught me having sex? She's always been of the opinion that telling us not to do something will just make us want to do it even more. As soon as my sisters and I got our periods, she marched us down to the doctor, put us on the pill and gave us a lifetime supply of condoms.

Still, knowing she heard Tyler and I having sex makes me feel dirty.

"That must have been a movie I was watching in my room. I'll make sure to keep the volume down from now on," I tell her, attempting to lie.

She scoffs and rolls her eyes at me. "Really? A movie? So you've taken up watching horse porn now, have you? Actually, I think I'd rather you were watching horse porn than sleeping with Tyler."

I ignore her and walk over to the counter to pour myself a cup of coffee.

"Mom, you can't be serious about hiring Tyler to work at Seduction and Snacks. He never shows up for work on time and he's got no work ethic," I complain.

"And yet, I hired you, didn't I?" she asks with a laugh.

"Oh, you're hilarious."

She's right, but it still sucks to hear it. How can I possibly show up on time and be expected to work when I don't care about what I'm doing? Shouldn't you be passionate about your career? The only thing I'm passionate about is spending my paycheck on a new Coach purse.

Just then I hear the front door open and a shout from my sister, Charlotte. "Hello? Is anyone home?"

"We're in the kitchen," mom yells back.

Charlotte walks in the room and gives mom a kiss on the cheek before walking up to me and taking the coffee cup out of my hand. "What's up, skank?"

"Nothing much, twat. I spit in that coffee, by the way," I inform her as she takes a sip.

"So that's why it tastes like rotten vagina," she tells me with a smirk.

"There's so much love in this room I almost can't stand it," mom adds, standing up from the table. "I have to run some errands. Play nice, you two. No fighting, no biting and no hair pulling. I still have bruises from the last time you two were alone in the same room together."

I love my sister, but we have a tendency to butt heads a lot. We always make up right away and never hold grudges against one another, but we've been known to break a few pieces of furniture and one of us usually ends up bleeding. My mom says we've been that way since we were old enough to walk. Our very first fight happened when Charlotte was five and I was two. Charlotte handed me a cupcake she'd made out of Play-Doh and told me to eat it. Being two, I did it without question and promptly puked up the Play-Doh cupcake all down the front of my favorite princess costume. I walked right up to Charlotte and kicked her in the cooch wearing my tiny, black patent leather Mary Janes. I'd seen my Uncle Carter do it to my Uncle Drew and it seemed like it hurt pretty bad, so I figured it would work on Charlotte. My mom said she thought two cats were eating each other's faces off by the sounds of the screams coming from our bedroom.

"So what's new with you? Still sleeping with Tyler the Turkey?" Charlotte asks with a laugh.

I made the mistake of telling Charlotte a little secret about something Tyler does whenever I'm giving him a blow job. Tyler is a talker in bed, and when I'm going down on him, it's even worse. He likes to coordinate said talking with whatever holiday is closest. The blow job in question was right before Thanksgiving. Tyler really got into the spirit of things, gobbling like a turkey while I had his dick in my mouth and yelling out "Yeah, baby! Suck on those giblets."

Do you see now why I kicked him out of my bed the other night? How can I possibly continue to sleep with someone who refers to his balls as turkey organs?

"I thought we agreed to never speak of that again? And no, I'm not sleeping with him anymore. I gave him the boot and told him to never come back," I tell her, pouring myself another cup of coffee.

"Didn't you tell him you would never sleep with him again after he told you to lick his little pumpkins on Halloween?" Charlotte laughs.

"Fuck off," I mutter. "Change of subject. How's married life?"

Charlotte rolls her eyes. "Shut up. We're not married."

"You're living in sin and finish each other's sentences – close enough. It's cute and disgusting all at the same time. He's probably going to propose on Christmas."

Her eyes widen and her mouth drops open. "Oh, my God. Do you think he will? No, there's no way! It's too soon! We've only been living together for a few months. Holy shit, what if he does? What should I wear?"

It's my turn to roll my eyes. She's so giddy and in love that it makes me want to punch her in the throat. I'm happy for her and Gavin, I really am. They have been friends since birth due to the fact that our parents are best friends and we all grew up together. A few months ago, they each decided it was time to admit their true feelings about one another. They both went about it the wrong way, making a list of ways to prove their love to each other instead of just coming right out and saying it. Charlotte's gay best friend pretended to be her boyfriend and Gavin pretended he was dating some bat shit crazy ex-girlfriend of his who wound up beating the shit out of a dude in the bar one night and calling him a Vaginaman. It was a hot mess, but it all ended well. They've been shacking up for the last few months and they work at Seduction and Snacks together. It's so perfect I want to gouge my eyes with a fork.

I'm woman enough to admit that I'm a little bit jealous. My only prospect for love is a man who lights his farts on fire and has a membership to a porn-of-the-month club. I really need to get back into the dating world and forget about Tyler once and for all.

"I'll take you shopping for the perfect proposal outfit, and I'll even buy it for you if you help me find a man," I tell her.

Even though Charlotte and I fight a lot, we still have one thing in common – our love of shopping. Her eyes light up at the idea of going to the mall and she holds out her hand.

I grab onto it and we shake, making a deal.

"Done. I have the perfect guy in mind for you. Don't make any plans for tomorrow night. Do you have something slutty to wear?"

She looks me up and down, focusing on the tight, low-cut shirt

I'm wearing that barely contains my boobs and the short, pleated skirt that stops right below my ass that I paired with black, knee-high stiletto boots.

"Never mind. I see you've already been shopping at Sluts R Us."

She leaves me no choice but to wrap my arm around her neck and put her in a choke hold.

"Goddammit, cut it out, asshole!" she yells at me as I bend over, taking her down with me.

She begins smacking my legs and I start pulling her hair, both of us screaming and cursing.

"STOP BEING SUCH A BITCH! I CAN'T BELIVE YOU– hey, is this the new Mossimo Pointe Stripe jacket?" I ask, pausing to pull the tag out of the neck of Charlotte's coat.

"Yes! I got it on sale at Target. Isn't it cute?" she asks, her head still down by my waist as I read the tag.

"You should have paired it with some skinny Seven jeans and those black Steve Madden pumps you wore to the DMV in August," I tell her, finally releasing my stranglehold so she can stand.

She smoothes down her hair that was mussed during our tussle and stares at me like I'm crazy. "How is it that you can precisely recall what I wore three months ago but you can't remember how to use the photocopier at work?"

I shrug, turning away from her to grab my keys off of the counter. "It's not that I'm incapable of remembering how that machine works, I just choose NOT to remember. It's boring."

"What was I wearing when we went to the Pink concert?" she asks.

"September 23rd? You had on a black Max and Mia drawstring waist dress with nude, Valentino couture bow platform pumps," I reply as I head out of the kitchen and towards the front door.

"October 15th?" she asks, following me outside towards my car.

"J Brand skinny stretch jeans, black Stuart Weitzman knee boots and a fitted, emerald green Donna Karan ¾ length t-shirt," I rattle off easily as I unlock my doors.

Charlotte stands next to the passenger side door, staring over the top of the car at me in awe. "Jesus Christ, you're like the Rain Man of fashion. Why the hell are you working at Seduction and Snacks? You should be taking over Nordstrom's."

I roll my eyes and laugh as we both get into the car.

"Believe me, if I could find a way to make money talking about clothes, shoes and purses, I would be all over that shit."

As we head towards the mall, I try not to think about Tyler or how much I hate my job. Charlotte is going to set me up with a new guy and maybe my life will finally start looking up.

Dating world, here I come.

Chapter 4

- You are NOT the Father -
Tyler

"I'D LIKE TO thank the Academy for this illustrious award," I speak into the mirror in my room, straightening my imaginary tie. "I'm humbled that so many of my peers thought I was deserving of the Dapper Dildo Award."

Do they give out awards at Seduction and Snacks? Eh, if they don't now, I'm sure they will after I've been in their employ for a few weeks.

I can't contain my excitement as I think about the fact that I have a real job. A real, honest to God job that I can be proud of and brag to people about on the street. I mean, The Gap was a pretty good gig – all the sweater vests I could handle and plenty of hot pieces of ass hitting on me every day. They were all gay dudes, but whatev. They appreciated a good thing when they saw it.

I've been trying to get my foot in the door at Seduction and Snacks ever since I found out Gavin's family owned the business. I make sure to keep myself current on all things sex. I've committed to memory the name, cup size and favorite sexual position of every female porn star of the last decade. I'm an expert on all things fetish, from sacofricosis and ederacinism to mucophilia and oculolinctus. I've even volunteered on more than one occasion to be a human guinea pig for new Seduction and Snacks products. I have the organic plaster they were tinkering with for penis molds to thank for the fact that I couldn't grow hair on my balls for three months. A few months of shiny, smooth balls were well worth the third degree burns I sustained on my taint when I tried to use a hair dryer to remove the plaster, especially if sacrificing a few pubes led to Liz realizing my full potential.

Maybe now that I have a good job, Ava will stop being such a bitch and sleep with me again. Grabbing my cell phone off of my dresser, I decide to shoot her a text and deliver the good news.

> *Hey there, loose labia. Wanna carpool in to work tomorrow? I'll let you give me a blow job in the parking lot.*

Satisfied that my news will thaw a little of the ice in her veins, I toss my phone back on my dresser and head upstairs to look for a good copy of my birth certificate.

Yes, I live in the basement of my parents' home. I get twenty-eight cable channels, access to all the porn my dad still has on VHS and meatloaf every Thursday night. Seriously, why would I leave?

Opening the door at the top of the stairs that leads into the kitchen, I stop in my tracks when I see my dad sitting up on the counter with his feet in the sink and my mom standing next to him shaving his legs.

"Oh, hi, sweetie! Do you need the sink?" my mom asks, smiling brightly as she squirts some extra shaving cream on my dad's shin.

Alright, maybe there's at least one reason to move out and get my own place.

"Mom, seriously? I just ate lunch. Do you want me to puke all over the floor?" I ask disgustedly as I avoid looking directly at them.

"Tyler, studies have shown that a man and a woman who share simple, every day experiences like this will have a long and fruitful sex life," my dad says, looking up from what my mom's doing and pushing his glasses up higher on his face.

"I shaved your father's balls for the first time when we were twenty-one and look at us now! We're still going strong twenty-six years later and our love making is more passionate than ever," my mom tells me with a smile.

Shaking my head at them, I keep my eyes averted as I head over to the built-in desk on the other side of the kitchen.

"I like the feel of smooth legs. I totally get why women have been doing this for centuries," my dad adds.

Really, their behavior shouldn't come as any surprise to me at this point. My parents, Donna and Nick Branson, are sex therapists. There was a time when I attributed my love of sex to their constant discussion of the topic, but now I worry all this "sharing" is going to one day seriously effect my ability to keep it up. Last week when I got home from work, I found them in the living room practicing their climax yells. Fully clothed, sitting on the couch, legs crossed like they were attending church services, screaming each other's names in different pitches to see which one sounded the best.

Ignoring my parents' giggles on the other side of the room, I dig through the desk drawers, tossing papers aside as I go. I grow more and more frustrated as I open drawer after drawer, and my parents' laughter gets more and more intimate. I know if I don't find what I'm looking for and get the fuck out of here, vegetables from the fridge will soon be added to the mix – and they won't be used for tonight's salad.

Where the fuck is it? I swear there was a copy in here.

"Sweetie, what are you looking for?"

Glancing up from the mess I've made on the top of the desk, I sigh, slamming the drawer closed. "I need something for my new job."

"Oh, no! Did you get fired from The Gap? Were you trying on all the clothes naked again? I told you they were going to be angry about that."

Geez, you have one runway show after hours and everyone loses their shit.

It's not my fault I didn't realize they had security cameras in the storage room. And really, they should have used that footage for a commercial. I worked the SHIT out of those boxer briefs and scarves.

"No, this time it wasn't my fault. They claim my birth certificate is a fake. Can you believe that? As if," I complain with a roll of my eyes. "I got hired at Seduction and Snacks. I start tomorrow and need to take a non-fake copy in."

My mom and dad look at each other nervously, sharing some silent communication shit before my dad hefts himself out of the sink.

"I think it's time, Donna," my dad tells her, grabbing a towel from the counter and wiping the shaving cream off of his legs.

"You're right. It's time for me to make dinner. Who wants meatloaf?" she asks with fake enthusiasm.

My dad grabs her arm before she can make it to the fridge, turning her to face him. I watch in confusion as he whispers a few words to her before they both turn to face me.

"Tyler, I think you should sit down," my dad begins.

"Dude, this isn't the end of the world," Gavin tells me as I continue splashing cold water on my face in his bathroom.

I showed up at his and Charlotte's apartment twenty minutes ago and have been in the bathroom the entire time trying to calm the fuck down.

"Not the end of the world? NOT THE END OF THE WORLD? I don't know who I am! I don't know where I came from. I'VE LOST MY IDENTITY!" I scream, shutting off the water and reaching blindly for a towel.

My hand brushes up against one and I quickly bring it to my face, wiping off the water that drips down my lips and chin.

"Oh shit, I wouldn't use that towel if I were you," Gavin mumbles.

I ignore him, scrubbing every inch of my face, hoping that maybe I can rub away the memory of the words my mother spoke to me.

"Tyler, your father isn't really your father. I, um… I don't actually know who your real dad is," my mom admitted. "I really wanted a baby and I wasn't seeing anyone at the time, so I went to a sperm bank. Also, when I say I wasn't seeing anyone, I mean I wasn't serious with anyone. I was still having lots of sex."

"Son, what your mother is trying to say is that she was sexually adventurous in her twenties," my dad added with a smile.

"If we're going to be honest with him, we might as well do it right," my mom cut in. "Tyler, I was a slut. Like, a really big one. I was young, though, and that's what you're supposed to do — sow your wild oats. I also went through a short lesbian phase, but that's beside the point."

I sank down into one of the chairs at the kitchen tabled and stared at them. "How in the hell did this happen?"

"Well, I picked out the sperm I wanted and then the doctor had me get on the table with my feet in the stirrups. Then he took a thing that looked like a turkey baster and shoved it up my-"

"NO! JESUS CHRIST, NO! Not that part! How the hell don't you know who my father is if you used a sperm bank? Don't they keep a record of that shit?" I asked in confusion.

"Well, normally that would be helpful, but I also had a foursome that same week. I'm pretty sure one of them was a woman I met in the food court of the mall, but the other two guys — no clue. I always made my partners bag it up, but something must have leaked because I found a little jizz in my-"

"MOM!" I screamed at her, shaking my head in disgust.

"Sorry, sweetie. Since sperm can live in a woman's vagina for up to five days, I can't be certain if it was donor sperm or…" my mom trailed off before glancing over at my dad with love in her eyes.

"Anyway, I met your father when you were a couple of months old and he adopted you. Sort of. We actually never filed the paperwork, but we made a very convincing copy of a birth certificate for you in Photoshop."

My dad walks over to me and pats me on the back. "I think the best thing *for us to do right now would be to sit down and talk about what we're feeling. I'll start. I'm feeling relieved that this is all finally out in the open."*

"I'm feeling like I want to puke all over this fucking floor!" I shouted.

My mom walked over to me and put her arm around my shoulder. "That's it. Let it all out, sweetie."

"Seriously dude, give me that thing," Gavin says, interrupting my thoughts.

I pull the towel away and glare at his reflection in the mirror. He's standing behind me with a look of disgust on his face and his hand out.

"What the fuck is wrong with you? I just found out that my mom was a slut and has no idea who my dad is and all you're worried about is your precious towel?" I ramble, my voice getting that hysterical squeak to it. "What's wrong? Is this one of Charlotte's 'good' towels, reserved for guests or some shit? Fuck, are you pussy whipped."

Gavin shakes his head at me and tries reaching over my shoulder to take the towel. I snatch it away and turn to face him.

"What is your fucking deal? It's a Goddamn towel!" I yell.

"Yeah, it's a jizz towel, dude."

I look at him in confusion, glancing down at the towel and back up at him when what he said finally sinks in. He's biting his lip and I can't tell if he's trying not to laugh or if he's trying to think of a way to run out of here as fast as he can.

"Hey, what are you guys doing in the bathroom?" Charlotte asks, suddenly appearing in the doorway. "Oh, my God! Did you just use that towel, Tyler?"

I quickly throw the towel away from me like it's on fire and it lands in the toilet.

"Dammit, don't throw it in the toilet, you'll ruin it!" Charlotte scolds.

"I'm pretty sure you ruined it by putting jizz on it!" I scream.

"Why the fuck would you leave a jizz towel on the sink where anyone could use it?"

Charlotte shoulders past us and uses the tips of her fingers to pull the towel out of the toilet and then tosses it into the sink.

"I'd never use it. I knew it was a jizz towel," Gavin replies with a shrug.

"Oh, my God! I scrubbed my fucking face with a towel that had your dry, crusty jizz on it!"

I can't believe this is happening right now. My mom had a foursome, my dad isn't my dad and now I have jizz face. Moving as fast as I can, I jump into the shower and turn on the water, not even caring that I'm fully clothed.

"Do you want us to leave so you can take your clothes off?" Charlotte asks, as the water rains down on me, soaking my t-shirt and jeans.

"I am NOT taking my clothes off. There could be trace particles of jizz on them! I'm going to have to burn these clothes!" I complain.

I keep my face under the scalding hot water, taking in large mouthfuls, swishing and then spitting on the shower floor.

"Eeeew, don't spit in our shower!" Charlotte scolds.

"I HAVE GAVIN'S JIZZ ON MY FACE! I WILL SPIT WHEREVER THE FUCK I WANT!"

Gavin grabs Charlotte's arm and pulls her towards the door. "How about we just give you a few minutes alone? We'll be out in the living room. There are *clean* towels under the sink."

I give him a dirty look when he mentions towels.

"Any and all jizz that was previously on those towels has been washed off, I swear," Gavin adds before exiting the room and closing the door behind him.

With a sigh, I stand under the water until it starts to get cold.

Chapter 5

— Dick Nipples —

Ava

"I CAN'T BELIEVE you're making me do this. I don't want to see him," I complain, flopping down on the couch.

"Stop being a bitch to him for two seconds. Tyler is having a really bad day and he could really use some support."

I bristle a little when she calls me out for being a bitch to Tyler. I mean, I know I can generally be a difficult person and I know that sometimes I'm not very nice to Tyler, but I don't think I'm a bitch when it comes to him, am I? He gives as good as he gets, so it never feels like I'm truly being horrible to him. Now that I think about what's going on his life, I actually feel bad for him.

Charlotte called me earlier and told me that Tyler showed up at her and Gavin's house having a meltdown because he found out his dad wasn't really his dad. I feel sorry for him, really I do. I just know that if I'm anywhere near him, I'm going to want to have sex with him. It's like a sickness. I think I need a Tyler Twelve Step Program. Or shock therapy.

"Fine. What's the plan? And where is he anyway?" I ask.

"He sort of jumped into the shower fully clothed. Gavin is getting him some dry clothes to put on. We don't really have a plan other than getting him drunk to cheer him up. I wouldn't normally suggest this, but maybe you could throw him a bone. Give him a little action. That would make him really happy," Charlotte suggests.

"I'm sorry, but did I just enter the fucking Twilight Zone? You can't stand Tyler! You've been telling me for months that I need to stay away from him," I remind her.

"I know, I know. It's just…I've never seen him like this. I feel awful for him. I know I told you I'd help you find a new guy, but maybe we should hold off on that for right now. Tyler really likes you and it might push him over the edge. I already called and cancelled your blind date for tonight."

Great. Now that my sister is on Team Tyler, I'm never going to be able to quit him.

With a sigh, I get up from the couch and head into the kitchen. I start opening cupboards and pulling out bottles of liquor, lining them up on the counter. If we're going to do this, we're doing it right. Maybe if I get Tyler drunk enough, he'll act like an idiot and I won't be tempted to rip his clothes off.

"I DON'T THINK I understand the game of this object. The game of this game. Fuck! I don't think I should have any more vodka," Charlotte slurs.

I've lost count of how many shots we've taken in the last hour. We decided to watch The Kardashians and take a drink every time one of them said 'like'. Gavin is trying to get us to play a different game now.

I watch from my spot on the loveseat as Charlotte curls into Gavin's side on the couch and he wraps his arm around her, pulling her close. Looking over at Tyler sitting on the floor in front of them with his chin resting on the coffee table, I wonder what it would be like to have the kind of relationship that Charlotte and Gavin have. They're so in love it's disgusting, but it's also kind of nice. They always have someone to talk to and lean on. They have a best friend in each other and someone to come home to every day. Maybe I've been too hard on Tyler.

"I think we should play 'Ava lets Tyler stick it in her ass'!" Tyler shouts excitedly.

Never mind.

"Exit only, moron," I remind him.

"I let Gavin have anal. You should try it, Ava. It's gooooooood," Charlotte says with a laugh.

I can't help but cringe. Seriously, there are just some things you should not know about your sister.

"See? Charlotte likes it. You should give it a try. Gavin, can we borrow your bedroom and a stick of butter?" Tyler asks, looking over his shoulder at Gavin.

"What the hell do you need butter for?" Gavin replies.

"Um, duh, for lube."

Gavin reaches for the bottle of vodka on the coffee table and pours four shots. "Moving right along. Okay, here's how this game works. Someone starts off by saying a phrase. It can be anything you want, no more than a couple of words. Everyone else has to scream that phrase as loud as they can without laughing. If you laugh, you take a shot."

"This sounds too easy and like no one will be drinking the rest of the night," I tell him.

"That's what you think. I am the master of this game," Tyler adds. "I'll go first."

The room is silent while he sits there thinking for a few minutes.

I'm about ready to complain that he's taking too long and my buzz is wearing off when he suddenly says, "Dick nipples."

We all stare down at him and then at each other, before we scream at the top of our lungs.

"DICK NIPPLES!"

Charlotte is the first to lose it, naturally. She starts laughing hysterically before she even gets to the word *nipples*.

"Down the hatch, baby!" Gavin tells her with a laugh, handing her a shot.

She tosses it back, half of it dribbling down her chin.

"Alright, since Charlotte lost, it's her turn," Tyler tells her, getting up from the floor and walking over to the loveseat. He sits down next to me, resting his arm on the back of the couch, his fingers brushing my shoulder.

It could be the vodka, but I suddenly feel really warm. I move as far away from him on the cushions as I can, but there's not very far for me to go. Who the fuck made loveseats so small? I can't really get up and move without letting him know he has some sort of effect on me.

Fuck you, hormones.

"ANGRY UTERUS!" Charlotte suddenly yells.

"Seriously, that's what you're going with?" I ask her. "And I don't think you're the one who is supposed to shout it."

"ANGRY UTERUS, ANGRY UTERUS, ANGRY FUCKING UTERUS!" she screams, bouncing up and down on the couch excitedly.

Once again, we all look at each other before shouting it back. This time, Tyler is the one who loses.

"Sorry, I couldn't help it. I just keep picturing a uterus with tiny little fists of fury screaming at people in a chipmunk voice, 'I'm a wee little uterus and I will fuck all of you up.'" Tyler says in a high-pitch voice before taking his shot.

I giggle and then clamp my hand over my mouth.

Jesus Christ, I don't giggle. What the hell is wrong with me? Tyler isn't funny. Tyler is annoying.

I feel the tips of his fingers graze my shoulder again and this time I shiver. Glancing over at him, I see him smirk and it takes everything in me not to reach over and smack him.

Fuck, why does he have to look so good? And smell good, too.

He's taller than me when I wear heels, which immediately goes in the 'plus' column. He's got blonde, surfer-boy hair that is long enough for me to grab onto, but not so long that he needs to put it in a ponytail. That's a deal breaker for me. If you need to borrow one of my ponytail holders, you need to pack up your vagina and leave. He's not big and beefy in the muscles department, but he's definitely cut. I've run my hands over his six-pack plenty of times. If he shaved every day, he'd have a baby face, but with the stubble he's always sporting, that face jumps right up into man territory. And good God, does that stubble feel good when it rubs up against my thighs...

"Alright, dude, it's your turn," Gavin tells Tyler, breaking me out of my fantasy.

I watch in horror as Charlotte moves her hand down to Gavin's crotch.

"We should go have some sex," she attempts to whisper in his ear.

I roll my eyes and take my shot.

"Hey, I didn't even say my phrase yet," Tyler complains as I slam my empty glass onto the coffee table and pour myself another.

Thankfully, the vodka starts to make my vision blur and I can easily ignore my sister as she continues to fondle Gavin through his jeans.

"Big dick titty fucker," Tyler states.

Gavin and Charlotte immediately start laughing before we even have a chance to repeat Tyler's choice phrase. They both do their shot and then Gavin stands up suddenly, pulling Charlotte with him.

"Alright, game's over. My dick has somewhere it needs to be," Gavin laughs.

Tyler and I stare after the two of them as they run from the room and down the hall, their bedroom door slamming closed behind them.

We sit here on the couch listening to laughter and moans coming from the bedroom, and after a few minutes, it starts to get really awkward. I do NOT need to listen to my sister having sex.

"So, what do you want to do?" Tyler asks.

Without thinking about what I'm doing, I push myself up, swing my leg over his thigh and straddle his lap, clutching onto handfuls of his hair.

"This is a one-time thing and I'm only doing this because I feel sorry about what happened to you today," I tell him honestly.

His hands grab onto my ass and he pulls me down against him, lifting his hips at the same time so that I can feel how hard he is.

"I can live with that," he replies.

Pulling his face closer, I crash my lips to his and pray to God that once my buzz wears off I'll forget this ever happened.

Chapter 6
– Accidental Anal –
Tyler

"OH, MY GOD. You're so wet and tight and—"

"Shut up. Stop talking," Ava pants as I pound into her from behind.

It's probably wrong that I've got her bent over the arm of the couch in my best friend's living room, but I don't give a fuck. If this is wrong, I don't wanna be right. I should still be freaking out about the bombshell my parents dropped on me this morning or the fact that Ava is only doing this because she pities me, but I don't have time for that right now. I've been dreaming about being inside of her again and I'm determined not to think about anything else.

My pants are around my thighs and Ava's skirt is bunched up around her waist. We didn't bother taking our clothes off out of courtesy for Gavin and Charlotte. Sure, we're defiling their couch right now, but at least we're being considerate by not being *naked* on their couch.

"You're pussy is like a warm Christmas cookie, fresh from the oven," I mutter as I slam into her harder.

"Jesus Christ, STOP TALKING! Oh, my God, harder," Ava demands.

I close my eyes and let my head fall back as I give her what she wants. God, she is such a bitch. I don't know what it is about her, but I just can't stay away from her. She hates me and I kind of can't stand her, but holy fuck is the sex good with her.

I can feel my balls start to tighten and I know I'm going to come any second. I know I should slow down and savor what could be my last time with Ava, but I can't. Her moans are getting louder and it just turns me on even more. She screams my name and smacks her hands down on the couch as she comes, which just throws me over the edge. Usually, she calls me 'mother fucker' or 'dick face,' so the sound of my name on her lips as she orgasms is enough to make me completely lose my shit. My hips are moving so fast against her ass that the couch starts sliding across the living room floor and, with one last thrust, I start coming. I'm completely oblivious to what I'm doing because it feels so fucking good.

That was my first mistake.

Wait for it.

"SON OF A MOTHER FUCKING BITCH!" Ava screams suddenly and I feel her entire body go rigid before she pulls away from me and scrambles over the arm of the couch.

I can tell by the sound of her voice that this is not a passion-filled 'son of a mother fucking bitch, I'm coming again' scream. It's more of a 'son of a fucking bitch, I'm going to kill you' scream.

It takes me a second to realize what's going on because I'm still in the process of coming, my hips moving all on their own, fucking nothing but air.

My eyes fly open and I find her huddled at the other end of the couch giving me a dirty look.

"What the hell?" I ask in confusion, pulling my pants up from around my thighs.

"What the hell? YOU PUT YOUR DICK IN MY ASS!" she screams.

I open the waist of my pants and glance down at my condom-covered dick in wonder, half expecting him to look up at me and wink for that sweet ninja move he pulled.

Holy shit, I just had anal!

I raise my eyebrows and smile.

Second mistake.

"This is NOT funny. Wipe that Goddamn smile off of your face RIGHT NOW! I was saving anal for my future husband!" she yells at me before reaching for one of the empty vodka bottles on the coffee table and chucking it at my head.

"JESUS CHRIST!" I yell, ducking down behind the arm of the couch just in time as the bottle goes sailing over me and *thumps* against the side of the island in the kitchen.

"It was a mistake, I swear." I raise my hands above my head and wave them back and forth like a white flag of peace. "Either you have a really tight vagina, or a really loose asshole because I didn't even notice."

Mistake número tres. In case you weren't keeping track.

She screams like a banshee and I have just enough time to wrap my arms around my head before she dives over my end of the couch and starts smacking every inch of face she can reach.

"I'm sorry! Jesus, I'm sorry. Stop hitting me! It was an honest mistake!"

"HONEST MISTAKE?!" she screeches. "An honest mistake is speeding, spilling a glass of milk or calling someone by the wrong name. It is NOT sticking your dick in the wrong hole!" she argues, her fist connecting with my cheek.

In between grunts of pain, I manage to grab onto her wrists and stand up. Her hair is a mess around her face and her cheeks are red from exertion and even though I'm pretty sure I should excuse myself to get rid of the jizz-filled condom I'm still wearing, I can feel myself getting hard again.

She tries to struggle out of my grasp but I hold on tight as I climb over the arm of the couch and push her onto her back on the cushions, resting my body on top of hers. Holding her arms above her head, I stare down at her face and try really hard to wipe the goofy smile off of my mine.

I don't know what she's so worked up about. It really *was* an honest mistake. There's only like a one-inch distance between the two holes. It could happen to anyone.

"You know, since I was already in there…"

Yep, you guessed it. I should probably just stop talking.

I may have her hands pinned, but her legs are still in working order. Her knee comes up between my legs and slams right into my balls.

I let out a scream and roll right off of her and onto the floor, clutching onto the boys as I curl up in the fetal position.

In between whimpers of pain, I watch as Ava gets up off of the couch and storms around the living room, picking up random objects: a shot glass, an empty bottle of vodka, the remote control and a huge jar candle. She cradles everything in her arms and then stalks over to me.

"I don't think Charlotte and Gavin expect you to clean up the living room," I groan, pushing myself up from the floor gingerly and wincing when it feels like my nut sack is going to explode.

"Oh, I'm not cleaning up. I'm going to shove these things up your ass and see how you like it," she tells me.

"I told you I was sorry," I remind her, using the edge of the couch to push myself up from the ground.

"We are never having sex again!"

I laugh and, with my hands cupping my balls, I start walking down the hall to Gavin and Charlotte's bathroom to dispose of the condom. I'm definitely too drunk to drive back to my parent's house. Hopefully Gavin and Charlotte won't mind if I crash here.

"You said that last week, Ava. Admit it, you can't get enough of me."

I hear her curse and I can't help but laugh as I use a wad of toilet paper to remove the condom and throw it in the trash before hobbling into the bedroom.

This day started off shitty and even though I can almost feel my balls up in my throat after that kick Ava gave me, it still ended on a good note. I kind of, sort of popped my anal cherry. Technically, I guess I popped *her* anal cherry, but semantics…I feel like I should tell someone about this. Is this the type of thing you post on Facebook or send out a mass text about? If not, it should be.

Tomorrow, I'm going to think about the fact that the man I grew up with isn't my father and pray my parents aren't hurt when I tell them I need to find out who he is. I have to know where I came from. Not just because it's imperative that I have an official birth certificate, but also because I need to know if my dad was a turkey baster or some asshole who slept with my mom and then never spoke to her again. When I do find out who he is, I'm going to beat his ass.

Climbing into bed, I slide my hands behind my head and stare up at the ceiling.

I have no idea who my father is.

I just had anal!

But I have no idea who my father is.

ANAL, MOTHER FUCKER!

Shit, I hate being so conflicted.

Chapter 7

– Ass Captain –

Ava

AS SOON AS the photo loads to the page, I do a quick preview of my blog post and smile. Something Charlotte said to me the other day when we went shopping struck a chord. She called me the Rain Man of fashion. Ever since I was a little girl I have always been obsessed with clothes and shoes, purses and jewelry. I would take playing dress-up to the extreme, reorganizing my mom's closet and putting outfits together for her for an entire year.

Everyone has a blog nowadays. They talk about their lives, their kids, and whatever else they have going on and it's all the same boring crap day after day. I've had a blog for a while and I rarely post on it. When I do, it's always about an outfit I wore or a sale I found at the mall and I always get a ton of hits, so I've decided to test something out and see where it goes. I'm starting an official fashion blog. I'll keep people up-to-date on current trends and where all the good sales are and post photos of myself wearing certain items so they can see how I pair things together. It's not something I'll be able to make a living doing, but at least it's something I'm excited about.

I hit 'publish' on the blog post and, while I wait for it to go live, my cell phone rings. When I see that it's my mom, I groan before answering it.

"There better be a damn good reason why you called off of work today," mom says, not bothering with 'hello'.

Letting out a little cough, I make my voice sound as weak as possible. "I'm really sick, Mom. Like, really. I think it's the flu."

She sighs through the line and I watch with a smile on my face as the views on my blog post already start adding up within seconds of it going live.

"Bullshit. You've been on your computer since dinner last night. In case you've forgotten, I know how to work the Internet. I just saw your blog post go live. Did you seriously call off of work to play around on your blog? You're messing up a perfectly good career opportunity, Ava. Even though I'm part owner of the company, I can't continue to cover for you when you do stupid shit like this," she complains.

I feel the butterflies of excitement about my blog post die a quick, painful death in my stomach when she calls what I'm doing 'stupid shit'. I love my mom, but she's never understood the fact that I don't want to be part of the family business, that I have other likes and interests apart from hers. I feel the sting of tears in my eyes and I have to squeeze them tightly closed to keep the tears from falling. No matter what I do, I just can't make her understand how important this is to me.

"I expect you to be back at work first thing tomorrow morning," she adds. "And for God's sake, call Tyler. He's decided that every time you ignore one of his voicemails or texts, he's going to forward them to me. Remember that song 'Accidentally in Love' from *Shrek*? Well, there is now a five-minute voicemail on my phone of him singing it, but he changed the lyrics to 'Accidentally in Your Ass.' I really do not need to know what *that* is about. Make him stop."

For right now, I decide the best thing is to just agree with my mom. If I try to explain to her once again how much I hate working at Seduction and Snacks, I'll never hear the end of it.

I hang up with my mom and scroll through all of the text messages from Tyler. He's been sending them to me non-stop for five days. Five days since he violated my ass. Okay, fine, it was an accident. I know he really didn't do it on purpose; he's not that kind of guy. He wouldn't just try to sneak his dick in there and figure I wouldn't notice.

Okay, he probably would, but he would be honest about doing it once I called him on it. He was adamant that it was a mistake and I'm pissed off that I believe him. I'm even more pissed off that, after the initial shock wore off, I was sorely tempted to demand he grab some lube and keep going.

As I read each message, I'm ashamed at myself for cracking a tiny smile.

> *I need to ASS you a question. Are you still mad at me?*
>
> *Dear Ava's Ass: I'm sorry. Please forgive me.*
>
> *Love, Tyler's Ginormous Dick.*
>
> *I bought a butt plug. You're right. This isn't very comfortable.*
>
> *Never mind. This isn't so bad.*
>
> *"I'm in love (with your ass), I'm in love (with your ass). Come on, come on, spin a little tighter" Wow, these lyrics are spot on. I think I found our new theme song.*
>
> *Check your voice mail.*

With a growl, I wipe the smile off of my face and finally reply to all of Tyler's nonsense.

> STOP TEXTING ME AND FOR FUCK'S SAKE,
> STOP TEXTING AND CALLING MY MOM!

He replies immediately, asking me if I've forgiven him yet and it makes me wonder if he's been sitting there for five days with his phone in his hand waiting for me to respond. This just makes me angrier because I kind of like the idea of a guy waiting around for me. I just don't like the idea that it's *Tyler* doing the waiting. He needs to go away.

Tossing my phone on my bed, I abandon my blog post, no longer as excited about it as I was, and make my way into the kitchen. Even though I'm not keen on being a part of the family business, I still like the things that are part of that business, namely, baking. I pull out all of the ingredients I need and get busy making some cupcakes. They say the way to a man's heart is through his stomach. I certainly don't want anywhere near Tyler's heart, but maybe a few dozen cupcakes dusted with rat poison will finally make him realize I don't want him.

The first batch of cupcakes is on a rack cooling and I'm whipping up some frosting, when I hear the front door open. Glancing up from the mixing bowl, I see my Aunt Claire walk into the room.

"I smelled baked goods as soon as I pulled in the driveway. Ooooh, cupcakes. What kind?" she asks, coming around the counter and bending down to look in the oven.

My Aunt Claire isn't really my aunt, just my mom's long-time best friend and business partner. She's the one who runs the sweet side of Seduction and Snacks and she taught me everything I know about baking.

"Chocolate chip cookie dough cupcakes with chocolate ganache icing," I tell her as I turn off the mixer and grab a spatula.

"Alright, out with it," Aunt Claire tells me as she turns around and perches on one of the bar stools across the counter from me.

"Out with what?" I ask her innocently, making sure not to make eye contact.

"You only bake when someone pisses you off or you're upset about something, so spill. Who pissed in your Cheerios?"

I should have known that Aunt Claire would realize something was wrong as soon as she walked in the door. She practically raised me and can read me like a book.

"Several people have pissed me off lately. My 'People to Kill' list has grown by leaps and bounds in the past few weeks," I admit.

"Well, that's nothing new. You hate people. Be more specific," she tells me, swiping her finger into the bowl of frosting and bringing it to her mouth. "Add a teaspoon of almond extract to that."

Turning away from her, I reach into the spice cabinet above the stove and grab the almond. I'm not really ready to discuss how disappointed I am in my mom for not understanding my future career choices with anyone, but especially not my mom's best friend. If I asked her to, she would keep my secret, but I don't want to have to put her in the position of keeping something from her best friend, so I go with the easier target.

"Tyler. He's gotten a little taste of the Amazing Ava and now he won't go away," I joke, adding the almond to the frosting and mixing it in.

"I'm assuming that's why you have six boxes of chocolate-flavored laxatives sitting here next to the container of sugar?" Aunt Claire asks, lifting up one of the boxes and raising her eyebrows at me.

I shrug. "We didn't have any rat poison. I figure if he's shitting his brains out he'll be too busy to bug me."

Aunt Claire gets up from the stool and starts rummaging through the pantry until she finds what she needs. With her arms full of pastry bags, decorator tips and pre-made frosting, she comes back to the counter and dumps everything on top.

"I'm going to kick your mom's ass for buying this shit frosting in a tub, but it will save us some time," Aunt Claire tells me as she scoops some of the vanilla frosting from the tub into a pastry bag and adds the standard round tip to the end of it.

"Let's give Tyler's ass a break and do something a lot more fun," Aunt Claire tells me.

I start to say something about how he didn't give *my* ass a break, but I'm not ready to get into that with her, either. I watch over her shoulder as she begins piping words onto the cupcakes. Her handwriting with frosting is flawless and beautiful, even with the words she's chosen to adorn the top of the cupcakes.

I read them out loud, confused a little at the last one. "Smelly crotch, dick biscuit, taint licker…shart fucker?"

Aunt Claire pauses and moves the pastry bag away from the cupcake. "Yeah, I'm running out of ideas."

She continues writing random things on the cupcakes and we're both silent for a few minutes as I watch her work, putting as much concentration into these cupcakes as she does with a wedding cake she makes for a stranger.

After a little while, she finally breaks the silence. "You know, Tyler might be immature, but he does have a little bit of sweetness in him, even if it's kind of fucked up. He's loyal to a fault and will do anything for one of his friends. Plus, his mom's more of a slut than your mom, so there's that."

I can't help but laugh and I'm thankful that my aunt decided to stop by. I still need to end things with Tyler once and for all, but maybe I can stop being such a bitch to him. After I give him these cupcakes, of course.

Aunt Claire finishes the last one, pulling back to examine her masterpieces. "There, all done. I have to stop by Seduction and Snacks after this. Want me to hand deliver them?" she asks.

I nod my head, my eyes zeroing in on the last cupcake. I quickly snatch it from the counter. "Yes, but not this one. He can't have this one."

She watches in shock as I shove the entire thing in my mouth. "Hey, that was my favorite one! What's wrong with Ass Captain?"

Chapter 8

– Pinky Pleasure or Butt Tower –
Tyler

"TYLER, WHAT THE hell are you doing?"

Looking up from the mess surrounding me, I see Gavin standing at the end of the aisle where I'm currently sitting on the floor. It's the end of my first week at Seduction and Snacks and really, I should be ecstatic. Every tour I did of the warehouse went smoothly, I answered all the questions thrown at me expertly and I started up a competition with the warehouse workers that's already starting to boost morale. I'm going to have to set a few ground rules for Vibrator Sword Fight Fridays so we don't almost lose an eye again, but other than that, I'm pleased with my performance. Shoving a handful of ice cubes into the penis-shaped pillow we carry went a long way towards calming Scott Jameson down after the Racing Rocket came close to making him a Cyclops. Obviously the penis pillow didn't make him happy, but we don't carry a vagina pillow. The ice brought down the swelling on his eye and he promised not to sue us for assault with a deadly weapon.

Unfortunately, I can't stop thinking about the fact that Ava won't return my calls or that I might find out today who my dad is.

"Well, Gavin, I'm sitting on the floor surrounded by vibrators and pocket pussies. Obviously I'm trying to think," I tell him, lying down on my back in the middle of the pile and swiping my arms and legs against the floor.

"Are you making a dildo angel?" Gavin asks, walking down the aisle until he's standing right next to me.

I sit back up and carefully stand, making sure not to disrupt my masterpiece. Jumping over the toys on the floor, I stand next to Gavin and we stare down at my pretty dildo angel.

"I heard you talked to my Aunt Liz about the whole birth certificate thing," he finally says.

"Yep. She told me to take my time getting her the real thing and that she'd pay me under the table until then."

I thought for sure Ava's mom was going to fire my ass when I told her I couldn't get her a copy of my birth certificate for the employment forms. She just smiled at me and told me not to worry about it, which is very unlike her. Obviously either Tyler or Ava had already explained the situation to her and she felt sorry for me. Awesome. Yet another person who pities me. I didn't mind it so much the other night with Ava because it meant she'd sleep with me. I don't like everyone else looking at me like I'm some sad, pathetic, fatherless dude.

"Did you tell your parents you called the sperm bank to have them pull the records?"

I nod and we turn to walk away from my angel, making our way into the offices. "I had to. The place wouldn't release any personal information unless my mom went in and signed a few papers saying she was okay with me finding out who my dad is. They're supposed to call me today with the guy's name and phone number so I can contact him."

Unfortunately, they can only give me the name of the guy who donated the sperm. That doesn't mean he's my real father since my mom was a slut.

Goddammit!

We walk into the break room and take a seat at the table.

"And how do you feel about that?" Gavin asks.

The thing about Gavin is, he's a genuinely good guy no matter how much I've tried to corrupt him. He's always been a good friend and I know he's worried about my mental health right now, but I don't feel like hashing this out with anyone. I just want to get this thing over with, find out who my dad is and beat the shit out of him. Then, I can go on with my life and never have to think about the guy ever again.

"Can we stop pretending like we have vaginas? I don't want to talk about my feelings, Dr. Phil. How about we talk about the fact that I got anal the other night at your house," I tell him proudly, leaning back in my chair and clasping my hands behind my head.

"Correction, you *accidentally* had anal and you barely got the tip in. You're forgetting that you're sleeping with my girlfriend's sister. They tell each other everything," Gavin laughs.

"Whatever. My dick still went into a hole that has been previously denied me. I don't care how much of it went in, it still went in. And she baked me cupcakes as a thank you."

Gavin shakes his head at me. "You mean the cupcakes that called you a Piss Drinker and a Turtle Fucker? I'm pretty sure that wasn't her saying thank you. That was her saying that none of her holes will be welcoming you inside anytime soon."

I wave my hand at him. "Mere technicalities."

The door to the break room opens and Gavin's dad, Carter, walks in with Ava's dad, Jim. Liz and Claire have to conduct a huge production meeting every Friday, so their husbands always stop by to pick them up and take them to dinner afterwards.

"Your mom said you boys might be in here. She and Liz have a few things to finish up before they're ready to go. How was work?" Carter asks as he pulls out a chair and takes a seat next to Gavin while Jim does the same next to me.

I've always liked Carter and Jim, even though Jim scares me sometimes. He's a quiet man, but I have a feeling if he knew the things I've done to his daughter, he'd chop off my balls and make me eat them. Gavin is a really great guy, treats Charlotte like a queen and he still punched Gavin in the face when he found out Gavin was in love with Charlotte. If he finds out his daughter has had intimate knowledge of my penis and I've secretly snuck in her bedroom on a few occasions, he will straight up murder my ass.

"Work was good. We were just talking about anal sex, care to add to the discussion?" Gavin tells them with a laugh.

I shoot him the middle finger and give him the stink eye. Jesus Christ, this is not something that should be discussed with Ava's dad two feet away from me. He's within punching distance.

"If you asking about anal sex has anything to do with my daughter, I think you should know that I'm perfectly fine with spending my life in prison," Jim warns him.

I gulp nervously and slide my chair a few inches away from Jim. The closer I am to the door, the easier it will be for me to run the fuck out of here if he finds out about me and Ava.

"Remember the words you're supposed to say to me whenever we're in the same room together?" Jim continues.

Gavin nods his head and speaks in a monotone voice like he's reading from a cue card. "Charlotte and I are waiting until marriage and we have separate bedrooms. We only kiss on Sundays after church and a thorough reading of the Bible."

Jim smiles in satisfaction and relaxes in his chair.

"Well, I myself don't care for anal that much, but Claire is pretty gung-ho about the whole thing," Carter admits, bringing the conversation back around.

"Oh, Jesus Christ, I didn't think this thing through. Stop it, stop it right now," Gavin tells him, covering his ears with his hands and cringing.

I can't help but laugh. He asked for it, thinking he could out me in front of Ava's dad. Now he has to deal with the image of his mom and dad having butt sex. Serves him right.

"If you have enough lube and porn on the television, anything is possible," Jim adds.

"I find that olive oil works much better," Carter explains, placing his elbows on the table and leaning forward.

"I CAN'T HEAR YOU! LA-LA-LA, I'M NOT LISTENING!" Gavin screams with his hands still over his ears.

The men ignore him and since I've got a couple of experts at my disposal, I, too, lean forward and suck in all of their knowledge like a sponge.

"Tell me about this olive oil thing you speak of," I say to Carter.

"Well, olive oil is a natural lubricant, it's good for your skin and it's always handy. However, you can't use it with condoms because it will break down the rubber and make them less effective," Carter explains.

Noticing a notepad and pen in the middle of the table, I grab both of them and slide them towards me. This is too good not to take notes. I start scribbling furiously as Carter and Jim go back and forth.

"Also, lots of alcohol. Liz is always more adventurous after a bottle of wine. We prefer Anal Eaze. It has a numbing agent that works wonders," Jim mentions, grabbing the pen out of my hand and adding that to my list of notes.

"No, no, no. You can't use that shit," Carter interrupts. "If she's numb, she has no idea if your tiny penis is hurting her. She has to feel what's going on so she can tell you to stop."

"LONDON BRIDGE IS FALLING DOWN, FALLING DOWN, FALLING DOWN. LONDON BRIDGE IS FALLING DOWN, MY FAIR LADY!" Gavin screams.

Everyone ignores him.

"Tiny penis, ha! Even after twenty some odd years together, Liz still walks funny after we have sex," Jim admits.

"That's because you're doing it wrong and probably fucked her thigh instead of her vagina," Carter laughs.

"What about you guys? Has either of you ever taken it up the ass?" I ask.

They stop their verbal sparring and stare at me like I'm insane. I don't see what the big deal is; it's a good question.

"I mean honestly, how can you know if what you're doing is any good if you don't experience it yourself?" I ask.

"Tyler, are you gay?" Carter asks.

"No! I'm not gay, I'm just saying. A little equal opportunity goes a long way when you're trying to get your woman to give you something she wouldn't normally. I am man enough to admit that I stuck a little something up my ass, and it wasn't so bad."

Jim stares down in horror at the pen in his hand that he took from me and then suddenly chucks it across the room. He jumps up from his seat and races over to the sink, dumping half the bottle of liquid soap into his hands before scrubbing them furiously.

I roll my eyes at him. "I didn't stick that pen up my ass, don't worry. You do know that we carry a very nice line of butt plugs here at Seduction and Snacks, right?"

Gavin lowers his hands from his ears. "Dude, seriously? Are we talking Pinky Pleasure or Butt Tower? Because there is a huge difference between those sizes."

"Bigger than a Q-Tip and smaller than a bread basket," I tell him with a smile.

"Huh. You might be on to something," Carter says, with a thoughtful expression on his face. "What aisle are butt plugs on again?"

Gavin screams, throwing his hands up over his ears.

"Wait a minute, are you asking all of these questions out of general curiosity or are you sleeping with someone?" Jim asks, drying his hands on a paper towel.

Don't look suspicious, don't look suspicious.

"Oh, you know, just keeping my options open. Hey, is that Liz? Hi, Liz!" I shout, looking through the glass doors next to Jim and waving at no one.

Jim doesn't turn around; he just narrows his eyes at me.

"I swear to all that is holy, if I find out this has anything to do with Ava, I will shove my fist up your ass," he threatens.

"Whoa, slow down there, Jim. I'm only on butt plugs. I'm not quite ready for fisting yet."

Carter leans closer to Jim. "I've got a better idea. How about we just unleash Cougar Claire on him as punishment?"

Jim gives me a sinister look and I feel a bead of sweat run down my back. Having a crush on Claire since college and always shooting perverted innuendos her way did not end well for me a few months ago. It's one thing to have a Mrs. Robinson fantasy about your best friend's mom in your spank bank, but it's something straight out of a fucking horror movie when she decides to act on it.

The sweet nothings she whispered in my ear quickly turned to threats about making me part of the next Human Centipede movie if I didn't cut that shit out. Now, whenever she walks in the room, I have PTSD flashbacks of that day in her house when she made me clean the kitchen floor on my hands and knees and then had me hand wash her period panties with the garden hose out back to teach me a lesson about flirting with older women.

Lesson learned.

Before Jim can threaten me any more, my phone rings. Reaching into the pocket of my jeans, I pull it out and check the display, swallowing nervously when I see it's the sperm bank calling me back.

Gavin notices the look on my face and slowly lowers his hands from his ears as I answer the call.

"Uh-huh. Yep. Sure. Okey dokey, thanks."

Ending the call, I set my phone on the table in front of me and stare at it.

"They found out who my dad is and he wants to meet me tomorrow at noon," I whisper.

Suddenly, getting fisted by Ava's dad sounds a whole lot more appealing.

Chapter 9
— Dolphin Rape —
Ava

"I WANT THIS blog to look really professional and, since you handle all of the media and design stuff for the Seduction and Snacks website, I thought you might be able to help me out."

Sliding my laptop across the table towards Aunt Jenny, I wait nervously as she scrolls through a couple of my posts.

Out of everyone, I figure Aunt Jenny would be the most supportive of my idea. She thinks everything is a good idea, even if she doesn't understand it most of the time.

"I don't get it. Is this going to be a porn site? You've got a bunch of pictures of your clothes all over your bed. Is that a Hermès scarf? Oh, please don't tell me you want to have sex on a Hermès," Aunt Jenny groans.

Closing my eyes, I take a deep breath and try to explain this to her again. "No, Aunt Jenny, this is not a porn site. I'm giving people fashion tips and stuff like that."

Uncle Drew walks into the dining room a few minutes later while Aunt Jenny is still staring in confusion at my webpage.

"Hey, baby, do these jeans make my butt look big?" he asks, turning around and sticking his ass out.

Aunt Jenny looks up and smiles. "No, but they make your penis look stupidest."

I groan and shake my head at her. "I think you mean stupendous and that's just gross."

Uncle Drew walks over to Aunt Jenny and leans down to kiss her cheek before checking out what's on the computer. "Thanks, babe. Hey, are you looking at porn without me? Where's the chick who took all those clothes off?"

I huff and cross my arms in front of me in irritation. "It is NOT a fucking porn site!"

Uncle Drew ignores me and reaches over Aunt Jenny's shoulder to click through some of the pictures. "I don't get it. Why aren't there any chicks in these photos? Oh, hey, there's Ava! Wait, are you doing porn? Your parents are NOT going to be happy about this."

Why did I think coming here was a good idea?

"I can definitely add some graphics to your blog and make it look nicer," Aunt Jenny tells me. "To be honest though, I think porn might be a better idea. You could totally make a lot of money doing that. I don't think anyone is going to pay just to look at your clothes and stuff. Ooooh, you should make some videos of you taking your clothes OFF instead of just having pictures of your clothes lying around AFTER you took them off. People would totally pay to see that."

"I would pay to see that," Uncle Drew adds.

"Eeeeew, seriously?" I ask in disgust.

"Dude, not you. That's just gross," he reassures me. "But Jenny? Totally. You should put Jenny on your site taking her clothes off. I've already got a few good shots of her ass on my cell phone I can send you."

He pulls his cell phone out of the back pocket of his jeans and starts scrolling through his pictures. "Oh, man, I forgot about this one. Remember when we rented the dolphin costume and recorded that public service announcement?"

Aunt Jenny forgets about my site and her face lights up. "Yes! The pasa! That was so much fun!"

"What's a pasa?" I ask in confusion, looking back and forth between them.

"She means PSA," Uncle Drew tells me.

"Right. PSA. It's pronounced pasa," Aunt Jenny adds.

"It's not pronounced anything, babe. It's just called a PSA. It's an acronym," Uncle Drew explains.

"Do I even want to ask what this dolphin PSA is about?"

Uncle Drew sits down at the table next to Aunt Jenny and looks at me seriously. "It's an epidemic that is spreading far and wide. People just have no idea what is happening right under their noses. It's scary and dangerous and they need to be aware. Jenny and I took it upon our selves to educate the world. I can't believe you haven't seen the video. It's been all over YouTube."

Aunt Jenny nods and grabs Uncle Drew's hands. "We read an article about it online and we just knew we had to do something. So, we made a video talking about the dangers of dolphin rape and we posted it online. We've received a ton of messages from people thanking us for our information."

"I'm sorry, did you say *dolphin rape*? Like, what? Dolphins raping other dolphins?" I ask in confusion.

I know I'm going to regret asking this.

"What? No! That would just be silly. Ava, this is about dolphins raping people. Surely you've heard the news," Uncle Drew adds.

"Every ninety-six seconds someone else is raped by a dolphin. Innocent men and women just enjoying a day at the beach and then BAM! A dolphin latches on and doesn't let go. They may seem like sweet and innocent creatures but let me tell you, they are not," Aunt Jenny says with a shiver.

Uncle Drew reaches over and wraps his arm around her shoulders, pulling her in close. "Your aunt had a close call with a dolphin last year on vacation. She doesn't like to talk about it very much."

"It was the worst day of my life," Aunt Jenny wails, burying her face in Uncle Drew's shoulder.

Every day I wonder how in the hell my parents became friends with Aunt Jenny and Uncle Drew. Today, I am completely baffled.

"Um, wow. That's... I don't even know what to say about that," I tell them, completely at a loss for words.

"It's okay, not many people know how to handle a situation like this. It's why we started D.R.A.W. It's a place where people like your Aunt Jenny can meet once a week and talk about their horrific experiences," Uncle Drew explains.

"And D.R.A.W. would stand for...." I prompt, even though I know I'm going to regret it.

"Dolphin Rape Awareness Workshop," Aunt Jenny finishes for me. "Although the meetings don't take place in a workshop. We just couldn't think of another word that started with W."

I'm not sure my brain can take much more information. I really need to bring this conversation back around to my reason for coming here.

"So, anyway. You said you could make some graphics for my site and make it look a little more professional?"

Aunt Jenny pushes away from Uncle Drew and sits up a little straighter. She turns back towards my laptop screen and studies it for a few seconds.

"Sure, no problem. It should only take me a few days. Just write down your password for me," she tells me.

"Well, if you two ladies will excuse me, I have a meeting to get to," Uncle Drew tells us, getting up from his chair and making his way to the front door.

"Meeting? What meeting? You didn't mention that you had a meeting today," Aunt Jenny says as she pushes a piece of paper and a pen towards me so I can write down my log-in information.

"Oh, it's nothing. I just have to see this guy... about a thing. Just... this... thing and a guy with a thing... that I need to see," Uncle Drew stammers as he grabs his keys from the side table by their front door.

"Okay, well have a good time!" Aunt Jenny tells him brightly as he rushes out the front door.

I stare at her as she clicks away at my computer. After a few seconds she looks up at me questioningly. "What?"

"He has to see a 'guy' about a 'thing'?" I repeat, using air quotes.

"That's what he said."

I continue to stare at her. "And you don't think that sounds a little bit suspicious?"

"Suspicious how? He knows lots of guys who have things that need to be looked at," she tells me seriously.

I decide to let it go for now, mostly because Uncle Drew isn't here to act as interpreter while I'm talking to Aunt Jenny. I have more important things to worry about right now, like how I can find a way to make money on this website so I can quit working at Seduction and Snacks without giving my mom a heart attack.

Chapter 10

– I Like Mushrooms –
Tyler

"DO YOU WANT me to come in with you or stay in the car?" Gavin asks as he pulls up to Quick and Delicious, the diner where I'm meeting my...father.

Jesus, it feels so weird so say that.

"Come in. No, stay in the car. Wait, no, come in. SHIT! I don't know what the fuck to do!" I complain as Gavin puts the car in park and shuts off the engine.

"Just take a deep breath, this is going to be fine. Just because you share the same DNA means nothing. Your dad who raised you is still your dad," Gavin reminds me. "Did the company send you that email with his name?"

I grab my phone from the center console and pull up the email app. They sent me an email after we hung up the phone yesterday, but I was too afraid to look at it then.

"This can't be right," I mutter, as I stare at the email from Cryobiology, Inc.

Gavin leans over and glances at the email I pulled up.

"His name is Dean O'Saur? That's got to be a typo," Gavin states.

I close out of the email and open it back up, hoping we both read something wrong.

"Dude, your dad is T-Rex. This may be the best news you've

gotten all week!" Gavin says with a laugh.

I groan and throw my head back against the seat.

"T-Rex be like, 'I can't make my bed with these tiny arms'," Gavin says, pulling his elbows into his sides and flapping his hands around.

"This is not funny," I complain.

He continues. "T-Rex be like, 'Raaaawr, that was a good performance, I'm going to clap now. Oh, wait.'"

He continues flailing his hands until I reach over and punch him in the arm.

Gavin finally drops his arms and sighs. "Just don't be a dick right off the bat. It's not like he got drunk and had a one-night-stand with your mom and then didn't speak to her again for like a ton of years."

I look over at him and raise my eyebrow.

"Fuck! I just described MY dad. Well, this sucks," he complains.

"I'm just going to go in there, see if we look anything like one another and then leave," I tell him.

Gavin nods. "Good plan. Get his medical history too. If there's a history of mental illness then at least you know your problems are hereditary, T-Rex, Jr."

"I'm going to drag you out of this car and beat the fuck out of you," I warn him, reaching for the door handle.

With one last fortifying breath, I shove open the door and step out of the car.

"Oh, you should give him some My Little Pony trivia questions. If he gets them wrong, you know he's not really your dad," Gavin shouts as I flip him off before slamming the door closed.

Really, what's the big deal with the fact that I like My Little Pony? I know for a fact I'm not the only one. I Googled it. There's an entire following of people just like me who appreciate that friendship is magic. If Gavin took one second to watch the videos I gave him, he would realize that they are relatable, endearing ponies that have meaningful developments in their lives. If more people liked

My Little Pony, world peace wouldn't be an issue, I guarantee it. You just can't watch that show without feeling happy. I also can't watch that show without getting horny.

I walk through the doors of Quick and Delicious, scanning the restaurant for a dude in his forties who looks like me. After a quick glance, I don't see anyone that fits the bill. I walk up to the hostess counter and wait for one of the waitresses to finish cashing someone out.

"Hi, I'm supposed to be meeting someone here. His name is Dean," I tell her. I refuse to give his full name to anyone ever, even a complete stranger. That shit needs to stay quiet.

She smiles at me as she comes around the counter. "Yep, he's been here for a few minutes. Right this way."

My palms start to sweat and I feel like I'm going to puke as I follow her through the restaurant. I get more and more nervous with each table we walk by and I contemplate turning around and running back out to the car.

Why the hell am I doing this? Gavin is right. Nick Branson is my father, for all intents and purposes. He taught me how to play catch, he bought me my first My Little Pony and he passed down his porn collection to me when I turned eighteen. I couldn't ask for a better father. I shouldn't feel like I don't know who I am just because I suddenly found out the man who raised me doesn't share the same DNA as me. It shouldn't matter.

And yet, it does.

What if I need a kidney transplant and the only match is this guy? What if my sperm doesn't work and the only way I can get my future wife pregnant with a baby who shares my DNA is by using *this* guy's sperm? I have to do this. I have to be strong and do this for the health of my kidneys and for the lives of my future children. It wouldn't be weird at all that their grandfather is also their father, right? I mean, people do that shit all the time and you never hear anyone say, "This is my grandpa-dad" when they're introduced. It will be fine. It will all be just fine.

"Here we go, I'll be right back to take your drink order."

The woman smiles at me and walks away and I get my first glimpse of my father. He's got the same blonde hair as I do, but that's about the only similarity I see.

The man smiles up at me as I slide into the booth.

"So, you're Dean," I state, breaking the silence after a few seconds.

"I like mushrooms," he replies.

Uh, okay.

"Did you know a female swine will always have an even number of teats? Usually twelve," he adds, the smile never leaving his face.

Thankfully, our waitress comes over and I'm saved from having to comment on pig nipples. She takes our drink orders and leaves us alone again.

"So, thanks for agreeing to see me. I know when you do this sort of thing you never expect to actually meet one of your kids," I tell him with a nervous laugh.

"I like to smell magic markers. Purple is my favorite smell," Dean says, his smile growing even wider.

Oh, my God. They really scraped the bottom of the sperm think tank for my mom, didn't they?

I guess it's random fact time at this Father-Son event.

"Yeah, well, I like to give my balls names that coincide with holidays," I admit, trying to get him to do something other than smile at me.

"Every time you lick a stamp, you consume 1/10 of a calorie. So far today I've had twenty-five calories. I like stamps."

The waitress drops off our drinks and as she turns to leave, I grab onto her arm and pull her close to me.

"Please tell me you made a mistake and sat me at the wrong table," I beg as I whisper in her ear.

She glances across the table and then back at me. "Nope, that's

Dean. He was really excited about meeting his son. But just so you know, he's already eaten four paper napkins and he's got one in his hand right now under the table."

She stands up and pats me on the back before walking away again.

"Dean, give me the napkin," I tell him, reaching across the table with my palm up.

He shakes his head at me and frowns.

"Give me the napkin right now. You can't eat napkins, Dean."

I give him a stern look and he slowly lifts his hand out from under the table, a small napkin clutched in his fist. He reaches towards my hand and right when he's about to drop the napkin into it, he quickly pulls his hand back and shoves the entire thing in his mouth.

I stare at him with wide, unblinking eyes as he chews.

"The average human can eat two pounds of paper before risking a bowel obstruction," Dean mumbles through his mouthful of paper.

As the waitress comes back to take our food order, I let my head drop to the table with a *thunk*.

Chapter 11
— I Will Not Have Sex With Tyler —
Ava

"Look, I told you it's fine with Gavin and I if you stay here until you can find your own place. But do you really think going out and getting drunk tonight is a good idea? You just got in a fight with mom. Maybe you should just stay in. We can pig out on ice cream and watch movies," Charlotte suggests.

I know she means well, but staying here is not going to happen. I'm depressed and pissed off and sitting around watching her and Gavin be all cutesy with one another is just going to push me over the edge.

I ignore her as she sits down on the bed in her guest room while I dig through my suitcase trying to find the perfect outfit for getting tanked and picking up a random stranger at a bar to help take my mind off of things.

I think of Tyler and a flash of guilt washes through me.

Shit! I have no reason to feel guilty. Tyler and I are NOT dating. We have sex every once in a while and, now that I've put an end to it once and for all, I need to get laid and blow off some of this steam. I'm not a slut; I just enjoy sex. Really, really enjoy sex and it's been seven days, thirteen hours and twenty-seven seconds since I last had sex. Not that I'm counting or anything.

"You know mom didn't mean anything that she said today,"

Charlotte continues as I pull a black, quilted, drop-waist skirt from Forever 21 out of my suitcase and hold it up.

"Do you still have that teal, bow-front, studded tube top from H&M that you wore to Molly's sixteenth birthday party?" I ask about our younger sister, ignoring what Charlotte said about mom.

I made the stupid mistake of showing her the finished blog after Aunt Jenny had worked her magic. I was so excited to show someone how great it looked and she shit all over it, telling me once again that I was wasting my time on something that had nothing to do with my future.

"Dude, seriously? Molly's sixteenth birthday was three years ago. How in the hell do you even remember that?" Charlotte asks.

"Do you still have that top or not? It would look great with this skirt and my black Nine West phantom peep toe ankle boots," I muse.

"It's under the box of dildos."

"JESUS CHRIST!" I shout, jumping in surprise and quickly turning around when I hear Molly's quiet voice.

"How long have you been standing there? And that door was closed and locked, how did you even get in?" I demand.

I swear to God, Molly should have been a ninja instead of a pastry chef. After being around her for nineteen years, you would think I'd be used to her stealth, but it still catches me off guard. Out of the three of us, she's the most quiet. And I'm not just talking about the way she can move in and out of a room like a ghost. I'm talking about the fact that we don't know anything about her life. She keeps to herself and never shares any personal information, but you can bet your ass she knows everything about everyone else.

Molly just shrugs. "I have my ways. As I was saying, Charlotte still has that shirt. It's on the top shelf of her closet under the largest box of vibrators I've ever seen."

With that little piece of information, she turns and walks out of the room.

"Jesus fuck, she scares me," I mutter before turning back to face Charlotte.

"I swear she can read minds or some shit," Charlotte adds as I pull off my jeans and slip into the skirt. "Did I tell you the other day I was looking all over the place for a twenty-dollar bill that I swore I left on the counter? My phone rang while I was tearing the kitchen apart and when I answered it, all she said was 'It's in the pair of jeans on your bathroom floor' and then she hung up. I think we need to ask mom just how much pot she smoked when she was pregnant with her."

Pulling up the zipper on the side of the skirt, I walk over to the full-length mirror hanging on the wall across the room.

"I'm sure our sister doesn't have special powers. She probably just has your house bugged," I say with a laugh as I check out my reflection. "Now, go get me that shirt. Or do you need some extra muscle to lift that giant box of dildos down off the shelf?"

Charlotte curses at me before getting up from the bed and walking out of the room. She comes back a few minutes later with the top. I slide it on and put the finishing touches on my make-up before blowing her a kiss and telling her not to wait up for me.

"SO, WHAT DO you say we get out of here? My van is parked outside."

Gulping down the rest of my vodka and Seven, I slam the glass on the top of the bar and turn to face the douche bag sitting next to me.

"Your van? What is this, 1987? Get your hand off of my thigh before I break your fingers," I tell him.

Why did I think going to a bar alone would be a great way to forget about my troubles? As soon as this guy sat down next to me I thought, perfect! A hot guy! And then he opened his mouth.

"Awwww, don't be like that, baby."

Alright, that's it. No one calls me baby.

Clenching my hands, I take a deep breath, not even caring that I'm most likely going to be kicked out of here the moment my fist connects with his face.

I turn my body on the barstool right as he lifts up his glass of beer, signaling to the bartender to get him another. He's so drunk that he can't hold his hand steady and the amber liquid in his glass sloshes all over the place while he waves his hand in the air. I watch in horror as beer splashes all over the top of my teal Taylor leather Bette Mini Coach tote.

"You got beer on my Coach," I whisper, unable to take my eyes off of my brand new purse.

"Yo! Bartender! Another beer!" douche bag shouts, completely ignoring me.

"YOU. GOT. BEER. ON. MY. COACH!"

My voice is much louder this time as the rage washes through me. It's one thing for this guy to grope me and talk like a moron, but no one defiles my Coach purse.

"Calm down, baby. It's just a purse-"

My arm flies out before he can even finish his sentence, my elbow connecting with his throat. He drops the glass, both hands flying to his throat and he clutches tightly to it while he coughs and sputters.

"You bitch!" he manages to shout in between coughs.

Before I can even think about threatening to cut off his balls, a hand shoots in between us, grabs onto the front of the guy's shirt and hauls him off of his barstool.

Swiveling around on my seat, I see Tyler pull the guy's face right up to his own and speak in a calm, cool manner.

"Apologize to the lady."

Douche bag looks over at me and gives me a dirty look.

Tyler's hand clutches tighter to the front of the guy's shirt and he roughly yanks him closer. "I said, apologize to the lady, before I shove my knee in your balls."

I should be irritated that Tyler just waltzed in here and took over a situation I could easily handle, but right now, watching him be this big, bad ass protector is making me so hot I can't sit still.

"Sorry," douche bag mumbles.

Tyler shoves the guy away and he stumbles backwards, tripping over his own feet and bumping into a couple of customers. Tyler turns to face me and closes the distance between us, sliding in between my thighs. Without a word to me, he grabs the drink the bartender refilled during the commotion and chugs it. I stare at his throat and watch his Adam's apple bob up and down as he swallows, biting my lip to stop myself from leaning over and licking his skin.

I will not have sex with Tyler, I will not have sex with Tyler.

"So, what's the deal? Were you on a date or something?" he asks, placing the now-empty glass back on the bar.

"Were you following me? I was doing just fine on my own, I didn't need your help," I snap, wincing when I hear how bitchy I sound.

He just shrugs, his hand reaching towards my face. I jerk back right before he touches me and give him a dirty look.

"Relax, princess, I was just going to move a piece of hair off of your cheek."

I hate it when people call me princess. I *really* hate it when Tyler calls me princess. So why the fuck do I feel like I'm on the verge of a spontaneous orgasm?

"And no, I wasn't following you. I had a bad day and didn't feel like going home. My parents are most likely there doing weird as fuck sex therapy shit and I'm not in the mood to see them," he explains. "Also, I know you can handle yourself. I stepped in for that dude's protection, not yours. I did it for my own sanity, too. I was afraid you'd break a nail on his face and then I'd have to listen to you bitch and moan all night long about your manicure.

I stare at him for a few minutes to see if he's telling the truth. When his gaze on me doesn't waver, I sigh loudly. "Well, I wasn't on a date. My mom pissed me off so I packed a bag and went to stay with Gavin and Charlotte. They were most likely getting ready to do some weird as fuck sex shit and I didn't feel like sticking around while Gavin licks my sister's ass."

Tyler laughs, resting his elbow on the bar, inching his way further between my legs until I can feel the material of his jeans rubbing against my inner thighs.

"What did your mom do to piss you off?"

And just like that, I open up to Tyler, the one person I never thought I would let my guard down around. I tell him about my fashion blog and how my mom shit all over my excitement with it. I tell him how much I hate working at Seduction and Snacks and how I hate where my life is going. He orders both of us another couple rounds of drinks without ever taking his eyes off of me, hanging on my every word and interjecting with little pieces of advice every now and then.

Before long, I'm buzzed and everything he says makes me laugh. My hands rest casually against his chest as he tells me about meeting his real father and something inside of me shifts. It happens so suddenly that I have to catch my breath. My heart speeds up and my hands start to sweat as I feel Tyler's heart beating under my palms. It takes me a minute to realize I'm not having a fucking heart attack. What I'm having is a moment of clarity – Tyler Branson is genuinely a nice guy. A nice guy with a huge penis, a six pack and eyes so blue they look like someone took a blue crayon and colored them in.

He's immature at times, a complete smart-ass and into some kinky shit, but he's nice to me no matter how much of a bitch I am to him; no matter how hard I try to push him away.

Son of a mother fucking bitch, I think I'm falling for Tyler.

Chapter 12

– Hot and Juicy Wiener –
Tyler

"OH, YEAH, THAT'S it. Right there! A little more to the left. Lick my Christmas ornaments."

Ava's mouth stills on my dick and she looks up at me. If my penis wasn't stuffed in her mouth, I have a feeling she'd be yelling at me for something. Her mouth is so warm and wet that I really couldn't care less what she yells at me about right now. She's giving me a blow job in the women's bathroom of the bar and I am not about to tell her to pipe down with the attitude, especially when I feel her graze my dick with her teeth. Nope, never piss off a woman who holds your manhood and the lives of your future children in between her chompers.

She sucks me hard into her mouth and I smack my hands down on the wall of the bathroom stall we're in. As good as this feels, I need to stop her. I'd much rather be between her legs when I come and I have a feeling she's already pissed about the fact that she's kneeling on a bathroom floor right now.

Leaning forward, I slide my hands under her arms and haul her up from the floor, pressing her back against the wall and sliding my hands up her bare thighs. I stare into her eyes as my hands continue to move until they are wrapped around the soft, smooth flesh of her ass.

"Fuck, you're not wearing any underwear?" I mutter as she leans forward and slides the tip of her tongue across my bottom lip.

"I was, but I took them off a little while ago when I went to the bathroom. I slipped them in the pocket of your coat that's still hanging over the chair by the bar," she tells me.

Ava reaches her hand in between our bodies and wraps it around my dick, stroking me while I knead her ass and pull one of her legs up around my hip.

Once her leg is secure, I quickly reach into my back pocket for one of the condoms I stuck in there before I left the house. I told her a little white lie when she asked me if I followed her. Charlotte called me after Ava left her and Gavin's place and asked if I'd keep an eye on Ava and make sure she didn't get into any trouble. Even though Ava swore she'd never have sex with me again, I knew she wouldn't be able to keep that promise.

I quickly rip open the condom with my teeth. Ava takes it from me and easily rolls the thin rubber down the length of my cock. I sigh in pleasure as she lines me up and in one hard thrust, I'm fully inside of her, both of us groaning. I don't waste any time – I immediately start pounding into her, the bathroom stall shaking with the force of my thrusts.

"Take that purse off of your shoulder, it's in my way," I complain, grabbing onto the strap as I hold myself still inside of her.

She smacks my hand away and gives me a dirty look. "Are you insane? Do you have any idea how much this bag cost? I'm not putting it anywhere near that floor. People have pissed on that floor."

I slowly grind my hips against her and try reaching for the purse again. She closes her eyes and moans, but even with her eyes closed she knows what I'm doing and her hand latches onto my wrist in a death grip.

"Touch that bag and you die. A slow, painful death where I cut off your balls and make you eat them."

Her eyes are still closed and she hums in approval when I jerk against her. This time, I'm not trying to distract her with my awesome sexual moves; I'm honestly fucking afraid of her. That little jerk was a reflex when I thought about my balls being detached from my body and force-fed to me. You can make all the jokes you want about balls being delicious and loving the feel of balls in your mouth, but it's not funny at all when we're talking about *my* sweaty, hairy balls.

I make a mental note to shave my balls as soon as fucking possible before I start moving inside of her again. I'm guessing if Ava does make good on her threat, balls would go down a lot easier if they weren't covered in pubes.

Ava's hands clutch onto my hair and she starts mumbling nonsense, telling me to move faster and harder as I bite and suck on the skin of her neck.

"Yeah, you like that? You like it when Big Papa gives you his hot and juicy wiener?" I pant, my hips hammering against her.

Her fists yank on my hair, pulling my head away from her neck so hard that I see stars.

"Ow! What the fuck?" I complain as she gives me a dirty look.

"You cannot say shit like that when we're fucking. You just can't," she warns me, letting out a low groan when I shift my hips and grind my pubic bone against her clit.

"What's wrong with a little dirty talk? I thought you'd like it."

Ava moves against me, matching me thrust for thrust and now it's my turn to groan.

"I like dirty talk. I LOVE dirty talk. What you're doing is not dirty talk. It's 'weird as fuck' talk. Repeat after me: I love fucking you, your pussy is so tight," Ava demands.

Well, damn, that was hot. I kind of wish I had a vagina right now.

Slowing down my movements, I start rolling my hips against her and do as she says.

"I love fucking you, your pussy is so tight," I tell her in a soft, low voice.

She moans her approval, so I continue.

"Your pussy is so tight, like trying to get a new My Little Pony out of the packaging. Like those fucking tight twisty ties-"

"Oh, my God, no! JESUS CHRIST" she interrupts.

I move my hand from her ass and slide it in between us, my thumb finding her clit and rubbing slow circles around it.

"Oh, God, oh, my God," she pants. "Okay, try this one: Your pussy is so wet and feels so good wrapped around my cock."

I hold myself inside of her and start moving my thumb faster against her clit.

"Your pussy is so wet and feels so good wrapped around my cock...like fucking a glass of warm water."

Ava grabs onto my ear lobe and yanks it as hard as she can, pulling my face towards her. "Stop fucking adlibbing!"

I pull out of her and then slam back inside, my thumb still working her over while she gasps and jerks her hips against me.

"I want to come inside you and then I want to fuck that tight little ass of yours," Ava mutters.

Pausing my hip thrusts, I stare at her in shock until she opens her eyes.

"When I told you I bought a butt plug, I didn't really think you'd take that to mean I wanted you to fuck me in the ass. Honestly, I don't even know how that works," I admit.

She rolls her eyes, moving her hands to my hips and forcing me to start pounding into her again.

"Hello? I'm giving you dirty talk suggestions. You're supposed to say that to me," she complains.

Once again, I completely stop moving.

"Wait, you want me to come inside you AND fuck your ass? You didn't talk to me for a week when I just put the tip in. I'm so confused right now," I tell her with a shake of my head.

"You know what? How about we just don't talk. At all. Just keep doing what you're doing with your thumb because I'm about two seconds away from coming," she moans.

Alrighty, that I can do.

Getting back to business, I keep my mouth shut and continue pounding into Ava, moving my thumb over her in tiny circles. Within seconds, she's screaming my name and I quickly follow right behind her. Who knew having sex in a bar bathroom could be so hot?

After we catch our breath, I pull out of her and dispose of the condom. Ava straightens her clothes and runs a hand through her long hair before we unlock the stall door and make our way back out to the bar.

"So, does this mean we can renegotiate the whole anal thing? Because I've been studying up with porn and I think I know what I did wrong last time," I tell her as we get to our seats.

"Shut up, Tyler," Ava replies.

My balls are still intact and we managed to spend a few hours together without killing one another.

I'd say this is progress.

Chapter 13
— Wood Chipper —
Ava

"JESUS CHRIST, THESE women are insipid fools who should just wear signs on their foreheads that say 'I'm a whore'," I mutter to myself.

Yes, I'm talking out loud to myself while watching *The Bachelor*. I can't help it. Even though these bitches make me want to throw myself off of a bridge, I continue to watch it. Ever since Aunt Jenny spruced up my blog, I've started writing little commentaries while I watch the show and I've noticed they get a ton of hits. Sure, I'm not talking about fashion on my fashion blog right now, but I'll do anything just to get people to click on the site.

Pulling up the app on my phone for my blog, I type up a quick post about tonight's show, letting everyone place bets on how long it will take for the first woman to start crying. The winner will get an open-knit eternity scarf from Urban Outfitters. One of the perks of having a fashion blog that's growing in popularity — designers will send me samples to try as long as I blog about them.

Social media is a crazy, awesome thing. The more I started posting on my blog, the more people started sharing my posts on Twitter, Facebook and Instagram. Pretty soon, companies got word of what I was doing and started contacting me about sending out some free stuff. Who was I to turn down free shit, especially clothes, purses and jewelry?

"Um, Ava? Could you come here for a minute?" Tyler shouts from down the hall.

Tyler has been crashing on Charlotte and Gavin's couch for the last couple of nights. After the night in the bar, I should be mad at him, but I couldn't bring myself to feel anything other than just a tiny bit happy. I knew he was lying when he said he hadn't followed me there. Charlotte told me that she let Tyler know I was going to a bar and most likely going to pick up some random dude to wash all of my sorrows away. Even though I don't do relationships, it was kind of nice to have him get a little jealous and come after me. I've never had a guy give a rat's ass about anything I do, mostly because the feeling is mutual. No guy has ever sparked my interest for longer than one night. Now that we're both living under the same roof, I'm sure whatever misguided feelings I have for him will be punched right in the face very quickly. There's no way we'll make it more than a week without killing each other.

"Ava? Are you out there?" Tyler yells again.

Case in point. I'm really fucking busy right now and he probably just wants sex.

"*The Bachelor* is on, can't it wait an hour?" I shout back.

Just then, one of the women on the show starts sobbing because she only got five minutes of alone time with that jackass they're fighting over like rabid women at a Hermes Birkin bag sample sale and now she's certain he'll never love her.

"Oh, my God, YOU JUST MET HIM!" I scream at the television.

I check my watch and realize that we have our first crier at exactly twelve minutes and seventeen seconds. Scrolling through the comments on my blog, I see that I have a winner who guessed twelve minutes correctly. Looks like she's getting a lovely scarf to commemorate the downfall of smart, independent women everywhere.

"Seriously, Ava, this can't wait!" I hear Tyler yell again.

With a roll of my eyes, I pause the DVR and toss my phone onto the couch cushions before getting up and heading down the hall.

Tyler meets me right outside the bathroom door with a towel wrapped around his hips while he chews on his bottom lip nervously.

It takes me a minute to compose myself when I see little droplets of water sliding down his chest. Thoughts of every single cheesy romance novel I've ever read float through my mind as I stand here like an idiot with my mouth open and stare at him, trying not to say things like "rock hard abs," "delicious six-pack" and anything with the words "manly" and "bulge".

Thank God Charlotte and Gavin went out for the evening. Now that I've fallen off the No Sex With Tyler Wagon, I plan on shifting that baby into high gear and riding him into the sunset.

"So, I need to show you something, but you have to promise not to laugh," Tyler says, pulling me out of my daze.

Before I can confirm or deny said promise of laughter, he yanks the towel away from his hips and drops it to the floor by his feet.

I didn't think it was possible for my mouth to open any wider than it already was. I've seen Tyler's penis before; I've had Tyler's penis in my mouth. While it's a pretty amazing sight to behold, for once that's not what has me in such a state of shock.

"Do you have a Band-Aid on your balls?" I ask incredulously as I tilt my head to the side to get a better look.

He's grabbed onto his penis at this point and pulled it up flush with his stomach so I can see what's going on. Sure enough, the area between his balls and his shaft is covered with a pink, My Little Pony Band-Aid.

"Yep, that's a Band-Aid. I sort of had an accident with the hair clippers I found under the sink in Gavin's bathroom," he admits, craning his neck to stare down at his own junk.

"You used Gavin's hair clippers to trim your ball hair? Are you insane?" I question, kneeling down to get a better look.

I should be walking away and not entertaining his odd behavior but really, how often do you get to see a dude with a Band-Aid on his balls?

"Under different circumstances, having you on your knees with your face by my cock would be so totally awesome," Tyler sighs.

I look up at him from the floor and scowl.

"But yeah, those clippers must have been from the 1950's or some shit. They sucked my pube hair into them like a fucking wood chipper and wouldn't let go. I can't believe you didn't hear me screaming from the shower. There was so much blood. Blood from my balls was everywhere. It was like Texas Chainsaw Ball Massacre."

He reaches down and starts peeling away the edge of the Band-Aid. I quickly jump up and move away, my back slamming into the wall in the narrow hallway.

"Oh, my God, what are you doing? Don't take that thing off! You're going to get your ball sack blood all over Charlotte's carpet!"

He ignores me, pulling the Band-Aid completely off and I cringe when I see the cut that goes straight up the underside of his penis. It looks like he tried to filet his junk like a fish.

"Why in the hell would you do that to yourself?" I question, shuddering when he taps his finger against the cut and then checks his finger for traces of blood.

"I just thought a little manscaping was in order. You're considerate enough to get waxed so I don't yack up a pube when I'm down there, thought I'd return the favor," he tells me with a smile.

Is it weird that I think this is kind of sweet? It's totally weird. I've lost my fucking mind.

"It's almost done bleeding," he continues, grabbing the towel from the floor and wrapping it back around his hips. "Man, I screamed like a bitch when the soap got on it in the shower. So, are we having sex tonight or what?"

Shaking my head, I turn and head back into the living room. "If getting soap on it hurt that bad, what the hell do you think my vagina is going to do to it?"

Tyler follows behind me. "Your vagina is sweet and kind and would never hurt my penis. Don't worry; it will be fine. It's way down at the bottom, so unless your vagina decides to suck up my balls, it will be okay. The bleeding should stop soon."

I turn around to face him when I get to the living room, crossing my arms in front of me. I can't help but stare back down at his crotch and feel a little sad that he covered it up. It really is a nice penis, even with a sliced scrotum.

"I am not earning my red wings with you tonight. Thanks, but no thanks," I tell him.

"Hey, I earned my red wings with YOU. It's only fair you reciprocate," he argues.

"That was an accident! You banged my period right out of me." Tyler laughs and puffs out his chest. "Yeah, I did. I should get that on a t-shirt. 'This guy bangs out Aunt Flo'."

He may be annoying, but he's phenomenal in bed. I have to clench my thighs together just thinking about how many orgasms he'll give me tonight.

"Fine, but if you get blood on Charlotte's sheets, you're explaining it to her," I warn him.

Chapter 14

— Hoity Toity —

Tyler

I INHALE DEEPLY and settle back into the couch next to Gavin just as Ava walks in from the kitchen with a glass of water in her hand.

"Did you just smell your fingers?" she asks me in horror.

Gavin and Charlotte got home from dinner as I stripped the condom off of my dick, leaving Ava in the bed blessedly silent after orgasm number four. You'll be happy to know there was no blood shed. Actually, Charlotte will be happy to know that since she does the laundry and won't have to worry about getting scrotum blood out of sheets.

I wiggle my fingers in the air at her and smile. "Yes, I did just smell my fingers, thank you for asking."

She looks at me in revulsion. "Why? Why would you do that?"

Gavin and I look at each other and shrug, speaking at the same time. "It's a guy thing."

Ava looks like she's going to puke. She mutters something about us being gross before heading down the hall to return to bed.

"I don't understand why women don't get that? You would think it's a compliment that I want to carry around her smell with me forever," I complain.

Gavin nods his head in sympathy.

"So, you haven't said a word about meeting your dad the other day. I know I kind of made fun of the fact that his parents hated him for giving him such a shitty name, but other than that, how was it?" he asks.

I let out a big sigh, the smell of my fingers forgotten for the moment. "Dude, I don't get it. I mean, my mom had to go through profiles to pick out the sperm she wanted. Out of every sperm in the book, that's who she picked?"

"Well, it's not like she was looking for a father figure, just a donor. Who cares if you guys have nothing in common," Gavin states.

"Um, nothing in common would be an understatement. The guy asked our waitress for crayons during dessert and then ate the blue ones because he said they taste like purple. I had to keep all of the napkins away from him because he tried to eat those, too, and when the bill came he asked if he could pay for it with red Skittles. It was like eating lunch with a toddler."

Gavin raises his eyebrow at me. "So, you're saying he was really immature? Wow, that doesn't sound anything like you."

I punch him in the arm and scowl at him. "I will have you know, I'm a fun, enthusiastic immature. This guy was just fucking weird."

"Did you talk to your mom about it?" Gavin asks.

I don't even want to think about my mom right now. When I went to the house to pack a bag and tell her I needed some time away to get my thoughts in order, she gave me a book on Kama Sutra and told me some new sex moves might cheer me up. I tested out the Inverted Cow and the Splitting Bamboo in the kitchen earlier and, while those did perk me up a little bit, The Deckchair and the Lustful Leg totally fucked up my thigh and now I have a pulled muscle. All I wanted from her was an explanation as to why she never told me the truth. All of those fucking sex ed homeschooling classes she made me sit through and she never once thought it would be a great idea to tell me she picked up some strange spunk at a drive-thru window?

"I'm done talking to my mom. Her answer to everything is sex,"

I complain.

"Um, your answer to everything is sex," Gavin reminds me.

"Well, yeah, but it's just gross when it's my mom suggesting it."

Gavin leans back into the cushions and we both kick our legs up on the coffee table. "Did you ever think that maybe the sperm bank made a mistake? I mean, I don't want to get your hopes up or anything, but I'm sure that sort of thing happens from time to time. Maybe they just pulled the wrong record or something."

That very thought crossed my mind right about the time Dean O'Saur started eating butter packets with a knife and fork without removing the foil wrapper.

"What if I find out that the sperm she used isn't even what got her pregnant? My mom told me herself she was kind of a slut and had a foursome the same week she went to the sperm back. God only knows who my father could be. Jesus God, what if it's someone worse than Dean O'Saur?"

Gavin laughs. "I don't think there is anyone worse than Dean O'Saur, unless he has a brother named Terry Dactyl."

"Actually, that's not a bad name. That would make me Tyler Dactyl. That's kind of bad ass," I consider.

"It doesn't have to be someone worse, you know. What if it's someone totally awesome? A rich, Hollywood actor or something. You could be a millionaire and not even know it."

The more I think about this, the more excited I get. "Oh, my God, what if my dad is Peter New?"

Gavin stares at me in confusion.

"Um, hello? Peter New? The voice actor for Big Macintosh on My Little Pony? God, it's like you live in a cave or something," I complain.

"I was thinking more along the lines of Brad Pitt or Robert Downey, Jr."

Now it's my turn to look at him like he's crazy. "Who?"

Gavin shakes his head at me and I ignore him. This idea has already taken root inside my brain and it totally makes sense. I mean,

Peter New is from Canada, which is like right by Ohio. I think. I could see him hanging out on college campuses and hooking up with my mom. I mean, I can't actually see *that* part or else I'd have to pour bleach in my eyes, but it has to be true.

"Even if it's not Peter New, it could definitely be Trevor Devall," I think aloud. "I mean, he's an older dude but my mom wouldn't care about that. She's an equal opportunity banger."

When Gavin doesn't reply, I turn my head to see he still has a blank look on his face.

"God, you are so out of the loop it's scary. Trevor Devall is the voice of Hoity Toity. Not one of my favorites, but still a great character in his own right. He always makes good choices, he's an Earth Pony and a major representative of the fashion world. Which would totally explain my attraction to Ava."

"Alright, slow your roll there, Pinkie Pie," Gavin interrupts. "I'm pretty sure your dad isn't going to be someone who does voices for My Little Pony."

"For your information, Pinkie Pie is a chick. It's not biologically possible for a chick to be my dad, nice try. And hello? You thought my dad could be Robert Pitt or Brad Downey, Jr. or whatever," I fire back.

"That's not...you know what? You're right," Gavin says, throwing his hands up in the in defeat. "Your dad could technically be anyone and you won't know for sure unless you contact the sperm back."

"I already contacted them."

"HOLY SHIT!" Gavin and I shout in surprise at the same time as we turn to see Molly standing at the end of the couch staring down at her cell phone.

"Where the fuck did you come from? How long have you been here?" I demand.

She just shrugs without taking her eyes off of her phone. "I've been here all night."

"Uh, all night?"

Molly finally looks up with a blank expression on her face. I swear to God she's a fucking robot or cyborg or some shit.

"Yes, all night. I was here for the wood chipper incident and listened to you cry about a My Little Pony butt plug. You know I'm only nineteen, right? I'm in the prime of my youth and you just scarred me for life."

Gavin turns away from Molly to look at me. "Wood chipper?"

I shake my head at him. "That's for another time, my friend."

Looking back at Molly, I get back to the important matter at hand. "You said you contacted them. Who did you contact?"

She rolls her eyes at me and if I wasn't afraid that she's a secret agent with the CIA and probably knows a hundred different ways to decapitate a man, I'd probably get lippy with her.

"I emailed the sperm back while you two Nancys were learning a new Friendship is Magic secret handshake," she deadpans.

"There's a secret handshake?" Gavin asks.

"NO! Ponies don't have hands! And the MLP's wouldn't reduce themselves to such trivial group activities," I inform them with disgust.

"Anyway," Molly continues. "They emailed me right back and apologized for the mix-up. Turns out you were right. Dean O'Saur isn't your real dad. They've been converting all of their old paper files to a new system and got your mom's information switched with someone else's. You have a meeting with them tomorrow at noon."

And with that, Molly shoves her phone in her back pocket and heads out the front door.

"Well, the good news is, you don't have to worry about sharing a meal of Crayolas at Dean's house for the holidays. The bad news is, when I marry Charlotte, I'll be related to Molly and I'll always have to sleep with one eye open," Gavin says with a sigh.

Looks like it's back to the drawing board for me. Fingers crossed that the sperm bank gets it right this time. Otherwise, I'm heading to BronyCon and finding my dad on my own.

Chapter 15
— Stripper Glitter —
Ava

"NO, NO, NO, you're doing it wrong. The Santa heads have to have blue eyes. Oh, my God, just let me do it."

Aunt Jenny, Charlotte, my mom and I all put down our knives and slowly back away from the table as Aunt Claire curses and scowls at us.

She invites us over every year to help her decorate the cookies for Christmas day, and every year she bitches at us for doing it wrong.

"For the love of God, slutbag, it doesn't matter if Santa has blue eyes or green eyes," my mom complains.

We all watch as Aunt Claire stalks towards her, waving a butter knife dripping with red frosting that looks a hell of a lot like blood.

"I don't tell you how to diddle yourself with vibrators, you don't tell me how to decorate my cookies, fuck face!"

Before this gets out of hand and frosting starts flying around the kitchen, Charlotte and I separate the two of them. Aunt Claire goes back to making her cookies perfect while my mom makes everyone some coffee.

For right now, the two of us have called a truce. I'm not ready to move back home yet and she's not ready to accept the fact that I don't want to spend my days filing order forms for Pocket Pussies, but at least she's stopped making snarky comments about my blog for the moment.

"So, any news on when my son is going to propose?" Aunt Claire asks nonchalantly.

I watch as Charlotte's face reddens in embarrassment and I can't help but be a little happy that she's in the hot seat for once instead of me.

"Um, I don't...uh, oh, my God," Charlotte stammers, looking at me with wide eyes and a look on her face that clearly says "Help me the fuck out".

I just shrug and smile at her. I'd like to know the answer to this question, as well. The two of them are already acting like they're married; they might as well make it official.

"I bet he'll do it on Christmas in front of everyone," I offer.

Charlotte shoots me a dirty look and I can't help but laugh. We've talked plenty of times over the years about the perfect proposal and Charlotte hates the idea of it going down on a holiday in front of a bunch of people. Especially people as insane as our family.

"Oh, thank God. If your Aunt Claire doesn't get to wear that blue dress she bought for the wedding soon, her ass is going to outgrow it," mom says as she pours herself a cup of coffee.

"Well, at least my tits won't be falling out of my dress like a cheap hooker," Aunt Claire adds, not looking up from her frosting work.

"Hey, I am a high priced hooker, get it right," mom fires back.

"I love you, bitch," Aunt Claire says with a smile.

Mom puts her hand over her heart. "Right back at you, skank."

Right then, Aunt Jenny burst into tears.

"What the hell, Jenny? You know we love you too," mom says in confusion, walking up behind her and patting her on the back.

Charlotte grabs a few tissues from the box on the counter and holds them out for Aunt Jenny to take. She blows her nose and takes a few minutes to calm down before she speaks.

"I think Drew is cheating on me," she tells us with a sniffle.

"I will cut off his dick and shove it down his throat," my mom states angrily.

Aunt Claire puts her frosting knife down and holds up her hands. "Wait just a minute. Why in the hell would you think Drew is cheating on you?"

"When we had sex the other night, he said he was too tired to use the nipple clamps and chip dip," Aunt Jenny complains, starting to cry again.

"Oh, gross. You two are almost fifty. Is there ever going to come a time when you have sex like normal people?" mom complains.

Ignoring her, Aunt Claire continues with her questions. "So, aside from that, is there anything else? I mean, maybe he really was just tired."

Aunt Jenny dabs at her eyes with a tissue. "He's been gone a lot lately and he keeps telling me he has meetings, but I think he's lying. Three times in the last week, I've found glitter on his clothes."

"He's probably just going to a strip club or something," Charlotte tells her with a shrug.

Aunt Jenny shakes her head. "No, it's definitely not stripper glitter. This glitter was thick and dark. Stripper glitter is fine and antidepressant."

"Well, I've always wondered if stripper glitter had anxiety issues," my mom mutters.

"Do you mean iridescent?" Charlotte asks Aunt Jenny softly.

"I don't know. I don't know anything anymore," Aunt Jenny sighs. "Just forget about it. I'm going to sit Drew down and make him tell me what's going on. I swear to God if he's having sex with another woman and didn't ask me to join, beds are gonna roll."

Mom groans. "HEADS are gonna roll, Jenny, HEADS."

"Okay, change of subject," Aunt Claire announces, turning to look at Charlotte. "I'm going to make a 'Congratulations on your Engagement' cake for you and Gavin to serve at Christmas dinner, so let me know what flavor you want. Oh, and your mom and I already picked out the invitations for the engagement party and I've got some great new cookie cutters of diamond rings we can use for favors-"

"Ava is falling for Tyler!" Charlotte suddenly shouts, cutting off Aunt Claire.

"What the fuck, Charlotte?" I yell back.

I get that she's freaking out about the prospect of getting engaged and everyone planning everything before it's even happened, but Jesus, she didn't need to throw me under the damn bus! Falling for Tyler...as if!

"Well, as luck would have it, we just got a new line of My Little Pony sex toys in at the shop," mom says with a sigh. "You'll never run out of gifts to celebrate your love. I'm particularly fond of the My Little Pony Fleshlight. They come in pretty colors."

Aunt Jenny finally perks up after her little meltdown. "I bought Drew one of those already! I also got him the Lyra Plushie and he can stick his penis in her ass. She's so cute. But word to the wide, make sure Tyler doesn't finish in her. Whatever she's made out of is a bitch to clean."

We all groan in disgust.

"I am not falling for Tyler and I will not be supporting his freaky My Little Pony habit by purchasing anything from that line of toys, thank you very much," I inform them.

Just because he has fabulous abs and a perfect dick, he's easy to talk to and occasionally says really nice things to me doesn't mean I'm falling in love with him. That's just stupid.

"Did you hear about what happened with the whole sperm bank mix up?" Charlotte asks.

Everyone nods and mutters words of compassion for Tyler while I stand there in confusion for several minutes until Charlotte notices.

"He didn't tell you? Dude, the sperm bank fucked up their records and gave him the wrong name. Now they can't figure out where his mom's records are so he has no idea who his dad is all over again. He's been really down about it," Charlotte explains.

What? Why didn't he tell me this?

I've been so busy worrying about my own problems that it didn't even occur to me to ask Tyler about his. I suck.

Wait, what? No, I don't suck. Who cares about his problems? He's a booty call, nothing more.

But shit, he must feel awful. I couldn't even imagine what it would be like to not know who my dad is. I don't like all of these conflicting feelings that are going on inside of me right now. All of a sudden I feel like doing something nice for him. I don't do nice. What the hell is wrong with me?

Shit, there is no way I'm falling for Tyler Branson.

Chapter 16

– *Pulsating Posey* –
Tyler

"WE NEED TO talk."

I quickly remove my hand from the My Little Pony butt plug I may or may not have been petting and turn around to face Ava.

"Does that sex toy have a pink horse tail on it?" she questions, tilting her head to the side to look around me.

"I wasn't touching it!"

She rights her head and raises her eyebrow.

"Ok, fine. I was touching it, but it's so soft and silky," I admit.

Ava shakes her head like she's trying to clear all thoughts of me playing with a butt plug with an attached tail.

"Anyway, I think we should talk," she tries again.

I don't like how serious she looks. Ava and I don't do serious. We do sex and we snap at each other and we do both quite well. This can only mean one thing – she doesn't want us doing the sex anymore.

Fuck.

"Can we go somewhere else? I feel dirty standing in an aisle of My Little Pony sex toys. Holy shit, does that vibrator have a My Little Pony head on it?" she asks in awe, stepping around me and reaching for the yellow and pink vibrator in the box next to the MLP Fleshlights.

"That's Pulsating Posey. On the show she's known for her garden of flowers. At Seduction and Snacks, she's known for titillating the petals of the flower between your legs," I explain.

She quickly tosses Pulsating Posey back into the box, turning back around to face me. If I'm not mistaken, I think PP might have turned Ava on just a little bit. If this chick suddenly develops a fondness for all things MLP, I'm going to have a hard time walking away from her.

"So, you want to talk, huh?" I ask her with a sigh. "Come on, let's go into my office."

I turn and walk down the aisle like a man going to the electric chair. I guess I should have known this was coming. Someone as beautiful and confident as Ava doesn't hang around a guy like me for that long. Sure, I have a better job and I'm not living in my parent's basement anymore, but I'm not exactly at the top of the "Great Catch" list either.

In the front corner of the warehouse, they've set up a small room for me to use as an office. It used to be a storage room and it doesn't have any windows, but it has a desk, a filing cabinet, a door that locks and a computer so I can watch porn in peace during my lunch hour. When we get inside, I close the door behind Ava and wait for her to drop the ax and bring an end to our magical time together of fucking like rabbits.

Ava perches her hip on the edge of my desk and I lean against the closed door with my arms crossed in front of me. I've had plenty of fantasies about screwing her on top of that desk and I'm a little sad that I won't get to fulfill them. Unless, of course, she's down with one last go for old time's sake.

"We've been spending a lot of time together and I realized that all we do is have sex," Ava starts, wringing her hands in her lap and cracking her knuckles nervously. "It's nice and all, but I thought we should talk. You know, try something new."

I can't stop the laugh that bursts out of my mouth. "Talk? You actually want to act like a nice human being?"

She winces, quickly looking back down at her hands and I immediately want to take my words back. I know we constantly bicker back and forth and can lob insults at each other with the best of them, but I can tell something is different with her this time. Here I was lamenting the fact that I'd never get to have sex with her again while she wanted to do something normal like talk and I go and fuck it up with my mouth.

"I didn't mean-"

Ava holds up her hand and cuts me off. "No, I get it, I'm a bitch."

"You're not a bitch."

She cocks her head and looks at me like I'm an idiot.

"Okay fine, you're a little bit of a bitch, but I don't care and obviously it turns me on," I admit, pushing away from the door and walking closer to her.

"I know I act like I don't care and that I'm just sticking around for the sex. I'm not used to someone like you. I've never been with anyone who I could tolerate for more than a day or two. I never expected for…*this*," she gestures between us. "To amount to anything. I never expected to *feel* things. I certainly never expected to be hurt when I found out something happened with your bio-dad situation and you didn't tell me yourself."

She lets out an uneasy laugh and I move even closer, sliding my body in between her legs and resting my hands on her hips. The only sides of Ava I've ever seen are sexy-hot and annoyed-bitchy. I didn't think it was possible to want her more than I already did, but I was wrong. Seeing her vulnerable and nervous as she opens up to me just the tiniest bit makes me want to rip all of her clothes off and make her mine.

"I think it's probably obvious to everyone that I'm unhappy with my life and where it's going. I took it out on you and I'm sorry about that," she says softly.

"You don't have to apologize. You drive me crazy, but I have more fun fighting with you than I've ever had getting along with anyone else," I explain, bring a hand up to the side of her face and cupping her cheek in my palm. "I have a My Little Pony fetish and I don't know any woman who would put up with that shit, but you sort of do and I like that about you."

She smiles at me and like a fucking chick, my heart skips a beat. I'm pretty sure I've never seen Ava smile unless she was plotting something evil and calculating. This smile is soft and lights up her entire face.

Yep, it's happened, folks. I've grown a vagina.

"Why are you so unhappy with your life? You've got a great job, the perfect family and you get boned by a dude with mad bedroom skills on a regular basis," I smirk.

Ava laughs and shakes her head at me, sliding her hands around my waist. "I do have a good job, but it's not the job I want. It doesn't make me happy."

I move my fingers under her chin and force her to look up at me. "What do you want, Ava? What makes you happy?"

She bites her lip before taking a deep breath and spilling everything to me. She tells me about her blog and how her mom is always putting it down. She uses words like "couture" and "fashion forecast" that I've never even heard of before. She gets more and more excited and animated as she talks and I can't help but smile. I've never seen her so passionate about something before and it makes me angry that her mom doesn't at least try to understand.

For the first time in my life, a chick is talking to me and I'm not zoning out and imagining what she would look like wearing only a unicorn headband.

Okay, fine. I lost concentration for a second when she mentioned "trunk show." Come on. What guy hears *trunk* and doesn't immediately think *ass*? For the most part, though, I'm right here with her, hanging on her every word. I want to see her happy like this all the time. I don't know what this blog thing entails, but I'm going to help her. If I can start a Bronies Support group in Ohio with only five members, my parents' garage, two VCR's and a poor, lost soul who was still in love with Rainbow Brite, then by God I will make this happen for her.

Even though Ava said all we did was have sex and she wanted to spend some time talking, we were alone in my locked office and I had a Pulsating Posey in my top desk drawer.

After our talk, I may have convinced Ava of the appeal of My Little Pony.

Three times.

Chapter 17
— Genital Flogging —
Ava

"YOU'LL NEVER GUESS who I just got off the phone with-"

I stop abruptly in Charlotte and Gavin's living room when I see Tyler on the couch with a book in his hands.

"Are you reading an erotic romance book?" I ask in shock after I got a peek at the cover.

Sticking an old receipt in between the pages to mark his place, Tyler sets the book down on the coffee table and looks up at me.

"Well, I heard this stuff is all the rage with the ladies so I thought I'd give it a go. I've decided that you should start calling me Master."

I roll my eyes and plop down on the couch next to him. "That's never going to happen."

I was a little worried moving in with Gavin and Charlotte that I'd never have any time to myself. Now that Tyler and I are sort of a *thing*, I figured we'd never get any alone time together either, but it's actually worked out in our favor. The two of them are never home. They're either working or going out together.

"It says in that book that women like to be dominated, so I think you should submit to me," Tyler states.

"Um, have you met me? I'm not like those women. There is no way I would let you walk all over me."

Tyler turns to face me on the couch. "Come on, be adventurous. I'll tie you to the bed and spank you. We just need a safe word," he muses.

"I've got a safe word. If you ever spank me and I scream 'DON'T FUCKING SPANK ME AGAIN', that's my cue for you to stop."

Tyler looks at me funny. "That's a really long safe word. I was thinking more along the lines of 'nipple' or 'pancakes'. Something simple."

"Tyler, focus! Stop thinking about BDSM for five minutes. I just got off the phone with Nordstrom's and they want to buy ad space on my blog."

After our talk the other day in Tyler's office, he asked me how many hits I got on my blog each time I post. When I told him the number, his mouth dropped open in surprise and he told me with numbers like that, I could definitely get a few sponsors that would pay me for advertising. I didn't think he was serious until he started making phone calls for me and the companies actually called me back. With this recent call from Nordstrom's, I now have five businesses paying me a monthly fee for advertising.

"See? I told you that you'd be able to make money off of this thing," he tells me with a smile. "Let's celebrate with some light bondage and role-playing."

I shake my head at him, grab his hand and pull him up from the couch. "I've got a better idea. I need to do a blog post today about a few of the items Charlotte Russe and Forever 21 sent me over the weekend and I need a model."

Tyler stops in the middle of the room and refuses to let me continue pulling him towards the bedroom. "Whoa, hold up there, missy. I don't know if I'm comfortable with this."

Putting on my best pouting face, I bat my eyelashes at him. "But they sent over a My Little Pony t-shirt. If you put it on and let me take a picture of you in it, I promise we can try out the whole bondage thing."

Tyler narrows his eyes. "Is this t-shirt bedazzled?"

"It's bedazzled AND it came with a multi-colored tail that attaches to the belt loop of your pants," I tell him.

Tyler grabs my hand this time and races towards the bedroom. "Damn woman! Next time, lead with that!"

"Ooooh that tickles, do it again!"

Smack.

"Okay, that one stung a little, not so hard."

Smack.

"FUCKING HELL THAT HURT! NOT SO HARD!"

Smack, smack!

"OH, MY GOD! I SAID NOT SO HARD!"

"Safe word, use the fucking safe word!"

"PANCAKES, PANCAKES, MOTHER FUCKING PANCAKES!" Tyler screams.

With a sigh, I drop the horsetail that came with the My Little Pony t-shirt and smile at his red ass. "You were right, this bondage stuff is fun."

Tyler looks over his shoulder at me and scowls. "Can you untie me now? It would be really awkward if Charlotte and Gavin come home early."

He starts to struggle against the pair of panty hose that I wrapped securely around his wrists before tying them to the curtain rod in the living room. I've got to say, seeing him trussed up to the window buck naked with his arms above his head is kind of a nice sight and it almost pains me to untie him.

"Honey, I'm home!"

I jump at the sound of Gavin walking through the door. The smile dies on his face as he takes in the scene in his living room.

"Well, this is unexpected," he mutters.

"Oh, hey, Gavin! In case you were wondering, your curtain rods are pretty sturdy," Tyler informs him.

"Things that can never be unseen," Gavin mumbles, unable to take his eyes off of Tyler.

"So, funny story. Tyler was helping me model some clothes for my blog, one thing led to another and we decided to try out some BDSM. You're lucky you got here when you did. Cock and ball torture was next on the list," I explain.

"Wait, what?" Tyler asks in horror, craning his neck even more to look at me.

"Oh, don't be such a baby. Surely Mr. We-Need-A-Safe-Word isn't afraid of a little genital flogging," I tell him, reaching up to untie his arms.

Arms free, he turns around, rubbing his wrists. "What are you doing home so early? And where's Charlotte?"

Gavin stares up at the ceiling. "Can you please put some pants on? I cannot have a conversation with you when your third leg is pointing at me."

Grabbing Tyler's jeans from the couch, I toss them at him. After he pulls them on, Gavin finally looks back down.

"Anyway, Charlotte had a meeting at work. I wanted to get home before her because I need some advice," Gavin explains, walking into the room.

He starts to sit down on the couch, but stops his descent with his ass hovering right above the cushions. "Did you guys have sex on this couch?"

Tyler shakes his head. "Nope."

Gavin drops the rest of the way, kicking his feet up on the coffee table.

"Not today at least, but we did yesterday. I think you're sitting in the wet spot."

Gavin jumps up from the couch like it's on fire and gives both of us a dirty look. "Seriously you guys? I think I liked it better when you two hated each other."

Tyler flips Gavin off and takes a seat on the love seat, pulling me down next to him and wrapping his arm around my waist.

"What kind of advice do you need? If it's about what you just witnessed here, make sure you and Charlotte are on the same page with the safe word. It's imperative for the safety of your scrotum," Tyler tells him.

"Jesus God, no. I want to propose to Charlotte and I have no idea how to do it," Gavin tells us.

I knew this was coming. I've been teasing Charlotte about it for weeks, but hearing Gavin come right out and say it is bittersweet. My sister has found the love of her life and he wants to marry her. She has her dream job, her dream man and everything is falling into place for her.

Looking over at Tyler, I see the huge grin on his face and I can't help but smile right along with him. My sister is getting married. My blog is starting to make money and I'm pretty sure I might be in love with Tyler.

"I've got the perfect proposal idea for you," Tyler tells Gavin. "We just need to find an Alpaca farm, a place that will let us use illegal fireworks and a working fountain we can add red Jell-O to."

I must be insane.

Chapter 18

— Sparkly Penis —

Tyler

"YOU HAVEN'T TALKED very much about the situation with your real dad. I know we're trying out this whole talking thing now, but all we seem to talk about is me," Ava says during our lunch break at work.

"I'm an open book. You already know everything. The sperm bank had a mix-up with the records and they have no fucking clue who the sperm donor was. My only hope at this point is that my mom remembers who she had the foursome with in college so I can try and contact those dudes," I explain to her.

"There's got to be something else you can do," she says, gathering up her trash and tossing it in the bin in the corner of the room.

"Oh, there is. I'm going to BronyCon to find my dad."

She turns to face me. "You're going to what?"

"Uh, hello? BronyCon, only the biggest My Little Pony convention in the entire world. They're having it in Cleveland this year the week after Christmas and I'm going."

Before I can further explain my epic plan and possibly ask her to go with me, the door to the lunch room opens and Gavin comes running in.

"I just saw Jim in the hall and I told him I was going to ask Charlotte to marry me and now I'm pretty sure he's going to kill me," Gavin says in a rush.

"I doubt Jim is not going to kill you because you want to marry his daughter," I laugh.

He ducks down behind my chair just as the door flies open again and Jim stalks in.

"Where is he? Where is that little maggot?"

Ava rushes up to her dad and throws her arms around him. "Hi, Daddy! It's so good to see you. Why don't we go find mom?"

Jim untangles her arms from around his neck and moves her to the side. "Not now, honey. I have a man to kill."

"See?!" Gavin whispers behind me.

I watch as Jim's eyes narrow when he catches sight of Gavin crouched down and rocking back and forth behind my chair.

"Dude, stand down. You aren't going to kill Gavin," Drew says, walking through the door and wrapping his hands around Jim's arms.

"Fine, I won't kill him. I just want to talk to him, loudly and with a few punches to his nut sack," Jim states quietly.

Standing up from my chair, I walk around the table to stand in front of Jim. "Mr. Gillmore, I'd just like to say that-"

"Move out of the way, fuck face, or I'll kick your ass instead," Jim interrupts.

I nod and step out of his way. "Very good, sir."

"Get your ass out from behind that chair," Jim yells to Gavin.

Ava inches towards the door. "I'm gonna go get help."

She turns and flees from the room and I have a sudden need to follow her. Jim is a scary motherfucker when he's angry and right now, he's pissed.

We watch as Gavin slowly stands up, his eyes darting all around the room, looking for a way out.

"What the hell is going on in here? Someone said there was a fight happening," Liz says as she walks into the room a few seconds later with Claire right on her heals.

"There's nothing to see here, ladies. How about you just go on back to work and let me handle this," Jim tells Liz. "Gavin and I are going to settle this like men."

Jim clenches his fists and brings them up in front of his face. "You want to marry my daughter? Then it's time for a little Fight Club."

Claire lets out a huff and puts her hands on her hips. "Oh, hell no! Fight Club is for Liz and me. You don't get to have Fight Club! The first rule of Fight Club is that you don't get to have fucking Fight Club!"

"Wait just a minute here," Liz interrupts. "Did Gavin seriously ask your permission to marry Charlotte? That is the sweetest thing I've ever heard!"

Jim sighs, never taking his eyes off of Gavin. "You're not helping. He is not marrying our daughter."

"Wouldn't you rather they get married so that the things he's currently doing to her that are illegal in ten states aren't frowned upon?" I ask.

"Boom! That just happened!" Drew shouts, holding his hand up for me to give him a high-five.

I reach up to smack it, quickly pulling my arm back down when I see Jim give me the look of death.

"Hey, is that glitter on your hand?" I ask Drew, taking a closer look at the sparkles on his palm.

Drew drops his arm and frantically tries to wipe his hand on his pants. "I'm not doing anything wrong or weird. Sometimes I like to cover my hand in glitter and then jerk off with it because it makes everything pretty like a rainbow, so you can all just shut up right now!"

Everyone stares at him, Gavin's pending beat-down momentarily forgotten.

"Even though I'm going to regret asking this, the glitter is seriously from you jerking off and not cheating on Jenny?" Liz asks.

"Cheating on Jenny? Why would I ever cheat on Jenny?" Drew

asks in shock.

"Well, she thinks you're cheating on her because you keep making excuses to leave the house and you come home covered in strange glitter that she swears isn't stripper glitter," Claire informs him.

"This is craft glitter. Everyone knows stripper glitter is more miniscule, comes in brighter colors and smells like vanilla," Drew tells us with a roll of his eyes.

I grab Drew's wrist and pull his hand close to my face. There's something familiar about this glitter but I can't wrap my head around it.

"I've seen this glitter somewhere before," I mutter.

Drew snatches his hand back. "No you haven't! You have no idea what you're talking about! It's my special glitter and all it does is make my penis sparkle!"

"I think I liked this conversation much better when we were discussing all the ways Uncle Jim was going to kill me," Gavin states with a disgusted look on his face.

"Yes, let's get back to that, shall we?" Jim asks, moving to the edge of the table, opposite Gavin. "Did you knock up my daughter?"

"Oh, for the love of God," Liz complains.

"What?! No!" Gavin shouts.

Jim starts to move around the table towards Gavin. "But you've been having sex with my daughter when the rules clearly state that I only let the two of you live together as long as you didn't touch her."

Gavin shuffles the opposite way around the table.

"Charlotte is NOT pregnant, I swear. We don't even want kids! I love her and she loves me. I want to spend the rest of my life with her," Gavin tells Jim, circling the table to get away from him.

"Jim, stop trying to kill Gavin. I have a meeting I'm late for," Liz complains.

"Calm down, Jim. They're probably just having anal. Anal

doesn't count," Drew announces.

Gavin laughs and Jim stops moving, glaring at him across the table.

I really feel like I should do something to stop this. Gavin is my best friend and I don't want to see him get the shit kicked out him by his future father-in-law. Glancing around the room I see that Ava never came back after getting Liz and her Aunt Claire so it's now or never.

The word-vomit starts flowing before I even think about what I'm doing. "I'm pretty sure I might be falling in love with Ava, I'm a certified Brony, I let Ava spank me with a My Little Pony tail and my safe word is pancakes."

Before I can recover my breath from my outburst, Jim's fist connects with my cheek and stars burst in front of my eyes. The next thing I know, I'm hitting the floor with a groan.

"Dude, my safe word is 'waffles.' I knew I liked you for a reason," Drew states, staring down at me.

He holds out his hand out and helps me up to my feet while I cradle one hand against my cheek that's screaming in pain.

Everyone stands around with their mouths wide open staring at Jim, waiting to see what he's going to do next. Hopefully he's not going to hit me again because Jesus fuck that hurt.

"Well, I feel better. Let's go plan this proposal," Jim states, shaking the soreness from his hand as he turns and walks out of the room.

Chapter 19

— Interstate —

Ava

I TRY TO steady myself on the sidewalk as Charlotte turns away from me to greet her best friend Rocco, but the entire street continues to swirl in front of me and I have a feeling I'm going to tip over if I don't grab onto something.

I've been a little out of sorts since I realized I might be in love with Tyler. I told Charlotte she needed to take me out tonight so I could spend some time away from him and get my head on straight. Unfortunately, I decided to get a head start with a few people from work. By the time Charlotte pulled up to the bar in a cab to get me, my head was long gone at the bottom of a few glasses of booze.

"Why is your sister sprawled on top of a stack of chairs?" I hear Rocco ask as the two of them walk towards me.

I lift my head and yep, I found a nice, comfy stack of chairs right outside the restaurant to lean against.

"I can't stand. Someone fucked up the sidewalk and it's all uneven," I complain as Charlotte grabs one of my arms and Rocco grabs the other, pulling me off of the chairs.

Rocco looks down at the ground and then back up at me. "Sweetie, why are you only wearing one shoe?"

I quickly look down and notice he's right. No wonder I can't walk. Why the hell do I only have on one shoe?

"I lost a shoe. Son of a fuck, I LOST A SHOE!"

I'm screaming. I know I'm screaming and there's nothing I can do about it.

Charlotte and Rocco hold onto me as they both examine my feet.

"How the hell did you lose a shoe?" Charlotte asks as I lift into the air a foot that's missing one nude Lauren Conrad platform heel, wiggling my naked toes.

"THAT FUCKING CAB STOLE MY LC SHOE! FUCK YOU CAB!" I shout, shaking my fist in the air at the cab that pulled away ten minutes ago.

Charlotte pushes me into Rocco and tells him to keep an eye on me for a minute as she runs inside a corner store next to the restaurant.

"You're really cute, Rocco. We should make out," I tell him, trying not to slur as I rest my head on his chest and he wraps his arms around me.

Rocco is a great guy and even though he's one of Charlotte's best friends, he's quickly become my friend, too. He endeared himself further when he pretended to be Charlotte's boyfriend a few months ago to make Gavin jealous. I wonder why Charlotte never dated him?

"You're really drunk, and I'm still gay," he reminds me.

Oh, that's right, he's gay.

"Plus, your sister already informed me that you're in love with Tyler. Is that why you're a hot mess tonight?" he continues.

I push away from him and put my hands on my hips. "I am NOT a hot mess, I'm FABULOUS!"

Rocco looks me over from head to toe. "Ghetto fabulous, maybe. You're wearing one shoe and that black eyeliner is staging a protest as it runs down your face in fear."

He puts his hands on either side of my face and uses his thumbs to swipe away the mess under my eyes.

"You know, there's nothing wrong with being in love with Tyler," he tells me softly. Before I can argue with him, Charlotte comes back outside with a bag in her hand. "Alright, dumbass, I got you a pair of shoes. Give me your foot."

Rocco holds me tighter as I let Charlotte remove my one, lonely shoe and replace it with a pair of flats. I'm too drunk to care that I'm letting a cheap pair of shoes from a corner store touch my feet.

"Alright, let's go get some food in you to sop up some of that alcohol," Charlotte announces as we make our way into the restaurant.

After we've been seated and our orders taken, Charlotte and Rocco sit across from me silently, waiting for me to start talking.

I don't want to talk. I don't want to think about the fact that I'm so totally in love with Tyler that I want to cry. I just want to drink more and forget all about it.

"WHOSE FUCKING SHOES ARE THESE?" I yell, staring down at the ugly black and white slip-on flats.

Charlotte shakes her head at me. "Dude, I just bought you those at the store, remember?"

Whatever, she's totally lying. Someone stole my shoes and replaced them with these monstrosities.

"So, let's talk. Why are you so afraid of falling in love?" Rocco asks, taking a sip of his wine.

I lean forward, smacking my hands down on the table so hard the glasses and plates clink together. "I am NOT afraid of falling in love! I love falling in love. Falling in love is lovely and I *love* love."

"She's never been in love before, that's her problem," Charlotte pipes up.

"I have too been in love before!" I argue.

She cocks her head at me. "Name one time."

I'd close my eyes and try to think but I'm afraid the room will swirl too fast and I'll fall out of my chair. After a few seconds, I snap my fingers excitedly.

"Two years ago, March 17th. It was a Monday and the time was exactly 8:54 pm. I fell in love so hard that it took my breath away. It was so hard and so good. Mmmmmm, hard and good and big and I felt so full...of love and stuff," I slur.

"I'm very uncomfortable with this conversation right now," Rocco mumbles.

"Didn't you get your first Michael Kors bag two years ago?" Charlotte questions suspiciously.

I shrug, slumping back in my chair as the waiter comes over to the table and begins setting plates of food down in front of us.

"Michael Kors will always be my first love. He gives great purse."

Rocco nods, picking up his glass of wine and tilting it in my direction. "Amen, sister."

Charlotte huffs. "Ava, stop being difficult and talk to us. I know it's a scary thing to be in love for the first time, but it's also amazing. Tyler is a nice guy. Sure, he's got a few kinky fetishes, but who cares? He's in love with you and he treats you better than any guy you've ever been with."

I will not drunk cry, I will not drunk cry.

"Who doesn't have kinky fetishes?" Rocco asks. "I once dated a guy who could only get it up if I played track ten on the *Oklahoma* soundtrack. Do you know what track ten is on the *Oklahoma* soundtrack? It's 'The Farmer and the Cowman.' As soon as he heard the words 'One man likes to push a plough, the other likes to chase a cow,' he would come like a wild man. He gave great head, so who was I to argue?"

My Little Pony suddenly doesn't seem so bad now.

"Who ordered this shit?!" I yell, staring down at my plate of pasta and refusing to talk about Tyler's fetishes.

"Be a good girl and eat your food," Charlotte tells me calmly.

I can't find my silverware and it suddenly occurs to me that I haven't eaten all day and I'm starving. I'm in love with hungry and I'm Tyler drunk.

Fuck it.

Rocco and Charlotte pause with their forks by their mouths to stare at me. I stare right back as I smack my hand down on the plate and scoop up and handful of rigatoni, splattering noodles and sauce all over the white tablecloth.

"I'm in love with drunk," I announce as I shovel noodles into my mouth.

"Is she seriously eating with her hands right now?" Rocco whispers in shock.

I ignore him, smacking my hand back down on the plate while I stare the two of them down. "I love hungry drunk!"

I notice a few patrons looking over at our table and I realize I'm probably being a little loud.

"This shit is delicious and I'm love drunk! Go fuck your face!" I shout at one woman in particular who is looking at me in disgust.

"Okay there, drunky, calm down," Charlotte says quietly, reaching over and placing her hand on my arm. "It's okay to admit it, you don't have to be afraid."

Rocco nods his head in agreement and all of a sudden, I feel like a weight has been lifted off my chest. Everything is going to be okay. I can be honest with my sister and my friend; they won't judge me.

I grab a few more noodles with my fingers and push them past my lips before taking a huge breath and letting it all out.

"I like to masturbate on the interstate!" I announce loudly.

Rocco's fork crashes to his plate and Charlotte starts choking on her glass of wine.

At this point, I can feel all eyes in the restaurant on me and I don't care. Fuck all of them!

"When I'm driving down the interstate, I just can't help it. All that open road and freedom makes me horny and I just have to do it. Every. Single. Time. Sometimes, I drive on the rumble strips at the edge of the road for miles because it makes me feel tingly."

I'm pretty sure I'm supposed to be talking about something else right now, but I don't remember what it is.

Fuck, this pasta is DELICIOUS.

"Oh, dear God," Charlotte whispers.

I smile at both of them and start licking sauce off of my fingers, lifting my feet up and resting them on Rocco's thigh.

"WHERE THE FUCK DID THESE SHOES COME FROM?" I yell, staring at my feet.

"I think it's time to get Interstate home to bed," Rocco announces, sliding my feet off of his lap as he stands.

Charlotte gets up from her chair, walks over to my side of the table and starts wiping my face with my napkin. "I know you're really drunk right now, but tomorrow when you're sober, you're going to be so happy that you finally realized you're in love with Tyler."

She helps me up from my seat and holds my arm as we walk out of the restaurant while Rocco pays the bill. I rest my head on her shoulder, letting her lead me out the front door. I can feel my throat getting tight and I squeeze my eyes closed to stop the tears from falling down my cheeks.

"Charlotte?"

"Yes, Interstate?" she replies with a laugh.

"I don't want these ugly fucking shoes on my feet!" I wail.

Chapter 20

– Fisting – For the Win –

Tyler

"YOU CAN'T PROPOSE to Charlotte by just handing her a puppy, it's boring. Big mistake. Big. HUGE!" I yell, taking a sip of my beer.

"I'm really concerned that you just quoted *Pretty Woman*," Gavin states with a shake of his head.

"Dude, that's every guy's dream. Get a hooker for the night and then keep her forever without having to pay by the hour."

Gavin sets his bottle down and stares at me. "That is NO man's dream."

"You're out of touch with reality, my friend. It's every man's dream, they just don't like to talk about it," I explain. "I'm breaking the silence! HOOKERS ARE PEOPLE TOO!"

While Ava and Charlotte went out with Rocco tonight for some girl time, Gavin and I decided to stay in so he could drum up some proposal ideas. So far, all of them suck ass, so I called in reinforcement to help him out. I mean really, this is going to be one of the biggest days of his life. He needs help.

"Alright, I've got jumper cables, ten quarts of BBQ sauce and a really nice rhinestone tiara that we could take apart and shape into a ring," Drew announces as he walks through Gavin's front door, his arms full of bags.

He kicks the door closed behind him and dumps everything in

the middle of the living room.

"I already bought Charlotte a ring, we don't need to make one," Gavin says, getting up from the couch to look through the bags.

"Fine, be a snobby little bitch. I'll have you know I make beautiful decoupage rings out of Polymer Clay, rubber cement and Mod Podge," he announces proudly.

Gavin ignores him, reaching into a bag and pulling out the largest flesh-colored rubber fist I've ever seen. He holds it up in the air staring at it while the thing flops back and forth.

"What the ever living fuck is this?" Gavin asks. "Please tell me this is not an actual FISTING fist."

Drew smiles and walks over to Gavin, grabbing the fist out of his hand. "This is Duke. He's a member of the family and he wants to help with the proposal."

Drew shakes the fist in front of Gavin's face. "Say hi to Duke."

Gavin scrunches up his face and moves away from the rubber fist. "I swear to God if that thing is one of yours and Aunt Jenny's sex toys I am going to puke all over this floor."

Drew pulls Duke close to his chest and looks at Gavin in shock. "I would NEVER defile Duke like that."

He holds the fist up to his face and speaks in a baby voice. "Don't you listen to big, bad Gavin, Duke. Daddy loves you."

"Where in the hell did you even get that thing?" I ask, staring in awe at Duke. If it wasn't so creepy looking, it really would be a thing of beauty. When I say it's a fist, I mean it's a fucking fist from elbow to fingers. That thing has got to be at least twelve inches long and six inches in diameter.

"Jenny and I rescued him from a sex toy mill," Drew tells us.

"I'm sorry, a what?" Gavin asks.

"A sex toy mill. It's like a puppy mill but worse. All of these sex toys crammed into boxes with no light or air, just waiting to die. It was so hard to just save one when there were so many who could use our help, but we saw Duke and we knew he had to come home with us," Drew explains, hugging Duke a little tighter to himself.

"Oh, sweet Jesus, that thing was a USED sex toy?" Gavin yells, scrambling up from the floor and moving as far away from Drew as possible.

Drew quickly sets Duke on the coffee table so he's standing straight up in the air and covers his hands over Duke's closed fist. "SHHHHHH! Not so loud, asshole! We don't like to talk about Duke's horrific past."

Drew goes over to the couch and flops down on the cushions. "So, I was thinking Duke could help you out with the proposal. He just had a manicure and he has an appointment for a facial tomorrow."

I laugh. "Let me guess, a cream pie facial?"

Gavin dry heaves and Drew shakes his head at me.

"He lived that long, lonely life for far too long, Tyler. Duke is on to bigger and better things."

Drew turns to Gavin who is currently pressed up against the far wall of the living room, as away from Duke as possible. "So, I was thinking. We could tie a ribbon around Duke's neck with the stupid ring you BOUGHT from a store and you could hold him out to Charlotte. We've been practicing his 'serene' face and I totally think he's got it down."

While Drew and Gavin start arguing about Duke being a part of the proposal, I pull my phone out of my pocket and try not to be disappointed that I don't have any drunk texts from Ava. Drunk texts are the best, especially when she totally forgets her aversion to anal and begs for it.

"Fisting is NOT romantic!" Gavin shouts from across the room, interrupting me from my thoughts.

"Duke is a very romantic person and it's going to hurt his feelings if he can't be part of this special day!" Drew yells back.

I pull up a video on my phone and walk over to Gavin. "See? Duke is a star. From the look on that chick's face, I'd say she's very happy to have Duke in her…life. And her vagina. Oh, look at that, and her ass!"

Gavin pushes my hand away. "That thing is not coming anywhere near Charlotte."

I stare at the video on my phone. "You're right, but I'm pretty sure *Charlotte* would be coming *everywhere* near that thing."

Drew laughs and rushes over to me for a high-five. "It's like we share a brain or something, dude."

Gavin groans. "You two are insane. I am getting a puppy and tying the ring on a ribbon around its neck, end of story."

Drew grabs Duke from the table and points it at Gavin. "You are a pussy. Duke is the most romantic person in the world. I can't believe you're saying no to him."

Gavin looks towards me for some help and I just shrug. "He's got a point. You are kind of a pussy and Duke is growing on me. I kind of want to take him out for drinks and sit him up in the middle of the table so he can wave at people that walk by."

"It might have to wait a few days," Drew informs me. "We were just at a club last night and Duke's still a little hung-over. He also wasn't happy that they had to stamp his hand on the way in. That ink was a bitch to scrub off this morning, wasn't it Duke?"

Gavin finally pushes away from the wall to cross his arms in front of him and glare at me. "If we're going to talk about pussies, how about we discuss the fact that you are in love with Ava but you're too chicken shit to tell her."

Drew stares at me with wide eyes, holding Duke up right in front of my face. "Oooooooh, burn!"

"I am NOT in love with Ava," I scoff.

Right? I'm not in love with Ava. Why would I be in love with someone who doesn't even like me?

"You've checked your phone fifteen times in the last half hour looking for a missed call or a text from her," Gavin accuses.

"Dude! I just don't want to miss out on drunk anal!" I argue.

Drew pulls Duke away from me and scratches the top of his head with Duke's fist. "Good call. Drunk anal is awesome."

"She told Charlotte you guys talked about your dad and that she opened up to you about how much she hates her job. Ava doesn't talk to people about shit like that unless she really trusts them and cares about them, and I'm pretty sure you wouldn't talk about your dad issues with just anyone," Gavin says.

"Awwww, do you have daddy issues?" Drew asks with a laugh.

I punch him in the arm. "Fuck you, I don't have daddy issues."

"He found out his dad isn't his real dad, and that his mom was a slut," Gavin tells Drew.

"Ahhhh, I love sluts," Drew muses.

"Why don't you just admit that you're in love with Ava?" Gavin questions, both of us ignoring Drew as he uses Duke to scratch his ass.

"Why don't you use Duke to propose to Charlotte?" I fire back.

"I'll make you a deal. I'll use Duke in my proposal if you tell Ava you love her."

The room is silent while Gavin and I stare each other down.

After a few seconds, I hold my hand out to him and he takes it. "Deal."

Drew places Duke on top of our joined hands and wraps his free arm around Gavin's shoulder.

Shit, what the fuck have I gotten myself into? I'm scared shitless to even think about the fact that I might be in love with Ava and now I have to come right out and tell her? I have to do it though. I have to get my feelings in check because it is absolutely imperative that Duke is a part of this proposal.

"This is the happiest day of Duke's life!" Drew announces as he squeezes Gavin's shoulder in excitement. "FISTING, FOR THE MOTHER FUCKING WIN!"

Duke – 1, Tyler – 0

Chapter 21
— All the Feels —
Ava

"Dude, get a camera."

"Is this heaven? Did we die?"

"Seriously, get a fucking camera!"

Whispers from across the room bring me awake and I immediately regret opening my eyes when I'm hit with the bright morning light streaming in through the window.

I am never drinking again.

"Don't make any sudden movements or they'll scatter like wild animals," I hear Tyler whisper.

Ignoring the pounding in my head, I squint and look down at myself.

"Why am I naked?" I speak with a raspy, hung-over voice.

Feeling an arm tighten around my waist, I look over my shoulder, watching Charlotte yawn before opening her eyes and staring right at me.

"Are you naked?" she asks in confusion, pulling back and looking between us. "Jesus Christ! Why am *I* naked too?"

Scooting away from her, I finally notice we're both curled up on the floor in between the couch and the coffee table. Empty bottles of beer and vodka are spread all around us, including one dead soldier of vanilla vodka shoved into the couch cushions. Memories of last night after we left the restaurant and came back here float through my mind. Charlotte, Rocco and I all got into a cab, stopped at a liquor store and then spent the rest of the night drinking ourselves into oblivion. Well, I was already there and by the state of undress between Charlotte and I, it looks like she followed very quickly. I have a vague recollection of Rocco telling us vaginas were gross and we felt the need to prove him wrong.

Where the fuck is Rocco?

"It's like porn and Christmas morning, all rolled into one," Tyler whispers in wonder.

Charlotte, finally realizing where we are and that we're not alone, screams so loud I have to cover my hands over my ears to stop my head from exploding.

"TYLER! Turn around! Turn around right now and stop staring at me!" she shouts, attempting to cover her boobs and crotch with her hands while she frantically yanks the couch cushions off and holds them in front of her.

"Jesus, could you guys keep it down? I've got the *worst* headache ever," Rocco complains, stepping out of the kitchen, holding his hand against his head.

"OH MY GOD WHY ARE YOU NAKED?!" Tyler screams, covering his eyes. "I JUST SAW A GAY PENIS! MAKE IT GO AWAY, MAKE IT GO AWAY!"

Oh, that's right. Rocco felt left out after Charlotte and I got naked.

Rocco laughs and leans against the doorframe. "Honey, my penis is the same as yours."

With his hands still shielding his eyes, Tyler shakes his head frantically back and forth. "FALSE! My penis prefers the pink and yours likes the stink. Put that thing away!"

Rocco sighs and goes in search of his pants.

Unlike my sister, I'm not one to shy away from nudity and I couldn't care less who's in this living room right now. I need water and aspirin STAT.

Pushing myself up from the floor, I work out the kinks in my neck resulting from a night spent on the floor and head towards the kitchen.

As I walk past Gavin and Tyler, Gavin averts his eyes from me and Tyler smacks him in the arm.

"I told you not to make any sudden movements. Now our chance of seeing real-life sister porn is ruined and filled with gay penis. RUINED!"

Gavin rushes over to Charlotte and helps her up from the floor and down the hall to their bedroom. While I rummage through their cupboards for a bottle of aspirin, Tyler comes up behind me and wraps his arms around my waist.

"So, I was thinking-"

"No, Charlotte and I will not recreate that scene for you later tonight," I interrupt him as I find the bottle, unscrew the top and shake three pills into my hand.

Tyler moves away from me, grabbing a glass from the counter and filling it up with cold tap water. He hands it to me and smiles. "Even though I believe you should seriously reconsider, I was actually going to suggest something else."

I pop the pills in my mouth, grab the glass from his hand and chug the entire thing. He takes the empty glass from my hands, refills it and hands it back. My heart stutters as he reaches out and slides his hand down the top of my head before cupping my cheek.

"Ava, will you go on a date with me?" he asks softly as he stares into my eyes.

Everything that happened last night with Charlotte and Rocco comes rushing back – the missing shoe, shoveling pasta in my mouth with my hands and the fact that I can't deny my feelings for Tyler any longer. Standing in the middle of my sister's kitchen without a stitch of clothing on, I suddenly feel more naked than I ever have in my entire life. I really do love this guy, as crazy as it sounds. I should tell him, I should just blurt it out like it's no big deal so we can move on and this moment won't be so uncomfortable anymore.

"A date? Are you serious?" I say instead.

Tyler nods, leaning in to place a kiss on my forehead. "Yep, a real date. I want to do something special with you, Ava. We can do whatever you want, as long as it's just the two of us."

I close my eyes as his lips leave my forehead and change my mind about blurting how I feel about him right now when I'm naked and have the hangover from hell. I suddenly realize I want to do something special for him, as well, something to show him how I feel so that when I do finally get the courage to tell him, it will be *extra* special.

Leaning up on my tiptoes, I kiss his cheek. "I think that's a great idea. Don't make any plans for tonight around seven o'clock."

PUTTING THE FINISHING touches on the table, I stand back to admire my work. Not too shabby for someone who just learned how to cook today, if I do say so myself.

"Alright, the lasagna has about five minutes left to cook. When the timer goes off, take it out and let it sit on the counter for about another fifteen minutes before you cut into it," Molly tells me as she comes out of our parent's kitchen.

Thank God for my baby sister. Being in culinary school, she was able to stop by in between classes and help me whip up dinner since I'm pretty much clueless in the kitchen unless I'm baking dessert. Molly is majoring as a pastry chef, but she's a genius with food no matter what she's making. She also let me know that our parents are out of town for two days so that I could sneak over here and have a quiet night alone with Tyler without having to worry about Gavin or Charlotte interrupting us.

I turn around to thank her for her help and she's already disappeared like the ninja she is. With a shake of my head, I look down at myself to make sure I didn't get any food on my new dress. All of this – having a romantic date, cooking dinner for someone I love so I can tell him I love him – it's all new to me, so obviously that required a new dress. Luckily, Nordstrom's sent over a new Jessica Simpson black and white scallop lace tiered dress for me to blog about yesterday. Not cut nearly low enough and far from slutty, it isn't a dress I would normally wear, but it's perfect for tonight. It's simple and elegant and I feel pretty. It's nice to feel pretty once in a while, especially when you're gearing up to pour your heart out to a guy and hoping he doesn't laugh in your face.

The doorbell rings and I take a moment to give one last look at the beautifully set table, ensuring everything is in place. I rush to the door and open it to find Tyler standing there in black dress pants and a white button-down shirt. I've never seen him in anything but a t-shirt and jeans and this is a sight to behold. It takes me a full minute to recover the breath he's stolen so I can speak, but he beats me to it.

"You take my breath away, Ava Gillmore."

I giggle like a little girl and for once, I'm not even ashamed to admit it.

"You're looking mighty fine yourself, Tyler Branson," I tell him, holding the door open for him.

Closing the door behind him, I take a few slow breaths to try and calm my racing heart. I am so out of my element here. I should have asked Charlotte to stand outside in the shrubs next to an open window so she could feed me my lines all night.

When I turn around, he's clutching a square box in his hands that has a big red bow on it.

"I figured flowers were a bit too tame for a woman with sex toys in her blood and the rubber fisting mitten is just better suited for a second date, so this will have to do," he explains, holding the box out for me to take.

With a smile I can't contain, I grab the box and untie the bow. Lifting the lid, my eyes widen in surprise and my jaw drops when I see what's inside.

"I hope those are the right ones. I remember you saying you'd been trying to get them for months but they were sold out everywhere," he tells me quickly, taking the box back and pulling out the most beautiful pair of shoes I've ever seen.

"Christian Louboutin black suede Strass Decorapumps with Swarovski crystals," I mumble in awe as I reach out and lovingly pet the shoes Tyler holds in his hands. "How in the hell did you find these?"

I watch as he gets down on one knee and wraps his hand around my calf, lifting my foot up to his bent leg so he can remove the black patent leather Mary Janes I put on earlier. He slides the Louboutin on my foot and I suddenly feel like Cinderella. He does the same with my other foot and then stands back up to admire his work.

"Damn, your legs look fucking hot in those things," he says with a whistle.

"Seriously, Tyler, how did you find these and how did you afford them?" I demand.

I don't mean to sound ungrateful or anything, but these shoes were even out of *my* price range and I'm a shoe whore.

"You'd be surprised what the guys in the warehouse at work can get their hands on," Tyler explains as I walk around the foyer, testing out my new shoes. "Bill knows a guy who knows a guy. I'm pretty sure they're stolen and quite possibly have the previous owner's blood on them, but I didn't figure you'd mind. Felicia asked me if I wanted any meth and Rob told me he could get his hands on some whale sperm. I passed on the meth but I'm seriously considering the whale sperm."

I don't even bother to question the absurdity of the need for whale sperm, instead launching myself into Tyler's arms and peppering his face with kisses.

"This is just...I don't even know what to say. I love... these shoes. I love them so much it scares the hell out of me," I tell him, completely chickening out.

I have the feels. I have all the fucking feels and I can't say it!

He wraps his arms around me and smiles. "It's okay, babe. My love for these shoes freaks me out a little bit, too. They are *fantastic* and totally hot shoes. I've grown really attached to the...shoes."

Oh, my God. What is he saying? Is he feeling all the feels with me?

Before I can analyze his statement, he pulls back and grabs my hand. "It smells amazing in here, what's for dinner?"

I can do this. I can totally do this. I'll wow him with my delicious food and when he's in a food coma, I'll tell him that I love him.

Piece of cake.

Chapter 22

− No Kink? No Problem. −

Tyler

"I NEVER MEANT to put him in an *actual* coma! Oh fuck, I killed him, didn't I?!"

Blinking my eyes open, I look up to see Ava pacing back and forth next to my hospital bed and I can't help but smile.

"He's going to be just fine. The important thing is that you got him here in time. As soon as we make sure he doesn't have any adverse reaction to the epinephrine we gave him, you can take him home and he'll be good as new."

I watch the doctor pat Ava on the back and give her a sympathetic look before leaving the room. She turns to look at me, her face lighting up when she sees that I'm awake.

"Tyler! Oh, thank fuck you're awake!" she exclaims, rushing to my side and placing her hands on either side of my face. "I'm so sorry. I swear I wasn't trying to kill you."

Laughing at her worry for me, I grab her arm and pull her closer until she's leaning over top of me. "Ava, it's fine. You had no way of knowing that I'm allergic to pine nuts."

She reaches up and runs her fingers through my hair and I have to fight really hard not to purr like a fucking cat.

"It's all Molly's fault. I had her help me make the lasagna and she had to be all fancy and shit with her sauce instead of just using something out of a jar," she says with a roll of her eyes.

I hate that Ava is so upset over this and I feel like shit for ruining the evening she planned. I knew as soon as I walked into the dining room and saw the table set with good china and lit candles that she put a lot of effort into making the dinner special and romantic. It's not her or Molly's fault that two bites of the delicious lasagna had me breaking out in hives and gasping for air as my throat closed up. Normally, I carry an EpiPen on me at all times because of this stupid allergy, but I was too worried about the gift I got her and trying to figure out a way to tell her that I love her to worry about a fucking nut allergy.

"Seriously, don't beat yourself up about it. It's not like I go around advertising the fact that eating pine nuts might kill me. Also, I'm really sorry about puking on your shoes in the parking lot," I tell her sheepishly.

She just shrugs and rests her head on my chest as she slides her body onto the small hospital bed next to me. "I don't care about the shoes, I'm just glad you're okay."

It's so quiet in the room you can hear a pin drop. Ava saying she cares more about me than a pair of fancy shoes is the equivalent of her telling me she loves me. I know it, and I'm pretty sure she knows it by the way she refuses to raise her head and look up at me. This is epic, like seriously mother fucking epic, and I really want to pull the curtain closed around us and strip her naked.

"So anyway," she finally says, ignoring the puke-stained shoes in the room. "The doctor said you'll be discharged within the hour, as soon as the I.V. bag of saline empties and you're feeling okay."

I clasp my hands together against her back and kiss the top of her head. I want to tell her I love her, but doing it in a hospital bed so soon after she had to see my body covered in red hives while I clutched at my throat gasping for breath doesn't seem appropriate.

"When we get out of here, we should take a shower," I tell her as she snuggles closer to me.

"Someone's obviously feeling better," she replies with a laugh.

"If you're talking kinky, I think you'll be just fine."

Resting my head back on the pillow while I hold her close, I contemplate the perfect way to tell her I love her.

"Kinky is definitely good, but…you smell a little like puke. We should probably take care of that first."

"SO, WHAT'S IT going to be tonight? Do I need to get out the lube or lay a drop cloth down?" Ava asks with a laugh.

After I was discharged from the emergency room with a reminder to avoid pine nuts in the future, we came back to Ava's parents' house and took a quick shower to wash away the smell of vomit. As hard as it was, I wouldn't let myself touch Ava in the shower no matter how much I wanted to. Shower sex is good and all, but not what I had in mind for tonight. Even though I ruined dinner by yacking all over her new shoes, I still want this night to end on a special note.

Resting my hands behind my head as I lay on her bed completely naked, I watch as Ava walks into the room with a towel wrapped around her. She rummages through the top drawer of her dresser and I lift up on my elbows to see what she's looking for.

"There's no point putting clothes on since I plan on ripping them right off in about five seconds," I laugh.

She steps into a pair of underwear and slides them up her thighs and under the towel. "Well, too bad. I bought new underwear for tonight so you're just going to have to suck it up."

I lick my lips as she reaches up and takes the clip out of her hair from the shower, her long hair tumbling down around her shoulders.

"Jesus, you are so fucking beautiful," I mutter as she runs her fingers through her hair.

She smiles at me, the tips of her fingers tracing over the cleavage peeking out of the top of the towel.

Anything else I might have said to her dies in my throat when she pulls the towel off and drops it to the floor.

I swallow thickly as she walks to the end of the bed in nothing but a black lace thong. She climbs up the end of the bed on her hands and knees, crawling over my body until she's straddling my thighs.

"You didn't answer my question," she says softly, leaning over me to rest her arms on either side of my head. "Ball gag, rubber body suit, Star Wars light saber dildo? What shall it be tonight?"

Her long hair falls around our faces like a curtain as I stare up at her. Removing my hands from behind my head, I grab onto her hips and roll us over without saying a word.

She gasps in surprise as I settle myself between her legs, shifting my hips so my cock slides right against the lacy material of her underwear.

"No toys tonight. Nothing weird, nothing kinky… just us," I tell her softly, holding myself above her.

Her brow furrows as she stares up at me. Reaching down, I slide one hand down the outer side of her thigh and pull it up over my hip. She places her hands on either side of my face, pulling me down to her lips. This kiss is unlike any kiss we've ever shared before and it suddenly occurs to me that maybe it's not that big of a deal if I don't have the words to tell her I love her. Actions speak louder and all that shit. Her tongue gently slides against my own and she tastes so fucking amazing that I groan and deepen the kiss.

Letting go of her thigh, I bring my hand between us, sliding my fingers through the edge of her thong at the juncture of her thighs and pulling it to the side. I thrust my hips slowly and slide my cock against her until I'm completely coated in her wetness and want to cry like a fucking baby at how good it feels.

Ava lifts her hips as she gently sucks my tongue into her mouth, forcing the tip of my cock to slide into her. I freeze, holding completely still and pulling my mouth away from hers.

"Condom, we need a condom," I gasp as she moves her hips again, pushing me a little deeper inside of her.

Her hands slide up into my hair and grasps onto chunks of it.

"In a minute. This feels really good. *You* feel really good," she whispers, pulling me back down to her mouth.

Making sure to keep myself still so I don't accidentally slam all of the way inside of her without protection, I kiss her again. Ava isn't having any of that, though, and she starts to move her hips frantically against me, trying to pull me in deeper, whimpering against my mouth.

"Fucking hell, Ava… your pussy feels so Goddamn good," I mutter, locking down every fucking muscle I have to hold still while she continues to lift her hips and the tip of my cock slides in and out of her.

"Say it again, fuck, say it again," she demands, raising her hips higher so my dick disappears a little further inside of her.

It's my turn to whimper as I feel more of her heat wrap around me. There's no fucking way I'm going to be able to move away from her body now. No fucking way.

"I love the way you feel. I don't want to stop," I tell her honestly.

She quickly moves her hands down to my ass and grabs on. I can't take the torture anymore and immediately relax.

"Then don't stop, it's okay, I'm on the pill and I trust you."

Her quietly whispered words and the way she's looking up at me is my complete undoing. I let out a shaky breath and slowly push my way inside of her.

We both groan when our hips meet and it takes me a minute to get used to the feel of being completely bare and completely inside of her. I've never felt anything this amazing in my life and I don't know how I'm going to last long enough to make this any good for her.

I bury my head in the side of her neck and breathe in the clean scent of her skin, pulling myself out of her and then sliding right back in. She runs her hands up my back and I shiver when I feel her nails lightly graze my skin. There's no way I can hold back at this point and I whisper words of apology to her as I start thrusting my hips. I should probably slow down long enough to remove the lace thong she put on for me, but I can't even be bothered with that. Now that I'm inside of her, I'm never leaving.

"Goddamn, baby," I whisper against her ear. This experience is so surreal that I just want to mumble and curse and call her every sweet name I can think of.

Ava wraps her arms around my back and locks her ankles together against my ass, using her heels to push me deeper inside of her as she lifts her hips to meet my thrusts.

I never thought vanilla sex would be something I'd like. I've always gotten off on crazy shit and scoffed at the simple stuff. I should have known sex with Ava, no matter what kind it is, would be anything but vanilla *or* simple. Listening to her chant my name as her orgasm approaches and dropping all of our barriers, the latex kind *and* the emotional kind, makes this the best fucking kind of sex in the entire world.

As I move faster and harder against her, she lifts her hands above her head, grabbing tightly to the wooden posts of the headboard. She tilts her head back and tightens her legs around me as she comes. Feeling her pulsing around my dick throws me right over the fucking edge. Smacking my hand down on the bed and clutching tightly to the sheet, I push myself as deep as I can go and lose myself inside of the woman I love.

This night could have turned to complete shit after everything that happened. As I collapse on top of Ava and we breathe heavily against one another, I smile, happy about the fact that some throw-up and a mild case of hives didn't ruin our first date.

If we can handle that, we can handle damn near anything.

Chapter 23

– I Made a Poopy! –

Ava

"THIS WAS THE worst proposal idea in the history of the world," I complain, kicking my boot through a pile of snow as we trudge through the back yard.

"Whose idea was this anyway?" Tyler grumbles, walking next to me.

"Aren't you glad your parents went on that swingers cruise and you got to spend Christmas with us instead?" I ask with a laugh.

"Do NOT remind me of all the disgusting things my parents are most likely doing out at sea," he complains.

"Gives new meaning to the words 'wet discharge' doesn't it?" Uncle Drew shouts.

We both stop and stare over at the edge of the lawn where a clump of bushes hides him.

"That's the name of my future boat, by the way," he adds.

Tyler and I both shake our heads in disgust and continue pacing around the yard.

After much consideration with the family, Gavin decided the perfect idea for proposing to Charlotte would be to buy her a puppy and tie the ring on a red ribbon around the puppy's neck. Super sweet idea until you realize that puppies are stupid and will eat anything. The trial run Gavin did resulted in the puppy eating the entire red ribbon and the fake, plastic ring he attached to it for practice.

Gavin promptly took the puppy back to the pet store and got a refund, failing to mention to the owner that there could be a shit surprise for him the next morning.

He decided to go with plan B, which sounded like a much better idea at the time. Unfortunately, no one passed that memo along to Uncle Drew.

"How long does it take you to shit, old man?" Tyler yells in the direction of the bushes.

I stare at him, trying to give myself an extra boost of courage to tell him that I love him.

It's not that hard, Ava, just fucking say it!

After what happened between us the other night after the trip to the emergency room, this should be the easiest thing in the world. I really thought life would Tyler would be all about the crazy, weird shit we'd do in the bedroom. He can definitely fuck like a boss when he gets kinky, but I feared it would get a little old, especially if I had to Google half the stuff he wanted to do. Knowing he can also make the sweetest love in the history of the world, as well as pull off the best dirty talk I've ever heard, solidified my feelings for him. If I didn't think it was completely cliché to tell him I love him during our post-coital glow, I would have done it then. I *should* have done it then. Having a few days to think about it and plan it out has just fucked with my nerves.

"A proper shit takes time, my friend. You just slow your roll and go grab me a magazine or something," Uncle Drew yells back, the branches of the shrubs rustle as he does God knows what back there.

Aunt Claire came up with the idea that Gavin should bake Charlotte cupcakes and hide the ring in one of them. Again, super sweet idea, until Uncle Drew saw them sitting on the counter and ate every single one. Whole. Just shoveled each one in his mouth until Gavin walked into the kitchen and started screaming. Tyler and I had to calm him down and get both him and Uncle Drew out of the house before Charlotte figured out what was going on.

"Just so you know, when he *does* go to the bathroom, I am NOT digging through his pile of shit for a diamond ring. There's a lot of things I'll do for diamonds, but that is not one of them."

Dammit! What is wrong with me? Just say it. Say, "I love you, Tyler."

"This problem could be solved in a minute if Duke were here," Tyler mumbles to himself.

"Duke? Who's Duke?" I question.

"Don't worry, Duke is right here helping things along," Uncle Drew shouts from the bushes.

Tyler takes a deep breath, sticks his hands in his pockets, pulls them back out and then starts pacing nervously.

"Shit. Shit fuck damn! Ava, I need to tell you something," he starts, turning to face me.

I watch him bite his bottom lip and a wave of desire washes through me so quickly I have to catch my breath. I really do love him. He's sweet and cute and he's good to me.

"I need to tell you something too," I tell him excitedly, moving closer to his body.

Tyler reaches for me and we both open our mouths to speak at the same time when Uncle Drew starts cheering and shouting across the yard.

"IT'S HAPPENING! IT'S REALLY HAPPENING! I'M SHITTING IN THE SHRUBS!"

We move away from each other and do everything we can to avoid looking in Uncle Drew's direction.

"Uuuggghh, I don't have time for this. I need to get on a computer and order my BronyCon tickets before they're gone," Tyler grumbles.

"You're serious about doing this? You can't possibly think some random guy that could be your father would even go to this thing.

How would you even know who he was when you got there?"

Tyler laughs and shakes his head at me. "Obviously if he's my dad, he'll be at this thing. I didn't just *turn* Brony, I was born this way."

"You're being absurd, Tyler. This isn't going to work," I tell him.

"This isn't about me finding my dad. This is about you not understanding me being a Brony. I knew you wouldn't be able to handle it."

Is he serious with this shit?

"Don't tell me what I can and can't handle. I think you're insane for believing you'll be able to go to some huge gathering of weird people and be able to immediately recognize your father," I argue.

Tyler crosses his arms in front of him and glares at me. "*Weird people*? Did you just call me weird? Oh, no you didn't!"

I hate that we're fighting outside in the freezing cold weather on Christmas, but his words hit too close to home and that pisses me off even more. I *don't* understand the whole Brony thing and I can't do anything but lash out.

"If the horse tail fits!" I fire back.

"You know what? At least I'm taking a risk. I'm going out on a limb and doing everything I can to find out who my father is so I can move on with my life. What about you, Ava? Are you just going to keep working at Seduction and Snacks for the rest of your life, making you and everyone else miserable in the process?"

I shake my head and turn away from him. "You don't understand."

Tyler grabs my arm and turns me around to face him. "You're right, I don't understand. You have enough sponsorship on your blog right this minute to quit the job you hate and do what you love. You can make a living off of this and yet you're still going in to your mom's office every day, hating every minute of it. You need to tell your mom what's going on."

I shrug out of his hold and take a step back. "My mom doesn't understand, I told you that."

"So MAKE her understand, dammit! Let her know how much this means to you."

I put more distance between us, walking backwards through the snow.

"Stay out of it, Tyler. This is *my* life."

He's quiet for a few minutes and I watch him stand there in the middle of the yard. He slides his hands in his pockets and puffs of cold air float out of his mouth.

"You're afraid. You're afraid to quit Seduction and Snacks because it's safe. It's easy to stay there, doing what you're told every day instead of taking a chance on something new," Tyler says quietly.

I'm pretty sure he's not talking about work anymore.

"I am NOT afraid! I take plenty of chances. I took a chance on you, didn't I? I completely changed myself for some GUY and look where it got me? I'm standing outside in the snow on Christmas waiting for my uncle to take a shit," I yell angrily.

"I never asked you to change anything for me. I like you just the way you are; I just want you to be happy. I'm so sorry being with *some guy* couldn't make you a little less of a bitch."

Before I can fire off another insult that will most likely make me feel even worse than I already do, the back door opens and Gavin comes rushing outside.

"Did he shit yet? I need that ring!"

Tyler glares at Gavin and I look away from both of them. Everything we said to each other is playing on a loop in my head and making me feel like the biggest asshole in the world.

"GAVIN! I MADE A POOPY!" Uncle Drew shouts as he comes running out from behind the bushes, buttoning his pants.

"Did you really just say that?" Tyler asks him with a shake of his head.

"Fuck your face! Now, who wants to dig through the epic dump

I just took and get the ring?" Uncle Drew asks.

Tyler walks up to Gavin and pats him on the back. "You should have went with my idea of riding in on an Alpaca. Alpacas won't eat diamond rings."

I quietly walk away from the three of them and make my way to the back door. I want to tell Tyler that I didn't mean what I said, but I don't even know if it's true. I *don't* understand the whole Brony thing and I really *do* think he's nuts for thinking he can go to this thing and find his real dad. It's probably better if I just walk away right now. I don't like thinking about the fact that he's right and I am afraid. I'm not the type of person who has ever been afraid of anything in my life. I go balls to the wall with everything I do and I never let anyone make me feel bad about the choices I make. Not having my mom's approval to do something different with my life has affected me more than I care to admit. I hate that Tyler might be right and that I'll continue doing what's safe because I'm too scared to put my foot down with my mom.

"Somebody get me a pair of tongs and some rubber gloves," Gavin demands as I open the door to the house.

"I'd tell you this is the weirdest thing that I've seen in a long time, but I've seen skat porn. Watching you dig through shit is nothing compared to that," Tyler states as I walk into the house and try not to think about the fact that I might have just screwed up the best thing that's ever happened to me.

Chapter 24

– Merry Kiss My Ass –
Tyler

"WHAT THE FUCK DID YOU DO TO MY COOKIES?!"

Gavin and I pause by the kitchen sink, staring at each other in confusion as Claire's angry voice carries from the living room.

"Dude, what's wrong with your mom?"

Gavin shrugs, returning to the task of removing all traces of human feces from Charlotte's engagement ring.

"Who the hell knows? Just keep an eye out for Charlotte. She can't see this ring until it's time."

"You're seriously still going to give that thing to her? Dude, you should just chuck it and call it a loss. You can't put a ring on her finger that at one point in time was in your uncle's colon."

Gavin ignores me and continues to furiously scrub the ring wearing a pair of rubber gloves, soap and water flying everywhere. I continue with my guard duty, standing between Gavin and the door so I can block what he's doing from anyone who enters. I'm not going to think about the fact that Ava and I just had our first fight and now she won't even look at me, or the fact that the gift I bought her for Christmas is now a total bust. She'll probably burn it and laugh at my lame attempt to try and get her to understand me a little better.

Gavin's hand is suddenly in my face, the two carat diamond

sparkling right by my nose. "Smell this. Does it smell like shit?"

"Eeeew! Get that thing away from me!" I shout, smacking his hand away as I turn to face him.

"Stop being a pussy and smell it!" Gavin argues.

"I don't want to smell it, YOU smell it!" I fire back.

"SMELL IT RIGHT NOW OR I WILL PUNCH YOU IN THE SACK!"

I hear a groan behind me and whip around to find Charlotte standing in the doorway with a disgusted look on her face. "Are you two smelling your fingers again?"

Throwing my arms out wide to cover Gavin, giving him time to pocket the ring, I smile at Charlotte. "Oh, my God, you caught us! We like smelling our fingers. What else would we smell? Smelling our fingers is fun. Do you want to smell my fingers?"

Gavin's elbow jabs into my spine and I quickly correct my last statement. "NO! Don't come over here. I'll come to you so you can smell my fingers."

Gavin curses quietly and Charlotte shakes her head. "You two are so weird. Gavin, you need to get in here. Your mom is having a breakdown about her Christmas cookies."

He sticks his head out next to mine. "Okay, honey! We'll be there as soon as we're finished in here!"

She gives us one last weird look before leaving the kitchen.

We both sigh in relief and I turn back around to look at Gavin.

"Smelling our fingers is fun?" he asks with a roll of his eyes.

"Hey, it got her out of here, didn't it?"

"I'M GOING TO KILL ALL OF YOU ASSHOLES!"

Another scream from Claire has us hustling out of the kitchen and into the living room. The sight before us is a little crazy, but nothing we haven't seen before in this family. Claire is holding a tray of frosted Christmas cookies in one hand and using the other to throw them at Drew, Carter and Jim, all of whom are huddled on the floor in front of the tree covering their faces and laughing hysterically.

I look over at Ava questioningly, but as soon as our eyes meet, she quickly looks away. I should never have said those things to her. I crossed the line and now she's never going to speak to me again.

"Honey, calm down, it's not that big of a deal," Carter laughs as a cookie bounces off of his nose.

"YOU RUINED CHRISTMAS!" Claire screams.

"Hey, can I get everyone's attention? I have something important to say," Gavin says loudly, trying to calm the situation.

Liz gets up from the couch, walks over to Claire and pats her on the back. "The cookies aren't that bad."

Claire turns and thrusts the tray into Liz's face. "Not that bad?! There are bloody frogs in Santa's bag."

I can't help it. A loud laugh bursts out of me, but I quickly cover my mouth when Claire looks at me with rage in her eyes.

Gavin tries again, walking into the middle of the room. "Seriously, can everyone stop talking?"

"Hey, it was your idea to let the three of us finish decorating those cookies. What did you expect?" Drew asks.

"What did I expect? WHAT DID I EXPECT? I certainly *didn't* expect you assholes to shit on tradition by writing 'Merry Kiss My Ass' on my Christmas cookies!" Claire screeches like a banshee as she lobs a handful of cookies across the room.

Gavin drops to the floor to avoid getting smacked in the face and Drew squeals like a girl when a cookie hits him square in the chest. "Heeeey, don't break this one! It's my favorite. Do you know how long I spent making flesh-colored frosting to turn these stockings in to penises?"

Claire lets out a feral scream and prepares to launch herself over the table to attack Drew but is thwarted by Liz, who grabs her firmly around the waist to prevent bloodshed.

"In our defense, Drew brought over some of his special cookies and we may or may not have eaten two dozen of them between us before we started decorating," Jim explains.

"You three idiots ate pot cookies before you decorated Claire's Christmas cookies? What is wrong with you?" Liz asks in amazement.

"See? Now you know why I want to kill them," Claire adds.

Liz lets go of her hold on Claire and crosses her arms in front of her. "Exactly. They had pot cookies and didn't share with us."

Claire smacks her in the arm and Liz backpedals. "I mean, you three should be ashamed of yourself for ruining those cookies."

From his spot on the carpet, Gavin reaches out and picks up one of the fallen cookies. "Does this present cookie say 'To Gavin, from Chuck Norris?'"

Claire and Carter make eye contact over Gavin's head and they both start laughing.

"Wait a minute. I remember when I was like ten, I got a bunch of presents for Christmas from weird people. Big Bird, Captain Spock, RuPaul and Satan," Gavin mutters.

This makes Claire and Carter laugh even harder.

"We may or may not have smoked a little pot that year under the Christmas tree while we wrapped your presents," Claire says in between giggles.

"Seriously, you guys? When I asked about it on Christmas morning you told me the elves were pissed at Santa because he didn't offer 401k," Gavin complains. "That's the year I stopped believing in Santa because you said he didn't have fair labor laws."

"We were probably high on Christmas morning, too," Carter says with a shrug.

Charlotte walks up to Gavin and offers her hand, helping him up from the floor.

"By the way, Claire, if you're looking for your rabbit vibrator, it's in the silverware drawer," Drew tells her casually as he gets up from the floor and drops himself onto the couch.

"What the hell are you talking about?" Claire asks. "Why were you anywhere near my rabbit?"

Drew shrugs and picks up a broken cookie resting on the cushion next to him. "Frosting cookies with a butter knife wasn't working for me so I went digging through the drawers in your bedroom. On the lowest setting with the beads swirling, the rabbit does a magical job of frosting cookies."

"I ate four of those cookies already!" Liz shouts, grabbing a napkin from the coffee table and wiping her tongue with it.

Gavin looks over at me and I'm fairly sure he's about ready to throw up. This is definitely not how he envisioned proposing to Charlotte, but he should have known better with his family.

"Dude, just do it. It can't possibly get any worse," I tell him.

Charlotte looks back and forth between us as Claire rushes over to the couch to strangle Drew. "Do it? Do what?"

Gavin takes a deep breath and gets down on his knee. The entire room goes silent and Charlotte's eyes go wide as Gavin digs into the front pocket of his pants.

He pulls out the ring and holds it up in front of him. "Charlotte, you are my best friend and I love you more than I ever thought possible. I want to spend the rest of my life kissing you goodnight and waking up to you every morning. Will you marry me?"

Charlotte doesn't miss a beat. She immediately starts jumping up and down screaming. "YES, YES, OH, MY GOD YES!"

She throws herself into Gavin's arms and everyone starts cheering and clapping as Gavin gets up from the floor.

"Well, what are you waiting for? Put the ring on her finger already!" Claire says excitedly.

Gavin looks down at the ring, up at Charlotte and then back down. "Um, I think I'll wait."

Charlotte holds her left hand out for him. "Don't be silly, put it on!"

Gavin pulls the ring in close to his chest. "No, really, I think you're going to want to wait to put this on."

She rolls her eyes at him, holding her palm out. "Give me the ring."

"No," Gavin shakes his head.

"Gavin, I want my ring."

He holds the ring tighter to his chest and continues shaking his head.

Oh, for the love of God.

"Charlotte, Drew shit out that ring about twenty minutes ago. It needs a good bleaching before it comes in contact with your finger," I tell her.

Gavin gives me a dirty look for spilling his secret and Charlotte's hand recoils in revulsion.

"Drew, I thought we decided a few years ago that putting jewelry up there was dangerous," Jenny scolds. "My mother still isn't happy that I haven't been able to return that strand of pearls I borrowed."

Everyone starts talking all at once while Gavin explains about Drew eating the cupcake with the ring inside. Ava has been quiet through this entire debacle and I can't help but stare at her across the room. She looks sad and I want to go to her, but I don't want to cause a scene in front of everyone right now. This is a happy moment for my best friend and I'm not going to ruin it by getting into another argument with Ava. I'm sure she just needs to cool off a little and then everything will be fine between us and we can go back to having amazing sex.

Chapter 25

— Whinny Like a Horse —

Ava

"JENNY, WHY DO you have photos taped all over your wall?" Aunt Liz asks.

She wanders over to the wall in Aunt Jenny's office at Seduction and Snacks that is covered in pictures she took at Christmas.

"That's my Facebook wall where I post my pictures. See? I tagged you in the pictures you're in," she explains, pointing to a picture with a sticky note attached to it that says *Liz*. "Here, I'm sharing the pictures, too."

Aunt Jenny grabs a stack of pictures from her desk and starts passing them out to us.

"Jenny, honey, you know that's not how Facebook works, right?" Aunt Claire asks, looking up from the paperwork on her desk as Aunt Jenny drops a few photos in front of her.

Fed up with the moping I've been doing for the last few days, my mom asked me to come in to the original Seduction and Snacks store and help with paperwork instead of going in to the main headquarters. I wanted to protest, but coming here would be better than going in to the office where I might run into Tyler.

"I don't understand most of Facebook, but this I totally get. I just need to get some addresses so I can mail the pictures I want to share with other people. I'm going to mail them a friend request, too," Aunt Jenny smiles excitedly.

Pulling my cell phone out of my purse, I check my messages and can't help but feel like shit when I don't see any from Tyler. I thought for sure he'd text me apologizing or asking if we could try anal again... *something*. I haven't heard from him in three days. Three long days without arguing with him, listening to him say stupid things, feeling his hands on me, kissing him, being annoyed with him... why hasn't he contacted me?

"Ava, either call the boy and make up or find someone else and move on. Quit pouting and help us file these invoices," my mom scolds.

I give her a dirty look as I shove my phone back in my purse. "I wasn't pouting, especially over Tyler. I don't know what you're talking about."

She laughs and shakes her head at me. "I'm not as stupid as your Aunt Claire looks."

Aunt Claire gives her the finger. "Shut up or I'll cut off your dick and make you eat it."

"Anyway," mom continues, "even though the guy irritates me the majority of the time and the sounds I've heard coming from your bedroom make my ears bleed, I don't like seeing you so sad over him."

If only she knew that he isn't the only reason I'm sad. With a deep breath, I decide to listen to what Tyler said and try talking to her again. She's got to understand how miserable I am at Seduction and Snacks.

"Drew likes to make horse noises during sex sometimes. I thought it was weird at first but it's kind of hot now," Aunt Jenny muses. "Look, I even shared it on my wall."

She points to a hand-written piece of paper taped to the wall that says '*My husband likes to whinny like a horse during sex*'.

"Can you guys tell me you like it? No one ever likes what I post," she complains.

We all ignore her and I walk up next to my mom as she unpacks and stocks a delivery of lube. "So, I've been thinking about giving my notice at Seduction and Snacks."

"Hey, Claire, did you ever get a reply back from Channel 5 news about the feature they wanted to do on us?" she yells over to my aunt, completely ignoring me.

"They're going to come out next Thursday to film some footage. The interview will be on Friday," Aunt Claire answers.

I try again, a little louder this time. "I don't want to work at Seduction and Snacks anymore."

"Fuck, Jenny! Will you stop poking me in the side?" Aunt Claire complains from the other side of the room.

Aunt Jenny huffs and crosses her arms in front of her. "Why the hell do they have poking on Facebook if no one likes it? I poked a customer the other day and she smacked my hand."

Taking a cue from Aunt Jenny, I shove my finger into my mom's side until she yelps. "What the fuck, Ava? Don't tell me I need to explain Facebook to you, too. Jenny, for God's sake, you've given my child the dumb. Stop fucking poking people."

My mom and Aunt Claire share a laugh and I reach the end of my rope.

"I HATE WORKING AT YOUR FUCKING COMPANY AND I QUIT!"

The room goes silent after my outburst and I take a step away from my mom when she glares at me.

"That *fucking company* has kept a roof over your head and put you in designer clothes since birth," she says in a low, menacing voice.

It's never good when my mom lowers her voice. Never.

"Mom, I didn't mean-"

She cuts me off. "Without that *fucking company*, you wouldn't know the difference between a Coach purse and a pile of shit."

I continue backing away from her until I bump up against my Aunt Claire. She wraps her arms around me in a comforting hug and leans down to whisper in my ear. "I'll distract her with a dildo to the face. When she's down, RUN!"

My mom continues walking until we're toe-to-toe and I swallow nervously. "Your Aunt Claire and I worked our fucking fingers to the bone to make this company what it is today. People would KILL for the job you have and you want to just throw it away because you're *bored*? You should be ashamed of yourself."

I choke back tears as my mom stares at me in disappointment. I *should* be ashamed. This *is* a job opportunity that anyone would be thankful for and I *am* throwing it all away. I just want her to understand that I'm not throwing my job away because I'm ungrateful or because I'm bored. I'm doing it because I have different dreams. Why the hell is it so hard to say that to her?

"Hey, ease up, Liz. Not everyone is cut out to work at Seduction and Snacks," Aunt Claire says softly from behind me, giving me a reassuring squeeze on the arm.

"Not everyone *should* be cut out to work there, but my kids damn well should be! This is my dream, this is what I've worked my entire life for and is it so wrong I want my family to benefit from the good fortune we've had?" my mom asks her.

Her dream, her dream, her dream... I wish she would listen to herself.

"It's not wrong, hon. I'm not going to lie about the fact that I love having Gavin here. I love it even more that working here has always been his dream. That's just it, though. It's what *he's* always wanted to do," Aunt Claire tells her.

My mom rolls her eyes and turns away from both of us, stalking to the other side of the room to angrily dig into a box of furry handcuffs. "Ava has no idea what she wants to do aside from shop. If she wants to quit, fine, but she better not ever come crying to me about how she made a mistake."

She won't even look at me now and she's talking about me like I'm not standing right here. This went just as well as I imagined.

So much for taking Tyler's advice.

I shrug out of Aunt Claire's hold, grab my purse from the desk and leave before anyone can see me cry.

"Hey, Ava, I just posted on my wall that you quit. I already got one 'like'!" Aunt Jenny shouts as I walk out the door.

"It doesn't count if you just *say* you liked it," Aunt Claire tells her with a sigh.

Screw everyone. I don't need my mother's approval and I certainly don't need Tyler. I'll be just fine on my own.

Chapter 26

— When You Wish Upon a Dildo —
Tyler

I PACE BACK and forth nervously outside of Liz's office, waiting for her to finish her conference call. I don't know what the fuck I'm doing, but I'm pretty sure I'm going to regret it.

Ava went back home to her parent's house Christmas night and we haven't spoken since. As much as I want to be pissed at her for the things she said, I can't. The more I thought about it, the more I realized she was probably right. I *was* delusional for thinking my dad could be some famous Brony and that I would be able to pick him out in a room filled with thousands of people. I wanted it to be true so badly that I didn't even stop to think about how far-fetched it sounds. I'm also in love with her and love makes you do asinine things.

After our fight in her parents' backyard, we stayed on opposite sides of the room for the rest of the night. We spent the remainder of the evening celebrating the holiday and toasting Gavin and Charlotte on their engagement before I walked out of there without even a wave good-bye from her.

That was a week ago. I was determined to walk away from her and chalk it up to us just not being meant for each other, but I know it's not true. Regardless of what I said to her, she's the strongest person I know. She's sweet and funny when she wants to be and I like being around her. No, fuck that. I love being around her. She gets my crazy fetishes even if she doesn't want to and she puts up with my childish behavior. I'm not about to let her wallow in her own misery.

"Come on in, Tyler," Liz shouts from inside the office.

I take a deep breath and walk through the doors, sitting down in one of the chairs on the other side of Liz's desk.

"If you came in here to demand I tell you where our masturbation room is, I'm going to stop you right there," she begins.

"Liz, one of these days you're going to be honest with me. I know this room exists and, as an employee of Seduction and Snacks, I think it's only right that you lead me to heaven."

She puts her elbows on her desk and her head in her hands.

"Actually, I'm here on a more important matter," I tell her.

She looks up and her eyes widen. "Wait, you actually want to talk about something other than the masturbation room that may or may not exist?"

I can't believe I'm doing this. Ava better appreciate this shit because I'm pretty sure I can get Liz to crack.

"I want to talk to you about Ava."

Liz sighs and leans back in her chair. "Well, good luck with that. I'm not too happy with Ava right now, so you're on your own with that one."

Gavin told me that Ava tried to talk to her mom the other day about quitting her job here and it turned into one big clusterfuck. I feel bad that I sort of pushed Ava into doing that and I want to make it right.

"Have you even looked at her blog lately?" I question her.

She picks up a pen and starts tapping it against her desk. "That jenky-looking thing she created on Wordpress with a couple of pictures of her in different outfits? Yes, I've seen it," Liz states sarcastically.

"It's not jenky anymore. She had Jenny create her a whole new site with graphics and it's pretty awesome. Did you know she gets more hits on that thing every day than the Seduction and Snacks website? I checked."

Liz stops tapping her pen and stares at me.

"She also has a shit ton of sponsors paying her for ads now. She's making more money on that blog than she makes here. This is what she's always wanted to do. Can you understand that?" I ask.

I hold my breath, waiting for her to vault over her desk and choke me out. Liz scares me just a little bit, but I need to keep going and say everything I came in here to say.

"Ava is smart and amazing and this blog she's doing, it's not just a hobby. It's something she really cares about and loves. She's been working her ass off on this blog. It's *real* for her. This is what she wants to do with the rest of her life. She loves shoes and clothes and all that other girly shit. Seduction and Snacks isn't her dream, it's yours. Her dream is to talk about all that girly shit and she's turned it into a good paying reality. She needs you to understand and to give her your approval. I'm sure not everyone was on-board with the whole sex-toy shop slash bakery when you and Claire dreamed it up. How would you feel if the most important person in your life belittled your dream?"

I stop and try not to wince as I brace for the explosion from Liz that I'm sure is imminent. Maybe I overstepped my bounds. Ava is *her* daughter and who the hell am I to tell her what to do?

Liz is quiet and still for so long that I'm a little worried I might have given her a heart attack. When she finally moves, it's to brush a tear off of her cheek.

Awwwww shit, I made her cry. This can NOT end well for me.

"She hates working here. I always thought it was because she was just being stubborn," Liz says quietly.

"Well, she is a stubborn ass, but that's not it."

Liz glares at me.

"I mean, she's an amazing, beautiful, wonderful, stubborn girl."

She leans forward and rests her elbows on her desk. "You're in love with her."

"WHAT? How do you know that? I just figured that out myself," I tell her in shock.

"Tyler, you came in here and pretty much told me I'm an idiot even though you knew there was a possibility I would beat the shit out of you for doing it," she explains. "If that isn't love, I don't know what is."

I smile at her. "See? I knew you'd totally understand how much of an idiot you've been."

"I can still cut off your dick and make you eat it," she states.

"Duly noted," I nod. "It doesn't matter, though, since I'm pretty sure she hates me."

Liz shakes her head in disagreement. "Ava has spent every day since Christmas crying in her room. I don't know what happened between you guys, but I'm pretty sure she's in love with you, too."

Ava's been crying? Ava knows how to cry? I don't even know how to process this information.

"I'm sure that has nothing to do with me. That's all your fault for shitting on her dream," I tell her.

"Don't ruin the good thing we have going on here, Tyler. I have a letter opener within reach that I'm not afraid to use on your balls," she threatens. "Even before we had our little fight the other day, she was a mess. I think she realized she's in love with you and screwed up."

Oh, God, please let her really be in love with me and I'll never jerk off to another episode of MLP ever again. Maybe. Probably. Shit. I'll try really hard.

"That fight was my fault. We got into it on Christmas and I sort of told her she was too scared to come out and tell you she doesn't want to work here anymore."

Liz lets out a low whistle. "Damn, and she didn't punch you in the throat for that? She's *definitely* in love with you if she let you get away with saying that to her."

She stares down at her hands for a few minutes before looking up at me. "She really doesn't want to work here?" Liz finally says with a sniffle.

I shrug. "No, she hates it here."

Her lip quivers and part of me wants to get up, walk around the desk and hug her, but there was this whole thing with Gavin's mom not that long ago where I sort of had the hots for her and that *really* didn't end well and I can no longer even *think* about the word 'cougar' without throwing up in my mouth just a little bit. I don't want Liz to get the wrong idea or anything.

I watch as Liz slides her laptop closer to her and starts clicking away on her keyboard. After a few seconds, her eyes widen and her mouth drops open.

"Oh, my God. This is her site? This thing is amazing," she says in awe.

I quickly get up and lean across the desk. "Yep, see all those ads on the right side of the page? Those companies are all paying her money to advertise on her site. And they send her free shit all the time to try on and tell people about."

Liz clicks through all of the pages and photos, making comments here and there. She stops when she gets to one picture and cocks her head to the side.

"Are you wearing a sparkly t-shirt, skinny jeans and black stilettos in this picture?" she asks.

"Hey, those pants were very slimming and if you'll look at all the comments, I was told those shoes made my calves look amazing," I tell her.

She clicks out of the picture and closes her laptop.

"I should probably cut off your balls for talking to me the way you did. I *do* have a reputation to uphold."

I slowly back away from the desk and cover my junk with my hands.

Liz gets up from her chair and rounds the desk as I continue to back up. She moves faster and grabs onto my arm, dragging me towards the door.

"Oh, God, what are you going to do to me? You know what? I probably deserve it, just try not to leave any scars on my face. I'd like to continue with my modeling career on the side if Ava ever forgives me. She just got in this great hat that I really think would look stellar on me."

We walk through the door and she continues to pull me down the hall and around a corner. She doesn't say a word to me until we get to the opposite end of the building and we're standing outside of a locked room. Liz pulls a set of keys out of her back pocket and unlocks the door.

"You are to tell NO ONE of this. This room doesn't exist and this never happened," she states as she pushes me into the room in front of her. "Tyler, welcome to the masturbation room."

It takes everything in me not to sink to my knees on the floor and start weeping.

"It's real. I knew it. I knew if I wished hard enough and thought about it long enough, it would come true," I whisper as I stare through the two-way mirror.

I'm so overcome with joy that all I can do is sing. "When you wish upon a dildo…"

"Oh, Jesus God," Liz mutters as she backs out of the room while I continue to hum.

Dreams really do come true.

Chapter 27
— Friendship is Magic —
Ava

"ALRIGHT, TIME TO stop being a vagina. Get your ass out of bed and take a fucking shower," Charlotte scolds as she barges in my room.

I stare at her in irritation as she goes digging through my dresser, tossing clothes at me.

"Oh, my God. I can't wear that shirt with these pants!" I complain.

Charlotte turns around to face me with a smile on her face. "There we go, that's the Ava I know and love."

I roll my eyes at her and flop back down on my pillows. I've done nothing but mope around the house since Christmas and then it just got worse after the fight with my mom. It's pathetic. I miss Tyler so fucking much and I want so badly to call him, but I'm sure he hates me. I haven't heard from him since we fought in the yard. I'm a bitch and I'm never going to change.

"I have some news for you. You're going to want to sit up for this," Charlotte informs me, jumping onto the foot of my bed and curling her legs up under her.

"If it has anything to do with the fact that I've called off of work the last three days, don't bother. I've already gotten an earful from mom about my responsibilities as an adult," I tell her.

"Jesus, stop feeling sorry for yourself, asshole! You know you brought this on yourself, right? All you had to do was sit mom down and be honest with her. You're good at telling people off and sticking up for others, why is it so hard to do it for yourself?"

I roll over and face the wall, not wanting to look at her while she tells me how much I suck. I already got that memo.

"Well, lucky for you, there's no need to worry about mom. Tyler took care of it for you."

I bolt up in bed and kick the covers off. "What? What are you talking about?"

Charlotte smiles and leans back against the wall casually. "Tyler marched into mom's office this morning and basically told her off. He told her how smart and amazing you are and how your blog is your dream and she should be more understanding of what makes you happy. He actually made mom cry."

My mouth drops open in shock.

"Why would he do that?" I whisper.

"Because he gets a sick thrill out of seeing her weep like a baby."

I shake my head in irritation. "Not the crying, dick face. Why would he talk to her for me?"

Charlotte sits forward and tilts her head. "Um, probably because he's in love with you, moron. He knew you needed a little push in the right direction, so he fought your battle for you."

Charlotte grabs my cell phone off of my nightstand and thrusts it towards me. "Now, be a good girl, call him and tell him thank you and that you owe him an unlimited amount of blow jobs."

I start to reach for the phone but then drop my hand. While I am absolutely grateful that he did something like this for me, that still doesn't solve our other problem.

"Charlotte, I don't know. I mean, I can handle a lot of things. I HAVE handled a lot of things, but the My Little Pony thing might be pushing it. He may have saved my ass with mom, but that still doesn't change the fact that this fetish or whatever you want to call it is just plain weird. There's a thing called BronyCon, Charlotte. BRONYCON. I might have to dress up as a horse and go to this thing every year for the rest of my life. I don't know if I'm ready for that," I admit.

Charlotte pushes herself up from my bed and grabs her bag that she dropped by my door. "I figured you would say something like that, so I brought something that might help."

She digs inside and pulls out a wrapped present, holding it up for me to see.

"You bought me another Christmas present?"

Charlotte rolls her eyes and tosses it to me. "No, that is the present from Tyler you never opened."

I blink back tears and stare down at the gift, afraid to open it. In all the commotion on Christmas, I totally forgot that he got me something. I shoved it under the tree to open later on and, after our fight, I didn't want anything to do with it.

"Well, open it!"

With a sniffle, I rip into the paper and stare in confusion at what I'm holding in my hand.

"Bronies: A Documentary," I read aloud. "Seriously?"

Charlotte pulls a folded piece of paper out of her purse and hands it to me. "This came with it too. Sorry, I already read it."

Snatching the paper out of her hand, I give her a dirty look before unfolding it and quickly reading through Tyler's hand-written note.

Dear Ava,

I know this isn't as awesome as another pair of fancy shoes, but I hope it will help explain things a little better. I want you to know everything about me - the good, the bad and the just plain fucking weird. I hope after you watch this, you'll understand me and where I'm coming from. I want to tell you that I adore you, but Gavin is looking over my shoulder and he told me that's too gay. So, I'll just end this note by telling you that you amaze me and I'm so glad you let me see you naked.

Love,
Tyler

"Look, I didn't get this whole thing either, but after I read that note, Gavin sat me down and explained everything to me and then made me watch Tyler's copy of that DVD. If I have to suffer through this documentary to try and understand a guy I'm NOT in love with, then it's only fair you do the same since you ARE in love with him."

Setting the note aside, I stare down at the DVD. "Charlotte, he thinks he can find his real dad at BronyCon. I want to support him, but that's just too crazy even for me."

She sighs and perches on the edge of my bed. "Ava, I think deep down he knows he's not truly going to find his real dad there. You need to understand how important this is to him. You need to realize how much he just wants to know and understand where he came from. It's a pipe dream that he'll find his dad out of all of those people, but it gives him hope. No one has ever understood the whole Brony thing he's got going on, aside from other Bronies. He just wants his real dad to be someone who understands him."

SIXTY MINUTES AFTER Charlotte left, I'm sitting on the floor in my room crying harder than I've ever cried in my life. Friendship IS magic. Tyler is part of a community that believes in friendship and being happy, why is that so bad? People only think it's weird because they don't understand it, but these horses are role models! Fluttershy represents people with crippling social anxieties and Twilight Sparkle embodies bookish people without making them look like nerds. It's genius!

It's about people trying to belong! Sure, they dress up like ponies and there's Cloppers and Furries and other things I don't understand, but that's not the point. These people don't want to have sex with ponies or do weird shit with them. Okay, some do, but not the majority. Most of them are simply looking for friendship and a place where they belong, a concept I'm very familiar with. All this time I've been looking for a place to belong. My mom tried to make it be Seduction and Snacks and I was miserable. Fashion is where I belong, and talking to other people about fashion. Tyler found his place to belong a long time ago and who am I to discourage that?

I immediately get out of bed and fire up my laptop. Hopefully I'm not too late and I can still do this. I'm going to show Tyler once and for all that I'm not afraid. He fought my battle for me with my mom, but I'm going to fight this one for him. I'm going to make sure everyone understands what I love about him.

As soon as I get what I need printed off of my laptop, I head towards my door just as my mom comes through it.

We stand there staring at each other awkwardly for a few minutes before she finally speaks. "I don't like apologizing."

I nod. "Me either."

Glad we established that.

"I forgive you for not wanting to work at Seduction and Snacks."

"And I forgive you for not understanding my dream," I tell her.

She leans in and wraps her arms around me. I slide my arms around her shoulders and hug her back.

"You're totally my favorite child," she whispers before pulling back.

"You just said that same thing to Charlotte a few minutes ago, didn't you?"

She shrugs. "Does it matter?"

"Nope."

I thrust my arm out and hand her one of the print-outs. "Now that we like each other again and Tyler made you cry, I expect you to be there."

She looks over the page and then gives me a questioning look. "You have got to be kidding me."

"I would never kid about something like this."

Mom looks back down at the paper. "If I go to this, can I make fun of people?"

I start to tell her no and then think better of it. If I tell her no, she definitely won't come and I need her to be there. "You can only make fun of people if they make fun of you first."

She thinks about this for a few seconds before nodding. "I can deal with that."

I walk out of my bedroom with a smile on my face, making plans in my head and hoping that everything works.

Chapter 28

– BronyCon –

Tyler

"I STILL DON'T understand why I have to be blindfolded. Are you going to do some weird, kinky shit to me?"

Gavin laughs and I feel his car come to a stop as he turns off the engine.

"Sorry, no kinky shit for you today, my friend. Today, your dreams are coming true," Gavin tells me.

I hear him open his car door and get out and, a few seconds later, he's opening my door and helping me out of the car.

"My dreams already came true. Liz finally showed me the masturbation room," I tell him as he slams my door closed and starts leading me away.

"I still can't believe she did that. Aunt Liz didn't even tell *me* about that room until a month ago," Gavin complains.

We walk in silence for a few minutes and I'm about ready to bitch at him again for the blindfold when I hear him speak to someone and a rustling of papers.

"Two adults? Very good. Have a magical day!"

Gavin thanks the guy and continues pulling me forward. We walk through a door and I'm suddenly assaulted with the sounds of hundreds of laughing people, a bunch of them bumping into me as we make our way through a crowd.

"Okay, I think it's safe to remove the blindfold now," Gavin announces.

I feel his hands at the back of my head and I'm blinking at the bright lights and colors that surround me a few seconds later.

This can't be happening. There is no fucking way this is real.

"Am I dreaming?" I whisper as a guy in a Twilight Sparkle costume walks by me and smiles.

There's My Little Ponies as far as the eye can see. MLP costumes, MLP toys, stuffed animals, games, signs and face painting. There are televisions lining the walls playing episodes of MLP, there are people acting out scenes on one side of me and voice actors from the show signing autographs on another. It's so beautiful I want to cry.

"Oh, fuck, it's Tara Strong, the voice of Twilight Sparkle," I say excitedly, pointing over to one table. "Shit, that's Peter New, the voice of Macintosh! Peter New is here, Peter New is here!"

I start jumping up and down, clapping my hands together like a fool, but I don't care! I'm at BronyCon, motherfuckers!

Gavin laughs, grabbing my arm to turn me around. When I see what's behind me, I really do start to get choked up. Standing in a group is everyone I love and none of them look the least bit uncomfortable surrounded by My Little Ponies.

My mom and dad are the first ones to approach me, both of them wrapping their arms around me.

"We just wanted to tell you that we love you and we accept you just the way you are," my mom tells me. "I've already been asked to speak on a panel about the negative implications regarding Bronies and perversion. Isn't that exciting?"

My dad pats me on the back and smiles. "Even though you're not my son by blood, you're the son of my heart and that's all that matters. Also, your mother now wants to try out one of those Brony butt plugs later on tonight, so thanks for that."

I cringe and back away from him as Liz and Claire both come up to me.

"We'd both like to thank you for your love of all things Brony because after being here for fifteen minutes, we've already been asked by BronyCon if they could be an official sponsor for Seduction and Snacks," Liz tells me.

Claire nods. "I was even asked to make a thousand pony-shaped cookies for next year's event."

Carter and Jim walk up to me next and my eyes widen in surprise when I see that they're both wearing MLP t-shirts.

"Oh, my gosh, are you guys going to be Bronies now? Do you want to come to my next meeting?" I ask them excitedly.

Jim holds up his hand. "Whoa, slow your roll. This shit is still weird as fuck, but I will admit that I like the way this shirt looks on me."

Carter shrugs, looking down at his own shirt that says 'BRONY' in big, black letters across the chest with a picture of Applejack under it. "I don't know, man, everyone here is so friendly. The guys at the face-painting booth told me I had nice bone structure. I could hang with them."

Even though I'm in the best place ever and all of these people have come to support me, there's still someone missing. Before I have a chance to dwell on it, I hear a throat clear behind me. I turn around and my jaw drops.

Ava stands there with her hands on her hips wearing a tight, pink bustier, a pink tutu and white, knee-high boots. She does a slow turn and attached to the ass of her skirt is a multi-colored tail that hangs down to her knees. She looks over her shoulder at me and shakes her ass and it takes everything in me not to throw her to the ground and climb her like a fucking pine tree.

I walk over to her as she completes her turn. She slides her hands up my chest and around my shoulders, clasping them together at the back of my neck.

"You are the hottest fucking woman I have ever seen in my life," I tell her softly as she smiles up at me.

"I hope this makes up for the fact that I was a total bitch to you. I should have never said the things I did."

I shake my head at her. "No, I was an asshole. I pushed you too far and I said some really shitty things when all I wanted to do was tell you that I love you."

Ava closes her eyes and sighs, pressing her lips to mine. She feels so right and so amazing in my arms that I let out a groan of disappointment when she moves away.

"I kind of like this look on me and I'm having a great time here. I think I'm going to like being in love with a Brony," she admits.

"Is this your way of telling me that you were completely wrong about Bronies and they aren't weird at all?" I ask with a laugh.

She thinks about it for a minute and then smiles. "I don't like apologizing, but when I'm wrong, I say I'm wrong."

I smile right back at her. "You looked wonderful out there. Nobody puts Ava in a corner."

We hear a groan and turn to see Drew and Jenny standing arm-in-arm.

"Did you two vaginas just quote *Dirty Dancing*?" Drew asks.

"Drew? What the fuck are you doing here?" Carter asks. "I thought you said you had a meeting today and couldn't get together with us."

"And what the mother of fucks are you wearing?" Jim questions, looking him up and down.

"You didn't tell me you guys were coming to BronyCon, you just said you were doing something to surprise Tyler," Drew explains. "And I'll have you know, this pony costume is one-hundred-percent fleece and the tail is made from genuine unicorn hair."

We all stare at Drew's pink, plush horse costume, complete with a giant stuffed horse head that he's currently carrying under his arm.

"My balls are sweating like a motherfucker in this thing, but it's totally worth it," he tells us with a smile.

"And the best part is, Drew hasn't been cheating on me!" Jenny announces with glee.

Drew sighs and takes a step forward. "I can't live with the shame and the guilt anymore, guys. I'm tired of lying by omission and not living my life the way I was meant to live it. Everyone, today I am officially coming out as a Brony."

A few passers-by stop when they hear Drew's announcement and start clapping and cheering for him.

"Shit! That's where I recognized the glitter from on your hand that day at work," I say suddenly. "That's the glitter we use at Brony meetings when we do the handshake. You've been secretly going to Brony meetings!"

Gavin leans in closer to me. "Dude, I thought you said there wasn't a handshake?"

I scoff at him. "Like I was going to admit all the Brony secrets to you. It's against the code, man."

My mom lets go of my dad's hand and walks up to Drew, staring at him for a few minutes. Drew stares right back, squinting like he's trying to get a better look at her.

"Don't I know you from somewhere?" Drew finally asks.

My mom nods. "You look familiar too, but I just can't place it."

I look back and forth between them, wondering what the hell is going on.

"Have you ever worked at the strip club Jennie's Juggs?" Drew asks.

My mom shakes her head. "Nope."

Drew brings one of his horse hoof hands up to his face and scratches his cheek. "What about Starbutts? They used to have this great show with two chicks and a couple of ping-pong balls. You sort of look like one of them."

My mom shakes her head again.

Drew eyes suddenly go wide and he lifts his hoof up in the air. "I REMEMBER! Aren't you the chick I had that foursome with in college? You're name's Debbie or Dinda or something, right?"

"Oh, my God," Gavin mutters next to me.

I'm still trying to figure out what the fuck is going on right now when I feel Ava squeeze my hand.

"Donna, my name is Donna," my mom tells him with a smile.

"That's it! Donna! Well, shit, it's good to see you again," he tells her before turning to Carter. "Dude, this was the chick I banged the night you met Claire, remember?"

"I thought you passed out in the bathtub the night we met?" Claire asks.

Drew and my mom laugh and the sound makes a little bit of vomit come up in my throat.

"I totally passed out in the tub, but that was after the foursome. Actually, now that I think about it, weren't you in the tub with me?" Drew asks my mom.

She laughs again and nods. "I was. I woke up the next morning curled up in that thing alone wondering what the hell had happened."

"Oh, holy fuck," Ava whispers.

No. No, no, no. This is not happening. This is NOT fucking happening!

Drew shakes his head in regret. "Damn. I didn't even realize I left you in there. I got up to take a piss and couldn't stop laughing about the fact that I still had the condom on, stuck to my penis."

I let out the breath I've been holding and send a prayer up to heaven.

"Too bad that fucker was totally broke and hanging in pieces around my junk," Drew continues. "Good thing nothing bad ever came from that, huh?"

Drew and my mom keep right on laughing, not even realizing that everyone is staring at them and I'm about ready to lose my shit all over this place.

Claire steps forward and looks back and forth between Drew and I. Her eyes widen and she does it again. Back and forth and back and forth until I want to run screaming out of this place.

"Oh, sweet Christ," she finally mutters.

My mom finally stops laughing and mimics Claire, looking between Drew and me.

"Oh. Oh, my," she whispers.

Drew puts his hoof hands on his hips and glares at the two of them.

"Well, you wanted to come to BronyCon and find your dad," Ava tells me. "Congratulations, sweetie."

I bend at the waist and rest my hands on my knees, taking in as many deep breaths as I can without passing out.

Drew huffs. "What? I don't get it."

Epilogue

Ava

Three months later...

"ARE YOU SURE you're using enough lube? I don't think you're using enough."

"Shut up, I totally know what I'm doing, I watched a couple of Youtube videos."

"You're not going to tell anyone about this, right? I mean, this is awesome and everything and I love you and trust you, but I don't need this shit getting out."

"Will you stop complaining? Do you want to do this or not?" I demand.

Holding the MLP butt plug up in the air, I glare at Tyler. He's clutching onto the table in the masturbation room at Seduction and Snacks, sticking his bare ass out, looking at me over his shoulder.

"Stop yelling at me! I can't relax if you keep yelling at me," he complains.

In hindsight, sneaking off to the masturbation room in the middle of Charlotte and Gavin's co-ed bridal shower probably wasn't the best idea, but we got bored watching them open up all of those stupid pots and pans and monogrammed towels.

Running my hand down Tyler's back, I lean in closer to him and whisper in his ear. "Calm down, baby, I totally know what I'm doing."

He sighs and turns his face, pressing his lips to mine. I glide my tongue across his bottom lip before pushing it between his lips. His tongue tangles with mine and I feel a gentle tug as he sucks it into his mouth. As the kiss continues, I can feel Tyler relaxing and I know he's getting excited.

"JESUS FUCKING CHRIST!" he suddenly screams, breaking the kiss and jumping away from the table.

"Sorry! Sorry, oh hell, I got a little carried away. I didn't mean to stick it all the way in!" I apologize, wincing at him as he gives me a dirty look.

He tries to twist and turn his body to look at his ass and when he does, the tail attached to the butt plug swishes back and forth across the back of his legs. I can't help it, I smack my hand over my mouth and start laughing.

"THIS IS NOT FUNNY! THIS IS NOT FUCKING FUNNY!" he yells, trying to grab for the tail to pull the entire thing out but it keeps swishing away from his reach. "GET THIS DAMN THING OUT OF MY ASS!"

I really wasn't sure I would ever be able to handle the weird shit Tyler likes to do in the bedroom but right now, I realize all of my fears were for nothing. Tyler's very good about throwing some normal, but equally hot sex into the mix every once in a while and I'm a strong, independent woman who can handle anything life throws at me. Including a hot guy dancing around a dark room trying to yank a horse tail out of his ass.

My website is still doing amazing and my mom even sponsored an ad on it for Seduction and Snacks. She's still a little sad that I won't be spending the rest of my life working in the family business, but she's accepted the fact that this is what I want to do and she's happy for me.

"Will you hold still? I can't get it out if you're going to keep flailing all over the place," I scold Tyler, walking over to him and grabbing his arms.

"I promise I will never, ever ask you for anal again. This is serious business right here and not for amateurs. I don't think I'll ever be able to take a proper shit again," he complains.

Standing up on my tiptoes, I kiss his lips and smile at him. "I love you, but you're a lying sack of shit. You know you're going to ask me tomorrow if it's Anal Friday yet."

"One of these days, it really will be Anal Friday and you'll be glad I asked," he tells me, turning around so I can get to his ass.

"You know, this tail really is quite pretty. I think you should leave it in for a while. I could brush it and maybe put a braid in it."

Tyler growls at me over his shoulder. "You made your point. From now on, I will think twice before calling you a wuss for not trying out a new toy."

I kiss the back of his shoulder and move to yank on the tail when the door to the room bursts open and Drew walks in.

"Come on, kid, it's time for us to play catch!"

After BronyCon, Drew and Tyler had a DNA test done and the results were fairly conclusive. Drew is now the proud father of another bouncing baby boy. Ever since the test results came back, he's been overcompensating the father thing just a little bit.

Tyler and I freeze and Drew crosses his arms in front of him, tapping his toe in irritation. "Son, I am really disappointed in you right now."

Tyler quickly reaches down around his ankles for his pants and pulls them up, the tail refusing to be hidden and, instead, drapes outside of his pants.

"It's not what it looks like," Tyler tries to explain, swatting at the tail to try and keep it out of sight.

Drew shakes his head at Tyler. "How many times do I have to tell you? When you're trying new, kinky shit, always get that stuff on camera. It's like you were raised in a barn or something."

Drew turns and walks back out of the room, throwing a parting comment over his shoulder. "Shake a tail feather, dick bag, I still need to teach you how to ride a bike!"

The door slams closed behind him and I slide my arms around Gavin's waist and look up at him. "Uncle Drew is aware that you already know how to ride a bike, right?"

Tyler pulls me in closer. "Who the fuck knows? Yesterday, he gave me the 'birds and the bees' talk and it included props and scenes he acted out with your Aunt Jenny. I can never look her in the eyes ever again."

I laugh, grabbing onto Tyler's face and pulling him down for a kiss. I'm pretty sure no one has a crazier life than I do, but that's okay. My closet is filled with couture and My Little Pony costumes, I have a job I'm ecstatic about, I'm in love with a crazy guy and my sister is getting married. It really doesn't get any better than this – or any stranger.

The door to the room opens up again and all we see is a very large, very creepy looking fist stick through the crack.

"Duke says get your horse's ass out here. It's time for cake!"

The fist disappears and the door quickly slams closed.

I look up at Tyler in confusion and he shakes his head at me. "Don't ask."

I take that back. The strange just never ends.

– The End –

Tattoos and TaTas

(Chocoholics #2.5)

by Tara Sivec

A Note to Readers

The idea for *Tattoos and TaTas* came to me about six months ago. It was a combination of things that made me want to write this story, first and foremost being that breast cancer awareness is something very near and dear to my heart. The second, it was the third anniversary of my mother's death from Leukemia. My family and I always reminisce about the time we spent together in hospital rooms, waiting rooms, emergency rooms and the ICU. Unlike most families, we're a bunch of assholes, so these memories are mostly happy, crazy, stupid ones.

I want everyone reading this to understand that I am in no way making light of breast cancer. It is a horrible disease that does not discriminate. It took my grandmother, one of my favorite cousins at a young age, infected several other family members and close friends and I myself had a scare a few years ago.

This story, as with the rest of the *Chocolate Lovers* and *Chocoholic* stories, is a way for me to share some real life events with all of you. It's my way of showing you that sometimes, it's okay to laugh, even when faced with something scary. Most of the events in this book are actual things my family and I did while my mom was sick. We're insane and we think we're funny when we're probably not, but it's our way of coping. I hope you enjoy *Tattoos and TaTas* and I hope it makes you laugh through the tears.

During the month of October, every single year, a percentage of proceeds from the sale of this book will be equally split between the Susan G. Komen Breast Cancer Foundation and Living Beyond Breast Cancer. During my research of this book, I found so many wonderful groups dedicated to breast cancer awareness that I decided to share the funds with more than one charity.

Research and statistics provided by the following sources:
www.breastcancer.org
www.komenohio.org
www.chemocare.com
www.lbbc.org
www.cancer.gov
www.cancerresearchuk.org
www.nationalbreastcancer.org

In memory of those we've lost and in support of the survivors, the fighters and everyone who loves them.

Prologue

HAVE YOU EVER met someone who you instantly knew was meant to be in your life forever? I'm not talking about the guy you took home from the bar one night after eleventy-seven rum and Cokes. You know, the one who disappeared after making your vagina sing a lovely melody. I'm not even talking about the person you're dating, engaged to or that you married. Sure, some people find that one person they know they want to spend the rest of their life with, making babies and growing old together with, but I'm not talking about that. I'm talking about your soul mate. Your REAL soul mate. The person who was put on this earth just to *get* you, not to breed with you.

I met the love of my life, Jim, in college and I did all those things that you're supposed to do with him. We fell in love, got married, had babies and lived happily ever after, but I found my soul mate much earlier than that. I met her in high school.

Oh, shut up, I'm not a lesbian. I'm talking about my best friend. My *person*. You might want to sit down for this next part because when I tell you how we met, I'm sure you'll fall over laughing your ass off. There will be no judging how Claire and I met or I will cut all of your mothers.

We met during cheerleading tryouts.

Shut up, I told you this is a judgment-free zone.

Commiserating over our fellow female students bouncing around and squealing exactly like cracked-out puppies brought us together, but our bond *kept* us together. We shared so many commonalities that it even freaked *us* out. Our parents shared the same wedding anniversary, somewhere in our ancient family tree we shared the same last name and family crest, my first name is her middle name and her first dog and I shared a name (I never met Liz the beagle, but I heard she was an asshole who licked her twat all the time. Sounds about right). We liked all the same movies and books and we finished each other's sentences. Claire and I met in the back of our high school gym, the only two girls in a group of thirty standing off on the sidelines with our arms crossed in front of us and similar resting-bitch faces plastered on.

We've been through everything together. Losing our virginities, college, starting a successful business, marriage, children, the imminent marriage *of* our children… through thick and thin and all the years in between, nothing could tear us apart.

Or so I thought.

Then that bitch had to go and give me the news that you never want to hear out of your best friend's mouth.

I can already hear all of you saying to yourself, "Awwwww shit, I wasn't expecting this; this is supposed to be funny and what you're about to put us through is NEVER funny." This is where I prove you wrong. The one thing this group has always had going for us is our sense of humor. Even when you get the worst news of your life, sometimes all you can do is laugh.

This is the story of the day everything changed, the day we all began looking at life a little differently than we did before.

It's also the story of how we almost got kicked out of a hospital, a funeral home, a tattoo shop and a small handful of bars.

So, basically just another Tuesday.

I feel like a little background is needed before we get into that whole crazy mess, though, so buckle up. It's going to be a bumpy ride.

Chapter 1
— Go Ducks! Rrraaawwwr! —

Tenth day of eleventh grade.
Too many years ago to count...

I HATE MY mother. This is probably a little bit of PMS and a whole lot of teenage-angst talking right now, but whatever. I hate her and I will continue hating her until the day I die. Or until the day I smother her in her sleep, whichever comes first. Not only did my parents ruin my life by deciding halfway through my high school career that we should move to some podunk town in Ohio, they are now forcing me to participate in extracurricular activities or suffer the consequences.

Their consequences usually entail an entire month of being confined to the house I'm forced to clean from top to bottom every single day. Being in a new school and not having any friends yet, I wouldn't normally care about the whole grounding bit, but it's the principle of the thing. My parents are under the illusion that if I become a sheep and follow around all the other stupid sheep with the added bonus of wearing a matching uniform, I'll instantly have friends and will no longer spend my hours at home locked in my room playing "Teenage Wasteland" on repeat as well as watching my new favorite movie—*Heathers*. My mother seems to think my obsession with a dark comedy about teenagers killing each other off is not healthy. I beg to differ. I tried to reason with her that the movie is set in Ohio so really, I'm supporting this shitty state they've forced me to live in, but it didn't work. She confiscated my VHS and it's on lockdown until I find an after school activity.

My goal this week wasn't really about finding a group that would be fun, because any situation where I'm forced to interact with other people is never fun. My goal was simply to pick the first thing I saw to shut my mother up and pray to God I wouldn't die from boredom or start passing out cups of Liquid Drano to my fellow students (See? A *Heathers* reference. That movie really is sanity saving).

As I was grabbing a few books from my locker at the end of the day and in a total panic that I still hadn't found a flock of sheep to join, a group of girls walked by all in a tizzy about some meeting going on in the gym and how they were going to have such a fun year going to all the football games. My ears immediately perked up at this information. I'm a football junkie. I love watching it, I love playing it every Thanksgiving with my cousins and, if my mother didn't think wearing a football helmet would ruin my hair, I'd have demanded to play on the school team. This, ladies and gentlemen, is the only sport/activity that I truly would have joined the masses for without one complaint. Deciding to see what all the fuss was about, I trudged behind the group of girls and tried not to gag on the smell of Love's Baby Soft wafting from each of them.

By the time I entered the gym and my brain caught up with what I was seeing in front of me, it was already too late to turn and run. I'd been spotted; honed in on like a raw steak thrown into a cage of rabid dogs. The mortification written all over my face was like a lighthouse in a storm to the she-devil who immediately bombarded me.

"Oh, my God, I LOVE your hair! It's so pretty and blonde!"

I watched in horror as the perky brunette bounced up to me, her hand coming towards me like she wanted to pet my hair. I smacked it away with a frown, but that didn't deter her.

"You are so cute! My name's Candace, but everyone calls me Candy!" she told me excitedly.

"Candy? That's a stripper's name."

She stared at me blankly for a few seconds and then began giggling as she wrapped one hand around my elbow and started dragging me closer to the large group of girls bouncing up and down in the middle of the gym, clapping their hands and squealing so loudly that I'm pretty sure my ears were bleeding.

"You are going to be perfect for the top of the pyramid. You're so tiny and cute and everyone is going to love you! And since I'm the captain, I get to decide who makes the squad and who gets cut, so you're in luck!" Stripper Candy babbled.

Pyramid. Squad. Captain… Oh, fuck.

"Tell me this isn't cheerleading practice," I mumbled as half the girls noticed us walking towards them and turned their clapping and squealing in our direction.

"EEEEEEK someone new!"

"Candy, you are a genius. She HAS to be on the squad!"

"I get to braid her hair first!"

I'm pretty sure at this point my brain went into self-preservation mode like those people who are in horrible accidents and wake up with temporary amnesia. My mind refused to process what was happening, which is the only explanation for why I wasn't running out of here screaming like my head was on fire.

In case you haven't already realized this, I'm not a girly-girl. Most of my friends are guys because I just can't stand the drama that comes with having girlfriends. I don't doodle my name with some dude's last name all over my notebooks with hearts around them, I don't spend two hours getting ready to go out in public, I hate pop music and the last time I wore a dress was… actually, I've never worn a dress. I don't squeal, clap my hands or bounce up and down when I get excited, so obviously I'm in the wrong place right now. I am NOT cheerleader material.

"Touch my hair and die," I deadpan to a tall blonde with her hands dangerously close to my head.

"Isn't she just the best?!" Candy shrieks. "Who wants some bubble gum lip gloss?"

I cover my ears as the group starts screaming and reaching for the pink tube of gloss Candy pulled out of her cleavage. When the tube finally makes its way to me, I stare at it with a look of disgust on my face.

"I am not putting anything near my mouth that has *her* tit sweat on it," I inform them with a point in Candy's direction.

Someone blows a whistle and my faux pas of refusing Candy's tit gloss is forgotten as the girls race to the other side of the gym. In the wake of all that hyperactive estrogen, I see a girl standing directly across from me with her arms crossed in front of her, looking just as miserable as I am. Now, I'm not one of those girls who goes out of her way to make friends, which I think is pretty apparent by now. I've never taken it upon myself to make the first move—people always seem to come to me and I am perfectly okay with that. For the first time in the history of my seventeen years, I feel the need to approach someone and share my pain with this girl. No sooner have I decided to do something completely out of character for me, when she drops her arms and I get a good look at the t-shirt she's wearing. It's white, off the shoulder and, in giant red letters across the front, it reads "BIG FUN." It's almost like the heavens opened up above her and a light from the gods begins to shine down. Or it's just the fact that she moved under one of the gym lights, but whatever. I'm calling it a sign, thank you very much. It can't be a coincidence that this girl is wearing a Martha Dumptruck, *Heathers* shirt. Well, I guess it could. I mean, maybe she used to be a big girl and she lost a bunch of weight and she's trying to tell everyone that even though on the outside she's small, on the inside she's still big and full of fun.

Fuck it, I'm going in.

I make it across the gym to her right about the time that all the perky cheerleaders start shouting some stupid chant about the football team.

"Is this school's mascot really the Ducks?" I ask in shock as I stand next to her and we stare at the synchronized movements across the way.

"Yes, yes it is," she replies. "Last year, Candy decided that shouting 'quack' wasn't tough enough. She changed all of the cheers to "Let's go Ducks—RRRRWWWAAAAR!"

"Candy made ducks growl?"

She nods. "Candy made ducks growl. Candy is a dumb fuck."

"Don't take this the wrong way, but you don't really seem like the cheerleader type," I inform her.

She lets out a sigh and turns to face me. "Yeah, I could say the same for you. Nice effort on the stripper comment. Unfortunately, that really is what she wants to be when she grows up, so she definitely took it as a compliment."

She finally turns to face me, sticking her hand out in front of her. "I'm guessing you're new here? My name's Claire Morgan. Welcome to hell."

After listening to the Ducks growl for two minutes, we decided our time would be better spent hiding in the locker room until practice was over. I know this isn't exactly what my mother had in mind when she told me to be a joiner, but it was safer for all those annoying cheerleaders if we were as far away from them as possible. One more growl and Claire and I were going to start throwing punches.

We had an immediate connection and neither one of us was afraid to admit that it was weird. Like me, she mostly hated other people and kept to herself and her father forced her into joining the cheerleading squad because her mother moved away to "find herself" and he was afraid that, without some other female influence in her life, she would turn into a crazy cat lady or open fire at a post office one day.

I quickly found out her shirt was, in fact, a tribute to *Heathers* and we spent twenty minutes trading our favorite quotes. We agreed that "Fuck me gently with a chainsaw" was probably the best sentence ever uttered in the history of the world and, from that moment on, we never spent more than a few hours apart from each other.

My parents and her father weren't too thrilled with the fact that we quit the cheerleading squad before we'd even technically made the team, but Claire and I were geniuses when we banded together for a cause. They quickly realized that our friendship wasn't to be messed with and that as long as we weren't spending every waking moment of the rest of our high school lives alone in our rooms wallowing in misery, wearing all black and listening to The Cure, we would be okay. We had each other and nothing else mattered.

And that, boys and girls, is how the dynamic duo of Liz and Claire came to be. Next comes the part where you might want to put on that seatbelt I mentioned. Or grab a nice giant cup of vodka. You're going to need it.

Chapter 2
– Who Wants Blistex? –

Present Day

"SO, I HAVE cancer. Who wants more wine?" Claire states with a big smile.

I know it's probably not the most appropriate response to the words that just left my best friend's mouth, but I laugh.

And once I start, I can't stop. It could be due to the amount of wine Claire, Jenny and I have consumed tonight at our favorite bar, Fosters, or it could be the fact that, while this is the worst joke in the history of jokes, it still has to be a joke since Claire is smiling.

"Ooooh, I have something for that!" Jenny announces as she reaches for her purse on the empty seat next to her. After a few seconds of rummaging around, she holds out a tube of Blistex in Claire's direction.

"Why in the hell are you giving me Blistex?" Claire asks as she tops off her wine glass and empties our third bottle of the night.

Claire used to work at Fosters back when she was a single mother and the owners still adore her, so they let her go behind the bar whenever we're here and help herself to whatever she wants. Sometimes, it's a little dangerous that we never have to wait for a waitress to refill our glasses and I'm guessing tonight is going to prove that point.

"It's nothing to be ashamed of. I get it all the time. Put a little bit of this on it and it will be gone in a few days," Jenny says cheerfully.

Claire turns away from her and gives me *The Look*. The one that we silently give each other whenever our friend Jenny speaks. The one that quietly shouts "HOW THE FUCK DOES SHE FUNCTION ON A DAILY BASIS???"

"I'm pretty sure if Blistex was the cure for cancer, someone would have mentioned it by now, but thanks for the offer," Claire says with a chuckle as she sips her newly filled glass of wine.

"Oh, you said cancer! Ha! I totally thought you said canker. You know, like herpes, but on your lip… Oh. OH. OH, MY GOD!" Jenny screams in horror when it finally sinks in.

A few of the other patrons look our way when Jenny shouts and Claire gives them an apologetic look, waving them off with a flap of her hand.

Claire barely has time to set her wine glass down before Jenny flies out of her seat and tackles her in a bear hug.

"This can't be happening! You're so young. It's lung cancer, isn't it? I told you we never should have smoked all that pot in our twenties!" Jenny wails, burying her face in Claire's shoulder.

It's right around this point that I stop laughing. Not just because I can see it written all over Claire's face that I need to do something to get Jenny off of her because crying chicks and Claire do not mix, but because I can see it written all over Claire's face that she's not kidding. This isn't some weird April Fool's joke in the middle of July. She isn't going to shove Jenny away and shout, "Ha ha, you bunch of gullible assholes! I'm totally messing with you!"

While Jenny cries out her frustrations all over the shoulder of Claire's t-shirt, I do nothing but sit here staring at her. *I* should be the one crying. *I* should be the one running to the other side of the table hugging my best friend. *I* should be the one cursing God and shouting about the unfairness of it all. The problem is, I know exactly what I should be doing right now, but I can't make any of it happen. My ass has become permanently attached to the chair and my feet are like giant cement blocks refusing to move.

"Stop it," Claire says quietly, staring right at me as she pats Jenny's back.

I look at her in confusion.

"There is only one overly emotional woman in this group and that's how it's supposed to be. If you started crying right now I would punch you in the throat," Claire states softly.

And just like that, I'm reminded just how well she knows me. She knows I don't do the whole touchy-feely thing just like I know that in about three seconds, she's going to start getting the shakes from having Jenny's arms wrapped around her along with the sounds of female sobbing so close to her ear. There has to be something wrong with me though, right? I mean, my best friend has cancer.

My best friend has *cancer*.

Why can't I feel anything? Why can't I do anything?

Finally, Claire pulls herself out of Jenny's death grip and grabs a couple of napkins from the table, handing them to a still sniffling Jenny.

"I'm going to make this short and sweet. I found a lump in my breast last week and Carter made me immediately call my gynecologist. After I saw her, she sent me to an oncologist for a mammogram just to be on the safe side. I had a biopsy done and two days later the oncologist called to tell me I have breast cancer. I'm going in a week for a double mastectomy, and then I'll have six treatments of chemo and finally, reconstruction surgery. Now, back to my original question, who wants more wine?"

Jenny raises her hand. "I do!"

Claire lets out a cheer and unscrews the top on another bottle. We're such classy bitches.

"You know, Drew and I play mammogram all the time. I read

about the importance of doing self-breast exams and of course Drew wanted to be helpful. He's so cute!"

Claire leans back against her chair as she shakes her head. "Do I even want to ask what exactly "playing mammogram" entails?"

"Well, Drew dresses up like a doctor and I put on a robe. Then, he takes two dinner plates from the kitchen and he smushes—"

"OKAY! Stop. That's enough. I'm going to puke up all this wine we've consumed. Never speak of that again. Ever," Claire warns her.

Reaching for the bottle Claire just opened, I opt out of pouring it into my glass and just chug it right from the bottle. Fuck it.

"Um, you can't do that."

With the bottle still close to my mouth, I turn to look at the judgmental waitress who is half my age.

"This is a bar," I tell her, holding the bottle of wine up in front of her face. "And THIS, is called alcohol. People like to drink it. IN A BAR."

The perky twenty-something puts her hands on her hips and glares at me. "You can't drink it straight out of the bottle."

"What are you, the wine police? Don't you have some Barbies that need to be played with somewhere?"

Jenny giggles, holding up her glass of wine. "Three cheers for Barbie! I learned what smithereens was with Gymnastics Barbie and Lifeguard Barbie."

"What the fuck is smithereens?" I ask, taking another swig from the bottle.

"You know, where two women lock their legs together and grind their hoo-has against each other," Jenny explains, making peace signs with both of her hands and then interlocking her fingers together.

"I think she means scissoring," Claire provides.

"Look, ma'am, I'm going to have to ask you to leave if you continue to drink out of the bottle," Slutty Waitress Barbie informs me.

"Awwwwww shit," Claire mutters as I slowly get out of my chair and stand in front of the girl.

"You did NOT just call me ma'am," I growl.

The waitress takes a step back and I feel good about the fact that even though I'm little, I'm mighty, and this bitch looks like she's afraid I'm going to punch her in the kidney.

"Steph, I promise I'll make sure she uses a glass," Claire tells the waitress kindly.

She smiles at Claire and nods. "Okay. Just, try not to scream or cry anymore either. Some of the other customers are getting nervous."

I clunk the bottle of wine on the table and take a step in Steph's direction. "You should probably run along now before I find a fun way to make *you* scream and cry."

Steph *literally* runs away from our table and I sit back down, snatching the wine glass from Claire's hand that she is holding out for me.

"We should shave your head tonight," Jenny suddenly announces, bringing us all right back to the matter at hand that I DO NOT want to think about. "You have great bone structure. You'll look great with no hair."

"You are not shaving my head tonight. I don't start chemo for two weeks, so how about we just wait and see what happens?"

Jesus Christ. Mammogram. Lump. Biopsy. Mastectomy. Chemo. WHAT THE FUCK IS HAPPENING RIGHT NOW?

"And let me just add one last thing," Claire announces. "No one in this room will be shaving their head in support of me. There will be no spaghetti dinners to raise money for my medical costs, you are banned from wearing anything pink or anything closely related to the pink family until this is all over and there will be no fucking candlelight vigils held for me. Can I get an 'Amen' from both of you?"

"Amen!" I deadpan the reply and Jenny shouts it excitedly but hey, at least we replied.

Jenny starts talking Claire's ear off about her first mammogram last year and I stare into my glass of wine wondering when the fuck I'll wake up from this bullshit nightmare I'm obviously having. I mean, how is it possible that one of us is even old enough to get breast cancer? I'm not stupid, I've seen the statistics and I know it can hit anyone at any time, but those are people I don't know. They are women who have nothing to do with my life and I can continue living each day with only a passing thought about all of those poor ladies and what they're going through. A friend of a friend's mother's sister on Facebook, your mom's college roommate's aunt, your dentist's neighbor's best friend. THESE are the people who get cancer, not someone I know and love.

This is happening right in my own backyard. Right in our motherfucking favorite bar! It's impossible to stay oblivious anymore. Cancer has jumped off the pages of a Facebook post of a friend of a friend of a friend's yoga instructor's Starbuck's barista and smacked me right in the face.

Wasn't it just yesterday that Claire and I were in college, lamenting about her pesky virginity and dreaming about someday owning a business together?

Chapter 3
— Sex and Cookies —

Sophomore Year of College.
Still too many years ago to count...

"YOU GUYS! THERE'S a party at Pi Kappa Phi tonight! You absolutely HAVE to go!"

Claire and I glanced up from our spot on the floor of our dorm room where we'd been looking through our pile of VHS movies trying to decide if it was a *Girls Just Want to Have Fun* or *The Lost Boys* kind of night. We tried not to groan when we saw Candy standing in the doorway.

After years of us telling her point blank to her face that she was entirely too fucking chipper to be friends with us, she still hadn't gotten the hint. Imagine our surprise when she enrolled in the same college as us two years ago and made sure we all lived in the same dorm.

"Wow, that sounds like a blast, but we have a project due on Monday testing the abhorrent amount of genetic mutations in certain female subjects with ecdysiast-related given names. Sorry," Claire told her with a shrug.

Candy stared at her in confusion for a few seconds before rolling her eyes and giggling. "I swear, one of these days I'm going to get you two to go to a Pi Kappa Phi frat party and it's going to change your lives."

"Yeah, that will be the day," Claire muttered under her breath as Candy blew us kisses and ran down the hall, shouting in excitement to a few poor souls who happened to be in her frat-party warpath.

"Remind me again why we didn't get an apartment off campus and away from that fuck-knob?" Claire asked.

"Because we're trying to be economical and save money for the sex club that we're going to open as soon as we graduate," I reminded her. "Also, ecdysiast-related given names?"

I raised my eyebrow at Claire as she pushed herself up from the floor and sat down on the bottom bunk.

"Ecdysiast means striptease performer. It was on my word-of-the-day calendar yesterday," Claire explained before she flopped onto her back. "Also, we're not opening a sex club. That's just gross."

Pushing the movies aside, I got up from the floor and joined her on the bed. We lie next to each other in silence, staring up at the wooden slats under my top bunk that I'd decorated with bumper stickers:

> What's your damage, Heather?
> CORN NUTS!
> Does Barry Manilow know that you raid his wardrobe?
> What's that smell? Vampires, my friend. Vampires.
> It's called a sense of humor.
> You should get one, they're nice.
> My Little Pony: Friendship is Magic

Where in the fuck did that MLP one come from?

"Do you think there's something wrong with us because we don't like people?" I asked Claire after a few minutes. I reached up and used my fingernail to start picking at the edge of that stupid My

Little Pony sticker.

Claire grabbed my wrist and pulled it away. "Don't take that one down, I like it!"

"Seriously? My Little Pony? What are we, ten?"

Claire shrugged, sliding her hands behind her head. "I have a feeling they're going to make a comeback someday. Leave MLP alone."

With an irritated scowl, I rolled onto my side to face her. "So, seriously. Are we weird?"

Claire turned her head to face me. "No, we aren't weird. We just have a low tolerance for bullshit. Who cares if we haven't gone to a Pi Kappa Phi party yet and made out with random douchebags? I mean really, those parties are crawling with STDs. You could probably get knocked up just by ringing the doorbell."

We both laughed at that thought and then it got quiet again.

Even though we'd been to plenty of frat parties during our two years of college, we'd avoided Pi Kappa like the plague. That was the house known for its jocks and snotty rich boys. It was also the house that threw the best fucking parties on the planet, though, and pretty much everyone at this school and every school within a seventy-five mile radius showed up. Except for Claire and I.

"Do YOU feel like we're weird because we haven't been to one yet? I mean, if that's the case, I would totally suffer through a Pi Kappa party to make you happy," Claire informed me. "Just because it isn't my idea of fun, doesn't mean it's not yours. Who knows? You could meet the love of your life there."

Claire moved her hands under her chin and fluttered her eyelashes at me. "Oh, you big, strong, frat boy! Please, do another keg stand to pledge your undying love for me!"

I punched her in the arm as I laughed. "Oh, shut up, you whore. I'm pretty sure I won't meet the love of my life or even someone worth a one-night stand at one of those things, but it might be nice to check one out and see what all the fuss is about. I mean, this is our sophomore year. We should do something memorable."

Claire looked at me in mock horror. "Oh, my God! You mean watching movies or going to the boring frat parties where they serve h'orderves and cups of tea every Friday night while we smuggle in Boone's Farm in our purses isn't memorable?"

Speaking of Boone's Farm...

I quickly scrambled off the bed and pulled two bottles of Boone's Farm Strawberry Hill out from under the bed and held them up.

Claire immediately started laughing, sprang forward and grabbed one of the bottles out of my hand and unscrewed the top. "Jesus, we're so fucking classy. It doesn't get much better than screw-tops."

She chugged a good amount of wine before letting out a loud, satisfied sigh and lying back down, resting the bottle on her stomach. I set the unopened bottle next to me in bed before grabbing Claire's and taking a sip.

"Okay, so frat parties aside, we should really talk about the sex club," I told her.

"You're going to have to ply me with something a hell of a lot stronger than wine with only four percent alcohol in it to get me to agree to that shit," Claire informed me, snatching the bottle back and taking another sip.

"Fine, it doesn't have to be JUST a sex club. Maybe we could pair it with something you're interested in. Make it sort of a joint company. What are you interested in, Claire?"

She thought about it for a minute while I curled up next to her and we passed the bottle of shitty but delicious wine back and forth.

"It would probably be easier to tell you what I'm not interested in. Like say, a club where people are doing gross things to each other in public," she told me, sticking her finger in her mouth and mock-gagging.

"You are such a fucking buzz kill. Fine. We can rethink the sex club aspect, but we WILL own a business together. Maybe if you'd finally give it up to someone, Virgin McVirginsen, you would be more agreeable to all things involving sex," I reminded her.

The virgin comment was Claire's cue to punch me in the arm. I loved this girl to death, but she was wound up entirely too tight, pun motherfucking intended. I'd been trying to convince her to get rid of that pesky virginity since high school, but she was dead set on finding "the one." She didn't need to find "the one." She just needed to find the one who would do for a few hours. Scratch that, we're talking college boys. A few minutes, tops.

"Stop talking out of your ass. I'll show you. Maybe I'll drag you to one of those stupid frat parties and have a one-night stand," Claire threatened.

I started laughing. And once I started I couldn't stop.

"Shut up! It could totally happen!" Claire argued.

"Right! It will happen just like My Little Pony will make a comeback. Give it a rest, Claire. You're not the one-night-stand type and that's perfectly okay. One slut in a friendship is one slut too many."

Claire shook her head at me. "You're not a slut. You're just equal opportunity. You buy eight pairs of shoes at one time because you can't stand the idea of leaving a pair in the store to get lonely. It's only natural you do the same with your vagina. You never want your vagina to be lonely. It's so beautiful."

I chugged half the bottle of Boone's while Claire laughed.

"Okay, in all seriousness, I really want to own a bakery some day. What if we sold like sexy lingerie on one side and cookies and cupcakes on the other?" she suggested.

I started to make fun of the idea, but then I thought about it. And thought about it some more. I thought about it while I polished off the rest of the bottle and then chucked the empty onto the floor.

"Heeeeey, wine whore!" Claire complained as I jumped up from the bed and started pacing the room.

"Sex and cookies," I muttered.

Claire paused in the process of opening the second bottle of wine. "Huh?"

"Sex and cookies. Oh, fuck, Claire! You're a GENIUS!" I shouted.

"Wait. Let me drink some of this and catch up to you before you shower me with more compliments."

She held her hand up in the air in the universal sign of "hold the fuck up" while she downed half the bottle. She wiped her arm across her mouth and belched loudly. "Okay, I'm ready. Tell me more. Make sure to add how pretty and nice I am."

I walked over to my desk and sat down, grabbing a pen and a notebook. I wrote "Sex and Cookies" really big at the top of a blank page.

"So, I like sex and you like baking. Jesus, this is brilliant. BRILLIANT!" I screamed as I made a list of things we could sell at this store and a rough estimate of how much money it would take to get something like this off the ground. Turns out my Business Administration classes were actually useful. Who knew?

"Fuck. They put more than four percent alcohol in this shit. I think I'm drunk," Claire mumbled as she squinted her eyes and tried to read the label on the bottle.

"Nah, I just roofied you."

Claire sniffed the opening of the bottle and then shrugged. "Cool. Make sure you take advantage of me when I pass out. Anyway, back to this Snack and Sex thing. Tell me more."

I scribbled a few more things on the paper before turning the chair to face her. "Sex and Cookies, asshole. It's the name of our future business endeavor, although we might have to tweak that a little. I'm not sure the city would allow us to put the word 'sex' on our sign, but whatever. You can have your bakery on one side and put people into sugar comas every day and I can sell sex toys and lingerie and shit like that and put people into erotic comas on my side. Then, we can make sure the building has a loft upstairs and live above our businesses and throw awesome parties every weekend.

WINNER!" I shouted.

Claire bolted forward on the bed so fast she smacked her head into the wooden slats of the top bunk.

"SON OF A BITCH!" she yelled, rubbing her hand on her head as she got up and walked over to me.

I got up from the chair and we stood staring at each other for a few minutes before both of our faces broke out into huge smiles. We grabbed onto each other and started screaming and laughing and jumping up and down in the middle of the room like a couple of assholes.

After we got that nonsense out of our system, we went to work making more lists.

"This is totally happening. We'll go to a Pi Kappa Phi party next weekend and make THAT dream come true, and then right after graduation in two years, we're opening this fucking business!" Claire stated.

We finished off the second bottle of Boone's Farm in celebration and popped our worn out copy of *Heathers* into the VCR on the dresser, reciting the words to the entire movie while we dreamed about our awesome future.

Chapter 4
— Hello, My Name is Zoltron —

I STOOD IN the corner of the room, staring at Claire and thinking about the day we came up with the idea for Seduction and Snacks as the nurse got her IV started. She doesn't look sick. How in the fuck is this happening? Sure, we're in our mid-forties, but we're still young. This does NOT happen to young people and it most certainly doesn't happen to one of MY people.

She met my eyes across the room and huffed. "Will you stop looking at me like that?"

"Like what?" I ask, pushing away from the wall and going to the edge of the bed.

"Like you're expecting me to start spewing green vomit or keel over."

I scoff and put my hands on my hips. "That's not funny. This is serious, Claire. You… you're…"

"I have breast cancer. It's okay, you can say it. My tits may be small, but they're deadly," she says with a laugh.

"The doctor just gave me this form she says you need to fill out," Drew interrupts, walking through the door.

For the first time since I met him, I'm actually glad to see Drew. Ever since Claire told us the news and we almost got kicked out of

Fosters, he's been the calm, rational one. We met Drew when Claire met her husband, Carter. Drew and Carter had just recently moved to our town and they worked at the same car manufacturing plant where my husband Jim worked. From day one, Drew was always the guy who said whatever he was thinking no matter how inappropriate or disgusting it was. He's the jokester in the group, the crazy dude you sometimes don't want to be seen in public with. Who am I kidding? You never want to be seen in public with Drew. The last few days, though, he's kept us all from falling apart and on a few occasions, I've actually thought about hugging him to thank him. Then I remember the story he told us last week about how he and his wife Jenny decided Tuesdays were now referred to as Taco Tuesday in their house. Something to do with salsa on his penis and Jenny wearing a sombrero. I've blocked out the rest of that story out of respect for my mental health.

"What's the form for?" Claire asks, craning her neck to look at the paper Drew holds out to her.

"It's all about your likes and dislikes and some 'getting to know you' shit. It's like the cancer version of Match.com. I think they want you to get a little action while you're here," Drew replies.

The nurse finishes up Claire's IV and smiles at us. "That's just a way for the staff to get to learn a little more about you. We want you to be as comfortable as possible and we feel that knowing some personal things about you helps us make that easier."

She fiddles with the IV machine, presses a few buttons and then leaves the room, telling Claire she'll be back in a little while to check on her and pick up the finished form.

"I don't have the energy to fill that thing out, will you guys do it for me?" Claire asks, closing her eyes and resting her head on the pillow behind her.

At this point, I would strip naked, light myself on fire and run screaming through the halls of this hospital if she asked. It's not easy for someone like me to feel helpless. I've spent my life being known as the bossy, take-charge one in this group. Having to stand off to the side and watch your person suffering and not being able to do a damn thing about it is sobering.

"Don't you worry your pretty little head, Claire. Jim and I will fill this out for you," Drew announces with a smile as my husband and Carter walk through the door, their arms loaded with coffee, bags of chips, Snickers, Pepsi and anything else they could find in the vending machine down the hall.

"Dude, they had pudding cups in the vending machine?" Drew asks, his eyes growing wide as he snatches a chocolate cup out of Carter's hand.

"Uh, not exactly. We found a fridge a few doors down and it was filled with a bunch of free stuff!" Jim explains.

I shake my head at them. "You guys, that's probably the nurse's lounge. You just stole someone's lunch."

Drew already has the top off of the pudding cup and we all watch as he reaches into the pocket of his jeans and pulls out a mini bottle of Kahlua. He unscrews the top and dumps the entire thing into the cup of pudding, using his fingers to stir the mixture around.

"Mmmmmm pudding shots," he mutters before tipping the cup back and slurping the entire thing down in one gulp.

Carter busies himself dumping all of the food on a table in the corner of the room, lining it up by size and then rearranging it by color. He huffs and then tries organizing the items alphabetically. Carter has been manically arranging things since Claire got the call from her oncologist last week. He started at Seduction and Snacks, putting all of the butt plugs with the ball gags because they both start with B. After that, he took every item out of their pantry at home and lined them up by expiration date. When he tried to rearrange Claire's baking cupboards, that's when she put her foot down and told him if he put the cinnamon near the coriander she would castrate him.

I feel for the guy, I really do. He needs to keep himself busy so he doesn't dwell on what's happening with Claire. I tried doing something like that after she told us. I decided it was a good idea to take up running. Jim found me an hour later, two blocks away from our house screaming about how no one in their right mind should run unless someone with a gun was chasing them. Even then, I might just let the guy shoot me. Running is dumb.

"Carter, stop diddling the applesauce cups and come help us fill out this form," Drew tells him, waving the piece of paper up in the air. "I have more yummy goodness in my pants and pudding cups to fill."

"Oh, Jesus," Jim mutters next to me. Still, it doesn't deter him from going over to Drew, grabbing one of the pudding cups and an offered mini bottle of vodka that Drew just pulled out of his back pocket.

I watch as Carter goes over to Claire's side, leans down and whispers something in her ear before kissing her on the head and disappearing out the door with Jim and Drew. This is the first time the two of us have been alone since we all got the news. It's also the first time I have no idea what to say to my best friend. Everything that runs through my mind right now is completely stupid.

"So, this kind of sucks, huh?"
"At least your oncologist is cute."
"Would it be wrong to ask if they have some extra morphine I can use?"
"Sorry if I can't stop staring at your boobs."

"Stop staring at my boobs," Claire deadpans, her eyes still closed on the pillow.

"How the hell did you know I was staring at your boobs?"

She opens her eyes and raises one brow at me. "Because the lump in there has a special homing beacon that can sense boob ogling."

I cross my arms over my chest and roll my eyes. "You are being entirely too flippant about all of this."

"What do you expect me to do, Liz? Scream and cry about the unfairness of it all? What good will that do me? Do you think the cancer will be like 'Well, shit. If she thinks it's unfair then we obviously need to skedaddle.'"

"Did you just say *skedaddle?*"

Claire nods her head. "Yes, yes I did. Now quit being a pussy, come over here and sit by me."

She pats the bed next to her. "It's not contagious."

"I know it's not contagious, asshole," I tell her as I gently climb into her bed and lean back against the pillows next to her.

We don't say anything, each of us staring up at the ceiling. I want to tell her how sorry I am, but that's so fucking cliché that I can't even form the words. I want to reassure her that whatever she needs, I'll be here for her, but what the hell could I give her right now to make this all better? I don't have a magic wand that will take this stupid fucking disease out of her body. In less than an hour, she's going into an operating room to have a double mastectomy for stage 2 breast cancer. I have nothing that will make any of this go away.

A half hour later, the boys walk back into the room, snickering and shoving each other, clearly a little tipsy from pudding shots.

"What did you guys do? How many of those cups of pudding did you have?" Claire questions.

"I have no idea what you're talking about, Zoltron," Jim replies with a laugh.

Drew chokes on his own laugh, bending over at the waist.

"Zoltron? Do I even want to know what you three idiots are talking about?" I ask as Jim walks over and hands me the questionnaire the nurse asked Claire to fill out.

I grab it from his hand and scroll through the questions, along with the answers the boys filled in.

"Question number one: Do you have any nicknames?" I read

aloud.

Claire leans forward to look over my shoulder, reading the answer that they wrote down. "My full name is Sheba, Princess of the Night, but I will only answer to Zoltron."

The boys start giggling like fools from the doorway.

"Keep going," Drew says in between laughs.

I sigh, moving on to question number two. "Do you have any hobbies?"

I feel Claire's rumble of laughter next to me as she reads the answer. "My hobbies include running a meth lab in my basement, throwing down gang signs, mailing underwear to members of Congress and breeding ferrets."

I quickly scan the rest of the questions and answers.

- **What is your favorite color?** Clitoris. A combination of clear, teal, orange and island blue.
- **What is your favorite song?** The Silent Song. I could sing it for you, but you wouldn't be able to hear it. Only alpacas and very rare mice have the ability to hear The Silent Song.
- **Do you have any children?** rufus, joseephus, artie choke, woody bush, pat may wiener, meowy, boopsie and bob.
- **What's your favorite movie?** It's a tie between "The Anal girls of tobacco road: vagina slimes" and "sex starved fuck sluts #22: stinky white women." The well-developed plot and range of emotions portrayed in vagina slimes far outweighs that of stinky white women, but at the same time, the complexity in the cinematic quality of stinky white women should not be overlooked.

The questionnaire goes on for two pages, each answer they wrote down worse than the last. The only thing stopping me from throttling the idiot men we married is the fact that Claire thinks it's funny and it's taken her mind off of the fact that her boobs are killing her. Those little bumps of fat sitting on her chest are literally sucking the life out of her. I keep running through every single memory of the two of us together. Every time we've made each other laugh, cry, snort, puke, trip down stairs or scream in frustration. Thirty years of going through everything together. I can't imagine living the rest of my life without her and I have no idea how to find the humor in any of this bullshit. We have so much more living to do, she and I. We have a business to run together, the wedding of our children to plan and future grandchildren to corrupt.

The nurse walks back in to grab the form, clearly irritated that there are three drunk men giggling like little girls in the room, trying on hospital masks that they drew smiley faces on the front of.

"There's no drinking of alcohol allowed on hospital premises," she tells them haughtily.

"Pudding shots do not equal drinking alcohol," Drew informs her, his voice muffled through the hospital mask that has a porn stache drawn on the front of it. "Pudding shots equal awesome. Can I call you 'Puddin'?"

"I'm going to have to ask you to leave," she tells him.

He throws his arm around her shoulders. "Awwww, don't be like that, Puddin. We'll share some with you."

As I wrangle the guys and get them out of the room to give Claire some peace and quiet and get Nurse Ratched off our backs, I suddenly wish I could turn back time. I'd go back to something better than this. A time when my best friend wasn't getting ready to go into surgery so they could try and cut out the part of her body that's killing her. A time when I was young and dumb. Those were the good old days…

Chapter 5
— Non One-Night Stand —

HERE'S A LITTLE secret that not too many people know: Claire wasn't the only one who had a one-night stand that one time at a frat party. Unlike my dumbass friend, at least I remembered the birth control and didn't get knocked up. Well, birth control that works. I guess it isn't her fault condoms break every once in a while.

That one time, at a frat party…

CLAIRE HAD DISAPPEARED with some really cute guy about twenty minutes ago and honestly, I was glad she walked out of the room. The two of them were trading lines from *Heathers* while they played a thousand games of beer pong and it had started making me feel stabby. *Heathers* was our thing. OURS. Now that whore decided to finally listen to me about losing her virginity with a dude who was going to steal her away from me. Some pretty boy with a sweet smile who was going to pop her cherry, ask her to marry him and then they would move away and I'd never see her again. Okay, I know I'm being dramatic, fuck your face. I'm a good friend, though. I stood watch over the guy all night long and made sure he wasn't some pompous frat boy who would slip a roofie in her drink and take advantage of her. The fact that he was actually *nice* made it harder to hate him for stealing my best friend. Thank God Claire strapped on a set of balls and took the lead, otherwise that guy would have just stared at her with those stupid googly eyes all night long and never manned up. That guy was two seconds away from kissing the ground she walked on. Really, I'm happy for her. If she's going to lose her virginity, at least it's with someone like that and not some douche who will hit it and quit it and she'll never see him again. I hope she at least remembers to get his damn name.

"You look bored. How can you possibly be bored at a frat party?"

I turned around so fast when I heard a voice close to my ear that my full cup of beer sloshed all down the front of the guy's clothes.

He let out a yell when the cold liquid hit his junk and I growled when I realized I'd just wasted a full cup of perfectly good beer. As he attempted to pull his wet shirt away from his body, I looked over at the keg that now had a red Solo cup covering the tap indicating it was empty.

Super. Just perfect. I have to stand here and wait for my best friend to finish doing the deed sober.

I started to move towards the kitchen in the hopes of finding something, *anything* to drink when a hand grabbed onto my arm. I had really good intentions, I swear. My mouth opened and I prepared to let a string of curse words fly, telling this asshole to get his hands off me before I kicked him in the balls, but my eyes met his and I forgot how to swear. I don't forget how to swear. I NEVER forget how to swear. Swearing is my favorite thing in the world and I always have some good ones on the tip of my tongue ready to fly just in case. Hazel eyes with a ring of green around them stared down at me and I swear to fuck they sparkled as he looked at me. Gorgeous eyes aside, the guy had the nerve to smile at me. Not smirk like a douche, but a full, showing all his teeth and the dimples in his cheeks *smile*.

"I promise I won't say something stupid like 'How about you

help me get out of these wet clothes,' but… I really need to get out of these wet clothes," he told me.

I just stood there staring at his lips as he spoke.

"I have an extra t-shirt and jeans out in my car, but I'm afraid if I go out and get them, you won't be here when I get back."

Finally, I tore my eyes away from his mouth and shook the cobwebs from my brain. I took a step back from him, putting some distance between us before I did something stupid like kiss the guy.

"What do you care if I'm not here when you get back? There are a hundred girls at this party," I replied lamely.

He shrugged. "You're the only one who looks like she doesn't want to be here and that intrigues me. It also doesn't hurt that you're the prettiest girl I've ever seen."

My mouth dropped open unattractively and I'm pretty sure he wanted to take that statement back immediately. I've been called hot, sexy, gorgeous and a bunch of other adjectives that I couldn't have cared less about, but no one had ever told me I was pretty. That word indicates sweet and nice and innocent—something I had never been. It also made my heart melt, which pissed me off. My heart never melts.

"My name is Jim," he told me with that fucking smile again.

He held his hand out in front of him and there was nothing I could do but take it. I mean, I didn't want the poor guy looking like a schmuck with his hand hanging there while I stared him down.

You know in all those romance novels how people feel 'sparks' the first time they touch? Yeah, totally stupid. And no, I didn't feel fucking sparks. Jim isn't a lightning rod and last time I checked I didn't have an electrical plug coming out of my ass connected to an outlet in the wall. I felt soft, warm skin and a hand that engulfed my small one and held on tight. I felt his handshake all the way up my arms and somewhere in my vagina. He held my hand and didn't let go even after the two second time limit for proper handshakes ended.

"I'm not having sex with you tonight," I blurted.

He squeezed my hand and leaned in close, his cheek brushing against mine until his lips were right by my ear.

"What makes you think I *want* to have sex with you?"

I should have been offended by his words, but I wasn't because I actually believed him. He seriously did NOT want to have sex with me. It was an anomaly and it made me want to know more about him. He pulled away from me and dropped my hand, sticking his own hands into the front pockets of his jeans.

"Look, I'm not into one-night stands. Sure, they're fun at the time but the next morning, you always wake up feeling used."

He started backing away from me, pushing his way through crowds of drunk college students.

"Besides, I don't even know your name!" he shouted before disappearing behind two drunk girls dry humping each other while a group of equally drunk guys cheered them on.

I looked behind me down the hall where Claire had disappeared, and then I stared off in the general direction of where Jim had been swallowed up by the group of idiots. Back and forth I looked, trying to decide which way to go. I know I should have ran down the hall and stood guard outside of the room Claire entered with Mr. Cherry Popper, but the thought of *listening* to what was going on behind that closed door made me want to throw up all the beer I'd consumed tonight. If I followed Jim out to his car while he got his change of clothes, I'd have to give him my name and actually *talk* to him. What he said about one-night stands was obviously true, but at least they were quick and painless. You found a guy, you had sex and then you went on your merry way and didn't have to deal with all the baggage and bullshit. In the end, I made the only choice I *could* make. I tossed my empty beer cup onto the ground and pushed the dry-humpers out of the way, running outside to try and find Jim and see what his deal was.

After ten minutes of jogging up and down the block, searching row after row of cars parked bumper to bumper for the party, I located Jim. He'd already changed into dry jeans and was in the process of pulling off his wet shirt.

I stopped at the front of his car and stared at his bare chest. I'm a sucker for muscular men. Give me a big, hulking beast of a man who can toss me over their shoulder any day. Jim wouldn't be cracking any walnuts with the sheer power of his biceps anytime soon, but he was in great shape. He was tall and lean and had a six-pack I wanted to run my fingers over. I may or may not have let out a whimper when he grabbed his clean shirt from the backseat and covered himself up.

He spotted me as soon as he got the shirt pulled down and that damn smile lit up his face again. I was going to swoon like those motherfuckers in romance novels. My legs were going to give out and I'd need smelling salts or some shit.

"So, before we get out of here and get some coffee, do you think I could get your name?" he asked as he closed his back door and walked up to me.

"Liz, my name is Liz. Just coffee, right?"

He nodded as he grabbed my hand and laced his fingers through mine.

"Yep, just coffee. I know a great place two blocks from here."

And that's how it all started. We walked to the coffee shop and spent three hours talking before heading to Jim's apartment and having the most amazing sex of my life. True to his word, though, Jim didn't do one-night stands. When I woke up the next morning and tried to quietly pull the covers back and sneak out, he jumped out of bed and started getting dressed.

"Are you hungry? I'm starving. The diner across the street makes the best pancakes. Breakfast is on me and then we can figure out what to do the rest of the day."

Normally, I would have found his assertiveness off-putting and told him to suck it, but I couldn't. I was fucking starving and the thought of a huge plate piled with pancakes made my mouth water. He held my hand the whole walk down two flights of stairs and across the street to the diner. When he excused himself to go to the bathroom after we ordered, he came over to my side of the table and kissed the top of my head. Over breakfast, we made plans to spend the rest of the day together taking a nap and watching movies. I eagerly arranged these things with him and didn't even realize what was happening. I was falling in love with a guy I just met. A guy who held open doors, pulled out my chair, asked me about myself and my dreams and refused to let our night together be something cheap.

I haven't spent more than a few nights apart from Jim in over twenty years and it's mostly thanks to Claire. After our day of cuddling and watching movies, I swear to God I started to break out in hives. I'd never had a relationship. I didn't know the first thing about spending more than a few hours with a guy. What in the hell would we even talk about? He'd get bored with me and walk away right when I got attached. I snuck into the bathroom during our movie marathon and made a frantic call to Claire. She told me to stop being an asshole and give him a chance to prove me wrong.

And prove me wrong he did. It was the best non-one-night stand I'd ever had. He tells me when I'm being an asshole and I tell him when he's pissing me off. He's my rock and he keeps me grounded. Aside from Claire, he's the only person who knows just by looking at me what I'm feeling. Sometimes it's a blessing, but with everything going on right now, it's a fucking curse.

Chapter 6
— Shaved Pussy —

AS SOON AS the doctor came out and told us that Claire's surgery went well and that she was resting comfortably, I left. Shitty thing to do, I know, but I couldn't take it anymore. I couldn't stand to drink one more cup of shitty hospital coffee and I was losing my mind pacing the shitty halls. I told everyone I was going to pick up some food so we didn't have to eat one more shitty meal in the cafeteria, grabbed the keys from Jim and ran to the parking garage. I've done nothing but drive around for an hour. I drove past Seduction and Snacks where we made our dreams come true, the park where Claire and I used to take the kids when they were little, the elementary school where we both got kicked out of the PTA for rolling our eyes at the president when she told us we needed to be more bubbly to be in the Parent Teacher Association, the high school where we met and then later sent our own kids, and finally, the hotel where Gavin and Charlotte had decided to have their wedding reception in six months.

Our kids are getting married, something we used to talk about when they were babies and it's actually happening. We've been fighting over what color dresses we're going to wear and who's going to cater the event and what song would be the perfect one to dance to when it comes time for the mother/daughter, mother/son dance. All the years of dreaming, all these months of planning and arguing and now I don't know if my best friend will even be there when our children tie the knot. There hasn't been one major event in my life that Claire hasn't been there for and now, the biggest one of all is coming and I might have to do it on my own. It's not fair. I can't do this without her. I can't do *anything* without her.

Before I head back to the hospital, I decide to stop by Claire's house and pick up a few things that she might need. I'm sure Carter packed everything in her closet, but I'm not ready to go back to the hospital just yet. I need some time to get my head on straight so I don't break down crying as soon as I walk into her room.

Pulling into the driveway, I see Carter's car parked in front of the garage and wonder what he's doing home. Figuring he had the same idea as me, I let myself into the house to look for him. When I get close to the kitchen, a can of green beans comes flying out into the hallway, denting the wall right next to my head. Crouching down, I peek around the kitchen doorway right as Carter reaches into the pantry and swipes his arm across every single shelf, sending cans of soup, boxes of Mac N Cheese, canisters of sugar and about a hundred other things crashing to the floor. When the pantry is empty, he moves on to the cabinets, yanking out pots and pans and tossing them across the room. Pans crash into the table, lids smack into the wall and he kicks a bag of flour out of his way as he moves across the room to wreak havoc on the cupboards under the island. Unfortunately, the toe of his shoe hits the bag of flour just right and the entire thing explodes, a cloud of white powder *poofing* all over the floor and the front of his jeans.

"MOTHERFUCKER!" he screams.

I've never seen Carter like this and for a minute, I'm afraid to approach him. I quickly pull out my phone and send a text to Jim and Drew, hoping they can get their asses over here and help me out.

Carter sees me cowering in the doorway and stalks over to me as I shove my phone in my pocket.

"I don't know what the fuck to do," he tells me angrily before turning and slamming his foot into a Tupperware dish, sending it flying across the room.

"I DON'T KNOW WHAT THE FUCK TO DO!" he screams.

He clutches his hands in his hair and I'm frozen in place as I watch him sink to the ground on his knees in the middle of the mess.

"FUCK YOU, GOD! FUCK YOU FOR DOING THIS TO HER!" he cries, his shoulders shaking with sobs as he completely breaks down.

I force myself to move, stepping over cans and boxes as I rush to his side and get down on my knees next to him, wrapping my arms around his heaving shoulders.

"This isn't fair! Goddammit, this isn't fair," he tells me angrily.

His entire body is shaking and for the first time since I found out about Claire being sick, I don't feel so helpless and alone. All this time, Carter has been a rock for Claire, doing whatever she needed and taking care of things when rage and fear were bubbling just under the surface. We share a love for Claire that is different in a lot of ways, but so alike in others. She is our soul mate and we are both caught in the middle of wanting to do everything we can to make her better, yet knowing there's not a damn thing we can do.

"I can't do this without her, Liz, I can't. Every part of my life is wrapped up in her. She's my wife, the mother of my children and my *everything*. How am I supposed to live without her?" he sobs.

I don't know how to answer him because everything I can think to say would be so fucking cliché. *She's going to be fine. You aren't going to lose her. She's strong and she's going to fight this.*

It's all bullshit. All of it. We *want* her to be fine. We *want* her to be with us forever, but that doesn't mean it's going to happen. How do you prepare yourself for a life without your soul mate, while at the same time holding onto hope that they will be okay? You have to walk a fine line between hope and reality, and every single day that line gets thinner and thinner. Eventually, you're going to have to tip one way or another and you have no way of knowing which way it will be. It's enough to drive you insane, to push you over the edge and make you question everything you thought you knew about yourself as a person.

"I'm so scared, Carter," I tell him honestly.

"I know, babe. Me too."

He keeps his arm slung over my shoulder as we move to the wall, resting our backs against it as we sit side-by-side with our knees pulled up to our chests. I can see some relief in Carter's face as we sit here in silence. It's like he just needed to scream and rage and get it out of his system in order to feel normal again. I wish I could do the same. No amount of trashing a kitchen is going to make me feel better, though.

I hear the front door open and shut and a few seconds later, Jim and Drew stick their heads in the kitchen, staring wide-eyed at the mess.

"Dude, have you been snorting cocaine without me?" Drew asks as he eyes the flour coating Carter's jeans.

"Why are you wearing shorts? Last time I checked it was twenty degrees outside," Carter asks him.

Drew waltzes up to us and sticks one of his legs in front of Carter. "Touch it. Go ahead, touch it."

Carter shakes his head back and forth and tries to move away from Drew's leg. Drew just sticks his leg closer to Carter's face until it's practically touching his mouth.

"TOUCH IT!" Drew shouts.

"What the fuck is wrong with you?! I'm not touching your leg!" Carter argues.

Drew bends over, running his hand up and down his leg and I swear I hear him purr. "Oh, yeah, silky smooth."

"What in the hell is happening right now?" I ask Jim, who's standing right behind Drew, shaking his head.

"Our friend decided to shave his legs in support of Claire. Don't ask," Jim tells me.

"I totally get why chicks do this," Drew mutters. "I can't stop touching myself."

"Please tell me you didn't shave *your* legs," I tell my husband.

He sits down next to me on the floor and shrugs. "Nah, my legs are still hairy. My balls on the other hand…"

"You shaved your balls?" Carter asks, leaning forward to look at Jim.

Drew nods, his hands still running up and down his leg. "Yep, Jimbo totally shaved his nut sack. His bathroom now looks like someone killed Sasquatch. You know, if Sasquatch was covered in pube hair."

"Uh, did you guys do this together or something?" I ask in disgust.

"Are you kidding? That would be totally gay," Drew scoffs.

"And shaving your legs isn't?"

He just shrugs. "I figured we should do something in honor of Claire and I also heard that you can donate your hair to cancer patients so they can make wigs out of it. How cool would it be if someone was wearing my leg hair on their head?"

"That is the most disgusting thing I have ever heard. You can't donate leg hair, idiot," I tell him.

"Why the fuck not? I'll have you know my leg hair was long and flowing. It would make a beautiful wig."

Carter laughs and even though the idiot I married and his friend are morons, at least they managed to make Carter laugh, which is exactly what I'd hoped for when I sent them a text.

"Don't laugh, dude. It's your turn now," Jim states.

"I'm not shaving my legs and for your information, my balls have been silky smooth for years," Carter informs them.

"Oh, you're not going to shave anything on *your* body," Drew says with a smile, pulling a pair of battery operated clippers from his back pocket. "Find your pussy."

Carter and I look at Drew in confusion until a few seconds later we hear a small "meow" from the corner of the room and Drew's face lights up with a huge smile.

"No. Absolutely not. You are NOT shaving Claire's cat," I tell them.

The guys sit perfectly still, looking back and forth between each other and I have a moment of hope that Drew was just kidding and that my husband and Carter aren't stupid enough to do something like this.

My hope is short lived, though. The poor cat lets out another "meow" and all three guys scramble up off the floor, shoving and pushing each other out of the way as they chase the cat through the house. Figuring there's no point in chasing after those morons, I start cleaning up the kitchen while listening to the guys screaming and laughing all through the house. Eventually, I hear the *whirr* of the clippers starting up and Drew lets out a war cry. "LONG LIVE SHAVED PUSSY!"

Thank God for good friends. Even though they have brains the size of peas, at least they got Carter's mind off of things for a few seconds. I wish the same could be said for me. I wish I could let my friends distract me and remember all the other stupid, silly things we've done together, instead of the sadness that is consuming our lives right now. I wish I could go back to a time when I actually knew how to make things better for my best friend.

Chapter 7

— Cow Ass —

Twenty-five years and nine months ago...
D-Day. Or is it P-Day?

"REMIND ME AGAIN why we decided to major in business? This business math bullshit is for the birds," I complained as I walked into our dorm room and tossed my backpack on my bunk. "Someone needs to get it through these professors' heads that we will NEVER need to use algebra to find X at any time other than in college. X can go fuck himself right in the face if he gets lost or can't figure out who he is."

When Claire didn't immediately reply back with an "Amen, sister!" I knew something was wrong. I saw her car parked downstairs, so I was pretty certain she was here. I'd been a shitty friend lately, not spending enough time with her since Jim decided to fuck with my head and my heart and I happily went along for the ride. I finally put my foot down today and told him I needed to spend some time with my girl. She'd been acting weird the last few weeks and I didn't like it.

"Claire?" I yelled as took off my coat and tossed it on top of my backpack.

I heard a sniffle come from the tiny bathroom in our dorm

room. Pushing the door open, I found her sitting on the shitty yellow tile, surrounded by pregnancy tests with tears and snot running down her face.

"What's going on? Is this some kind of experiment for one of your classes?" I asked dumbly.

"I drank an entire gallon of milk in less than three minutes and did you know cows don't take pregnancy tests? A farmer sticks his hand up a cow's ass and feels around for a little ball of baby cow in her uterus. You have no idea how glad I am that I'm not a cow. No one needs to be up to their elbows in my anus," Claire rambled as she wiped the tears from her face.

"What in the actual fuck are you talking about right now?" I asked in horror, trying to get the image of an entire human arm shoved up a cow's ass out of my head.

"No need to fear, pasteurization does NOT mess with the hormone called human chorionic gonadotropin, or in layman's terms, HCG. This hormone is produced right after a fertilized egg attaches to the wall of a woman's uterus and OH, MY GOD I feel like I'm in fifth grade health class all over again and I WANT TO DIE!" she wailed as a fresh set of tears started pouring from her eyes.

Kicking the pile of plastic tests out of the way, I got down on my knees next to Claire and pulled her into my arms. She sobbed and mumbled random facts about sperm and I reminded myself to tell her at a later point to stay the fuck away from the library reference books. No good can come from those things.

I reached down with one hand and picked up a test from the pile and sure enough, a big, fat pink plus sign was right smack in the middle of it. My heart dropped to my toes and I felt like crying myself all of a sudden.

"Maybe the tests are wrong. They could be wrong, right? Women get false positives all the time. I saw it on Oprah," Claire rambled as she snot all over the shoulder of my shirt. "This one woman thought she was pregnant and when it came time to deliver, she found out it was a giant tumor. Maybe I have a tumor? A tumor masking itself as a baby. Both of them could suck the life right out of me and make me want to die, but I think I'd rather have a tumor. You can remove a tumor and never have to see it again. You can't do that with a baby, right?"

I tossed the pregnancy test down onto the pile of others and rested my cheek on top of her head. "I hate to break it to you, but I'm pretty sure it's not a tumor. I don't think you'd get twenty-seven positive pregnancy tests out of a tumor."

"Thirty-two," Claire mumbled. "I took five at the grocery store while I drank the milk."

We sat on the floor of our dingy bathroom and I let her cry it out for a few minutes before I spoke again.

"Are you going to tell me who the rat bastard is so I can chop off his balls?"

That just started a whole new round of wailing and crying from Claire and I did my best to calm her down, but nothing worked.

"I'm a slut! I'm a dirty, dirty slut! I had a one-night stand at a frat party and I didn't even get his name! I'm the girl parents warn their daughters about. They're going to put my face on a billboard telling teenage girls what NOT to do. MY LIFE IS OVER!"

I turned to face Claire and grabbed her shoulders, forcing her to look at me. "Stop it, right now. No one talks about my best friend like that, got it? I shouldn't have pushed you so much to lose your virginity to the first guy who came along. It's that douchebag's fault for not using a fucking condom! We are going to get through this, Claire. You're going to dry your eyes and stop the girly crying shit. You're stronger than this! You are a total badass and I am not about to let you wallow in misery. We're going to get up, get out of this bathroom and go hunt this motherfucker down."

She nodded her head during my speech, so hopefully I was doing *something* right. I didn't even bring up adoption or abortion because even though Claire never ever wanted to have kids, she was definitely pro-life and one of those women who owned up to her mistakes and took whatever consequences came her way, including having a baby.

Jesus Christ, my best friend was going to have a baby.

"First thing we're going to do is feed you. Have you even eaten anything today?" I asked as I got up from the floor and pulled her up right along with me.

"Are we counting the milk, because I'm pretty sure an entire gallon should be considered its own food group."

I shook my head at her and she sighed.

"Well, I had seven sticks of string cheese and an entire loaf of bread before I went to the store to buy the tests," she replied. "Also, we're out of bread. And string cheese."

I wrapped my arm around her shoulder and led her out of the bathroom. "I'm going to call Jim and see if he can do some detective work to find out who this guy is. If anything, we'll just go back to the frat house during the day when there's a chance of them being sober and see if they know who he is."

"Just promise me you won't kick his ass," Claire begged.

"Why the hell shouldn't I kick his ass? He knocked you up and never even told you his name," I argued.

"We were drunk! It's not like I told him my name either," she fired back. "He was nice, Liz, really nice. I was the idiot who snuck out of the bedroom the next morning and did the walk of shame out of the house."

I really couldn't argue with her at that point. When I finally made it home after spending the day with Jim the day after the party, I was completely ecstatic that she'd finally done the deed. I almost shed a few tears when she told me how she hit it and quit it and never looked back. My girl was finally all grown up and taking a page out of my book. Minus the whole getting knocked up at a frat party thing.

"Fine, so he was a nice guy. I still think he needs his ass kicked on principle alone. For your sake, we'll do this nice and civilized. We'll ask around and we'll find him. I mean, how hard can it be? Ohio University isn't that big. We're bound to find someone who knows who this guy is."

Claire took a few deep breaths and wiped the remaining tears from her face. She put her chin up and had a look of determination on her face. "You're right. How hard *can* it be?"

I grabbed Claire's purse from the desk next to our bunks and handed it to her, throwing my own over my shoulder as we headed for the door to pound pavement and find her baby daddy.

"No matter what happens, I'm going to be here for you, okay? I know it really sucks right now, but you're not alone. That baby is going to be the coolest kid in the entire fucking world because he has you for a mom and me for an aunt."

Claire smiled at me as I held the door open for her. "We should probably try cutting back on our swearing before this thing gets here. I don't think its first words should be 'fuck' or 'kiss my ass'."

I shrugged as I locked the door behind us and we headed downstairs. "Could you imagine having a kid who repeated everything we say? Kid would be a Goddamn genius, I'm telling you."

Chapter 8
– Rack of Ribs –

"YOU CAN'T IGNORE her forever."

I look up from a pile of paperwork at my desk and scowl when I see Jim standing in the doorway of my office at Seduction and Snacks. Now that Gavin and Charlotte both worked at headquarters, Claire and I had been able to spend more time lately in our flagship store, our baby and where we loved to be.

"I have no idea what you're talking about," I tell him.

I look away from him and back down at my paperwork so he can't see my eyes and know I'm lying. It's stupid. I know it's stupid. He knows I'm lying, I know I'm lying, EVERYONE knows I'm lying.

Claire has been home from the hospital for three days and I haven't gone to see her. I'm ashamed of myself but what the fuck am I supposed to do? I'm scared to death. I have no control of this situation and it makes me want to scream.

"I talked to Carter last night. He said she's doing really good and sleeping a lot," I tell him.

"Hon, you have to go see her. She *needs* you," Jim reminds me.

I slam my pen down on top of the desk and stare at him. "She doesn't need me! She needs a fucking cure for what's happened to her and I can't give that to her. For the first time in our friendship I can't do anything to help her and it's fucking killing me!"

I swallow back the tears, refusing to cry. I know once I start, I'll never be able to stop. I've been working like a maniac since Claire got out of surgery and the doctor told us she was stable and the surgery went well. I didn't know what else to do. After Carter's breakdown in their kitchen and the shaved cat incident, I drove right to Seduction and Snacks and buried myself in work. Working takes my mind off of things I can't control. Work is the only thing keeping me sane right now. Who knew that organizing orders of butt plugs and anal beads would actually keep my insanity at bay?

"She doesn't need you to fix her, Liz. She just needs you to be there for her," Jim tells me softly as he walks across the room and squats down next to me.

He grabs onto the seat of my chair and spins me so that I'm facing him.

"It's too hard," I whisper.

Jim rests his hands on my thighs and rubs his thumbs comfortingly over my skin. "I know it is, babe. You guys have been through a lot together but this is the worst. Through thick and thin, isn't that what best friends are all about? What would Claire do if the situation were reversed? I'm guessing she'd be all up your ass and pissing you off so much that you forgot all about what was happening. That's all she needs from you right now. She just needs to know that you're there and you care."

Of course I care. It's absurd for anyone to think otherwise. She's my person, my other half. I care so much that it's killing me right now not to be there for her, but I don't know what to say and I don't know what to do. That whole saying about actions speaking louder than words runs through my mind and just like that, I know exactly what to do. It will most likely piss Claire off, but maybe it will take her mind off of things and in my own way, I can show her that I'm sorry for flaking on her the last few days.

I give my husband a quick kiss and grab my phone, calling Jenny and getting her on board with my plan.

"DO YOU KNOW how hard it was to get an appointment at the last minute?" Jenny complains as we walk up the sidewalk to Claire and Carter's front porch.

When I called her earlier, she was about two hours away meeting with a new marketing company and said she wouldn't be able to make it back in time to join me for my own appointment. I wouldn't let myself get discouraged though and told her to just do it on her own and then we'd meet up later tonight at Claire's house.

"Quit your bitching, Claire is going to love this," I tell her as I knock a couple of times on the door to announce our presence before walking inside.

"Are you sure she's going to like this? It makes absolutely no sense," Jenny complains.

I have no idea what she's talking about and I don't have time to argue with her because as soon as we get in the house, I see Claire sitting on the couch under a pile of blankets.

She looks pale and tired and I panic for a minute. I shouldn't want to run away from my best friend, but I do. I want to turn around and run out the door and pretend like this isn't happening. I want to close my eyes and walk back into the house and imagine that it's three months ago when I walked through the door to celebrate her birthday and she was already halfway to being trashed, her face flushed and her smile bright as she called me a bag of dicks and thrust a beer in my hand.

"Claire, you look like shit," Jenny tells her.

I smack Jenny's arm as Claire laughs.

"I feel like shit too," Claire informs us with a low, raspy voice.

Carter walks into the living room from the kitchen with a glass of ice water and sets it down on the coffee table in front of her. I watch him slide his arms behind her and help her sit up and I want to scream. She's the strongest person I've ever met and she needs help sitting up on the couch. I should have been the one to race over there and help her. I should have instinctively known she needed help but I didn't. Or maybe I did but I'm just too fucking scared to get close to her.

"We have a surprise for you!" Jenny announces as Carter fusses over Claire's blankets and she smacks his hands away.

Carter starts to walk away but immediately stops in his tracks when Jenny pulls her shirt all the way up until her tits pop out.

"Is that the surprise, because I like it," Carter says with a nod.

"Oh, for God's sakes," I mutter, grabbing onto the hem of my shirt and tugging it up just enough to show off the skin over my ribs.

Claire stares back and forth between Jenny and I, a look of confusion on her face.

"One of these things is not like the other," Claire sing-songs.

I lean forward to get a look at Jenny's side, trying to avoid her tits hanging out for the world to see.

"What in the fuck is that?" I shout, pointing to whatever the hell it is.

Jenny looks down at herself and then back at me. "It's what you told me to do! I'll admit, it sounded a little weird when you told me on the phone, but I kind of like it and it totally makes sense."

Carter cocks his head to the side and squints. "I believe what we're looking at is a rack of ribs tattoo. Awesome!"

I turn to face her, pointing to my own tattoo. "Pink ribbon on our ribs, Jenny! PINK RIBBON ON OUR RIBS! How in the hell does a rack of ribs make any kind of sense right now?"

Jenny stares at me in confusion for a few minutes and then the light goes on. "Ohhhhhhh, yeah. I guess that makes sense. But, I mean, it's a rack. Get it? Save your rack? I really think mine is better."

Jesus Christ, when I called Jenny and told her we should get matching tattoos of a pink ribbon in support of Claire, I should have known she'd get it all wrong. I never should have let her do it on her own.

"Well, the sentiment was nice," Claire tells us with a shrug, trying to hide her laugh.

"Dammit, now I'm hungry for ribs," Carter complains.

Jenny finally pulls her shirt down and walks over to the couch, flopping down next to Claire. "Drew has been driving me insane since I got the tattoo earlier. He keeps wanting to lick it because he's convinced it will taste like barbeque."

Carter scrunches up his face in disgust. "And now I'll never be hungry for ribs ever again. Thank you for that."

Carter leaves us alone, most likely to go throw up somewhere and an awkward silence fills the room when he's gone.

Thankfully, Jenny doesn't know how to shut up for more than two seconds so she starts rattling on and on about barbeque sauce in places one should NEVER put barbeque sauce and I tune her out.

Claire stares right at me like she's waiting for me to say something. I know I should apologize for not coming over sooner, but I can't make the words come out. Is there a book called *How to Talk to Your Best Friend When She Has Breast Cancer For Dummies?* I might need that. I've always been there for her when she needed me. I've always known the right things to say, why should now be any different? Maybe because all the times in the past weren't life or death situations. To quote *The Breakfast Club*, when Claire messed with the bull, I shoved my horns up someone's ass to make them pay. Okay, I'm paraphrasing there, but whatever.

If Claire had a problem, I fixed it. End of story. Why in the fuck can't I fix this? Why can't we just go back to when things were crazy and fun and I could make everything better for her?

Chapter 9
— Meat Curtains —

Twenty-five years ago...

"THIS IS FUCKING BULLSHIT! If you don't have drugs then get the fuck out of my room!" Claire screamed at the poor nurse who came in to take her vitals.

The nurse took one look at Claire, told her she'd come back later and ran from the room.

"Oh, that was really nice. Great attitude, Miss Exorcist. Will there be green vomit spewing from your mouth for your next trick?" I asked as I handed her a cup of ice chips.

She snatched the cup out of my hand and snarled at me. "Eat. A bag. Of Dicks."

"Classy. I hope those are your son's first words," I told her as I pulled a chair up to the edge of the bed and sat down.

"Where the hell is Jim? He left like three hours ago to get me a grape Popsicle. I WANT MY FUCKING GRAPE POPSICLE!" Claire screamed.

"He left five minutes ago, cranky ass," I reminded her.

Claire had been in labor for exactly one hour. ONE HOUR and she was already losing her shit. I feared for anyone within a mile radius of this woman when she actually had to start pushing that thing out of her.

"Come on, it can't hurt *that* bad," I joked, dodging out of the way when her hand flew up to smack me. "I'm kidding! Jesus, you know I'm kidding. Lighten up, dude. After today, you'll finally be able to see your feet. And just think of all the booze you can drink in the middle of the night when you can't sleep because he's screaming his fool head off."

Claire started to curse at me, but thankfully another contraction ripped through her and she had to concentrate on breathing instead of kicking my ass.

I grabbed onto her hand and let her squeeze the life out of it, watching the contraction monitor next to her bed and letting her know when it was almost over.

"You're doing good, keep breathing, just a few more seconds."

When it passed, she let out a huge sigh and slumped back against her pillows.

She turned her head and stared at me, tears filling her eyes. "I'm so scared, Liz."

I knew immediately she wasn't talking about the whole pushing a human out of her body-thing. While that thought was scary and more than a little bit gross, I knew she was thinking about what happened *after* he was here. She was a strong woman who could handle a few hours of pain, but I could tell just by looking at her that she was second-guessing her ability to be a mom.

"You're going to be fine. He's going to come out and he's going to be perfect and you're going to be FINE. It's going to suck for a while and you're going to miss out on a lot of sleep and you'll probably never take another uninterrupted shower or piss again, but it's going to be okay, I promise you. You are amazing and you're strong and you're going to get through this. You've got me and Jim and your father and we're going to be there every step of the way. No matter what you're worrying about right now, just remember that you aren't alone. You will *never* be alone. I've got you, babe."

Another contraction hit and I stood up, brushing her hair off of her face and helping her count through the pain. I felt so helpless that I couldn't make the pain go away, but it didn't matter. For the first time in our lives, this was something she had to do on her own. All I could do was be there for her and help her any way I could. I decided that humor was always the best medicine. I couldn't take the pain from her, but I could make her laugh.

"So, have you thought about how horrific your vagina is going to look after you push that little guy out? Like meat curtains flapping in the breeze every time you walk. Man, your poor vagina."

Claire attempted to call me an asshole, but she couldn't get the words out. She started laughing instead. "Oh, my God! It's going to look like a wilted, roast beef sandwich."

"Jesus, I'm never going to be able to eat at Arby's again. Thank you for THAT visual," I told her with a shudder. "On the bright side, it could be a great pick-up line. 'Hey, there hot stuff. Do you like beef? I've got some in my pants just for you.'"

Claire rested her hands on her huge stomach as she continued laughing. "Vagina, the other white meat."

"Beefy vagina: it's what's for dinner!" I shouted.

The doctor chose that moment to walk in the room. He looked at both of us, laughing so hard we were crying and I shrugged my shoulders. "Just giving her a little encouragement, Doctor. Would you like to place your vagina bet? I've got ten to one odds right now that her vagina will resemble ground zero of a bomb blast. What say you?"

The doctor ignored us, pulling the privacy curtain around the bed to block the doorway. "I'm just going to check on you and see how things are progressing. How are the contractions?"

"They hurt like a motherfucker," Claire told him honestly.

"Good, good. That means things are moving along."

I quickly reached over and grabbed onto Claire's legs when I saw a look of murder in her eyes. She was about one second away from kicking the good doctor in the face.

Once he got the blanket pushed up over her knees, he snapped on a pair of rubber gloves and went to town between my friend's legs.

"Don't look. Whatever you do, you are NOT allowed to look down there," Claire threatened.

She winced at whatever the doctor was doing and I winced right back in sympathy. "No need for *that* warning. I wasn't about to stick my head down there to get a look at the crime scene you've got going on between your legs."

The curtain suddenly slid open. "Who wants a grape Popsicle?!"

Claire and I both looked up at Jim and watched the smile on his face fall.

"Oh, no," he muttered as the Popsicle dropped out of his hand and hit the floor.

"OH, MY GOD! GET OUT! STOP LOOKING!" Claire and I both shouted at the same time.

My poor fiancé didn't budge.

"Monster. Help. Popsicle scary," he mumbled.

Claire tried to close her legs but the doctor was knee deep in vagina and there was nothing she could do.

"GET OUT RIGHT NOW!" we both screamed in unison again.

His eyes were glazed over at this point and I was thanking God we were in a hospital because I was pretty sure he was going to pass out any minute now.

"I like Popsicles. And puppies. Just think about puppies," he muttered to himself.

When I realized that my poor man was in a pregnant woman vagina daze-slash-nightmare, I took action. I hustled around to the end of the bed and stood in front of him, blocking his view.

"Breathe, Jim. BREATHE!" I reminded him.

He took a huge breath and finally blinked. "I'm just gonna leave."

I nodded at him and turned him around, pushing him back towards the door. "That's a great idea, honey. How about you just go back into the waiting room with Claire's dad and never, ever step foot in this room again, okay?"

"Never step foot in this room again?" he questioned as I walked him to the door.

"That's right, never step foot in this room again. Good boy."

I patted him on the back and shoved him into the hallway, closing the door to the room behind me before going back to Claire's bedside.

"Your future husband saw my vagina," Claire stated.

"Better him than me."

The doctor stood up, pulling his gloves off and tossing them into the trash next to the bed. "Well, you haven't dilated at all, but it's still early. We're going to put a fetal heart monitor on the baby just to make sure he's handling the contractions okay and I'm going to have one of the nurses give you some Pitocin to try and move things along. I'll come back to check on you in a little while."

A few hours later, long after the Pitocin and Claire threatening to kill everyone who came near her, the doctor decided it was time for an emergency C-section. Claire was scared to death. I was scared to death. Everything started happening so fast at that point. Doctors and nurses were running around, making calls and before we knew it, Claire was being wheeled out of her room and down the hall to the operating room.

I jogged next to her bed and never let go of her hand the entire way. I knew she was freaking out and I didn't know what the hell to do other than make sure she understood that I'd always be here for her.

"You're not going to leave, right?" Claire asked when we got into the brightly lit OR and they transferred her to another bed.

I squeezed her hand tighter as one of the nurses handed me a pair of scrubs and a hospital mask. "I'm *never* going to leave you. I'm going to be here the entire time. It's just you and me, Claire, you and me."

She nodded her head as the nurses started putting up sheets around her body so we couldn't see what was going on below her chest.

"You and me," she agreed.

"You can do this. You've totally got this. It's going to be over soon and Gavin is going to be here and he's going to be healthy and perfect and we're going to start teaching him how to swear before he shits his pants for the first time."

Claire laughed and I quickly threw on the scrubs over my clothes and took my seat next to Claire's bed.

Right at that moment, I knew that I would do anything for my best friend. I would hold her hand when she was in pain, scream at my catatonic fiancé when he saw her vagina and sit by her side when she became a mom. There was nothing I wouldn't do for her and I knew that's how it would always be.

Chapter 10
— It's All About You —

"I HAVE LAURIE running things at the bakery for the next six weeks and you don't have any weddings or big events coming up, so I think she can handle it. Jenny is going to take over ordering baking supplies and she's going to help Laurie and your two part-time girls do all the baking," I explain, going down the list of items I put in my notepad app on my phone. "If any big orders come in, we can always get some more help in, but I think we'll be fine. We'll have to put the Friday Freebie cupcake sale on hold for the time being, but I don't think too many people will mind."

Claire grabs my cell phone out of my hand and I finally look up at her. I wish I hadn't. I wish I still had my phone in my hand to give me something else to stare at, something to keep myself occupied so I don't have to see what is happening to her. I'm a shitty friend and an even shittier person because I can't bear to look at my best friend and see what the chemo has done to her hair. Every time she runs her fingers through her hair or brushes up against the back of the couch, more strands come out, but she just shrugs her shoulders like it's no big deal. One round of chemo almost three weeks ago and she's already losing her hair. She still has five more rounds to go and I'm scared to death she's just going to keep fading away until there's nothing left of her.

"I've hired some extra help at my store so I'll be able to pop over to your side as much as I want," I continue. "We were supposed to do that interview with the local television station next week, but I called them and told them to postpone it. I'll keep a file with all your invoices and bring them over when you need to sign something so you won't need to—"

"Will you shut up already?" Claire interrupts. "Stop talking about work when we both know there's something a little more important we need to discuss."

I shake my head and grab my phone back from her. "No, it's fine. We don't need to talk about it. You don't need to think about it. We can just talk about fun things like work and how Jenny has decided to start breeding ferrets now that the kids are in college and she's bored."

"As disturbing as that is, I don't want to talk about the damn ferrets," Claire tells me. "Wait, she was serious about breeding ferrets?"

I nod my head. "You don't even want to know where she got that idea. There's something called Fur Fest that she and Drew want to attend and she thinks she needs to breed something exotic and furry in order to fit in. I Googled Fur Fest. I can never get back those five minutes. So anyway, things are running smoothly at the shop and I don't foresee any issues with—"

Claire reaches over and presses her hand over my mouth.

"Stop. Talking. About. Work. I had a double mastectomy four weeks ago and a round of chemo that is kicking my ass and I can count on one hand how many times I've seen you during all of this. I get it; it's scary. What I don't get is why you won't even fucking *talk* about it with me."

I move my face away from her hand and get up from the couch to pace around the room. I can't sit still for this. I need to keep moving or I'm going to completely break down and that's not what she needs right now.

"You need to accept the fact that this is happening. It's real. You can't keep pretending like everything is okay," she tells me softly.

I stop pacing and make myself look in her general direction. It hurts too much to look right at her—my best friend, so small and tired and run down, sitting on the couch with blankets tucked around her as her beautiful brown hair is quickly disappearing. "I'm trying, Claire. I don't want to talk about it all the time and keep reminding you about what's happening."

Claire throws her hands up in the air in irritation. "You don't think I'm reminded of this fucking disease every damn time I take a breath or look in the mirror? Every time I open my eyes, every time I MOVE it's there, trying to bring me down. It's all I fucking think about and you pretending like it's not real is what's really killing me."

Her words cut right through me and I can't help but gasp.

"Jesus Christ, you just compared me to…"

"CANCER! Fucking say it, Liz. I compared you to cancer. I have cancer. You can't even fucking say it!" Claire screams.

"NO! I can't fucking say it because you're right! I don't want it to be real. I don't want this to be happening right now. I don't want you to be sick. I can't stand the fact that there is absolutely NOTHING I can do to make this better!" I shout back.

She flings the blankets off of her and gets up from the couch, stalking over to me.

"You still don't get it! This isn't about YOU! You can't fix it, you can't make it better, you don't know what to say, you don't know what to do. YOU, YOU, YOU! This is happening to ME, Goddammit, and I just need my fucking friend! Why can't you just be my friend? This is out of everyone's control, especially yours. If you can't deal with that then you need to get the fuck out of my house."

We stand toe-to-toe, both of us wearing equal looks of anger. As much as I don't have the right to be mad at her, I can't help it. This was never supposed to happen. Our friendship was solid and I thought nothing could ever break it. She's pissed at me for not being a good friend and I'm pissed at her for not understanding that I don't know HOW to be a good friend if I'm not the one making things better. She knows I'm a control freak, how can she possibly expect me to not feel helpless about this?

"I'm sorry I'm not perfect!" I fire back. "My friend gets sick and I don't know what the fuck to do, so sue me! I'm trying here and you're not making it any easier. You want to talk, talk, talk about this horrible thing that's happening and I can't do that. I can't just act like it's the most natural thing in the world to talk about my best friend having breast cancer! I'm not a sappy, talk about my feelings kind of person and you should damn well know that by now. I got a fucking tattoo to show you I cared, I'm taking care of your shop so you can rest and I'm trying to take your mind off of things because I don't know what else to do!"

Claire takes a step back and crosses her arms across her chest. "I never asked you to get a tattoo, nor did I ask you for help with the shop. All I needed was my best friend to tell me everything will be okay and you can't even do that. I know it's horseshit. I know we don't know if everything will be okay, but I need YOU to believe that. How the hell am I supposed to believe it if you don't? You can't even LOOK at me!"

I realize I've been staring at a button on her shirt the entire time she spoke and quickly look up to meet her eyes. I don't know what she sees on my face but it's enough for her to shake her head at me.

"Just get out," she tells me sadly.

I'm so pissed that she's ordering me out of the house I don't even think about the fact that this is the first real fight we've ever had in thirty years of friendship and I'm not sure if we'll ever be able to recover from it.

"Fine! I'm out of here!" I scream back.

I walk away from my best friend and let the front door slam behind me. I get to my car and let the anger flow through me as I pull out of the driveway and head home. My anger festers and builds until I get inside my house, throw my purse across the kitchen and head to my bedroom. It all disappears as soon as I flop down on my bed and realize what just happened. I curl my legs up to my chest and, for the first time since Claire told us what was going on, I let myself cry. I cry so hard and for so long that I can't breathe. I keep right on sobbing when I feel the bed dip behind me and Jim curls up against me, wrapping his arms around me and holding me close. He doesn't say a word, he just lets me cry.

I can't believe I screamed at my best friend. She's got cancer, she's sick and she's scared and I stood in her living room and yelled at her. What kind of person does that? I should have just taken what she threw at me. She deserves to scream and yell and let it all out. She's right, it's not all about me. It was never about me, it was always about her. This is *her* battle and *her* illness and as much as I want to, I can't fight it for her. I was supposed to be the one who always understood her, but at the first sign of trouble, I forgot everything about being a good friend and what she would need from me. I didn't talk about what was going on with her because it was too hard for me, but it shouldn't have mattered. What she's going through is a thousand times worse than what I'm going through. I am a selfish person and I let Claire down.

I was so scared of losing my best friend to this disease that I never stopped to think that I might just loser her because of my own pig-headedness instead. She's been there through all of my good times and I let her down during one of her worst times. I just want to go back to the good times. It was so much easier then.

Chapter 11
— Balloon Fucker —

Twenty-two years ago, in a balloon galaxy far, far away…

JIM AND I planned getting pregnant, so it wasn't much of a surprise when the stick turned pink. It wasn't a huge secret because we'd been talking about it and trying our hardest to make it happen for months, but I still wanted to do something special to break the news to him. I hate surprises and being the center of attention, but Jim loves it so I really wanted to plan something special to tell him. I would have been perfectly fine just blurting it out over dinner and being done with it, but Jim is a romantic and he wouldn't be too pleased with that.

I asked Jim to meet me at Seduction and Snacks one night under the guise of helping me with inventory. When he walked in, his face took on a look of confusion when he saw the entire place filled with balloons. Piles of green, purple, red, blue and orange balloons littered the floor and every available surface of the shop and hundreds more filled with helium covered every inch of the ceiling. I could have gone with pink and blue, but I didn't want to make it too obvious.

Jim kicked balloons out of the way, making a path as he walked towards me. He opened his mouth to speak, but was immediately interrupted by Drew, who came running in from Claire's side of the store.

"This is the best day EVER!" Drew shouted, holding the largest balloon I had ever seen in his hands.

Jim looked at me questioningly.

"Sorry, this was kind of his idea, so I told him he could help," I explained.

I watched as Drew raced back and forth among the balloons like a two-year old on crack. "Tell him the best part! TELL HIM THE BEST PART!"

I grabbed my husband's hands and squeezed them. "I have a surprise for you. Drew thought it should be something fun. So, if you want to know what your surprise is, you'll need to pop the balloons until you find the one it's hidden in."

I managed to slide the positive pregnancy test into one of the balloons before we blew it up and it was somewhere in this room, although I'd lost track of it ever since Drew came barreling in here.

"OH, MY GOD! POP THEM! POP THEM!" Drew shouted as he swatted at balloons that floated up and down from the ceiling.

Before I could question how much caffeine Drew had ingested to make him so excitable, Claire, Carter and Jenny stepped in from Claire's side of the store and made their way over to the counter where the cash register was.

"Don't mind us," Claire announced. "We're just here to huff some helium."

Jenny immediately grabbed a ribbon attached to a balloon on the ceiling, yanked it towards her and went to work untying it while Drew finally stopped running to stand in front of Jim. He held the giant balloon he'd been racing around with out to him. "Please, pop this one first."

Jim laughed before taking the balloon from Drew's hand.

"Mmmmmm yeah, pop that balloon," Drew moaned as Jim started squeezing it.

Jim paused and looked up at him. "Why are you moaning?"

Drew didn't answer. His eyes glazed over as Jim squeezed harder and when the balloon popped, I swear to God his legs almost gave out and his eyes rolled to the back of his head.

Since Jim didn't find the pregnancy test in that balloon, he went to work walking around the store, stomping on balloons as he went. I couldn't help but notice that Drew was following close behind Jim. Every time he popped another balloon, Drew's voice got deeper and more sexual as he cheered him on and it really started to creep me the fuck out. I couldn't even complain to my friends, though, because they were all sucking helium and cracking each other up.

"We represent, the Lollypop Guild, the Lollypop Guild, the Lollypop Guild!" Carter sang in a squeaky, high-pitched voice. Everyone laughed while Drew got right up by my ear.

"Tell Jim he should pop that red one next. It's so round and full and when it pops it's going to make this great noise and the smell of rubber will fill the air…" he trailed off and his entire body shuddered.

"What in the actual fuck is happening with you right now?"

Drew ignored me, bending down to grab a red balloon. He rubbed it over his chest and sighed before handing it to Jim.

"I am not touching that thing now that you fondled it," Jim told him.

His eyes widened. "Can I pop it? Please, please, please, can I, can I, can I?!"

"You can pop every fucking balloon in here if it means you'll stop looking like you want to have sex with the damn things," Jim told him in disgust as Drew hummed while he squeezed the balloon.

"Drew is a Looner," Jenny yelled over to me in a helium-filled voice.

"What the hell is a Looner?" Claire asked in the same munchkin-like, helium tone.

"A Looner is a very complex individual who revels in the popping of balloons," Carter informed us, sounding like a cast-off from Wizard of Oz.

When everyone looked at him funny, he just shrugged. "I Googled it."

"Ha! Now I know why Drew wanted to fill this place with balloons," Claire announced before taking another hit of helium. "Drew is a balloon fucker!"

Now, one would think that hearing the words "balloon fucker" coming from the mouth of my best friend who sounded like she was from Munchkin Land would have been hilarious. However, Drew was now on all fours down by my feet, dry humping a balloon.

"OH, MY GOD! WHAT ARE YOU DOING?!" I screamed at him.

"I'm only doing what comes naturally! My balloon fetish is a form of sexual imprinting! YOU CAN'T STOP ME FROM SEXUALLY IMPRINTING ON THIS GREEN BALLOON!" Drew shouted as he thrust roughly against the balloon until it popped.

As soon as it exploded, I heard the *click-click-click* of a plastic pregnancy test bouncing across the floor.

"WOOOHOOO! You found the balloon with the surprise in it! Pick it up and show it to Jim!" Carter squeaked with his fists pumping in the air.

"If you think I am going to touch something that Drew just humped out of a balloon, you are sadly mistaken," I told him.

"Whew, that was exhausting. I think I need a nap," Drew announced, grabbing onto an orange balloon and sticking it under his head like a pillow.

Jim ran across the room, shoving balloons aside until he found the test on the floor a few feet away. He picked it up, stared at it in awe for a few minutes before walking back to me.

"Liz, are you serious?! Are you—"

"WE WELCOME YOU TO MUNCHKIN LAND!" Jenny

sang loudly, dissolving in a fit of giggles as she quickly grabbed another balloon from the ceiling while Claire and Carter took a big huff of the balloons in each of their hands.

I sighed, turning back to Jim to finally tell him out loud what he already knew was true. "I love you. We're going to have a—"

"Tra la la la la la la la la la la la!" Carter and Claire squeaked at the top of their tinny voices.

"When you guys are finished, can I spend some time alone here in the shop?" Drew suddenly questioned.

"Ashtray! You little bitch ass motherfucker! Come over here and give your grandma a hug!" Carter shouted in his helium voice, because quoting *Don't Be a Menace* while huffing helium is always a fine idea.

"Bitch ass motherfucker!" Jenny repeated.

"I'VE HAD IT WITH THESE MOTHERFUCKING SNAKES ON THIS MOTHERFUCKING PLANE!" Claire shouted.

Jesus Christ, it sounded like Munchkins gone wild in this place.

"How about we just cut to the chase?" I asked Jim, wrapping my arms around his shoulders. "We're going to have a baby. As soon as he or she is born, we are getting as far away from these idiots as possible."

Jim wrapped his arms around me and we stared at our friends who were now trading Samuel L. Jackson quotes back and forth in between sucking on the balloons.

"Awwww, come on, our friends are fun. Just think about how interesting your baby shower will be. We can have Drew do balloon animals for the kids," Jim laughed.

"Except that would turn into Drew actually DOING balloon animals," I reminded him.

"Well, one thing's for certain—our life will never be boring with these people in it," Jim told me.

As Carter wrapped his arms around Claire and whispered high-pitched sexual innuendos in her ear, Jenny ran over to Drew and flopped down on the floor next to him and they both started rubbing balloons all over themselves.

"You're right, life will never be boring with any of them," I agreed.

Chapter 12
— Say Cheese! —

MY FAMILY AND I are pretty lucky in that we've never had to deal with losing someone close to us. My kids still have all four grandparents and our extended family of aunts, uncles and cousins are alive and kicking. It's probably hard to believe, but we've only attended one funeral. Ever. It was for one of our neighbors a few years ago. She was a nasty old woman who screamed at my kids if they so much as *looked* at her yard when they walked by and she had a habit of stealing people's Christmas decorations if she thought they were too gaudy. We only went to the funeral for her husband, who was the exact opposite of the old bat. Also, we were hoping our blinking "Santa Stops Here" sign might be perched in front of the casket so we could take it back. I loved that cute little sign.

Looking back on it now, I'm kind of glad that was our one and only experience with a funeral because we did not behave well. We tried, we really did, but it was no use.

Six years ago, when a funeral home suddenly became the best place on earth...

"I'VE GOT A camera on my cell phone!"

My daughter, Charlotte, and I looked up at the little boy standing next to my chair. He was around seven years old and he proudly held an old school flip phone in his hand.

I glanced around at the other mourners who filled the room in row after row of folding chairs, but no one seemed to be looking for their lost child.

"That's a great phone," I whispered to the boy. "You should probably go take some pictures or something."

Jim leaned forward in his seat on the other side of Charlotte and gave me a questioning look. I just shrugged. I didn't know who the hell this kid was, but I was pretty sure he needed to leave me alone. I had three teenage daughters who were lucky I even liked them, let alone loved them. I didn't do well with other people's children.

"My name is Luke. I like chocolate!" the kid announced.

"I can see that. You've got it smeared all over your damn face," I replied, scrunching up my nose in disgust as he leaned his dirty face closer to me.

"You said a bad word!" he whispered.

"I'm going to keep on saying bad words if you don't go away."

Charlotte snorted and Jim just shook his head.

"That's my grandma up there," Luke said, pointing to the open casket at the front of the room. "She's dead."

This just made Charlotte laugh harder for some reason. She covered her mouth with her hand to stifle the noise and I elbowed her to shut up. I'm pretty sure this room of sad people wouldn't be too happy to hear her laughing like a hyena.

"Okay, dude, run along now. Go take some pictures."

I was starting to get a little uncomfortable with this kid. He was a regular Chatty Cathy and this was supposed to be a quiet time of reflection for the deceased or some shit before the priest came in and said a few words.

I was so busy trying to shush Charlotte that I didn't notice that the stupid kid decided to listen to me. He ran along, and he definitely took some pictures. You know how those old flip phones would make noises when you took a picture like the clicking of a camera or something else equally annoying? Well, in the middle of "quiet time," when half the room was crying softly and the other half was deep in prayer or whatever, at the front of the room, right in front of the casket was our little buddy Luke. He had his flip phone open, pointed directly at the dead body of Mrs. Lyons. I'm pretty sure we were the only people in the room who saw what he was about to do, but that all changed as soon as he hit the "take picture" button. In the quiet, somber room filled with death and sadness, the mechanical, overly cheerful voice of the flip phone said "SAY CHEEEEEEEESE!" followed by the *click* of the shutter releasing.

"Jesus Christ, did he just take a picture of his dead grandma?" Jim whispered.

Charlotte was laughing so hard at this point she started choking. I couldn't believe what the fuck had just happened and for some reason, it became the funniest shit in the entire world. I clamped my hand over my mouth to keep the giggles contained, but that didn't stop my shoulders from shaking as Charlotte and I huddled together, both of us whispering, "Say cheese!" in between our snorts of laughter.

Luke's mother finally got her head out of her ass and came running down the center aisle, snatching the phone out of his hand as she gave us a dirty look.

"We did NOT put him up to that!" I whispered as she made her way down the aisle past us, dragging Luke behind her.

Charlotte let out a cough/snort/laugh that was so loud, the entire room was now looking at us. Our very first funeral and we were going to get kicked out of it. Everything just became funny at that point and it didn't help that Charlotte kept whispering "say cheese" and "I wonder if I could get a five by seven of that shot?" We decided to make things easy on everyone and excused ourselves from the funeral before they asked us to leave. Really, I think that little bastard Luke should have been the one to get kicked out. He started it.

I FIND MYSELF thinking about that funeral and how my children have no idea how to deal with death and sadness or something awful happening to someone close to them. Charlotte sits across from me at the kitchen table looking miserable and I'm at a loss on how to help my child. How can I help her when I don't even know how to help myself? She's no longer a fifteen year old at the funeral of the mean neighbor lady. Her fiancé's mother, the woman she herself thinks of as an aunt, is sick and it's scary and that little asshole Luke isn't here to diffuse the situation with inappropriate pictures of his dead grandmother. My daughter needs my help and I need to find a way to give it to her.

"What should I do, mom? Gavin is trying to act all strong and he keeps telling me he's fine, but I know he's not. I know he's freaking out and I don't know what to do," Charlotte tells me as tears fill her eyes.

"Honey, all you can do is let him know that you're there for him. He's going to continue being strong and not showing any emotion in front of Claire because he doesn't want his mom to see how much he's hurting," I explain. "He's a guy. Guys don't want anyone to know they're scared. Look at his father. Carter has been rearranging their house and putting everything in alphabetical order. That's his way of coping."

Charlotte lets out a sigh and I move my chair to her side of the table, wrapping my arms around her.

"He's my best friend, mom. I don't want him to be scared. I just want to make everything better for him, but I can't. I hate feeling so helpless."

I always thought my oldest daughter and I were so different. She was always the bubbly, happy girl who made friends easily and looked at life with rose-colored glasses. Right now, I realize we're more alike than I ever knew.

"All of this is out of everyone's control and it sucks. Maybe he just needs you to tell him how you're feeling and that he's not alone. Be honest with him. Be there for him. That's all you really *can* do right now."

Guilt overwhelms me as I hold my daughter and let her cry. It's easy for me to give her this great advice. Why isn't it easy for me to follow it myself?

"I don't want Aunt Claire to die," Charlotte whispers.

My throat tightens and I squeeze my eyes closed to keep the tears from falling.

"Do you remember the first time I got my period, you guys both showed me how to put a panty-liner in my underwear?" Charlotte suddenly asks with a laugh.

We both sniffle through our laughter, remembering that day.

"Now there's a story you could tell Gavin to lift his spirits. We were at your Aunt Claire's house in her bedroom, sitting on the floor next to a laundry basket of clean clothes. She reached in and grabbed the first pair of underwear she could find and it was one of Gavin's Spiderman Underoos," I chuckle.

"Shut up, it was not!" Charlotte exclaims, pulling away to look at me.

I nod my head. "Yep, totally was. Your Aunt ripped off the paper backing of the pad and slapped it on the crotch of Spiderman tighty-whities. We decided Kotex was Spiderman's new weapon of choice. Instead of a web shooting out of his wrist, maxi pads would fly out, rendering all of his enemies helpless."

Charlotte and I sat at the kitchen table, reminiscing about the funniest things that have happened over the years and an idea started forming in my head. The one good thing about our group of friends is that we're never short on laughter. Someone is always doing something stupid or inappropriate and no matter what's happening in our lives at that point in time, laughter has always been the cure for everything.

I don't know if I can repair the damage that's been done to my friendship with Claire, but I'm not going down without a fight. We have too many years and too many memories to just give up. Claire has always believed in me and I need to show her that she still can.

Chapter 13

— Atom Machine, For the Win! —

Nineteen years ago...

"WHERE IN THE hell is Jenny?" I asked Claire, glancing around the casino floor.

She shrugged and put another twenty into the machine in front of her. "I don't know and I don't care. I have found my *Sex in the City* machine and all is right with the world."

When I found out Jim had a meeting for work right next to the casino in Cleveland, Claire decided we should tag along and have a "girls" weekend. We needed it. Claire was running ragged with seven-year-old Gavin and three-year-old Sophie and I was losing my mind with Charlotte, who's also three, Ava who just turned one, and my newborn, Molly, who is six weeks old today. Jenny, being a new mom of only four weeks with her daughter, Veronica, jumped at the chance to get out of the house for a night.

We had entirely too many fucking kids and we needed a break.

We'd only been here for a few hours and we'd already lost Jenny. She had been way too excited about the prospect of free booze while she played. After six rum and cokes during one hand of Black Jack, Claire and I had walked away and pretended like we didn't know her. Luckily, Jim's meeting wasn't until tomorrow morning, so we put him on babysitting duty to make sure she didn't get kicked out of the casino. Bringing a first-time mom who hasn't had a drink in over nine months to a place where you could drink for free as long as you were gambling probably wasn't our brightest idea.

After a few vanilla vodka and diet cokes, I started to feel warm and fuzzy. When I felt warm and fuzzy, I spoke about things that I normally wouldn't when I was sober. Like about how being a mom of three little girls scared the ever living shit out of me.

"So, I'm thinking I'm not cut out to be a mom of three girls. Do you think Jim would be mad if I packed up my things and moved to Lithuania?"

Claire paused with her hand above the "repeat bet" button and turned to look at me. "What in the hell are you talking about?"

I shrugged, smacking my hand down on the closest button on my machine just to give myself something to do. "I mean, this shit is hard. What in the hell ever possessed me to have three kids?"

Not only did I have three kids all under the age of three, I also ran my own business that had turned into several chains across the U.S. and had a husband I liked to pay attention to every once in a while. I was drowning in invoices and baby formula and interviewing preschools and managers for the chains, not to mention the fact that I hadn't gotten more than two consecutive hours of sleep in at least two years.

"Of course it's hard. Being in a mom is the hardest job in the entire fucking world. I'm not going to tell you that 'it's all worth it in the end' or some stupid shit like that because who knows if it will be worth it? Who knows if when our kids finally grow up we'll have done a good job or if they'll need therapy for the rest of their lives? All you can do is the best that you can and believe me, you are doing great. Your kids are all still alive, that's all that matters. If I'm having a shitty day, the kids are crying, the phone is ringing off the hook and Carter and I are arguing about something, all I do is look at my kids and say 'Well, at least they're still alive'," Claire explained.

"I feel like I'm losing my mind. Why didn't you tell me being a mom would make me go insane?"

Claire laughed and shook her head at me. "Sorry, those are trade secrets in the mom world. And if I remember correctly, you were there for the first four years when I was a single mom to a boy who liked to talk about his penis in public. He's seven now and still likes to talk about his penis to strangers, but at least now I have Carter to help out, just like you have Jim. You're doing a great job, Liz. Your girls adore you and someday, they'll be grown and have kids of their own and you can point and laugh at *them* when they come crying to you. Full circle, baby. Full circle."

"DAAAAAAAAADDDY! I need more money!"

Claire and I turned in our seats when we heard Jenny whine behind us. She stood in front of Jim with her hand out while he shook his head at her.

"Uh, hey guys. Why is Jenny calling you daddy?" Claire asked Jim.

Jenny looked up and her sad face immediately went away when she saw us.

"You guys!! I am having the BEST time! But Daddy here took my money and he won't let me have any more," she said with a pout as she pointed at Jim.

My husband stared at her with a blank expression on his face, which usually meant he was trying his hardest to keep his mouth shut before he said something he'd regret.

"Why won't 'DAAAAAADDDDYY' let you have any money?" Claire asked, doing a perfect imitation of Jenny's whiny voice.

"If one more person calls me Daddy, you're all going to die," Jim stated in a monotone voice.

"Daddy isn't being fair!" Jenny complained with a stomp of her foot.

Jim growled and I put a hand on his arm to keep him from choking Jenny.

"Hey, Jenny. How about you tell them why I'm not letting you have your money," Jim suggested.

We looked at Jenny and she rolled her eyes. "I was winning! I put my gambling card in the machine and it gave me two hundred and fifty dollars!"

"What machine is this?" Claire asked, looking around for the machine that was obviously a winner.

"Oh, please tell them what machine," Jim begged, his face suddenly taking on a look of pure delight.

Jenny pointed to the other side of the room. "See? That one over there. The Atom game."

Claire and I squinted, trying to find this Atom game she spoke of, but we couldn't see anything through the mess of people, blinking lights and gaming tables.

"What Jenny is pointing out to you would be the ATM machine," Jim informed us.

"You win every single time!" Jenny announced happily.

"And this is why she is no longer allowed to have her 'gambling card' or her money," Jim added, using his hands to finger-quote gambling card. Which we suddenly realized was her bank card.

"Come on, Daddy! I want to win more money!" Jenny shouted, grabbing Jim's arm and dragging him away.

He gave us a pleading look, but Claire and I waved happily at him as they disappeared in the crowd.

"Well, the good news is, Jenny is giving him tons of babysitting practice for your kids," Claire stated as I sat back down next to her at my machine. "Would now be a bad time to tell you that I made you and Jim the guardians of Gavin and Sophie if something were to happen to us?"

My hand paused mid-air as I got ready to hit a button on the machine. I stared at her with wide eyes and an open mouth for so long that she finally had to snap her fingers in front of my face to pull me out of my daze.

"Don't worry, it's not like something is going to happen to us," Claire explained. "Carter and I just figured we should update our wills and it's not like I want my dad to get the kids. Could you imagine? They'd spend their childhood watching the Gameshow Network, taking naps and brushing up on their skills of stringing swear words together. Actually, that might not be a bad thing."

"Why in the hell would you ever think it was a good idea to make *me* the guardian of your kids? Did you not just hear me complaining about how I suck as a mother and I don't know what I'm doing?" I reminded her.

Claire turned her chair to face mine. "Listen, going into that lawyers office and having to talk about your children being raised by someone who isn't you is the most depressing thing in the world. I couldn't even get through two minutes of that meeting without crying. My kids drive me insane, but they're still my kids. My *babies*. The thought of not being here to watch them grow and to teach them about life… it really sucks. But as soon as the lawyer asked me for a name, I knew there was no one else in the world I would want to raise my kids if I couldn't do it."

I refused to fucking cry in the middle of a casino, but it was no use. My eyes filled with tears and I was honored that Claire trusted me enough to make me the guardians of her kids, but I still didn't get it.

"But why me? I mean, you have Carter's parents and your dad and, even though Jenny and Drew are fucking crazy, they're fun and young at heart and great parents so far. Why in the hell would you ever pick me?"

Claire cocked her head at me and leaned closer. "No one could ever replace me as my kid's mom. But when you're looking at the people in your life who might just have to take on that role someday, you try to find someone who will give your children a taste of their mother when she's gone, someone who reminds them of you. I can't imagine someone else raising my children. No one seems like the right choice because they're not *me*, so I chose someone who is as close to 'me' as I could get. You're my person, Liz. You're my other half. If I'm not here, there is no one else in the world who could remind my kids of me and give them the same kind of love I did."

"DAAAAAAAADDDDY! GIVE ME MY GAMBLING CARD! The Atom Machine is hot! Someone just won on it!" we heard Jenny shout over the noise of ringing machines and people cheering.

"And on that note, I think it's time for another drink," Claire announced.

Chapter 14
— Aggressive Vagina —

IT'S NOT OFTEN that I find myself apologizing to someone, mostly because I make sure I'm never wrong. Just ask my husband. It's tough for someone like me to realize she was an asshole and made a huge mistake. It's even tougher to admit something like that out loud, in front of actual people. Armed with a bag full of tricks, I make my way inside the Cleveland Clinic and head to the Oncology Department on the third floor, prepared to do whatever I can to fix things with Claire. I've spent these last few weeks thinking about our history together and through the good and bad, funny and insane, one thing always remained constant—the fact that Claire and I were meant to be in each other's lives. We were better when we were together. I forced her to be more outgoing and helped her realize her dreams, and she taught me how to not be such a hard ass all the time and take a chance on things like falling in love and being a mother.

After asking a nurse for directions, I finally find the chemo treatment room. Taking a deep breath and making sure the baseball cap is pulled down far enough on my head, I walk inside. I see Carter on the other side of the room, sitting in a chair next to Claire reading a magazine. Claire is curled up under a blanket in a recliner, hooked up to an IV that I'm assuming is the chemo. She's busy doing something on her phone, so I have a second to stare at her without her noticing me. I'm ashamed at myself for not wanting to look at her before because I felt bad or because I was scared. Seeing her now, with a scarf tied around her head and a determined look on her face regardless of what's happening to her, I am so proud to call her my friend. Where before I only noticed her sickness, the pallor of her skin and the loss of her hair, now I see strength. I see what I should have seen all those weeks ago. A woman who takes whatever is thrown at her and pushes through, determined to survive no matter what. A woman who is the strongest person I have ever known. She survived getting pregnant in college and raising a child on her own for four years, she managed to build a thriving business and make her dreams come true, she took care of her family and she always, *always* took care of me. She pushed me to give Jim a chance when I knew nothing about love and relationships, she convinced me I was a good mother and she trusted me to be a good friend no matter what life threw at us.

I walk across the room with my head held high even though I feel like the lowest person in the world. Claire looks up at me in surprise when I drop my bag next to her chair and doesn't say a word as I dig through it for the first item I need. I pull out the piece of paper I printed from the computer this morning, grab a roll of scotch tape and walk over to her IV.

"What are you doing?" Claire finally speaks.

I ignore her for the time being as I tape my sign to the clear bag of fluid hanging from the steel pole next to her chair. When it's finished, I take a step back and study my work.

Carter gets up from his chair and walks over to stand next to me, reading the sign out loud. "This is probably vodka."

He nods his head and pats me on the back. "Fitting. Very fitting."

I walk back to my bag and pull out another sign, taping it to the footrest on her recliner so that it hangs down by Claire's feet. Once again, Carter walks over to me and reads the sign. "Beware: I have an aggressive vagina."

Carter laughs and Claire shoots him a dirty look.

"What?" he asks her. "Your vagina is kind of aggressive."

Next, I pull out a couple of t-shirts, handing one to Claire. She holds it up in front of her, reading the text printed on the front of it in pink. "Itty Bitty Titty Committee—President".

I hold up my own shirt and she reads it. "Itty Bitty Titty Committee—Secretary."

The third shirt comes out and I turn it around for Claire to read as well. "Itty Bitty Titty Committee—Director of Foreign Affairs."

She looks at me questioningly and I finally speak. "Jenny is the only one of us with a big rack. Obviously she's in charge of Foreign Affairs."

Claire is trying really hard not to smile through her pursed lips and I feel a little better about my plan.

Carter walks over to her side, leans down and kisses the top of her head. "I'm going to head over to the lounge and see if I can find some coffee. Do you need anything?"

Claire shakes her head and Carter gives me a one-armed side hug before he leaves the room, letting me know that he's happy I came.

When we're finally alone, aside from the two other people currently hooked up to their own chemo treatments that are napping on the other side of the room, I stick my hands in my pockets and step closer to Claire's side.

"I'm just going to cut right to the chase and apologize for being an asshole," I tell her. Claire crosses her arms across her chest, not saying a word. "I know nothing that is happening right now is about me, I *know* that, but you're my person, Claire. What happens to you, happens to me. I'm a fixer, I like to make things better, take charge and get shit done. I have never felt so helpless in my life. It killed me that I couldn't do anything to make you better."

Claire opens her mouth to argue with me, but I hold up my hand to stop her. "I know it wasn't up to me. I know it was out of my hands and I should have realized that all you needed was a friend. You needed me and I wasn't there for you. I was too scared, too ashamed, too worried about my own problems to think about what you might need."

I squat down next to her chair and grab her hand, pulling it away from her chest and squeezing it between my two hands. "It's going to be okay, Claire. You're going to be okay. You are a fucking fighter and you're going to beat this."

Her chin quivers and she swipes at a tear that is falling down her cheek and I continue.

"Fuck cancer. Fuck not having your tits anymore because you're going to get bigger and better tits in a few weeks and those fuckers won't try to kill you. You're going to be fine because you *have* to be fine. I refuse to let you NOT be fine because I need you here with me. You are going to beat this thing because you are strong and amazing and you aren't going to let some stupid shit like cancer stop you from growing old with me so we can corrupt our grandchildren. Shit, we have a wedding to finish planning and I have a hotter dress than you to wear to it. You have to be fine because we need to walk down the aisle together so everyone can judge us and realize that I look amazing in my mother of the bride dress."

Claire laughs through her tears and shakes her head at me. "Fuck your face. I'm going to have new tits for this wedding. Obviously I'll be the hotter one."

We stare at each other in silence for a few minutes before she speaks again. "I'm still pissed at you, but I'm glad you're here."

"I'm pissed at me, too. I give you permission to call me an asshole for the rest of our lives," I tell her.

"I was already planning on calling you an asshole forever, this just makes it more fun," Claire says with a shrug. "What else do you have in that bag?"

She leans over the side of her chair and stairs down at my duffle bag.

"There may or may not be some pot Rice Krispies Treats in there."

Claire stares at me wide-eyed, quickly glancing around the room before lowering her voice. "What the fuck are you waiting for? Give me one of those damn things."

Reaching into my bag, I pull out the Tupperware container and hand it to her. She tears open the lid, grabs one of the huge marshmallow squares and shoves the entire thing it into her mouth.

"Um, I don't think you're supposed to eat the whole thing at once. Didn't you learn your lesson a few years ago with Drew's pot cookies?"

Claire narrows her eyes at me, her cheeks stuffed full of Rice Krispies Treat as she chews slowly. When she finally swallows the thing, she lets out a sigh and smiles at me. "If these things prevent the constant diarrhea and projectile vomiting I'm plagued with after treatment, I will eat the entire fucking container of them. Tunnel vision and licking walls be damned."

"Diarrhea, seriously?" I ask as she grabs another treat and starts chowing down on it.

"Dude, you have no idea. I swear to God I shit out my intestines last time," she informs me. "So, what's been going on since we last talked? I think Carter is losing his shit, but he swears he's okay."

I reach into the container on Claire's lap and take a treat. Friends who get high together, stay together, or some shit like that.

"Your husband absolutely lost his shit all over your kitchen a few weeks back. You'll be happy to know that your non-perishables are no longer in alphabetical order," I tell her. "He's okay though. I think he just needed to get it out of his system. You know, screaming, yelling, cursing God. The boys stopped by and took his mind off of things."

Claire stops chewing. "Is that why my cat now has the word

"Fuck Canker" shaved into her side?"

I nod sadly. "Unfortunately, yes. Drew claims she wouldn't sit still for him long enough to get it right, but I'm pretty sure he thinks that's how you spell cancer. Also, he shaved his legs and my husband shaved his balls. I know you said no one was allowed to shave their heads, so they decided to take a different approach."

Claire shakes her head in irritation. "I'm still holding firm on the spaghetti dinner and candlelight vigil. If any one of you tries that shit, I will stab you in the neck."

"Noted," I tell her with a nod of my head. "Move over."

I stand up as she slides to the other side of her chair, crawling into the recliner next to her.

"Your ass is too big for this chair," she informs me.

"Fuck off, I have a great ass and it's the perfect size," I reply as I get comfortable. "You keep inhaling those Rice Krispies Treats and we're going to have to grease the door to get your giant ass out of here."

Reaching up, I take the baseball cap off of my head, holding onto the scarf I tied underneath to keep it in place.

"So, there's one more thing I have for you and it's really going to piss you off."

Claire looks up from the bowl of treats and stares at my head. Her smile falls and she starts shaking her head frantically back and forth.

"No, you didn't. Fuck your face, NO, YOU DIDN'T!" she yells.

The patients who were previously sleeping wake up immediately and look in our direction. Reaching up, I squeeze my eyes closed and pull the scarf off of my head, waiting for her to call me an asshole again. When entirely too much time passes without her saying a word, I slowly open my eyes to find Claire outright sobbing. She lifts her hand and runs her palm over my now-bald head.

"I know you hated the tattoo and you're really hating this right now, but it's something I had to do. I realize I can't fix you, but at least I can support you. If you are going to walk around without any hair, then so am I."

Claire continues to rub her palm over my head while she wipes the tears off of her cheeks. "I didn't hate the tattoo, but this is insane."

All I can do is shrug. "Yep, it's totally insane. You need to know that regardless of my actions the last few weeks, there is nothing I wouldn't do for you."

Claire drops her hand into her lap but continues to stare at my shaved head. "I hate to tell you this, but you look like a total asshole, baldy."

I laugh, reaching for the scarf to put it back on my head. Claire puts her hand on top of mine and shakes her head. "Oh, no. Scarf stays off. Also, when I'm done here, we're going to parade you through the grocery store so people will roll their eyes and make snap judgments about your fashion style. I'm going to tell people you're in a gang and make you bark at them."

Claire rests her head on my shoulder and I set my chin on top of her head. We both stare at the IV, the bag of chemo almost empty. We watch the liquid slowly flow through the tube connected to her PICC line. With each drop that falls, I say a prayer that everything I said to Claire today will come true—that she'll be okay and she'll never leave me.

"I'm sorry," I whisper.

Claire tucks herself in closer to me, grabbing onto my hand and squeezing it. "I know you are."

Carter walks back in the room and does a double-take when he sees my bald head. "Dammit, I knew you'd outdo me. Shaving my balls and pussy isn't as cool anymore."

We ignore the strange stares from the other patients as Carter makes himself comfortable in his chair next to Claire and me.

"You're going to be okay," I remind her.

Claire nods her head. "Yep, I'm totally going to be fine."

For the next half our while she finishes her treatment, our high kicks in and everything suddenly seems so funny that we can't stop giggling. Claire makes me practice my barking for when she takes me to the grocery store and I make her meow like a cat in honor of her poor, shaved pussy at home. I'm pretty sure it's the one and only time someone almost got kicked out of their own chemo treatment.

Things are finally back to normal and aside from the pot flowing through me, there's also hope. Pot and hope... it doesn't get much better than that.

Chapter 15
— Porn Star Tits —

Five months later...

"DREW, WHAT THE hell is in that bag?" I ask as he walks into Claire's hospital room, hefting the largest duffle bag I have ever seen on top of the table next to her bed.

"This, my friends, is to prove my theory that size DOES matter," he tells us as he unzips the bag and digs around inside. "I like to call it my Bag O' Boobs."

"Wait, since when did anyone EVER say that size doesn't matter?" Claire asks as we all stare at Drew.

"Since we started talking about your new rack," Drew informs us, pulling out two lemons and holding them up in front of his chest.

Claire finally finished with all of her chemo treatments two weeks ago and is now undergoing reconstruction surgery. During her mastectomy, the doctor inserted a tissue expander under her skin, but he wanted to wait until her chemo was finished before completing the reconstruction and giving her new boobs. He said that chemo and radiation could sometimes affect implants, so it was easier to just expand the skin on her chest during treatment and then go back and put the implants in when she's done.

"What you have here is your basic A cup. It's budding and beautiful, a perfect small handful and it can get the job done. Since you'd never let me touch your old ones, I'm going by sight alone and I've determined that you were a generous A cup, correct?" Drew asks Claire.

"Oh, good Lord," she mutters.

"Now, why go with what you had before when you can get something new and improved? This is your time, Claire. Your time to make all of my boob dreams come true."

Carter reaches into the bag and pulls out a honeydew melon. Drew immediately snatches it out of his hand and puts it off to the side of the table.

"Now, now, let's not get ahead of ourselves," he scolds.

Drew goes back to the bag and pulls out two oranges. "This here is the next step up. A lovely B cup that is not only ample but alluring."

My husband eyes the oranges and then looks at my chest, nodding his head. "True story."

I roll my eyes as Drew continues, setting the oranges down and pulling out two grapefruits.

"Next we have the C cup. Full and fabulous. A little more than a handful, but looks great in a bikini."

"I'm suddenly hungry for fruit salad, anyone else?" Jim asks.

Drew ignores him, pulling two cantaloupes out of the bag next.

Jenny walks over and grabs one of them, holding it up to her own boob. "This is me! I have candy loop boobs!"

Drew kisses her cheek, taking the melon back. "Yes, you have lovely candy loops, sweetie pie."

He turns back to face Claire. "D cup. Voluptuous and va-va-voom! More than a handful, more than a mouthful and has a delicious, juicy center."

"Eeeeew," I complain.

Jim picks up the honeydew on the table while Drew reaches into the bag and pulls out its match.

"Behold, the double D," Drew says in awe. "Bountiful and bodacious, porn star tits and the star of many a man's fantasy."

Carter and Jim rub their hands over the honeydew with a glazed look in their eyes. I smack the back of both of their heads since Claire is hooked up to an IV in bed and can't reach Carter.

"I love you, your boobs are perfect," Jim tells me sweetly.

"Fuck off," I growl at him.

When the doctor walks in a few minutes later, the boys are in the middle of a heated fruit argument and I'm trying to wrestle the honeydew out of Drew's hands and back in the bag.

"So, Claire. Have you decided on the size? The tissue expander has given us enough skin to work with a full C cup, but it's completely up to you," he explains.

"She'll be going with the honeydew today, doctor," Drew informs him.

This time Carter was the one doing the hitting and Drew let out a yelp when Carter's fist connected with his arm.

"What do you think?" Claire asks Carter.

He shrugs his shoulders. "Babe, I love you exactly the way you are. It is completely up to you."

She narrows her eyes at him and I shake my head. "Stop lying to your wife. Pick a boob size and man up."

Very slowly, Carter leans over to the table and picks up a grapefruit, looking at Claire sheepishly. "Um, this is kind of nice."

I give him a pat on the back. "Well done, sir."

Claire lets out a sigh and smiles. "I guess we'll be going with the grapefruit today, doctor."

The doctor spends a few minutes chatting with Claire about the procedure and making notes on her chart before he leaves the room. Jenny, Drew, Jim and Carter go in search of coffee while Claire moves over in bed, patting the empty spot next to her. I hop up beside her, grabbing the extra grapefruit and holding it up in front of her chest.

"I'm going to have to fire you from your position as president of the Itty Bitty Titty Club. This is a sad, sad day in Titty Club history," I tell her sadly.

"I'd like to say I'm sorry for stepping down from this illustrious position, but I'm not. I'm going to have FANTASTIC tits!" Claire announces.

"I hate you. You're going to look so much better in your mother of the groom dress next month."

"Fuck the dress, I'm going to walk around naked from now on. Show my tits to people when I'm walking down the street. I might even ask random strangers to touch them," she tells me.

"You could even make up a new cupcake for the store. Tantalizing Titty Cakes."

She nods her head. "Creamy C Cup-Cakes. With a milky filling."

I dry heave and shake my head. "Too far. Jesus God, too far."

"Will you still love me even when I have a better rack than you?" she asks.

I wrap my arm around her shoulder and nod. "I love you when you're an asshole, I love you when I'm an asshole, I love you when you have no hair and I love you when you call me on my shit. Of course I'll still love you when you have better tits than me. I'll secretly hate you on the inside, but it will be fine."

We settle back into the pillows and stare up at the ceiling where I taped random notes while she was in the bathroom earlier changing into her hospital gown. It reminds me of that time in college when we got drunk on Boone's Farm and curled up on our bunk bed, staring at my stickers taped to the bottom of the bunk.

"I think the one that says 'Hot Tits or Bust' is my favorite," Claire states.

"I don't know, I'm particularly fond of the My Little Pony with the huge rack," I tell her. "Pinky Pie Porn Star is all the rage."

Claire laughs. "I told you My Little Pony would make a comeback."

"And I told you that you would be okay, didn't I?" I remind her.

"You did. And you were right," she tells me with a nod.

"I'm always right. Except with the whole shaving my head thing. That was probably a bad move."

I run my hands over my short, spiky blonde hair that Claire would not let me continue shaving after the first time. She demanded that I let it grow back out immediately. I now resemble that chick from the movie *The Legend of Billie Jean* and I'm pretty sure Claire just wanted me to start growing it out so she could quote that damn movie every time she saw me.

She puts her fist in the air and shouts, "FAIR IS FAIR!"

I roll my eyes. "Stop being an asshole."

"Shut up, YOU'RE an asshole," she counters.

"But I'm your little asshole and I promise, I will never get spooked again," I tell her solemnly.

"Now you're REALLY an asshole for quoting *Cocktail*. Just sit there and be quiet and let's dream about my new, pretty boobs," she tells me as she closes her eyes.

"I get to touch them first," I remind her.

She scoffs. "Obviously."

Epilogue

NOT EVERYONE HANDLES bad news the same way. Some people scream and cry and rage about the unfairness of it all, others turn all emo and clam up and refuse to accept reality and some continue to have hope and fill their days with rainbows and unicorns and never let the man bring them down.

Then you have me. I thought I could fix everything until life gave us something unexpected that I could do nothing about. My friendship with Claire was tested and I'm happy to say we came out stronger on the other side. Claire now has a better rack than me and her hair is finally starting to grow back.

The doctors are confident that they removed all of the cancer from her body during the mastectomy and the chemo was done as a preventative measure for insurance. There's always a chance that some of the cancer cells traveled elsewhere in her body and we won't really know anything definitive for a while, but Claire is happy, she feels great and that's good enough for all of us. We have a wedding next month to finish planning and we're not going to let a little bit of cancer get in our way. Claire's illness forced us all to realize just how fragile life really is and that we can't take one minute for granted. She went with me last week to get my first mammogram and I've already scheduled my next follow-up appointment. Jenny and Drew continue to play "mammogram" at home in between her own appointments. Even though just the thought of it is disgusting, at least she's being proactive.

Tantalizing Titty Cakes have been a huge hit at Seduction and Snacks. We give them away for free on days when Claire has a doctor's appointment and she also has a stash of "special" Titty Cakes hidden under the counter for cancer patients and cancer survivors. They get an entire dozen for free, along with a warning to only eat a little bit at a time unless they want to start crawling on countertops, thinking the wallpaper tastes like Snozzberries and barking like a dog in the middle of chemo treatments.

Through it all, we're staying positive and we are absolutely keeping our sense of humor.

I think people sometimes forget just how powerful laughter is. I know I did for a little while. It took a trip down memory lane to remind me that the best thing about our group of friends is our ability to make each other laugh, even in awful situations. Sometimes you just need to pretend like your IV is filled with vodka, get a horrible rack of ribs tattoo on your body and almost get kicked out of a hospital for filling out their information form with porn titles. Life is filled with enough bullshit and drama, why make it worse? Tell me something. What makes you feel better, crying and complaining or laughing and making fun of a situation? It's an easy answer and one we all need to remember from time to time. Cancer definitely isn't a laughing matter, but what are a few giggles and a couple of inappropriate comments going to hurt? Sure, you might get some funny looks when you're at a funeral or in an ICU ward at a hospital, but that's just because those people haven't learned what *you* have—laughter makes everything better. It might not cure cancer, but it sure makes it a hell of a lot more bearable.

Fuck Cancer. Save second base. Fight like a girl. Do it all and do it with a few laughs because you are amazing, you are strong and you are a fighter, just like my best friend.

- The End -

Baking and Babies

by
Tara Sivec

Prologue

THERE IS A phrase in the English language that I believe should be banned for all of time. Two little words that will fuck up life as you know it and make everyone around you certifiably insane.

"I'm pregnant."

You just shuddered a little didn't you? A small chill wound its way up your spine, your eyes got wide, and you looked over your shoulder like a monster might be standing there waiting to rip your head off. Maybe you even put your hand to your stomach and said, "Awe, shit." It could be out of sympathy for the words you just read or maybe it's real. You could be knocked up right now and not even know it. If you are currently with child…my condolences are yours for the taking. I mean, sure, once the baby gets here you'll probably be happy, but you have nine months—give or take—of people riding full speed ahead on the crazy train and dragging you with them.

I had a good life. No, I had a GREAT life before I uttered those stupid words. Twenty years old, almost finished with my two-year accelerated program in culinary school, and perfectly content staying hidden in the background around my nut-job family. I learned at an early age to keep my mouth shut so I'd have a good chance at never being publicly humiliated by them. It worked great until a couple of months ago when I just HAD to open my mouth and make my presence known.

My older sister, Charlotte, seems to think all of this is a great "learning experience" for me. Of course she would say that considering everything that happened is HER fault, but I guess she sort of has a point. I definitely came out of my shell in the last eight weeks. For the past two years I'd done nothing but eat, sleep, and breathe culinary school. When I finished and finally had some free time, I got a life. It was a fake life for the most part, but hey, at least it was a life.

Unfortunately at this point, I'd much rather still be the girl who spent two years secretly daydreaming about her pastry chef instructor and what he would do if she walked up to him and swiped the flour off of his cheek that always seemed to be there.

Luckily, I got to find out what would happen when I did that. I also got to find out a lot of things about my instructor and what he would do, like lie right to my face about something extremely important—and after I let him make me a non-partial virgin, too! But at least we had a few good weeks. That poor guy put up with a lot—a black eye, everyone knowing how he masturbates, me puking on his brand new chef coat, learning things about afterbirth he probably never, ever wanted to know, eating an actual bag of dicks…oh yeah, and telling everyone he was the father of my baby that wasn't really my baby without even knowing that the baby wasn't my baby because he's just a damn good guy. You know, if he wasn't such a liar-face liar pants.

So, this is the story all about how my life got flipped-turned upside down…no, seriously, it is. Stop singing, you heartless bastards.

I'm pregnant.

Those words can just fuck right off.

Chapter 1

– Can I Get A Woohoo?! –

Molly

"IF YOU WHIP and fold in the egg whites last, you'll get the best volume in your finished soufflé."

Listening to the deep timber of my pastry instructor's voice as he wanders around the test kitchen, I pause with my whisk in my hand and imagine Marco Desoto naked for probably the thousandth time. Today.

"Very nice, Molly," he speaks softly right behind me.

He continues watching over my shoulder, and I don't even care that I'm the only one in the class who already had the foresight to add my egg whites in last. Everyone else is scrambling around to start their soufflés over while I'm just standing here with a kitchen utensil in my hand thinking about slathering his body with the egg whites and licking them off. Shaking away my lust-filled thoughts and the idea of consuming raw eggs and the possibility of Salmonella, I go back to manically whipping my whisk through the fluffy white mixture in my bowl until I have perfect, soft peaks.

"You have beautiful peaks, Molly," he adds quietly.

Usually, nothing breaks my concentration in the kitchen, and even though I know I have perfect egg white peaks in the bowl in front of me, hearing my instructor say the words right by my ear turns me into an idiot.

"Do you think so? They're a nice, full B-cup, but I've never thought of them as beautiful before," I ramble.

"Did you say something, Molly?" he asks.

I notice he moved a few feet away and didn't hear me talk out of my ass like...someone in my family. Quickly shaking my head, I concentrate on the peaks in my bowl instead of the ones on my chest.

For two years I've had to try and be stealthy about my obsession with our student-teacher, Marco Desoto, and I can tell I'm losing my edge. He's caught me staring at him more than once, and the few times (okay, more than a few) I've quietly walked up behind him just to smell him while he was busy at the stove, he knew I was there and called me out on it. I can't help it. He smells like the best damn cookie in the world. Like vanilla and almond dipped in brown sugar and butter. Girls buy *lotions* to smell like that crap and this guy oozes it from his pores.

I was once the queen of stealth. I walked through our house completely naked because I realized we were out of towels right when I was getting into the shower and I had to grab one from the dryer. Our living room was filled with all the adults in our family, and no one even noticed me strolling bare ass across the carpet to the laundry room off the kitchen. That was the day I found out my Aunt Claire smoked pot and licked the walls at Seduction and Snacks.

Another time, I stood over my sister, Ava's, shoulder and spent fifteen minutes watching her text her boyfriend, Tyler. I learned about "accidental anal" and a bunch of other shit I can never scrub from my mind, but hey, I got some more dirt to add to my ever-growing laundry list of things about my family I've titled "Things I need to know in case anyone ever tries to fuck with me". It's not that I don't love my family, I just like to cover all my bases. I like being the only quiet person everyone forgets about until I speak up, and then they all look at me like they're trying to remember who I am and what I'm doing there. It's not their fault. I've spent the last two years living and breathing culinary school studying to be a French Pastry Chef.

"I thought I heard you say something about cups, my mistake," Marco says with a smile.

"Nope! No cups here. Just beautiful, firm peaks that will not drop no matter how old and wrinkly they get!"

Marco Desoto is turning me into the princess of bumbling idiots and my family will never let me live it down if I don't get my shit together. Uncle Drew was disappointed when I told him I was going to culinary school and had to inform him that there was no such thing as "ninja school". He truly thought he would get to tell all of his friends that he had a niece who was a real-life ninja. I'm pretty sure that was the first day I ever saw him cry.

Monday through Thursday, every day including summers for twenty-four months, I've been up at school from six in the morning until eleven at night. I'm lucky my family even remembers my name at this point. Even before that though, I usually kept to myself. My family is plenty loud and annoying enough to make up for my lack of enthusiasm.

It makes this unhealthy obsession with Marco all the more annoying. Even though I remembered the whole egg white thing today, I've been flakey and off my game the last few weeks. Being a pastry chef is my dream and I'm on the verge of making it a reality. Tomorrow is my last final exam and I will finally be done with school. I need to stop thinking about Marco covered in eggs and concentrate on what I'm supposed to be doing. I have to finish writing an essay about the history of soufflé's, and then all day Monday, I have to do my final presentation, which includes making eight different desserts and showcase them in an exhibit. I've already spent over twelve hours researching my paper and getting most of it typed up, but I still have a few more things to add as well as doing a few practice baking runs when I get home so that everything is perfect. It *has* to be perfect. Nothing can distract me, especially Mr. Sugar Cookie, who I can't stop staring at as I fold my egg whites into my other mixing bowl.

Why did he have to show up in one of my classes two years ago? WHY? Ever since then I've made sure that I sign up for whatever courses he's teaching that corresponds with my schedule like some kind of creepy stalker. I stare at him instead of concentrating on my food, and for God's sake, I started talking to him about my BOOBS a minute ago.

As everyone finishes up what they are doing and Marco reminds us what time we all need to be here in the morning to start our final, I am determined to do absolutely nothing for the rest of my night but think about Monday and my dreams finally coming true. In just a few more days, I will be a classically-trained French Pastry Chef with a bachelor's degree in Baking and Pastry Arts. I will be able to bring some classiness to Seduction and Snacks and maybe get a life. I really, really need to get a life.

THE SCREAM FROM the bathroom across the hall is deafening and so loud that I can hear it through my earbuds as I blast Mozart's Piano Concerto No. 21 while flipping through *The Baking Bible*. Charlotte stopped by to do a load of laundry since hers and Gavin's washing machine is on the fritz, and I'm assuming she found a red sock mixed in with her whites. Oh, the horror.

Turning the volume up, I go back to writing down a few notes to add to my final paper, leaving my sister to the domestic bliss of washing her soon-to-be husband's tighty whities.

Gavin and Charlotte have been up each other's asses ever since they got engaged and started planning their wedding. I'm pretty sure she only asked me to be a bridesmaid out of family obligation. We're not really that close and it's probably my fault. I haven't had time for anyone ever since I started taking college courses my sophomore year of high school and then went right into culinary school after graduation. On top of that, I like to keep to myself. My family is crazy, loud, and so inappropriate that most of the things they say and do border on being illegal. I've wondered many times if I was adopted, but I'm just too chicken shit to ask anyone. I've never felt like I belong in this family.

Sure, I have a sense of humor, but it's more sarcastic and dry instead of in-your-face like everyone else. Charlotte and Ava have much more in common with each other than with me. They care about love and guys and fashion…all that shit you read about in women's magazines. But me? I just care about baking. Cookies, cakes and pastries never let you down. People think it's all about recipes, but it's so much more. It's the science and chemistry of using exact measurements and the right temperatures, and when you follow the rules everything comes out perfectly. I like knowing exactly how something will turn out. I know if I do what I'm supposed to, it will be exactly how I want it. Even if you plan it all out and follow everything to a T, life will fuck you right up the ass. Without lube.

Just as the genius idea pops in my head for making an apple-chutney-stuffed soufflé to add to my presentation tomorrow, another scream breaks through my concentration. With a huff, I yank my earbuds out and quietly make my way across the hall to the bathroom, gently turning the handle and slowly peeking my head inside. Sure, I probably could've stomped across the hall and angrily flung the door open so that it banged against the opposite wall, but that's not my style. Remember, queen of stealth. It's much more productive to sneak up on someone. There isn't all that wasted time of asking things like, "Are you okay?" or "What's wrong?" Standing silently behind them for a few seconds usually gives you all of the information you need. Like right now, for instance. Charlotte is standing in front of the sink staring in horror at a pregnancy test in her hand.

"Look at you, with a bun in the oven," I tell her, pushing the door open wider and leaning my shoulder against the doorframe.

She jumps and turns to face me, then lets out another God-awful scream. I wince and shake my head at her. "I think the screaming part comes at the end when you're trying to push that thing out of you."

Charlotte starts shaking her head back and forth and begins muttering to herself. "This can't be happening. I'm getting married in four weeks. Oh, my God, what am I going to do?"

"Well, clearly we're going to have to take you into town for a back alley abortion since only trollops and floozies get in the family way before marriage," I deadpan as I step further into the bathroom.

She opens her mouth to scream again and I quickly smack my hand over her lips. "It's not 1912. Who cares if you're pregnant? Your fiancé was the product of a one-night stand at a frat party. Do you really think anyone in this family is going to judge you?"

Charlotte grabs onto my wrist and pulls my hand down. "I don't care about that shit! It's Gavin! He doesn't want kids. We've talked about this and we both decided it wasn't something we wanted. He's not going to want to marry me now. I'm going to be pregnant and alone and no one will ever want me! I smell bread. Were you baking bread? Does my stomach look fat to you?"

The speed with which she changes subjects makes my head spin, and all I can do is stare at her as she pulls up her shirt and touches her perfectly flat stomach.

"Yes, you look like a heifer and you'll never fit your fat ass into that wedding dress. You should just call it off."

She nods her head in agreement. "I have to call it off. This whole wedding is a sham now."

"Oh, for fuck's sake, stop being so dramatic. How about you

just act like an adult and tell Gavin. Clearly it was an accident, and I do believe it was his dick that did this to you," I remind her.

"I'm going to wind up on *MTV's Real Life: I'm a Crack Whore in Love With a Brony*," she mutters to herself.

"Um, what?"

She looks up at me and pulls her shirt back down. "Well, you know, I'll be alone and I'll be so depressed without Gavin that I'll turn to crack to take the pain away. At that point I'm sure Tyler will start looking pretty good to me so I'll most likely steal him away from Ava and then she'll kill me. I'll wind up a crack whore dead in an alley. It's what I deserve!"

This, right here, is why Charlotte and I have never been close. She's certifiably insane.

"HON! ARE YOU UPSTAIRS?"

Gavin's shout from downstairs immediately throws Charlotte into more of a panic than she's already in. Her eyes grow so wide I'm surprised they don't pop right out of her head. I hear stomping up the stairs and I know it's only seconds before Gavin walks in here and sees Charlotte holding the positive pregnancy test in her hands.

"Oh, my God, oh, my God, oh, my God!" Charlotte whispers frantically. "I'm not ready! I can't do this! OH, MY GOD!"

Gavin is at the top of the stairs now and the thump of his shoes echo on the hardwood floors.

"Char? You in the bathroom?" he calls.

Her eyes immediately fill with tears, and I sort of feel bad for her until she thrusts the pregnancy stick towards me.

"Take it!" she insists in a hushed voice.

I throw my hands up in the air and take a step back. "Eeeew, you peed on that!"

"TAKE IT!" she snarls through clenched teeth as she presses the purple and white stick up against my stomach.

"Get your pee stick away from me!" I whisper back in horror.

Her bottom lip starts to quiver and her eyes fill with tears as she looks over my shoulder.

"Hey! What are you guys doing in here?" Gavin asks from behind me.

Without giving it a second thought, I grab the test from her and quickly twist around to face him, hiding the thing behind my back and trying not to think about the fact that my sister's pee is most likely touching my hand.

"Oh, you know. Just girl stuff," I reply with a nonchalant shrug.

Gavin looks back and forth between us and then cranes his neck to try and look around me. "What's behind your back?"

"Nothing. It's nothing," Charlotte tells him in the guiltiest voice imaginable.

I silently curse her and her inability to lie in a believable fashion. Every time she lies, her voice goes up at least twenty octaves until she sounds like a mouse being stepped on by someone wearing stilettos.

Gavin laughs. "Nice try. Seriously, what's going on?"

He keeps trying to get a look behind my back and I keep turning my body in the opposite direction. Too late, I realize we're standing in front of a fucking mirror. Gavin looks up into it and his jaw drops open.

"Is that what I think it is?"

"I don't know. Do you think it's a hot new shade of lipstick that Charlotte was just about to put on me?" I ask innocently.

"No, no I don't. That's a fucking pregnancy test," he replies in a low, slightly angry voice.

In that moment, I see now why Charlotte was freaking out. Gavin does NOT look happy about the possibility that she could be pregnant. I love this guy like a brother. I've known him since birth and in four weeks he WILL be my brother through marriage, and I've never wanted to punch him straight in the mouth more than I do right now.

I always think before I speak. Always. I carefully process every word to make sure I get the desired outcome.

Until now.

"I'm pregnant!" I blurt out.

Charlotte starts to cry loudly and Gavin's eyebrows rise up into his hairline.

"Yep, I'm knocked up. With child. In the maternal condition. Preggers. Can I get a woohoo?!"

I raise my arms in the air and shake them around, wondering what the hell is wrong with me. Who the hell says *woohoo*?

"Why is Charlotte crying? Hon, why are you crying?" Gavin asks gently.

She sniffles and wraps her arms around my waist from behind. "I just love Molly so much."

I lower my arms and shrug, trying not to roll my eyes.

"Charlotte is just overcome with excitement about the love child in my womb."

I pat my stomach for added emphasis, figuring I might as well make this a stellar performance for Charlotte's sake. She is seriously going to owe me for this shit. Like, name her damn kid after me or something.

Gavin sighs and runs his hand through his hair. "I don't know what to say. I mean, are you happy about this? I didn't even know you were dating anyone. Shit, ARE you dating someone? Who is he? I'll kick his fucking ass."

Gavin goes back to being pissed and now I don't know what the hell to do. I didn't exactly think this whole thing through when I blurted out I was pregnant to save Charlotte. Everyone is going to see right through this charade. Shit. Everyone is going to KNOW. There's no way Gavin is going to keep his mouth shut. Oh, my God, my parents are going to kill me.

"It's horrible, Gavin! He's a horrible man! He got her pregnant and now he doesn't want anything to do with her!" Charlotte wails dramatically.

I look over my shoulder at her and give her the most evil eye I can muster.

"Seriously?" I whisper in irritation.

I turn back around to see Gavin looking at us in confusion.

"I mean, SERIOUSLY. She's serious. It's horrible. I'm so distraught."

With a sniffle, I rub my eyes and curse Charlotte to hell.

Gavin reaches out and pats my shoulder. "Don't worry. You're not going to go through this alone. We all love you, and we're going to find this guy and make him pay."

Awwwww, shit. What the hell have I done? Why didn't I just stay in my room and ignore the blood curdling scream from down the hall like any sane person would have done? When I said I needed to get a life, this isn't really what I had in mind.

Chapter 2

– *Satisfaction and Sugar* –
Marco

"Hey, Ma! What was that secret ingredient you use in your Zeppole filling again?" I shout from the living room, trying to finish up a few last minute questions on my laptop to add to the final exam for the students tomorrow.

I should know the answer to this question considering I've been helping my mom make her favorite Italian dessert since I was five, but just like everything in my brain lately, it's turned into a pile of mush thanks to one beautiful, shy student I haven't been able to stop thinking about for the last two years. Stupid fraternization rules.

My mom pokes her head out from the kitchen doorway and points her wooden spoon covered in red sauce at me. "Get off that gadget and help your sisters set the table before I whoop you with this spoon."

She disappears back into the kitchen and I shake my head, closing the lid to my laptop and pushing myself up from the couch. I'm twenty-four years old and I still tuck my tail between my legs and run when my mother scolds me. It's not like I'm sitting in her living room writing porn on the Lord's Day. Well, not really. I guess it could be considered food porn to some people.

Walking into the dining room, my ears are immediately assaulted

BAKING AND BABIES

by the sounds of my two older sisters arguing.

"You're just jealous because I can date whoever I want and you're an old married hag at twenty-six!"

"And by date, you mean screw anyone with a penis. Give me a fucking break," Tessa groans, placing a fork next one of the plates.

"Contessa Maria Desoto! Watch your mouth!" mom scolds, setting a huge bowl of pasta in the middle of the table. "We are going to have Sunday dinner like normal, civilized people for once. No swearing, no fighting, and no throwing food."

She looks directly at me as she says the last part. You throw one dinner roll six months ago when your sister calls you a *tool* and you never live it down. It's not my fault it ricocheted off her shoulder and up into the ceiling fan before one of the blades sent it flying into our mother's face.

Rosa looks across the table at me and sticks out her tongue. I slyly flip her off without our mom seeing as we all take our seats. Even though it might not look like it, we really do love each other. We're your typical loud, eating, breeding Italian family, although our mother likes to remind us on a daily basis that we aren't doing our part in the breeding department. She met our father (God rest his soul) when they were sixteen years old, got married at eighteen, and popped out my oldest sister Contessa nine months later. Rosa followed a year after that, and I came screaming into the world a year after her.

"Alfanso, honey, say grace."

My mother folds her hands in front of her and closes her eyes, thankfully before she can see the scowl on my face and the laughter my sisters are just barely holding in.

"Ma, how many times do I have to tell you not to call me that?" I complain, trying not to whine like a little girl.

I spent my entire childhood saddled with that name and constantly being teased—mostly from my sisters, and when I left middle school behind and started high school, I refused to let anyone call me by anything other than my middle name of Marco. Sadly, my mother continues to ignore my request.

"Alfanso is a strong, Italian name and you should be proud you share—"

"The same name as my mother's father's uncle's brother from Sicily," my sisters and I cut her off and finish in unison.

"And by Sicily, we mean the planet Melmac, Alf," Tessa snorts, earning a one-eyed glare from my mother who still has her head bowed, eyes closed, and hands together in prayer.

I bow my head and close my eyes, refusing to take my sister's bait when she uses the same, tired joke comparing my name to some furry creature on a TV show long before any of us were born.

"Rub-a-dub-dub, thanks for the grub. Yay God!"

Mom's hand smacks me upside the head as soon as I finish and Tessa kicks my shin under the table. One of these days I should try not being an asshole, but it's just too much fun.

We all start digging into our food and the only sounds that fill the room for a few minutes are forks scraping plates and ice cubes clinking in glasses. It reminds me of every single Sunday dinner we've ever had, even if it is surprisingly quiet for the time being. Regardless of my sisters and I being adults with our own lives and our own homes, it's an unwritten rule that no matter where we are or what we're doing, that we always come home for Sunday dinner.

"So, Alfanso, when are you going to bring a nice woman home to meet the family?" mom asks casually as she slathers butter on a slice of homemade bread.

"He doesn't know any nice women; he only knows skanks." Rosa laughs.

"Skanks with the I.Q. of a banana," Tess adds.

I glare at both of them with my fork halfway to my mouth. "Hello? I'm sitting right here. They aren't skanks and they aren't stupid. I prefer to call them 'scantily-clad ladies with limited vocabulary.'"

Mom sighs. "All of my friends have photos of grandchildren on their bookshelves. Do you want to know what I have on my bookshelves? I have porn."

In a moment of insanity and a little bit of depression after my father passed away, I got the genius idea to write a cookbook, filled with my family's favorite Italian dessert recipes. When the publishing house I sent it to told me it was too boring, instead of getting drunk and crying about it, I got drunk and added a bunch of tips for men on how they could get any woman they wanted just by making those recipes. It included the best recipe for Italian buttercream that wouldn't leave grease stains on their sheets after they smeared it on their girl, as well as how to give a woman an orgasm using only cannoli filling and a spatula.

"Hey," I bristle at her porn comment. "That's a signed copy of *Satisfaction and Sugar.* If you announce on Facebook you have that, women will start clawing each other's eyes out for it."

I don't mean to sound conceited, but it's true. I get emails from a ton of women on a weekly basis, thanking me for spicing up their sex life while teaching their significant other how to bake and asking if I give in-home demonstrations. It's really great for the ego and it's made my popularity grow so much in the book world that the publisher has requested another cookbook from me.

Rosa snorts. "Try not to break your arm patting yourself on the back there, little brother."

My family really is proud of my accomplishments, even if they don't sound like it sometimes. They are my biggest supporters and always tell me how impressed they are of everything I've done at such a young age, but to them, I'm just Alfanso Marco Desoto. The son and brother who refuses to settle down, gets a cheap thrill out of teasing his older sisters, and had to grow up real fast when our father died suddenly of a heart attack three months before I was supposed to go to Paris to be the head pastry chef for one of the most popular restaurants in the city. I'll never regret the decision to stick close to home to teach at my alma mater and take care of my family, but I'm not going to lie and say that I don't still dream about Paris, although helping men all over the land get laid with desserts does take the sting out of things.

"What's the deadline for your next cookbook? Do you still want me to edit?" Tessa asks, wiping her mouth with a napkin.

Tessa is a copy editor for our local newspaper. It's nice to have someone in the family with editing skills that I can trust my cookbooks with, who won't dry heave when I confirm that I try out every piece of advice I give before putting it in a book.

"I want to have this thing finished in a few months. If all goes well, and I don't have any distractions for the next four weeks, this puppy could be on shelves in bookstores by early next year," I tell everyone proudly.

"Rosa, put your phone away at the dinner table," Mom chastises.

Rosa ignores her, scrolling through something on her screen and laughing. "It's Marco's phone and I'm just checking the notifications on his cookbook page. You really pissed this chick off."

Rosa has floundered between jobs ever since she graduated college, never quite being able to figure out what she wanted to do with her life. When my cookbook started gaining popularity a couple of years ago, I was spending more time answering emails and dicking around on Facebook, instead of doing lesson plans and preparing finals. So when I offered her a job as my social media assistant, she jumped at it. I might be regretting the decision of giving her my Facebook password right now though.

Tessa leans closer to Rosa and looks over her shoulder. "What did he do?"

"Some guy on the page asked if all of the tips and recipes still gave you the same outcome if you had kids, and Marco told him that his first mistake was *having* kids," Rosa snorts with a chastising shake of her head.

"ALFANSO MARCO DESOTO!" Mom yells, bringing out my

full name for extra, angry emphasis.

I hold my hands up in surrender. "Ma, it was a joke. I was just being my usual charming, sarcastic self."

I turn back to Rosa. "Who commented and what did she say?"

Tessa grabs the phone from her hand. "Her name is Molly and she said, 'You're an ass. You probably don't even know how to bake and just copied all these recipes from your mommy. Cut the cord and get a life.'"

Rosa takes the phone back and Tessa smacks her in the arm. "Ooooh, burn! She's got your number, Marco!"

I roll my eyes and help myself to another serving of pasta. "Whatever. She's obviously got a stick up her a..." I glance quickly at my mom and correct myself. "...foot, and doesn't have a sense of humor."

"Her name is Molly Gilmore, and it says she's from Ohio too," Rosa continues, completely ignoring me.

The spoon slips out of my hand and drops with a loud *clatter*, splattering red sauce all over the table.

"Ooops, slippery little bugger." I laugh uncomfortably, grabbing a handful of napkins and sopping up the mess, hoping no one notices I lost all bodily functions as soon as I heard that name.

Tessa gasps and points at me with wide eyes. "Oh my Gosh, you know her! You know her and you like her and she thinks you're an ass!"

Seriously, how does she *do* that? People drop spoons all the time; it doesn't mean they like someone. How does she know my hand didn't go numb? Maybe it's early onset Parkinson's or a stroke. I could be dying and she doesn't even care.

"I have no idea what you're talking about," I mutter as I wad up the dirty napkins, getting up from my chair and heading into the kitchen. "Who wants dessert? I brought my special Tiramisu!"

Not even chocolate, mascarpone, and the special thing I do with the Lady Fingers can deter the three women in my family when they smell something fishy.

They bum rush me in the kitchen so fast all three of them get stuck in the doorway pushing, shoving, and arguing until one of them manages to break free and get to me first.

"Is she pretty? Can she cook? When are you bringing her to dinner so I have enough time to bring out the good china and your grandmother's lace tablecloth?" Mom asks in a rush of excitement.

Figuring there's no point in lying to them since I already planned on making my move with Molly as soon as she finished her final tomorrow and will no longer be my student, I grudgingly answer my mother's questions, hoping it will shut her up.

"Yes, yes, and never."

She puts her hands on her hips and my sisters do the same, standing behind her and giving me equal looks of annoyance.

"So, you know who this Molly Gilmore person is, but clearly she has no idea you're the same Alfanso D. whose Facebook page she was on, cookbook author and the guy she just knocked down a few pegs," Tessa states. "What does she look like? How old is she? Where did you meet her?"

I roll my eyes at all the questions that just won't stop. When I first found out my cookbook was going to be published, I spoke with the school I worked for to make sure it wouldn't be a conflict of interest. They suggested using some sort of penname just in case and since I'm only known as Marco Desoto at work, Alfanso D. was born. None of my students know I'm the author of that widely-popular cookbook and only a very small handful of the faculty knows.

"She's got long dark hair and pretty blue eyes, she's twenty, and ooooooooh, she's one of Marco's students! You naughty boy, you." Rosa giggles with her eyes glued to the phone in her hand. "Forget writing cookbooks, you could write one of those *'I Bent the Rules and Bent Her Over My Desk'* taboo student/teacher romances."

Mom turns around and flicks Rosa's ear, causing her to yelp and complain loudly, distracting her enough for me to reach around my mother and snatch my phone from her hand. Glancing down at it, I see that Rosa found Molly's Facebook page and was knee-deep in her investigation, going by the fact that she was in a photo album dated five years ago.

"After tomorrow, she will no longer be my student, so there won't be anything taboo about it," I inform them, clicking out of her Facebook page even though all I want to do now is sit and scroll through her pictures. "If any of you say one more word about this, I will pack up that Tiramisu, go home, and eat the entire thing myself."

I can see each of them struggle to keep their mouths closed, their nosiness at war with their stomachs.

"Did you soak the Lady Fingers in hazelnut coffee?" Tessa asks with wide, hopeful eyes.

I nod.

"Did you put vanilla AND almond extract in the mascarpone?" Rosa questions with a dreamy sigh.

I nod again, crossing my arms in front of me and refusing to budge until they all agree to stay out of my love life. Or what I hope will be a love life and not a complete disaster when Molly finds out I'm the ass she thinks can't bake.

After a few seconds, they concede reluctantly.

"Fine," Tessa mutters. "But if that tiramisu sucks, all bets are off."

I laugh, long and hard, as they trudge back into the dining room and I grab dessert from the fridge, knowing without a doubt I would never make a sucky tiramisu. I'm insulted she would even suggest such a thing.

The rest of the night continues with only a few more minor arguments and no more violence from my mother for my behavior. With a kiss on her cheek and three Tupperware containers filled with leftovers, I leave my childhood home and head across town to my apartment to put together a plan of charming the pants off of Molly Gilmore, and hope my comment about kids on my Facebook page doesn't come back to bite me in the ass.

Chapter 3
— Soup —
Molly

STARING PROUDLY AT my soufflé display that still sits on the middle of the stainless steal counter in the kitchen at school, I look around the huge room, making sure I'm alone. Confident that the rest of my classmates have long since gone home after receiving their pass or fail grades, I start shaking my ass and dancing around the counter. When I get to the other side, I pause my celebration long enough to grab the sheet of paper next to my display that officially declares me a French Pastry Chef, waving it around above my head as I resume my horrible moves.

"What are you doing?! You can't be dancing like that in your condition!"

I freeze mid hip thrust with my arms in the air and watch Charlotte stalk across the room, snatching my final exam out of my hand and smacking it on the shiny surface.

"Shaking your hips like that could hurt the baby," she continues. "It could also hurt my reputation if anyone else witnessed that horrible display that resembled white girl wasted drunk moves."

With a sigh, I drop my arms and start unbuttoning my pastry coat. "In case you forgot, you're the one with the fertilized egg in your uterus, not me. What are you even doing here at my school?"

She crosses her arms in front of her as I toss the white fabric onto the countertop. "I didn't forget, Molly. It's hard to forget something like that when you're constantly puking. If this is going to work, you have to be one hundred percent dedicated and that means behaving exactly like a pregnant woman would. I wanted to catch you here at school before you got home."

Reaching into the giant purse she has slung over her shoulder, she pulls out a thick book and thrusts it at me.

"Here, I got you this. Skim through it and pay close attention to the things I marked with post-it notes."

Taking the book from her hand, I stare in irritation at the picture of the happy pregnant woman on the cover and the big bold words that say *"What to Expect When You're Expecting"*. My hopes that Charlotte would forget this shit, come to her senses, and tell Gavin the truth was clearly a waste of time. Going by the fact that there are post-it notes in a multitude of colors sticking out of practically every page in the book, she still hasn't grown a brain and has instead boarded the crazy train to La La Land and offered to drive.

"Charlotte, this is insane. I am not going to learn about…" I flip through the book and pause on a random page, realizing *this* thing is probably the cause for her puking. "Growing hair on your nipples and hemorrhoids."

I close the book with a *snap* and shove it back at her. "I did you a favor by taking one for the team yesterday when you panicked. That doesn't mean I'm going to keep up with this charade just because you're too chicken shit to tell Gavin."

Her bottom lip starts to quiver and her eyes fill up with tears.

"Oh, no," I scold, pointing my finger in her face. "Don't even try that shit with me. I know for a fact you can cry on command, and you do it every time Dad tells you no."

The tears immediately disappear and she huffs, moving on to a different tactic.

"Molly, please," she begs. "Just do me this one favor. Just until after the wedding and I have enough time to ease Gavin into the news. I've never asked you for anything in your entire life…"

She trails off and I laugh, shaking my head at her audacity.

"Took the blame for the dent in Mom's car when the mailbox magically jumped out in front of you so you wouldn't get grounded and miss prom. Took responsibility for the vodka you puked all over the bathroom floor the day AFTER prom so you could still go to a pool party. And let's not forget the week I spent in my room after I falsely admitted to dying the cat's hair pink so you wouldn't miss Stephanie Johnson's birthday party," I remind her, ticking the items off on my fingers.

"Oh my GOD, that happened when you were six! Get over it already!" she complains. "See? Look how good you are at making Mom and Dad believe whatever you say. What's one more tiny little favor?"

I roll my eyes at her as I turn away and pull my display to the edge of the counter. It's a three-foot-long thick piece of cardboard covered in foil with my different soufflés resting neatly on top. It's heavy and awkward, but I need to move it to the display case in the lobby with the rest of the pastry student's projects.

"It's hilarious that you can call this a tiny favor, Char," I tell her as I slowly lift the makeshift tray with both hands and turn to face her. "You're asking me to tell our parents I'm pregnant. To lie to our entire family for four weeks, have them spend that whole time being disappointed and upset with me, just because you couldn't remember what a condom looked like."

Tears fill her eyes again and I can tell she's not faking them this time. I hate that I actually feel sorry for her. She's the most selfish person on the planet, and I feel sorry for her stupid ass. She hasn't even asked about finals when she knew what a big day this was for me. Two years of not having a life and working my ass off and she comes in here thinking only about herself.

"You don't understand, Molly," she whimpers. "I love Gavin more than anything else in this world. You have no idea how dead set he is against having kids. I thought I felt the same way until I took that test. I know it will just take him time to get used to the idea. I just need a little while to convince him how good it will be."

I close my eyes and count to ten, trying really hard not to give in.

"Mom made me clean up your vodka puke," I remind her, trying at the same time to remind myself all the reasons why I shouldn't cave. "I had to listen to a forty minute lecture about knowing my limits, and then she made me watch fifteen episodes of *Intervention* with her."

Cleaning up Charlotte's puke wasn't as bad as my mother trying to convince me that vodka was a gateway drug to meth and I should think about how embarrassing it would be if she put me on a reality show where the entire world would see me huffing air dusters and sleeping with eighty-year-old men to pay for crack.

"I know, I'm sorry," Charlotte whispers. "I'll make it up to you this time, I promise."

My arms are starting to get heavy, and if I don't agree to this, she's never going to leave me alone. It's not like I have anything else going on in my life now that I'm finished with school. I start working full-time at the Seduction and Snacks headquarters in a few days, but that's a regular job with regular hours and nothing like the time I had to put in for school. And it's not like I'll be busy having a hot romance since I was too much of a chicken to finally try and have a real conversation with Marco instead of just sniffing him. He didn't say one word to me when he studied my project earlier, made several notes on his notepad, and then walked away. He didn't even look in my direction when we came back into the kitchen a few hours later and he handed out our final scores. Now that I'll be walking out of this school for the last time, I'll probably never see him again, and I completely blew whatever opportunity I had to flirt with him and see if he might be interested. My life sucks. It's only four weeks, I guess I can handle a month of this nonsense to save Charlotte's marriage.

"I want every baking item and pastry utensil you get at your shower. Including the KitchenAid mixer I know Aunt Claire already bought off your registry," I inform her.

Charlotte squeals and claps her hands together happily. "Deal!"

"I also want ten percent of your profits from cards at the actual wedding."

Her smile falls and she glares at me.

"Five," she counters.

"I'm fake carrying your baby for four weeks, and you know Mom is going to want to talk about nipple hair! TEN!" I argue.

She stomps her foot and huffs. "Fine! Ten. But you better be the most convincing fake pregnant woman in the history of the world."

"I'll even dump a can of soup in the toilet when I have fake morning sickness," I reassure her.

Charlotte quickly clamps her hand over her mouth.

"Dnsh shtak ashtok shtup," she muffles against her palm.

The look of confusion on my face makes her pull her hand away, swallowing a few times to keep, what I'm assuming is a little vomit, in her throat.

"I said, don't talk about...soup."

She whispers the word *soup,* and I can actually see her face turn an interesting shade of green.

"You are so weird," I mutter, shifting the display in my hands as my arms start to cramp. "So, what's the plan?"

It's her turn to look confused and she's lucky I'm holding twenty-five pounds of soufflé's or I'd smack that look right off of her face.

"How and when am I supposed to tell Mom and Dad this joyous news?" I growl in annoyance.

"Well, I told Gavin not to say anything until you could talk to them, but he might have already said something to Tyler who probably told Ava. So you should do it really soon. Like, as soon as you get home," she tells me, having the decency to wince delivering the news that our sister and her weird boyfriend might already know about my fake delicate condition.

"So, I'm supposed to just walk into the house and say 'Hey, Mom and Dad, good news! I passed all my exams, I'm finally done with school, graduation is Friday at seven, I made a chocolate cake to celebrate, and oh, by the way, I got knocked up by a guy I never told you about and who you'll never meet because Charlotte already told Gavin he was a horrible man that wants nothing to do with me. What's for dinner?" I ramble, picturing my father's head literally exploding all over the living room wall if I said that.

"Perfect!" Charlotte says with a nod, not hearing the sarcasm in my voice.

I open my mouth to call her a range of creative names, but a male voice coming from the doorway cuts me off.

"That won't work at all. What if I go home with you and pretend to be the father?"

I jump and turn so fast towards the doorway that my display slips right out of my hand and splats to the floor, sending pastry crust and pounds of different flavored fillings all over mine and Charlotte's shoes.

"Eeeeeew, it looks like tomato soup," she whines, probably talking about the cherry filling dripping from her shins.

I ignore the gagging sounds coming from her and stare with my mouth wide open at Marco as he lounges against the door jam, not even caring that I just ruined my display that I spent weeks agonizing over and all day today baking and perfecting.

"You're not doing this alone, Molly. Let me help you out," he tells me softly.

I'm too mesmerized by the sound of his voice and how his eyes got all sweet looking when he said my name, that it takes me a couple of seconds to process what he said. He cocks his head and smiles at me, and it finally hits me that he must have overheard the last part of my conversation with Charlotte and he's offering to help me. He thinks I'm pregnant with another guy's child and he just volunteered to walk right into the lion's den of my parent's house and take some of the heat off me.

Butterflies flap around in my stomach and a giddy grin starts to take over my face, realizing I didn't blow my opportunity with him and he clearly likes me a little bit if he's being so sweet and offering to stand in as the baby daddy for me.

OH, MY GOD HE'S OFFERING TO BE MY BABY DADDY BECAUSE HE THINKS I'M PREGNANT WITH ANOTHER GUY'S CHILD!

"Yes. YES!" Charlotte shouts next to me in between gags as she shakes her leg to try and get the cherry filling off. "This is perfect! I don't know who you are, but you are a very nice and generous guy to help Molly out like this."

I'm still unable to form words as she takes over speaking for me, telling Marco about the fake horrible man that fake knocked me up whose name she can't even bare to utter (BECAUSE HE'S FAKE) and how he left me in this condition and it would be just awful if I had to face it alone.

Marco nods in understanding while she prattles on, wrapping her arm around my shoulder and giving it a sympathetic squeeze when she tells him how much she loves me and how she feels so much better now that I won't be going through such a trying time alone.

When she finally finishes her long-winded, TMI explanation to the guy I've had a crush on for what feels like forever, who is now looking at me like he wants to give me a supportive hug instead of ripping my clothes off like I always dreamed, I finally find my voice.

Turning away from Marco's sad smile, I look right into my sister's eyes and whisper the words I know will hurt the most.

"Soup, soup, soup. Cream of mushroom soup, green pea soup, chunky gelatinous globs of soup from a can. Soup."

Our faces are so close I can literally hear the vomit fly up into her mouth. Her cheeks puff out to keep it in, her eyes widen in fear, and without another word—thank God—she turns and runs from the room as fast as she can, bumping into Marco on her way out.

"She has a thing about soup; so weird," I tell him with a shrug as the clack of her shoes running down the hall to the closest bathroom fades away.

"Listen, Marco, you don't have to—"

"Molly, stop," he cuts me off, moving out of the doorway and walking towards me. "I know I don't have to, I want to. I've wanted to get to know more about you for a while now, so I guess this will give me that chance."

He stops when he gets to the counter, resting his palms on top and leaning across it towards me. I can't help myself from leaning towards him as well, the smell of cookie dough filling my nose and making my knees weak.

"Let me do this for you. We can go get some dinner to get our stories straight, and then I'll give you a ride home so that we can talk to your parents together," he suggests.

All I can do is nod in agreement when he gives me another smile. I've waited two years to be alone with this guy and now I'm getting my chance. By making him the father of the baby I'm not really pregnant with.

"How about I clean up this mess on the floor and you check on…?"

"My asshole sister," I mutter as he comes around the counter to grab some towels from near the sink.

Marco laughs as he bends down and begins cleaning up the floor.

"She's probably still got the soup pukes, she'll be fine," I tell him.

He smiles up at me as he stands and drops the dirty towels into the sink. When he finishes washing his hands, he walks to my side and threads his fingers through mine, pulling me gently to the door of the kitchen.

We walk through the school and out into the parking lot, and all I can think about is that Marco Desoto is holding my hand. Marco Desoto is taking me on a date.

I mean, a date where we'll talk about hairy nipples, hemorrhoids and afterbirth, and how my father's brain matter will stain his blue dress shirt when his head explodes, but still.

If being the pretend father of my pretend child is the only way I can get him to spend time with me, so be it. I'll just ask Charlotte if I can catch a ride on that crazy train of hers when this is all over.

Chapter 4

— Toxic Sporge —

Marco

I STARE AT Molly across the table as she picks at her food, wondering if she's going to puke. Do pregnant chicks puke at night too or just in the morning? Should I go sit next to her and hold her hair back just in case? What if she doesn't have pregnancy sickness but Marco sickness? Maybe I disgust her. I kind of disgust *myself* right now that I opened my mouth without really thinking about what I was doing.

The girl I've been fantasizing about for two years is having some other guy's baby, and instead of doing what any normal guy would do, I offered to pretend to be the father. I've lost my goddamn mind. I can't be a fake dad to someone else's kid, even if I AM hot for the woman carrying said kid. My dreams of Molly included seeing her naked and asking her to help me test out a few new ideas for my next cookbook, not watching her hot body turn into an alien WITH SOMEONE ELSE'S KID.

She didn't say much on the drive over to the diner aside from letting me know the girl with the long, dark brown hair who has a strange aversion to soup was her older sister, Charlotte. She pretty much gave me one-word answers to every question I asked, or flat out refused to answer them. Dinner isn't going much better, no matter how hard I try to get her to talk. As much as I *don't* want to know about the other guy she was seeing, I still think she'll feel better if she talks about it, and it will give me a way to ease into telling her I made a big mistake.

"I can't do this," Molly suddenly mutters, dropping her fork onto her plate.

Oh, thank God. Thank the good sweet lord I don't have to go back on my word and tell her I changed my mind.

"You're the sweetest guy in the world for doing this, but...I can't," she whispers with a shake of her head.

Good, because I still want to put my penis in her, but I don't think I can stomach it knowing some other dude's baby would be looking at it, judging it and saying something like, "My dad's was bigger than yours, asshole." She still looks like she might throw up. I need to say something nice and comforting.

"Okay. Want to order dessert?"

Yeah, real smooth, buddy.

Molly sighs and I wonder if she's mad I gave in so easily or because the diner's dessert selection sucks. What self-respecting diner doesn't serve apple pie?

"Stupid, selfish, irritating moron..." she mumbles, resting her elbows on the table and dropping her head into her hands.

So, I guess it's me, then.

"Look, I'm sorry, Molly. I really like you. Like, *really* like you. You're smart, beautiful, and the most amazing pastry chef I've seen come through that school. I like you too much to be able to just sit back and be okay with you....you know."

I wave my hand and move my eyes down in the general direction of her stomach.

"I think my services would be better served if I...I don't know, beat the shit out of the guy who did this to you," I continue, talking faster so she doesn't hate me too much for going back on my word to help her. "Give me his name, and I'll make sure he steps up to the plate for you. I can roundhouse punch his face and give him a nice left hook kick to the kneecaps."

She slowly lifts her head from her hands and stares at me.

"Have you ever been in a fight?" she asks skeptically.

"Uh, hello? Have you seen these guns?" I ask, flexing my bicep and giving it a nice little pat for emphasis. "I'm a fighting machine."

She doesn't need to know the one and only fight I participated in happened in the fourth grade with Tommy Knittle when he called me a sissy for bringing in a plate of cookies I'd made to share with the class. I showed him, though. He said he'd give me two black eyes if I didn't eat all three dozen cookies myself in front of everyone on the playground. It only took *one* black eye, thank you very much.

"That's sweet, but it's roundhouse *kick* and a left hook *punch*," she informs me, trying to hide a smile.

"I'm Italian. We do things a little more hardcore where I come from."

"Aren't you from Ohio?" she asks skeptically.

"I meant my mother's house. If you can dodge a wooden spoon, you can dodge a fist," I inform her, trying to maintain as much coolness as I can. "Enough talk about me, let's talk about the scum bag who put you in this situation."

So what if I haven't been in a fight since elementary school? I can beat the shit out of bread dough and I'm sure it's the same thing as some guy's face.

"Did you mean it when you said you liked me?" she whispers.

I can't believe that hasn't been obvious over the last few years, especially from the number of times I leaned over her shoulder to compliment whatever she was making just so I could smell her hair. She always smells like cinnamon and apples and it drives me crazy. Now she's going to smell like cinnamon, apples and someone else's sperm. I don't know who this loser is, but I'm sure his spunk smells like toxic waste. I shouldn't have waited so long to make my move. She stuck with toxic waste spooge when she could have had pineapple spooge. (Page 35, Section 2 of *Seduction and Sugar: Pineapple Dump Cake and Making Your Jizz Taste like a Tropical Island Getaway*)

"Yes, of course I meant it," I tell her, saying good-bye to my fantasy of Molly telling me I taste like a Piña Colada while I take a big sip of ice-cold water to cool my libido.

"Why do you have to be such a nice guy? Why can't you be a jerk like that cookbook author, Alfanso D., who hates kids?" she complains. "I bet the D. stands for dickhead."

The water immediately goes down the wrong pipe, and I start choking and coughing, slamming the glass onto the table to smack my fist against my chest. Molly jumps up from her seat and races around to me, sliding into my side of the booth to pat me on the back through my coughing fit.

Even hacking up a lung of ice water, I can't avoid the scent of cinnamon apples as she leans in close to me and asks if I'm okay. Dammit, why couldn't she smell like ass and toxic jism instead of a delicious dessert?

"I'm fine, I'm fine," I tell her between coughs, subtly scooting a little bit away from her on the bench.

Her hand drops from my back and she smiles. "It's good to know I'm not the only one who almost chokes to death at just the mention of that guy's name. If you aren't following him on Facebook, you should, just to see what asshole thing he'll say next."

She laughs and if I wasn't the dickhead in question, I'd probably laugh right along with her. Molly turns to face me on the bench, tucking one leg up underneath her. My eyes glance down to her flat stomach and I try picturing it all ginormous and gross with arms and legs kicking through the skin trying to claw their way out, instead of how her laugh makes my dick tingle and how if I told her I'm the one saying asshole things on Facebook she'd give me one of those left hook kicks to the nut sack instead of another smile.

"Sorry, I know I'm being weird. Evading your questions, changing the subject, and talking about some idiot on Facebook that pissed me off," she explains. "I can't lie to you when you're being so honest and nice."

Honesty is my middle name. Right after Lying Dickhead Asshole.

She looks away for a minute, blows out a huge breath, and then turns her head back to me, nervously chewing on her bottom lip.

"Marco, I'm not pregnant."

Now my eyes move to the general region of her crotch area, and I wonder if I should have paid better attention in health class since I'm guessing she must have lost the baby somewhere between Third Street and the second refill of our drinks, and I had no idea it could happen so fast and without my knowledge.

"Um, do you need to go to the hospital or something?" I ask lamely. "Boiling water or clean towels…I could flag down the waitress."

I don't know much about losing a baby, but I'm guessing it's not as simple as losing your car keys and she probably needs medical assistance at the very least. And why do they call it *losing* a baby? You didn't misplace it. I'm pretty sure you know where that thing is at all times.

Molly laughs again and shakes her head, and I'm a little surprised she isn't more torn up about this. I cried when I lost my favorite star frosting tip. I mean, allegedly. Like I'd really cry over a little piece of stainless steel I found by chance at a garage sale three years ago that made the perfect fleur-de-lis I haven't been able to recreate with another tip since it disappeared months ago.

"I didn't lose the baby, Marco. I was never pregnant to begin with."

Her words make my mouth drop open and save me from the embarrassment of telling her the tears in my eyes are from allergies and not a frosting tip whose loss I can neither confirm nor deny still haunts me to this day.

"I'm sorry. I should have told you the truth as soon as you offered to help me. I'm not pregnant, and I understand if you hate me for lying to you," she tells me sadly.

All thoughts of the perfect fleur-de-lis fly from my brain and it's all I can do not to pinch myself to see if I'm dreaming.

"Come again?" I whisper.

No, really. I'm pretty sure I just came in my pants when you said you weren't pregnant and I'd like to do that again, please.

"I'm not pregnant and I never was. I was lying for Charlotte," she explains. "She's getting married in a month and just found out she's pregnant and it's this whole big mess I got roped into because she doesn't want her fiancé...never mind. It's not important. It's my mess to deal with and I'm sorry you got pulled into it."

I can hear sadness in her voice and I feel bad she thinks I'd hate her over something that just made me the happiest man on the earth. I can still fantasize about having sex with her without feeling gross. I can still *have* sex with her without worrying another man's fetus is giving my penis the side-eye.

Finally pulling my eyes away from her crotch where a baby didn't somehow escape between courses, past her flat stomach I no longer have to worry about alien limbs trying to claw out of, taking a moment to pause on her tits and only feeling a little ashamed that the one thing I might have enjoyed about this entire shit show is seeing them get huge from the douchebag fetus (because that was something I definitely paid attention to in health class), my eyes finally land on her face.

"So, what you're telling me is I can ask you out on a date now and not feel weird about you carrying another man's child?" I ask happily.

She raises her eyebrow and glares at me. "Seriously? That's all you got out of my confession?"

I quickly backpedal, realizing I still need a way for her to see I'm a good guy and only pretend to be a dick online to sell more cookbooks. I can't tell her I'm Alfanso D. until she knows the D. stands for something much better than dickhead. Like decent, dependable, desirable, daring, and hopefully delicious (pineapple dump cake jizz, here I come!).

"What I meant to say is, I could never hate you for doing something so selfless for your sister," I explain, doing my best to let the whole decent and dependable part shine. "How long are you supposed to help her out with this?"

Molly rolls her eyes and turns away from me, flopping her body against the seat back. "Just until the wedding. So roughly four weeks. It's not *that* long I guess, but it's an entire month of my family being disappointed and ashamed of *me* instead of her. I mean, my family is cool and understanding and they wouldn't come right out and tell me any of this, but I know they'll feel it deep down inside whenever they look at me. This is supposed to be the best time of my life. I just graduated and I have my whole life ahead of me, and instead of celebrating, I'm going home to lie to my family. I keep trying to tell myself it's for a good cause. I'm helping my sister, as selfish as she is, get her shit together and figure out a way to break the news to her fiancé so they can live a long, happy life together. Right now, it doesn't feel like a good idea thinking about what will happen when I walk in that door."

Now that I know there's no chance of her pregnant-puking on me, and I don't have to fight the delectable smell of her skin and how it makes me want to lick every inch of it, I slide across the bench until our thighs are touching. A month is perfect. It's plenty of time for me to charm the pants off of her and hopefully *take* the pants off of her, blinding her with passion and bedroom skills until she has no other choice but to fall for me AND Alfanso D.

"I'm still in, if you are," I tell her softly, leaning in until her long, dark hair tickles my nose and I can take a big, completely innocent inhale of her scent.

"Did you just sniff my hair?" she asks softly, her face turning towards me and our noses are almost touching since I moved even closer while I got a whiff.

"Yes, yes I did smell your hair, and I'm not ashamed to admit it," I inform her, hoping she'll see this as *daring* that I didn't cover up my obsession with her sweet fragrance. "I've noticed you always smell like cinnamon and apples and I like it."

She runs her hand nervously through her hair and I watch as the cutest blush highlights her cheeks.

"It's an essential oil I use for stress. Apple cinnamon oil. You're supposed to put it on the inside of your wrists and the back of your neck to relieve stress and anxiety," she rambles. "I took to bathing in it the last two years of school just so I wouldn't lose my mind."

I stare into her eyes and smile when I see the color on her cheeks deepen and she laughs uncomfortably, pulling her face back from mine and scooting away from me this time. She shakes her head and huffs in annoyance.

"Stop distracting me with your stupid dimples and tell me if I heard you correctly a minute ago, or if you've been sneaking hits of crack under the table," she speaks, a little snark mixed in with her words.

I've caught a few glimpses of her fiery attitude over the past couple of years when she didn't know I was watching, and it's something I looked forward to seeing and hearing whenever I was around her. I like a woman who speaks her mind and doesn't get all giggly and shy with a guy. I like a little ball-busting from a woman, as long as it doesn't result in the *actual* busting of balls because I kind of need those things to live.

"Did you really tell me you're still in if I am?" she continues, looking at me like I've lost my mind.

I probably have. I'm sure I lost it somewhere after the meatloaf and before I found out she didn't really lose a baby in between the seat cushions and realized she was no longer chock full of infested, smelly-ass sperm from some no-name douchebag I'd no longer have to hire someone else to beat up.

"I did, and I am," I reiterate. "I have two sisters myself that drive me insane, but I'd still do anything for them. If you want a baby daddy to take some of the heat off of you, I'm am ready, willing, and able to be your baby daddy."

She shakes her head rapidly back and forth. "I can't let you do that, Marco. I know I said my family is cool and understanding, but they're straight up insane. You have no idea what you'd be walking into with them. Hell, I've known them my entire life and *I* don't even have a clue."

Unable to help myself, I reach up and brush her hair off of her shoulders, mentally sending words of warning to my dick that now is NOT the time to jump around with his hands in the air when I find out her hair is as silky and soft as I thought it would be.

"Molly, I want to do this. Believe me, my family is certifiable," I tell her with a laugh. "There is nothing I haven't seen or heard before when it comes to family. I can handle whatever they dish out."

For a second there she looked like she might bite off my hand when I touched her, and I'm not gonna lie, that it turned me on. My mind starts churning out ideas of adding a little BDSM to the next cookbook, maybe some light whipping while your partner whisks egg whites into cream...

"You don't have to do something like this just because you feel sorry for me," she says in irritation, pulling my head out of the gutter where Molly was wearing a black leather apron and nothing else while I held a riding crop in my hand.

"Did you miss the part where I told you I like you?" I ask her, realizing she thinks I'm still offering to help her out of some sort of guilt. "I *really* like you, Molly, and I'd like to spend more time with you. If that means I have to be the fake sperm donor to your fake baby, then so be it."

I wisely leave out the part where my dick is now handing out "It's not a boy OR a girl" cigars to my balls in celebration that they still have a chance with this girl.

"You have no idea what you're agreeing to…." she tells me, trailing off as she scrunches up her face while she thinks it over.

The waitress drops off our check and I leave Molly to her thoughts as I pull out my wallet and count enough for the bill and a hefty tip, even if I'm still pissed about them not having apple pie. Smelling Molly's hair cured me of my need for it anyway.

Pushing against Molly's hip with my own to get her to move out of the booth, she slides out and stands next to the table to wait for me to follow. Returning my wallet to my back pocket, I grab her hand and slide my fingers through hers, giving her hand a reassuring squeeze.

"Come on, let's go tell your family the happy news." I smile, tugging her towards the door. "I can practice my apologetic looks and fake happiness over this pretend blessing on the ride over and you can tell me more about your family."

When we get out to the parking lot, I add a little more decency to the D. in my name by holding the passenger door open for her, quickly realizing I might have pushed it a little too far when I made a grand, sweeping gesture with my arm and called her *m'lady*, going by the annoyed snort and eye roll she gave me.

Making a mental note that she doesn't seem to like being treated like a princess, I round the hood of the car and get in behind the wheel, looking over at her as I pull my car keys out of my front pocket.

"So, what's the first thing I should know about your family?" I ask, sticking the keys in the ignition.

"Don't do all that mushy, girly stuff like hold my hand or open doors," she begins. "My family will know you're lying right away because I'm not into all that PDA shit," she begins. "When my dad starts cracking his knuckles and talking about how he trained as a kickboxer for twenty years, don't show any signs of weakness. But if he gets his gun out of the hall closet, run."

Silence fills the car for a few moments until a high-pitch,

screeching noise hits my ears and I realize my fingers are still clutched tightly to the key in the ignition and I've continued to turn it in a daze even though it started twenty seconds ago.

"Heh, heh," I laugh uncomfortably, yanking my hand away from the key to clutch the steering wheel. "That's hilarious, Molly. Good work trying to scare me out of doing this."

She laughs as I put the car in gear and pull out of the parking lot, her laughter letting me know she really *was* kidding and her father isn't going to try and kill me.

"You can't blame me for trying," she says with a shrug as I pull out into traffic and head in the direction she points. "My dad's never taken a kickboxing class in his life, so you don't have to worry about that."

Well, that's good to know. If I couldn't fight that little shit, Tommy Knittle, there's no way I could take on a pissed off father who thinks I knocked up his little girl. I'm a baker, not a fighter.

We both share a laugh until she suddenly stops and looks over at me. "But seriously, you can run, right? Because he really does have a gun."

I can still bake with a gunshot wound, right?

Chapter 5
– Thug Mug –
Molly

As Marco follows my directions home, I throw out a few random facts about my family on the way, doing my best not to freak him out too much. I mean, aside from the whole gun thing, but I feel like I would have done him a disservice by leaving that part out. It's bad enough I let him think I was pregnant, even if was only for thirty minutes tops before my conscience got the best of me. I don't want him to be completely blindsided by my family when he's doing something so amazing for me, but maybe I said too much. He stopped talking and started looking like he might throw up about ten miles ago. Maybe telling him about how my Uncle Drew and Aunt Jenny never shut up about their sex life is where I lost him. Or it could have been when I tried to explain what a Brony is and promised him I'd never let Ava and her boyfriend Tyler force him to wear a horse tail. It was probably when I said that stupid shit about not liking PDA. Normally, I cringe if a guy tries to kiss me or hold my hand in public, but when Marco does it I want to rip his clothes off. Which is why it's probably for the best that he stop doing it altogether. My family doesn't need another reason to be freaked out.

"Turn left at the next stop sign," I tell him, twisting my neck to stare at his profile as he flips on the blinker and slows to a stop.

He's so good looking it's almost sickening. With his Italian genes that give him a gorgeous olive complexion, thick dark brown hair he keeps short on the sides with a messy spike on top, and so many muscles it's a wonder he doesn't bust out of every shirt he puts on, it's very hard not to drool in his presence. The fact that he told me he *likes* me should make me feel better that my crush isn't one-sided, but it just makes everything worse. It makes me act like a *girl* around him – a stupid, giggly, shy girl who forgets how to speak when he smiles at her. I might be known as the quiet one in the family, but I've never been shy until I met Marco Desoto. Now, not only do I have to worry about what's going to happen with my family in the next couple of weeks and if I'll be able to pull this whole thing off, I have to worry about Marco witnessing all of it and hoping he still likes me when it's over.

My phone vibrates in my hand and I stop gawking at Marco long enough to look down and see I have a Facebook notification. Opening the app, I laugh out loud when I see what the notification says and who it's from.

"What's so funny?" Marco asks, taking his eyes off the road long enough to see that I'm looking at my phone.

Since he's finally talking again, and no longer looks like he's going to yak all over the dashboard, I figure I might as well share this with him and give him a good laugh to ease the tension of what's about to happen.

"So, remember that douchebag I mentioned at the diner? Alfanso D., the supposed cookbook author? I called him out in front of all of his adoring fans, and he just replied to my comment."

"HE WHAT?!" Marco shouts, the car swerving off the berm and onto the gravel before he hastily rights the wheel and gets us back onto the road.

He gives me a quick look of apology and mutters something about a cat in the road before continuing. "There's no way he replied. Are you sure? Maybe you're confused."

I laugh, wondering why the hell he looks so freaked out when we're not even talking about my family, but some idiot on Facebook.

"I'm definitely not confused, and yes, I'm sure he replied. Here, listen to this," I tell him, clearing my throat and reading the pathetic comment. "'Dearest Molly, I am deeply sorry if anything I said angered you. Please accept my apology and know I will do my best not to make such offensive comments going forward.'"

It's even funnier reading it out loud so I do it one more time, but make my voice high-pitch and very feminine this time.

"There's no way this guy wrote that thing himself. I bet the comment I made about cutting the cord from his mommy made him go running right to the poor woman and he made *her* type this," I chuckle.

"His mother tries to text people using the TV remote. I doubt she'd know her way around Facebook," Marco mutters.

I look at him questioningly and he laughs. "I mean, I'm *assuming* that's how his mother is. You know, because he's a douchebag and all that…"

Figuring he's probably right and that the mother of Alfanso Douchebag has got to be as dumb as *he* is, I point out the next street Marco needs to turn down and which house is mine before looking back at my phone.

"He even put a heart and smiley face emoji at the end of his reply. How sad is that?" I ask. "This guy definitely has a small penis. Or no penis at all."

Marco pulls the car to the curb, mumbling under his breath so quietly I can barely hear what he says. The only words I catch are *anaconda penis* and something about *sisters wishing they'd never been born*, but before I can ask him to repeat himself, I look up and realize we're in front of my house. My hands start to sweat and my stomach flip-flops all over the place as he turns off the ignition and we sit in silence.

"Deep breaths, it's going to be fine," Marco reassures me as he pockets his keys. "I'm going to be right here the whole time. You're going to do great, they're going to believe every word you say, and they're going to surprise you by being happy and supportive and making this a hell of a lot easier on you."

I do what he says and take a few deep, calming breaths. I just need to keep my eye on the prize. A whole new set of baking utensils, a KitchenAid mixer, and ten percent of Charlotte and Gavin's wedding money. That will be more than enough for a deposit on my own apartment so I can move out of my parent's home and finally have some privacy. Privacy that will hopefully include a lot of naked time with the man next to me, as long as he hasn't changed his name and fled the country after dealing with my insane family for the next few weeks.

"And if things start to heat up, I'll just tell them about my incredibly huge penis, and how I'm without a doubt decent, dependable, desirable, daring and delicious," he says with a smile, leaning across the console to give me a quick peck on the cheek.

He's out of the car and around to my side, holding my door open for me before I can do something stupid like cradle my cheek in my hand and vow to never wash it again after he kissed it.

"Didn't I tell you to stop doing stuff like that?" I growl, pretending like I'm annoyed instead of two seconds away from asking him to take his pants off on the front lawn.

"Well, stop having such a kissable cheek then," he replies easily.

Marco continues to tell me how everything will be fine as we make our way up the sidewalk and onto the porch. I start to feel a bit more confident until I open the front door. The quiet peacefulness of the neighborhood outside is immediately ruined as we step into the foyer and the sounds of screaming, arguing, and cursing coming from the living room explode through the house.

"What in the hell?" I murmur as I start to move down the hall to the direction of the noise, the sound of Marco's shoes on the hardwood echoing behind me as he quietly follows.

When we're a few feet from the living room and the noise has reached ear-piercing level, Charlotte suddenly flies out of the room and around the corner, sliding across the floor in her stocking feet and quickly latching onto my arms to stop herself from slamming into me.

"What is going on in there?" I ask her when I can finally make out one of the shouting voices and it's my mother's, who just told someone to *"Shut the fuck up before I fucking make you shut the fucking fuck up, you fucking fuck!"*

Not her cleverest of curses, but certainly not one I haven't heard before.

"What are you doing here?" Charlotte whispers frantically. "I sent you a text! Didn't you get my text?!"

The shouting in the other room goes back to blending all together into one big noise as I pull my phone out of my back pocket and see I did indeed miss a text from Charlotte.

"Sorry, we were talking on the ride over and I missed it. Oh my gosh, wait until I tell you about the douchebag who—" I stop mid sentence when I open up the missed text and see what has Charlotte in such a panic and World War III happening in our living room.

THEY KNOW! OMG THEY KNOW! TXT ME ASAP!

I look up at Charlotte in sympathy and awkwardly pat her shoulder. "I'm sorry. Obviously the adults aren't taking it very well, but what did Gavin say? Are you guys okay?"

She winces and shakes her head back and forth. "No! They know about YOU, not about me!"

"Would you guys just shut the hell up so I can think? Drew, go get my gun. And the brass knuckles. Oh, for fuck's sake, don't look at me like that. A coffee cup with brass knuckles as the handle does too count as actual brass knuckles, so you can fuck right off."

My dad's voice is loud and clear over everyone else's this time, and I hear Marco whimper softly behind me. I wish I had time to remind him again that my dad's bark is usually worse than his bite, but I have more pressing concerns right now.

"What do you mean they know? How in the hell did they find out?" I whisper-shout as Charlotte suddenly realizes Marco is standing behind me.

Her eyes widen and she not-so-subtly jerks her head in his direction before moving her face closer to mine.

"Oes-day e-hay now-kay?" she mumbles, still shooting worried glances over my shoulder.

"*Does he know?*" Marco asks in confusion. "Does who know what?"

Charlotte gasps. "He knew what I said!"

"You spoke in Pig Latin, Charlotte," I say with a roll of my eyes. "That's not exactly a foreign language no one understands. And yes, he knows everything."

She clutches my upper arms tightly, jerking my body with each of her words. "Why would you tell him?! Before you know it, the whole world will know!"

"I am not afraid to smack a pregnant chick, so let go of my arms," I threaten through my gritted teeth, shrugging out of her tight hold on me. "In case you're forgetting, this is my life too, and I will tell whomever I want, especially the guy agreeing to be your baby's fake baby daddy that I'm now pretending to carry."

Can this get anymore confusing???

"Can we get back to a more pressing matter right now?" I continue once Charlotte has the decency to look sorry for being an asshole to someone going through a hell of a lot of trouble to help save her marriage. "How did mom and dad find out already?"

Charlotte winces and shrugs.

"I told Gavin not to say anything, but I guess he mentioned it to Tyler, and you know Tyler can't keep his mouth shut so he told Ava and she called mom and dad, thinking they already knew!" Charlotte quickly spits the words out in one breath. "But hey, look at it this way, at least you don't have to come right out and tell them, and that's the worst part!"

A bright smile lights up her face, and if she wasn't pregnant, I'd punch her right in the ovaries.

"Really, Charlotte? THAT'S the worst part?" I scoff. "Do you even hear the shit coming out of that room right now?"

"I don't care if it's been a while and I am NOT too old for Fight Club," my mother yells at someone. *"Claire, get over here and punch me in the stomach so I can get warmed up for that asshole responsible for this shit."*

My eyes widen in fear. I've heard stories about my mom and Aunt Claire's Fight Club and it isn't pretty. Forget having Marco fear my dad's gun, he really needs to fear my mother's fists.

"It will be fine once you get in there and tell them everything," Charlotte reassures me. "They still think you got pregnant by a loser who walked away. I tried explaining how that was a misunderstanding, but they won't stop screaming long enough to listen to me."

Charlotte looks over my shoulder and smiles. "Besides, I'm sure as soon as they meet Marco and see how sweet and nice he is, they'll forget all about wanting to kill him."

Marco puts his hands on my hips and his face next to my ear, the heat from his body against my back making my brain short-circuit.

"So, I'm rethinking that whole talk-about-my-huge-penis idea, and I've decided crying might be the best way to go," he informs me. "They wouldn't hit a guy who's crying, right?"

Sounds of a scuffle and something falling off a table and thumping to the floor comes from the living room.

"Are you CRYING? There's no crying in Fight Club!" my mother yells.

"That HURT, you dick-nose slut-box! I HAD CANCER!" Aunt Claire responds.

"Oh, fuck right off! You HAD cancer, you don't have it anymore and you

should be able to take a punch, you pussy!" my mother shouts back.

Marco gasps and his hands fall from my hips. "Jesus Christ. They hit people with cancer? I'm a dead man."

He starts pacing nervously behind me and I ignore him, strapping on the set of balls I'm going to need to make it through this without killing my sister.

"Marco, what's the going rate for a convection rack oven?" I ask, talk of anything that involves baking taking his mind off of his impending doom.

He stops pacing and comes to stand next to me, looking down at me while he contemplates my question as Charlotte looks back and forth between us in confusion.

"For a good rack oven? I'd say around three grand, give or take," he tells me as I look back at Charlotte and put my hands on my hips.

"All the baking utensils at the shower, the KitchenAid mixer, ten percent of your wedding profits, AND a three thousand dollar bonus that you will hand over before you leave here tonight," I demand.

Marco whistles and Charlotte's narrows her eyes at me.

"Three thousand? Are you kidding me? Where in the hell am I supposed to get three thousand dollars TODAY?" Charlotte asks in irritation.

"Hey, Marco, how much do you think an ice sculpture of a heart with two doves kissing on top of it costs?" I ask casually.

Charlotte gasps and her hand flies up to her chest. "You wouldn't?!"

I've heard Charlotte and my mom talking about that stupid ice sculpture for months and how proud Charlotte was that she saved the money herself so our parents would have one less thing to pay for.

"Would you rather have a block of ice at your reception that people are going to dare each other to lick all night long after they start drinking, or a reception that actually has a groom in attendance who didn't freak out about being a father and head for the hills?" I demand.

"What kind of wedding receptions have *you* been attending lately?" Marco asks in wonder.

Charlotte stomps her foot and crosses her arms in front of her with an angry huff. "FINE! I'll write you a check later. But I don't want to hear one complaint out of you for the next four weeks."

I make a crisscross over my heart with my finger and then hold my hand up. "Cross my heart. I'll be a better fake pregnant girl than a slutty college co-ed trying to trap her boyfriend into not breaking up with her."

Charlotte rolls her eyes, turns and stomps back into the chaos of the living room.

"If this works and we both make it out alive in a month, you can have all that extra stuff she promised me. It's the least you deserve for not running right back out the door as soon as we got in here," I tell Marco as he tries to grab my hand, but I quickly jerk it away and roll my eyes at him as we head towards the shouting. "I was going to use the extra money to get an apartment, but I don't care about ever moving out of this house as long as I have that rack oven."

Marco laughs as we pause in the doorway of the living room and takes in the scene in front of us. My mom and Aunt Claire are over by the couch trading punches to the stomach, Uncle Drew is sitting on the couch staring at them with a bowl of popcorn in his lap, Aunt Jenny is sitting on the arm of the couch filing her nails, and Uncle Carter is pacing in front of the fireplace. I find my dad sitting in a chair next to the fireplace, holding his hand out in front of him and admiring the brass knuckle coffee mug hanging from his fingers that says "Thug Mug" on it.

"If I'm still breathing in the next twenty minutes, you can keep it all," Marco whispers, finally responding to my offer of letting him have everything I'd negotiated from Charlotte. "The only thing I want in return is a promise that whatever happens at the end of these four weeks, you'll keep an open mind no matter what I say to you."

His words confuse me, but I'm so happy and shocked he still wants to go through with this that nothing else matters right now.

"I'd also like for you to remember at the end of these four weeks how brave it was of me to take a bullet for you and your unborn fake baby," he finishes, flashing me that damn dimpled smile that turns me into an idiot.

Instead of blushing and giggling, I go with the snark that makes me comfortable.

"No one is going to shoot you," I whisper back to him with another roll of my eyes.

"Fine, maybe I won't be taking a bullet tonight," he concedes, "but I'm pretty sure your dad plans on shoving that Thug Mug into my skull, and I can guarantee you it's not going to be pleasant."

I glare at Marco and his dramatics, refusing to let him know that everything he says just makes him look even more adorable and sweet in my eyes. I take another glance around the room, realizing we still haven't been spotted in the doorway when Gavin suddenly jumps out from the other side of the wall where he must've been lurking. A flash of panic rushes through me, wondering if he overheard Marco's comment about my unborn fake baby, but it's pretty clear Gavin is still in the dark as soon as he opens his mouth.

"So, this is the guy," Gavin states loudly, punching his fist repeatedly into his opposite palm as he tries to look intimidating.

His voice causes every head in the room to jerk in our direction, including my mother's, which unfortunately happens at the exact moment whens Aunt Claire pulls her arm back and slams her fist into mom's stomach.

"Wow! That was a nice roundhouse punch, Mrs. Gilmore!" Marco shouts happily across the room as my mother clutches her waist and drops to her knees.

"Roundhouse *kick*, left hook *punch*!" I remind him out of the corner of my mouth. "And the woman jumping up and down in victory is *not* my mother. The one on the floor groaning in pain is!"

Marco winces as my mother starts crawling on all fours across the room towards us, smacking Charlotte's hand away when she rushes over to her and tries to help her up.

Leaning closer to Marco's side, I figure it's probably best to just introduce him and get it over with, and quickly, before my mother makes it over to us and starts biting his ankles or something.

"Everyone, I'd like you to meet my…um…" I pause in a panic, realizing Marco and I never discussed what he'd be in this whole charade. Friend, boyfriend, nice guy who got me pretend pregnant who doesn't want a relationship, but wants to be in the pretend baby's life?

"Boyfriend," Marco finishes, smiling down at me. "I'm Molly's boyfriend."

Gavin continues punching his palm while he looks Marco over from head to toe. "And does this *boyfriend* have a name?"

Tearing my eyes away from Marco's sweet smile, I glare at Gavin and send him a silent warning to back the fuck down because no one is going to believe he could beat up a guy twice his size, even if the poor guy keeps confusing fight terms.

"Yes, he has a name," I inform Gavin through clenched teeth before looking away from him to address the rest of the room.

I paste a happy smile on my face and point in Marco's direction. "Everyone, this is Marco."

Uncle Drew jumps up from the couch so fast that his bowl of popcorn goes flying, dumping the entire thing all over the floor. He kicks the bowl and some of the popcorn out of the way to bounce back and forth on the balls of his feet.

"Honey, do you have to pee?" Aunt Jenny asks as she gets up from the arm of the couch and puts a worried hand on his elbow.

"I'm sorry, I'm usually better prepared for situations like this," Uncle Drew mutters, ignoring my aunt and smiling so big and with so much excitement he looks like a kid on Christmas morning. "Could you just tell us what his name is, one more time?"

Marco and I share a confused look, but I just shrug. I stopped trying to figure out my Uncle Drew a long time ago, and really, he'll be the easiest person in this room to deal with, so I don't even care about the point of this right now.

I give Marco's arm a squeeze to let him know it's okay to speak and unfortunately, he does.

"Marco."

"POLO!" Uncle Drew screams, throwing both of his arms up in victory. "Oh, my God, this is the best day EVER!"

Everyone turns and shoots him a dirty look. He drops his arms, bends down, and grabs a handful of spilled popcorn from the floor, shoving it into his mouth as he stands back up.

"You know, without the whole *Molly-is-knocked-up-by-some-dude-we've-never-met-before* thing," Uncle Drew says with a shrug as he licks popcorn salt from his fingers.

Chapter 6

— Cream Puff Balls —
Marco

"SO, ANYWAY, THIS is my boyfriend, Marco—"

"POLO!" the guy munching on popcorn shouts again, cutting her off.

I try not to roll my eyes because going by the description Molly gave me in the car, I'm guessing he's her Uncle Drew, and after what she told me he can do with a cheese grater, waffle iron, and a two pound bag of Skittles, I'm thinking he could be a lot of help with this next cookbook. Also, it's hard to be irritated when my penis is happy after hearing Molly call me her boyfriend. It's too conflicting and it's always best to go with whatever emotion my penis wants, and my penis wants me to be happy, dammit.

Molly grabs my arm and starts squeezing it so hard I'm not sure if it means I should speak or let her do the talking for now. I'm too busy watching her mother continue to crawl across the floor with her hair draped down over her face like that freaky little girl in the movie *The Ring*, while eyeing the coffee mug in her dad's hands that he's now puffing his breath on and then buffing against his chest. I'm sure it will feel so much better smashing into my skull if it shines.

"Desoto," Molly continues, giving them my last name and wisely ignoring her Uncle Drew. "We've been dating for..."

"Six months," I finish for her when she pauses, figuring six months sounds like a good number. Not too short where they'll think I defiled their little girl on the first date, and not too long where they'll think we're in a really serious relationship and drag us to the courthouse, demanding we get married immediately.

"Oh, aren't they just the cutest thing, finishing each other's sentences like that?!" Charlotte asks happily, trying to get everyone's minds off of all the different ways they could kill me and make it look like an accident.

The woman I mistook for Molly's mother walks across the room, sidestepping the real Mrs. Gilmore as she pauses on her hands and knees in the middle of the room to catch her breath from all that crawling.

She stands in front of me and holds out her hand. "I'm Claire Ellis, Molly's aunt. It's nice to meet you, Marco."

"POLO!" Uncle Drew shouts again and the room lets out a collective groan. "I'm sorry! I just can't help myself. It's like a sickness."

Aunt Claire gives me an apologetic smile and a quick reassuring squeeze of my hand before letting go. She seems really sweet and nice and not at all scary like Molly warned me in the car. Some of the tension immediately leaves my body, and I decide the best course of action right now is to suck up to someone who seems to be on my side and hopefully, the rest of these people will follow.

"Claire Ellis," I repeat, returning her smile. "I thought you looked familiar. I can't believe Molly never told me she had such a famous and talented aunt."

I quickly realize I'm on the right track when Molly's death grip on my arm loosens and I see the appreciative smile on her aunt's face. I don't even have to pretend how cool it is to find out Molly is related to THE Claire Ellis. We use several of her recipes in our classes at school, and there's even a chapter in one of the first-year textbooks on business management about how she went from being a single mother and waitress to co-owning one of the largest business chains in the United States.

"You're one of the reasons I became a pastry chef," I boast proudly, hoping it'll win me more brownie points. "My mother bought me your first cookbook for Christmas, I can't even remember how long ago now, and your tip about chilling eggs before separating them changed my life."

She laughs, her smile widening as she listens and basks in the glory of every compliment I throw at her like it's my job.

"That is so sweet of you to say," Claire tells me before giving Molly a wink. "Handsome, a pastry chef, *and* an outstanding suck-up. Looks like you picked a good one, Molls."

Molly rests her cheek against my shoulder, forgetting about her no PDA rule, and I can practically feel the happiness and pride radiating off of her.

Yeah, that's right Mr. Thug Mug over there, I'm good at this shit so pay attention! You too, Mrs. Ankle Biter trying not to have a heart attack on the carpet. Your best friend thinks I'm a good one! Back off, haters, I'm on a roll.

To firmly secure my excellent standing with Molly's Aunt, I give her one last, perfect compliment I know she'll appreciate, holding my hand out to her for another shake to seal the deal.

"Seriously, though. It's an honor to meet you, ma'am."

There's a gasp from someone in the room, but I have no idea who it came from or why.

"Awwwww, shit," Molly mutters, lifting her head from my shoulder.

The guy standing to the side, who I think is Gavin and just moments ago looked like he wanted to pummel my face, suddenly looks like he fears for his life as he begins backing away. With a quick glance around, I realize *everyone* has backed away as far as possible and they're all studying different objects in the room like they've never seen them before. Uncle Drew has dropped to the ground and rolled under the coffee table to stare at the underside of the damn thing, and even Molly's dad has his head stuck up the chimney, looking all around the inside like he expects to find a nest of birds in there.

When my eyes make it back to Molly's aunt's face, I realize the smile is completely gone and I'm still standing here holding my hand out that she's refusing to take for some reason.

What in the hell did I do wrong?

"Forget everything I said about my dad," Molly whispers. "You should probably start running now."

Right when I start to drop my hand and apologize for God-knows-what, Claire's smile suddenly reappears and she grabs my hand, squeezing it so hard I can feel my bones pop and rub together. I start to wonder if I imagined what just happened when Claire yanks me towards her so forcefully that I stumble and catch myself right before I slam into her.

"Wow, you are curiously strong," I mutter as she leans her face so close to mine I can count each individual eye lash.

"You seem like a nice guy, Marco—"

"POLO!" Uncle Drew shouts from under the coffee table.

Claire continues in a low, threatening voice, like she didn't even hear him. "But if you ever call me *ma'am* again, I will chop off your testicles and use them as cream puffs."

My formerly happy penis shrivels up in fear, taking my balls with him.

Claire gives me a big smile that no longer comforts me, and I have a feeling I'll be seeing this smile in my nightmares in the coming days, waking up in a cold sweat and clutching my balls.

She drops my hand and turns away, walking over to Molly's mom. "Get up, fuck-face. I didn't hit you that hard."

Claire grabs Molly's mom's elbow and hauls her up from the floor.

"Kiss my ass, twat-licker!" her mom replies, yanking her arm out of Claire's grasp, pushing her hair out of her face and straightening her clothes. "I'll have you know I got carded buying wine the other day. The cashier told me he thought for sure I was only twenty."

Claire snorts. "Yeah, maybe in dog years. Don't worry, as soon as I buy you a *Worlds Greatest Nana* sweatshirt, no one will ever mistake you for being anything but old as fuck."

Right when I think I can relax and have a few seconds without any attention on me while these two are busy bickering, everyone in the room suddenly grows balls again, crawling out from under tables and pulling their heads out of chimneys to give me the evil-eye now that Claire has mentioned the elephant in the room.

"Wait, did we decide on Nana, Granny, or Mee-Maw?" Claire asks, poking the bear that is Molly's mom even harder. "Personally, I think Granny suits you. Granny Liz has a nice ring to it."

Newly-crowned Granny Liz sticks her finger right in Great-Aunt Claire's face, glaring at her without saying anything for a few seconds.

"I'll deal with you later," she finally threatens with a growl, flicking the tip of Claire's nose before turning and stalking across the room to stand in front of me.

She crosses her arms over her chest and taps her foot against the ground, obviously waiting for me to speak first. After the mistake I made with Aunt Claire, I know I need to step my game up the next time I open my mouth. This is Molly's *mom*. I cannot piss off the mother of the woman I want to date or say anything stupid that will come back to haunt me even after everyone finds out the truth.

Be smart, be cool. You've totally got this, Marco.

"You're really pretty and young and don't look like a grandma at all. I'm sorry I made you a grandma when you're so young and pretty and did I mention young? It was an accident, I swear. I mean, no, not an accident because this is kind of a happy thing and an accident is usually a bad thing where people die or bleed profusely and well, I guess there will probably be blood from what I remember of those high school health class videos but I'm pretty sure no one will die unless you or your husband decide to kill me and can I just say if I go missing my family would probably notice when I didn't show up for Sunday dinner and if I miss a Sunday dinner, my mother would find where you buried my body and dig it up just to kill me again for missing dinner. Please, please don't kill me and then make my mother kill me again because she'll probably use a wooden spoon to beat me and that kind of thing will take a really long time to kill me and I don't do very well with pain and—"

I feel a smack against the back of my head, cutting off the shit I couldn't stop spewing, and I jump in fear wondering if my mother is somehow here and I really am about to die.

"I have a big penis, and I think I'm going to cry," I mumble.

That earns me another smack to the back of my head and I realize Molly is the one channeling my mother when this time, she adds a threat to the smack.

"Stop talking. Please, for the love of GOD, stop talking," she whispers loudly.

"Mom, I'm so sorry for—"

Molly doesn't have a chance to finish her apology because her mother suddenly bursts into tears, moves away from me and wraps her arms around her daughter.

"I love you, Molls. Everything is going to be okay, even if you've been impregnated by an idiot," her mother sniffles, rocking them both back and forth. "At least he's pretty and you'll have a pretty baby."

I feel like I should take offense to that statement, but I wisely keep my mouth shut this time since I'm still feeling lightheaded after that long, run-on sentence of pure dog shit.

"So, is it okay for me to be happy about this now?" the woman who I guess to be Aunt Jenny shouts from across the room.

I'm assuming that's Aunt Jenny since Molly told me a little bit about the woman in the car, and judging by the fact that she's the only one in the room still pretending to be engrossed in something else, and that something else being a spot on the wall she's had her nose pressed up against since I first made the mistake of using the word *ma'am* with Aunt Claire, I'm going to go out on a limb here and say I'm right.

"I can't handle all of the yelling and fighting, it's messing with my Aurora," she complains, turning away from the wall and rubbing her nose.

"I think you mean *aura*," Charlotte informs her.

"No, it's *Aurora*. She's the one in charge of my chalks, which are the centers of spiritual power in my body. If Aurora is upset, all of my chalks are upset, and then my day is just ruined. *Aura*," she scoffs. "That's not even the name of a real person, Charlotte."

Yep, that's definitely Aunt Jenny.

"Get used to it, pretty boy," Molly's mom advises as she continues holding tightly to her daughter, but finally gives me a smile. "It's best to just let Jenny talk. She'll tire herself out eventually."

I let out a sigh of relief, hoping she's forgiven me for everything I said and what I allegedly but not really did to her daughter, praying it will help with her husband, who has gone back to shining his Thug Mug as he casually saunters over to one of the windows and glances outside.

"That your car out there parked by the curb?" he finally speaks without turning around.

Molly and her mother move out of their embrace, but keep one arm around each other's waist as they look over at Molly's father.

"Um, yes. Yes, sir, it is," I reply, hoping to God he doesn't have the same aversion to *sir* that Aunt Claire has to *ma'am*.

"GT Mustang Fastback, manual transmission with a five-point-oh-liter V6 engine?" he asks quietly.

The man definitely knows his cars and described my baby to a T just by looking at her parked on the street. I saved up for two years to buy that car and she is the most important thing in my life, after my mother and sisters, of course. Oh, and I guess this pretend baby that I'm the pretend father of. That should probably go somewhere towards the top of the list I suppose.

"That's correct, sir," I confirm, starting to get a little nervous that he might be having thoughts about bashing in my car's skull instead of my own.

He finally turns away from the window and thankfully sets the Thug Mug down on the table next to the couch.

"Drew, Carter, how about we take Marco—"

"POLO!" Drew quickly screams happily.

Molly's dad purses his lips in annoyance at the interruption, letting out a sigh before continuing.

"How about we take Marco-I-Swear-To-Fuck-If-You-Say-Polo-One-More-Fucking-Time-I-Will-Shove-My-Foot-Up-Your-Ass, for a little drive?" he asks, glaring at Drew as he turns my name into one long curse word.

"Jim, everything's fine, honey," Molly's mom tells him. "There's no need to do anything stupid."

Jim smiles at her. "We're not going to do anything stupid. Are we, boys?"

Drew and Carter walk up to either side of him and all three of them smile at me. Three evil smiles that don't quite reach their eyes and obviously scream, "We're going to fuck this Marco Polo asshole up until his face looks like raw hamburger meat and he no longer has the use of his legs."

What the hell am I doing? Is some hot chick I've fantasized about really worth all of this? I can't believe I actually thought MY family was crazy. They look like the damn Brady Bunch compared to these people.

I look away from the evil triplets long enough to glance at Molly. Her smile is so big it takes my breath away and that's all it takes for me to realize she's worth it. No woman has ever made me want to jump through hoops just to get her to smile. I've never felt so tied up in knots around anyone like I feel whenever Molly looks at me.

Call it a gut feeling, call it plain old stupidity, but whatever it is, I'm not about to give up now. I knew the moment she told me she wasn't really pregnant and I thought my heart would burst out of my chest that I would do whatever it takes to see where this thing goes. I want to know everything about her, even if it means dealing with her insane family. What's a little blood in my urine and drinking my food through a straw as long as she's there to give me sponge baths?

"Keys?" Drew asks, holding his hands out.

I tell myself everything will work out in the end as I pull the keys to my baby out of my front pocket and toss them across the room to Drew. As soon as he catches them, he runs towards me, ramming into my shoulder as he races through the doorway of the living room and down the hall behind us.

"SHOTGUN, BITCHES!" he shouts right as the front door slams closed behind him.

"Carter, don't you *dare* let him shoot any guns while he's driving!" Jenny warns.

Carter walks over to her and pats her on the head like a puppy without saying anything. He then makes his way to Claire, giving her a kiss on the cheek.

"Don't wait up, honey," he tells her with a smile as she runs her palms down the front of his chest.

"Please try not to get any blood on this shirt. Blood stains are such a bitch to get out," she informs him with a sigh.

Everyone seems to think this is funny and they all laugh. I don't find this funny at all. It's so NOT funny that I think a little pee might have come out of me.

Carter casually sticks his hands in his pockets and whistles jovially as he too rams his shoulder into mine when he walks through the doorway and down the hall to the front door.

Molly pulls away from her mother and rushes in front of me when her father starts to make his way in this direction, and there's no sense in denying it, I'm pretty positive I'm going to pee my pants.

"Daddy, don't hurt him," she warns, blocking him from me and throwing both her hands up in the air to stop him from coming any closer.

"I'm not going to hurt him, Molls," he promises softly with a smile that's faker than the baby I didn't knock Molly up with. "Marco Polo here has nothing to worry about, aside from the fact that the man who currently has the keys to his brand new Mustang felt the need to call shotgun just to make sure he sat in the front seat."

I forget all about my own well-being and hope my car insurance policy covers three lunatics who purposefully slam a vehicle into every tree they encounter before shoving it over a cliff.

Jim kisses the top of Molly's head, lingering there for a few seconds before telling her softly that he loves her no matter what. Charlotte starts sobbing loudly from across the room, breaking up the heartfelt moment with huge sniffles and gasping breaths.

When Jim pulls away from Molly and looks over at Charlotte with a raised eyebrow at her outburst, she quickly puts a big smile on her face and waves away his concerned look.

"It's fine, I'm fine, no big deal," she says with a hiccup and a smile. "I'm just so happy you still love Molly, even if she screwed up and made a huge mistake that will probably ruin her life, because she's going to really need you to love her when she gets fat and ugly and no one else will love her anymore!"

She starts crying louder this time and Gavin rushes across the room to console her. Molly doesn't have any reason to worry about *our* ability to pull this off since it looks like it will only be a matter of time before Charlotte completely cracks and ruins her own stupid plan.

While Molly and her mother are busy watching Charlotte lose her shit, Jim takes that opportunity to sneak around Molly and her attempt to protect me from bodily harm. He slings his arm around my shoulders casually and leads me quietly away from the women and Gavin.

Maybe he really is all talk, just like Molly told me. I mean, he wouldn't really hurt the fake father of his fake unborn grandchild, would he?

"Um, I'm sure you already know this, sir, but my car isn't really big enough for four large men," I tell him as he opens the front door and we walk through it together.

He takes his arm off my shoulders to pat me on the back good-naturedly, giving me a friendly smile.

"Oh, that's not going to be a problem at all," he says with a chuckle.

His good humor is contagious, and I laugh along with him as we make our way down the steps of the front porch and across the lawn to my car. I try not to cringe when I see Drew sitting on the open window ledge of the driver's side door with his feet inside the vehicle and his fists pounding on the roof to the beat of the rock song he has playing loud enough to shake the entire car.

"Let's go, fuckers!" Drew shouts to us over the music. "Happy hour at the strip club is over in thirty minutes, and then I'll have to pay full price for lap dances. Ain't nobody got time for full-price lap dances!"

Jim puts his hand on my shoulder and leads me to the back of the car, rapping his knuckles against the top of the trunk twice, and I see Carter through the back windshield lean in between the two front seats from his spot in the back. The trunk suddenly pops open and Jim gives me another big smile.

"Nope, no trouble at all with this small, fancy car of yours," Jim tells me as he grabs the edge of the trunk lid and lifts it open wide. "We'll all fit just fine because your daughter-impregnating ass is riding in the trunk."

With a hard shove from both hands against my back, I fly face-first into my own trunk and the lid quickly slams shut on top of me.

"Hold on tight, asshole, it's going to be a bumpy ride!" Jim's muffled voice shouts through the closed trunk as he laughs at his own joke.

I hear a car door slam and my engine rumbles to life through the trunk. My body slams against the inside as we take off like a shot, the squeal of tires against the street punctuating how fast we're going.

Molly's mom might not be very good at removing blood stains from clothing, but I hope to God she knows how to get the smell of urine out of the trunk of a car.

Chapter 7

"MOLLY, STOP STARING out the window, he'll be fine. I'm sure your father will wait until after the baby's born to kill him," my mother says with a laugh as I move away from the kitchen window where I've spent the last twenty minutes silently brooding.

"Very funny," I tell her as I lean against the edge of the kitchen sink and watch her rapidly move around the island in the middle of the kitchen. My mom likes to feed people whenever there's a tragedy, and going by the sheer volume of cold cut sandwiches she's been putting together since the guys left, she's preparing for the end of the world.

"It's the least your father can do," she continues as she slathers mustard on sandwich number thirty-seven. "Maybe the baby won't even look like Marco and it turns out to be someone else's. Then he's just gone and killed a man for no reason."

Aunt Claire laughs and I shoot her a dirty look before aiming it in my mother's direction. "Seriously, mom? Did you just insinuate that I'm a slut?"

"If it looks like a slut and quacks like a slut!" Aunt Jenny pipes up from the kitchen table.

"Oh, don't give me that look, young lady," mom warns. "I never said the word *slut*. It's not like you got drunk and knocked up at a frat party and never got the guy's name until four years later."

"Heeeeeeeeey!" Aunt Claire yells, from her seat next to Aunt Jenny.

Mom sets her mustard-covered knife on the counter and glances over at Aunt Claire.

"Really?" she deadpans.

Aunt Claire sighs. "Okay, yeah, that was kind of slutty. Carry on."

Mom goes back to her work, moving from turkey sandwiches to salami.

"I'm just saying, Molly, we don't know this guy, nor did we have any idea you were even dating someone. Forgive me for being a little suspicious about your sexual activity."

I shudder, grabbing the sandwich she just finished and tossed on top of the giant pile. "Please, never say the words *sexual activity* again."

The funniest part about this entire mess is that I have no sexual activity for her to be suspicious of. I wonder if she'd go easier on me if I told her I'm the world's first official pregnant virgin. Well, aside from that whole mother of God thing, but that happened a long time ago, and I'm pretty sure it's a bit more rare in this day and age.

Figuring I should just shovel food in my mouth before I'm tempted to say something I shouldn't, I wrap my lips around the sandwich filled with lettuce, cheese and extra salami, just the way I like it. As soon as my teeth sink into the bread, the sandwich is smacked out of my hand and it goes flying across the kitchen.

"WHAT THE HELL ARE YOU DOING?" Charlotte yells, wiping bread crumbs off of her sandwich-smacking hands.

"What am *I* doing? What are *you* doing? I was going to eat that!" I argue, staring longingly at my sandwich scattered across the floor.

I barely ate two bites of my spaghetti at dinner with Marco earlier because my stomach was tied in knots and every forkful of pasta I tried to choke down threatened to come right back up.

"You can't eat lunchmeat, Molly!" Charlotte scolds with a huff. "Everyone knows you can't eat lunchmeat."

I didn't know I can't eat lunchmeat. Since when did this become a rule around here?

I really think this pregnancy has made my sister lose her mind completely so I grab another sandwich from the pile and ignore her.

"I'm starving. Go away," I mutter.

Charlotte rips the sandwich right out of my hands and starts to shake it in front of my face, meat and lettuce falling out of the bread and onto the counter.

"Pregnant women can't eat lunchmeat. Everyone knows it can cause Listeriosis," Charlotte complains.

"Isn't that the stuff you wash your mouth with?" Aunt Jenny asks.

"Sweet mother of pearl…" Aunt Claire mutters.

Charlotte's face quickly changes from irritation to revulsion as she stares at the parts of the sandwich still clutched in her hand. She swallows thickly, but manages to keep talking. "Lunchmeat is dangerous. And smells. And….smells like…meat."

She stops mid-sentence, shooting a look of panic at me. "You look sick, Molly. Are you going to throw up?"

I look at her like she's as insane as I believe her to be and shake my head. "Uh, no. I'm fine."

"No, you really look sick. You should go to the bathroom right now."

She's still holding the sandwich in her hand, but now she's fisting it into a ball and I can see beads of sweat dotting her forehead.

Awwwww shit.

"You know, now that you mention it, I'm feeling a little pukey," I announce, quickly pressing my hand to my stomach. "Uuughhh, yeah, definitely gonna throw up."

Charlotte nods, still holding the mangled mess of a sandwich in one hand while she grabs my hand with the other. "I should go with you and hold your hair back just in case."

"Yes, yes, wise decision. Wouldn't want to get puke in my hair," I laugh awkwardly before realizing I probably wouldn't be laughing if I really felt like throwing up. I quickly change my laugh to a groan as Charlotte drags me from the kitchen while our mom and aunts stare at us wordlessly.

"Don't use the Listeriosis on the bathroom sink after you throw up, Molly! I have a mint you can use instead," Aunt Jenny shouts after us as we race out of the room and down the hall to the bathroom.

As soon as I shut the door behind us, Charlotte drops to her knees in front of the toilet and tosses not only her cookies, but from the looks of it, everything she's eaten in the past week. I don't know how one person can have so much bile in their body, and now I really am starting to feel sick listening to the sounds that are coming out of her as well as the smell of vomit that quickly fills the small space.

"Oh, my God, what did you eat?!" I complain, covering my nose with my hand.

"The salami! It smells so bad! Like meat!" she cries in between heaves.

"Then why are you still holding it in your hand?!" I screech.

"I DON'T KNOW!" she cries, leaning her head closer to the bowl as more vomit comes flying out.

A knock at the door makes me jump and Charlotte choke in the middle of a gag.

"Everything okay in there?" mom asks softly.

Charlotte groans loudly and I quickly cover it up with an even louder groan.

"UUUUGGHHHHHHH, so sick!" I yell through the door. "Be out in a minute!"

Moving behind Charlotte, I hold my breath while grabbing onto her hair and hold it away from the toilet while she continues throwing up. "You will be done soon, right? Good God, woman. How does someone so small have that much puke in her?!"

She rests her head on the arm draped over the toilet seat and sighs.

"I'll just make you some soup to settle your stomach when you're finished," mom says through the door.

"Oh, no," I whisper as I hear her footsteps moving her away from the bathroom.

"SOUP!" Charlotte wails, moving her head back over the bowl and gagging even harder.

"Don't worry, I'll eat it in another room or something," I promise.

Five minutes later, after Charlotte cleaned herself up while I messed up my hair and splashed water all over myself to look like a recent puke victim, we walk back into the kitchen where my mother has wisely hidden all of the sandwiches and bags of lunchmeat.

"So, no one answered me before when I asked if we can be happy about this now. So, can we?" Aunt Jenny asks.

Mom shrugs and gives me a small smile. "Sure, Jenny. I guess we can be happy about this as long as Molly is happy."

Charlotte wraps her arm around my shoulder and gives me a squeeze. "Molly is very happy. She's just scared and nervous and worried, but she's so happy."

"Thank you for telling us how Molly feels," Mom laughs. "How about we let Molly tell us?"

I stare at everyone dumbly as they wait for me to say something.

"Um, yeah. What she said," I reply with a forced smile.

"Sweet! Pound sign, Molly's pregnant!" Aunt Jenny cheers, holding her fist out for someone to "pound."

"Don't you mean *hashtag*?" Aunt Claire asks.

"No. It's pound sign. Twitter stole it from math," Aunt Jenny replies with a roll of her eyes.

"Wow, I actually can't argue with that," Aunt Claire says with a shrug, giving in and pounding her fist to Aunt Jenny's.

"Alright, who wants chicken noodle soup?" Mom asks happily, holding up a can of Campbell's.

"Oh, God. Molly's going to be sick again!" Charlotte yells, grabbing my hand and dragging me back out of the kitchen.

Chapter 8
– Bag of Dicks –
Marco

"I can't believe I missed half-price lap dances," I hear Drew grumble as I make my way into the house a few minutes after everyone else.

My shoes squeak and squish against the floor as I go, and thankfully, the women seem to be more interested in what Drew is saying than what I look like and I can stand in the doorway of the kitchen unnoticed.

"You guys went to a strip club? Are you kidding me?" Molly's mom complains.

"Do you see stripper glitter on my face? Do I smell like desperation and bad life choices?" Drew asks, pausing to lift his arm & smell his pits. "Wait, don't answer that."

"We didn't go to a strip club; don't worry," Molly's dad reassures her, walking over to the fridge and opening the door. "Ooooh, you made sandwiches!"

I see Charlotte slide against the wall in my direction, quickly covering her mouth when Jim brings the plate, heaping with sandwiches, out of the fridge and sets them in the middle of the island. Gavin moves to her side and puts his arm around her, quietly asking if she's okay.

"The meat," she whispers with a shell-shocked look in her eyes. "Uh, Molly can't stand the smell of meat and she threw up earlier. Seeing the sandwiches again just made me think of all that puke."

I feel a hand on my arm and look away from the couple to see Molly staring at me in confusion.

"Why are you all wet?" she asks, taking in my wrinkled, damp t-shirt I wrung out and put back on and my jeans that are now dripping onto the kitchen floor.

I notice her wet, gnarled mess of hair hanging around her face that is also dripping with water and return her own question. "Why are YOU all wet?"

"She had the meat sweats," Jenny informs me, giving Molly a pat on the back as she walks behind her and over to Drew.

"What the hell are meat sweats?"

Molly winces, pushing a clump of hair out of her eyes. "I really don't want to talk about the meat sweats."

I force myself to keep my eyes off of Charlotte even though I can see out of the corner of them that she's got her back pressed up against a wall next to us, watching her father nervously as he takes a big bite out of a salami sandwich.

"I really like salami, too," Molly mutters sadly before looking back at me. "But seriously, why are you all wet?"

Drew and Carter start laughing as they each grab a sandwich from the insanely large pile from the plate on the counter.

Molly leans in close to me and sniffs. "And why do you kind of smell like pee?"

I groan and throw my hands in the air, shooting an annoyed look at the three men now giggling like little girls. Little asshole girls. "You guys said the smell was gone!"

"It's not our fault you couldn't handle the low pressure hot wax," Drew says through a mouthful of food. "If I can handle a little candle wax on my balls every third Friday, you can handle a hot wax treatment on your undercarriage."

"I really don't want to know what you're talking about, but I'd still like to know why Marco is all wet," Molly informs him, wisely choosing not to comment on the candle wax on the balls subject. I learned much more about Drew's balls tonight than I ever needed to know, thank you very much.

"You can't get clean going through a car wash if you're in the trunk. Obviously riding on the hood made more sense," Jim smirks.

"Jim Gilmore!" Liz scolds.

"What? We had to get the pee smell off of him somehow."

So much for thinking this night couldn't get any more uncomfortable after Drew felt the need to show me the scars on his balls from when he let Jenny shave them.

"Do you want to talk about the pee smell?" Molly asks me.

"Do you want to talk about the meat sweats?" I fire back.

"So, what else did you guys do?" she asks, looking away from me and back to the guys.

"Marco, why don't you take her and the rest of these lovely ladies outside and show them what else we did?" Carter suggests.

I forget about my embarrassment over the whole pee situation and get excited all over again about what we did. Grabbing Molly's hand, I pull her towards the front door while the rest of the women follow behind, leaving the men in the kitchen to stuff their faces.

"Wait until you see it, Molly. It's the coolest thing in the world!"

"It sounds like you had a good time. And there aren't any noticeable bruises on your face, so that's a plus," she tells me.

"Aside from the incident in the trunk that we are never to speak of, and the scalding hot water from the car wash, I had a good time. Although you could've warned me that your Uncle Drew likes to whip his balls out in public."

She shrugs. "He only shows them to people he likes, so that's a good sign."

I press my hand to the small of her back, guiding her outside and down the steps of the front porch, stopping in the yard and pointing proudly to the curb.

"Well, what do you think?"

Molly stares out at the street, my new beauty perfectly spotlighted under one of the blazing street lamps right in front of it.

"What do I think about what?" Molly asks, looking everywhere but at the lovely little lady in front of her house.

"Do you not see what's parked right in front of you?" I ask with a laugh.

"I see a mom van. Where's your Mustang?"

Claire walks around us to check out my new set of wheels with Liz, Jenny, and Charlotte following right behind her. "Oh, my God, did you buy a minivan?"

I scoff and put my hands on my hips.

"It's not a mom van OR a minivan. That is a state-of-the-art, safest thing with four wheels, family car," I announce proudly as the four other women walk around the brand new red, Chrysler Town and Country.

"I repeat, where is your Mustang?" Molly asks, not sounding anywhere near as excited as I thought she'd be.

"The guys told me it wasn't safe or practical for a family man," I explain. "It didn't even have the proper hook-up in the backseat for the six-point harness system car seat or side airbags, and we can't have our baby riding around in a death trap like that."

I realize as soon as the words leave my mouth that I sound crazier than anyone in Molly's family. I'm a twenty-four-year-old single dude helping the woman I want to sleep with fake a pregnancy. It does not require trading in my chick-magnet Mustang for a mom-magnet van, but it was peer-pressure, dammit! I couldn't exactly refuse to trade in the Mustang for a family car with Molly's dad and uncles cracking their knuckles and staring me down. Besides, this thing has plenty of room, and I didn't have to ride in the trunk on the way home.

"Wow, it has built-in DVD players in the seat backs!" Claire shouts to us as she slides open the side passenger door and sticks her head inside.

"Marco, how much alcohol did my dad and uncles give you? Do you feel strange or lightheaded? Is there a tingling in your arms and legs? They could have roofied you," Molly tells me nervously. "Never leave your drink unattended around them, wasn't that one of my warnings on our way over here earlier?"

I laugh, patting her softly on the back. "I'm not drunk and I haven't been roofied. I traded in the Mustang for safety reasons."

"Are you forgetting the one little fact that you aren't going to be a family man?" she whispers. "You don't need a mom-mobile with a six-point whatever or extra air bags. Did they hypnotize you? What's your name? What year is it?"

She leans up on her tip toes and uses the pad of her fingers to pry my eyes open wide so she can stare into them.

Even after the pretend meat sweats or whatever the hell happened to her while I was gone, she still smells like apple pie and I smell like I pissed my pants. Which I will neither confirm nor deny happened after Drew drove to an abandoned parking lot, did a hundred donuts at roughly ninety miles an hour, and then from my fetal position in the trunk, I heard the guys screaming about Drew playing chicken with an oncoming semi and how he'd never be able to jump the gap in the bridge at such a slow speed. How was I supposed to know they were fucking with me when I was trapped in a dark trunk?

"It's not my fault and it happens to everyone!" I shout, realizing I said that out loud by mistake.

"You've definitely been hypnotized," Molly says with a slow shake of her head. "I know it sounds weird, but my Uncle Drew learned how to do it on the Internet. No one believed it until Aunt Jenny volunteered to let him do it to her. Whenever he said the word *moist* she'd bark like a dog and try to shit on the carpet. It wasn't pretty."

She drops her hands from my face and I'm surprised I'm not even shocked by the things I continue to find out about her family at this point. Claire, Jenny, Charlotte, and Liz are all busy looking in the front seat and talking about the GPS and other bells and whistles and luckily can't hear us.

"Is that a car seat in the back?" Molly asks in shock.

"We went to Babies R Us after the dealership and the guys all chipped in. Wasn't that nice of them?" I tell her excitedly as I push the sliding back door open wider. "We went to the fire station after so one of the firemen could properly install it. I had no idea you couldn't just buckle one of those things in and call it a day."

Molly grabs both of my arms and turns me around to face her. "I knew it. My family made you lose your mind. I thought you'd be able to make it out unscathed in four weeks, but I was wrong."

I laugh and shake my head at her. "I know it's crazy, but I didn't lose my mind. That Mustang really was impractical."

"It was not impractical for a single, twenty-four-year-old guy who is NOT going to be a father," she whispers, echoing my earlier thoughts.

"Well, maybe I am going to be a father. I've been thinking about getting a puppy for a while now and I'm going to need something safe to transport him in," I explain.

"I don't think a puppy needs a mom-van," Molly laughs with a shake of her head.

The puppy thing was a stupid, spur-of-the moment answer to try and explain away how crazy I'm behaving just because I'm afraid of a few guys twice my age and twice my size, but hearing her laugh makes me go with it.

"You can't be too safe with puppies, Molly, and stop calling it a mom-van. It's a Town and Country which sounds much more manly," I inform her. "The puppy can be nice and safe while we cruise around town AND he can watch Animal Planet on the built in DVD player that also has a satellite cable hook-up."

Molly stares at me with a smile and I'm not sure if it's because she still thinks I'm crazy or because I did something so *decent* and *dependable* to try and score more points for that dipshit Alfanso D. I know trading in my Mustang is the most insane thing in the world and I probably *have* started losing my mind after only a few hours with the men in Molly's family, but after the first half hour of torture when they finally let me out of the trunk, they taught me a hell of a lot.

Like how having a child is the most important thing you will ever do in your life. And how it makes you grow up fast and changes your entire view on life. How it's scary and nerve wracking and the hardest job you'll ever have, but it's also the most rewarding. I had to grow up a lot after my father died, but I've still spent the last few years refusing to settle down and jumping from one girl to the next because I thought that's what I needed to do to be happy. Spending one day with Molly and her family has made me see there is a lot more to life than that and it makes me want more.

Jesus, maybe I really have gone insane.

"Good choice on the leather seats," Claire says with approval as the women all move out of the front seat and over to us. "Cloth seats are a bitch to get amniotic fluid out of."

"Amni-what?" I ask in confusion.

"Amniotic fluid," Liz repeats. "It's a yellowish liquid that surrounds the baby and gets all over the fucking place when your water breaks. Leather seats will be a plus if it happens while Molly's in the car. You can just wipe the stuff right off."

I nod, my eyes glazing over with thoughts of yellow, pee-like liquid pouring out of someone and getting all over my new seats.

"Plenty of leg room too, in case she goes into labor in the car and you have to pull over on the side of the road and deliver the baby yourself," Claire adds.

Liz nods and it's a good thing Charlotte is standing behind them and they can't see the deer-in-the-headlights look in her eyes.

Claire smacks her hand a couple of times against the side of the van. "This baby definitely has enough room for Molly to spread her legs and push that baby out into your hands. You should probably throw a couple of towels in the back to clean up all the blood and the afterbirth."

"Don't forget the poop," Liz adds. "There's always a chance she'll shit all over the place pushing that thing out."

I know none of these things are really going to happen in my new vehicle, and definitely not to Molly, but that doesn't stop my brain from seeing it all, clear as day and want to run down the street screaming at the top of my lungs.

Charlotte looks like she's going to start crying and it would appear that I might get to see what these meat sweats are, going by the disgusted look on Molly's face as her mother and aunt continue talking about bloody placentas and other things I would've been able to continue living out the rest of my days knowing nothing about, but I need to get out of here. It would probably be best if I go back inside the house and get away from all this womanly talk before I never want to have sex again.

"I think I hear Drew calling my name," I suddenly announce, cutting of Claire when she starts talking about people who eat placentas for the nutrients and vitamins.

Dropping a kiss on Molly's cheek and ignoring the dirty look she shoots me for PDA'ing her, I back away as quickly as I can. She watches me go with a look of annoyance on her face that I'm making an escape while she's stuck out here listening to her aunt rattle off placenta recipes. I realize she'll probably kick my ass for the easy and natural way I kissed her cheek in front of her family, like it was something I do all the time in the six months we've been fake-dating. Just like trading in my Mustang, I know it's crazy, but it feels right. I can't explain how after only spending a few hours with her I feel like I've known her forever instead of just fantasizing about her for two years from a distance. I didn't even think about kissing her cheek, I just did it automatically, her aversion to public displays of affection be damned.

When I'm halfway across the yard and the older women start talking again, I see Molly mutter the words *"chicken shit,"* and I laugh, giving her a wink before turning around and jogging up the steps and back into the house.

After all the gross childbirth talk and girly feelings I've been having all evening, I need some intelligent, manly conversation. I need to talk about something intellectual and macho like politics or war.

"You cannot justify your reasoning because of an article you read online," I hear Carter complain as I enter the house and head towards the living room where the voices are traveling from.

"The facts are right in front of you, man. You can't shut down my theory just because you don't share the same views as I do," Jim argues.

Perfect! Just what I was looking for. A nice, civilized manly discussion that has nothing to do with the goo that comes out of a woman when she gives birth or anything else that will make me vomit.

"I'm telling you, I've seen the stats and maybe I'm in the minority here, but I'm going to have to side with Carter on this one," Drew says with a sigh as I enter the room and find them seated around the coffee table.

"Perfect timing, Marco Polo," Drew greets me with a smile. "You can settle this debate once and for all."

I drop into the remaining empty chair and lean forward, resting my elbows on my knees and clasping my hands together between them.

"Lay it on me. What's the topic? Presidential candidates? War climate?" I ask.

Drew looks at me like I've grown two heads. "Uh, no. We're talking dicks."

"Bag of dicks, to be precise," Jim adds.

I sit up slowly, wondering if I should walk back out of the room and pretend like I was never here.

"I'm sure you've heard the expression 'eat a bag of dicks', correct?" Carter questions seriously.

Drew rolls his eyes when I continue to sit here, planning my escape without answering the question.

"You know, like, 'Eat a bag of dicks, you piece of shit!'" Drew yells in an angry voice. "Tell me you've heard it or I'm going to seriously regret giving you the privilege of seeing my amazing balls."

Not wanting him to mention those bald, wrinkly, scarred pieces of flesh again, I nod in agreement. "Yeah, sure. I've heard the phrase. Why?"

"We need you to settle this argument once and for all," Jim states.

"Okaaaaaay," I drag the word out cautiously and a little bit in fear.

"I mean, how big of a bag are we talking here? Like, Ziploc baggie or Hefty garbage bag? Because size really does matter when it comes to eating dicks," Drew states.

"That is false and you know it!" Carter argues. "Eating a bag of dicks is eating a bag of dicks whether you eat ten or a hundred and ten. You're still eating dicks!"

Jim nods, his face a mask of complete seriousness. "And if size really does matter, is this bag of dicks hot-dog-sized dicks, or cocktail-weenie dicks? Because I think I could handle a bag of cocktail weenies, no problem."

"Of course you could, cock sucker," Drew laughs. "We all know how much you like to gobble up those dicks. Nom, nom, nom!"

Carter lifts his hand and silently gives him the finger.

"I think it makes much more sense if people would just say 'Eat a dick', rather than an *entire bag* of dicks," Jim says with a sigh. "It would cut down on so much confusion, and then we wouldn't even be having this debate. Marco, what are your thoughts on the situation?"

I think I'd rather be talking about placentas right now.

Chapter 9

"I'M SORRY, MINIVAN means WHAT? And how do you even know this?" Charlotte asks loudly.

A few people in the waiting room look in our direction and mom shushes us. I lean in closer to Charlotte, speaking as softly as I can.

"When I walked back into the house the other night, I heard Uncle Drew explaining it to Marco. I can't even repeat it, just look it up on Urban Dictionary," I explain.

Of course she immediately pulls her phone out of her purse, goes to that stupid website, and starts reading the definition out loud.

"The act of putting two fingers in the vagina and a fist up the ass. Called the *minivan* because you can fit two in the front and five in the back."

I shudder just imagining it, and Charlotte can't decide between being disgusted along with me or laughing, the noise she makes coming out as some sort of gag-snort-cough that makes everyone look at us again.

"Sorry!" she apologizes loudly. "Just discussing minivans and their amazing rear capacity!"

I smack her in the arm and she tucks her phone back in her purse, still laughing.

"That still doesn't explain why dad, Uncle Carter, and Uncle Drew keep calling Marco, *Mo* and then laughing like idiots the rest of the night," she says in confusion as she turns to face me.

I sigh, thinking about all the abuse Marco took the other night and realizing it's probably why he hasn't called since then.

"Not *Mo*, like the name. M. O. – *M* period, *O* period, for Minivan Operator."

Charlotte giggles and I glance down at my phone instead of punching her for laughing at poor Marco. This is the hundredth time I've checked my phone today and I try not to feel like an idiot for doing so when I don't see any new messages or missed calls. I will not be like one of those stupid girls who powers the phone off and on just to make sure it's working. And not because I already called Charlotte four times in the last half hour and made her call me twice to confirm I can in fact still receive incoming calls, but because I have more dignity than that, dammit.

It's bad enough I have that whole minivan fisting image in my head, now I have to deal with anxiety about not hearing from Marco since the text he sent me yesterday morning, the day after the strangest day of my life that ended with my dad and uncles daring Marco to eat a quart-sized Ziploc bag of hot dogs in under a minute to prove some point I didn't even want to ask about. On top of not hearing from him since he texted me to say he now knew what the meat sweats were and he'd been puking up hot dogs since he got home from my house, I've been forced to go to the doctor to confirm my fake pregnancy.

"I can't believe it's taking this long," Mom complains as she flips through an old magazine. "When I called to make the appointment they told me they had a bunch of cancellations and could get you right in today."

Yes, my wonderful, loving mother took it upon herself to call up the doctor and make an appointment for me without my knowledge, informing me when I woke up this morning that I had fifteen minutes to get dressed and get out the door. Thank God Charlotte answered her phone on the first ring as I raced around my bedroom getting dressed and trying not to panic. She got to the doctor's office before we did and mom only seemed a little bit surprised when I told her I asked Charlotte to come for moral support.

"He'll call, don't worry," Charlotte whispers while I stare in annoyance at my phone.

I quickly shove it into my front pant's pocket and roll my eyes. "I have no idea what you're talking about."

Charlotte snickers. "Nice try. You might be pretty good faking a pregnancy, but you suck faking noninterest in a guy."

I glance nervously at Mom sitting across from us and see she's still engrossed in the magazine, not paying any attention to us or preparing to ask a hundred questions about what we're whispering about. She's got to wonder why Charlotte and I are suddenly spending more time together considering we've never kept it a secret that we haven't been able to stand each other for most of our lives. Even though I've always felt like an outsider with my two sisters and have nothing in common with them, I've always been a little closer to Ava. She has the same sarcastic, brash attitude that I do and it's just easier to talk to her than Charlotte. I have no idea why our mother hasn't asked why Charlotte is the one I called for the supposed moral support today, but I guess I should be glad that it's one less thing I have to lie about.

"I'm not faking noninterest in Marco," I tell Charlotte. "I just don't want to be one of those girls who drops everything for a guy and acts stupid whenever he's around. This isn't exactly how I pictured us together the first time he finally noticed me and it's confusing and weird and I don't like it."

Charlotte laughs softly and shakes her head at me. "I'm pretty sure this is not the first time he's noticed you. He definitely has much stronger feelings for you than you realize. No guy would go through all of the shit he's gone through in one day for a girl he just 'likes'. You need to have more faith in yourself, Molls. You're smart and beautiful and talented. If he hasn't noticed those things long before now, he never would have set foot in Mom and Dad's house the other day, let alone put up with all that torture from Dad and the guys."

I'm pretty sure I still remember the last time my sister said anything this nice to me. I was seven and she was nine; it was the first day of school and mom forced me to wear this frilly pink dress that I hated. Charlotte stared for a few seconds and then said, "It's fine. You don't look *that* gross."

These compliments throw me for a loop, and it's not until Mom gets up from her chair and leans across the coffee table to tap my knee, that I realize the nurse was calling my name.

"Molly Gilmore?"

I raise my hand meekly and the nurse smiles. "You can come on back. You're family is welcome to join you."

Shit! How the hell do we keep Mom out of the room?

Before I can go into a full-blown panic trying to come up with a plausible reason to give my mother on why she needs to be blindfolded and wear earplugs, Charlotte quickly speaks up.

"Mom, if you don't mind, can I go back with Molly alone?" she asks so sweetly that I start to wonder if that baby inside of her has some sort of magical powers. "It's just...I know I haven't been the best sister to her growing up, and I'd really like to do something important like this with her, just the two of us."

Mom practically melts into a puddle of goo right on the floor of the waiting room, her eyes filling with tears as she looks back and forth between the two of us.

"I've been waiting twenty years for you two to stop being assholes to each other and all it took was one of you getting knocked up," she sniffles. "If only getting pregnant when you're a teenager wasn't frowned upon, we could have solved this problem years ago."

The nurse gives her a funny look and Mom rolls her eyes. "Oh, don't judge me. *You* try giving birth to three spawns of Satan who constantly try to kill each other."

With those parting words to the shocked nurse, Mom wipes a stray tear from her cheek and waves us away, sitting back down in her chair and grabbing the magazine she previously tossed onto the coffee table.

Charlotte and I leave her in the waiting room and follow the nurse down the hall. She weighs me on the scale in the hallway and takes my temperature with an ear thermometer before leading us further down the hall, pushing open a door and handing me a small plastic cup with an orange lid.

"I just need you to give us a urine sample. I'll be right over there at the nurse's station so you can bring it out when you're finished," she explains with a smile before looking at Charlotte. "If you'd like to come with me, I can show you to the exam room and you can wait for her to finish."

I quickly grab Charlotte's arm and the cup from the nurse.

"It's okay, she can come in with me. I need her to hold the cup for me," I blurt without thinking.

The nurse gives me a quizzical look, and I laugh nervously. "I'm a little freaked out and my hands are shaking and if I try and hold the cup I'll probably pee all over the place so I need someone with steady hands and Charlotte's are rock steady. She'll make sure the pee goes where it needs to go."

Charlotte nods, confirming my crazy explanation and then pulls me into the bathroom, slamming the door closed in the poor, confused nurse's face.

I hand her the little plastic cup and lean against the wall, bending forward with my hands on my knees to take a few calming breaths while Charlotte goes to work.

"I think I'm going to hyperventilate," I tell her. "Do you think I could go to jail for insurance fraud from filling out all those medical forms when we got here? I can't go to jail; I'd never survive. In theory I feel like I have enough balls to make someone my bitch, but I don't know if I could actually do it. I can make an amazing sugar display, but I don't know if that will translate well when I need to make a toothbrush shank."

I realize I'm rambling and it suddenly occurs to me that I might not be as different from my sisters as I always thought considering I'm acting just as insane as they usually do. None of this makes me feel any better about what is happening right now.

"You're not going to jail. Stop freaking out or you're going to make me freak out, and it's not good for the baby," Charlotte tells me as she flushes the toilet and washes her hands. "Personally, I think you'd make a great badass in jail. You'd have plenty of bitches offering to make toothbrush shanks for you."

I stand up and scowl at her. "You're not helping."

She picks up her cup of pee, walks over to me, and holds it out in front of her.

"Eeeew, get that thing away from me," I complain, scrunching up my nose.

"You have to take it out there to the nurse. Technically, this is your pee," she reminds me.

With a sigh, I tentatively reach out and take the cup from her, trying not to drop it as soon as my hands wrap around it. Charlotte opens the bathroom door and I walk as slowly as I can behind her, holding the cup out as far away from me as possible.

"Oh, my God, it's so warm," I whisper in disgust. "And why does my hand feel wet?"

Charlotte glares at me over her shoulder as we make our way down the hall to the nurse's station.

"I might have dribbled a little down the sides, it's fine," she whispers back to me like it's no big deal.

"I have your pee on my hands?!" I hiss a little too loudly and she stops quickly, almost causing me to slam into her with my pee-covered hands holding her warm cup of pee.

"Will you keep your voice down?" she scolds quietly. "It's just a couple tiny drops of liquid. Just pretend it's water."

"But it's *not* water, it's your warm, wet pee! And it's touching me!" I reply, wondering if I'll ever be able to look at my hand again and not picture Charlotte pissing all over it like a dog marking its territory. "I cook with this hand, and now it's a pee hand! You had one job to do—piss in a fucking cup without getting pee on my hand. This is why we can't have nice things, Charlotte, because you piss all over everything, and now I smell like pee!"

She rolls her eyes and grabs my wrist holding the cup, dragging me the rest of the way down the hall to the waiting nurse. I sigh in relief when the nurse takes the cup from my hand and tells us to head right across the hall to examine room number four, letting me know she'll be in as soon as she processes the urine sample.

I run to the room without saying a word, racing to the sink in the small room and start scrubbing my hand as Charlotte follows me and closes the door behind her.

When I'm satisfied that there are no lingering traces of Charlotte pee on my skin, I dry my hands, and the door opens right as I'm throwing away the paper towel.

"Okay, Molly, I just need you to get fully undressed and put on the paper robe on the exam table," she explains as she walks to the table and starts pulling the stirrups out of their hiding spots inside it.

I shoot a worried look at my sister and she just shrugs, her expression mirroring my own as we watch the nurse move to a side table and start extracting things out of the drawers.

"Um, I thought I'd just be peeing in a cup today," I mutter.

The nurse turns around and Charlotte and I both gasp loudly when we see the world's biggest vibrator in the nurse's hand. And that's saying a lot considering my mother owns one of the largest sex toy stores in the world and I've been around those things since birth. I still have nightmares about Chocolate Thunder.

"What the hell is that for?" I ask, pointing at the huge, white phallic object in her hand that the nurse is busy putting an equally huge condom over top of.

She laughs sympathetically.

"It's an internal ultrasound wand. According to the date of your last period you put on the medical form, you're not very far along in your pregnancy. Ultrasounds done on the stomach won't be very accurate at this point, so the doctor will use this internally to get a better reading," she says with a smile.

"That thing has to go inside me?!" I screech loudly.

"Believe me, it looks much worse than it actually is," she explains. "It's really no different than having sex, maybe just a tad more uncomfortable, but it won't hurt."

I'm willing to do a lot of things for a KitchenAid mixer and money for an apartment, but having a tree stump shoved up my vagina is not one of them.

While I try my best not to hyperventilate again, the nurse finishes setting everything up for the doctor and leaves Charlotte and I alone to wait for him.

"That thing is not going in me, Charlotte," I warn her as soon as the door closes behind the scrub-clad woman. "You better figure something out before the doctor gets in here, or I will lose my shit all over this exam room!"

Charlotte starts to pace next to the paper-covered table.

"Well, obviously you can't let him give you that ultrasound or he'll figure out right away you're not pregnant," she says. "I don't know why *you're* freaking out. It's not like you've never had a penis in there before, and like the nurse said, it's not much different than that."

My silence immediately gives me away and Charlotte stops pacing to stare at me. "Holy shit, there's no way you're still a virgin.

What about prom and Quinn Curtis?"

I growl at her and point an accusing finger her way. "I *knew* you read the texts on my phone that weekend, you lying slutbag!"

The morning after that disastrous prom night I walked into my bedroom after taking a shower and caught Charlotte standing by my dresser with my phone in her hands. She told me she accidentally erased all her contacts and needed Gavin's number.

"How else was I supposed to find out how it went? You refused to answer any of my questions, dick-face vagina-hole!" she fires back.

"Maybe because it wasn't any of your business, you asshole fuck face!"

We stare at each other angrily for a few minutes before we both burst into laughter.

"Oh, my God, we sound like Mom and Aunt Claire," Charlotte giggles.

"Dick-face vagina-hole?" I ask through my laughter.

"Oh, please, like asshole fuck-face was any better," she smiles. "Grandpa George would be so disappointed in our lack of follow through with strings of curse words."

Charlotte hops up on the examine table, the paper cover crinkling noisily under her. When the room is silent again after she gets situated, I sigh heavily and move to lean against the table next to her.

"According to Quinn, it was amazing," I tell her. "According to me, his picture is now in the dictionary next to the words 'just the tip.'"

Charlotte laughs, looking at me questioningly.

"Seriously. He barely got the tip in before he came, screaming to God about how good it felt. Tampons have gone in my body further than that boy's tiny penis," I complain.

"So, technically you're a pregnant virgin," she smiles.

"Just call me the Virgin Mary," I reply sarcastically.

"What are the chances the doctor is really old and senile, and we can switch vaginas without him noticing?" Charlotte asks right as the door opens.

A very handsome, very young man who doesn't look a day over forty walks in wearing a white lab coat and a nametag that reads *Dr. Christenson.*

"Not good at all," I whisper as he looks up from his clipboard and smiles.

"How's your vision, doc?" I ask casually. "Twenty-twenty or blind-as-a-bat?"

He looks puzzled at my question and I don't blame him. I don't even understand half the things coming out of my mouth lately myself.

"Do you have the results from the urine sample?" Charlotte asks.

"I do and congratulations," he tells me with a smile. "You are definitely pregnant. I just need to do an internal ultrasound so we can nail down how far along you are and discuss your next couple of visits."

Charlotte hops down from the table and slides her hand through the crook of my arm. "Actually, doctor, I'm really sorry about this, but my sister isn't feeling very well so we're going to have to reschedule. She's already thrown up twice, so we really need to be going."

I put my hand over my mouth and make some pretend gagging noises as we walk to the door.

"Morning sickness…can't stop puking," I mutter behind my hand in between gags, giving him an apologetic look.

"Yep, so much puking," Charlotte agrees, a loud gag coming out of her own mouth.

"What are you doing?" I whisper as we move through the door. "I'm the one fake gagging, not you!"

"I."

Gag

"Can't."

Gag

"Help it," she finishes as we rush down the hall towards the bathroom instead of the waiting room.

"Your fake gagging made me real gag!" she complains, dropping her hand from my arm and running the rest of the way to the bathroom and right to the toilet.

Once again, I'm stuck in a small, enclosed space listening to my sister upchuck the contents of her stomach while I hold her hair back.

While I hold my breath and try to ignore the smell and sounds coming out of Charlotte, I feel my phone vibrate in my pocket. Holding Charlotte's hair with one hand, I pull my phone out with the other and smile when I see a text from Marco.

"Marco apologized for not calling," I tell Charlotte.

She lifts one arm from the bowl and gives me a thumb's up while she sits back on her feet and sighs in relief.

"Oh, and good news," I continue, reading the second text he just sent. "He's finally finished throwing up hot dog pieces and feels much better."

Charlotte whimpers, quickly sitting up and sticking her head back over the toilet bowl, another round of gagging overtaking her.

"You hairy-ball-sack-whore-of-a-whale's-dick!" she curses in between gags.

"Oh, pipe down you smelly-ass-giant-vagina-scrotum-licker!" I shout back, quickly shoving my phone back into my pocket and holding her hair back with both hands.

There's nothing quite like the love between two sisters.

Chapter 10

- Titillating Tube Socks -

Marco

"TODAY'S MY DADDY'S birthday. He farts a lot."

I don't even get my mother's front door closed all the way before a squeaky little voice starts rattling off strange, random facts.

"My dog Ralphie pees on all of our pillows. Daddy called it *humping* but mommy said I can't say that word and I'm 'upposed to say he's peeing."

Valerie, my four-year-old niece and the spitting image of my sister Tessa with her long, curly black hair and big blue eyes, starts running around in circles in front of me.

"Hump-hump-hump, I'm gonna pee on you!" she chants loudly as I pat her on the head awkwardly and walk towards the noise I hear coming from the kitchen. I love my niece, especially now that she can walk, talk, and take a dump without assistance, but I'm not really that great with kids. I love kids, don't get me wrong. I'd like to have my own some day, I just don't know what to say or do when I'm around them. At least I got a weekend off from getting yelled at for teaching her new swear words at Sunday dinner last week, since Valerie spent the night at Tessa's husband's parent's house. Hopefully, I can remember to watch my mouth today and avoid my mother's wrath. Tessa should be the one getting in trouble, since she hasn't taught her offspring to stop repeating everything people say.

I find Rosa carefully ladling sauce from a giant pot into mason jars spread all over the island in the middle of the room.

"Canning sauce for the winter?" I ask, walking up to the opposite side of the counter from my sister and dipping my finger into one of the mason jars, bringing it up to my mouth for a taste test.

"Don't put your dirty fingers into the sauce," Rosa scolds, smacking the top of my hand. "God only knows where you've put those fingers lately."

I know where I'd *like* to put my fingers, but after Molly had to watch me throw up in her parent's bushes the other night after proving it was possible to eat an entire bag of dicks, I'm not sure these digits will be going anywhere near the Promised Land any time soon.

"Hump-hump-hump, I'm gonna pee on you!" Valerie shouts happily into the kitchen as she races by to head to one of the spare bedrooms my mother converted into a toy room for her only grandchild.

Rosa gives me a dirty look and I put my hands up. "Hey, don't look at me like that. I did NOT teach her those words. Where is Tessa anyway? Shouldn't she be keeping an eye on her spawn?"

"She asked us to watch Valerie for a few hours so she could get some work done while Danny is out of town at a conference," Rosa explains distractedly as she starts putting lids on the already-filled mason jars.

I've been friends with Tessa's husband Danny since high school, and I don't hold it against him that he broke the cardinal rule of Guy Code by dating my sister. Mostly because when he's in town, he breaks up all the estrogen in this house so I don't feel like I'm starting to grow a pussy being surrounded by women all the time.

"Where's Ma?"

"Grabbing more supplies from the basement," she replies, finishing with the last jar and letting out tired breath.

"Good. Since we're alone, I can kick your ass in peace for the shit you pulled on Facebook," I tell her.

"I have no idea what you're talking about," she says, unable to hide the smirk on her face as she crosses her arms in front of her and stares at me.

"You made me sound like a giant pussy. A smiley face? Really?"

Rosa laughs. "Hey, I did you a favor with that Molly chick. I'm trying to make you look like less of a dick so when she finds out you're Alfanso D., she won't hate you so much. Wait until you see what I posted today."

My jaw drops and I quickly pull my phone out of my back pocket, immediately going to Facebook. The Alfanso D. page has over two-hundred notifications and I hold my breath as I click on the post pinned at the top.

"What did you do?! Oh, sweet Jesus on a jelly bean…you asked her on a date?!" I screech.

I read the post out loud because clearly reading it in my head wasn't torture enough.

"Dear Molly Gilmore," I pause and give my sister a little growl of annoyance. "Gee, thanks so much for tagging her in this post."

She takes a bow and I remind myself that hitting a girl, even if she's your annoying older sister is frowned upon, and turn my attention back to the post that is sure to ruin my life. "In case you didn't see my previous apology, I'd like to take this opportunity to publicly apologize to you in front of all my readers. I would also like to officially ask you to have dinner with me so I can prove to you that the D. in my name does not stand for *dick, douchebag, dummy or dipshit.*"

Rosa quietly mouths the words along with me, smiling happily when I get to the end.

"Poetry. Pure poetry," she murmurs. "Now you can profess your love to her and tell her you want to make babies with her."

A hysterical laugh flies out of my mouth, but it's quickly cut off and exchanged for screams of pain when something hard starts smacking repeatedly against the back of my shoulder. I'd know that stinging pain anywhere, and when I whirl around with my hands up to block my face, sure enough, my mother is standing there with a wooden spoon in her hand, hitting every part of me she can reach.

"HOW COULD YOU DO THIS TO ME, ALFANSO? I HAD TO HEAR ABOUT IT FROM THE WOMEN AT THE BEAUTY PARLOR!" she screams, the wooden spoon slapping against the side of my arm.

"Ma! Cut it out!" I yell back, dodging her flailing arm wielding the spoon of torture, the same spoon she's been using on my sisters and I since we were mouthy little asshole kids.

"I could have had a heart attack!" she screeches, chasing me around the island with the spoon above her head. "I could have died and you don't even CARE!"

Luckily, Rosa snatches the spoon from mom's hand when she races by her, so at least I can stop running away from my mother and her wooden spoon like a wuss. Unfortunately, when I stop and stand next to my sister, my mother doesn't even notice the spoon is missing and her hands start wind-milling against my arm like she's in a catfight with a chick.

"It's like you don't even love me!" she wails, her little hands reigning hellfire against my forearms while I shield my face. "I went through thirty-seven hours of labor with you, and I had to find out from a stranger!"

Not knowing what else to do, I start whipping my own hands against hers until we're having the world's most pathetic slap fight in the middle of her kitchen.

"It was two hours of labor and you got an epidural after the first contraction!" I remind her, our hands still smacking rapidly together.

"Well, it FELT like thirty-seven hours!" she argues. "How could you not tell your own mother that you're going to be a father?!"

"WHAT THE FUCK?!" Rosa and I yell at the same time.

My mother manages to end our slap fight and whack both of us upside the back of our heads at the same time.

"YOU GOT SOMEONE PREGNANT?"

"WHO TOLD YOU THIS?"

Once again, Rosa and I shout at the same time, her at me and me at our mother. We turn to face each other and both point a finger in each other's faces.

"WHO THE HELL DID YOU KNOCK UP?!"

"STAY THE HELL OUT OF THIS!"

I groan in frustration when we do it again, and before I can try once more to speak on my own, our mother grabs both of our earlobes and yanks our heads close to her face.

"Ow, ow, ow, ow, ow!" Rosa and I whine, neither one of us caring when our words overlap this time because it fucking hurts!

"Ho intenzione di spingere il cucchiaio finora nel culo verrà fuori dalla tua bocca!" Our mother shouts in rapid-fire Italian.

Rosa and I immediately clamp out mouths shut. We only truly fear our mother when she does two things: Screams our full names or speaks in Italian. I can't speak fluently, but I know enough to get by and I'm pretty sure she just said something about shoving her spoon up our asses until it comes out of our mouths.

When Rosa and I remain silent for a few seconds, mom finally releases our ears and we back away from her, rubbing our earlobes while shooting each other accusatory looks.

"How could you do this to me, Alfanso?" Mom starts in again, stomping away from me and out of the kitchen before I have a chance to explain.

I have no choice but to race after her as she storms across the hall into living room, muttering in Italian under her breath while she begins grabbing giant plastic shopping bags from the couch and starts placing them at my feet.

"Mom, I didn't do anything. Will you just let me explain?" I ask as she makes five trips back and forth between the couch and me until there are at least ten bags lying at my feet.

"I distinctly remember your father showing you how a prophylactic works when you were thirteen and I started finding crusty socks under your bed," she starts.

"Jesus, mom!" I yell.

"Eeeeeew, you did it into socks?" Rosa says in disgust as she comes up next to me.

"I was thirteen!" I shout, wishing Molly was here to see that my family could give hers a run for their money in the crazy department. Then I realize I'm talking to my mom and my sister about my masturbation habits when I was a teenager, and I immediately erase that thought.

"You should have done it in the shower like a normal teenager!" Rosa argues.

"Yes, because I got so much bathroom time living with three women!" I fire back. "It's not like the sock thing happened all the time, only when it was more convenient."

"I bought you a twenty-pack of tube socks every other week when you were in eighth grade," Mom adds. "I thought you had a foot fungus problem until I found sixty-two pairs stuck to the floor under your bed."

Just a few minutes ago, I thought my mom finding out about this thing with Molly would be the worst thing that could possibly happen to me. Clearly, I was wrong.

"Uuugghhh, I will never be able to look at another pair of tube socks without throwing up in my mouth," Rosa complains.

"Can we please get back on track here?" I ask with an annoyed shake of my head.

Mom reaches into the front pocket of her apron and pulls out a banana and a condom, holding them out to me.

"Fine. You're going to demonstrate the proper way to use protection, and you're going to keep doing it until you get it right," she informs me. "Take the banana and the prophylactic. I had to ask the pharmacist to show me where to locate these things, and then he had to explain all the different kinds. It's no wonder you screwed this up. Ribbed and magnum and tingling sensation…I do not understand today's youth and why they make things so difficult. Your father and I managed just fine with the 'pull-out-and-pray' method."

Rosa starts laughing and I start wondering what the possibilities are that I'm adopted.

"I'm not going to demonstrate anything and stop saying *prophylactic*; it's freaking me out!" I complain, crossing my arms like a child and refusing to take the things in her hand.

Picturing my mother going to the pharmacy and asking where the condoms are is bad enough. Having to hear her continue to say that word over and over will make me never want to have sex again.

"We're not leaving this room until you put this on the banana!" she argues. "I got glow-in-the-dark so we can be here all night!"

Grabbing the items from her hands so she stops shaking them in my face, I toss them over my shoulder and the banana thumps on the floor out in the hallway.

"I know how to use a condom, we are never speaking of my childhood masturbatory habits ever again, and I did NOT get anyone pregnant!" I yell at the top of my voice.

"I'm confused," Rosa states.

I sigh, realizing I've reached a new low when I'd rather go back to talking about jerking off into gym socks than trying and explain this to them.

"It's a long story," I mutter.

Both of us stare at our mother as she bends down and starts pulling things out of the bags by my feet.

"There's no sense in lying about it now, Alfanso. I had a nice long chat with that Molly girl's aunt at the beauty parlor, and then we went shopping together," she tells me happily, her mood doing a complete one-eighty as she digs through one of the bags and the sound of crinkling plastic fills the room.

Rosa's head whips up from watching Mom dig through the bags and she stares at me in shock. "Wait, Molly as in *'Cut the cord from mommy'* Facebook Molly? The Molly you just publicly asked out on a date on social media? That's who you knocked up?"

"YOU asked her out on a date, not me! And yes, *that* Molly," I reply, quickly backpedalling when Rosa opens her mouth to most likely call me a bunch of names. "But I did NOT get her pregnant!"

Mom stands up and begins shoving things at me, one after another until my arms are full of....

"Are these bibs? And bottles and baby socks and...what the hell is THIS?" I ask, staring at the box she just put on top of the pile I'm trying not to drop.

"It's a breast pump," Mom says with a huff, like I'm a moron for not knowing. "I also got ten packs of diapers, three receiving blankets, four different styles of pacifiers because you never know what the baby will like, diaper rash cream, and a baby monitor."

Her face scrunches up in concentration for a minute and while she thinks, I try to force my brain to process what is happening.

"Oh!" she announces excitedly, clapping her hands together. "I knew I forgot something. Rosa, go out to my trunk and get the Diaper Genie."

"What the hell is a Diaper Genie? Is that like, a guy who changes all the diapers? Why didn't Tessa have one of those?" I ask, my brain clearly not catching up as fast as I'd like.

"I think now would be a good time for that long story you mentioned before Mom starts building an addition on the house for a nursery," Rosa whispers, as my mom hands her a tiny little baby shirt.

"Awwww, look," Rosa says, holding it up in front of her. "It says *World's Greatest Aunt!*"

I finally get my head out of my ass, opening my arms and letting everything my mom shoved at me fall to the floor, snatching the shirt from Rosa's hands that she's cooing over.

"Heeeey! Give me my aunt shirt back!" she complains.

"You don't need a damn aunt shirt because you aren't going to be an aunt again!" I argue, holding it out of her reach as she tries to grab it back. "And I don't need a magic genie to change diapers, or any of this other stuff, because I'm not going to be a father! I didn't get anyone pregnant."

Bending down to avoid the evil-eye both of the women in the room are now giving me, I start shoveling all the items I dropped back into the bags.

"Molly is doing a favor for her sister, and I'm not kidding when I say it's a long story," I explain, wondering if I could have Molly give all this stuff to Charlotte and earn me a few more brownie points so she'll forget about the whole puking in the bushes thing the other night. "She's pretending to be pregnant and I'm pretending to be the father because her sister wants to wait until after her wedding in a few weeks to break the news to everyone. I'm sorry I didn't tell you, but I honestly never thought you'd run into one of Molly's relatives and find out. It's not that big of a deal, but you guys absolutely CANNOT tell anyone about this."

Rosa pats me on the back when I stand back up. "Damn, I guess you don't need my help clearing Alfanso D.'s name. You could tell her you're Satan at this point and she'd probably shrug it off since you're going through so much trouble for her family. You actually *do* have a brain."

I ignore the brain comment instead of saying something sarcastic because I don't like how quiet our mother is, and if Rosa and I start firing insults at each other, she might make good on that threat of shoving a spoon up our asses.

"Look, Auntie Rosa! I put a dress on the 'nanana!"

Rosa and I turn around and find Valerie sitting in the middle of the hallway behind us, proudly holding up the banana I threw, now covered in a florescent green condom.

Our mother pushes her way between us, walking over to Valerie, squatting down in front of her and taking the condom-covered banana from her hand.

"What a pretty dress for the banana!" Mom exclaims. "I have thirty-nine other dresses, in all the colors of the rainbow. Why don't you teach Uncle how to put a dress on the banana, since he doesn't seem to care about me at all?"

I roll my eyes at her dramatics as she stands back up and helps Valerie up from the floor as well.

"How could you do this to me?" she whispers as my niece starts making airplane noises and flying the condom banana around the hallway. "Is it too much to ask that my son give me another grandchild? What am I supposed to tell the women at the beauty parlor now?"

One minute she's beating me with a spoon when she thinks I got someone pregnant, and now she's bitching at me for NOT getting someone pregnant. I need a drink.

"If you'll excuse me," she says with a haughty lift of her chin. "I'm going to rearrange my bookshelf to make room for your next porn cookbook, now that I know I won't need the space for pictures of my new grandchild."

I think I'd prefer having the spoon shoved up my ass right about now...

"I believe this would be a good time to get drunk and tell me the rest of the story," Rosa informs me as Valerie races up to us and starts smacking me in the leg with the banana.

"Hump-hump-hump! Banana's gonna pee on you!"

Rosa laughs, walking away from me as I try to get the phallic-shaped fruit away from our niece.

"Hey! A little help here!" I shout to her as she keeps going.

"Hump-hump-hump!" Valerie shouts. "Uncle, why is the green dress all slippery? It's making my hands yucky!"

Rosa's laugh echoes down the hallway as she gives me a wave over her shoulder.

"I'll have the wine ready when the four-year-old finishes teaching you how to dress a banana!" she shouts, disappearing into the kitchen.

I finally manage to wrangle the banana out of Valerie's hand, hearing the front door open and shut while I try to keep it out of her reach.

"GIVE ME BACK MY HUMPY!" she screams.

Tessa walks up behind her daughter, staring at the banana I'm now holding above my head.

"I think Uncle needs Humpy more than you, Val," Tessa tells her daughter, running her hand over the top of her head. "Grandma sent mommy a text and said Uncle doesn't know how to properly dress a banana so he needs to practice."

Yep, I'd definitely prefer being locked in a trunk and covered in pee.

Two hours and four bottles of wine later, I find myself lying on my mother's kitchen floor next to Rosa, while my mom and Tessa sit at the kitchen table talking about me like I'm not even here.

"It's like he doesn't even care, Tessa," my mother says with a sigh.

"Hey, give me your phone, I've got the best idea EVER!" Rosa tells me, holding her hand out above my face.

"Okay," I tell her, letting my wine buzz speak for me as I slap my phone into her hand.

She's had just as much wine to drink as I have, it's not like she's sober enough to do anything *that* bad.

Chapter 11
— Handy —
Molly

"I CAN'T BELIEVE I took a red-eye flight home for this shit," Ava complains, shaking her head at me in disappointment as she perches on the edge of our mother's desk at Seduction and Snacks.

"Hey, I told you on the phone last night what was going on. It's not my fault you felt the need to get the first flight out," I argue.

Today was my first official day at the headquarters of our family business in the test kitchen. I had a glorious day working alone in the huge industrial kitchen while I got busy tweaking some of the old recipes, and then Ava had to come in and ruin my good mood by dragging me away from my happy place and into mom's empty office on the other side of the building while she was out running errands.

"Charlotte tore me a new asshole for spilling the beans to Mom and Dad so I figured coming home early in your time of need was the least I could do," she informs me. "I still can't believe she's making you do this shit for her, and I can't believe you actually agreed to it."

I was so busy trying to decipher a bunch of weird, random text messages Marco sent last night that when my cell phone rang, I quickly answered it without checking caller I.D., hoping it was him. Ava screamed at me for fifteen minutes about getting pregnant and how she had to find out from Tyler instead of me. When I finally managed to shut her up and tell her the truth, she said she was coming home and hung up before I could say anything else.

"It seemed like a good idea at the time, and did you not hear me when I told you everything she agreed to give me?" I ask.

"Who cares about that shit? Tell me more about this hot teacher of yours that's standing in as the baby daddy," she says with a wicked smile. "Charlotte said his name is Mo or something."

Rolling my eyes, I push myself up from the chair in the middle of the room and start to pace. "His name is Marco, not Mo, and he's not my teacher. Not anymore at least, you know, since I *graduated*."

I pause, wondering if she'll acknowledge my big accomplishment since no one else seems to have remembered now that they have my fake baby on the brain. I'm trying not to let it get to me that no one in my family has said a word about how all of my hard work for the last two years has successfully come to an end. Even today, my first official day of work, which was temporarily scheduled six months ago barring I passed my final, went unnoticed. When I announced I was going to work this morning and waited for it to click in with my mother, all she did was hand me a prenatal vitamin and told me not to take it on an empty stomach.

"Mmmmmm, Marco," she purrs. "Me likey. He already sounds hot, tell me more."

Feeling stupid for thinking Ava of all people would be the one to congratulate me, I continue pacing.

"All guys name their penis, so don't be embarrassed about that. Although Humpy the Wonder Penis is a little much," she muses, causing me to stop pacing.

"Where the hell did you get my cell phone?!" I yell, trying to take it from her, but she moves quickly and smacks my hand away.

"I grabbed it from the kitchen counter before I dragged you in here," she laughs, continuing to read the string of weird texts I got from Marco last night. "You should know better than to leave your phone lying around for just anyone to take."

I haven't even had a chance to try and decipher those texts, and now Ava is going to make it worse.

"Humpy likes to wear green dresses and bananas are delicious," she reads one of the texts out loud. "Yikes, how much time did you say he spent alone with Uncle Drew?"

I finally manage to overpower her and snatch my phone out of her hands. "Your boyfriend dresses up like a horse, your opinion is invalid!"

She hops off of her desk and puts her hands on her hips. "It's not a horse, it's as PONY, show some respect!"

There are so many things I could say right now, but I decide to keep them to myself because spending any amount of time thinking about what Ava and her Brony boyfriend do when they're alone makes me was to dunk my head in a tub full of bleach.

"I see what you're doing by trying to turn this around on me," she says casually, dropping her hands from her hips to lean back against the edge of the desk. "You're avoiding the real issue."

I scoff. "Really? I'm pretending to be pregnant because our sister is too afraid to tell her fiancé the truth. I'm fucking up my life, so she can live happily ever after. How is that avoiding ANY subject?"

She waves me off with a flap of her hand.

"Pshaw, b-o-r-i-n-g," she says in a sing-song voice. "I'm much more interested on you being a pregnant virgin. Let's discuss *that*."

"Oh, my GOD, is nothing sacred in this family?!" I shout in irritation.

And here I thought Charlotte and I finally had a moment in the doctor's office. She probably called Ava five seconds after we left.

"Sacred? You're kidding, right?" she laughs. "Uncle Drew puts a picture of his balls on their Christmas card every year, and forever ruined Taco Tuesday night at mom and dad's when he told us Aunt

Jenny's vagina can hold two taco shells without spilling the contents. The *sacred* ship sailed long before we were born."

I cringe, remembering there are much worse things to have floating around in my brain aside from Ava and her pony-loving boyfriend.

"I think we need to discuss when you plan on telling this Marco guy that you haven't lost your virginity," she smirks.

I feel my face heat with embarrassment as she stares at me. Forget the whole fake pregnancy thing. That is a piece of cake compared to *this* torture.

"And don't bother trying to make up some lie about how he's just a guy and it's no big deal," she warns me. "Charlotte already told me how cute you two are together and how you've been all girly and emo that he hasn't called since he met the family."

My mouth drops open in indignation. "I have NOT been girly and emo!"

"So you haven't been checking your phone every two minutes and kept yourself locked in your bedroom playing the soundtrack from *The Virgin Suicides* on repeat?" she asks with a knowing smile.

First Charlotte and now my mother. Forget moving across town, I'm moving to Mexico.

"It's a good soundtrack!" I argue lamely.

"From a movie about five sisters who commit suicide!" she replies. "I repeat, girly and emo."

I groan, throwing my hands up in the air.

"Fine! I really like the guy, and he said he really likes me too which I guess is obvious considering that he agreed to do something so crazy to help me out, but then all the idiots we're related to got ahold of him and he traded in his macho sports car for a mom van, came home smelling like pee and threw up hotdogs for the next two days where I only heard from him twice until last night when he kept sending me texts about bananas wearing dresses, and I'm pretty sure our family ruined him permanently and I'll never see him again," I ramble so fast I barely comprehend what is coming out of my mouth.

Fortunately, Ava speaks fluent rambling nonsense and nods her head in understanding.

"Yeah, Charlotte told me about the bag of dicks thing, too. Bravo to Marco for finally putting an end to *that* argument so we don't have to listen to it at yet another Thanksgiving dinner," she says. "He's not completely ignoring you, so obviously they didn't scare him away for good. The poor guy had to deal with a lot in one day, so cut him some slack. He took his own life in his hands, and you didn't even put out when it was over. That guy is a saint."

Even though my life is on the verge of imploding all because of Charlotte, I can't deny that it was sort of nice when we did have that little moment in the doctor's office, and she's called and texted me nonstop since then checking to see if I've heard anything more from Marco, like she actually *cares*. And I'm more than a little surprised that I actually *like* it.

If Charlotte is the sister I can talk about stupid girl stuff with like my feelings, and it doesn't make me break out in hives, I suppose I can suck it up and give Ava a chance to give me *her* expertise—sex.

"There's no way he expected to get sex after that…" I mutter, biting my bottom lip as I think it over. "Right? I mean, sure we've known each other for two years, but that was the first time we ever hung out and said more than a handful of words to each other."

She laughs and shakes her head at me. "Oh, little sister, you have so much to learn. Tyler expects sex if he remember to put the toilet seat down. Marco met your family on the first date AND had to put up with everyone looking at him the entire time while they pictured him sticking his penis in their little girl. He had to deal with the fact that our parent's brains gave his dick more action than his dick actually got. You're right, sex might have been a bit much, but you could have thrown the guy a bone and given him a handy or something."

I'm pretty sure studying Urban Dictionary would be more beneficial than asking for Ava's advice on sex.

"Can you be serious for one minute?" I ask in irritation. "I don't need you making fun of me for not jerking him off at the end of the night. I'm sure touching a guy's penis when he's throwing up six pounds of hotdogs is no big deal for you, but it's just a little bit out of my comfort zone."

She crosses her arms and speaks to me matter-of-factly. "I am always serious when it comes to sex. While it's true that I happen to have some experience with the aforementioned during a recent bout of the stomach flu and Tyler insisting it was the only way he could stop throwing up, I assure you it wasn't the easiest thing I've ever done."

I never thought I'd see the day when I'd rather talk about Bronies...

"I'm not making fun of you, Molly," she continues. "To avoid any confusion, my advice would be to tell Marco the truth. If he knows you're a virgin, his expectations won't be as high and you won't constantly be worrying that he's waiting for you to do something."

I shake my head at her and roll my eyes. "I can't just come right out and tell him something like that, it's embarrassing."

"Really?" she scoffs. "More embarrassing than our father picturing Marco spraying his seed all up in your business whenever he looks at you?"

"Eeeeeew!" I groan in disgust. "Come on!"

"It's not like you have to give him all the details about Quinn Curtis in the back of his dad's Honda Civic and explain that you sort of had sex, but you're still a virgin because they guy has a micro penis," she informs me.

"Jesus, is there anything Charlotte DIDN'T tell you?" I complain.

"Oh, Charlotte didn't tell me that. I read your texts two days after prom," she informs me with a shrug. "Don't feel bad. I dated his older brother for a week in high school and gave him a blowjob after a football game. I open my mouth wider when I whistle. It runs in the family."

I close my eyes and start rubbing the tips of my fingers against my temples, wondering if it's possible for a brain to literally explode.

"Here, let's practice," she announces. "Repeat after me. Marco, I haven't lost my virginity yet."

I drop my hands from the side of my head and glare at her.

"I'm not just going to blurt out that I haven't lost my virginity. I didn't lose it, I know exactly where it is. It's in my vagina where it will remain until the right time comes along," I tell her indignantly.

"This guy has seen Uncle Drew's balls!" she argues. "In a Walmart parking lot, for God's sakes! There is no such thing as the right time when Uncle Drew's balls have already made an appearance. Do you want to have sex with this guy?"

I roll my eyes and sigh. "Yes."

"Then be loud and be proud!" she shouts, throwing her fist in the air. "I haven't lost it yet, but I want to lose it with you!"

Since I made the mistake of staying in the room and letting Ava give me her stupid expertise instead of plugging my ears and running away as fast as I could, I might as well get this over with so I can pretend like it never happened.

"I haven't lost it yet, but I want to lose it with you," I mumble under my breath.

"I'm sorry, I can't hear you," she says, holding her hand to her ear.

"I HAVEN'T LOST IT YET, BUT I WANT TO LOSE IT WITH YOU!" I yell at the top of my lungs.

"Lost what? Do you need help finding something?"

I scream and whirl around, wishing immediately that the whole brain explosion thing would have happened a few minutes ago. I'd kind of like to be dead right about now.

"Sorry for interrupting, but the woman at the front desk told me you were in here." Marco smiles at me before glancing over my shoulder. "Hi, I'm Marco Desoto. You must be Molly's other sister, Ava."

"Ooooh, an Italian Stallion," she whispers. "You won't have to worry about an inchworm penis with this one."

"I heard you yelling about losing something, need some help?" Marco asks, his eyes roaming around the office.

Ava snorts unladylike and I'm too busy waiting for the floor to open up and swallow me to care.

"I'm pretty good at finding things," Marco announces. "Did you lose your keys? Wallet? Cell phone?"

I'm unable to make my mouth work or form words, and all I can do is watch in mortification as he starts digging through the couch cushions of the love seat against the wall.

"Am I hot or cold?" Marco asks as he moves to a side table and pulls open the drawer.

"I don't know, what do you think, Molly?" Ava laughs.

"I know it's stupid, but did you try your pants?" Marco asks, oblivious to how much enjoyment Ava is getting out this. "I think I lose things all the time and then find them in the most obvious places."

He walks right up to me and starts patting my hips while my sister tries to stifle her giggles behind me.

"I think you're getting warmer, Marco. I'm sure you'll find what you're looking for in her pants," Ava informs him.

Even though the combination of wanting to die and the feel of Marco's warm hands running up and down my hips has turned me stupid, I finally manage to recover enough bodily function to turn my head and glare over my shoulder at Ava.

"I will murder you in your sleep," I whisper through clenched teeth.

She ignores me, grabbing an old-fashioned calligraphy dip pen from the top of mom's desk that she found at an antique store a few months ago, holding it up in the air.

"Oh, look! I found it!" she announces with a big smile. "It's a gift for you, Marco. Molly tried to give it to someone else a few years ago, but he didn't know what to do with it."

I snarl at her as Marco drops his hands from my hips and reaches around me to take the pen from her outstretched hand.

"Wow, this is pretty cool," he muses. "I actually know how to use one of these, too. I took a calligraphy class as an elective in college."

"Awwww, did you hear that, Molly? He knows what to do with this gift you're giving him," she says happily.

"You just have to be careful. It can get really messy if you go too fast or don't know what you're doing," Marco adds.

"Very messy, especially the first time. Never use it on a bed with white sheets," Ava says with a nod.

"A bed?" Marco laughs. "On top of a table is a better idea."

Her eyes light up. "Ooooh, kinky. I like you already, Marco."

Grabbing Marco's hand before this gets even more out of hand, I drag him to the door, staring at Ava as I go, making sure my eyes convey that she should sleep with one eye open for the rest of her life.

"It was nice meeting you, Ava!" Marco shouts as I pull him out the door.

"See you soon, Humpy banana penis!" she yells back.

Marco groans as I hustle him down the hall and as far away from my sister as possible.

"Oh, God, she saw the texts I sent you? This is mortifying," he complains as I push open the front doors of the building and pull him outside.

"Don't talk to me about mortifying until your sister tells you about giving her boyfriend a hand-job to make him stop puking," I mutter.

"Wait, that's a thing? I can't believe I've wasted all these years asking for 7-up when there was a much better alternative," he says in awe.

I can't believe the things that come out of your mouth remind me of something my family would say, and it makes me like you even more.

I need therapy.

Chapter 12

– Dammit, Ian –

Marco

I KNOW IT would be wrong to ask Molly to say "hand-job" again just so I can stare at her lips as they form the words, but that doesn't stop me from silently wishing upon a star.

Spending two days away from her was the worst decision I've ever made. She didn't look as happy to see me as I'd hoped when I walked in on her and Ava a few minutes ago. I don't know if it's because she's pissed at me for my disappearing act, pissed at me for the God awful drunk texts Rosa sent to her after I'd passed out on our mother's kitchen floor, or pissed at me that I didn't find what she'd lost back in the office. Right when I opened my mouth to apologize for all three just to cover all the bases, she had to go and say "hand-job," and now my dick and my brain are doing shots and partying it up in the gutter instead of paying attention.

"So, what brings you to Seduction and Snacks today?" Molly asks, stopping next to my van I left parked at the curb in front of the building.

"You look really pretty today," I tell her with a smile, knowing all women appreciate compliments. It should be a piece of cake to soften Molly up and make it easier for her to look beyond my avoidance of her the last couple of days.

"Sucking up to me will get you nowhere," she deadpans.

Or not.

"It's okay if my family was a bit too much for you," she continues, without giving me a chance to say anything. "I get it. Not everyone can handle their unique brand of hazing someone new. If you want out, just be honest with me. I'll tell them you changed your mind or something. Ava is pretty good with computers, I'm sure she can make sure your home address isn't easily accessible anywhere on the internet until everything blows over."

Shit, Rosa was right with all that advice she gave me before I passed out. By staying away from her in the hopes that the image of me hurling in her parent's shrubs would disappear from her mind, all I did by avoiding her was make her second-guess me. I'm just going to pretend I didn't hear the home address thing. Knowing the men in her family would hunt me down and shank me like a thug in the prison yard if they thought I left a pregnant Molly all alone is enough to give me nightmares.

I step right up in front of her until our toes are touching, hoping she notices I smell like Cool Water cologne instead of Cold Water and Piss.

She has a dusting of flour on her right cheek that my hands have been itching to brush off ever since I first walked into that office a few minutes ago. I silently bring my hand up to the side of her face and graze the tips of my fingers against her skin. I keep touching her long after the flour is gone because she feels like velvet—warm and soft and smooth.

"They weren't too much for me, I promise," I insist quietly as she lifts her chin and searches my eyes to see if I'm telling the truth.

"I'll admit, the thirty-eighth hot dog was too much, and I should have tapped out somewhere around thirty-four, but I haven't changed my mind and I'm sorry for being a dick the last few days," I apologize.

"You don't have to say you're sorry," she says with a shake of her head. "I'm the one who's sorry for bringing you into this mess. I know it's crazy, and you probably think I'm the biggest idiot in the entire world for faking a pregnancy for my sister…"

Her voice tapers off and she sighs heavily, looking away from me to stare out towards the street.

"I've spent my whole life feeling like an outsider with my entire family, but mostly with my two sisters," she explains softly. "Growing up, they were always boy-crazy and fashion-crazy and just plain fucking crazy, and I couldn't relate to them. The only thing I've ever been crazy about is baking. Until now. Now, we have something in common and something to talk about and I actually *like* it. It's girly and it's dumb and I'm sure they're going to want to get pedicures and do my hair and watch reality TV together now, but I don't care."

Molly laughs softly before turning her face back to mine, and I can tell by the way she had to force the laugh out that she hates sharing her feelings and acting, like she said, *girly*.

"Can you be a little more specific on the thing you guys have in common now?" I ask with a raise of my eyebrow.

Her cheeks flush in embarrassment and that gives me my answer, but I still want to hear her say it.

"It's the fashion-crazy thing, isn't it?" I tease. "I bet you're going to start demanding everyone in the kitchen at work has to wear designer chef jackets. You're such a fashion whore."

She smacks my chest and laughs.

"You know that's not the crazy I'm talking about and if you make me say it, I will help my mother turn your balls into cream puffs," she warns.

"As long as you like to *eat* cream puffs, I'm okay with my balls *being* cream puffs," I tell her with a wink and a smirk. "Come on, just say it. There's no shame in admitting you're boy-crazy. But you should probably amend it to *man*-crazy because, I mean, look at me."

I put my hands on my hips, puff out my chest and give her my best smoldering look.

"What are you doing with your eyes?" she questions.

I try harder, narrowing my eyes and imagining I'm that Ian Somerhalder guy from *Vampire Diaries*. He has a good smolder. I mean, from what I've heard. From people who actually watch that dumb show because I clearly never would, especially since he had to go and get married and now Team Delena is dead forever.

"I'm smoldering you. It's totally working," I murmur.

"It looks like you have one of those eye-twitch things happening."

Dammit, Ian. You ruin everything.

I relax, softening my face and placing my hands on her shoulders.

"I get why you're doing this and you're right, it's completely insane, but I get it." I knead her shoulders gently. "Doing something like this makes you feel close to your sisters for the first time in your life and you want to hold onto that. I think that makes you brave and amazing, not stupid or crazy."

Silence stretches between us as we stand on the sidewalk staring at each other. I can smell her cinnamon apple skin and there's a glossy sheen on her lips that makes me wonder if she's wearing lip gloss and if it will taste as good as she smells. My dick takes a time-out from the gutter party to rise up and toast me, threatening to bust right through the zipper of my jeans when Molly licks those damn shiny lips.

I want to kiss her more than I want to breathe, but I don't want to do it in front of her place of work while employees come and go all around us. I want to be alone, in a quiet place where maybe I can fake an illness and the kiss can lead to her showing me how to cure nausea by putting her hand down my pants.

"I'm sorry I didn't call or make plans to see you that last few days," I apologize again. "I was a little embarrassed that the first day we spent together ended with me regurgitating hotdogs."

She laughs and rolls her eyes at me, something that has suddenly become one of my favorite things to see.

"I accept your apology, but you owe me," she threatens, jabbing her finger into my chest. "I had to get my fake pregnancy confirmed at the doctor."

My eyes widen in shock, wondering how in the hell she pulled *that* off.

"So I'm guessing somewhere in town there's a roofied doctor waking up with a really bad headache?" I ask with a laugh.

"I wish. Luckily, they confirmed the pregnancy with pee. I had to carry a cup of Charlotte's pee." She scrunches her cute little nose up in disgust, her body shuddering under my hands that are still resting on her shoulders.

She waves her arm in the air and changes the subject.

"If you see me wash my right hand until the skin starts falling off, don't ask any questions," she informs me.

I try not to let it bother me that she takes a step back so I have no choice but to let my hands drop from her shoulders. One of these days I'm going to get this girl to let me touch her and not freak out about it.

"Enough of this mushy crap. Let's move on to Humpy and why your penis likes to wear green dresses," she says with a smirk. "I really don't know if green is a good color for you."

Remind me to never get drunk with Rosa again. Even if she did give me good advice before I passed out in a puddle of my own drool on our mother's linoleum.

"My sister sent those texts, not me. She pumped me full of wine and then stole my phone. Like I'd really name my penis Humpy," I scoff.

His name is Thor, obviously. He's strong and slams it like a hammer. BOOM!

"I'll explain the whole green dress banana thing in the car," I promise, glancing down at my watch. "Right now, we have somewhere to be."

Molly looks at me questioningly as I push her aside and open the passenger door to the van, holding it open for her.

"Get in, don't ask any questions, and don't give me that look for holding your door open like a *decent* gentleman," I warn her. "It's a surprise."

I'm not kidding when I said Rosa gave me some good instructions, after she punched me repeatedly in the arm for staying away from Molly. She called me every curse word she could think of before she told me I was an idiot for being introduced as the baby daddy to her family and then leaving her alone to deal with that shit by herself. It never even occurred to me that her family would probably wonder where I'd been or ask her a million questions about why I hadn't been around, and I knew I had to do something to make up for being such an idiot.

"I don't like surprises," she mutters as she gets into the passenger seat and pulls the seat belt around her.

"Suck it up, buttercup. You'll like this one, I promise," I assure her before shutting the door and walking around the front of the van to get behind the wheel. After spilling my guts to Rosa and telling her everything I knew about Molly and asking her for ideas on how to make myself look like a good guy and other romantic shit I could do to win her over, Rosa pointed out something so obvious that I wanted to punch *myself* in the arm that I didn't come up with it first.

When I called a few people this morning, they were really excited about my idea and even let me make them feel guilty as shit for not doing it themselves. Listening to them kick themselves in the ass over the phone made me forgive them for the car wash ride and bag of dicks contest.

"You're not going to get in trouble for leaving work early, are you?" I ask, even though I already know the answer.

"Nope, as a matter of fact, my mom sent me a text a half hour ago and told me to go home and put my feet up," Molly explains. "My poor fake baby had a rough day."

As I pull out of the parking lot and onto the street, I sneak a glance at Molly as she looks away from me to stare out the window. I really hope this doesn't turn out to be a bad idea. I'll never be able to console Thor if he doesn't get to meet her.

Chapter 13

— Shocker Honor —

"SURPRISE!"

I freeze in the middle of my parent's backyard when Marco and I round the side of the house and twenty-five people jump up from chairs and tables set up all around the yard.

Everyone starts clapping, hooting, whistling and chanting my name. Marco squeezes my hand and I tear my eyes away from the chaos to look up at him.

"If this is a pregnancy party or a stupid baby shower, I'm baking your balls at 500 degrees instead of the required 350," I growl.

He laughs, letting go of my hand to wrap his arm around my shoulder and pull me against his side. I'm in too much shock to move away from him, and he smells so delicious and his body feels so good pressed against mine that I forget about my family wondering if I've lost my mind by letting a guy get all grabby-hands in public.

"No, silly girl. This is a graduation party."

Looking around the yard again, I see what I missed during my initial shock from the shouting and seeing the yard filled with my entire extended family. A giant *Happy Graduation* sign hangs between two trees, a couple dozen cardboard graduation hats hang from all the branches, and the centerpieces on all the paper-covered tables are bouquets of sugar cookies cut out and frosted to look like pastry hats, wooden spoons, whisks and other baking items.

"You threw me a graduation party?" I whisper in awe as a few members of my family start walking across the yard towards us.

"I felt bad that this fake pregnancy thing overshadowed the biggest accomplishment of your life. Just so you know, they all felt really horrible they forgot," he tells me.

It's the sweetest thing anyone has ever done for me, and I have to bite down on my bottom lip to stop myself from crying like a baby.

"I was starting to feel like Molly Ringwald in *Sixteen Candles* when her family forgot her birthday," I whisper.

"Well then, you'll be happy to know I did not sell a pair of your panties in the boy's bathroom," Marco announces proudly.

"Never, ever say the word *panties* again," I warn him as my mom gets up to us and pulls me in for a hug.

"We are the worst people ever and I'm so sorry Molly," she apologizes, raining kisses all over both my cheeks. "You should have smacked us in the face when we forgot to ask you about finals."

She pulls away and holds me at arm's length and I can see tears welling up in her eyes. Mom hates to cry in front of people just as much as I do, so I go easy on her before she starts snotting all over the place and embarrassing herself.

"Brace yourself, Mother. I'm joining Fight Club," I announce, making two fists and bringing them up between us.

"I was being facetious. Don't even think about punching me. I brought you into this world and I can—"

"Ooooh, bad call quoting Bill Cosby," Dad interrupts. "Unless you plan on slipping a roofie in your daughter's drink to make it more authentic."

He pats Mom on the back and then moves her out of the way so he can give me his own hug. "Congratulations, baby girl. You worked your ass off, and I couldn't be more proud."

Uncle Carter, Aunt Claire, Uncle Drew, and Aunt Jenny each take their turns congratulating me, giving me hugs and apologizing for being assholes.

"It's good to see you came back, M.O.," Uncle Carter tells him, giving him a pat on the shoulder. "I thought for sure those hot dogs killed you, or at the very least you got a brain aneurism from the brushes at the car wash. You're like a fucking cat!"

Aunt Claire looks at her husband in confusion. "Because he's selfish and licks his own ass?"

"I meant because he has nine lives, but sure, you're way is good too," he tells her with a shrug.

"Why did you call him Mo?" Aunt Jenny asks Uncle Carter.

"Minivan Operator," Uncle Carter replies. "You know, minivan? From Urban Dictionary."

Aunt Jenny smiles and nods her head in understanding. "Oh, I get it! Because you can fit four people in the front and nine people in the back!"

Uncle Carter shakes his head. "I don't think it means what you think it means."

Aunt Jenny rolls her eyes. "Yes I do. Drew and I have done the minivan and he can definitely fit nine in the back."

Everyone groans and Marco leans down close to my ear.

"I'm ashamed to say I really thought you were kidding about them," he whispers.

"Since we're all here, we need to discuss something important," Mom announces as Marco moves away from my ear. "Grandpa George is on his way and he doesn't know about the pregnancy."

Grandpa George is actually Aunt Claire's father. Even though he's not blood-related, I've known him all my life, and he's always been Grandpa George to my sisters and I.

Mom turns to Marco. "George is…how should I say this?"

"He's old school and even though he was pretty good about me getting pregnant in college, that was a while ago, and I don't know how he'd take something like this in his old age," Aunt Claire explains. "Plus, I'm pretty sure he was the one who shot a man in Reno, just to watch him die."

Everyone nods silently in agreement.

"So, can everyone promise they will not tell George about the pregnancy until we absolutely have to?" Mom asks.

Everyone raises their hands and mumbles their agreement.

"Shocker honor!" Uncle Drew shouts, holding his hand in the air with his thumb holding down his ring finger, his pointer and middle fingers pressed together, and his pinky sticking out to the side.

"What the fuck is shocker honor?" Uncle Carter asks.

"I was never a Boy Scout, so it would be sacrilegious to say scout's honor," Uncle Drew explains. "Since I'm not only a member, but also the president of Shocker Nation, this makes more sense."

Dad shakes his head. "It makes no sense. Shocker honor isn't a thing and you can't swear on it."

"Shocker honor is too a thing and it's a very important thing," Uncle Drew argues. "There is nothing more serious than two in the pink, one in the stink."

"He's right, there isn't," Aunt Jenny adds with a serious nod. "It's more important than a pinky swear."

Aunt Claire looks over my shoulder and waves. We all turn around to see Grandpa George and his wife Sue coming around the side of the house.

"Another thing you guys should know, Sue had some sort of accident the other day that affected her ear drums," Aunt Claire quickly explains. "I guess she can't hear very well, so you might have to talk a little louder."

She walks around Marco and I to greet them. "Hi, Dad, thanks for coming. Can I get you something to drink, Sue?"

"OH, NO THANK YOU! IT'S TOO HOT FOR SOUP!" Sue shouts with a smile as Aunt Claire leads them over to our group.

Grandpa George, not one for public displays of affection, gives me an awkward one-armed side hug and hands me a card.

"Congratulations, Molly. There's fifty bucks in there. Don't spend it on anything stupid," he warns me as I take the card from his hand.

"There goes your plans of spending your graduation money on booze and sex," Uncle Drew laughs.

"NO, IT'S NOT A ROLEX, BUT THANKS FOR ASKING!" Sue shouts, holding up her wrist and pointing to her gold watch.

"Care to tell me how Sue lost her hearing since you were a little vague on the phone yesterday?" Aunt Claire asks her dad.

"Eh, I let off a couple M-80's in the backyard and she was standing too close," he says with a shrug.

"Why in the hell were you lighting M-80's in your backyard?" Aunt Claire furrows her brow in dismay.

"That's the dumbest question you've ever asked me," Grandpa George mutters, shaking his head. "I found them in a box in the garage. One does not just leave M-80's in a box when they find them. Have I taught you nothing?"

Before Aunt Claire can scold him, Gavin and Charlotte walk over to our group to say hello.

"What's new, Grandpa George?" Charlotte asks, kissing him on the cheek and giving Sue a quick hug.

"PIGEON FORGE? NEVER BEEN, BUT I HEAR IT'S NICE!" Sue yells.

Aunt Claire smacks Grandpa George on the arm when he chuckles.

"I can't believe you're laughing at her!" she whispers. "You should be ashamed of yourself."

He shrugs, sticking his hands in his pockets. "I asked her this morning if we had anything to fix a drain clog and she thought I asked for a blow job. I picked up ten cases of M-80's on the way home from the hardware store."

Aunt Claire makes a gagging noise and covers her ears while Uncle Drew gives grandpa a high five.

"You kids ready for the wedding?" Grandpa asks Gavin and Charlotte. "You gonna wear a fancy tux or get a new suit?"

"I ALREADY TOLD CLAIRE I DIDN'T WANT SOUP, GEORGE," Sue shouts with a frown.

I watch as Charlotte's eyes widen in horror and her face starts to turn green.

Aunt Claire and Uncle Carter both start talking very loudly about how there isn't any soup, making sure to enunciate that word and drag it out each time they say it so Sue can understand them. The more they say it, the more Charlotte starts to look like she's going to puke right here in front of everyone.

"Uuuggghhh," I moan loud enough to make them stop talking. I put my hand on my stomach and grimace. "Please don't say that word, it makes me sick."

Grandpa George looks at me questioningly. "Why in tarnation would that word make you sick? Soup is delicious and good for you. We just had split pea soup with ham last night for dinner."

Charlotte's hand flies up to cover her mouth and Grandpa George notices out of the corner of his eye, turning his head in her direction.

"And what the hell is wrong with you? Don't tell me soup makes you sick too? Has everyone in this family turned stupid?" he asks.

"WHY WOULD CUPID BE HERE? I THOUGHT YOU SAID THIS WAS A GRADUATION PARTY, NOT A VALENTINE'S DAY PARTY?" Sue yells to Grandpa George.

"Charlotte thinks she's coming down with the flu," Gavin explains, rubbing his hand soothingly against her back. "But Molly's pregnant and *that word* makes her throw up."

Everyone groans and Aunt Claire smacks Gavin's arm. "Did you not hear me when I told you as soon as you got here that we weren't going to tell grandpa about Molly right now?"

Gavin winces. "Oops, sorry. I totally forgot. Charlotte told me she cancelled the ice sculpture for the wedding and I got distracted."

Uncle Drew throws up his hands and huffs. "No ice sculpture? Are you kidding me with this shit? What the hell am I going to lick at the reception? You guys ruin all the fun."

I give Charlotte a knowing look and she rolls her eyes at me, her face finally returning to a normal color now that all the soup talk is finished.

"I was wondering if any of you girls would follow in your Aunt Claire's footsteps," Grandpa says with a sigh. "I hope you were smarter than her and at least know the guy's name."

"Heeeeeeeey!" Aunt Claire protests, putting her hands on her hips.

"Oh, I'm sorry, I didn't realize we were able to change history. If that's the case, I can tell all the guys at the VFW my daughter got married and THEN got knocked up, like a good daughter should," Grandpa states. "No offense, Molly."

"None taken," I reply, grabbing Marco's arm and pulling him closer to my grandfather. "This is Marco, my boyfriend. Marco, this is Grandpa George."

Marco holds out his hand and gives my grandfather a smile. "It's nice to meet you, sir."

Grandpa stubbornly keeps his hands in his pockets for a few seconds, finally removing one slowly. Instead of grabbing Marco's hand, he sticks a toothpick in his mouth and starts to chew on it. After a few tense moments, he removes the toothpick and holds it up in front of Marco.

"See this here toothpick?"

Marco nods silently.

"If you don't do right by my granddaughter, I will gouge out your eyes with it, then rip off your scalp and skull-fuck you," he says quietly, sticking the toothpick back in his mouth.

"SOMEONE'S MOVING TO SUFFOLK?" Sue asks loudly.

"Well, this has been fun," I mutter, grabbing Marco's hand again before he passes out or runs away in fear. "I need a drink, who wants a drink?"

Everyone raises their hands and we all move towards the coolers my parent's set up by the food tables. Opening the first one, I find it filled with ice and beer. Quickly grabbing two of the bottles, I hand one to Marco and then twist the top of mine, sighing happily when I hear the seal *pop*.

I bring the cold bottle up to my lips, my mouth watering for some much needed alcohol. The beer is an inch from my mouth when it's quickly snatched out of my hands and replaced with a cup of apple juice.

"That baby already has enough problems with our family's DNA flowing through it, don't make it worse by getting it drunk," my mother scolds, chugging the beer she just took from me.

I watch longingly as she downs half the bottle before she saunters off to greet more family members.

"So, hey, thanks again for the graduation party," I tell Marco, trying not to glare at him while he drinks *his* beer. "If we ever do this again, let's do it when I'm not fake pregnant and I can get wasted and pretend like I'm not related to any of these people."

Marco laughs and leans forward, pressing a quick kiss to my lips. Just like with everything he does with me, it's easy and natural and he makes it feel like he's done it a million times before. I love that he organized this party for me, and I love that he made my family feel bad about not acknowledging my graduation, but would really love it if we were alone right now so he could kiss me again. I know that makes me sound all stupid and girly and exactly like my sisters, but I'm so distracted by his lips that I don't care.

"I'll make you a deal. I'll distract everyone so you can sneak a few beers if you promise you won't let your grandfather skull-fuck me," he negotiates alcohol for protection like he's been a part of this family for years.

I hold up my hand, putting my fingers in the same formation as Uncle Drew did earlier.

"Shocker Honor, I promise I will never let my grandfather skull-fuck you with a toothpick."

Chapter 14

- I Have a Vagerie -

Marco

I CAN'T BELIEVE I agreed to this. What the hell was I thinking? Oh, I know. I was thinking that I'd do whatever Molly asked of me after she protected me from imminent skull-fuckage at her graduation party the other day. I was so happy to have my brain non-fucked with a toothpick that I told her I wanted to take her on a date. As much as I like her family now that they've decided not to kill me, I wanted to do something with her away from their prying eyes where we didn't have to watch what we say about this whole pregnancy business. I made the mistake of telling her we could go wherever she wanted.

"Your mom likes this brand of wine, right?" Molly asks as we walk up the steps of my mother's front porch.

Yep, Sunday dinner. Molly decided our first official date should be Sunday dinner with my family. I am so screwed.

"My mom likes anything with the name wine in it," I joke. "Don't worry about the wine. You should really be more concerned with my mother hitting you with a wooden spoon because I didn't knock you up, while at the same time complaining I almost killed her when she thought I *did* knock you up."

After the graduation party ended, I drove Molly back to Seduction and Snacks so she could get her car, and I told her all about how I had to come clean with my mom and sisters about what's going on.

"I still can't believe she goes to the same salon as my Aunt Claire," Molly mutters. "And that the two of them went baby shopping and my aunt never said a word to me about it."

Opening the door and motioning for her to go in ahead of me, I call for my mom as soon as we get inside.

Three sets of feet pound against the floor like a herd of elephants as my mom, Tessa, and Rosa all come racing out of the kitchen and down the hall.

Mom goes right up to Molly and pulls her in for a tight hug, kissing both of her cheeks before pulling back to look her up and down.

"You're prettier than your pictures on The Facebook," she exclaims with an approving smile.

"It's just Facebook, Mom," Rosa tells her. "Hi, I'm Rosa."

Mom moves out of the way so Rosa and Molly can meet.

"You know I don't understand that interwebs thing," Mom complains. "And you still haven't fixed the remote so I can send those text message things and—"

"Molly, this is my other sister, Tessa!" I interrupt, hoping Molly doesn't remember what I said in the car on the way to meet her family when I mentioned how Alfanso D.'s mother probably tries to send text messages from the television remote.

My sisters take turns giving Molly hugs as well and my mother ushers all of us into the living room.

"I thought we could have a nice little chat while the lasagna is baking," she says, taking a seat on the couch.

"Wow, you have so many books," Molly exclaims, walking over to the bookshelf and glancing at all the titles.

"I usually prefer autobiographies, but my daughters keep buying me romance novels," Mom tells her as Molly walks the length of the built-in bookshelf along the back wall. "I really enjoyed that *Fifty Hues of Black*. It was quite spicy."

My sisters laugh and I try not to let this information ruin my appetite.

"Mom, it's called...you know what? Never mind, I'm just glad you enjoy them," Tessa laughs.

"Oh, my God. I can't believe you have a copy of this," Molly states.

I watch in horror as she pulls *Seduction and Sugar* off the shelf and turns around, holding it up.

Oh, fuck. Please let these crazy women remember that Molly doesn't know I'm the author yet. Please, for the love of God. I promise I'll go to church more than just on Christmas and Easter. I promise not to masturbate more than two...make that four, times a week. I will let Grandpa George skull-fuck me AND give me a minivan and I'll say ten Hail Mary's for saying the word 'skull-fuck' in this prayer.

"Wow, you even have a signed copy," Molly muses as she flips open the front cover.

Thank fuck I wrote that dedication in Italian because I knew it would make my mother forgive me for writing a dirty cookbook.

"What does it say?" she asks.

"It says, 'Thank you for loving this cookbook and for your kind email telling me I'm the most decent, dedicated and delightful man you've ever known.'" I quickly tell her before my mother can open her mouth.

My sisters both cover their mouths to hide their laughter and my mother gives me the stink eye. She was not happy when I told her she needed to keep quiet about this until I had a chance to tell her myself.

"Well, that's...nice. And unexpected," Molly mutters, turning around to slide the cookbook back on the shelf. "I've had a few exchanges with the author on Facebook and he's a real piece of work."

She turns back around and my mother pats the spot on the couch. Molly sits down and when I move to take the spot next to her, my mother quickly slides up against Molly, forcing me to sit on the other side of my mother. I plop down with a sigh as my sisters both sit down across from us on the love seat.

"Marco, did I tell you that guy asked me out on a date on Facebook?" Molly asks with a laugh.

"You don't say?" I reply, glaring over at Rosa while she beams at me.

"I happened to be on the author's page the other day and saw your comment to him," Rosa tells her. "He really does sound like a momma's boy. Nice job on the cutting the cord comment."

If I glare at my sister any harder, I'm going to pop a blood vessel in my forehead.

Molly laughs and rests her elbow on the arm of the couch. "Thanks, I was pretty proud of that one. Of course the guy had to go and apologize and be all nice. I'm sure it was just a publicity stunt. Now I don't know what to think about the whole date thing."

"I think you should go," Tessa pipes up.

"Um, hello?" I mutter in irritation, waving my hand in the air. "Person she's already dating, sitting right here."

Sure, we haven't been on an official date yet and we haven't had a chance to talk about being exclusive, but I think fake knocking her up and being a fake baby daddy gives me the right to call this thing between us whatever I want.

"You and that Alfanso D. sound a lot alike," Rosa muses. "I bet if Molly agrees to go out with him, she'd probably find out you're almost like the same person."

Why couldn't I have been an only child?

"I think I have enough on my plate right now, so I think I'll stick to just dating your brother," Molly laughs, looking behind my mother's head to give me a wink.

"Marco tells me you just graduated from the school where he

teaches," my mother states, pulling Molly's eyes from mine. "I hope my son was a good teacher."

Mom gives me a dirty look, a nice little warning that she will kick my ass if she hears anything bad about me, quickly turning and smiling at Molly like she didn't just silently threaten to end my life.

"He was a very good teacher, one of the best," Molly tells her.

I'm too busy patting myself on the back to predict the next words out of my mother's mouth.

"I wish he'd spend more time focusing on teaching instead of writing that porn," she complains.

If we were in a bar, I'm pretty sure you'd be able to hear the screech of a needle sliding across a record as the entire place goes silent.

Molly chuckles. "I'm sorry, I thought you just said writing porn."

It's like we've all started playing a game of freeze tag and the person who's "it" is being a major asshole and refusing to unfreeze everyone. My sisters aren't moving or blinking, my mouth is stuck in a blow-up doll "Oh" face, and I'm wondering how long a person can hold their own breath before passing out.

I'm pretty certain that *I'm* the asshole and I know I should say something—*anything*—to change the subject, but words are potatoes and four is a purple cat.

Molly realizes she's the only one laughing and looks around the room at everyone's shocked expressions.

"Um, Marco?" she asks softly.

"Ha ha, so, funny story," Rosa pipes up and I finally breathe, taking back my wish to be an only child as long as she does something to fix this fucking situation.

"Marco here writes porn!" she announces. "Well, he likes to call them *erotic stories*, but whatever."

So, I'll just go ahead and die right about now.

"He's quite good at it too," Tessa adds, playing along with Rosa. "He writes fanfiction. *Vampire Diaries* fanfiction to be more specific.

You should let her read the m/m one you did with Damon and Stefan."

Tessa winks at me and I vow to make sure Valerie goes to her first day of preschool with a backpack filled with condom-covered bananas for show-and-tell.

I can see by the confused look on Molly's face as she looks back and forth between my sisters, and I that she's not sure if she should believe what they're saying. I hope to God she doesn't think I'd write a story like that. I mean, come on. Damon and Stefan are brothers, that's just disgusting.

"Let's talk about something else," my mother suggests, folding her hands in her lap.

At least my mother loves me enough to stop this insanity before my sisters make it worse.

"Molly, has Marco ever told you about when he was thirteen and I found all of his socks stuck to the floor under his bed?" she asks Molly sweetly.

"I think we should talk about Molly and the awesome thing she's doing for her sister," I proclaim, stopping my mother before she goes off on a masturbation tangent.

Seriously, it's like they get a sick thrill out of making me look like an asshole. A porn-writing, tube-sock-masturbating asshole.

"You must really love your sister," Mom states. "Your Aunt Claire told me over lunch the other day that your family is very close."

Molly nods. "I do, and we are. They drive me crazy, but I'd do anything for them. Clearly, since I'm lying to all of them just to make sure my sister gets to marry the man she's been in love with since she was a little girl."

The pounding of little feet echoes out in the hallway and a dark-haired ball of energy flies into the room and dives onto Tessa's lap.

"Aren't you supposed to be taking a nap, little girl?" Tessa asks Valerie as she wraps her arms around her daughter's waist and pulls

BAKING AND BABIES

her back against her chest.

"Naps are dumb," Valerie announces. "Who are you?"

She points at Molly and then squirms out of Tessa's hold to march over and stand in front of her.

"I'm Molly," she greets her with a smile.

"My name's Vagerie."

Everyone laughs when she says her name wrong and mom shoots Tessa a questioning look.

"Why is my granddaughter calling herself *Vagerie?*"

We hear a laugh from the doorway and I let out a sigh of relief when I see my brother-in-law standing there.

"Sorry, that's my fault," Danny explains. "Tessa told me we need to start using proper words for body parts whenever Val asks about them, and her new favorite word is vagina."

Valerie nods excitedly, moving right up to Molly until she's pressing her little body against Molly's knees.

"I have a vagerie and are you the Molly that Mommy says Uncle wants to hump?"

I immediately cough and choke at the same time and my mother reaches over and pats me on the back.

"It's okay, hump means pee, but I don't think people are 'opposed to pee on each other," Valerie informs her before turning her head towards me. "Uncle, you aren't gonna pee on her, are you?"

Jumping up from the couch, I grab Valerie's hand and pull her towards the doorway.

"Come on, Val, let's go run with scissors and light some matches." I ignore the laughter coming from all four women in the room. "When we're done, I'll pour you a bowl of sugar and give you some Red Bull to wash it down."

"YAAAAAAY I love sugar!" Valerie cheers as we walk passed Danny and I call him a traitor for laughing with everyone else.

"Make sure she gives you another lesson on how to properly dress a banana," my mother calls after me. "You wouldn't even know how to take care of a pretend baby, let alone a real one."

I walk faster with Valerie, knowing it's probably not wise to leave Molly alone with those people for any length of time, but I have to get out of that room before I lose my shit.

"My cat licks his butt hole. Can you lick your butt hole, Uncle? Mommy says everyone has nipples, but I think she's lying. My Barbie's don't have nipples. Do you have nipples?" Valerie rambles as we make our way to the spare bedroom.

Kids are so weird.

Chapter 15
— Ganja Grandma —
Molly

LEANING AGAINST THE door frame of my parent's living room, I watch my uncles and Marco all huddled together, deep in conversation. It's so crazy how well he fits in with my family that it's hard to believe he hasn't been around them more than a handful of times. I'm trying to not let it get to me that we haven't had more than a few minutes alone since this insanity started, but I only have myself to blame. Marco asked me out on a date and I chose dinner with his family instead of going somewhere alone. It was nice to witness someone else's family be embarrassing instead of my own, but I should have consulted one of my sisters before immediately deciding on a family dinner for our first real date.

"How you feeling, honey? You up for tonight?" my mom asks, coming up next to me.

"Feeling great and I can't wait for tonight," I tell her, even though I'd rather have a root canal than participate in the activities my mother and aunts have planned.

Tonight is Charlotte's bachelorette party, and while I'll be busy watching everyone get white-girl-wasted and make bad choices as I sip on fucking apple juice, the guys are going to hang out here.

Gavin decided he'd rather have a more relaxed bachelor party, much to Uncle Drew's dismay, especially since mom made the whole "No Strippers in the House" rule after my dad's bachelor party. Obviously I wasn't born yet, but I've heard the stories. Aunt Claire warned all of us kids years ago to never mention my mom's favorite couch and how she dragged it out into the front yard and lit it on fire, screaming about "stripper juice stains" for the whole neighborhood to hear.

"What if we put plastic on the furniture?" Uncle Drew asks, leaning out of the huddle to shout to my mother.

"What if I light your balls on fire?" she replies.

"Wouldn't be the first time," he mutters, going back to the guys.

"So, what's this big announcement you have for us?" I ask my mom.

We were originally all supposed to meet at Charlotte and Gavin's place and go from there, but my mom called everyone this morning and said she had something to tell us and wanted everyone to come here first.

"It's a surprise. Something needs to be set up first so it shouldn't be too much longer," she tells me. "Oh, Grandma Madelyn decided to join us tonight, so prepare yourself."

I let out a surprised laugh. My Grandma Madelyn is my mom's mom and she's a tad uptight, a tiny bit snobby, and a control freak when it comes to any kind of big event. She's been driving mom and Charlotte insane lately, calling ten times a day to check on the wedding plans. I don't really see her letting loose or boozing it up with everyone else in the hotel suite we booked downtown Cleveland for tonight. At least I'll have one sober person to keep me company though. Well, besides Charlotte, but she has to act drunk and that's going to be just as bad. She's been freaking out all week about how she's going to make it look like she's drinking in front of everyone, so I filled up five flasks with water and stuck them in my purse. Ava packed three of her own filled with orange juice, and we plan on shoving them at her any time someone else tries to give her a real drink.

"I DON'T WANT YOUR HUSH MONEY!"

The front door slams shut and my mom and I turn our heads to see what the hell is going on.

Tyler, Ava's boyfriend, stands in the entryway with Grandma Madelyn, holding out a wad of bills to her.

"It's not hush money, Madelyn, it's gas money," Tyler explains. "You already offered to take the stuff to my dad's house and I want to pay for your gas."

Grandma looks at the money in his hand with disgust while mom and I make our way towards them.

"That's drug money! I don't want your drug money!" Grandma shouts, crossing her arms over her chest.

"Drug money spends just as well as regular money!" Tyler argues. "What do you think I used to pay for that new TV Ava and I got you for your birthday last year?"

Tyler told me a few months ago that he started growing pot to sell to his friends so he could make some extra cash to buy Ava an engagement ring. I'm not a prude and I've smoked it a time or two, but I told him he was an idiot and nothing good could come from that endeavor since the stuff still isn't legal in Ohio.

"What the hell is going on?" Mom asks.

"Um, well, you see, one of my friends overheard our landlord talking to someone about there being pot in a some of the apartments," Tyler explains. "I got a little freaked out there would be a raid or something, so I packed everything up in my trunk and got it out of there just in case."

Mom sighs and shakes her head.

"I was pulling it out of my trunk to put in Dad's car when Madelyn came up and asked if she could help," he says with a shrug. "When she asked what was going on, I told her I was just moving some of my stuff back to Mom and Dad's, and she offered to help so they wouldn't have to."

Mom sighs again and I wonder if she's lost the ability to speak or if she's just letting out all the pissed off air so she doesn't start screaming obscenities in front of her mother.

"Is your father aware you planned on putting illegal narcotics in his car?" Mom asks.

"You've met my father, right? He offered to smoke it all so the cops wouldn't find it," Tyler replies.

Tyler found out not too long ago that his biological father is my Uncle Drew. It's a long story that involved a drunken one-night stand in college, but there you have it. This information, while a tad shocking, at least gave all of us a reason for why Uncle Drew and Tyler are so strangely similar.

"I thought it was just clothes and nick-knacks until I smelled skunk. I know that smell. I've smoked the ganja a few times in my day, but I've never seen so many pounds of the ganja in one place," Grandma tells us, whispering the word "ganja" each time she uses it.

"Please tell me you did not bring a trunk load of marijuana to my house," Mom finally speaks.

"Of course not," Tyler replies. "I'm not an idiot. It's just two totes of marijuana, not an entire trunk load."

Mom and I both shake our heads and I wonder if I should start restraining her now or wait until she makes a lunge for his throat.

"The dried buds are all carefully sealed in zip lock bags, don't worry."

Grandma drops her arms to her sides and studies Tyler for a few seconds.

"Buds as in flower buds? Like house plants?" she asks.

"Sure, just like house plants," Tyler nods, deciding it's best to humor her so she stops screaming about hush money.

"Well, in that case, put them in my trunk and I'll take them to my house," she informs him.

"Mom!" my mother yells.

"Oh, Liz, it's fine. You know Drew and Jenny don't have green thumbs and they'll just kill the plants. I can water the ganja on Thursday when I water my ferns and lilies," she informs her.

"Excuse me, could you say that one more time, a little louder? Stan, get a mic on her, would ya?"

We all turn and see a guy standing behind us in the hallway with a huge camera on his shoulder, while another guy stands next to him holding a long metal pole with a giant microphone attached to the end.

"Surprise!" Mom says with fake enthusiasm. "The big announcement is that Claire and I were asked to do a documentary about our daily lives and running a business."

Grandma quickly smooths her hair back and straightens her clothes, smiling brightly for the camera.

"I don't know if I'm comfortable being on television, Liz," she whispers through her smile.

"It's a little late for that, Ganja Grandma," Mom mutters.

The front door opens and Tyler jumps out of the way as Ava pokes her head inside.

"The limo is here, bitches!" she shouts. "Any female who plans on being a drunk whore tonight should immediately report to the driveway!"

Mom groans, closing her eyes and dropping her head.

"What's with the camera?" Ava asks, staring at the two strangers in the hallway, happily recording the shit show in front of them.

"Oh, no big deal. They're just filming a documentary on our family," I inform her. "You're just in time for the episode about Grandma becoming a drug dealer."

The camera and sound guy quickly turn away from us when the guys walk out of the living room in the middle of a heated argument.

"I jerked-off into socks when I was a teenager, for Christ's sake. It's not like I still do it now!" Marco yells loudly, coming to a quick stop when he sees the camera and microphone.

Dad, Uncle Drew, and Uncle Carter all slam into the back of

him when he stops so suddenly.

"What the hell, M.O.? Did your crusty socks stick to the floor or something?" Uncle Drew asks with a laugh. "Hey, are we on TV?!"

I quickly skirt around the camera crew and up to Marco, going up on my tiptoes to give him a kiss on the cheek and a sympathetic pat against his chest.

"It's fine, I'm sure this thing isn't going to air on any major networks or anything," I whisper.

"Actually, it's probably going to be syndicated on the Discovery Channel in all fifty states," the guy holding the microphone informs us.

"So, I just told a few million people I used to masturbate into my socks," Marco mutters.

"But you looked good doing it!" I say cheerfully.

"Can we please get moving? All this standing around is killing my buzz," Ava complains.

Charlotte comes bounding down the stairs just then, stopping at the bottom and looking around at everyone. "Sorry I took so long getting ready. What did I miss?"

"Jizz socks!" Uncle Drew shouts.

"Anyone have a preference on where we go tonight to film?" the camera guy asks. "Stay with the guys or go with the ladies?"

Drew walks around the guys and throws his arm over the cameraman's shoulder. "Might as well stay with us, man. I can't promise you strippers, but I *can* promise a turtle porn snuff film, and I have a guy from the zoo stopping by in an hour to let us play with a meerkat. Should make for good television entertainment, especially if we can get the meerkat to watch the turtle porn."

Charlotte grabs my arm and drags me away from Marco while everyone else says their good-byes. Once again, poor Marco is suffering at the hands of my family and I can't help but wonder how much more he's going to able to take before he heads for the hills. Not to mention the fact that I just kissed him in front of everyone, including a camera crew.

While the women pile into the stretch limo parked in the driveway, my sisters and I stand outside the vehicle for a few private minutes. Ava pulls one of the flasks out of her purse and hands it to Charlotte.

"Start chugging it in the limo," Ava tells her. "Make sure to giggle and yell a lot."

Charlotte takes the flask and rolls her eyes. "I've been drunk before, Ava. I think I know what I'm doing."

"And I've seen you drunk before. It's not pretty," Ava replies. "You go from telling everyone you love them to sobbing in two-point-three seconds. As a fake drunk, I expect better of you."

Aunt Claire leans her head out of the limo and looks at the three of us.

"Let's go, assholes. There's a bottle of vodka on ice at the hotel with my name on it and it's not gonna drink itself," she announces before pulling her head back inside.

"You people better not get on my nerves tonight," I mutter as I wait for Ava and Charlotte to get in the limo. "Drunk people are complete idiots when you're sober."

I hold onto the door and listen to Ava start up a chant with the rest of the women until the sounds of ten females screaming "Drunk bitches" repeatedly fills the quiet night. As I bend down to get in the limo and seal my fate, I hear my name shouted from the house. Quickly pulling back from the open door, I turn around to see Marco jogging down the front porch and across the yard.

All these years of making fun of my sisters for losing their heads over guys…is this what it was like for them? The nerves, the sweaty palms, and racing heart whenever you're in the same vicinity as him? The constant anxiety that you aren't smart enough, good enough or pretty enough to keep the interest of someone like him? I spent so much of my life making fun of how Charlotte and Ava behaved and I thought they were sad and pathetic. I get it now, and I'm ashamed of myself for being so hard on them. I watch Marco's face light up as he rushes towards me and I want to crawl under a rock because I don't feel worthy of that look in his eyes. The one that says he likes me, in spite of my family, and that I make him happy. The pressure of this is so much worse than anything I did in culinary school.

I move towards him in a trance, meeting him in the middle of the front yard. It's not fair for someone to be so good-looking without even trying. Even in a tight, long-sleeved grey t-shirt and worn jeans he looks just as good as he would if he were wearing a tux.

"I'm glad I caught you before you left," he smiles, the dimples in his cheeks making my knees weak.

"What's wrong?" I whisper, hoping he didn't race out here to ask for advice on how to make Uncle Drew stop dropping his pants and showing everyone his balls.

"Nothing's wrong, I just forgot something."

I open my mouth to ask if he forgot to write down the number to Poison Control in case Tyler gets into the nail polish remover again, but before I can take a breath, his hands are cupping my face and his lips are on mine. With my lips still parted to speak, his tongue slides easily into my mouth. All the blood in my body rushes to my nether regions and with every brush of his tongue against mine, I feel myself getting lightheaded. My hands fly to his chest and I grab onto handfuls of his shirt to hold myself steady as he kisses me soft and slow and the world around me disappears. He tastes like peppermint and smells like cookies, and I want to jump into his arms and wrap my legs around his waist. My heart thumps rapidly in my chest as our tongues swirl together until I'm not sure where he begins and I end. Our mouths have become one and have replaced everything in my brain with cheesy romantic poetry and dreamy Jane Austen quotes.

I need to stop this kiss before I turn completely stupid.

I never want this kiss to end and I don't care if it turns me into

Uncle Drew.

Marco slowly ends the kiss, gently biting my bottom lip as he pulls his mouth from mine. With my face still cradled in his hands, he presses his forehead to mine and sighs.

"Sorry, I tried to wait until we were alone to do that, but I think hell might freeze over before then," he laughs softly.

"GET A ROOM, YOU WHORES!"

The lust-filled excitement in my body quickly vanishes when I hear Ava yell to us from the limo.

"Wrap it up before you knock her up on the front lawn! Oh, wait…" Ava adds with a loud giggle.

"I should probably go. The drunks are getting restless," I tell him softly, wishing I never had to move and his warm, soft hands never had to drop from my face.

"Be careful," Marco says as his hands slide from my face and down the sides of my neck to rest on my shoulders. "Never take a drink you didn't pour yourself, and if you're being attacked, always scream 'fire' instead of 'help'."

I snicker, unclenching the death grip on his shirt to rest my hands on top of his on my shoulder.

"I'm hanging out with my aunts, sisters, and cousins all night," I remind him.

"You're forgetting I've met those women. You should be more afraid of *them* giving you a roofie and trying to rape you," he responds with a serious expression on his face.

"I'll call you later to make sure you're still alive," I tell him, regrettably taking a step back from him.

He laughs and sticks his hands into the front pocket of his jeans. "Don't worry about me, I'll be fine."

"Hey, Minivan Fuck Nugget! Do me a favor and grab the blow torch, edible underwear, Christmas tree tinsel, and the bag of goldfish from my trunk on your way in," Uncle Drew shouts from the open front door.

"Goldfish, as in goldfish crackers?" Marco yells back.

"Uh, no. Twenty-four *live* goldfish. Why in the world would I have goldfish *crackers* in my trunk? I thought you said he was smart, Molly?" Drew complains before going back inside.

Marco shakes his head and starts backing away from me as I do the same, refusing to take my eyes off of him as I move towards the limo.

"My mom keeps a cookie jar on top of the fridge with bail money in it, just in case," I inform him as my butt bumps against the side of the limo.

"Good to know," he replies with a wave, turning to jog to Drew's car parked in the driveway.

I take my time climbing backwards into the limo, staring at Marco's ass as he leans into the trunk of Uncle Drew's car. After that kiss, there is no way I'm waiting another second when this night is over to be alone with that man. Maybe I can sneak a few shots of liquid courage when no one is looking and have Ava and Charlotte give me some more advice. I don't know the first thing about flirting or seducing a guy, and judging by that stellar kiss, I'm going to need all the skills I can get. It's time for me to consult the experts.

"Don't knock it until you try it; pony play is very erotic," Ava informs the group as I sit on the comfortable leather bench next to Charlotte, closing the door behind me. "The plastic hooves are a little hard to get used to at first, but once you add the tail and the unicorn horn, you really get into it."

Did I say experts? I meant mental patients.

Chapter 16

- Fuck Betty White -

Marco

"SORRY, NO TAKE backs. You already said you'd kill Demi Moore, marry Taylor Swift, and fuck Betty White," Drew reminds me.

"I blurted it out without thinking!"

"Hide yo wives, hide yo grannies!" Drew cheers.

"My wife is going to be your child's grandmother. Do you want to fuck her too? Or are you more selective with your grandmother fucking?" Jim asks.

Oh, for the love of all that is holy…playing Fuck, Marry, Kill seemed like a much better idea than being forced to watch that weird as shit turtle porn video again. Who knew turtles were so vocal during orgasm?

"I do not want to sleep with any grandmothers!" I protest.

Thankfully, the camera crew decided to pack it up and go home after Drew tried to get the meerkat to eat live goldfish out of the edible underwear he put on, and none of this is being recorded for the world to see.

"Alright, I've got *Friendship Rocks*, *Call of the Cutie*, and *Dog and Pony Show*. Which one will it be, boys?" Tyler asks, walking into the room with three DVDs in his hands.

"Ooooh, definitely *Dog and Pony Show*," Drew says with smile and a nod.

"We are not watching that stupid My Little Pony shit," Jim tells Tyler, grabbing the DVDs from his hands and chucking them across the room.

"Wait, MLP movies? Wow, that is NOT what I thought *Dog and Pony Show* was," Drew mutters.

"What the hell else are we going to do, then? Thanks to Drew we don't have a meerkat to play with anymore," Tyler complains.

"How the hell was I supposed to know? Jesus, you give a meerkat one sip of beer and you'd think I tried to poison him with the way that stick-up-his-ass zookeeper acted," Drew mutters.

"I'm pretty sure beer IS poisonous to an animal like that," Carter tells him.

"Excuse me for not being up-to-date on my meerkat knowledge," Drew grumbles. "It's not my fault the little guy liked it and wanted more. He was thirsty after all of that underwear candy. Fucking Tom Brady…"

Drew notices all of us staring at him in confusion and he shrugs. "I didn't feel like Sunshine Wiener Schnitzel was a good name for him, so I changed it to Tom Brady. It's always Tom Brady's fault."

We sit here for a few quiet minutes, staring into our bottles of beer.

"This is pathetic. Are we really this old that we don't know how to throw a good bachelor party anymore?" Carter asks.

"It's all Liz's fault for not letting me have strippers," Drew complains. "Stupid strippers and their stupid snail trails…"

"I think we should watch some student/teacher porn in honor of Marco and Molly," Tyler suggests with a wag of his eyebrows. "I bet you could tell us a few stories about bending that one over your desk and spanking her with a ruler, am I right?"

He nudges Jim with his elbow and gives him a smirk.

"I bet I could tell a story about how I shoved my entire arm up your ass, how about that?" Jim replies.

"Awww, no fair!" Drew complains. "I was going to tell that story later. No matter what anyone tells you, KY Tingling Jelly shouldn't go in your ass. I was shitting fire for three days, let me tell you."

I quickly chug the rest of my beer, hoping the alcohol kicks in soon and erases everything from my mind that happened tonight. Well, except the kiss. Damn, that fucking kiss almost made me come in my pants. As soon as Molly walked out the door all I could think about was kissing her. Shit, from the moment I open my eyes every morning until I fall asleep, that's all I think about. I couldn't stand going one more second without knowing what kissing her would be like instead of just dreaming about it. I ran outside as fast as I could and I couldn't wipe the goofy grin from my face seeing her still standing next to the limo.

God, those lips. That tongue. That fucking mouth that tasted like sweet, crisp apples, just like I wondered. I think I might've been better off not knowing. Now that my suspicions are confirmed, I'm never going to be able to get rid of my hard-on. I want to strip her naked and taste every inch of her skin. I want to bury myself inside of her until we both lose our minds. I want to hear her scream my name and claw at my back until…

"What are your immediate future plans with my daughter?" Jim asks, pulling me out of my horny thoughts and hoping I didn't mutter any of them out loud.

"Um…to spend time with her, and…uh, yeah. Hang out and stuff," I tell him uncomfortably. I don't really think he'd appreciate me telling him all the ways I want to fuck his daughter.

"I mean, are you planning on making an honest woman out of her and proposing?" he questions. "It's the least you could do after you defiled her and ruined her for any other man."

Wow, really? And here I thought Jim was starting to take a liking to me. What the hell is wrong with my dick and sperm that he thinks it would defile Molly? I'll have you know my sperm is very nice, and

I've gotten quite a few compliments on how appealing to the eye my penis is.

"She's not defiled," I grumble. "The Desoto sperm is filled with all sorts of good stuff."

"My sperm is filled with pineapple. I eat two pineapples a day leading up to blow job day," Drew comments.

"She's twenty years old and just finished college. What man is going to want a woman tied down with another man's child?" Jim asks, folding his arms and glaring at me.

"Um, how about me, the father of the child?"

The fake child, but whatever. I know I freaked out in the beginning and couldn't imagine being with her if she were having someone else's kid, but things have changed since then. If Molly really were pregnant by someone else, it wouldn't matter. I'd find a way to deal with the knowledge that she had someone else's gross spooge all up in her, and I'd deal with everything that comes along with helping her raise that child, because in the end, she's still the same girl I've wanted for two years. She's still Molly and even if we don't know each other well, even if tonight was the first time I kissed her and there's still so much I need to learn about her, she's gotten into my heart and under my skin, and I'm not going to let anything ruin that.

"At least Gavin has the good sense to wrap his dick up to prevent shit like this, because he and Charlotte are smart and they don't want kids," Jim informs me.

"That's what you think," I laugh, realizing immediately I should have kept my mouth shut.

Everyone looks at me funny and I quickly blurt out the first thing I can think of.

"I mean, I wrap my shit up too, but accidents still happen. I even double-bag it. That's right, I wear two condoms so suck it!" I tell them. "But you know what, sperm is conniving and vindictive, and if they want to chew their way through two layers of latex, they will sure as shit gnaw through that stuff and give you the finger while their little spermy tails are moving them right along. Fucking sperm and their spermy tails..."

Realizing I sound like a complete moron, I slam my empty bottle on top of the coffee table and grab another beer from the ice bucket in the middle. I down the entire thing, wiping my hand across my mouth when I finish.

Tyler decides to break the tension in the room by walking over to Jim and getting down on one knee in front of him.

"Jim, give me your hand," he states, holding his palm out.

"What the fuck are you doing?" Jim complains.

"Just give me your hand, I need to ask you something."

Jim looks at him in disgust, and then smacks Tyler's hand away.

"Fine," Tyler huffs. "We'll do it your way."

He clears his throat and lifts his chin, resting his hands on top of Jim's knees.

"Jim, I'd like to officially ask for your daughter's hand in marriage," Tyler tells him confidently.

"Fuck, I think I'm going to cry," Drew mumbles with a sniffle, rubbing his fists against his eyes.

"Get the fuck off your knee and remove your hands from my legs," Jim growls.

"I'm sorry, Jim, but I need to do this the right way. I want you to see that I will spend as much time on my knees as it takes to please you."

Drew laughs and holds out his fist for Carter to bump. "Ha ha, that's what she said!"

Jim glares at him and Drew gives him the finger.

"Oh, fuck your face. Like I was the only one thinking it."

"I can't believe you're going to get married," Gavin says quietly. "What happened to bros before hos?"

Tyler snorts. "Really, dude? You're getting married in like, a few weeks. You already made the decision to quit me for a ho so it's time for me to get my own life and my own ho."

Jim snaps his fingers in front of Tyler's face. "Hey, asshole. The hos you're referring to are my daughters."

Gavin and Tyler ignore him and continue with their own weird conversation.

"I didn't quit you, I just asked the love of my life to marry me. I'm sorry if that gets your panties in a twist," Gavin complains.

"I wore Ava's panties ONCE and you were supposed to keep that a secret, fucker!" Tyler yells angrily. "You're my best friend, and in some circumstances you will come first, but not when it has to do with marriage, which you should understand. I'm sorry, but I'm picking the ho this time."

Jim punches Tyler in the arm and pulls back his fist to do it again when Tyler holds up his hands in surrender. "I'm sorry, I'm sorry! Ho is a term of endearment, I swear!"

"Whatever," Gavin grumbles. "It's not like I'd marry you anyway. It just would have been nice to be asked."

Tyler gives him a smile, pounds his fist against his heart and points at Gavin. "You're my boy, Blue Balls."

Gavin does the same with his fist and Tyler turns back around on his knees to face Jim.

"So, do I have your permission to marry Ava? I've already made the calculations and I only need to sell two more ounces of weed to be able to buy her the ring she wants, and since I have roughly thirty ounces heading to Madelyn's house—"

"Twenty-five," Drew interrupts. "Sorry, that shit is full of sorcery. It kept calling my name and I couldn't resist. Speaking of that, you're out of Cheetos and Fruity Pebbles."

Jim sighs, shoving Tyler's hands off his knees. "You didn't knock her up, did you? Do I have to get my shotgun?"

Tyler quickly shakes his head. "No, sir. We are extremely careful. I always wear a condom, and when I don't, I pull out faster than a roadrunner speeding away from dynamite. No sperm has touched your daughter's ovaries, I can promise you that."

Tyler looks over his shoulder and gives me a smirk. If he wasn't so much like a girl and hitting girls is frowned upon, I'd punch him right in the face.

"Get off your damn knees, dumbass. I'll let you marry Ava as long as you never use the words *sperm* and *your daughter's ovaries* in a sentence again. Ever. If you even think those words in my presence, I will kill you and make it look like an accident," Jim threatens.

Tyler pushes himself up from the floor and leans in to hug Jim, who immediately holds his hand up and presses it against Tyler's face to hold him off.

"Stop trying to hug me."

"Can I call you dad, then?" Tyler asks, his words muffled behind Jim's palm.

"Not if you want to keep your dick from being shoved down your throat."

My phone vibrates in my back pocket and I quickly pull it out and step out of the room while Drew runs over to Jim and Tyler and tries to make a group hug happen.

When I get out the hallway, I look down and smile when I see a text from Molly.

Send me a penis of yur picture :)

I laugh when I see she screwed up her words and must have managed to sneak some alcohol at the party, and then my laughter dies when I realize what it is she's trying to ask. She wants me to send her a picture of my penis. My heart starts racing and my palms start sweating as I run down the hallway to the closest bathroom.

Flipping on the light switch and locking the door behind me, I turn in circles trying to figure out where I can stand that will give me the best lighting. It's not very bright in here and there are too many dark shadows. This is not going to make my penis look the best that he can be, dammit! I need a spotlight or a bulb with a minimum of seventy-five watts for optimum photographic beauty.

Realizing I'm not going to get what I need in here, I see another door by the shower. Walking across the large bathroom, I open the door and see that it leads into a bedroom. Poking my head into the room, I see exactly what I need in the far corner. I move quickly across the carpeted floor, unbuttoning my jeans as I go. I don't have a lot of time to do this before the guys will wonder where I am.

I close my eyes and play back the kiss out in the yard, remembering the feel of Molly's tongue against mine and the soft little moans she made into my mouth. I need a chubby for this photo to really impress Molly and a chubby is what I'm now holding in my hands thanks to that quick little trip down memory lane.

It would be great if I could say that my girlfriend's father didn't walk in on me two minutes later sitting at his wife's make-up table with the bright lights lining the mirror highlighting my dick in one hand while I held my cell phone pointed down at it in another, staring at a framed photo of his wife which I swear was a total accident, but that would be a lie.

While I apply pressure to my bloody, split lip and wonder if I still have the ability to eat solid foods, Drew sits down next to me on the floor of the bedroom. He hands me a bag of frozen peas to hold against my eye, giving me a sympathetic look.

"Don't feel bad, dude, we've all spanked it a few times to a picture of Liz, she's hot."

Fucking Betty White. I blame her for all of this.

Chapter 17

— Lips, Tongue, Penis, Suck —
Molly

"OH, MY GOD! Are you drunk?!" Charlotte whispers hysterically.

I sway a little bit as the room spins, grabbing onto the edge of the bar in the kitchen of the ginormous suite we've been celebrating in.

"Bugger off, you daft cow!"

"Why are you speaking with a British accent? What the hell is happening right now?" Charlotte complains, grabbing my arms and giving me a little shake.

"I'm practicing for when I travel the world. I want to fit in with the locals in London. Top o' the mornin' to ya, eh?!"

Charlotte shakes her head at me, all three of them. "That was Irish and I think Canadian. How much alcohol have you snuck?"

I hold up one hand and spread out all five fingers.

"Seven many," I mumble, trying to focus on my fingers and wondering why we have so many. Why five and not four? Do we really need a ring finger? It holds no purpose aside from giving us a place to put rings.

"You're lucky mom and Aunt Claire haven't come back yet from apologizing to the strippers and aren't witnessing this right now," she mutters.

"Why aren't *you* out there with them?" Ava asks, coming up beside us. "You're the one who puked all over the poor guy's stomach."

Charlotte rolls her eyes and puts her hands on her hips. "I already apologized to him and offered to pay for a new thong. He was just so greasy and he kept slapping his flaccid junk against my knee, and it reminded me of bologna and I couldn't help it."

Luckily Charlotte was able to play off her stripper-inducing puke by batting her eyelashes and giggling about being soooooo drunk. I had already snuck into the bathroom for the tenth time to take a shot by the time the three hip-thrusting, dick-dangling men showed up so watching her vomit made me run right to the bathroom and purge the demons. Everyone had a good laugh about how my "baby" didn't like strippers.

"WOOOHOOO bring back the naked men! Charlotte, why aren't you drinking?!" Grandma Madelyn yells, dancing her way past us and sloshing her drink all over the floor.

Charlotte holds up her flask of water and takes a sip, which makes Grandma throw her arms up in the air and shout again, throwing the contents of her drink all over the wall in front of her.

"Jesus, who knew Grandma was like a Gremlin? You feed her booze after midnight and she turns into crazy drunk monster," Charlotte mutters.

"So, did you text Marco? What did you say?" Ava asks, looking away from grandma as she gets up on the coffee table and starts thrusting her hips to the loud music blaring through the sound system in the living room.

"I said I'd like a spot of tea while I get snookered," I giggle.

"Why do you have a British accent? Charlotte, why does she have a British accent?" Ava asks, looking away from me to question our sober sister.

Charlotte shrugs. "It appears our sister turns British when she gets drunk."

"Oh, are you guys talking about foreign languages?" Aunt Jenny asks as she stumbles over to us, drinking the last bit of martini from her glass before smacking it down on the bar behind me.

"I don't get why we can't just all speak American," She complains. "You've got British and Alaskan and Canadian and Texan...why do we need all these different languages mucking everything up?"

Charlotte puts her arm around Aunt Jenny and gives her a squeeze. "Oh, Aunt Jenny. You always know how to make me feel like the smartest person in the room."

Aunt Jenny beams at Charlotte and gives her a sloppy kiss on the cheek. "I love you too, Charlotte!"

The three of us watch her stumble over to Grandma and get on top of the coffee table with her.

"Alright, back to the important matter at hand," Ava says, turning back to face me. "What did you say to Marco? Did you text him what I told you to?"

I pull my phone out of my back pocket and hand it to her without a word. She presses a few buttons and her eyes widen in shock.

"You asked him for a picture of his penis?!" she shouts.

"I tried to do what you said and tell him to come up here because I got us a hotel room, but I couldn't figure out how to type all those words," I tell her with a shrug.

"Did he send the picture? Let me see!"

Charlotte leans over Ava's shoulder and we both stare at her.

"What? I'm getting married, I'm not dead. Marco is hot and I'm sure he has an equally hot penis," Charlotte explains.

"Sorry, no Italian sausage for you tonight, Char. But he did send a close-up picture of a bloody lip, which is a little confusing," Ava tells us, turning the phone around for me to see.

"Shit. Did dad beat up his face?!" I yell, trying not to sway so I can get a better look at the photo. "Oh, no. His poor, pretty face. I really like that face."

Ava turns the phone back around and starts rapidly punching buttons.

"What are you doing? Are you telling him to send the picture penis again?" I ask, leaning forward to see what she's typing.

"Forget about the penis picture, you drunk slut. I'm doing what you were supposed to do and telling him to come up to the hotel."

My phone makes a *whooshing* sound, signaling that she sent it. She sets it down on the counter and walks around the bar, grabbing a glass from one of the cupboards and filling it up with water. She slides it across the counter to me and points at it.

"Chug it. Time to sober up, bitch."

I grab the glass and drink, half of it dribbling down my chin.

"I don't think this is a good idea. Should she really try and seduce him when she's drunk?" Charlotte asks as I slam the empty glass down and ask for a refill.

"She needs to be a little drunk or she'll chicken out. Some liquid courage is always good the first time you touch a penis," Ava announces, sliding another full glass of water towards me.

"Hey, I've touched a penis before. It was the size of a piece of Pez candy, but it was still a living, breathing penis," I inform them, bringing the glass up to my mouth.

"That doesn't count. Quinn yanked your hand away as soon as you touched it. Haven't I always told you guys that it's never a good idea to have sex with a virgin?" Ava sighs. "They're so wound up with years of pent-up sperm they'll blow their load if the wind changes direction. Always go with someone who has experience."

The water starts churning in my stomach and I quickly put the glass down.

"Marco has experience," I whisper nervously. "And he's older. He knows what he's doing, and I've only touched a Pez Penis. What the fuck am I doing?!"

Charlotte smacks my cheek, grabs both of my arms, and turns me to face her. "Snap out of it, woman! There is no instruction manual for this shit. No one knows what they're doing. You just go with the flow and do what feels right."

I nod even though everything she's saying just makes me more nervous. Why isn't there an instruction manual? Sex For Partial Virgins 101.

The ding of my cell phone sounds from the counter, and I watch as Ava picks it up and smiles.

"Buckle up, slut. There's a penis with your name on it headed this way. He was already headed down here to see if you needed rescuing so he's right around the corner. There's also a partially melted bag of frozen peas and a raw steak coming as well, whatever that means," Ava states. "I really hope Uncle Drew hasn't been teaching him anything weird tonight."

My eyes widen and I whip my head back to face Charlotte.

"What if he wants to have sex with the steak? What if he wants to use the peas on me? Is that a thing? Like some sort of tiny Ben Wa balls or something?" I ask her in a panic. "I knew I never should have left him alone with Uncle Drew! Now he's got ideas. Weird, kinky ideas that involve frozen food and I don't know how to have regular sex, let alone frozen food sex!"

My scalp starts to get itchy and sweaty and I can't remember if I put on deodorant before I left the house. At least I put on good underwear.

"Speaking of Ben Wa balls, did you hear Aunt Jenny had to go to the emergency room AGAIN last week because she got them stuck up in her?" Ava laughs. "Uncle Drew asked if they could have their own parking space. I guess after the nurses spent so much time watching Aunt Jenny waddle across the parking lot while doing lunges, the doctor submitted the request to the hospital board for safety reasons."

I whimper and my lip starts to quiver.

"I don't want to go to the emergency room because frozen peas get stuck in my vagina!" I wail.

"Oh, for the love of God," Charlotte mutters. "Ava, stop freaking her out. Molly, no one's putting frozen peas up your who-ha. No one says you have to have sex with him tonight. You two need to be alone. Maybe start with something simple. Get to know his penis. See what he likes and take it slow."

I look at Ava to see if she agrees and find her nodding in approval.

"Slow is good. Try a blowjob. It's pretty impossible to screw those up. As long as your mouth is on his dick, he's not going to care about anything else."

Okay, I can do this. I can put my mouth on a penis. I've seen porn and I know how it's done. In theory.

"Why is it called a blowjob? Don't you just suck on it? There's no blowing involved, right?" I ask.

"Since you're a beginner, just stick with the sucking for now. When you graduate to the advanced class, we'll discuss the use of popsicles and lube that heats up when you blow on it. For now, just focus on the basics. Lips, tongue, penis, suck. The end," Ava explains.

"Lips, tongue, penis, suck," I repeat.

"I thought it was lick, slam, suck?" Grandma asks, dancing by us again and overhearing what I said. "Have I been doing tequila shots wrong tonight?"

She turns away from us when the hotel door opens and my mom and Aunt Claire walk back inside.

"Girls, you didn't send those strippers away, did you?" Grandma shouts across the room. "I need to borrow one of those boy's wieners to lips, tongue, penis and suck with my next tequila shot. I guess that's what the kids are doing these days."

There's a loud knock at the door, saving mom and Aunt Claire from trying to respond to Grandma. Aunt Claire moves to the side while my mom opens the door, holding it wide so Marco can come in.

"Oooooh, forget the stripper! I'll use *his* penis!" Grandma announces.

"You better get over there and get him to your room before Grandma ruins him," Charlotte whispers. "There is no coming back from false teeth falling out on your dick during a blow-job."

She pats me on the back and Ava gives me a thumb's up. "You got this. Embrace your inner slut."

I can do this. I can totally do this.

"Did someone order a hot piece of man-meat?" Aunt Claire shouts, sliding her hand around Marco's elbow and leading him into the room.

Mustering up as much confidence as I can, I raise my hand and smile.

"That would be me. Looks like my delivery came in thirty minutes or less."

Aunt Claire deposits Marco in front of me, grabbing Charlotte's arm and waving Ava over to join them as they head into the living room area.

I look up into Marco's face and I gasp.

"Holy shit! You have a black eye!"

Reaching my hand up, I gently touch the purple area on his upper cheekbone, jerking my hand away when he winces and gasps.

"Oh, no, your lip," I mutter, my fingers tracing over the crusted blood on his bottom lip.

The picture Ava showed me on my phone didn't come close to how bad it looks in person. His poor, perfect lip that rocked my world with that kiss earlier is now out of commission.

"It's okay. It looks worse than it is," he tells me, placing his hands on my hips and pulling me closer. "Just promise me if your dad asks you to search my place for pictures of your mom that you'll ignore him and not ask any questions."

I have no idea what he's talking about and I don't care. I'm sad I won't be getting any more kisses from him tonight, but that just makes what I'm about to do easier. No kisses means I won't be distracted and I won't attempt to waste time or try to chicken out before getting to the good stuff.

I'm putting Marco's penis in my mouth tonight and nothing is going to stop me.

Chapter 18

- Hairball -

Marco

THE DOOR CLOSES behind Molly and I watch her stalk towards me, looking so confident and beautiful that I almost can't breathe. It's deathly quiet in this room, especially compared to the one we just left filled with drunk women screaming and dancing on tables and loud, techno music that made my ears bleed. It's too quiet and I can hear my heart pounding in my chest. I don't want Molly to know I'm nervous to be alone with her. I want her to see me as strong and confident, not a pussy with sweaty palms. I was already on my way down here to see if she needed saved from bachelorette party hell, and as soon as I got her text telling me she got us a hotel room, I knew it was time for me to come clean about Alfanso D. Even if nothing happens in this room tonight, I can't keep this from her any longer. It makes me sick to my stomach to keep lying to her whenever she talks about him. Me, him, me…what the fuck ever. I've never felt this way about anyone before and I don't want to fuck things up before they even really begin. She deserves better and on top of that, Rosa liked Molly so much after dinner the other night that she told me if I didn't tell her soon, she'd do it herself and it wouldn't be pretty.

"It's so quiet in here," I mumble lamely, trying to fill the silence and build up the courage to come clean.

Molly doesn't say a word, just walks right up to me and shoves her hands against my chest, sending me flying backwards. I bounce on top of the king-sized bed, and she jumps on top of me and straddles my thighs. I reach up to grab her hips and she quickly stops me, wrapping her hands around my wrists and pulling my arms above my head as she leans forward. Her tits press against my chest and her hair forms a curtain around our faces as she looks down at me.

"Keep your hands up here and don't move them until I say so," she demands, letting go of my wrists and sliding down my body.

"Holy shit this is hot," I whisper as she trails her hands down my chest and stomach, stopping when she gets to the button of my jeans. Maybe I'll wait until after she finishes whatever she's planning to do to me to tell her the truth. I mean, what's another couple of minutes in the grand scheme of things?

"Just so there's no confusion, we don't have to do anything tonight. We can talk or watch TV or do whatever you want," I tell her.

I will legit cry like a baby if she stops, but it's impossible for me to be an asshole with her. I didn't come over here with any expectations aside from finally being alone with her. Sure, I'm a dude and I always want sex, but I don't expect it, especially with Molly.

"Watch TV or let me put my mouth on your penis, your choice," she replies.

Her fingers pause on the zipper of my jeans and my jaw drops open as I stare at her while she waits for me to remember how to speak.

"Penis mouth," I mumble. "Definitely penis mouth."

She nods, her hands going back to work as she unzips my pants. "Wise decision."

I watch in awe as she sits up on her knees, swiftly yanking my jeans over my hips and to the middle of my thighs. She scoots her body down my legs until she gets to my knees, bending forward over my legs until her face is right above the crotch of my boxer briefs. I can feel her warm breath puff against the thin cotton material and it's like a mating call to my dick. He jerks and twitches and struts his stuff like a peacock showing its feathers.

"I'm serious, Molly. We really don't have to do anything. I know you've been…uuuhhhh…drinking and I don't want to take…holy fuck…advantage of you," I tell her, tripping over my words, moaning and cursing when she slips her fingers in the waistband of my briefs and tugs them down until my penis is on full display.

"I think you're confused," she says softly, her breath warming my dick, making it jerk with excitement again. "I'm taking advantage of *you*. Just close your eyes and don't move."

I do as she says, afraid she'll change her mind if I don't follow her orders. My head flops back onto the bed and I close my eyes and hold my breath, waiting for the heavenly feel of her lips on my cock.

Waiting.

Waiting.

Still waiting.

I open one eye and lift my head to see her staring down at my penis with a look of concentration on her face. Maybe the women I've been with lied. Maybe I don't have a pleasing penis. What if it's ugly? What if Molly is repulsed by it? I knew I should have just taken the damn picture in the bathroom and sent it immediately. At least then she would have been prepared and had time to get used to it. Damn my need for good lighting!

"Everything okay?" I ask, chuckling nervously.

She nods without looking up. "Just getting to know your penis. Charlotte suggested it so I'm giving it a try."

I should be embarrassed that she was talking about my penis with her sister, but I spent the evening telling her father how good my sperm was and then had to explain to him I wasn't masturbating to a picture of his wife in their bedroom while he beat the shit out of me. She can discuss my penis with whomever she likes.

"Take your time. Whatever you need," I tell her, dropping my head back to the bed and relaxing now that I know she isn't disappointed that I have an ugly penis.

"Feel free to…holy mother of God," I mutter with a groan when I feel her hand wrap around the base of my cock.

I try to come up with something more to say, something hot and sexy like, *Yeah, that's it baby, harder,* but as soon as I open my mouth, her warm, wet lips are sliding over the head of my cock and all I can manage is, "Fuuuuuuuuck-shit-damn-good-God-almighty-mouth-penis."

I've had plenty of blowjobs over the years. Some good ones and some bad ones, but I can't for the life of me remember anything about them once I feel Molly's mouth on me. I can't even remember my name or what day it is when she starts bobbing her head up and down, sucking on me and swirling her tongue around the head of my dick each time she gets to the tip.

Grabbing handfuls of the blanket above my head, I hold on for dear life when her hand tightens around the base of my cock and she moves it up and down the length along with her mouth. Each time she goes down, she takes me in her mouth a little further until I see stars behind my closed eyes and I'm a little embarrassed at how fast my orgasm starts to approach. I'm pretty proud of the fact that I can last as long as a woman needs and I've never been a two-pump-chump, even as a teenager, but I've never had a woman's mouth on my dick that I fantasized about for two years and it's overwhelming. Pushing aside the shame of my weakness, I realize I should warn her I'm dangerously close to coming. I learned my lesson back in high school with Michelle Johnson, but I was a rookie then, figuring if she was going to put her mouth of my dick, she should know the only possible outcome would be me having an orgasm, and therefore she should expect it to happen at any moment, moving away if needed. I kept my lips sealed and started coming in her mouth with a smile on my face. She jerked away from my dick mid-orgasm and the mistake of not warning her resulted in screaming, crying, and jizz in the eye. Michelle wasn't too happy either.

As soon as I feel the head of my dick touch the back of Molly's throat, my balls tighten, my legs start to tingle and I open my mouth to give her the required warning in case she's not a swallower.

Before I can say anything, I hear her gag and the words die on my tongue. One might think the sound of a chick gagging on your dick would be a turn-off, but one would be wrong. Feeling bad that I'm disobeying one of her rules, I open my eyes and lift my head to watch. There's nothing hotter than watching a girl go to town on your dick.

Unfortunately, her long hair is hanging down over her face and I can't get a good view of her mouth, but at least I can imagine what it looks like as I feel her take me deeper, another small gagging sound coming from her.

I smile and give myself a mental pat on the back for having such a monster dick that it makes her gag. I'm so busy giving myself a high five and enjoying the way her tongue feels sliding up and down my cock that it takes me a second to realize she's still gagging. There's a musical rhythm to it now—*slurp, gag, slurp, gag, slurp, gag.* I admire her determination and her refusal to quit, and it almost makes me wish I wasn't seconds away from coming so I could make it last all night.

Then, something horrific happens. It's so horrific that I should look away, but it's like driving up on a car accident and slowing down to see if there are any bodies lying in the road. It's wrong and you feel dirty for doing it, but it's impossible not to stare. My eyes are glued to Molly's body and I can't force myself to look at something else. Anything else, for fuck's sake.

She gags harder and louder and her back bows while she continues trying to swallow my dick. The sounds coming from her mouth immediately stop being hot and move right into something out of a scary movie. She's choking and gagging so violently that her back keeps arching with every sound she makes until she starts to resemble a cat trying to cough up a fur ball. I've had a few pet cats over the years. I've watched them stop what they're doing to choke and heave and bob their head until they manage to yak up whatever was stuck in their throat. That's what is happening right at this moment and there's nothing I can do to stop it.

I'm so conflicted. Molly's giving me a blow-job.

My dick is making her choke like a cat trying to bring up a wet, slimy ball of hair.

But Molly's giving me a blow-job!

"Hey, are you okay? It's fine, you can stop," I mutter, my ears ringing with the sounds of her retching and my eyes glued to her back as it continues to spasm.

She shakes her head *no* as much as she can with my dick still stuffed in her mouth and works through the pain like a trooper. I'm ashamed to say that even with how horrified I am right now, my dick is still hard as a rock and my orgasm continues teetering close the edge.

She tries to speak, but her voice comes out garbled and muffled. It sounds like she's saying "I'm not a quitter," but it's impossible to know for sure since she refuses to remove her mouth from my dick and tries to say the words again.

The vibrations from her voice are like a bolt of electricity shooting right to my balls and while she does her best impression of a hairball yacking cat straddling my thighs, I come so hard and so quickly it takes the breath from my lungs and I lose the ability to think. My hips jerk and my mouth opens wide with a pathetic, high-pitch squeak instead of a manly shout as I experience the best, and possibly weirdest, orgasm of my life.

My happiness at learning the girl of my dreams is in fact a swallower is short-lived. With the pleasure of my orgasm still floating through my dick and balls, Molly's back arches one last time and she finally gets that pesky hairball up. Or the gallon of vodka she must have downed before I got here. For the first time in my life, and hopefully the only time, a girl pukes on my dick.

Oh, Jesus Christ! Not only is there puke on my dick, there is puke filled with jizz on my dick. I don't give a fuck if it's my own jizz, it's jizz-puke and it's ON MY FUCKING DICK!

She finally removes her mouth from me as the last of the puke trickles out onto my penis and I prepare myself to give her as many words of comfort as I can so she isn't embarrassed because Jesus fucking Christ she just puked on my cock!

Don't worry about me and my dick covered in vomit mixed with mucusy spooge. It's fine; it's totally fine that I can feel it dripping down my balls and into my ass crack. I need to play it cool or she'll never want to put her mouth on my penis again.

Molly quickly sits up on my legs and drags the back of her hand across her mouth. I give her a second to compose herself and pretend like the puke sliding down my hips and between my legs is just warm water. Slimy, jizzy water. It's fine, puke washes off of balls, no biggie. As long as Molly is okay, I can handle pukey balls.

She finally lifts her head to look at me and I give her a small smile.

"It's okay, no big deal," I reassure her.

Without a word, she slides off my lap and crawls up to the top of the bed, flopping face-first into the pile of pillows.

I watch her quietly for a few minutes and she doesn't move.

"Molly? Are you okay?"

Instead of getting an answer, I hear a tiny little snore and then the deep sounds of her breathing.

As carefully as I can, I scoot myself to the edge of the bed, trying to keep the puke contained to my lap as I contort my body and quickly shuffle to the bathroom to shower. Once I'm cleaned off, I wrap a towel around my waist and strip the covers out from under Molly's passed out body. I toss them in the corner of the room and grab the extra blanket from the top shelf of the closet, crawling into bed next to her. Turning off the lamp on the bedside table, I unfold the blanket to cover us both. Gently turning her body to the side so I can press myself against her back, I wrap my arms around her waist and pull her snugly against me.

Closing my eyes, I nuzzle my nose into her hair and breathe her in. Partially because I love the way she smells, but mostly because it masks the smell of vomit lurking in the air. Maybe I should be freaked out that my first sexual encounter with Molly ended with her puking on my dick, with said dick still in her mouth. I'm sure any other guy would have left her alone in this hotel room and gotten the fuck out of dodge, but I'm not just any guy. I'm a sick fuck and I don't care if my balls smell like puke for the next couple of days. I don't even care if my jizz going down her throat was the cause of her upchuck instead of the booze she drank. I'll let her cough up a hairball on my dick any time, as long as she still wants to put her mouth on it again after tonight.

I drift off to sleep with a smile on my face that my night ended better than I thought it would after Molly's dad introduced me to his fists.

Who knew vomit balls would trump a black eye and a bloody lip?

Chapter 19
— Poop Sex —
Molly

"ARE YOU EVEN listening to me?" I whisper angrily, peeling back the curtain just enough to make sure mom is still busy talking to the seamstress.

"Molly, I don't have time to hear the dick puking story again. I have bigger problems right now," Charlotte complains, huffing and grunting as she tries to suck everything in as hard as she can as I go back to trying to zip her into her wedding dress.

"I threw up all over the first penis I ever put in my mouth!" I whisper-shout angrily, planting my feet wider and tugging on the zipper as hard as I can. "Does that not sound like a huge fucking problem to you?"

It's been two weeks since the night I became the Incredible Dick Puking Molly, and I've tried to get Charlotte to help me since then and she's brushed me off every time. It's bad enough I passed out right after it happened and Marco had to clean up my puke by himself. It's even worse that I woke up the next morning feeling like I'd been run over by a truck with only a vague memory of what had occurred the previous night. Even the feel of Marco's arms holding me and how good it felt to have him curled up around me couldn't stop the feeling of dread in the pit of my stomach, knowing something horrible happened even if I couldn't remember everything. Marco tried to pretend like everything was fine, but not even his hot body wrapped in just a towel could distract me from the overwhelming smell of puke in the room. After twenty minutes of me arguing with him to tell me what happened, he finally did and I immediately wished I'd ignored the puke smell and let my brain keep what I did a nice little secret locked away forever.

"Maybe the zipper is broken. That's probably what it is, just a broken zipper," Charlotte mumbles.

"The zipper isn't broken, tubby. How is this possible when you're only like five minutes pregnant? How does this dress not fit when you've been puking every day since the stick turned pink?" I complain, immediately regretting my use of the puking word since it just makes me remember what I did the first time I had a penis in my mouth.

"Shut the fuck up, dick-bag!" she yells through clenched teeth. "You call me tubby one more time and I will punch you in the throat!"

The curtain slides open and Ava sticks her head in the dressing room. "Everything okay in here? Why is it taking so long for you to put on a fucking dress?"

I drop my hands from the zipper and back away from Charlotte. There is no way that zipper is going to budge.

"Fatty here doesn't fit into her wedding dress anymore," I tell Ava.

Charlotte's arm flies back and her forearm smacks against my throat. I start choking and wrap my hands around my neck, giving Charlotte a dirty look.

"I warned you," Charlotte growls, returning my dirty look as she stares at me over her shoulder.

"You told me not to call you tubby, you didn't say anything about fatty, you fatty-fat-ass-dick-head," I growl back in between coughs.

"You seriously can't zip the dress?" Ava questions, stepping inside the small room and pulling the curtain closed behind her.

She steps forward and tries to zip it herself, giving up after a few hard tugs.

"Nope, not gonna happen. This size two no longer fits your size eight ass," Ava informs our sister. "Maybe you should have eased up on that entire box of Twinkies you inhaled for breakfast this morning."

Charlotte stomps her foot and whirls around, the dress billowing out around her as she turns. It really is a beautiful dress and she looks stunning. From the front.

"They're the only things that I can keep down so shut the fuck up!"

The curtain slides back again and this time, Aunt Claire pokes her head in. "They're getting a little stingy with the free champagne out here, can we speed things along?"

Charlotte quickly moves in front of me so the huge gap in the back of her dress can't be seen in the full-length mirror behind her.

"This isn't a bar, Aunt Claire. I think five glasses is enough," Charlotte tells her.

"I had cancer! Have you no shame?" she argues.

"There is a statute of limitations on how long you can keep using that to make us feel bad," Ava says. "It's not going to work because you want more booze."

Aunt Claire gives her the finger. "You're mean and I don't like you very much right now."

"Why am I the only adult in this room?" Ava complains with a roll of her eyes.

"I *am* acting like an adult, you're just being a meanie doo-doo head," Aunt Claire states, sticking out her tongue as she pulls her head back and yanks the curtain closed.

"We'll just tell them you've been stress-eating," Ava says with a shrug. "Weddings are stressful, it's easily believable. It's not like they didn't witness you inhaling that box of snack cakes in the car. Oh, wait. They didn't because you hunkered down in the back seat and made Molly hold the box and pretend like she was the one eating them."

I nod in agreement. Not my finest hour pretending to chew every time our mother looked in the rearview mirror or Aunt Claire turned around to look at the three of us.

"Oh, just so you know, Marco hasn't said a word to Tyler about the night of the great penis purge," Ava tells me while Charlotte reaches behind her to try and zip up her dress on her own. "Don't worry, I didn't tell him, I just nonchalantly asked what they talked about when he got home from grabbing a beer with Marco last night. If Tyler knew, it would have been the first thing out of his mouth since that man cannot keep a secret. Not only can your man handle a little vomit on his junk, he doesn't gossip about it. You've got yourself a keeper."

I close my eyes in mortification as she laughs, refusing to give her a high-five when she holds her hand up in the air.

Even though I wanted to lock myself in my room and never face Marco again after the night in the hotel room, he made that impossible to do. He wouldn't let one day go by without seeing me, and as much as I wanted to hide from him so I never had to think about what I did, I wanted to be around him even more. He came up to work every day and took me to lunch, he planned dates and things for us to do almost every night and he never let more than a few hours go by without calling to tell me he just wanted to hear the sound of my voice. My two year crush and only a handful of weeks with him has shot me right up the hill of *falling* in love with him to tumbling over the edge and head over heels, madly, passionately *in* love with him.

"What am I going to do if I can never give him another blow-job? What kind of a relationship can we possibly have if I can't put his penis in my mouth without throwing up?" I ask, trying to keep my panic at a minimum before I curl up in the fetal position and cry.

"Stop being a drama queen, for fuck's sake. So you threw up on his dick? Come back to me when you've had accidental anal," Ava says with a sigh. "At least you had the luxury of passing out after you threw up. I couldn't sit down for a week and I was afraid to take a shit for four days."

I grimace and throw my hands up.

"Seriously, you have *got* to stop with the over-sharing," I complain.

"Maybe I should give Gavin anal and then tell him about the baby," Charlotte thinks aloud. "Anal can make anything better, right?"

Ava nods. "Sure. Anal is pretty much the sexual duct tape of the world—it fixes everything. I should put that on a t-shirt."

While Ava ponders her idea, I turn my focus to Charlotte.

"Have you even tried talking to Gavin about kids yet or are you just planning on dropping this huge bomb on him as soon as he says *I do*?" I ask, trying not to sound annoyed.

"You can't rush something like this, Molly. It's a very delicate situation."

Her annoyance comes through loud and clear and it pisses me off.

"Oh, by all means, take your time. In fact, why don't you wait until you go into labor to break the news? I'm having so much fun fucking up my life and having mom and dad upset and disappointed in me instead of enjoying what should be the best time of my life. As long as you're happy, Charlotte, that's all that matters," I bite out sarcastically.

Ava pats me on the back in sympathy and Charlotte immediately bursts into tears.

"I'm so fat and Gavin is going to leave me, and now you hate me and I'm going to be pregnant and alone and this baby is going to hate me for ruining it's life!" she wails.

"Oh, give me a fucking break!" Ava complains. "Turn off the fake waterworks. I am not afraid to punch a pregnant chick so cut that shit out."

Charlotte huffs in annoyance, the tears in her eyes immediately disappearing, proving that Ava was correct and she was faking it. She almost had me feeling sorry for her pathetic ass.

"Jesus, are you even human?" I mumble.

"It's a gift," she shrugs, resuming her struggle to try and zip her dress. "I just imagine someone I love dying in a really horrible way."

"You need to be medicated. If Gavin doesn't dump your ass when you tell him about the baby, he sure as shit will when he figures out you're psychotic," Ava states.

"Your boyfriend can't get it up unless you dress up like Mister Ed so fuck off," Charlotte replies. "I think I've almost got it."

Charlotte pants as she twists and turns with her arms still behind her back. Her face is red and glistening with sweat as she struggles for a few more seconds before dropping her arms and sighing in relief. "I did it!"

She turns to show us, Ava and I sharing a quick look behind her back.

"Yep, you did it!" Ava cheers as Charlotte turns back around with a smile. "You moved the zipper a whole centimeter. Well done, fatty."

Charlotte lunges at Ava and I quickly jump forward, wrapping my arms around her and holding her back while she pulls and struggles and curses.

"You dick-bag-whore-fuck-ass-licking-twat!" Charlotte screams, not even bothering to keep her voice down.

"Fuck right off, you selfish cunt!" Ava yells back.

Charlotte stops struggling and I let out a low whistle.

"Damn, going right for the C U Next Tuesday, huh? That's harsh," I tell her.

Ava shrugs. "It couldn't be helped. Can we call a truce for now and get this shit show over with? Aunt Claire is going to start throwing punches if she goes much longer without champagne."

I drop my arms from around Charlotte and she takes a deep breath for courage. I decide to keep my mouth shut for now and suck this crap up a little longer. I'm pissed and I'm frustrated and I just want this whole thing to be over with, but I know it's just as bad for Charlotte. She's nervous about everything running smoothly with the wedding she's been planning since she was a little girl, she's pregnant and scared and now her dream dress that she loved the minute she first tried it on six months ago doesn't fit. And least I have one good thing in my life that makes all of this bullshit better, even if I'm now afraid of his penis.

Ava and I leave the dressing room first and I hold the curtain open for Charlotte to walk through. Mom, Aunt Claire and Aunt Jenny stop talking and stare at Charlotte as she walks out of the room.

Mom immediately bursts into tears and Aunt Claire silently grabs a box of Kleenex from the table next to her, shoving it into mom's stomach.

"Oh, honey, you look so beautiful," Mom gushes as Charlotte smiles at the praise, lifting up the skirt of her dress and doing a little twirl.

"Why isn't your dress zipped?" Aunt Claire asks when Charlotte stops twirling.

"I'm stressed. I've been stress-eating and gained a little weight, and it's no big deal and it happens to every bride," Charlotte rambles.

"Oh, my gosh, you too?" Aunt Jenny asks. "I'm so nervous and excited about the wedding I've been eating in my sleep. I'm sleep-walk eating."

Mom blows her nose and Aunt Claire holds up her empty champagne glass, signaling to the owner of the shop. "Something tells me I'm going to need a refill."

Aunt Jenny continues as Mom tosses her tissue and box of Kleenex to an empty chair. She walks behind Charlotte to try and zip the dress, glancing at the camera man and sound guy standing next to Aunt Claire with their equipment pointed right at Aunt Jenny.

"Do you guys ever take a lunch break or anything? Now might be a great time for that," Mom informs them.

Daren the camera guy, or Dicky Daren as Uncle Drew likes to call him, who has been recording our family's every move for the last two weeks, tilts his head to the side of the camera and shrugs.

"Sorry, folks. Producer says I have to get everything. Don't worry, they'll edit out anything they don't think is interesting."

At this point, the documentary their filming will be approximately 85,000 hours long instead of a two-hour special. Our family doesn't know how to do anything uninteresting.

"Does that mean you'll include the footage of you letting Drew fondle your wanker? Because that was pretty interesting, Dicky Daren," Aunt Claire says with a wink.

"He didn't fondle it; he grazed it on accident when he tripped over the microphone chord! I have never let a dude fondle my penis!" Daren argues. "I mean, not that it's wrong or anything. I'm down with the gays and they're cool and everything, but I prefer chicks on my dick."

Stan, the sound guy, elbows him in the side and nods to the camera.

"Fuck! Of COURSE I didn't stop recording," Daren mutters, shifting the camera more securely on his shoulder and moving his face back behind the eye piece.

"You should be loud and proud about that shit, Dicky Daren," Aunt Claire says with a laugh. "You got at least an hour of footage of Drew going on and on about how big your penis is and how he's pretty sure it's the size of his forearm. Do you know how many women you could bang if that airs? Seriously. You'd have to beat them off with a stick."

Mom laughs, her fingers still trying to pull up the zipper that won't budge. "Forget the stick, he could just beat them off with his python penis."

Daren starts muttering to himself behind the camera, something about crazy women and how he doesn't get paid enough for this shit, and we go back to pretending like he's not there.

"Okay, back to what I was saying," Aunt Jenny continues. "I couldn't understand why I gained like ten pounds in two weeks until I woke up one morning with an empty box of Ho Hos on my pillow and chocolate smushed on the sheets. Drew assumed it was poop and thought I wanted to try some skate play. I tried for over an hour to convince him it was just chocolate, but he didn't believe me. Now he won't shut up about it and keeps telling me there's no shame in admitting I like poopy sex."

The shop owner who was on her way to Aunt Claire with a freshly opened bottle of champagne immediately turns on her heels and runs away.

"I believe you mean *skat* play, not skate play, Jenny," Aunt Claire mutters. "And can we please get out of here so I can find the closest drug dealer? I'm gonna need to shoot up some meth or something to erase that information from my mind."

Mom gives up on trying to zip Charlotte's dress, telling her not to worry and that she'll just have the seamstress sew a piece of fabric in to hide the problem.

Ava and I help Charlotte out of her dress and we all head out to the car to leave the poor owner in peace so she can cry alone after what she just witnessed, while Daren and Stan load the equipment in their van to follow behind us. Aunt Claire tried to lose them last week just for fun and it ended in a high-speed chase, three annihilated mailboxes, one flat tire, two dead squirrels, and my mom never letting Aunt Claire behind the wheel of a car again.

My phone beeps as Mom pulls out of the parking lot while Aunt

Claire complains there's a guy with a walker moving faster than we are. I smile when I see a text from Marco and block out the sounds of my mom and my aunt arguing from the front seat.

> *Clear your calendar tonight and plan on getting naked. Puking permitted, but not required.*

He always knows just the right thing to say to make me feel better.

Chapter 20

- Pez Penis -

Marco

"IT'S FINE. IT happens to a lot of guys."

Molly rubs the palm of her hand in slow circles against my back and gives me a sympathetic smile.

"It's not *fine* and it doesn't happen to me!" I yell, immediately feeling bad for raising my voice when she's being so nice and understanding. She shouldn't be nice. She should be laughing and making fun of me and storming out of here in disgust. It's what I deserve.

"Seriously, it's no big deal. Stop beating yourself up about it."

She leans in closer and kisses the top of my shoulder.

"This is embarrassing. I swear to God this has never happened to me before, ask anyone," I mutter.

All I wanted was to give Molly a perfect, romantic, wonderful night. Was that too much to ask? Am I being punished because I still haven't told her about Alfanso D.? It's not like I can just blurt it out. I thought if I turned on the charm and left her feeling satisfied, she'd have no choice but to forgive me. I can't do anything right.

"Marco, it's nothing to be embarrassed about. We can try again later," she encourages, running her fingers through my hair.

Her touch makes my dick stir, and I'm honestly a little surprised

I can still get it up at this point.

"It won't be the same," I mumble. "The first time is always special and now I've ruined it."

She sighs and wraps her arms around my waist, squeezing me tight.

"It's because of me, isn't it? You're off your game because every time you look at me you remember the worst blowjob you've ever received," she whispers sadly.

Quickly turning towards her, I cradle her face in my hands and stare into her eyes.

"Stop it. This has nothing to do with you, I swear," I reassure her. "You turn me on just by breathing. I promise you, that blowjob was stellar, and regardless of the puke, your determination and won't-quit attitude scored you a lot of blowjob points in my book."

She smiles at me, and I drop my hands from her face to wrap them around her back and pull her closer.

"It really does happen to everyone, it's not that big of a deal."

I scoff and raise one eyebrow at her. "Has this ever happened to *you* before?"

She bites her bottom lip, but doesn't say anything.

"See?! It's just me! I'M the problem!"

"No you're not," Molly says with a sigh. "I just haven't been doing it as long as you."

She drops her arms from around my waist as I turn towards the kitchen counter, picking up the ruined soufflé with a scowl.

"Exactly my point," I tell her, walking over to the garbage can and dumping the dessert angrily inside. "I'm a pro. I've been baking soufflés since I was in elementary school, and I have NEVER had one collapse. This is mortifying."

I could blame Molly for ruining the dessert, but that's not exactly fair. I'm the one who was holding the oven door open to check on it when she got here twenty minutes ago and I'm the one who let the handle slip from my hands and slam shut when she walked into the kitchen wearing a tiny, blue strapless dress that clung to her tits, hugged her curves and fit her like a second skin. Her long, shiny black hair was curled into soft waves that hung around her shoulders, and don't even get me started on the matching blue fuck-me heels she had on that made her tall enough for her lips to be perfectly aligned with mine when she stood in front of me.

Maybe the soufflé could have survived the slamming of the oven door, but I definitely killed it when I grabbed her hips, turned her around and repeatedly pushed her body against the double oven to kiss her. And then I made sure it would never survive by continuing to hump her against the damn oven while I lost my mind between her legs with my tongue in her mouth.

Not only was she so fucking hot it made me want to drop to my knees and thank God for bringing her into my life, she looked so worried and nervous standing in the middle of my kitchen while she fidgeted with the dress and nervously shifted back and forth on her feet. When she shyly whispered that Ava picked out her clothes and did her hair and that she felt stupid, I knew I had to do something to erase that panicked look from her face like she was waiting for me to laugh at how she looked.

"So, now that my plan of making you fall madly in love with me as soon as you took a bite of my world famous soufflé that I never share with students is ruined, what do you want to do?" I ask, deciding to stop being a baby over a stupid dessert and concentrate on the gorgeous woman standing in my kitchen.

I spent all day cleaning this place up so it didn't look like a pigsty bachelor pad, and I made sure any evidence of Alfanso D. was safely hidden out of sight. I am determined to come clean with her tonight, but I want it to come from *me* and not have her find out by seeing all of my notes for the next book lying around. Since I trade working summers every year with another teacher, this is my summer to be off for three months and every minute I haven't been with Molly, I've been working on the book. My entire apartment was littered with sheets of notebook paper with scribbled ideas on them, post-it notes with recipes stuck to all the walls, and several copies of *Seduction and Sugar* lying all over the place so I could go back and reference whatever I needed. Now that everything has been shoved into the spare bedroom closet, I don't have to worry about her finding something before I can explain it myself. Which WILL happen before this night is over.

"Hmmmm, what should we do?" Molly ponders, tapping a finger against her lips. "I believe you mentioned something about getting naked in your text."

Tell her right now before she gets naked. Molly naked will result in you turning stupid.

"Yes, I believe I did say something to that effect. Why don't we sit down and talk first," I suggest as she walks slowly around me and heads into the living room.

Perfect, she wants to talk. Chicks always want to talk before getting to the good stuff. Just pretend like she never mentioned getting naked and everything will be fine.

I follow behind Molly, unable to move my eyes away from her ass as her hips gently sway while she walks into my living room. When she turns around in front of the couch, I'm still staring and now my eyes are glued to her crotch.

Focus, dammit! Don't think about what her pussy looks like. Don't drool wondering if it's shaved or full-on bush, trimmed or cut into a neat little design like a lightning bolt or arrow pointing down. Move your eyes up, asshole!

"We could talk, sure," Molly says softly, her fingers playing with the hem of her dress that stops at the top of her thighs.

Fuck, her legs are so long and smooth with just a hint of muscle definition that assures me she could wrap them around my shoulders and hold on for dear life.

GAAAAAAAAAH, FOCUS! I'm Alfanso D., I'm Alfanso D. Just get it over with!

"Great! Perfect," I reply with a clap of my hands, entirely too excited to sit down and talk instead of sitting down and burying my face in her vagina. "How about we sit on the couch and talk."

And then I'll bury my face in your vagina.

"How about you start talking and I'll get comfortable."

Mentally screaming at my dick to take a nap for a few minutes instead of trying to claw his way through my zipper, I smile and take a step towards the couch, figuring Molly is going to take her shoes off and put her feet up on the coffee table to get comfortable or something.

I barely take one step towards the couch before my feet refuse to move and I freeze like a deer caught in headlights.

When Molly said she'd get comfortable, she really meant it. In one smooth, quick motion, she grabs the hem of her dress and quickly slides the material up and off her body, tossing it to the side where it lands in a puddle on the carpet.

"Sweet baby back ribs," I whisper.

Molly crosses one leg in front of the other and casually clasps her hands together behind her ass, the motion pushing her tits out until I'm pretty sure I feel a little drool dripping down my chin.

She's wearing a black lace thong and a matching black lace strapless bra, the material so sheer I can see her nipples. And Land O'Lakes what wonderful nipples they are.

"Do you still want to talk or is there something else you'd rather do?" she asks innocently.

Talk? What's talk? Who said talk? Do I know the word talk?

"I might have a few ideas, but I think I need a little more inspiration," I tell her quietly, surprised I'm able to unglue my tongue from the top of my mouth and remember how to string words together.

Her hands move up behind her back and she expertly unclasps the hook of her bra, the sheer black lace dropping from her body to land at her feet.

"Damn, you're like a ninja with that thing," I whisper, unable to remove my eyes from her naked tits. "It takes me at least five tries to unhook a bra. It's like I have giant gorilla fingers whenever I get near those damn things."

Okay, I know I said I wanted to talk, but this is just pathetic. Why am I rambling about gorilla fingers when there's a half-naked woman in my living room with the best pair of tits this side of the Mississippi. And the other side of the Mississippi. And all down the fucking Mississippi.

STOP THINKING ABOUT MISSISSIPPI AND START THINKING ABOUT TITS, YOU PUSSY!

While I'm busy standing in the middle of my living room having an argument in my head, Molly walks towards me until she's right in front of me. She slides her hands around my waist and presses her naked body against me. I can feel her nipples poking into my pecs, and I swear I hear the sound of my zipper ripping to shreds as my dick tries to hulk his way out of my jeans and into the Promised Land.

My head finally catches up with my body and I move my hands to her hips, sliding them around to clutch her smooth, perfect ass.

"I'm just going to apologize ahead of time for ruining this," I whisper.

"Why would you ruin this?" she asks, pressing her hips against mine and gently kissing my chin.

"I mean, *I* wouldn't ruin it, but I'm pretty sure my dick will," I mutter, moaning softly when she kisses a trail across my jaw and to my neck.

"My dick is an asshole and never listens to me. You're so fucking hot and beautiful, and I'm pretty positive he's going to ignore all the baseball stats and college football teams I can name in alphabetical order and come in about five seconds if you keep doing that," I ramble in one long incoherent sentence, moaning again when she wraps her lips around my earlobe and gently tugs on it with her teeth. "Fucking hell, you're so good at this."

Her lips immediately disappear from my ear and she leans back just enough so I can see her face. Gone is the confidence and determination I love so much and in its place is the same nervous and scared look she had when she first walked into my kitchen.

"Hey, what's wrong? Was it the dick thing? I was just kidding. Sort of. I mean, I've always been able to last as long as I need to, but I've never been with someone I fantasized about for two years. I'm having a hard time believing this isn't a dream, but I promise I'll try my best to keep my dick in line," I over-explain.

She laughs softly and shakes her head. "It's stupid, but I need to tell you something. Ava told me to tell you but Charlotte told me to keep my mouth shut because it would ruin everything, but I can't do it. I am really out of my element here and Ava even made me practice this in front of the mirror until I could do it without rolling my eyes or covering myself up but I still feel like a liar and a hypocrite and I don't want to keep this from you because I really like you. I more than like you. I'm just going to spit out and if you want me to leave, I'll understand."

I don't feel so bad anymore about the whole gorilla fingers thing when Molly rambles without taking a breath and it just makes me want to stick her in my pocket and keep her forever. You know, if Harry Potter were a real person and he'd let me borrow his wand to make her tiny. But there would have to be a reverse spell where I could make her big again so she'd have normal-size hands and a normal-size mouth and a normal-size vagina because I might not have a dick the size of a python, but I'm pretty sure it could still kill a teeny tiny Molly that fits in my pocket.

Mental patient, party of me, your padded cell is now available.

Removing one hand from her ass, I bring it between us and under her chin, tipping her face up so she'll stop staring at a spot in the middle of my chest and look at me.

"No matter what you tell me, I would never make you leave, Molly. Don't you get it? Don't you see what you've done to me?" I rasp. "I've never been this crazy or this tied up in knots before and it's all because of you. Because you're just as amazing as I thought you'd be when I first saw you in the school kitchen with powdered sugar on your cheek and more talent in your pinky finger than the entire class put together."

I see tears pooling in her eyes and it makes my heart skip a beat, which I'm pretty sure might be a sign of a stroke or possibly a heart attack but since I still have feeling in my left arm, I'm just going to ignore it.

"I think I've been in love with you since that very first day when the entire class groaned after I said we'd be starting with sugar sculptures and your eyes lit up in excitement," I tell her with a smile. "I know it's crazy, and I know we're in the middle of a shit show situation with your family, and I *know* we've only spent a few weeks together, but I'm falling in love with you Molly Gilmore. I love how much you care about your insane family, even if you try to deny it. I love your talent in the kitchen, and I love that you're a hard ass with everyone but me. I love your smile and your laugh and how you smell like apples and cinnamon and how being with you is as easy as breathing."

She closes her eyes to stop the tears from falling, opening them right back up to roll them at me in that fucking adorable way I love so much.

"You're crazy and wonderful, and I think I'm falling in love with you too, and I'm still a virgin, but technically I've kind of, sort of had sex, so I use the term partial-virgin because it was one time and he only partially got his penis in before he finished, and his penis was literally the size of a piece of Pez candy and my sisters like to call him Pez Penis now and make fun of me because now I'm a pregnant partial-virgin, and I just wanted you to know because I don't want to keep any secrets from you."

She finally stops talking and takes a deep breath, letting it out slowly.

I know I should have paid really close attention to every word she said, but she talked incredibly fast and my brain shut down after the words "falling in love with you too" and "virgin". Then it came right back to life when she said she didn't want to keep any secrets from me. Now is my chance. Now is the perfect opportunity to tell her who I am. It doesn't get any better than this moment, right here.

"Say something so I don't feel like even more of an idiot because I'm half-naked in your living room, talking like a dumb girl about dumb feelings and other dumb girl stuff that gives me hives," she complains.

I open my mouth to spit it out, I swear I do. The words are right there on my tongue and I even take a deep breath, full of confidence now that I know she loves me back. Then Molly has to go and move her hips, doing this incredible little swirling motion that rubs her lace-covered vagina against my dick.

I'm such a cheap whore with a one-track mind.

"So, when you say partial-virgin, it's because you and some fuck-for-brains were naked and something resembling sex occurred, correct?" I ask.

You know, just to clarify and make sure we're on the same page.

"Sure, I guess you could put it that way," she nods, still moving her hips the tiniest bit, just to make sure my dick is paying attention. "His penis, was legit the size of the head of your penis. My fingers have gone deeper than his Pez dispenser."

And that's it, folks. My brain is tapping out and my dick is now in charge. When a chick talks about fingering herself, there's no coming back from that shit.

In one quick motion, I keep one arm behind her back and bend down to slide the other one behind her knees, scooping her up into my arms as I charge through the living room, down the hall and into my bedroom.

"If you're okay with this, I'd like to release you of your partial-virgin status," I tell her as I gently lay her on top of my bed and move on top of her, holding myself up on my arms so I don't crush her.

"I think I'm more than okay with that," she whispers, sliding her fingers through my hair at the back of my head and pulling my face down to hers.

"You should probably start reciting those football teams now," she breathes against my lips. "Don't forget I was raised in a sex shop. I took my first steps in the lesbian porn aisle and my first word was orgasm."

She wraps her legs around my hips, locking her ankles together against my ass and uses her muscles to pull the lower half of my body closer until my denim-covered dick is nestled right against the heat of her soon-to-be no longer a partial-virgin vagina.

Her hips start rocking against mine, and I tell myself it's totally fine if I wait one more day to tell her about Alfanso D. She is in need of my expertise and who am I to let a woman in need down?

"Air Force, Akron, Alabama, Appalachian State, Arizona," I begin chanting softly between kisses as I move down her neck and across her chest before wrapping my lips around one of her perfect nipples.

Molly's back arches and she lets out a low moan that makes my dick twitch and with excitement.

"Arwiwona Fate, Arwansas Fate, Wamy," I recite with a muffled voice, refusing to remove my mouth from her nipple.

"God I love football," Molly says with a sigh.

Chapter 21

- Drunk Babies -

Marco

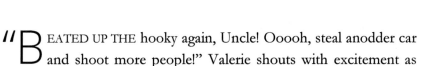

"BEATED UP THE hooky again, Uncle! Ooooh, steal anodder car and shoot more people!" Valerie shouts with excitement as she bounces up and down on the couch next to me.

"It's pronounced *hooker*, not hooky, and I don't need to steal another car right now, sweetie," I explain, jerking my body to the left as I aim the PlayStation controller at the screen and make my car swerve around a pedestrian.

Letting my four-year-old niece watch me play Grand Theft Auto for the last hour probably wasn't the best decision I've ever made, but at least it kept her in one place instead of screaming and climbing the walls.

No, seriously, she actually climbed the wall in my bedroom like fucking Spiderman. It's Tessa's fault. She told me to give her a piece of chocolate every time Valerie goes to the bathroom on her own. No one gives me a Snicker's when I take a shit without assistance, but whatever. Valerie must have a bladder the size of…I don't know, something really fucking small because she has gone to the bathroom every two minutes for the last three hours. I'll let her swim in the sugar bowl as long as she doesn't piss on the carpet.

"Shoot him in the head! Make his head explode!" Valerie

screams, clapping her hands together when I shoot a cop trying to arrest me.

"Do you remember what I told you, Val?" I ask, pausing the game to look down at her.

"Grand Feft Auto isn't real life. It's bad to shoot people, even hookies. I mean hookers," she tells me with a serious face.

"You've learned well, Grasshopper," I reply with a nod and a pat to the top of her head.

Once I finally found something to hold her interest for more than two seconds that wouldn't cause death or dismemberment and a seriously pissed off sister, it actually hasn't been so bad hanging out with my niece. When I asked Tessa if I could babysit her for a few hours today, I thought she was going to choke to death she laughed so hard. After she finally stopped laughing and realized I wasn't laughing with her and I was totally serious, I had to sit there for an hour while she gave me a quick course on Babysitting for Dummies. When she finished and gave me a list of telephone numbers for every person she's ever met in her entire life, including the numbers of ever hospital in a three-hundred mile radius, she made me sign a piece of paper stating she has permission to cut off my balls with a pair of rusty scissors if anything worse than a paper cut happens to her child under my care.

I've had a goofy fucking grin on my face ever since I successfully took care of that pesky partial-virgin status for Molly, but at the same time, I feel like the biggest jerk in the world that she trusted me and gave something so important to me and I still haven't managed to tell her the truth. The more time we spend together and the longer I wait, the worse I feel, yet I keep coming up with one excuse after another to keep putting it off.

Molly's giving me a blowjob—it can wait.

Molly's naked in my living room—what's one more day?

Molly wakes me up with her head under the covers and her mouth on my dick—she needs to rebuild that confidence and overcome the penis puke, I can't ruin that.

Molly takes me on a tour of Seduction and Snacks and asks me to fuck her in the warehouse in the vibrator aisle—I swear I'll do it after her orgasm when she's relaxed but one orgasm turned into four and I needed a nap.

Molly asks me to help her with a troubling recipe, and before I know it, there's chocolate sauce on my penis and dripping off her tits—chocolate on tits is delicious. No explanation needed.

Molly brings home toys from work and asks if I want to watch her use them—I AM JUST A MAN, STANDING IN FRONT OF A WOMAN, ASKING HER TO GET HERSELF OFF!

Before I knew it, the day before the wedding was upon us and I knew I needed to wait until it was over. Charlotte has turned into a bridezilla, and Molly is stressed about her parents finding out the real truth and them being mad at her for lying. She has too much on her mind right now that it wouldn't be right to add one more thing that I know will upset her.

Since there's no use denying how much of an asshole I am and I'm scared to death Molly will never trust me again or let me put my penis inside her which would be a tragedy I'll never recover from, I'm doing whatever I can to show her I'm not that person anymore. I overheard her talking to Ava on the phone last week when she thought I was sleeping and I still can't get her words out of my head. She was on her iPad going back through every damn post I made on the Alfanso D. page for the last six months. Even though I couldn't hear what Ava was saying, it wasn't too hard to figure out whenever Molly would say, "I know, right? He's such a pig" or, "You've got to be a pretty stupid woman to ever sleep with someone like that."

Yes, I was a pig. Yes, I was a bit of a man whore and yes, I exploited my sexcapades in a cookbook. I put up posts about how easy it was to sleep with any woman you wanted as long as you fed her chocolate. I made comments putting women down, putting relationships down and putting people down who had kids. I was *that* guy. The frat boy who refused to grow up.

Well, I'm assuming my behavior was like a frat boy since I was never actually *in* a frat, even though I tried to join one and was asked to never come back when I suggested we all go to a cooking class instead of doing keg stands.

And this leads us to where I am now, the day before Charlotte and Gavin's wedding where Charlotte will finally break the news to her betrothed (after he says I do of course, so he's less likely to leave the country), Molly will finally get to stop pretending she's pregnant, and I'll get to stop flinching every time her father jumps out at me and screams "BOO!". Actually, that will probably always happen even after he finds out I didn't impregnate his daughter since he still thinks I like to beat-off to photos of his wife.

I spent the last few days going back and forth with my publisher about this next cookbook and a new idea I came up with, trying to convince them I can make it just as good as the first one. They finally agreed last night, which brings me to the reason I am currently teaching my niece fun new vocabulary words and how to properly execute a kill shot while in a high-speed chase. Molly changed everything and I want her to know that even if she never trusts me again. What was originally going to be a sequel to *Seduction and Sugar* with even more over-the-top sex stories and matching recipes, is now: *Baking and Babies: How to Spice it Up in the Kitchen AND the Bedroom When You Have Kids.*

I've listened to Molly's aunts and uncles and her mom and dad tell stories over the last few weeks about what it was like after they added kids to the mix and how they managed to keep the romance alive. Some were funny, some were sweet, and some were downright horrifying. Pampers really needs to get their act together if babies can manage to shit so much that it leaks out of their diaper, up their back and sometimes in their hair. I'm a grown ass man and even *I* can't produce that much shit at one time.

All these stories were perfect for this cookbook, but I knew I needed real-life experience. The people who loved my first cookbook loved it because I shared a big piece of myself and my life on every page, even if I did it in a really slutty way and was never afraid to admit it on social media. A few hours with my niece seemed like the perfect way to get some experience as well as spend some time with her and learn how to not be so afraid of kids. They're not so bad once you get the hang of it. They really are like tiny drunk people and I've been around my share of enough drunk people to know the following rules apply to both:

1. Be prepared to make a Taco Bell run for the border. They will scream for Taco Bell (can be substituted for McDonalds) until you have no choice but to give in and go to the drive-thru in your pajamas in the middle of the night if you want them to shut up.

2. Never let them out of your sight, especially around sharp objects, things that are flammable or anything they might trip over and hurt themselves.

3. Smile and nod no matter what they mumble, slur, scream, or cry. Pretending like you understand them will eliminate arguments and or more crying.

4. If they say they're going to puke, do not hesitate to move your ass. Carry them like a football, drag them by the arm or toss them over your shoulder. Do whatever it takes to get them to a toilet, bush, sink or in some cases, the side of the road.

5. Know that accidents *will* happen. They can and will pee their pants, shit their pants and if you ignore number 4, puke on you and themselves. Keep a change of clothes and a container of wipes on hand at all times.

6. Watch what you say. If it's something you don't want repeated very loudly to everyone within shouting distance, don't say it. Everything you say can and will be very hilarious

to them and they take enjoyment in your misery.

7. Some of them like to be naked. They have no shame and don't see the problem with taking their clothes off in public. Understand that clothes can sometimes annoy them. The clothes make them hot, make them itch, are too tight, too loose, or too ugly. Calmly tell them they have to put their clothes back on and offer assistance. If that doesn't work, some may become argumentative and may even lash out by kicking, screaming, biting and or hitting. If that happens, throw your coat or the closest blanket around them and drag them away.

8. Always be firm and speak slowly, enunciating each word carefully. They don't always understand the words coming out of your mouth so try not to lose your temper or get frustrated. Don't be afraid to use a loud voice or threaten punishment, especially if their life could be at risk.

9. Never let them use your cell phone, iPad, iPod, laptop, or any other device that will connect them to your social media. They can and will post very bad things, but just know they aren't doing it on purpose. It's very easy to punch a few random buttons and the next thing you know, there's a dick pick you sent to your girlfriend and forgot to erase on Facebook and your mother has been tagged.

10. Memorize the number for Poison Control.

I really should buy Valerie a pony or something. A few hours with her and this book practically wrote itself.

Valerie suddenly jumps down from the couch and runs out of the room.

"Hey! Where are you going?" I shout.

"I GOTTA PEE!" she replies.

Tessa really needs to get that shit checked. I haven't even given her anything to drink since she's been here just to try and prevent any accidents. While I listen to the sounds of the toilet flushing and the sink running and know Valerie didn't somehow escape from a window, I quickly send a text to Tessa and tell her to call Valerie's pediatrician.

Tessa immediately replies with a comment about how I just might make a good dad someday, and I pat myself on the back until she sends another text immediately after, telling me to just make sure I pick the right woman and not try to fertilize the entire state.

It's annoying, but I deserve it. I'm going to prove to everyone with this cookbook that I've grown up and it's all because of Molly.

Tossing my phone onto the coffee table, I watch Valerie come racing back into the room and hop back up on the couch next to me.

"Did you wash your hands?" I ask.

She reaches up and wipes her wet hands on my cheeks.

"That better be water and not pee," I mutter, wiping the wetness off my face.

"Hump-hump-hump, I just peed on you!" she shouts, falling back into the couch in a fit of giggles.

Her laughter stops abruptly and she quickly sits back up, holding her hand out in front of me.

"I went poop. Gimme chocolate," she states.

I reach for the bag of Hershey Kisses on the table next to the couch and try not to panic when I realize it's empty. Valerie looks at the empty bag in clutched in my hand, her eyes filling with tears and her bottom lip starting to quiver.

"Hey, it's okay! Don't cry," I beg. "How about a box of cereal? Or some grapes. Grapes are really yummy!"

Valerie isn't buying it and she crosses her arms in front of her angrily.

"Chocolate! I poop and I get chocolate, mommy says so!" she yells.

Shit, rule number three, just remember rule number three.

I smile and nod, exaggerating my enthusiasm. "I know! You're such a big girl for shitting all by yourself. I mean, dropped a deuce. No, that's bad too. You pooped! Yaaaay you pooped on the potty!"

Valerie isn't amused even when I wave my hands in the air above my head.

"How about I let you beat up some hookers, rob a bank, and shoot up a strip club?" I ask with a sigh, dropping my hands into my lap.

Her eyes light up and she starts bouncing up and down on the couch again.

"I wanna drive the black car and run people over, and can I stab someone wif a knife? I like it when the blood squirts all over and they fall down!"

Shaking my head, I hand over the controller and un-pause the game.

"Have at it, kid. Just remember—"

"Grand Feft Auto isn't real life," she cuts me off in a robotic voice, her eyes never leaving the TV.

Look how easy it was to teach a four-year-old something new? Maybe I will make a good father someday. Hopefully Molly will agree.

Chapter 22
— Pumpkin Roll Punany —
Molly

"SEE? THAT'S WHERE you went wrong. You have to separate the eggs first and only use the egg whites. You're such an amateur," Uncle Drew complains, shaking his head at Tyler as I walk by them.

"Hey, Molly! You're, like, a cook and shit, right? You can answer this question for us," Tyler says, grabbing my arm to stop me from walking right on by them and pretending like I don't know them.

"I'm actually a classically trained French Pastry Chef," I remind him.

They both stare at me in confusion and I sigh.

"Yes, I cook and shit."

Tyler smiles and Uncle Drew lifts his beer bottle and gives me a wink.

"Egg yolks or egg whites? Which is better?" Uncle Drew asks.

"Um, it depends what you're making," I reply, shocked and a bit happy that these guys recognize and understand my passion and career expertise. "If you're talking about making whip cream, you never used the yolks, but if you're making, say a nice béarnaise you would-"

Uncle Drew puts his hand on my arm and snorts. "Imma let you finish but…"

"But, we're talking about which works better as a substitute for sex latex, obviously," Tyler finishes for him with his own snort and eye roll.

"Please tell my idiot son that only egg whites harden when brushed on the nipples so you can gently peel it off," Uncle Drew states, turning away from me to glare at Tyler. "I even dog-eared that chapter in the porn book for you AND highlighted it."

Tyler throws his hands up in the air in annoyance. "Do you know how long I had to sleep on the couch after mixing up Pumpkin Roll Punany and Baking Bread and Butt Bumps? That book you gave me had half the pages stuck together and I fucked everything up. It turns out, spanking a woman with a pumpkin roll is very messy and mixing fresh bread ingredients in a vagina really DOES cause a yeast infection."

I close my eyes and wonder why I ever thought our family could have a nice, dignified evening out in public for once as Uncle Drew and Tyler continue arguing back and forth. Not even the beautiful, fancy atmosphere of one of the nicest restaurants in town could make these people behave.

My eyes slowly open when I feel a pair of warm lips press to the side of my neck. I smile even though my uncle and Tyler are still arguing, but now it's over who can successfully use the word *nipples* in every sentence in regards to dinner.

"My nipples get hard just thinking about the chicken parm they're serving."

"I can see cousin Rachel's nipples through her white shirt."

"OVERRULED!"

"On what grounds?!"

"Incest is only legal in porn and erotic fiction!"

"Fine. Sustained, but I'll need to see you in my chambers."

I turn away from the idiots in front of me and wrap my arms

around the waist of the smart, beautiful man behind me.

"Do I even want to ask?" Marco laughs, running one of his hands up and down my arm.

"Not unless you want to lower your I.Q. by about a hundred points."

Pushing up on my toes, I give him a quick kiss, pulling back to smile. "Thank you for coming to the rehearsal dinner tonight."

His hand continues moving up my bare arm and over my shoulder, wrapping its warmth softly around my neck so he can slide his thumb back and forth over my cheek.

"Free booze and a five course meal? Like I'd say no to that!" He laughs. "Or a chance to see your sexy ass in a hot dress again."

I let Ava dress me again for Gavin and Charlotte's rehearsal dinner since the last time she did, Marco couldn't keep his hands off me. Tonight, she stuffed me into a skin-tight red halter dress that I have to say, makes my boobs look amazing.

"Marco! Just the man I want to see," Tyler yells from behind me as Marco keeps his hand in place on my neck and takes a sip of his drink with the other.

"You look like the type of guy that's used *Seduction and Sugar* on a few women before. What's your take on the Tiramisu and Titty Twister chapter?" Uncle Drew asks.

Marco's drink goes down the wrong pipe and he immediately starts choking and coughing. I quickly move to his side to pat his back, giving my uncle a dirty look.

"Seriously, Uncle Drew? I think Marco has a bit more class than that."

Marco starts coughing harder, and I take the drink from his hand as he bends at the waist and puts his hands on his knees. Uncle Drew and Tyler finally walk away, muttering something about how no one appreciates good porn anymore.

After a few minutes of rubbing my hand soothingly against Marco's back, he finally stands up and takes a deep breath.

"I should have know *those two* would consider that stupid book their bible," I laugh. "Are okay?"

Marco takes his drink glass from my hand and sets it on a nearby empty table, turning back to grab both of my hands.

"I need to tell you something," he whispers.

"My family is full of idiots?" I ask with a laugh. "I'm aware."

"I'm an idiot too. A really, really big idiot. I need to—"

Glancing over Marco's shoulder, I see Charlotte finally alone, standing in the corner of the room on the other side of the restaurant and I hold my hand up distractedly.

"Sorry, can you hold that thought?" I ask, my eyes glued to Charlotte as she checks something on her phone. "Charlotte is finally alone and I need to talk to her really quick."

Marco looks a little frustrated that I interrupted him, and I immediately feel bad. I thought he was going to tell me something stupid my dad and Uncle Carter said to him since he'd been busy talking to them over by the bar before he came over here, but maybe I was wrong.

"Never mind, I'll talk to her later."

He shakes his head and gives me a quick kiss on the cheek. "No, it's fine. It can wait. Does this have anything to do with the private little conversation I saw you and Gavin having a little bit ago?"

It has *everything* to do with that talk my soon-to-be brother-in-law had and if I'm lucky, we can finally be finished with this stupid charade once and for all.

"That it does," I tell him with a smile. "Brace yourself, Marco. If all goes well, I should be un-knocked up by the third course."

He quickly gets down on one knee, grabs my hips, and presses his lips to my stomach.

"What the hell are you doing?" I whisper loudly, looking around in embarrassment when a bunch of people start staring.

"If this whole thing is coming to an end, I feel like I should go out with a bang," he explains. "Really put everything I've got into this role to make it memorable. Besides, I've gotten to know this little fake fetus the last few weeks. We've bonded. I'm going to be sad to see the little bugger go."

I clutch onto the shoulders of his dress shirt and try pulling him up from the ground, but he's not budging.

"No matter what you hear tonight, Cletus the Fetus, Daddy loves you," he speaks softly to my stomach. "We've had some good times, we've had some bad times, and we've had some times where you've needed to cover your little fake fetus ears because your mommy is a screamer."

I smack his arm, shooting a nervous smile to all the people watching us with sappy looks on their faces.

"Oh, my God, get up!" I whisper through my embarrassed smile.

"I know, Cletus the Fetus, Mommy confuses me too. Oh, my God is usually followed by *'Go down!'* when she screams it," Marco tells my stomach.

"If you don't get up right now, I will tell everyone your soufflé couldn't get it up," I growl.

He quickly stands and gives me a shocked look. "You wouldn't? It was ONE time and you said it happens to everyone!"

With a laugh, I grab his tie and yank him down to my lips, pressing my mouth to his. When the people standing closest to us start to clap and cheer, I pull my lips from his before I get too carried away.

"Save me a seat, I'll be back in a few," I tell him, smoothing his tie down before heading in Charlotte's direction.

"I'll miss you Cletus! Remember me fondly," Marco calls after me.

I ignore him and charge through the crowd, standing quietly behind Charlotte while she's still staring at something on her phone. I lean over her shoulder and immediately regret it when I see she's watching some sort of horror movie, the screen filled with what looks like bloody roast beef falling out of a wound in someone's body that has blood and guts and internal organs spilling out of it.

"What the fuck are you watching?"

Charlotte screams, dropping her phone as she whirls around to face me.

"Dammit, Molly! I thought you'd finally gotten tired of sneaking up on people. It's like you get some sort of sick thrill out of making people scream," Charlotte complains with a sigh, bending down to grab her phone.

"It's true, I do. I keep your screams in a jar in my closet next to the severed heads," I explain with a shrug. "Want to tell me why you're watching the world's most disgusting horror movie right before dinner?"

"It wasn't a horror movie, it was a Youtube video of a live birth," she tells me, setting her phone on the table next to her.

"That was a vagina?" I ask in shock. "I knew they were pretty resilient, but how the hell do they come back from something like that? It looked like it went through a meat grinder. Your vagina is going to look like a raw hamburger patty covered in ketchup and thrown at a wall."

She glares at me, her hands on her hips and her foot tapping against the floor. "Thanks a lot. Like I'm not freaked out enough as it is."

I pat her shoulder comfortingly. "Well, you'll be happy to know I have one less thing for you to be worried about. I had a nice little chat with Gavin earlier. He wanted to apologize for being a dick and so angry when he walked in on us in the bathroom that day and also for avoiding me since then."

Charlotte's eyes widen in fear and her hands drop to her sides. "Did you tell him? What the fuck did you say to him?!"

"Calm the fuck down, burger vag," I sigh. "I didn't tell him anything, but you definitely will before this night is over. It turns out, Gavin wasn't angry, he was jealous. Because he's decided he wants kids and he's afraid to tell you since you guys both agreed not to have them. So, now you can tell him tonight and not have anything at all to worry about tomorrow."

I smile happily, waiting for her to tell me how amazing I am and how it's all thanks to me that she can marry the love of her life without having any secrets between them.

"Are you insane?!" She screeches. "I can't tell him now, at our rehearsal dinner! He'll want to tell everyone and then mom and dad will know and it will start a huge argument and this perfect night will be ruined!"

"Did you even hear what I said?" I yell back. "Your fiancé wants kids. You can finally stop telling him you have the flu and that your ass isn't the size of Texas now because of stress-eating. This is a *good* thing, dumbass!"

She huffs, snatching her phone from the table as the owner of the restaurant announces for everyone to take their seats so they can begin serving the first course.

"You bitches want to tone it down a little? People are starting to stare," Ava tells us as she walks up next to us.

"I'll tone it down when meaty vagina here tells Gavin the truth," I announce petulantly.

Charlotte grimaces and Ava sighs.

"I'm just going to pretend I understand the meaty vagina reference before Charlotte pukes on my shoes. I thought we were waiting until after the wedding?" Ava asks.

"We ARE," Charlotte growls. "I don't want anything to ruin tonight or tomorrow. What's the big deal, anyway?"

"The big deal is that I just told you your fiancé wants kids and all you care about is having a perfect wedding!" I argue.

"Wait, Gavin wants kids?" Ava asks in shock.

"Not only does he want kids, he's been jealous of my fake pregnancy this entire time and is freaking out about telling Charlotte he's changed his mind," I inform her.

The pissed off and annoyed look on Charlotte's face immediately disappears and she smiles brightly at something behind me.

"We saw you guys having a little argument. Don't mind us, just carry on," Dicky Daren tells us as he aims the camera in our direction.

Charlotte laughs nervously. "Oh, no, we're not arguing! We're...ummmm, excited. Molly just told us she felt the baby kick!"

The camera flies in my direction and I can hear it clicking and whirring as it zooms in on my stomach.

"Right, Molly? You felt the baby kick because that would be sweet and awesome and wouldn't cause anyone like Mom and Mad to scream and fight and ruin this entire night, right?" Charlotte asks, her eyes wide and pleading with me as she presses her hands to my stomach.

"You are such an asshole," Ava mutters to Charlotte, as the camera pans to Ava's face. "I mean, an asshole for getting to feel that little spawn kicking before me!"

Ava's hands also fly to my stomach and all three of us look into the camera with fake smiles while I silently curse Charlotte.

"Yaaaaay, it kicked," I cheer in a monotone voice with fake enthusiasm.

Someone clangs their silverware against a glass across the room and Dicky Daren finally finds something more interesting to record as he walks away from us.

All three of us let out a sigh when we're alone again.

"I'm sorry," Charlotte whispers. "I just don't want anything to mess this up. Please, Molly, just until after the wedding. I know I'm being selfish and I know you hate me, but this is the only wedding I'll ever have and I want it to be perfect."

With an annoyed growl, I point my finger at Charlotte's face. "You better hope this is your only wedding because if there's a second one, I will fuck that shit up."

Charlotte squeals, throwing her arms around me to squeeze me so tight I can't breathe. "You are the best sister in the whole world!"

Ava clears her throat. "Um, hello? What about me?"

Charlotte finally releases me and scowls at her. "You sent me that birthing video and told me it was a cute kitten compilation."

"Well, it *was* about pussies, so technically I didn't lie. I just forgot to mention it was about pussies that look like a serial killer got ahold of them," Ava shrugs.

Leaving them to bicker, I turn and make my way to the table where Marco is sitting. He sees me coming and pulls my chair out for me, resting his arm on the back when I sit down.

"Everything go okay?" he asks softly as the servers come out of the kitchen and start putting plates in front of everyone.

"Super," I tell him with a bright smile. "You'll be happy to know Cletus kicked for the first time. It was a joyous event."

Marco slides a glass of orange juice across the table to me and gives me a sympathetic smile.

"Yum, more mommy juice," I grumble, bringing the glass to my lips and taking a huge swallow.

My throat burns and my eyes water as soon as the liquid slides down my throat and I slam my fist against my chest as I cough.

"I guess I shouldn't have asked the bartender to put enough vodka in there to choke a horse," Marco whispers in my ear as he pats my back. "Fetal Alcohol Syndrome for our baby it is!"

I get my coughing under control and manage a small laugh. "Thanks for sneaking me a drink. I'm going to need about ten more to get through this night."

Clinking my glass against Marco's beer bottle, I hold it up for a toast.

"Here's to one more night with our little bundle of joy. May our baby have your good looks and my charming personality, minus the swearing and underage drinking."

A server's arm that was sliding between us suddenly drops the plate of food right into Marco's lap.

"YOU'RE having a baby?!"

Marco's chair flies backwards as he pushes his feet against the floor to quickly remove the boiling hot shrimp scampi appetizer from his crotch, and I turn around to look at the woman who just yelled and dropped the plate.

I practically motorboat the woman standing between us since her giant fake boobs that are popping out of her shirt are right at my eye level.

"Megan, I didn't know you worked here," Marco says with an uncomfortable laugh while he swipes away the food with his cloth napkin. "It's been a while. How've you been?"

I look back and forth between Tits McGee and Marco, wondering how they know each other, hoping they're neighbors or cousins. Please, God, let them be related.

"Did I really hear you say you're having a baby? I think I'm going to be sick," Bimbo Barbie says with a grimace, tossing her perfect blonde hair over one shoulder.

"Um, Molly, this is Megan Levine. Megan, this is my girlfriend, Molly," Marco says without looking up, suddenly very interested in getting the stains out of the crotch of his pants.

She doesn't even glance in my direction, and if I didn't already hate her because of her fake tits, big hair, tiny waist and all around perfect body, I sure as shit would now. She looks right over my head like I'm not even sitting here.

"It must take a lot of skill to say the word *girlfriend* without laughing," she says with a smile that is definitely not friendly. "Looks like nothing has changed and you're still sleeping your way through another stupid porn cookbook. If you decide to include another story about me in this one, at least get the facts straight. The Chocolate Sauce Suckfest was *my* idea, and I'm the one who told you to use milk chocolate instead of semi sweet. The least you could do is put my name in the acknowledgements."

So, not a cousin, unless it's recently become acceptable to blow your relative.

I try really hard to say something awesome and sarcastic to make her feel like an asshole, but I'm too busy wondering why Marco would ever want someone like me when he had someone like *her*. Also, what in the holy fuck is she talking about? Porn cookbook? Acknowledgements? Is everyone a fan of that stupid *Seduction and Sugar* book but me?

"Oh, how cute," Megan purrs. "I think your *girlfriend* is in shock. You might want to do something about that, Alfanso. Or is it Marco? I can never remember which is the right one."

What in the actual fuck of all fucks is happening right now? Am I on drugs? Is *she* on drugs? Is the documentary they've been filming really some kind of hidden camera show where they play jokes on people? Maybe it's an episode of *Intervention* and mom was right. Vodka really is a gateway drug to meth and I became an addict without even knowing it.

I need to say something since it appears as if Marco has become mute. Tell her to go fuck herself. Tell her to take her porn star tits and go back to the stripper pole where she belongs. Tell her she's a liar and snotty bitch.

Wait, did she say Alfanso?

"I puked when I gave him a blowjob," I mutter.

"Blowjob puking?" Uncle Drew pipes up from across the table. "There's porn for that. It's a little disturbing, but surprisingly good quality. Hold on, I have it bookmarked."

Uncle Drew pulls out his phone, and I stare at Marco, waiting for him to explain what the hell is going on before I lose my mind.

"Ava almost did that once, but she made it to the toilet right after she swallowed," Tyler muses. "That's why my pet name for her is Cum-Bubble. She had this adorable little bubble of snot and jizz in one nostril. I think I still have the picture somewhere on my phone."

Why isn't Marco saying anything?

"Holy shit! Are *you* Alfanso D.?!" Tyler suddenly shouts across the table in excitement, staring wide-eyed at Marco. "Dude, Chocolate Sauce Suckfest changed my life!"

He elbows Uncle Drew.

"Hold on, I almost found it. I saved it after the link for grandma banging and before the one for midget anal," Uncle Drew mutters, finally looking up from his phone when Tyler keeps nudging him.

"Dad, we've been in the company of porn royalty this entire time and didn't even know it," Tyler says in awe.

"I'm not a partial-virgin anymore," I mumble stupidly.

"Oh, I KNOW I've got virgin porn on here. You're gonna need to be more specific about the partial thing, though," Uncle Drew says, going back to his phone.

"Molly, I can explain," Marco whispers, finally deciding to speak.

"Oh, this should be good," Blondie mutters with a sarcastic laugh.

I finally clear my head enough to notice the guilty look on Marco's face, and I realize he hasn't said one word about how this bitch is lying or confused or a homeless meth addict posing as a server.

"How about you just fuck right off, Giant Jugs?" I growl, my eyes narrowing at the slut who refuses to walk away.

She gasps and then huffs, looking at Marco like she expects him to come to her defense. When he wisely keeps his mouth shut and his eyes stay glued to mine, she finally storms away, leaving a cloud of fruity perfume in her wake that makes me nauseous.

"Molly, please—"

"Was she telling the truth?" I ask, cutting him off.

I don't know why I'm even asking since I can see it written all over his miserable face. I can't decide if I want to cry or smack him.

Calmly pushing my chair back, I stand and toss my napkin on top of the table.

"I lied. It IS a big deal and it doesn't happen to every guy!" I yell, channeling Rachel from *Friends*.

Marco gasps, but I'm too upset and heart broken and pissed to let the hurt look on his face get to me.

"Ooooh, got yourself a wilting wiener problem, huh?" Uncle

Drew asks him with a sympathetic smile. "Don't worry, I've got just the porn for that. Shit, where did I put the link to the toe fucking website..."

On that note, I turn and walk away from the table. I keep my head down as the tears start to fall when I realize Marco isn't going to chase after me, a shout from Uncle Drew making this night even more sad and pathetic.

"Shit! I can't believe someone erased my toe-fucking link. Dammit, Tom Brady!"

Chapter 23

– Smell the Meat –

Marco

LIKE THE FUCKING coward I am, I left the rehearsal dinner last night with my tail tucked between my legs as soon as Molly walked away from me with tears in her eyes. Well, as soon as Drew made me watch twenty minutes of foot fetish porn and Tyler told me he knew a guy who knew a guy who could get me Viagra, but it would involve me stripping at something called BronyCon that I was afraid to ask about.

I knew this would happen and I knew it would fuck up everything, but like an idiot, I just kept putting it off until it all blew up in my face. And blow up it did when a blast from my man-whore past showed up and ruined my life.

Fucking Megan Levine…that chocolate sauce chapter wasn't even about her, but the one with the recipe for a strawberry sauce to add to your bath water for a fresh smelling vagina was. That chick had a nice rack, but her pussy smelled like ham, and not delicious, Easter Sunday ham either. Like ten-day-old rancid lunchmeat ham.

Stupid Megan Levine and her stupid ham vagina.

"Did you call my guy's guy about the dick drugs?"

Tyler comes up next to me and hands me a beer while I stare across the room at Molly. I tried to talk to her earlier at the wedding ceremony, but she pretended like I didn't exist and refused to even look at me. I'm not leaving this reception until she lets me apologize and explain.

"I don't need dick drugs, Tyler, we were talking about a soufflé," I clarify, watching Molly duck down under the head table again for probably the tenth time in the last few minutes.

What the hell is she doing?

"Is that like, French or something? I kind of like it. It sounds more dignified to say *I fucked a soufflé,*" he muses. "Is that gonna be in the next book? Can I get an advanced copy?"

I chug my beer for some liquid courage and prepare to head over to Molly, dragging her out of here if I need to.

"The next book is called *Baking and Babies* and has nothing to do with the fucking of desserts," I tell him with a sigh.

"Baking babies? Dude, that's hard-core. I mean, I know kids are annoying and shit, but cooking them? Can you even do that?" he asks.

I watch Molly pop back up from under the table and stand, wobbling a little as she clutches onto the back of her chair. She's so fucking beautiful it makes me want to cry. I've heard women complain about being forced to wear ugly bridesmaid dresses, but there is nothing ugly about the short purple, satin strapless dress clinging to Molly's body. Her hair is up in some fancy do with a few pieces hanging down around her face and my hands have been itching all day to pull out the pins holding it in place so I could watch the silky dark locks spill around her naked shoulders.

"I guess you can slather BBQ sauce on just about anything and it will taste good, but I just don't know if I could stomach eating an actual baby, no matter what you baste it in."

While Tyler continues to talk to himself, I shove my empty bottle at him start walking towards the head table.

"What about Ranch?" Tyler shouts after me. "I might eat a baby if you put Ranch on it."

A few people try to stop and talk to me, but I ignore them and keep my eye on the prize. When I'm a few feet away from the head table, the DJ comes up behind Gavin and Charlotte and speaks into his microphone.

"If everyone could have a seat, we're going to get started with the toasts before dinner is served," he announces to the room.

The reception hall is filled with the sounds of chairs scraping across the floor as everyone sits down. With a quick glance around me, I realize I'm the only one still standing so I quickly grab an empty seat at the nearest table as the DJ hands the microphone to Molly.

She grabs it and moves to stand behind Gavin and Charlotte, swaying a little when she stops and I immediately realize what she was doing each time she disappeared out of sight under the table.

"This is going to be amazing. She's so wasted," Ava whispers with a laugh as she pulls up a chair next to me and flops down.

"Shouldn't you be up there with the rest of the bridal party? And why the hell did you let her drink so much?" I ask in a quiet, angry voice.

Molly blows loudly into the microphone, the speakers screeching with feedback as everyone in the room winces from the ear piercing noise.

"I didn't realize until five minutes ago that she's been inhaling a bottle of vodka under the table since she got here," Ava tells me while Molly giggles into the microphone and apologizes to everyone. "I went to get her some black coffee from the kitchen, but they haven't brewed any yet."

"I'd like to thank everyone for coming out tonight to celebrate the joyous union of my perfect sister and her perfect Gavin," Molly starts, holding her champagne glass in the air.

"I hope someone is filming this," Ava laughs.

"Aren't they just sooooooooo perfect?" Molly asks sarcastically.

"We need to do something. This is not good," I mutter.

"Are you kidding me? This is amazing. Charlotte has been a raging bitch to us all day, reminding us to keep our mouth's shut every five minutes so we wouldn't ruin her *perfect* day," Ava explains while Molly starts to pace behind a nervous-looking Charlotte and a confused-looking Gavin. "I love Charlotte, but I fully support whatever Molly is about to do. Charlotte has been so concerned with having the perfect wedding that she doesn't even realize none of this shit matters in the long run."

I definitely agree with Ava, but I really don't want Molly doing something she's going to regret. Giving a drunk speech in front of two-hundred friends and family when half of them think she's pregnant might be a bad idea.

"Also, you're lucky I'm wearing a dress and not kicking your ass right now," Ava tells me with a glare while Molly instructs everyone to hold up their glasses for her toast. "I don't know what you did to my sister last night, but it must have been pretty bad for her to cry. I've never seen that bitch cry. She collects jars of *other* people's tears under her bed, she never sheds them herself. What did you do?"

I open my mouth to tell her it's a long story and I plan on doing whatever I can to fix it when the sound of loud, heavy breathing echoes through the room.

"Hold on a second. I need to take these fucking heels off, my feet are killing me," Molly says, the words sounding even more garbled since she has her mouth pressed right up against the microphone while she leans against the wall and quickly removes her shoes.

She chucks them right over Charlotte and Gavin's head and they land in the middle of the front table where her parents and aunt and uncles are seated.

"WOOOHOOOOO TAKE IT OFF!" Drew shouts, grabbing one of her shoes and waving it around above his head.

Claire punches him in the arm and I hear her yell at him about Molly being his niece, Drew quickly lowering his arm and his lips form the words, "Oh, yeah. I forgot."

Molly starts walking behind the bridal party, stopping when she gets to a small table at the end that holds trays of appetizers.

"So, I guess you guys all heard that I'm knocked up," she speaks into the microphone, setting her glass down on the table.

"Did she say she's getting locked up? I didn't know Molly was going to prison," someone whispers loudly.

I turn my head and realize I sat down at Molly's grandfather's table and he's currently giving me the stink eye while Sue shakes her head sadly and he chews on a toothpick.

"Skull-fucker," Molly's grandpa mouths silently, pulling the toothpick out of his mouth and pointing it at me.

I swallow nervously and turn back around to watch the train wreck in front of me, wondering if I should go up there and take the microphone away from Molly or if that would just make things worse.

One of the groomsmen leans to the side and holds his hand out for the microphone and Molly smacks him on the hand with it.

"Fuck off! I'm in the middle of something here," Molly shouts when she brings the mic back up to her mouth. "Where was I?"

Yep, going up there would probably be worse.

She grabs one of the trays from the appetizer table and unsteadily carries it back to her original spot behind the bride and groom.

"Oh, yeah," she continues, dropping the tray onto the table next to Charlotte. "So, this one day I was minding my own business, and then BAM, I was suddenly knocked up. And here's the funny thing, I hadn't even had sex! I know, right?"

Charlotte drops her head to the table and Molly laughs.

"Well, I mean, there was this one time with Pez Penis but that doesn't count, and then like, fifteen times with a guy I thought loved me and those TOTALLY count and they were awesome because he doesn't have a Pez Penis, but he's a liar and he lied and I threw up on his penis and everything and he still lied," Molly says with a sniffle.

"Did she say she threw up on a penis?" Sue whispers.

"God dammit, you heard that? There goes my Wednesday blow jobs," Molly's grandfather grumbles.

"DAMN YOU, TOM BRADY!"

I don't even need to turn my head to see who yelled *that*, especially when I hear Jenny tell him to shut the hell up because Molly is trying to confess her sins to cleanse Aurora.

"I'm so happy my sister married the love of her life and had the most perfect wedding ever," Molly continues. "I'm so glad she gets to live happily ever after when my life sucks and it never would have sucked in the first place if I didn't have Cletus the Fetus and a liar liar-pants baby daddy who can't get it up!"

This half of the room all whip their heads in my direction with shocked expressions on their face and I throw my hands up in the air.

"It was a soufflé, dammit! I collapsed a soufflé," I tell them.

"Say it with a French accent, dude! It doesn't sound as pervy that way!" Tyler shouts from the back of the room.

"Is Molly drunk? Isn't that bad for the baby?" Uncle Carter asks his wife.

"Oh yeah, she's trashed. Just wait for it," Claire tells him with a smile.

"Is there something I need to know?" Jim questions Liz.

"You just sit there and look pretty, honey," Liz says with a smile, patting the top of his hand.

"I'd like everyone to raise their glasses and toast the happy, perfect couple sitting right here looking all happy and perfect," Molly tells the room.

While everyone awkwardly lifts their glasses, Molly grabs a huge handful of something from the tray she dropped to the table and then taps Charlotte on the head with the microphone.

Charlotte slowly lifts her head as Molly sticks her hand right up to her face.

"What the hell are you doing? Get that away from me," Charlotte whines, the microphone just barely picking up her words.

"What's wrong, Charlotte? It's just some cured meats from your antipasto appetizer. Mmmmmmm, meat. Don't they smell good? Like meat. Mmmmmmm lunchmeat," Molly says into the microphone, waving a fist full of cold cuts in front of Charlotte's nose.

Charlotte covers her mouth with one hand and shakes her head back and forth frantically.

"Smell the meat, Charlotte, SMELL IT!" Molly yells.

"This is a very strange wedding toast," one of the guests whispers loudly from another table.

Charlotte tries to back away from Molly's meat holding hand, but Molly moves right along with her and smacks her hand full of cold cuts against Charlotte's chest. They stick to her skin as Molly pulls her hand away and laughs into the microphone.

Charlotte takes one horrified look down at the meat stuck to her chest and her cheeks puff out as she leans forward and throws up all over the table.

The room explodes in a chorus of groans and a couple of gags, but Gavin's voice can still be heard above the noise.

"Shit! I thought you said your flu was finally gone?" he asks his new bride, grabbing a napkin to help her wipe her mouth.

"She doesn't have the flu, you dumbass!" Molly informs him. "She's got the meat sweats, isn't that right, Charlotte?"

Charlotte's hand flies back to her mouth, and she turns her head to glare at Molly.

"Stop talking about meat!" she screams behind her hand.

"Fine. SOUP, SOUP, SOUP! CREAMY SOUP, CHUNKY SOUP, GREASY, LUMPY, SOUP, SOUP, SOUP!" Molly yells into the microphone.

Charlotte's eyes get so wide I'm surprised they don't pop out of her head. Sweat drips down from her forehead and she quickly presses her other hand on top of the first one, holding them both as hard as she can against her mouth.

"Honestly, Molly, if you want soup that bad just ask the caterer, there's no need to yell," Gavin complains while he continues consoling his wife.

As soon as Gavin says the word *soup*, Charlotte's body jerks with a heave and she presses her hands harder against her face to keep the vomit in.

"I know I should go up there and do something, but it's like I'm watching a bus full of people slam into a brick wall," Ava mumbles. "It's horrifying and mesmerizing at the same time."

Molly holds the microphone against her mouth and leans in close to Charlotte.

"Say it, out loud," Molly growls.

"Who is Edward, from Twilight?!" Drew shouts excitedly.

"Oh, I get it now. This is like a wedding version of Jeopardy. Soup and meat, soup and meat…" Jenny says, scratching her head as she thinks. "Oh, I know! What are astrophysicists?!"

Drew looks at her in confusion and she rolls her eyes.

"You know, like chocolate and oysters and other stuff that makes people horny," Jenny explains.

"Say it, or I will!" Molly yells at Charlotte.

"Fine!" Charlotte shouts back, dropping her hands from her face and turning to look at Gavin.

"Molly was never pregnant. It was me the whole time, and I'm sorry for lying to you, but I was afraid you wouldn't want to marry me and I love you so much, and I didn't want to lose you and I just wanted us to have the perfect wedding, and I know you probably hate me now and Molly hates me and my parents hate me, and I just threw up in front of everyone I know and I'm sorry I made Molly do this for me, but it's not my fault your boyfriend lied to you about writing porn and WHY THE FUCK DOES THIS SALAMI SMELL LIKE ROTTEN ASS?!" Charlotte screams at the end of her rambling explanation.

"Pumpkin Roll Punany, bro!" Tyler shouts, pounding his fist against his heart and then pointing at me with a wink and a big smile.

"Cheers, mother fuckers!" Molly yells as she leans back from Charlotte. "Gilmore, OUT!"

With that, Molly throws her arm out in front of her and drops the microphone as it screeches with more feedback, thumping loudly through the speakers when it hits the floor.

Everyone mumbles a confused "cheers" in response, but they don't get a chance to drink when all of a sudden a loud, banshee-like scream comes out of Charlotte's mouth as she jumps up from her chair and lunges at Molly.

Ava and I fly up from our chairs as Charlotte quickly grabs the tray of antipasto salad, jerking it in Molly's direction as she charges her. Huge piles of salami and thinly sliced ham soar through the air and smack against the front of Molly's dress.

"Let's see how YOU like the meat sweats!" Charlotte screams as Molly reaches down the front of her dress and pulls out a fist-full of ham.

"I happen to LOVE the meat sweats! Too bad we don't have any ground meat so I could shove it in your fat ass granny panties and you can see what it will be like to have a slimy, meaty vagina in a few months!" Molly screams back.

"I think *I'm* going to puke now," Gavin mutters, pressing his hands to his stomach.

The parents and aunts and uncles all jump up from their table and join Ava and I in a race around the bridal table as Molly and Charlotte scream in unison and start whipping lunch meat at each other's faces.

"EAT THE SLIMY HAM, YOU SLUTTY PREGNANT DICK!" Molly yells, snatching a clump of meat from the table and shoving it against Charlotte's mouth with one hand while she grabs a handful of Charlotte's veil and holds her head still with the other.

"*YOU* EAT IT, YOU PENIS-PUKING-PORN-WRITER-FUCKER-WHORE-FACE!" Charlotte screams back, jerking her face from side to side as Molly keeps trying to shove ham in her mouth.

Ava and I get to Molly first and we both wrap our arms around her, pulling her away from Charlotte as she kicks and screams and curses. Liz and Jim do the same to Charlotte, and we all manage to separate the girls as they continue to fling cold cuts at each other while we drag them apart.

Tyler quickly grabs the microphone from the floor where Molly dropped it, tapping on it a few times before addressing the crowd.

"And that concludes the dinner theater portion of the reception! How about we give these guys a hand for their amazing and artistic portrayal of a white trash family?!" Tyler says, clapping his hand against the microphone as the room slowly joins in. "Help yourself to the open bar and stay tuned for the next show in forty-five minutes. The famous author, Alfanso D. will be cooking up some tasty babies as a special treat for everyone!"

He sets down the microphone and the confused guests start getting up from their tables to head to the bar where hopefully there's enough booze to make all of them black-out.

"You take care of this one, I'm going to help Mom and Dad," Ava tells me, shoving Molly into my arms. "Fix her, or I will use the box of toothpicks in my grandfather's pocket to filet your dick like a trout and shove it down your throat."

My dick tries to claw its way up inside my body in fear when Ava gives me the two-finger warning, point at her eyes and then my crotch area before walking away.

Taking a deep breath, I turn Molly around to face me and quietly begin pulling pieces of ham and salami out of her hair.

"I ruined my sister's wedding and you ruined my heart," she whispers sadly.

Glancing behind her, I see Gavin down on his knees talking to Charlotte's stomach with a huge smile on his face while the rest of her family laughs and jokes with each other around them.

"Only one of those things is true," I tell her quietly as I peal off a slice of ham stuck to her shoulder and toss it to the floor. Gently turning her body around, I point to her family a few feet away.

"I can't believe I'm going to be a dad!" Gavin says happily, placing another kiss to Charlotte's stomach before jumping to his feet and pulling her in for a hug.

Charlotte nestles her face into the side of his neck and mumbles an apology.

"I'm sorry I lied to you. I should have told you the truth, I was just so scared of losing you. I'm such an idiot..." she trails off.

"You're both idiots," Claire tells them, glaring at Gavin. "How in the hell did you not realize your fiancé was pregnant when you live together?"

Gavin shrugs. "I mean, I knew she was acting different, but you always told me if I didn't have anything nice to say that I shouldn't say anything at all. What kind of a man would I be if I told the woman I love that I thought her ass was getting a little big?"

Charlotte starts crying and Gavin quickly backpedals. "I didn't mean it like that! You have a GREAT ass!"

Drew steps forward and nods enthusiastically. "It's true, you do. Tom Brady always grabs the gherkin when he looks at your ass."

Molly turns away from them and I press my hands to her cheeks, tilting her face up to me.

"You have no idea how sorry I am."

She sniffles, swiping angrily at a tear on her cheek. I hate myself for making her cry, but at least she's not running away, refusing to listen. Judging by what just happened, I'm pretty sure she polished off more vodka than everyone in this room combined and who knows if she'll even understand or remember what I'm about to say, but I know it's the only chance I have to explain and I'm taking it whether she passes out or throws up.

Giving up on the meat since there seems to be a hell of a lot stuck to her and down the front of her dress, I grab her face and tilt it up so I can see her eyes.

"I'm sorry for lying to you," I whisper. "It killed me to keep it from you, and I swear on my mother and sister's lives that I've tried to tell you so many times the last few weeks. I'm sorry I'm such an asshole and kept putting it off because I was so afraid of losing you."

She sighs loudly and I start talking faster before she walks away.

"I was a jerk before we got together, and yes, I said and did a lot of stupid shit online just to get people to laugh and buy that stupid cookbook. You changed everything, Molly. You and your crazy family made me want things I never thought I did before. I've never been so tied up in knots or so scared or crazy. You make me crazy, and it's the best thing that's every happened to me," I tell her softly.

"I was so scared to tell you the truth because I know how much you hate that guy. I hate him too but you have to know I'm not him anymore, and it's because of *you*. It kills me knowing I hurt you and it breaks my heart that I'm the reason for your tears. Please, forgive me, Molly. If you give me one more chance, I promise I'll never make you cry again. I'll spend every day showing you I'm not that same jerk who exploited women for a stupid cookbook. Give me a chance to earn your trust again. I love you. I've waited my whole life for someone like you. Stay with me, say you'll forgive me, and I will do anything. Whatever it takes."

I stop talking and hold my breath until she finally speaks.

"You'll do anything?" she asks.

My heart beats faster with excitement even though I shouldn't get my hopes up. There is no way she'll forgive me this easily and I don't blame her.

I nod my head quickly in response.

"Whatever I ask?" she questions.

I nod again and she pushes up on her tiptoes and whispers softly in my ear. When she's finished, she pulls away and I drop my hands from her face with a soft groan.

"Really? Right now?"

She takes a few steps back and grabs the microphone from the table where Tyler left it, her eyes never leaving mine as she comes back to me and holds it out in front of her.

"I'm covered in meat grease and announced to everyone I know that I puked on a dick because I drank half a bottle of vodka to try and stop my heart from hurting," she tells me, pointing towards the room full of people. "Right here, right now."

With a sigh, I bring the microphone up to my mouth.

"Excuse me, could I have everyone's attention, please?"

The low hum of conversation in the room immediately quiets down and all eyes turn to me. I glance at Molly to see if she might change her mind, but she just crosses her arm and waits for me to do what she asked.

I look back out at the crowd and smile nervously.

"So, um, hello everyone. My name is Marco and I just want to thank you all for coming and tell you I masturbate into my socks. Like, a lot."

I laugh uncomfortably at the silence in the room, looking over at Molly again to see her pull a piece of salami out of the front of her dress and take a bite. She motions to me with the half-eaten slice to continue, the meat flopping around in her hand as I look back out at the crowded room.

"I like how the soft, fuzzy cotton of tube socks feels against my penis. I am a tube-sock-masturbator, and I'm not ashamed to leave crusty, jizz-filled socks under my bed for my mom to find," I say in a rush, quickly pulling the microphone away from my mouth.

"WE LOVE YOU, MINIVAN!" Drew screams.

The guests immediately go back to their drinks and conversation, no longer shocked about anything that happens at this point.

Tossing the microphone on top of the table, I wrap my arms

around Molly's waist and pull her against my body. "Am I forgiven now?"

She presses her hands against my chest and looks up at me.

"Not yet, but that definitely earned you a few bonus points," she tells me with a smile.

I can finally start breathing normally again and I lean my face down to hers, needing to feel her lips against mine to reassure myself that everything will be okay.

Her hand comes up between us and she presses it against my lips right before they touch hers.

"I really want to kiss you even thought I'm still kind of pissed at you, but I think I'm ready to throw up all the vodka now. Eating that meat was a bad idea," she whispers, moving her hand from my mouth to hold it over her own.

"Oooooh, does Molly have the meat sweats now?" Charlotte laughs as her and Gavin walk up to us with their arms wrapped around each other.

"I think it's the vodka sweats," I tell her as Molly bends forward and puts her hands on her knees while I rub her back.

"Oh, that's nothing. Try having the night sweats because you're becoming a changeling," Jenny announces, walking over with Drew while Claire and Carter and Liz and Jim follow.

"Jesus, Jenny, how many times do I have to tell you it's called *going through the change*, not becoming a fucking changeling?" Claire tells her.

Drew shakes his head sadly and pats her back. "Sweetie, you don't have to make up stories about menopause. It's okay to admit you've been waking up with hot flashes because you're having sex dreams about poop sex. You're amongst family and no one will judge you. I've accepted your fetish, and I promise to take a dump on you the next time I've got one ready."

Molly groans down by my knees and I feel her pain as my stomach rolls with the need to puke right along with her.

"I'm going to pretend I never heard those words come out of your mouth and just say I'm glad you girls finally got your shit together and came clean," Liz says. "Do you have any idea how hard it's been to keep a straight face the last few weeks? Jesus, Claire and I deserve a fucking medal."

Molly's head pops up and she looks quickly between her mother and her aunt. "You knew? This entire time you knew we were lying?"

Liz and Claire share a look and start laughing.

"Duh. Do we look like idiots?" Liz asks.

"Do you think maybe you should have clued me in on this information?" Jim complains.

Liz glares at him. "I was going to until I found out that stain on my living room carpet is actually meerkat jizz and not chip dip, like you swore it was."

Jim groans and Drew starts laughing. "Fucking Tom Brady. That little guy sure did appreciate turtle porn, let me tell you. I've never seen so much spooge come out of such a tiny animal."

Molly immediately turns her head and relieves herself of that pesky vodka, all over my shoes while Charlotte does the same down the front of Gavin's tux.

"But seriously," Liz continues, like the pukefest isn't even happening. "I kind of just wanted to see how far you guys would take it before putting you out of your misery, but then you three girls started getting along like real sisters and that seemed more important than the shit-show you were putting on for us."

I'm not sure who is more shocked right now since Charlotte, Ava, Molly and I all share the same jaw-dropping looks of surprise.

"So, Molly's not pregnant?" Drew asks.

Liz shakes her head. "Nope."

"But she had sex, right? You had sex?" Drew asks, turning to look at Molly, still bent over down by my knees.

"Uh, yes?" Molly replies uncertainly.

"WOOOHOOO, Molly had sex!" Drew cheers, punching his fists in the air.

A painful '*oof*' comes out of him when Jim punches him in the stomach. When Drew recovers, he holds his hands up in front of her to stop Jim from hitting him again.

"I know, I know! She's my niece, and it's disgusting I'm happy, but…it's sex, dude!" Drew explains. "Sex is awesome! But, she's my niece and I should be pissed. But sex is awesome!"

Drew crosses his arms and shakes his head. "I hate being so conflicted."

Liz grabs Charlotte and Ava, pulling them over to Molly as she finally stands back up and takes a deep breath to calm her churning stomach.

"I almost smothered the three of you when you were toddlers and couldn't get along. Then, I tried to sell you on eBay when all three of you had your periods at the same time and almost killed each other," Liz tells them. "Now that you're adults, I'm not ashamed to admit I've done research on turning you into mail-order brides and shipping you off to another country to make you someone else's problem. Can you girls finally admit you love each other and stop acting like assholes?"

The three sisters look at each other quietly for a few minutes before they all smile.

"I'm sorry I ruined your wedding," Molly tells Charlotte.

"I'm sorry I made you lie to everyone and carry my baby," Charlotte replies with a shrug. "I'd hug you, but you still smell like meat."

Molly nods, leaning her head on my shoulder as I shake her puke off my shoes.

Charlotte, Molly and Liz turn their heads towards Ava and wait for her to apologize.

"I'm sorry I've had to put up with you two slutty cock-knobs my entire life."

Liz sighs and Ava rolls her eyes.

"Fine! You know I hate all this touchy-feely shit," she grumbles. "I love you fuckers. I'm sorry I couldn't be less of an asshole than you two and it took *this* shit to bring us together."

Satisfied with the apologies and the love in the room, Liz drops her arms from around Ava and Charlotte, motioning towards the back of the room.

"It's T-Time, assholes. I need a drink."

Everyone cheers and they all follow Liz as she leads them to the bar, leaving Molly and I alone.

I wrap my arms around Molly and hold her tight as we watch Gavin and Charlotte bring up the rear holding hands, staring at each other lovingly despite the crazy train their wedding turned in to.

"I love you and I really like your family, but we're eloping when we get married," I tell Molly.

"Oh, there is no fucking way we're inviting any of these lunatics," she agrees, wrapping her arms around my waist as we make our way across the room to continue celebrating with all the crazies.

Epilogue

One year later...

"GOD DAMMIT, TOM BRADY," Uncle Drew mutters, shaking his head at the meerkat he has on a leash. "Your dick is going to fall off if you keep it up."

Mom's face curls up in disgust as she stares at the new stain on her carpet.

"Drew, get that damn animal out of my house. That's the third time today he's jerked-off on my carpet. What the fuck is wrong with him?"

Uncle Drew bends forward in his chair and quickly covers the animal's ears. "Don't yell at Tom Brady! It's not his fault he has a healthy libido."

After the night of the bachelor and bachelorette parties, Uncle Drew got a call from the zookeeper informing him that due to the trauma the meerkat sustained, he was suffering from PTSD and his behavior was scaring the zoo guests. To save the animal from being shipped back to Australia and placed in a home for wayward meerkats, Uncle Drew adopted him. I don't know how that's legal and I don't want to know. It's always best to never ask questions in this family.

"Alright, in honor of this momentous occasion, I think we need a T-Time," mom announces as she goes around the living room handing out shot glasses and filling them with cherry vodka.

I look around the room and smile as my family laughs and jokes with each other while my mom finishes her bartender duties. They're certifiably insane and drive me crazy, but I wouldn't trade them for the world. I spent so long being an outsider that I never felt like I fit in and often wondered if I was adopted. All I needed to do was go a little crazy myself and realize we aren't that different. We might not all be blood, but we're all family and we found each other because of one crazy decision my Aunt Claire made at a frat party all those years ago. We've stuck by each other through crazy situations and continue to love each other because that's what families do, and I wouldn't have it any other way.

"I can't believe you actually want to watch this," Aunt Claire complains when my mom finishes with everyone's shots and sets the empty bottle on the coffee table.

"I feel bad all that footage went to waste. We owe it to Dicky Daren for what he went through," mom explains, taking a seat in between Aunt Claire and dad.

After six months of following our family around and another three months of the production company editing the hundreds of hours they filmed down to two, they were unable to sell it to any network. It's a sad, sad day when even the adult film networks passed because our documentary was just too inappropriate for television.

"I bet it was Tom Brady that put them over the edge," Uncle Drew announces sadly.

"I'm pretty sure it was the audio recording of Molly regurgitating a dick," Ava laughs.

Everyone joins in and my face heats in embarrassment.

"Have I apologized for not remembering to take my mic off that night?" Marco whispers close to my ear.

I turn my face towards him and the tips of our noses touch.

"Don't worry, you'll be making it up to me later tonight. I brought home a few new samples from work for us to try."

His eyes light up and he kisses the tip of my nose.

"I hope it's those satin wrist ties. You'll look so hot tied to my bed so I can have my way with you," he tells me with a wink.

Reaching my hand up between us, I pat my palm against his cheek. "Actually, it's a ball gag and butt plug. You'll look so hot when I violate you on my bed."

His eyes widen in fear and I leave him to his worry when my mom instructs everyone to hold up their glasses.

Uncle Drew puts Tom Brady back on the floor by his feet, wrapping his arm around Aunt Jenny's waste as she sits on his lap and they both raise their shot glasses in the air.

Dad and Uncle Carter, on either end of the couch, hold their arms high while mom and Aunt Claire, squished in between them, tilt their heads together and raise their own glasses.

Gavin stops pacing behind the couch and shifts Molly Marco Ellis, his five-month-old sleeping daughter, to his other shoulder to grab the shot Charlotte hands him. When he takes it, Charlotte softly rubs Molly's back, places a kiss on her daughter's head and holds up her own shot.

"Hey, Marco, I forgot to tell you Ava and I tried out chapter twelve of *Baking and Babies* when we were watching little Molly Marco the other day," Tyler tells him, throwing his arm around Ava's shoulders as they lean against the side of the coffee table on the floor. "Bouncy Seat Brownies and Blowjobs was a hit, man. Well done!"

Tyler points his shot glass in Marco's direction and smiles. He catches Charlotte glaring at him from across the room and shrugs.

"You had sex while you were babysitting our child?" Gavin scolds.

"She was safely strapped into her bouncy seat facing the wall, just like the cookbook instructed," Tyler tells them with a roll of his eyes.

"Remind me again why we let him watch our daughter?" Gavin asks Charlotte.

"Because you wanted to practice chapter nine—Naptime Noodles and Nipples, to make sure we could really do it in thirty minutes or less," Charlotte whispers.

Marco's second cookbook took off bigger and better than the first one and he managed to save enough money to buy his own home. Since I decided it wasn't right to take any of Charlotte and Gavin's wedding money even though I earned it, I stayed with my parents until Marco closed on the house and asked me to move in with him.

By baking me a soufflé, that I'm happy to say he was able to get up, and keep up.

Mom leans forward on the couch and glances around the room with a confused look on her face.

"What's up, slut? I thought we were doing T-Time?" Aunt Claire asks her.

"I just feel like we're missing a few people," mom mutters.

"Well, we did have a shit ton of kids, it's hard to keep track of them all," Dad tells her.

"It's easy to forget what's-their-names since we hardly ever mention them. Wait, isn't one of them our daughter?" Uncle Carter asks.

"Shit, Sophia! That's her name!" Aunt Claire shouts. "I think she's away at college, right?"

Everyone shrugs and mumbles in agreement.

"Don't forget Billy and Veronica, our two precious spawns of Satan," Uncle Drew adds. "I haven't heard from them since they joined the circus. I'm sure they're fine."

We all share a moment of silence for the three people we've mentioned once or twice before but never heard from again. Mom finally raises her glass, waiting for everyone else to do the same.

"Here's to you, here's to me, fuck you, here's to me," she states.

We all toss back our shots and dad grabs the remote from the arm of the couch next to him and aims it at the flat screen TV above the fireplace.

"Alright, you dirty fuckers, let's see what Dicky Daren was nice enough to put together for us," he says, pressing play on the DVD player.

My parents received a package in the mail yesterday with an apology letter from the production company about our documentary not airing on TV and enclosed a DVD that Dicky Daren put together just for us. We all sit back and quiet down as the DVD starts to play, opening up on an interview with mom and Aunt Claire.

"So, yeah, I guess it all started when I got drunk at a frat party one night and gave my virginity to a random guy and then found out I was pregnant," Aunt Claire says into the camera. *"I became a single mom, found the guy four years later and then Liz and I opened the first Seduction and Snacks. It took off like crazy and here we are now with stores and bakeries all over the country. That's about it."*

The camera pans to mom laughing, sitting next to Aunt Claire.

"Yeah, there's a lot more to the story than that, slut bag. I think you left out a few things."

Mom reaches down next to her chair and pulls five photo albums onto her lap, opening the cover of the first one and sliding a picture out of the page to hold up for the camera. It zooms in to a picture of Mom and Aunt Claire in college with their arms wrapped around each other, holding up red Solo cups. As the camera rolls, she begins going through all the pictures in the albums. There are photos for every event in our lives, quotes that go with every photo and the two of them share the stories for each one. They laugh on camera, they cry on camera, they punch each other several times on camera, and they curse so much it's pretty obvious why no networks wanted to air this thing. Their bleep button would have broken in the first ten seconds.

"Your tits are like Bounty. The quicker dick picker upper."

"Well, fuck me gently with a chainsaw."

"Aaarrrggg, ahoy me matey, thar's a great grand vagina over yonder." Penises talk like pirates when I'm drunk.

"Papa says your friends Johnny, Jack and Jose maded you sick. Friends shouldn't do stuff like that, Mommy. If Luke maded me sick, I'd punch him in the nuts!"

"I wanna eat her Snickers finger but my arm teeth won't feel."

"There is no way you were even remotely as surprised as me. If I woke up tomorrow with my tits sewn to the curtains, I wouldn't be this much in shock."

"In the words of the great Maury Povich, 'You ARE the father'."

"Rule number one: P.O.R.N. is more fun with friends, invite them. Otherwise, you just look pitiful engaging in P.O.R.N. alone. Rule number two: Sharp objects should never be used in P.O.R.N. Poking someone's eye out will ruin the moment. Rule number three: Sneak attacks or 'back door action' must come with advanced warnings or have prior approval. Rule number four: Only two balls allowed in play at all times to avoid ball-confusion, unless approved by the judges. Rule number five: P.O.R.N. is over when the other player(s) say it's over. Otherwise, someone is left holding useless balls."

"Bad boys, bad boys, whatcha gonna do, whatcha gonna do when they cut your wiener."

"Vajingo. As in 'maybe the vajingo ate your penis'."

"Stop by Seduction and Snacks for the grand opening tomorrow and try some of Claire's boobs. They're delicious!"

BAKING AND BABIES

"You are a gigantic, stinkotic, vaginastic, clitoral, liptistic whore dizzle."

"You're a dick. Go fuck your face."

"FUCK YOU, SAM I AM!"

"No nut shots before lunch."

"These snozzberries taste like SNOZZBERRIES!"

"Wait, maybe it was the nuts. Is Claire allergic to nuts? She might be going into anal flaccid shock."

"I want to teach inappropriate things to our children with you forever. Claire Donna Morgan, will you please, please marry me and love me for the rest of your life?"

"A. SEX. SWING. From the Latin words, 'you are supposed to fuck in it, not rock your kid to sleep'."

"My toilet is your toilet; your spoop is my spoop. I'm on this train, but just so you know, I don't want to be the caboose."

"It's the fucking zombie virus! Son of a bitch, I told you this day was coming! No one believed me and you all laughed. Well, who the fuck is laughing now?! If I go first, you kill me before I eat ANYONE'S face off, do you hear me?"

"Vagina Skittles are delicious."

"You spidermanned the one you love."

"It's fucking Meerkat Manor in my pants."

"I roofied you because I wanted you naked .... and afraid."

"*RUN, VAGINAMAN, RUN!*"

"*Just say NO to weird sex, Gavin!*"

"SON OF A BITCH, TAYLOR SWIFT! I TOLD YOU, NOT UNTIL THE CHORUS!"

"*No, YOU shut your prancing face, Twilight Sparkle, before my parents hear you.*"

"*HONEST MISTAKE?! An honest mistake is speeding, spilling a glass of milk or calling someone by the wrong name. It is NOT sticking your dick in the wrong hole!*"

"*My tits may be small, but they're deadly*"

"*Right at that moment, I knew that I would do anything for my best friend. I would hold her hand when she was in pain, scream at my catatonic fiancé when he saw her vagina and sit by her side when she became a mom. There was nothing I wouldn't do for her and I knew that's how it would always be.*"

The video ends with a picture of my mom and Aunt Claire standing in front of Seduction and Snacks on the day it opened and fades to black with a picture of them standing in front of a map of the United States filled with red dots indicating every Seduction and Snacks store open today.

Dad stops the DVD and the room is silent aside from a few sniffles every couple of seconds.

"Are you assholes crying? There's no crying in Vagina Skittles!" Uncle Drew shouts. "Dammit, Tom Brady! Get your hand off your dick!"

He quickly grabs the animal from the floor and continues scolding him softly.

"We've been through a lot, haven't we, Slutbag McFuckstick?" Mom whispers to Aunt Claire as she rests her head on her shoulder.

"I wouldn't be where I am today if it wasn't for you, ass face," Aunt Claire whispers back, resting her cheek on Mom's head. "You told me I had nothing to lose by taking a chance and you were right. Everything I have is because of you. Thank you for being my person."

Mom wipes a tear from her cheek and the two best friends, who started us all on this crazy ride, wrap their arms around each other on the couch.

"How about one more toast?" Uncle Carter suggests, grabbing another bottle of cherry vodka from the coffee table and unscrewing the cap.

Everyone quickly passes it around and refills their shot glasses, raising them in the air when the last person's glass is full.

"To Seduction and Snacks—where it all began," Uncle Carter says.

"To Seduction and Snacks!" we cheer, toasting each other and tossing the shots back.

"Alright, enough of this sappy shit or I'm going to grow a vagina," Uncle Drew complains, setting his empty shot glass on the coffee table and pushing himself up from the couch, promptly dumping Aunt Jenny onto the floor. "Who's in the mood for a little Ceiling Fan Baseball?"

Mom jumps up from the couch. "I'll get the dinner rolls!"

"I'll get the frying pans and cutting boards!" Aunt Claire adds, following my mom into the kitchen.

"Can I be up to goal first? Maybe shooting a basket will unstick these Benjamin Balls from my vagina," Aunt Jenny says as she waddles behind everyone else.

Marco stands and holds out his hand to help me up from the couch.

"Does your family ever do anything normal?" he asks as he wraps his arm around me and we head towards the dining room.

"Dammit, Tom Brady! Not in the mashed potatoes!" Uncle

Drew shouts from the kitchen.

Marco laughs and I shake my head.

"Normal is overrated. They're bat-shit crazy every day of their lives and that's just the way it should be," I tell him with a smile.

Many, many, many, many, many years later...

CLAIRE AND CARTER Ellis went on to live a long and happy life together. Just like in a cheesy romantic movie, they died together in their home, peacefully in their sleep on their 75th wedding anniversary, after a celebratory game of Metamucil pong. Well, Carter snored up until the end and Claire gave him one last kick to the shin before she joined him.

LIZ AND JIM GILMORE passed away the weekend after their 78th wedding anniversary, suffering heart attacks at the same time when they decided to test out an entire new shipment of vibrators in one evening. They died quickly and without pain, in the porn room of the flagship Seduction and Snacks store.

JENNY AND DREW PARRITT died in the parking lot of the emergency room, next to their personalized parking space, when Jenny slipped on a sheet of ice trying to dislodge a whisk from her vagina and hit her head, which caused her to swallow the ball from the ball gag Drew's arthritic fingers were unable to remove and she choked to death. Drew passed away shortly after, overexerted himself giving CRP. To her vagina. He choked on the whisk lodged in his favorite place.

CHARLOTTE AND GAVIN ELLIS went on to have two boys after Molly Marco, and Gavin has enjoyed every minute being a father, teaching his children not to give nut punches before lunch and making sure they understand just how dangerous to your life beer pong can be.

AVA AND TYLER BRANSON got married a few years after the birth of their niece, Molly Marco, at BronyCon, in front of all of their friends and family. They bought a horse farm in the country where they went on to host their very own BronyCon every year, spreading the *friendship is magic* message. They too went on to have three children and Tyler is still holding a grudge that Ava wouldn't let him name them Pinky Pie, Shutterfly and Applejack.

MOLLY AND MARCO DESOTO enjoyed a quiet, non-crazy elopement on the island of St. Thomas on Molly's twenty-fourth birthday. Even though they enjoyed the few weeks they spent with Cletus the Fetus, they decided never to have children of their own, fearing that Molly's vagina would one day resemble an Arby's Beef and Cheddar, minus the cheddar. Instead, they adopted two baby boys from broken homes who grew up to be Grand Theft Auto experts, and thanks to their mother, have never, ever collapsed a soufflé.

SOPHIA, BILLY AND VERONICA…uh, yeah. We still have no idea what happened to them, but we assume they had good lives and lived happily ever after, just like the rest of the family.

The End.

Seriously.

Totally not kidding. This is it. Forever.

They're kind of all dead now, so, there's that.

I mean, they could all come back as zombies and I guess that might be kind of funny, but, like, not an entire book funny.

Sorry. This is really the end. Hug it out, bitches.

Acknowledgements

I guess I should probably thank my family first and foremost. It's their fault the majority of the scenes and quotes in this entire series are true. Thank you for being crazy and giving me plenty of material to write about.

A HUGE thanks to Ana's Attic Book Blog for being such a huge supporter of this series and these insane characters. I'm so glad I made you piss yourself all those years ago, which led to the awesomeness that is Wicked Book Weekend, which then led to us making out. Thank you for being a great friend, blogger and all around awesome person (a.k.a. good kisser).

Thank you to EVERY SINGLE reader who took a chance on Seduction and Snacks and continued to follow these characters through all of their stupid decisions. It's because of YOU this series is loved (and disgusted) by so many. Thank you for continuing to tell your friends about it, thank you for refusing to speak to friends who won't read it, and thank you for being so amazing.

For my FTN girls, thank you for always being so supportive and wonderful. I'm honored to call you friends and co-workers and to have people in my life I can happily lose my mind with.

Thank you to Stephanie Johnson and Michelle Kannan for being the best beta readers in the world. I'm sorry for what I put you through with this book, but it was Tom Brady's fault. I love your faces.

As always, saying "thank you" will never be enough for ALL the bloggers out there. You guys work tirelessly to pimp me and support me, and I will be forever grateful for all that you do.

To my Slappers. I love you and I will never forget that you were the first ones to believe in me and support me. Twilight nerds forever!

Lastly, to the entire Twilight fanfiction community, it's because of you I'm able to live my dream and do what I love. Thank you for letting me test my skills with The Vagina Monologues, and thank you to those who have continued to follow me on this crazy train!

CPSIA information can be obtained
at www.ICGtesting.com
Printed in the USA
FFOW04n1940100517
35366FF